THE CONFIDENCE-MAN:
His Masquerade

AN AUTHORITATIVE TEXT
BACKGROUNDS AND SOURCES
REVIEWS · CRITICISM
AN ANNOTATED BIBLIOGRAPHY

W. W. NORTON & COMPANY
also publishes

THE NORTON ANTHOLOGY OF AFRICAN AMERICAN LITERATURE
edited by Henry Louis Gates Jr. and Nellie Y. McKay et. al

THE NORTON ANTHOLOGY OF AMERICAN LITERATURE
edited by Nina Baym et al.

THE NORTON ANTHOLOGY OF CONTEMPORARY FICTION
edited by R. V. Cassill

THE NORTON ANTHOLOGY OF ENGLISH LITERATURE
edited by M. H. Abrams et al.

THE NORTON ANTHOLOGY OF LITERATURE BY WOMEN
edited by Sandra M. Gilbert and Susan Gubar

THE NORTON ANTHOLOGY OF MODERN POETRY
edited by Richard Ellmann and Robert O'Clair

THE NORTON ANTHOLOGY OF POETRY
edited by Margaret Ferguson et al.

THE NORTON ANTHOLOGY OF SHORT FICTION
edited by R. V. Cassill

THE NORTON ANTHOLOGY OF WORLD MASTERPIECES
edited by Maynard Mack et al.

THE NORTON FACSIMILE OF
THE FIRST FOLIO OF SHAKESPEARE
prepared by Charlton Hinman

THE NORTON INTRODUCTION TO LITERATURE
edited by Carl E. Bain, Jerome Beaty, and J. Paul Hunter

THE NORTON INTRODUCTION TO THE SHORT NOVEL
edited by Jerome Beaty

THE NORTON READER
edited by Linda H. Peterson, John C. Brereton, and Joan E. Hartman

THE NORTON SAMPLER
edited by Thomas Cooley

THE NORTON SHAKESPEARE
edited by Stephen Greenblatt et al.

⇻ A NORTON CRITICAL EDITION ⇺

HERMAN MELVILLE

THE CONFIDENCE-MAN:
His Masquerade

AN AUTHORITATIVE TEXT
BACKGROUNDS AND SOURCES
REVIEWS · CRITICISM
AN ANNOTATED BIBLIOGRAPHY

Edited by

HERSHEL PARKER

UNIVERSITY OF SOUTHERN CALIFORNIA

W · W · NORTON & COMPANY

New York · London

W. W. Norton & Company, Inc., 500 Fifth Avenue, New York, N.Y. 10110
W. W. Norton & Company Ltd., 10 Coptic Street, London, WC1A 1PU

Copyright © 1971 by W. W. Norton & Company, Inc.

Library of Congress Catalog Card No. 71-141591
ISBN 0-393-04345-2 {Cloth Edition}
ISBN 0-393-09968-7 {Paper Edition}
PRINTED IN THE UNITED STATES OF AMERICA

5 6 7 8 9 0

Contents

Foreword

After the extravagant style and unconventional psychoanalysis of *Pierre* (1852) lost him his British publisher and much of his American reputation, Melville began writing magazine stories for *Putnam's* and *Harper's*. In the next years he mastered a sort of secret writing in which he palmed off upon his genteel publishers a series of innocuous tales which concealed highly personal allegories not meant to be understood. *The Confidence-Man* (1857), while containing little of that kind of private writing, would not have been published by the circumspect firm of Dix & Edwards if its religious meanings had been obvious. For his first readers those meanings were concealed by an elaborately indirect style and by a bewildering series of characters who debate all manner of philosophical and theological issues. Dozens of references to journalistic commonplaces of the day, such as confidence men, Western robbers, P. T. Barnum's freaks, Jeremy Diddlers, land frauds, water cures, prowling Jesuits, Indian-haters, and counterfeit bill detectors, gave some early readers the illusion that the book was merely a picaresque satire on the hazards of Western travel and the peculiarities of American manners and morals, but these references only make the book harder for present readers to understand. Most inaccessible of all, to many modern readers, are the Biblical echoes through which Melville commented on the state of Christianity in the America of the 1850's. In short, *The Confidence-Man* profits well from the kinds of materials that can be assembled in a Norton Critical Edition.

Recent criticism of *The Confidence-Man* is notoriously confused, yet in preparing this edition it seemed easy enough to discern a standard line of interpretation, even though certain segments of that line had been tumbled over or imperfectly shored up and certain small gaps remained. Mysteries have dwindled steadily since the mid-forties, when Egbert S. Oliver demonstrated that Melville had brought at least three real people into the book as targets of his satire: Fanny Kemble, Ralph Waldo Emerson, and Henry David Thoreau. In 1951, John W. Shroeder located the events in the book "geographically and spiritually" by his "literary cross references" to Hawthorne's "The Celestial Railroad." He demonstrated that the book is a satiric allegory in which the Devil comes aboard the world-ship to swindle its passengers, and he identified two of the major satiric targets: "nineteenth-century optimism and liberal theology." Three years later Elizabeth S. Foster confirmed Shroeder's most important discoveries in her Hendricks House edition of *The Confidence-Man* (she had anticipated many of them in her 1942 Yale dissertation) and explicated many passages. She showed, for instance, that certain episodes satirize specific varieties of "optimistic philosophies which assume that the universe is benevolent and human nature good." On a few major points she was mistaken, I believe, but for the most part her interpretation was admirably cogent and gracefully argued. Oddly, many recent scholars have ignored her work, but others have confirmed and supplemented it, helping to fill out that "standard line" of interpretation.

The text of this edition is a slightly corrected reprinting of the first American edition. The footnotes identify the more obscure historical, literary, and Biblical allusions and occasionally comment on Melville's strategies. Such annotations could hardly have been made without Miss Foster's long Introduction and her Explanatory Notes. Following the text, a brief Textual Appendix contains a complete list of emendations and a transcription of Melville's manuscript of "The River." The next section, Backgrounds and Sources, prints main sources such as the New York *Herald's* account on July 8, 1849, of the "*Arrest of the Confidence Man*," "The Celestial Railroad," and James Hall's chapter on Indian-hating, as well as other influences and parallels. Both in the Backgrounds and Sources section and in a later section, Criticism, the first selections are general and the later ones are arranged in the order of the chapters they are relevant to. Essays have been chosen to emphasize genuine consolidated gains in interpretation, not provocative topics of critical debate, although some diverse opinions on the style, for instance, are included. The last section is An Annotated Bibliography, especially prepared for this book by Watson G. Branch, the author of the Historical Note in the Northwestern-Newberry Edition of *The Confidence-Man*. More elaborately annotated than any bibliography yet published for one of Melville's books, it sets forth the multiplicity of critical insights, influences, and antics.

The largest debt of any editor of this book must still be to Elizabeth S. Foster. Johannes D. Bergmann generously shared with me his then-unpublished discovery of the original Confidence Man. My friend Robert R. Allen, a Renaissance scholar, lent his fresh eyes to the manuscript of "The River." For consistent support, as well as for specific contributions, I am grateful to Watson G. Branch. At W. W. Norton & Company, Inc., Carol Paradis and John Benedict were unfailingly lucid in their criticism and lavish with their help. The text is preceded in this edition by its own unofficial dedication to victims of auto-da-fe, a perhaps whimsical note Melville made on a page of trial titles for chapters; the first edition bore no dedication. My part of this book is dedicated to my wife, Heddy Parker, who believes with me that the scrupulous reader of *The Confidence-Man* is rewarded by an intensity of intellectual and aesthetic exhilaration comparable to almost nothing else in our literature except some early Swift (such as *A Tale of a Tub*) and some late Nabokov (such as *Pale Fire*). To share that exhilaration is the purpose of this Norton Critical Edition.

HERSHEL PARKER

The Text of
The Confidence-Man

(Dedicated to victims of Auto da Fe)

Contents of *The Confidence-Man*

Chapter 1

A MUTE GOES ABOARD A BOAT ON THE MISSISSIPPI

At sunrise on a first of April,[1] there appeared, suddenly as Manco Capac at the lake Titicaca,[2] a man in cream-colors, at the waterside in the city of St. Louis. His cheek was fair, his chin downy, his hair flaxen, his hat a white fur one, with a long fleecy nap. He had neither trunk, valise, carpet-bag, nor parcel. No porter followed him. He was unaccompanied by friends. From the shrugged shoulders, titters, whispers, wonderings of the crowd, it was plain that he was, in the extremist sense of the word, a stranger.[3]

In the same moment with his advent, he stepped aboard the favorite steamer Fidèle, on the point of starting for New Orleans. Stared at, but unsaluted, with the air of one neither courting nor shunning regard, but evenly pursuing the path of duty, lead it through solitudes or cities, he held on his way along the lower deck until he chanced to come to a placard nigh the captain's office, offering a reward for the capture of a mysterious impostor, supposed to have recently arrived from the East; quite an original genius in his vocation, as would appear, though wherein his originalit consisted was not clearly given; but what purported to be a careful description of his person followed.

As if it had been a theatre-bill, crowds were gathered about the announcement, and among them certain chevaliers,[4] whose eyes, it was plain, were on the capitals, or, at least, earnestly seeking sight of them from behind intervening coats; but as for their fingers, they were enveloped in some myth;[5] though, during a chance interval, one of these chevaliers somewhat showed his hand in purchasing from another chevalier, ex-officio a peddler of money-belts, one of his popular safe-guards, while another peddler, who was still another versatile chevalier, hawked, in the thick of the throng, the lives of Measan, the bandit of Ohio, Murrel, the pirate of the Mississippi, and the brothers Harpe, the Thugs of the Green River

1. April Fools' Day, appropriate for the Devil to spend testing nominal Christians by preaching or parodying genuine Biblical Christianity.
2. An allusion to the mysterious advent of the founder of the Inca empire, sent to earth by his father, the sun.
3. See Isaiah 53:7: "He was oppressed, and he was afflicted, yet he opened not his mouth: he is brought as a lamb to the slaughter, and as a sheep before her shearers is dumb, so he openeth not his mouth."
4. *Chevalier d'industrie*: sharper, swindler, engaged here in picking pockets.
5. This peculiar use of "myth" is probably not what Melville wrote. Watson G. Branch's suggestion of "night" is plausible.

1

country, in Kentucky—creatures, with others of the sort, one and all exterminated at the time, and for the most part, like the hunted generations of wolves in the same regions, leaving comparatively few successors; which would seem cause for unalloyed gratulation, and is such to all except those who think that in new countries, where the wolves are killed off, the foxes increase.

Pausing at this spot, the stranger so far succeeded in threading his way, as at last to plant himself just beside the placard, when, producing a small slate and tracing some words upon it, he held it up before him on a level with the placard, so that they who read the one might read the other. The words were these:—

"Charity thinketh no evil."[6]

As, in gaining his place, some little perseverance, not to say persistence, of a mildly inoffensive sort, had been unavoidable, it was not with the best relish that the crowd regarded his apparent intrusion; and upon a more attentive survey, perceiving no badge of authority about him, but rather something quite the contrary—he being of an aspect so singularly innocent; an aspect, too, which they took to be somehow inappropriate to the time and place, and inclining to the notion that his writing was of much the same sort: in short, taking him for some strange kind of simpleton, harmless enough, would he keep to himself, but not wholly unobnoxious as an intruder—they made no scruple to jostle him aside; while one, less kind than the rest, or more of a wag, by an unobserved stroke, dexterously flattened down his fleecy hat upon his head. Without readjusting it, the stranger quietly turned, and writing anew upon the slate, again held it up:—

"Charity suffereth long, and is kind."

Illy pleased with his pertinacity, as they thought it, the crowd a second time thrust him aside, and not without epithets and some buffets, all of which were unresented. But, as if at last despairing of so difficult an adventure, wherein one, apparently a non-resistant, sought to impose his presence upon fighting characters, the stranger now moved slowly away, yet not before altering his writing to this:—

"Charity endureth all things."

Shield-like[7] bearing his slate before him, amid stares and jeers he moved slowly up and down, at his turning points again changing his inscription to—

"Charity believeth all things."

6. The words on the slate are from I Corinthians 13.
7. In this book laced with bits of the Pauline epistles, probably a reminder of "the breastplate of righteousness" (Ephesians 6:14).

and then—

"Charity never faileth."

The word charity, as originally traced, remained throughout uneffaced, not unlike the left-hand numeral of a printed date, otherwise left for convenience in blank.

To some observers, the singularity, if not lunacy, of the stranger was heightened by his muteness, and, perhaps also, by the contrast to his proceedings afforded in the actions—quite in the wonted and sensible order of things—of the barber of the boat, whose quarters, under a smoking-saloon, and over against a bar-room, was next door but two to the captain's office. As if the long, wide, covered deck, hereabouts built up on both sides with shop-like windowed spaces, were some Constantinople arcade or bazaar, where more than one trade is plied, this river barber, aproned and slippered, but rather crusty-looking for the moment, it may be from being newly out of bed, was throwing open his premises for the day, and suitably arranging the exterior. With business-like dispatch, having rattled down his shutters, and at a palm-tree angle set out in the iron fixture his little ornamental pole, and this without overmuch tenderness for the elbows and toes of the crowd, he concluded his operations by bidding people stand still more aside, when, jumping on a stool, he hung over his door, on the customary nail, a gaudy sort of illuminated pasteboard sign, skillfully executed by himself, gilt with the likeness of a razor elbowed in readiness to shave, and also, for the public benefit, with two words not unfrequently seen ashore gracing other shops besides barbers':—

"No TRUST."

An inscription which, though in a sense not less intrusive than the contrasted ones of the stranger, did not, as it seemed, provoke any corresponding derision or surprise, much less indignation; and still less, to all appearances, did it gain for the inscriber the repute of being a simpleton.

Meanwhile, he with the slate continued moving slowly up and down, not without causing some stares to change into jeers, and some jeers into pushes, and some pushes into punches; when suddenly, in one of his turns, he was hailed from behind by two porters carrying a large trunk; but as the summons, though loud, was without effect, they accidentally or otherwise swung their burden against him, nearly overthrowing him; when, by a quick start, a peculiar inarticulate moan, and a pathetic telegraphing of his fingers, he involuntarily betrayed that he was not alone dumb, but also deaf.

Presently, as if not wholly unaffected by his reception thus far, he went forward, seating himself in a retired spot on the forecastle, nigh the foot of a ladder there leading to a deck above, up and down which ladder some of the boatmen, in discharge of their duties, were occasionally going.

From his betaking himself to this humble quarter, it was evident that, as a deck-passenger, the stranger, simple though he seemed, was not entirely ignorant of his place, though his taking a deck-passage might have been partly for convenience; as, from his having no luggage, it was probable that his destination was one of the small wayside landings within a few hours' sail. But, though he might not have a long way to go, yet he seemed already to have come from a very long distance.

Though neither soiled nor slovenly, his cream-colored suit had a tossed look, almost linty, as if, traveling night and day from some far country beyond the prairies, he had long been without the solace of a bed. His aspect was at once gentle and jaded, and, from the moment of seating himself, increasing in tired abstraction and dreaminess. Gradually overtaken by slumber, his flaxen head drooped, his whole lamb-like figure relaxed, and, half reclining against the ladder's foot, lay motionless, as some sugar-snow in March, which, softly stealing down over night, with its white placidity startles the brown farmer peering out from his threshold at daybreak.

Chapter 2

SHOWING THAT MANY MEN HAVE MANY MINDS

"Odd fish!"

"Poor fellow!"

"Who can he be?"

"Casper Hauser."[1]

"Bless my soul!"

"Uncommon countenance."

"Green prophet from Utah."

"Humbug!"

"Singular innocence."

"Means something."

"Spirit-rapper."

"Moon-calf."

"Piteous."

1. A "wild boy" (1812?–1833) who was found in the marketplace of Nuremberg in 1828. By his accounts, he had been kept in a hole until finally taught to stand and walk by a man who abandoned him—and who five years later gave him a mortal wound. See the references to Peter the Wild Boy in Chapter 21 and to Hairy Orson in Chapter 26.

"Trying to enlist interest."
"Beware of him."
"Fast asleep here, and, doubtless, pick-pockets on board."
"Kind of daylight Endymion."[2]
"Escaped convict, worn out with dodging."
"Jacob dreaming at Luz."[3]

Such the epitaphic comments, conflictingly spoken or thought, of a miscellaneous company, who, assembled on the overlooking, cross-wise balcony at the forward end of the upper deck near by, had not witnessed preceding occurrences.

Meantime, like some enchanted man in his grave, happily oblivious of all gossip, whether chiseled or chatted, the deaf and dumb stranger still tranquilly slept, while now the boat started on her voyage.

The great ship-canal of Ving-King-Ching, in the Flowery Kingdom, seems the Mississippi in parts, where, amply flowing between low, vine-tangled banks, flat as tow-paths, it bears the huge toppling steamers, bedizened and lacquered within like imperial junks.

Pierced along its great white bulk with two tiers of small embrasure-like windows, well above the water-line, the Fidèle, though, might at distance have been taken by strangers for some whitewashed fort on a floating isle.

Merchants on 'change seem the passengers that buzz on her decks, while, from quarters unseen, comes a murmur as of bees in the comb. Fine promenades, domed saloons, long galleries, sunny balconies, confidential passages, bridal chambers, state-rooms plenty as pigeon-holes, and out-of-the-way retreats like secret drawers in an escritoire, present like facilities for publicity or privacy. Auctioneer or coiner, with equal ease, might somewhere here drive his trade.

Though her voyage of twelve hundred miles extends from apple to orange, from clime to clime, yet, like any small ferry-boat, to right and left, at every landing, the huge Fidèle still receives additional passengers in exchange for those that disembark; so that, though always full of strangers, she continually, in some degree, adds to, or replaces them with strangers still more strange; like Rio Janeiro fountain, fed from the Corcovado mountains, which is ever overflowing with strange waters, but never with the same strange particles in every part.

Though hitherto, as has been seen, the man in cream-colors had by no means passed unobserved, yet by stealing into retirement, and there going asleep and continuing so, he seemed to have courted oblivion, a boon not often withheld from so humble an applicant as he. Those staring crowds on the shore were now left

2. The contrast is with the nocturnal dreaming of the hero of Keats's *Endy-* *mion.*
3. Genesis 28:11–15.

far behind, seen dimly clustering like swallows on eaves; while the passengers' attention was soon drawn away to the rapidly shooting high bluffs and shot-towers on the Missouri shore, or the bluff-looking Missourians and towering Kentuckians among the throngs on the decks.

By-and-by—two or three random stoppages having been made, and the last transient memory of the slumberer vanished, and he himself, not unlikely, waked up and landed ere now—the crowd, as is usual, began in all parts to break up from a concourse into various clusters or squads, which in some cases disintegrated again into quartettes, trios, and couples, or even solitaires; involuntarily submitting to that natural law which ordains dissolution equally to the mass, as in time to the member.

As among Chaucer's Canterbury pilgrims, or those oriental ones crossing the Red Sea towards Mecca in the festival month, there was no lack of variety. Natives of all sorts, and foreigners; men of business and men of pleasure; parlor men and backwoodsmen; farm-hunters and fame-hunters; heiress-hunters, gold-hunters, buffalo-hunters, bee-hunters, happiness-hunters, truth-hunters, and still keener hunters after all these hunters. Fine ladies in slippers, and moccasined squaws; Northern speculators and Eastern philosophers; English, Irish, German, Scotch, Danes; Santa Fé traders in striped blankets, and Broadway bucks in cravats of cloth of gold; fine-looking Kentucky boatmen, and Japanese-looking Mississippi cotton-planters; Quakers in full drab, and United States soldiers in full regimentals; slaves, black, mulatto, quadroon; modish young Spanish Creoles, and old-fashioned French Jews; Mormons and Papists; Dives and Lazarus;[4] jesters and mourners, teetotalers and convivialists, deacons and blacklegs;[5] hard-shell Baptists and clay-eaters; grinning negroes, and Sioux chiefs solemn as high-priests. In short, a piebald parliament, an Anacharsis Cloots congress of all kinds of that multiform pilgrim species, man.[6]

As pine, beech, birch, ash, hackmatack, hemlock, spruce, basswood, maple, interweave their foliage in the natural wood, so these varieties of mortals blended their varieties of visage and garb. A Tartar-like picturesqueness; a sort of pagan abandonment and assurance. Here reigned the dashing and all-fusing spirit of the West, whose type is the Mississippi itself, which, uniting the streams of the most distant and opposite zones, pours them along, helter-skelter, in one cosmopolitan and confident tide.

---

4. The rich man and the beggar in Jesus's parable (Luke 16:19–31).
5. Professional gamblers.
6. Anacharsis Cloots led a multi-racial and multi-national deputation into the French National Assembly in 1790 to symbolize the support of the French Revolution by all mankind.

Chapter 3

IN WHICH A VARIETY OF CHARACTERS APPEAR

In the forward part of the boat,[1] not the least attractive object, for a time, was a grotesque negro cripple, in tow-cloth attire and an old coal-sifter of a tamborine in his hand, who, owing to something wrong about his legs, was, in effect, cut down to the stature of a Newfoundland dog; his knotted black fleece and good-natured, honest black face rubbing against the upper part of people's thighs as he made shift to shuffle about, making music, such as it was, and raising a smile even from the gravest. It was curious to see him, out of his very deformity, indigence, and houselessness, so cheerily endured, raising mirth in some of that crowd, whose own purses, hearths, hearts, all their possessions, sound limbs included, could not make gay.

"What is your name, old boy?" said a purple-faced drover, putting his large purple hand on the cripple's bushy wool, as if it were the curled forehead of a black steer.

"Der Black Guinea dey calls me, sar."

"And who is your master, Guinea?"

"Oh sar, I am der dog widout massa."

"A free dog, eh? Well, on your account, I'm sorry for that, Guinea. Dogs without masters fare hard."

"So dey do, sar; so dey do. But you see, sar, dese here legs? What ge'mman want to own dese here legs?"

"But where do you live?"

"All 'long shore, sar; dough now I'se going to see brodder at der landing; but chiefly I libs in der city."

"St. Louis, ah? Where do you sleep there of nights?"

"On der floor of der good baker's oven, sar."[2]

"In an oven? whose, pray? What baker, I should like to know, bakes such black bread in his oven, alongside of his nice white rolls, too. Who is that too charitable baker, pray?"

"Dar he be," with a broad grin lifting his tambourine high over his head.

"The sun is the baker, eh?"

"Yes sar, in der city dat good baker warms der stones for dis ole darkie when he sleeps out on der pabements o' nights."

1. Where the mute was last seen.
2. Evidently a semi-private hint of the diabolic nature of the Black Guinea: James Hall in *Notes on the Western* *States* mentions a Mississippi bluff called the Devil's Bake-oven. See the reference to a bluff called Devil's Joke at the end of Chapter 22.

"But that must be in the summer only, old boy. How about winter, when the cold Cossacks come clattering and jingling? How about winter, old boy?"

"Den dis poor old darkie shakes werry bad, I tell you, sar. Oh sar, oh! don't speak ob der winter," he added, with a reminiscent shiver, shuffling off into the thickest of the crowd, like a half-frozen black sheep nudging itself a cozy berth in the heart of the white flock.

Thus far not very many pennies had been given him, and, used at last to his strange looks, the less polite passengers of those in that part of the boat began to get their fill of him as a curious object; when suddenly the negro more than revived their first interest by an expedient which, whether by chance or design, was a singular temptation at once to *diversion* and charity, though, even more than his crippled limbs, it put him on a canine footing. In short, as in appearance he seemed a dog, so now, in a merry way, like a dog he began to be treated. Still shuffling among the crowd, now and then he would pause, throwing back his head and opening his mouth like an elephant for tossed apples at a menagerie; when, making a space before him, people would have a bout at a strange sort of pitch-penny game, the cripple's mouth being at once target and purse, and he hailing each expertly-caught copper with a cracked bravura from his tambourine. To be the subject of alms-giving is trying, and to feel in duty bound to appear cheerfully grateful under the trial, must be still more so; but whatever his secret emotions, he swallowed them, while still retaining each copper this side the œsophagus. And nearly always he grinned, and only once or twice did he wince, which was when certain coins, tossed by more playful almoners, came inconveniently nigh to his teeth, an accident whose unwelcomeness was not unedged by the circumstance that the pennies thus thrown proved buttons.

While this game of charity was yet at its height, a limping, gimlet-eyed, sour-faced person—it may be some discharged custom-house officer, who, suddenly stripped of convenient means of support, had concluded to be avenged on government and humanity by making himself miserable for life, either by hating or suspecting everything and everybody—this shallow unfortunate, after sundry sorry observations of the negro, began to croak out something about his deformity being a sham, got up for financial purposes, which immediately threw a damp upon the frolic benignities of the pitch-penny players.

But that these suspicions came from one who himself on a wooden leg went halt, this did not appear to strike anybody present. That cripples, above all men, should be companionable, or, at least, refrain from picking a fellow-limper to pieces, in short, should have a little sympathy in common misfortune, seemed not to occur to the company.

Meantime, the negro's countenance, before marked with even more than patient good-nature, drooped into a heavy-hearted expression, full of the most painful distress. So far abased beneath its proper physical level, that Newfoundland-dog face turned in passively hopeless appeal, as if instinct told it that the right or the wrong might not have overmuch to do with whatever wayward mood superior intelligences might yield to.

But instinct, though knowing, is yet a teacher set below reason, which itself says, in the grave words of Lysander in the comedy, after Puck has made a sage of him with his spell:—

"The will of man is by his reason swayed."[3]

So that, suddenly change as people may, in their dispositions, it is not always waywardness, but improved judgment, which, as in Lysander's case, or the present, operates with them.

Yes, they began to scrutinize the negro curiously enough; when, emboldened by this evidence of the efficacy of his words, the wooden-legged man hobbled up to the negro, and, with the air of a beadle, would, to prove his alleged imposture on the spot, have stripped him and then driven him away, but was prevented by the crowd's clamor, now taking part with the poor fellow, against one who had just before turned nearly all minds the other way. So he with the wooden leg was forced to retire; when the rest, finding themselves left sole judges in the case, could not resist the opportunity of acting the part: not because it is a human weakness to take pleasure in sitting in judgment upon one in a box, as surely this unfortunate negro now was, but that it strangely sharpens human perceptions, when, instead of standing by and having their fellow-feelings touched by the sight of an alleged culprit severely handled by some one justiciary, a crowd suddenly come to be all justiciaries in the same case themselves; as in Arkansas once, a man proved guilty, by law, of murder, but whose condemnation was deemed unjust by the people, so that they rescued him to try him themselves; whereupon, they, as it turned out, found him even guiltier than the court had done, and forthwith proceeded to execution; so that the gallows presented the truly warning spectacle of a man hanged by his friends.

But not to such extremities, or anything like them, did the present crowd come; they, for the time, being content with putting the negro fairly and discreetly to the question; among other things,

3. *A Midsummer Night's Dream*, II, ii, 115.

asking him, had he any documentary proof, any plain paper about him, attesting that his case was not a spurious one.

"No, no, dis poor ole darkie haint none o' dem waloable papers," he wailed.

"But is there not some one who can speak a good word for you?" here said a person newly arrived from another part of the boat, a young Episcopal clergyman, in a long, straight-bodied black coat; small in stature, but manly; with a clear face and blue eye; innocence, tenderness, and good sense triumvirate in his air.

"Oh yes, oh yes, ge'mmen," he eagerly answered, as if his memory, before suddenly frozen up by cold charity, as suddenly thawed back into fluidity at the first kindly word. "Oh yes, oh yes, dar is aboard here a werry nice, good ge'mman wid a weed, and a ge'mman in a gray coat and white tie, what knows all about me; and a ge'mman wid a big book, too; and a yarb-doctor; and a ge'mman in a yaller west; and a ge'mman wid a brass plate; and a ge'mman in a wiolet robe; and a ge'mman as is a sodjer; and ever so many good, kind, honest ge'mmen more aboard what knows me and will speak for me, God bress 'em;[4] yes, and what knows me as well as dis poor old darkie knows hisself, God bress him![5] Oh, find 'em, find 'em," he earnestly added, "and let 'em come quick, and show you all, ge'mmen, dat dis poor ole darkie is werry well wordy of all you kind ge'mmen's kind confidence."

"But how are we to find all these people in this great crowd?" was the question of a bystander, umbrella in hand; a middle-aged person, a country merchant apparently, whose natural good-feeling had been made at least cautious by the unnatural ill-feeling of the discharged custom-house officer.

"Where are we to find them?" half-rebukefully echoed the young Episcopal clergyman. "I will go find one to begin with," he quickly added, and, with kind haste suiting the action to the word, away he went.

"Wild goose chase!" croaked he with the wooden leg, now again drawing nigh. "Don't believe there's a soul of them aboard. Did ever beggar have such heaps of fine friends? He can walk fast enough when he tries, a good deal faster than I; but he can lie yet faster. He's some white operator, betwisted and painted up for a decoy. He and his friends are all humbugs."

"Have you no charity, friend?" here in self-subdued tones, singularly contrasted with his unsubdued person, said a Methodist minister, advancing; a tall, muscular, martial-looking man, a Tennessean by birth, who in the Mexican war had been volunteer chaplain to a volunteer rifle-regiment.

"Charity is one thing, and truth is another," rejoined he with the wooden leg: "he's a rascal, I say."

"But why not, friend, put as charitable a construction as one can upon the poor fellow?" said the soldier-like Methodist, with increased difficulty maintaining a pacific demeanor towards one whose own asperity seemed so little to entitle him to it: "he looks honest, don't he?"

"Looks are one thing, and facts are another," snapped out the other perversely; "and as to your constructions, what construction can you put upon a rascal, but that a rascal he is?"

"Be not such a Canada thistle," urged the Methodist, with something less of patience than before. "Charity, man, charity."

"To where it belongs with your charity! to heaven with it!" again snapped out the other, diabolically; "here on earth, true charity dotes, and false charity plots. Who betrays a fool with a kiss, the charitable fool has the charity to believe is in love with him, and the charitable knave on the stand gives charitable testimony for his comrade in the box."

"Surely, friend," returned the noble Methodist, with much ado restraining his still waxing indignation—"surely, to say the least, you forget yourself. Apply it home," he continued, with exterior calmness tremulous with inkept emotion. "Suppose, now, I should exercise no charity in judging your own character by the words which have fallen from you; what sort of vile, pitiless man do you think I would take you for?"

"No doubt"—with a grin—"some such pitiless man as has lost his piety in much the same way that the jockey loses his honesty."

"And how is that, friend?" still conscientiously holding back the old Adam in him, as if it were a mastiff he had by the neck.

"Never you mind how it is"—with a sneer; "but all horses aint virtuous, no more than all men kind; and come close to, and much dealt with, some things arc catching. When you find me a virtuous jockey, I will find you a benevolent wise man."

"Some insinuation there."

"More fool you that are puzzled by it."

"Reprobate!" cried the other, his indignation now at last almost boiling over; "godless reprobate! if charity did not restrain me, I could call you by names you deserve."

"Could you, indeed?" with an insolent sneer.

"Yea, and teach you charity on the spot," cried the goaded Methodist, suddenly catching this exasperating opponent by his shabby coat-collar, and shaking him till his timber-toe clattered on the deck like a nine-pin. "You took me for a non-combatant did you?—thought, seedy coward that you are, that you could abuse a Christian with impunity. You find your mistake"—with another hearty shake.[6]

"Well said and better done, church militant!" cried a voice.

"The white cravat against the world!" cried another.

"Bravo, bravo!" chorused many voices, with like enthusiasm taking sides with the resolute champion.

"You fools!" cried he with the wooden leg, writhing himself loose and inflamedly turning upon the throng; "you flock of fools, under this captain of fools, in this ship of fools!"

With which exclamations, followed by idle threats against his admonisher, this condign victim to justice hobbled away, as disdaining to hold further argument with such a rabble. But his scorn was more than repaid by the hisses that chased him, in which the brave Methodist, satisfied with the rebuke already administered, was, to omit still better reasons, too magnanimous to join. All he said was, pointing towards the departing recusant, "There he shambles off on his one lone leg, emblematic of his one-sided view of humanity."

"But trust your painted decoy," retorted the other from a distance, pointing back to the black cripple, "and I have my revenge."

"But we aint agoing to trust him!" shouted back a voice.

"So much the better," he jeered back. "Look you," he added, coming to a dead halt where he was; "look you, I have been called a Canada thistle. Very good. And a seedy one: still better. And the seedy Canada thistle has been pretty well shaken among ye: best of all. Dare say some seed has been shaken out; and won't it spring though? And when it does spring, do you cut down the young thistles, and won't they spring the more? It's encouraging and coaxing 'em. Now, when with my thistles your farms shall be well stocked, why then—you may abandon 'em!"

"What does all that mean, now?" asked the country merchant, staring.

"Nothing; the foiled wolf's parting howl," said the Methodist. "Spleen, much spleen, which is the rickety child of his evil heart of unbelief: it has made him mad. I suspect him for one naturally reprobate. Oh, friends," raising his arms as in the pulpit, "oh beloved, how are we admonished by the melancholy spectacle of this raver. Let us profit by the lesson; and is it not this: that if, next to mistrusting Providence, there be aught that man should pray against, it is against mistrusting his fellow-man. I have been in mad-houses full of tragic mopers, and seen there the end of suspicion: the

6. However admirable by secular standards this representative of muscular Christianity is, by Melville's Biblical standards he is weighed and found wanting. See *Pierre*, Book XIV, "The Journey and the Pamphlet," where Melville contrasts ideal, cheek-turning obedience to Christ's Sermon on the Mount (Matthew 5) with the worldliness of "professed Christian nations."

cynic, in the moody madness muttering in the corner; for years a barren fixture there; head lopped over, gnawing his own lip, vulture of himself; while, by fits and starts, from the corner opposite came the grimace of the idiot at him."

"What an example," whispered one.

"Might deter Timon,"⁷ was the response.

"Oh, oh, good ge'mmen, have you no confidence in dis poor ole darkie?" now wailed the returning negro, who, during the late scene, had stumped apart in alarm.

"Confidence in you?" echoed he who had whispered, with abruptly changed air turning short round; "that remains to be seen."

"I tell you what it is, Ebony," in similarly changed tones said he who had responded to the whisperer, "yonder churl," pointing toward the wooden leg in the distance, "is, no doubt, a churlish fellow enough, and I would not wish to be like him; but that is no reason why you may not be some sort of black Jeremy Diddler."⁸

"No confidence in dis poor ole darkie, den?"

"Before giving you our confidence," said a third, "we will wait the report of the kind gentleman who went in search of one of your friends who was to speak for you."

"Very likely, in that case," said a fourth, "we shall wait here till Christmas. Shouldn't wonder, did we not see that kind gentleman again. After seeking awhile in vain, he will conclude he has been made a fool of, and so not return to us for pure shame. Fact is, I begin to feel a little qualmish about the darkie myself. Something queer about this darkie, depend upon it."

Once more the negro wailed, and turning in despair from the last speaker, imploringly caught the Methodist by the skirt of his coat. But a change had come over that before impassioned intercessor. With an irresolute and troubled air, he mutely eyed the suppliant; against whom, somehow, by what seemed instinctive influences, the distrusts first set on foot were now generally reviving, and, if anything, with added severity.

"No confidence in dis poor ole darkie," yet again wailed the negro, letting go the coat-skirts and turning appealingly all round him.

"Yes, my poor fellow, *I* have confidence in you," now exclaimed the country merchant before named, whom the negro's appeal, coming so piteously on the heel of pitilessness, seemed at last humanely to have decided in his favor. "And here, here is some

---

7. The misanthrope of Shakespeare's *Timon of Athens*, called by Melville in his essay on Hawthorne's *Mosses* one of the "dark characters" through whom Shakespeare "craftily says, or sometimes insinuates the things, which we feel to be so terrifically true, that it

were all but madness for any good man, in his own proper character, to utter, or even hint of them" (Norton Critical Edition of *Moby-Dick*, pp. 541–542).
8. A type name for a swindler.

proof of my trust," with which, tucking his umbrella under his arm, and diving down his hand into his pocket, he fished forth a purse, and, accidentally, along with it, his business card, which, unobserved, dropped to the deck. "Here, here, my poor fellow," he continued, extending a half dollar.

Not more grateful for the coin than the kindness, the cripple's face glowed like a polished copper saucepan, and shuffling a pace nigher, with one upstretched hand he received the alms, while, as unconsciously, his one advanced leather stump covered the card.

Done in despite of the general sentiment, the good deed of the merchant was not, perhaps, without its unwelcome return from the crowd, since that good deed seemed somehow to convey to them a sort of reproach. Still again, and more pertinaciously than ever, the cry arose against the negro, and still again he wailed forth his lament and appeal; among other things, repeating that the friends, of whom already he had partially run off the list, would freely speak for him, would anybody go find them.

"Why don't you go find 'em yourself?" demanded a gruff boatman.

"How can I go find 'em myself? Dis poor ole game-legged darkie's friends must come to him. Oh, whar, whar is dat good friend of dis darkie's, dat good man wid de weed?"

At this point, a steward ringing a bell came along, summoning all persons who had not got their tickets to step to the captain's office; an announcement which speedily thinned the throng about the black cripple, who himself soon forlornly stumped out of sight, probably on much the same errand as the rest.

Chapter 4

RENEWAL OF OLD ACQUAINTANCE

"How do you do, Mr. Roberts?"

"Eh?"

"Don't you know me?"

"No, certainly."[1]

The crowd about the captain's office, having in good time melted away, the above encounter took place in one of the side balconies astern, between a man in mourning clean and respectable, but none of the glossiest, a long weed on his hat, and the country-merchant before-mentioned, whom, with the familiarity of an old acquaintance, the former had accosted.

1. The chapter has a loaded title, since Roberts has just met the Confidence Man in the guise of the Black Guinea. See the double entendres just below, such as "Poor fellow, I know him well."

"Is it possible, my dear sir," resumed he with the weed, "that you do not recall my countenance? why yours I recall distinctly as if but half an hour, instead of half an age, had passed since I saw you. Don't you recall me, now? Look harder."

"In my conscience—truly—I protest," honestly bewildered, "bless my soul, sir, I don't know you—really, really. But stay, stay," he hurriedly added, not without gratification, glancing up at the crape on the stranger's hat, "stay—yes—seems to me, though I have not the pleasure of personally knowing you, yet I am pretty sure I have at least *heard* of you, and recently too, quite recently. A poor negro aboard here referred to you, among others, for a character, I think."

"Oh, the cripple. Poor fellow, I know him well. They found me. I have said all I could for him. I think I abated their distrust. Would I could have been of more substantial service. And apropos, sir," he added, "now that it strikes me, allow me to ask, whether the circumstance of one man, however humble, referring for a character to another man, however afflicted, does not argue more or less of moral worth in the latter?"

The good merchant looked puzzled.

"Still you don't recall my countenance?"

"Still does truth compel me to say that I cannot, despite my best efforts," was the reluctantly-candid reply.

"Can I be so changed? Look at me. Or is it I who am mistaken?—Are you not, sir, Henry Roberts, forwarding merchant, of Wheeling, Pennsylvania? Pray, now, if you use the advertisement of business cards, and happen to have one with you, just look at it, and see whether you are not the man I take you for."

"Why," a bit chafed, perhaps, "I hope I know myself."

"And yet self-knowledge is thought by some not so easy. Who knows, my dear sir, but for a time you may have taken yourself for somebody else? Stranger things have happened."

The good merchant stared.

"To come to particulars, my dear sir, I met you, now some six years back, at Brade Brothers & Co.'s office, I think. I was traveling for a Philadelphia house. The senior Brade introduced us, you remember; some business-chat followed, then you forced me home with you to a family tea, and a family time we had. Have you forgotten about the urn, and what I said about Werter's Charlotte, and the bread and butter, and that capital story you told of the large loaf. A hundred times since, I have laughed over it. At least you must recall my name—Ringman, John Ringman."

"Large loaf? Invited you to tea? Ringman? Ringman? Ring? Ring?"

"Ah sir," sadly smiling, "don't ring the changes that way. I see you have a faithless memory, Mr. Roberts. But trust in the faithfulness of mine."

"Well, to tell the truth, in some things my memory aint of the very best," was the honest rejoinder. "But still," he perplexedly added, "still I—"

"Oh sir, suffice it that it is as I say. Doubt not that we are all well acquainted."

"But—but I don't like this going dead against my own memory; I—"

"But didn't you admit, my dear sir, that in some things this memory of yours is a little faithless? Now, those who have faithless memories, should they not have some little confidence in the less faithless memories of others?"

"But, of this friendly chat and tea, I have not the slightest—"

"I see, I see; quite erased from the tablet. Pray, sir," with a sudden illumination, "about six years back, did it happen to you to receive any injury on the head? Surprising effects have arisen from such a cause. Not alone unconsciousness as to events for a greater or less time immediately subsequent to the injury, but likewise—strange to add—oblivion, entire and incurable, as to events embracing a longer or shorter period immediately preceding it; that is, when the mind at the time was perfectly sensible of them, and fully competent also to register them in the memory, and did in fact so do; but all in vain, for all was afterwards bruised out by the injury."

After the first start, the merchant listened with what appeared more than ordinary interest. The other proceeded:

"In my boyhood I was kicked by a horse, and lay insensible for a long time. Upon recovering, what a blank! No faintest trace in regard to how I had come near the horse, or what horse it was, or where it was, or that it was a horse at all that had brought me to that pass. For the knowledge of those particulars I am indebted solely to my friends, in whose statements, I need not say, I place implicit reliance, since particulars of some sort there must have been, and why should they deceive me? You see, sir, the mind is ductile, very much so: but images, ductilely received into it, need a certain time to harden and bake in their impressions, otherwise such a casualty as I speak of will in an instant obliterate them, as though they had never been. We are but clay, sir, potter's clay, as the good book says,[2] clay, feeble, and too-yielding clay. But I will not philosophize. Tell me, was it your misfortune to receive any concussion upon the brain about the period I speak of? If so, I will with pleasure supply the void in your memory by more minutely rehearsing the circumstances of our acquaintance."

2. Isaiah 64:8. On the *Fidèle*, as in much satanic lore, the Devil regularly quotes Scripture for his own purposes.

The growing interest betrayed by the merchant had not relaxed as the other proceeded. After some hesitation, indeed, something more than hesitation, he confessed that, though he had never received any injury of the sort named, yet, about the time in question, he had in fact been taken with a brain fever,\ losing his mind completely for a considerable interval. He was continuing, when the stranger with much animation exclaimed:

"There now, you see, I was not wholly mistaken. That brain fever accounts for it all."

"Nay; but—"

"Pardon me, Mr. Roberts," respectfully interrupting him, "but time is short, and I have something private and particular to say to you. Allow me."

Mr. Roberts, good man, could but acquiesce, and the two having silently walked to a less public spot, the manner of the man with the weed suddenly assumed a seriousness almost painful. What might be called a writhing expression stole over him. He seemed struggling with some disastrous necessity inkept. He made one or two attempts to speak, but words seemed to choke him. His companion stood in humane surprise, wondering what was to come. At length, with an effort mastering his feelings, in a tolerably composed tone he spoke:

"If I remember, you are a mason, Mr. Roberts?"

"Yes, yes."

Averting himself a moment, as to recover from a return of agitation, the stranger grasped the other's hand; "and would you not loan a brother a shilling if he needed it?"

The merchant started, apparently, almost as if to retreat.

"Ah, Mr. Roberts, I trust you are not one of those business men, who make a business of never having to do with unfortunates. For God's sake don't leave me. I have something on my heart—on my heart. Under deplorable circumstances thrown among strangers, utter strangers. I want a friend in whom I may confide. Yours, Mr. Roberts, is almost the first known face I've seen for many weeks."

It was so sudden an outburst; the interview offered such a contrast to the scene around, that the merchant, though not used to be very indiscreet, yet, being not entirely inhumane, remained not entirely unmoved.

The other, still tremulous, resumed:

"I need not say, sir, how it cuts me to the soul, to follow up a social salutation with such words as have just been mine. I know that I jeopardize your good opinion. But I can't help it: necessity knows no law, and heeds no risk. Sir, we are masons, one more step aside; I will tell you my story."

In a low, half-suppressed tone, he began it. Judging from his auditor's expression, it seemed to be a tale of singular interest, involving calamities against which no integrity, no forethought, no energy, no genius, no piety, could guard. At every disclosure, the hearer's commiseration increased. No sentimental pity. As the story went on, he drew from his wallet a bank note, but after a while, at some still more unhappy revelation, changed it for another, probably of a somewhat larger amount; which, when the story was concluded, with an air studiously disclamatory of alms-giving, he put into the stranger's hands; who, on his side, with an air studiously disclamatory of alms-taking, put it into his pocket.[3]

Assistance being received, the stranger's manner assumed a kind and degree of decorum which, under the circumstances, seemed almost coldness. After some words, not over ardent, and yet not exactly inappropriate, he took leave, making a bow which had one knows not what of a certain chastened independence about it; as if misery, however burdensome, could not break down self-respect, nor gratitude, however deep, humiliate a gentleman.

He was hardly yet out of sight, when he paused as if thinking; then with hastened steps returning to the merchant, "I am just reminded that the president, who is also transfer-agent, of the Black Rapids Coal Company, happens to be on board here, and, having been subpœnaed as witness in a stock case on the docket in Kentucky, has his transfer-book with him. A month since, in a panic contrived by artful alarmists, some credulous stock-holders sold out; but, to frustrate the aim of the alarmists, the Company, previously advised of their scheme, so managed it as to get into its own hands those sacrificed shares, resolved that, since a spurious panic must be, the panic-makers should be no gainers by it. The Company, I hear, is now ready, but not anxious, to redispose of those shares; and having obtained them at their depressed value, will now sell them at par, though, prior to the panic, they were held at a handsome figure above. That the readiness of the Company to do this is not generally known, is shown by the fact that the stock still stands on the transfer-book in the Company's name, offering to one in funds a rare chance for investment. For, the panic subsiding more and more every day, it will daily be seen how it originated; confidence will be more than restored; there will be a reaction; from the stock's descent its rise will be higher than from no fall, the holders trusting themselves to fear no second fate."[4]

3. Possibly a recollection of the scene in *The Autobiography* in which Mr. Whitefield's sermon progressively enlarges the amount Franklin decides he will donate to a Georgia orphanage. Franklin was much in Melville's mind in the mid-fifties, as *Israel Potter* (serialized 1854–1855) shows.
4. As Henry F. Pommer showed in *Milton and Melville* (1950), this is an echo of *Paradise Lost* (II, 14–17): "From this descent / Celestial vertues rising, will appear / More glorious and more dread then [than] from no fall, / And trust themselves to fear no second fate . . . ." Stock in Hell is so good that holders should weather out any temporary panics, such as those during religious revivals.

Having listened at first with curiosity, at last with interest, the merchant replied to the effect, that some time since, through friends concerned with it, he had heard of the company, and heard well of it, but was ignorant that there had latterly been fluctuations. He added that he was no speculator; that hitherto he had avoided having to do with stocks of any sort, but in the present case he really felt something like being tempted. "Pray," in conclusion, "do you think that upon a pinch anything could be transacted on board here with the transfer-agent? Are you acquainted with him?"

"Not personally. I but happened to hear that he was a passenger. For the rest, though it might be somewhat informal, the gentleman might not object to doing a little business on board. Along the Mississippi, you know, business is not so ceremonious as at the East."

"True," returned the merchant, and looked down a moment in thought, then, raising his head quickly, said, in a tone not so benign as his wonted one, "This would seem a rare chance, indeed; why, upon first hearing it, did you not snatch at it? I mean for yourself!"

"I?—would it had been possible!"

Not without some emotion was this said, and not without some embarrassment was the reply. "Ah, yes, I had forgotten."

Upon this, the stranger regarded him with mild gravity, not a little disconcerting; the more so, as there was in it what seemed the aspect not alone of the superior, but, as it were, the rebuker; which sort of bearing, in a beneficiary towards his benefactor, looked strangely enough; none the less, that, somehow, it sat not altogether unbecomingly upon the beneficiary, being free from anything like the appearance of assumption, and mixed with a kind of painful conscientiousness, as though nothing but a proper sense of what he owed to himself swayed him. At length he spoke:

"To reproach a penniless man with remissness in not availing himself of an opportunity for pecuniary investment—but, no, no; it was forgetfulness; and this, charity will impute to some lingering effect of that unfortunate brain-fever, which, as to occurrences dating yet further back, disturbed Mr. Roberts's memory still more seriously."

"As to that," said the merchant, rallying, "I am not—"

"Pardon me, but you must admit, that just now, an unpleasant distrust, however vague, was yours. Ah, shallow as it is, yet, how subtle a thing is suspicion, which at times can invade the humanest of hearts and wisest of heads. But, enough. My object, sir, in calling your attention to this stock, is by way of acknowledgement of your goodness. I but seek to be grateful; if my information leads to nothing, you must remember the motive."

He bowed, and finally retired, leaving Mr. Roberts not wholly without self-reproach, for having momentarily indulged injurious thoughts against one who, it was evident, was possessed of a self-respect which forbade his indulging them himself.

Chapter 5

THE MAN WITH THE WEED MAKES IT AN EVEN QUESTION WHETHER
HE BE A GREAT SAGE OR A GREAT SIMPLETON

"Well, there is sorrow in the world, but goodness too; and goodness that is not greenness, either, no more than sorrow is. Dear good man. Poor beating heart!"

It was the man with the weed, not very long after quitting the merchant, murmuring to himself with his hand to his side like one with the heart-disease.

Meditation over kindness received seemed to have softened him something, too, it may be, beyond what might, perhaps, have been looked for from one whose unwonted self-respect in the hour of need, and in the act of being aided, might have appeared to some not wholly unlike pride out of place; and pride, in any place, is seldom very feeling. But the truth, perhaps, is, that those who are least touched with that vice, besides being not unsusceptible to goodness, are sometimes the ones whom a ruling sense of propriety makes appear cold, if not thankless, under a favor. For, at such a time, to be full of warm, earnest words, and heart-felt protestations, is to create a scene; and well-bred people dislike few things more than that; which would seem to look as if the world did not relish earnestness; but, not so; because the world, being earnest itself, likes an earnest scene, and an earnest man, very well, but only in their place—the stage. See what sad work they make of it, who, ignorant of this, flame out in Irish enthusiasm and with Irish sincerity, to a benefactor, who, if a man of sense and respectability, as well as kindliness, can but be more or less annoyed by it; and, if of a nervously fastidious nature, as some are, may be led to think almost as much less favorably of the beneficiary paining him by his gratitude, as if he had been guilty of its contrary, instead only of an indiscretion. But, beneficiaries who know better, though they may feel as much, if not more, neither inflict such pain, nor are inclined to run any risk of so doing. And these, being wise, are the majority. By which one sees how inconsiderate those persons are, who, from the absence of its officious manifestations in the world, complain that there is not much gratitude extant; when the truth is, that there is as much of it as there is of modesty; but, both being for the most part votarists of the shade, for the most part keep out of sight.

What started this was, to account, if necessary, for the changed air of the man with the weed, who, throwing off in private the cold garb of decorum, and so giving warmly loose to his genuine heart, seemed almost transformed into another being. This subdued air of softness, too, was toned with melancholy, melancholy unreserved; a thing which, however at variance with propriety, still the more attested his earnestness; for one knows not how it is, but it sometimes happens that, where earnestness is, there, also, is melancholy.

At the time, he was leaning over the rail at the boat's side, in his pensiveness, unmindful of another pensive figure near—a young gentleman with a swan-neck, wearing a lady-like open shirt collar, thrown back, and tied with a black ribbon. From a square, tableted broach, curiously engraved with Greek characters, he seemed a collegian—not improbably, a sophomore—on his travels; possibly, his first. A small book bound in Roman vellum was in his hand.

Overhearing his murmuring neighbor, the youth regarded him with some surprise, not to say interest. But, singularly for a collegian, being apparently of a retiring nature, he did not speak; when the other still more increased his diffidence by changing from soliloquy to colloquy, in a manner strangely mixed of familiarity and pathos.

"Ah, who is this? You did not hear me, my young friend, did you? Why, you, too, look sad. My melancholy is not catching!"

"Sir, sir," stammered the other.

"Pray, now," with a sort of sociable sorrowfulness, slowly sliding along the rail,[1] "Pray, now, my young friend, what volume have you there? Give me leave," gently drawing it from him. "Tacitus!" Then opening it at random, read: "In general a black and shameful period lies before me." "Dear young sir," touching his arm alarmedly, "don't read this book. It is poison, moral poison. Even were there truth in Tacitus, such truth would have the operation of falsity, and so still be poison, moral poison. Too well I know this Tacitus. In my college-days he came near souring me into cynicism. Yes, I began to turn down my collar, and go about with a disdainfully joyless expression."

"Sir, sir, I—I—"

"Trust me. Now, young friend, perhaps you think that Tacitus, like me, is only melancholy; but he's more—he's ugly. A vast difference, young sir, between the melancholy view and the ugly. The one may show the world still beautiful, not so the other. The one may be compatible with benevolence, the other not. The one may

1. An early link between the Confidence Man and the serpent which was "more subtil than any beast of the field" (Genesis 3:1). See the allusion to Genesis 3:14 at the end of Chapter 23.

deepen insight, the other shallows it. Drop Tacitus. Phrenologi-
cally, my young friend, you would seem to have a well-developed
head, and large; but cribbed within the ugly view, the Tacitus view,
your large brain, like your large ox in the contracted field, will but
starve the more. And don't dream, as some of you students may,
that, by taking this same ugly view, the deeper meanings of the
deeper books will so alone become revealed to you. Drop Tacitus.
His subtlety is falsity. To him, in his double-refined anatomy of
human nature, is well applied the Scripture saying—'There is a
subtle man, and the same is deceived.'[2] Drop Tacitus. Come, now,
let me throw the book overboard."

"Sir, I—I—"

"Not a word; I know just what is in your mind, and that is just
what I am speaking to. Yes, learn from me that, though the sor-
rows of the world are great, its wickedness—that is, its ugliness—is
small.[3] Much cause to pity man, little to distrust him. I myself
have known adversity, and know it still. But for that, do I turn
cynic? No, no: it is small beer that sours. To my fellow-creatures I
owe alleviations. So, whatever I may have undergone, it but deepens my confidence in my kind. Now, then" (winningly), "this
book—will you let me drown it for you?"

"Really, sir—I—"

"I see, I see. But of course you read Tacitus in order to aid you
in understanding human nature—as if truth was ever got at by
libel. My young friend, if to know human nature is your object,
drop Tacitus and go north to the cemeteries of Auburn and Green-
wood."

"Upon my word, I—I—"

"Nay, I foresee all that. But you carry Tacitus, that shallow Tacitus. What do I carry? See"—producing a pocket-volume—"Akenside—his 'Pleasures of Imagination.'[4] One of these days you will
know it. Whatever our lot, we should read serene and cheery books,
fitted to inspire love and trust. But Tacitus! I have long been of
opinion that these classics are the bane of colleges; for—not to hint
of the immorality of Ovid, Horace, Anacreon, and the rest, and the
dangerous theology of Eschylus and others—where will one find

---

2. As Miss Foster says, "not an exact
quotation but apparently a way of referring the reader to a passage in Ecclesiasticus 19 that suits the colloquy
between the man in mourning and the
sophomore." See verses 25–26: "There
is an exquisite subtilty, and the same
is unjust; and there is one that turneth
aside to make judgment appear; and
there is a wise man that justifieth in
judgment. There is a wicked man that
hangeth down his head sadly; but inwardly he is full of deceit."
3. The "man of feeling, the graveyard

sentimentalist, appropriately extols the
sentimental optimism of the eighteenth
century. His aesthetic definition of evil
is conveyed in the Shaftesburyan parallel of wickedness and ugliness" (Foster). She also cites arguments in Lord
Shaftesbury's *Characteristics* to the
effect that "morality, like art, is a
matter of Taste."
4. A way of linking the man with the
weed with "eighteenth-century sentimental optimism," since Akenside's
book "presents a benevolent universe in
which whatever is is right" (Foster).

views so injurious to human nature as in Thucydides, Juvenal, Lucian, but more particularly Tacitus? When I consider that, ever since the revival of learning, these classics have been the favorites of successive generations of students and studious men, I tremble to think of that mass of unsuspected heresy on every vital topic which for centuries must have simmered unsurmised in the heart of Christendom. But Tacitus—he is the most extraordinary example of a heretic; not one iota of confidence in his kind. What a mockery that such an one should be reputed wise, and Thucydides be esteemed the statesman's manual! But Tacitus—I hate Tacitus; not, though, I trust, with the hate that sins, but a righteous hate. Without confidence himself, Tacitus destroys it in all his readers. Destroys confidence, paternal confidence, of which God knows that there is in this world none to spare. For, comparatively inexperienced as you are, my dear young friend, did you never observe how little, very little, confidence, there is? I mean between man and man—more particularly between stranger and stranger. In a sad world it is the saddest fact. Confidence! I have sometimes almost thought that confidence is fled; that confidence is the New Astrea[5] —emigrated—vanished—gone." Then softly sliding nearer, with the softest air, quivering down and looking up, "could you now, my dear young sir, under such circumstances, by way of experiment, simply have confidence in *me*?"

From the outset, the sophomore, as has been seen, had struggled with an ever-increasing embarrassment, arising, perhaps, from such strange remarks coming from a stranger—such persistent and prolonged remarks, too. In vain had he more than once sought to break the spell by venturing a deprecatory or leave-taking word. In vain. Somehow, the stranger fascinated him. Little wonder, then, that, when the appeal came, he could hardly speak, but, as before intimated, being apparently of a retiring nature, abruptly retired from the spot, leaving the chagrined stranger to wander away in the opposite direction.

Chapter 6

AT THE OUTSET OF WHICH CERTAIN PASSENGERS PROVE DEAF TO THE CALL OF CHARITY

—"You—pish! Why will the captain suffer these begging fellows on board?"

These pettish words were breathed by a well-to-do gentleman in a ruby-colored velvet vest, and with a ruby-colored cheek, a ruby-

5. Greek goddess who fled to heaven to escape the impiety of mortals.

headed cane in his hand, to a man in a gray coat and white tie, who, shortly after the interview last described, had accosted him for contributions to a Widow and Orphan Asylum recently founded among the Seminoles.[1] Upon a cursory view, this last person might have seemed, like the man with the weed, one of the less unrefined children of misfortune; but, on a closer observation, his countenance revealed little of sorrow, though much of sanctity.

With added words of touchy disgust, the well-to-do gentleman hurried away. But, though repulsed, and rudely, the man in gray did not reproach, for a time patiently remaining in the chilly loneliness to which he had been left, his countenance, however, not without token of latent though chastened reliance.

At length an old gentleman, somewhat bulky, drew nigh, and from him also a contribution was sought.

"Look, you," coming to a dead halt, and scowling upon him. "Look, you," swelling his bulk out before him like a swaying balloon, "look, you, you on others' behalf ask for money; you, a fellow with a face as long as my arm. Hark ye, now: there is such a thing as gravity, and in condemned felons it may be genuine; but of long faces there are three sorts; that of grief's drudge, that of the lantern-jawed man, and that of the impostor. You know best which yours is."

"Heaven give you more charity, sir."

"And you less hypocrisy, sir."

With which words, the hard-hearted old gentleman marched off.

While the other still stood forlorn, the young clergyman, before introduced, passing that way, catching a chance sight of him, seemed suddenly struck by some recollection; and, after a moment's pause, hurried up with: "Your pardon, but shortly since I was all over looking for you."

"For me?" as marveling that one of so little account should be sought for.

"Yes, for you; do you know anything about the negro, apparently a cripple, aboard here? Is he, or is he not, what he seems to be?"

"Ah, poor Guinea! have you, too, been distrusted? you, upon whom nature has placarded the evidence of your claims?"

"Then you do really know him, and he is quite worthy? It relieves me to hear it—much relieves me. Come, let us go find him, and see what can be done."

"Another instance that confidence may come too late. I am sorry to say that at the last landing I myself—just happening to catch

1. The many heroic virtues of the historical Seminole Indians are irrelevant here. In Melville's joke, which depends upon Cotton Mather's standard equation of Indians with Devils, the Devil canvasses Christians for the support of widows and orphans of devils.

sight of him on the gangway-plank—assisted the cripple ashore. No
time to talk, only to help. He may not have told you, but he has a
brother in that vicinity."

"Really, I regret his going without my seeing him again; regret
it, more, perhaps, than you can readily think. You see, shortly after
leaving St. Louis, he was on the forecastle, and there, with many
others, I saw him, and put trust in him;[2] so much so, that, to convince those who did not, I, at his entreaty, went in search of you,
you being one of several individuals he mentioned, and whose personal appearance he more or less described, individuals who he said
would willingly speak for him. But, after diligent search, not
finding you, and catching no glimpse of any of the others he had
enumerated, doubts were at last suggested; but doubts indirectly
originating, as I can but think, from prior distrust unfeelingly pro-
claimed by another. Still, certain it is, I began to suspect."

"Ha, ha, ha!"

A sort of laugh more like a groan than a laugh; and yet, somehow, it seemed intended for a laugh.

Both turned, and the young clergyman started at seeing the
wooden-legged man close behind him, morosely grave as a criminal
judge with a mustard-plaster on his back. In the present case the
mustard-plaster might have been the memory of certain recent
biting rebuffs and mortifications.

"Wouldn't think it was I who laughed, would you?"

"But who was it you laughed at? or rather, tried to laugh at?"
demanded the young clergyman, flushing, "me?"

"Neither you nor any one within a thousand miles of you. But
perhaps you don't believe it."

"If he were of a suspicious temper, he might not," interposed
the man in gray calmly, "it is one of the imbecilities of the suspicious person to fancy that every stranger, however absent-minded,
he sees so much as smiling or gesturing to himself in any odd sort
of way, is secretly making him his butt. In some moods, the move-
ments of an entire street, as the suspicious man walks down it, will
seem an express pantomimic jeer at him. In short, the suspicious
man kicks himself with his own foot."

"Whoever can do that, ten to one he saves other folks' sole-
leather," said the wooden-legged man with a crusty attempt at
humor. But with augmented grin and squirm, turning directly upon
the young clergyman, "you still think it was *you* I was laughing at,
just now. To prove your mistake, I will tell you what I *was* laughing at; a story I happened to call to mind just then."

2. Melville is probably alluding
obliquely to John 20:29: "Jesus saith
unto him, Thomas, because thou hast
seen me, thou hast believed: blessed are
they that have not seen, and yet have
believed."

Whereupon, in his porcupine way, and with sarcastic details, unpleasant to repeat, he related a story, which might, perhaps, in a good-natured version, be rendered as follows:

A certain Frenchman of New Orleans, an old man, less slender in purse than limb, happening to attend the theatre one evening, was so charmed with the character of a faithful wife, as there represented to the life, that nothing would do but he must marry upon it. So, marry he did, a beautiful girl from Tennessee, who had first attracted his attention by her liberal mould, and was subsequently recommended to him through her kin, for her equally liberal education and disposition. Though large, the praise proved not too much. For, ere long, rumor more than corroborated it, by whispering that the lady was liberal to a fault. But though various circumstances, which by most Benedicts[3] would have been deemed all but conclusive, were duly recited to the old Frenchman by his friends, yet such was his confidence that not a syllable would he credit, till, chancing one night to return unexpectedly from a journey, upon entering his apartment, a stranger burst from the alcove: "Begar!" cried he, "now I *begin* to suspec."

His story told, the wooden-legged man threw back his head, and gave vent to a long, gasping, rasping sort of taunting cry, intolerable as that of a high-pressure engine jeering off steam; and that done, with apparent satisfaction hobbled away.[4]

"Who is that scoffer?" said the man in gray, not without warmth. "Who is he, who even were truth on his tongue, his way of speaking it would make truth almost offensive as falsehood? Who is he?"

"He who I mentioned to you as having boasted his suspicion of the negro," replied the young clergyman, recovering from disturbance, "in short, the person to whom I ascribe the origin of my own distrust; he maintained that Guinea was some white scoundrel, betwisted and painted up for a decoy. Yes, these were his very words, I think."

"Impossible! he could not be so wrong-headed. Pray, will you call him back, and let me ask him if he were really in earnest?"

The other complied; and, at length, after no few surly objections, prevailed upon the one-legged individual to return for a moment. Upon which, the man in gray thus addressed him: "This reverend gentleman tells me, sir, that a certain cripple, a poor negro, is by you considered an ingenious impostor. Now, I am not unaware that there are some persons in this world, who, unable to give better proof of being wise, take a strange delight in showing what they think they have sagaciously read in mankind by uncharitable

3. Newly married men, especially those who have long been bachelors.
4. An echo of Hawthorne's description of Apollyon in "The Celestial Railroad."

suspicions of them. I hope you are not one of these. In short, would you tell me now, whether you were not merely joking in the notion you threw out about the negro? Would you be so kind?"

"No, I won't be so kind, I'll be so cruel."

"As you please about that."

"Well, he's just what I said he was."

"A white masquerading as a black?"

"Exactly."

The man in gray glanced at the young clergyman a moment, then quietly whispered to him, "I thought you represented your friend here as a very distrustful sort of person, but he appears endued with a singular credulity.—Tell me, sir, do you really think that a white could look the negro so? For one, I should call it pretty good acting."

"Not much better than any other man acts."

"How? Does all the world act? Am *I*, for instance, an actor? Is my reverend friend here, too, a performer?"

"Yes, don't you both perform acts? To do, is to act; so all doers are actors."

"You trifle.—I ask again, if a white, how could he look the negro so?"

"Never saw the negro-minstrels, I suppose?"

"Yes, but they are apt to overdo the ebony; exemplifying the old saying, not more just than charitable, that 'the devil is never so black as he is painted.'[5] But his limbs, if not a cripple, how could he twist his limbs so?"

"How do other hypocritical beggars twist theirs? Easy enough to see how they are hoisted up."

"The sham is evident, then?"

"To the discerning eye," with a horrible screw of his gimlet one.

"Well, where is Guinea?" said the man in gray; "where is he? Let us at once find him, and refute beyond cavil this injurious hypothesis."

"Do so," cried the one-legged man, "I'm just in the humor now for having him found, and leaving the streaks of these fingers on his paint, as the lion leaves the streaks of his nails on a Caffre. They wouldn't let me touch him before. Yes, find him, I'll make wool fly, and him after."

"You forget," here said the young clergyman to the man in gray, "that yourself helped poor Guinea ashore."

"So I did, so I did; how unfortunate. But look now," to the other, "I think that without personal proof I can convince you of your mistake. For I put it to you, is it reasonable to suppose that a man with brains, sufficient to act such a part as you say, would take

5. A running irony in "The Celestial Railroad" is that the liberal, modern—and unchristian—narrator is courteous even to the Devil.

all that trouble, and run all that hazard, for the mere sake of those few paltry coppers, which, I hear, was all he got for his pains, if pains they were?"

"That puts the case irrefutably," said the young clergyman, with a challenging glance towards the one-legged man.

"You two green-horns! Money, you think, is the sole motive to pains and hazard, deception and deviltry, in this world. How much money did the devil make by gulling Eve?"

Whereupon he hobbled off again with a repetition of his intolerable jeer.

The man in gray stood silently eying his retreat a while, and then, turning to his companion, said: "A bad man, a dangerous man; a man to be put down in any Christian community.—And this was he who was the means of begetting your distrust? Ah, we should shut our ears to distrust, and keep them open only for its opposite."

"You advance a principle, which, if I had acted upon it this morning, I should have spared myself what I now feel.—That but one man, and he with one leg, should have such ill power given him; his one sour word leavening into congenial sourness (as, to my knowledge, it did) the dispositions, before sweet enough, of a numerous company. But, as I hinted, with me at the time his ill words went for nothing; the same as now; only afterwards they had effect; and I confess, this puzzles me."

"It should not. With humane minds, the spirit of distrust works something as certain potions do; it is a spirit which may enter such minds, and yet, for a time, longer or shorter, lie in them quiescent; but only the more deplorable its ultimate activity."

"An uncomfortable solution; for, since that baneful man did but just now anew drop on me his bane, how shall I be sure that my present exemption from its effects will be lasting?"

"You cannot be sure, but you can strive against it."

"How?"

"By strangling the least symptom of distrust, of any sort, which hereafter, upon whatever provocation, may arise in you."

"I will do so." Then added as in soliloquy, "Indeed, indeed, I was to blame in standing passive under such influences as that one-legged man's. My conscience upbraids me.—The poor negro: You see him occasionally, perhaps?"

"No, not often; though in a few days, as it happens, my engagements will call me to the neighborhood of his present retreat; and, no doubt, honest Guinea, who is a grateful soul, will come to see me there."

"Then you have been his benefactor?"

"His benefactor? I did not say that. I have known him."

"Take this mite. Hand it to Guinea when you see him; say it comes from one who has full belief in his honesty, and is sincerely sorry for having indulged, however transiently, in a contrary thought."

"I accept the trust. And, by-the-way, since you are of this truly charitable nature, you will not turn away an appeal in behalf of the Seminole Widow and Orphan Asylum?"

"I have not heard of that charity."

"But recently founded."

After a pause, the clergyman was irresolutely putting his hand in his pocket, when, caught by something in his companion's expression, he eyed him inquisitively, almost uneasily.

"Ah, well," smiled the other wanly, "if that subtle bane, we were speaking of but just now, is so soon beginning to work, in vain my appeal to you. Good-by."

"Nay," not untouched, "you do me injustice; instead of indulging present suspicions, I had rather make amends for previous ones. Here is something for your asylum. Not much; but every drop helps. Of course you have papers?"

"Of course," producing a memorandum book and pencil. "Let me take down name and amount. We publish these names. And now let me give you a little history of our asylum, and the providential way in which it was started."[6]

Chapter 7

A GENTLEMAN WITH GOLD SLEEVE-BUTTONS

At an interesting point of the narration, and at the moment when, with much curiosity, indeed, urgency, the narrator was being particularly questioned upon that point, he was, as it happened, altogether diverted both from it and his story, by just then catching sight of a gentleman who had been standing in sight from the beginning, but, until now, as it seemed, without being observed by him.

"Pardon me," said he, rising, "but yonder is one who I know will contribute, and largely. Don't take it amiss if I quit you."

"Go: duty before all things," was the conscientious reply.

The stranger was a man of more than winsome aspect. There he stood apart and in repose, and yet, by his mere look, lured the man in gray from his story, much as, by its graciousness of bearing, some

6. A wry allusion to the "providential" founding of Hell in *Paradise Lost*, Book I.

full-leaved elm, alone in a meadow, lures the noon sickleman to throw down his sheaves, and come and apply for the alms of its shade.

But, considering that goodness is no such rare thing among men—the world familiarly know the noun; a common one in every language—it was curious that what so signalized the stranger, and made him look like a kind of foreigner, among the crowd (as to some it make him appear more or less unreal in this portraiture), was but the expression of so prevalent a quality. Such goodness seemed his, allied with such fortune, that, so far as his own personal experience could have gone, scarcely could he have known ill, physical or moral; and as for knowing or suspecting the latter in any serious degree (supposing such degree of it to be), by observation or philosophy; for that, probably, his nature, by its opposition, imperfectly qualified, or from it wholly exempted. For the rest, he might have been five and fifty, perhaps sixty, but tall, rosy, between plump and portly, with a primy, palmy air, and for the time and place, not to hint of his years, dressed with a strangely festive finish and elegance. The inner-side of his coat-skirts was of white satin, which might have looked especially inappropriate, had it not seemed less a bit of mere tailoring than something of an emblem, as it were; an involuntary emblem, let us say, that what seemed so good about him was not all outside; no, the fine covering had a still finer lining. Upon one hand he wore a white kid glove, but the other hand, which was ungloved, looked hardly less white. Now, as the Fidèle, like most steamboats, was upon deck a little soot-streaked here and there, especially about the railings, it was a marvel how, under such circumstances, these hands retained their spotlessness. But, if you watched them a while, you noticed that they avoided touching anything; you noticed, in short, that a certain negro body-servant, whose hands nature had dyed black, perhaps with the same purpose that millers wear white, this negro servant's hands did most of his master's handling for him; having to do with dirt on his account, but not to his prejudice. But if, with the same undefiledness of consequences to himself, a gentleman could also sin by deputy, how shocking would that be! But it is not permitted to be; and even if it were, no judicious moralist would make proclamation of it.

This gentleman, therefore, there is reason to affirm, was one who, like the Hebrew governor, knew how to keep his hands clean,[1] and who never in his life happened to be run suddenly against by hurrying house-painter, or sweep; in a word, one whose very good luck it was to be a very good man.

---

1. Pontius Pilate, who washed his hands to disclaim responsibility for the fate of Jesus (Matthew 27:24). This unfavorable allusion complicates the problem of just how Melville meant the gentleman to be judged.

Not that he looked as if he were a kind of Wilberforce[2] at all; that superior merit, probably, was not his; nothing in his manner bespoke him righteous, but only good, and though to be good is much below being righteous, and though there is a difference between the two, yet not, it is to be hoped, so incompatible as that a righteous man can not be a good man; though, conversely, in the pulpit it has been with much cogency urged, that a merely good man, that is, one good merely by his nature, is so far from thereby being righteous, that nothing short of a total change and conversion can make him so; which is something which no honest mind, well read in the history of righteousness, will care to deny; nevertheless, since St. Paul himself, agreeing in a sense with the pulpit distinction, though not altogether in the pulpit deduction, and also pretty plainly intimating which of the two qualities in question enjoys his apostolic preference; I say, since St. Paul has so meaningly said, that, "scarcely for a righteous man will one die, yet peradventure for a good man some would even dare to die;"[3] therefore, when we repeat of this gentleman, that he was only a good man, whatever else by severe censors may be objected to him, it is still to be hoped that his goodness will not at least be considered criminal in him. At all events, no man, not even a righteous man, would think it quite right to commit this gentleman to prison for the crime, extraordinary as he might deem it; more especially, as, until everything could be known, there would be some chance that the gentleman might after all be quite as innocent of it as he himself.

It was pleasant to mark the good man's reception of the salute of the righteous man, that is, the man in gray; his inferior, apparently, not more in the social scale than in stature. Like the benign elm again, the good man seemed to wave the canopy of his goodness over that suitor, not in conceited condescension, but with that even amenity of true majesty, which can be kind to any one without stooping to it.

To the plea in behalf of the Seminole widows and orphans, the gentleman, after a question or two duly answered, responded by producing an ample pocket-book in the good old capacious style, of fine green French morocco and workmanship, bound with silk of the same color, not to omit bills crisp with newness, fresh from the bank, no muckworms' grime upon them. Lucre those bills might be, but as yet having been kept unspotted from the world, not of the filthy sort. Placing now three of those virgin bills in the applicant's hands, he hoped that the smallness of the contribution would be pardoned; to tell the truth, and this at last accounted for

2. The English philanthropist (1759–1833), leader of the agitation against the slave trade, which was finally abolished in 1807; looked upon as the conscience of the nation.
3. Romans 5:7.

his toilet, he was bound but a short run down the river, to attend, in a festive grove, the afternoon wedding of his niece: so did not carry much money with him.

The other was about expressing his thanks when the gentleman in his pleasant way checked him: the gratitude was on the other side. To him, he said, charity was in one sense not an effort, but a luxury; against too great indulgence in which his steward, a humorist, had sometimes admonished him.

In some general talk which followed, relative to organized modes of doing good, the gentleman expressed his regrets that so many benevolent societies as there were, here and there isolated in the land, should not act in concert by coming together, in the way that already in each society the individuals composing it had done, which would result, he thought, in like advantages upon a larger scale. Indeed, such a confederation might, perhaps, be attended with as happy results as politically attended that of the states.[4]

Upon his hitherto moderate enough companion, this suggestion had an effect illustrative in a sort of that notion of Socrates, that the soul is a harmony; for as the sound of a flute, in any particular key, will, it is said, audibly affect the corresponding chord of any harp in good tune, within hearing, just so now did some string in him respond, and with animation.

Which animation, by the way, might seem more or less out of character in the man in gray, considering his unsprightly manner when first introduced, had he not already, in certain after colloquies, given proof, in some degree, of the fact, that, with certain natures, a soberly continent air at times, so far from arguing emptiness of stuff, is good proof it is there, and plenty of it, because unwasted, and may be used the more effectively, too, when opportunity offers. What now follows on the part of the man in gray will still further exemplify, perhaps somewhat strikingly, the truth, or what appears to be such, of this remark.

"Sir," said he eagerly, "I am before you. A project, not dissimilar to yours, was by me thrown out at the World's Fair in London."[5]

"World's Fair? You there? Pray how was that?"

"First, let me—"

"Nay, but first tell me what took you to the Fair?"

"I went to exhibit an invalid's easy-chair I had invented."

"Then you have not always been in the charity business?"

"Is it not charity to ease human suffering? I am, and always have

4. Written in the middle of the inflamed decade of the 1850's, this can hardly be unironic.
5. The "Exposition of the Industry of All Nations" (1851), housed in the famous "Crystal Palace" that covered almost nineteen acres. Among the innovations displayed was the Colt repeating pistol, referred to in Chapter 29.

In 1854 P. T. Barnum briefly accepted the presidency of New York's blatant imitation of the London fair, which also included a Crystal Palace. The publisher G. P. Putnam invited Melville to attend a "Complimentary Fruit & Flower Festival" there on September 27, 1855 (Log, p. 507).

been, as I always will be, I trust, in the charity business, as you call it; but charity is not like a pin, one to make the head, and the other the point; charity is a work to which a good workman may be competent in all its branches. I invented my Protean easy-chair[6] in odd intervals stolen from meals and sleep."

"You call it the Protean easy-chair; pray describe it."

"My Protean easy-chair is a chair so all over bejointed, behinged, and bepadded, everyway so elastic, springy, and docile to the airiest touch, that in some one of its endlessly-changeable accommodations of back, seat, footboard, and arms, the most restless body, the body most racked, nay, I had almost added the most tormented conscience must, somehow and somewhere, find rest. Believing that I owed it to suffering humanity to make known such a chair to the utmost, I scraped together my little means and off to the World's Fair with it."

"You did right. But your scheme; how did you come to hit upon that?"

"I was going to tell you. After seeing my invention duly catalogued and placed, I gave myself up to pondering the scene about me. As I dwelt upon that shining pageant of arts, and moving concourse of nations, and reflected that here was the pride of the world glorying in a glass house, a sense of the fragility of worldly grandeur profoundly impressed me. And I said to myself, I will see if this occasion of vanity cannot supply a hint toward a better profit than was designed. Let some world-wide good to the world-wide cause be now done. In short, inspired by the scene, on the fourth day I issued at the World's Fair my prospectus of the World's Charity."

"Quite a thought. But, pray explain it."

"The World's Charity is to be a society whose members shall comprise deputies from every charity and mission extant; the one object of the society to be the methodization of the world's benevolence; to which end, the present system of voluntary and promiscuous contribution to be done away, and the Society to be empowered by the various governments to levy, annually, one grand benevolence tax upon all mankind; as in Augustus Cæsar's time, the whole world to come up to be taxed; a tax which, for the scheme of it, should be something like the income-tax in England, a tax, also, as before hinted, to be a consolidation-tax of all possible benevolence taxes; as in America here, the state-tax, and the county-tax, and the town-tax, and the poll-tax, are by the assessors rolled into one. This tax, according to my tables, calculated with care, would result in the yearly raising of a fund little short of eight hundred millions; this fund to be annually applied to such objects, and in

6. Miss Foster showed that at the London fair in 1851 were exhibited reclining chairs for invalids made by a Philadelphia manufacturer, "so constructed that the degree of inclination is regulated with facility by the weight of the body." A Protean easy chair would be as delusively lulling to the conscience and intelligence as a Celestial Railroad.

such modes, as the various charities and missions, in general congress represented, might decree; whereby, in fourteen years, as I estimate, there would have been devoted to good works the sum of eleven thousand two hundred millions; which would warrant the dissolution of the society, as that fund judiciously expended, not a pauper or heathen could remain the round world over."

"Eleven thousand two hundred millions! And all by passing round a *hat*, as it were."

"Yes, I am no Fourier,[7] the projector of an impossible scheme, but a philanthropist and a financier setting forth a philanthropy and a finance which are practicable."

"Practicable?"

"Yes. Eleven thousand two hundred millions; it will frighten none but a retail philanthropist. What is it but eight hundred millions for each of fourteen years? Now eight hundred millions— what is that, to average it, but one little dollar a head for the population of the planet? And who will refuse, what Turk or Dyak even, his own little dollar for sweet charity's sake? Eight hundred millions! More than that sum is yearly expended by mankind, not only in vanities, but miseries. Consider that bloody spendthrift, War. And are mankind so stupid, so wicked, that, upon the demonstration of these things they will not, amending their ways, devote their superfluities to blessing the world instead of cursing it? Eight hundred millions! They have not to make it, it is theirs already; they have but to direct it from ill to good. And to this, scarce a self-denial is demanded. Actually, they would not in the mass be one farthing the poorer for it; as certainly would they be all the better and happier. Don't you see? But admit, as you must, that mankind is not mad, and my project is practicable. For, what creature but a madman would not rather do good than ill, when it is plain that, good or ill, it must return upon himself?"

"Your sort of reasoning," said the good gentleman, adjusting his gold sleeve-buttons, "seems all reasonable enough, but with mankind it wont do."

"Then mankind are not reasoning beings, if reason wont do with them."

"That is not to the purpose. By-the-way, from the manner in which you alluded to the world's census, it would appear that, according to your world-wide scheme, the pauper not less than the nabob is to contribute to the relief of pauperism, and the heathen not less than the Christian to the conversion of heathenism. How is that?"

"Why, that—pardon me—is quibbling. Now, no philanthropist likes to be opposed with quibbling."

7. French social reformer (1772– 1837) who advocated a Utopian system of communistic association in "phal- anxes." His views influenced the reformers at Brook Farm.

"Well, I won't quibble any more. But, after all, if I understand your project, there is little specially new in it, further than the magnifying of means now in operation."

"Magnifying and energizing. For one thing, missions I would thoroughly reform. Missions I would quicken with the Wall street spirit."

"The Wall street spirit?"

"Yes; for if, confessedly, certain spiritual ends are to be gained but through the auxiliary agency of worldly means, then, to the surer gaining of such spiritual ends, the example of worldly policy in worldly projects should not by spiritual projectors be slighted. In brief, the conversion of the heathen, so far, at least, as depending on human effort, would, by the World's Charity, be let out on contract. So much by bid for converting India, so much for Borneo, so much for Africa. Competition allowed, stimulus would be given. There would be no lethargy of monopoly. We should have no mission-house or tract-house of which slanderers could, with any plausibility, say that it had degenerated in its clerkships into a sort of custom-house. But the main point is the Archimedean money-power that would be brought to bear."

"You mean the eight hundred million power?"

"Yes. You see, this doing good to the world by driblets amounts to just nothing. I am for doing good to the world with a will. I am for doing good to the world once for all and having done with it. Do but think, my dear sir, of the eddies and maëlstroms of pagans in China. People here have no conception of it. Of a frosty morning in Hong Kong, pauper pagans are found dead in the streets like so many nipped peas in a bin of peas. To be an immortal being in China is no more distinction than to be a snow-flake in a snow-squall. What are a score or two of missionaries to such a people? A pinch of snuff to the kraken. I am for sending ten thousand missionaries in a body and converting the Chinese *en masse* within six months of the debarkation. The thing is then done, and turn to something else."

"I fear you are too enthusiastic."

"A philanthropist is necessarily an enthusiast; for without enthusiasm what was ever achieved but commonplace? But again: consider the poor in London. To that mob of misery, what is a joint here and a loaf there? I am for voting to them twenty thousand bullocks and one hundred thousand barrels of flour to begin with. They are then comforted, and no more hunger for one while among the poor of London. And so all round."

"Sharing the character of your general project, these things, I take it, are rather examples of wonders that were to be wished, than wonders that will happen."

"And is the age of wonders passed? Is the world too old? Is it barren? Think of Sarah."

"Then I am Abraham reviling the angel (with a smile).[8] But still, as to your design at large, there seems a certain audacity."

"But if to the audacity of the design there be brought a commensurate circumspectness of execution, how then?"

"Why, do you really believe that your World's Charity will ever go into operation?"

"I have confidence that it will."

"But may you not be over-confident?"

"For a Christian to talk so!"

"But think of the obstacles!"

"Obstacles? I have confidence to remove obstacles, though mountains.[9] Yes, confidence in the World's Charity to that degree, that, as no better person offers to supply the place, I have nominated myself provisional treasurer, and will be happy to receive subscriptions, for the present to be devoted to striking off a million more of my prospectuses."

The talk went on; the man in gray revealed a spirit of benevolence which, mindful of the millennial promise, had gone abroad over all the countries of the globe, much as the diligent spirit of the husbandman, stirred by forethought of the coming seed-time, leads him, in March reveries at his fireside, over every field of his farm. The master chord of the man in gray had been touched, and it seemed as if it would never cease vibrating. A not unsilvery tongue, too, was his, with gestures that were a Pentecost of added ones,[1] and persuasiveness before which granite hearts might crumble into gravel.

Strange, therefore, how his auditor, so singularly good-hearted as he seemed, remained proof to such eloquence; though not, as it turned out, to such pleadings. For, after listening a while longer with pleasant incredulity, presently, as the boat touched his place of destination, the gentleman, with a look half humor, half pity, put another bank-note into his hands; charitable to the last, if only to the dreams of enthusiasm.

Chapter 8

A CHARITABLE LADY

If a drunkard in a sober fit is the dullest of mortals, an enthusiast in a reason-fit is not the most lively. And this, without prejudice to

---

8. Genesis 17:17: "Then Abraham fell upon his face, and laughed, and said in his heart, Shall a child be born unto him that is an hundred years old? and shall Sarah, that is ninety years old, bear?"

9. I Corinthians 13:2: "though I have all faith, so that I could remove mountains, and have not charity, I am nothing."

1. The day of Pentecost is described in Acts 2:1–40.

his greatly improved understanding; for, if his elation was the height of his madness, his despondency is but the extreme of his sanity. Something thus now, to all appearance, with the man in gray. Society his stimulus, loneliness was his lethargy. Loneliness, like the sea-breeze, blowing off from a thousand leagues of blankness, he did not find, as veteran solitaires do, if anything, too bracing. In short, left to himself, with none to charm forth his latent lymphatic, he insensibly resumes his original air, a quiescent one, blended of sad humility and demureness.

Ere long he goes laggingly into the ladies' saloon, as in spiritless quest of somebody; but, after some disappointed glances about him, seats himself upon a sofa with an air of melancholy exhaustion and depression.

At the sofa's further end sits a plump and pleasant person, whose aspect seems to hint that, if she have any weak point, it must be anything rather than her excellent heart. From her twilight dress, neither dawn nor dark, apparently she is a widow just breaking the chrysalis of her mourning. A small gilt testament is in her hand, which she has just been reading. Half-relinquished, she holds the book in reverie, her finger inserted at the xiii. of 1st Corinthians, to which chapter possibly her attention might have recently been turned, by witnessing the scene of the monitory mute and his slate.

The sacred page no longer meets her eye; but, as at evening, when for a time the western hills shine on though the sun be set, her thoughtful face retains its tenderness though the teacher is forgotten.

Meantime, the expression of the stranger is such as ere long to attract her glance. But no responsive one. Presently, in her somewhat inquisitive survey, her volume drops. It is restored. No encroaching politeness in the act, but kindness, unadorned. The eyes of the lady sparkle. Evidently, she is not now unprepossessed. Soon, bending over, in a low, sad tone, full of deference, the stranger breathes, "Madam, pardon my freedom, but there is something in that face which strangely draws me. May I ask, are you a sister of the Church?"

"Why—really—you—"

In concern for her embarrassment, he hastens to relieve it, but, without seeming so to do. "It is very solitary for a brother here," eying the showy ladies brocaded in the background, "I find none to mingle souls with. It may be wrong—I *know* it is—but I cannot force myself to be easy with the people of the world. I prefer the company, however silent, of a brother or sister in good standing. By the way, madam, may I ask if you have confidence?"[1]

"Really, sir—why, sir—really—I—"

1. Melville's satire is directed toward the bluff directness of American evangelical Protestantism that became embodied in the tag, "Brother, are you saved?"

"Could you put confidence in *me* for instance?"

"Really, sir—as much—I mean, as one may wisely put in a—a—stranger, an entire stranger, I had almost said," rejoined the lady, hardly yet at ease in her affability, drawing aside a little in body, while at the same time her heart might have been drawn as far the other way. A natural struggle between charity and prudence.

"Entire stranger!" with a sigh. "Ah, who would be a stranger? In vain, I wander; no one will have confidence in me."

"You interest me," said the good lady, in mild surprise. "Can I any way befriend you?"

"No one can befriend me, who has not confidence."

"But I—I have—at least to that degree—I mean that—"

"Nay, nay, you have none—none at all. Pardon, I see it. No confidence. Fool, fond fool that I am to seek it!"

"You are unjust, sir," rejoins the good lady with heightened interest; "but it may be that something untoward in your experiences has unduly biased you. Not that I would cast reflections. Believe me, I—yes, yes—I may say—that—that—"

"That you have confidence? Prove it. Let me have twenty dollars."

"Twenty dollars!"

"There, I told you, madam, you had no confidence."

The lady was, in an extraordinary way, touched. She sat in a sort of restless torment, knowing not which way to turn. She began twenty different sentences, and left off at the first syllable of each. At last, in desperation, she hurried out, "Tell me, sir, for what you want the twenty dollars?"

"And did I not—" then glancing at her half-mourning, "for the widow and the fatherless. I am traveling agent of the Widow and Orphan Asylum, recently founded among the Seminoles."

"And why did you not tell me your object before?" As not a little relieved. "Poor souls—Indians, too—those cruelly-used Indians. Here, here; how could I hesitate? I am so sorry it is no more."

"Grieve not for that, madam," rising and folding up the banknotes. "This is an inconsiderable sum, I admit, but," taking out his pencil and book, "though I here but register the amount, there is another register, where is set down the motive. Good-bye; you have confidence. Yea, you can say to me as the apostle said to the Corinthians, 'I rejoice that I have confidence in you in all things.' "[2]

2. II Corinthians 7:16. The register the man in gray refers to is the one kept, according to Christian lore, by the Recording Angel.

Chapter 9

TWO BUSINESS MEN TRANSACT A LITTLE BUSINESS

—"Pray, sir, have you seen a gentleman with a weed hereabouts, rather a saddish gentleman? Strange where he can have gone to. I was talking with him not twenty minutes since."

By a brisk, ruddy-cheeked man in a tasseled traveling-cap, carrying under his arm a ledger-like volume, the above words were addressed to the collegian before introduced, suddenly accosted by the rail to which not long after his retreat, as in a previous chapter recounted, he had returned, and there remained.

"Have you seen him, sir?"

Rallied from his apparent diffidence by the genial jauntiness of the stranger, the youth answered with unwonted promptitude: "Yes, a person with a weed was here not very long ago."

"Saddish?"

"Yes, and a little cracked, too, I should say."

"It was he. Misfortune, I fear, has disturbed his brain. Now quick, which way did he go?"

"Why just in the direction from which you came, the gangway yonder."

"Did he? Then the man in the gray coat, whom I just met, said right: he must have gone ashore.[1] How unlucky!"

He stood vexedly twitching at his cap-tassel, which fell over by his whisker, and continued: "Well, I am very sorry. In fact, I had something for him here."—Then drawing nearer, "you see, he applied to me for relief, no, I do him injustice, not that, but he began to intimate, you understand. Well, being very busy just then, I declined; quite rudely, too, in a cold, morose, unfeeling way, I fear. At all events, not three minutes afterwards I felt self-reproach, with a kind of prompting, very peremptory, to deliver over into that unfortunate man's hands a ten-dollar bill. You smile. Yes, it may be superstition, but I can't help it; I have my weak side, thank God. Then again," he rapidly went on, "we have been so very prosperous lately in our affairs—by we, I mean the Black Rapids Coal Company—that, really, out of my abundance, associative and individual, it is but fair that a charitable investment or two should be made, don't you think so?"

"Sir," said the collegian without the least embarrassment, "do I understand that you are officially connected with the Black Rapids Coal Company?"

1. In this involved byplay, the Confidence Man in his fifth disguise cites himself in his fourth disguise about the whereabouts of himself in his third disguise.

"Yes, I happen to be president and transfer-agent."

"You are?"

"Yes, but what is it to you? You don't want to invest?"

"Why, do you sell the stock?"

"Some might be bought, perhaps; but why do you ask? you don't want to invest?"

"But supposing I did," with cool self-collectedness, "could you do up the thing for me, and here?"

"Bless my soul," gazing at him in amaze, "really, you are quite a business man. Positively, I feel afraid of you."

"Oh, no need of that.—You could sell me some of that stock, then?"

"I don't know, I don't know. To be sure, there are a few shares under peculiar circumstances bought in by the Company; but it would hardly be the thing to convert this boat into the Company's office.[2] I think you had better defer investing. So," with an indifferent air, "you have seen the unfortunate man I spoke of?"

"Let the unfortunate man go his ways.—What is that large book you have with you?"

"My transfer-book. I am subpœnaed with it to court."[3]

"Black Rapids Coal Company," obliquely reading the gilt inscription on the back; "I have heard much of it. Pray do you happen to have with you any statement of the condition of your company?"

"A statement has lately been printed."

"Pardon me, but I am naturally inquisitive. Have you a copy with you?"

"I tell you again, I do not think that it would be suitable to convert this boat into the Company's office.—That unfortunate man, did you relieve him at all?"

"Let the unfortunate man relieve himself.—Hand me the statement."

"Well, you are such a business-man, I can hardly deny you. Here," handing a small, printed pamphlet.

The youth turned it over sagely.

"I hate a suspicious man," said the other, observing him; "but I must say I like to see a cautious one."

"I can gratify you there," languidly returning the pamphlet; "for, as I said before, I am naturally inquisitive; I am also circumspect. No appearances can deceive me. Your statement," he added, "tells a very fine story; but pray, was not your stock a little heavy a while ago? downward tendency? Sort of low spirits among holders on the subject of that stock?"

2. That is, to convert Earth into an office for transferring souls to Hell, as the Devil is dedicated to doing.
3. The court is God's, although the oc-casion is not necessarily the Last Judgment. See Job 1:6 for the casualness with which Satan comes among the sons of God.

"Yes, there was a depression. But how came it? who devised it? The 'bears,' sir. The depression of our stock was solely owing to the growling, the hypocritical growling, of the bears."

"How, hypocritical?"

"Why, the most monstrous of all hypocrites are these bears: hypocrites by inversion; hypocrites in the simulation of things dark instead of bright; souls that thrive, less upon depression, than the fiction of depression; professors of the wicked art of manufacturing depressions; spurious Jeremiahs; sham Heraclituses, who, the lugubrious day done, return, like sham Lazaruses among the beggars, to make merry over the gains got by their pretended sore heads— scoundrelly bears!"

"You are warm against these bears?"

"If I am, it is less from the remembrance of their stratagems as to our stock, than from the persuasion that these same destroyers of confidence, and gloomy philosophers of the stock-market, though false in themselves, are yet true types of most destroyers of confidence and gloomy philosophers, the world over. Fellows who, whether in stocks, politics, bread-stuffs, morals, metaphysics, religion—be it what it may—trump up their black panics in the naturally-quiet brightness, solely with a view to some sort of covert advantage. That corpse of calamity which the gloomy philosopher parades, is but his Good-Enough-Morgan."[4]

"I rather like that," knowingly drawled the youth. "I fancy these gloomy souls as little as the next one. Sitting on my sofa after a champagne dinner, smoking my plantation cigar, if a gloomy fellow come to me—what a bore!"[5]

"You tell him it's all stuff, don't you?"

"I tell him it ain't natural. I say to him, you are happy enough, and you know it; and everybody else is as happy as you, and you know that, too; and we shall all be happy after we are no more, and you know that, too; but no, still you must have your sulk."

"And do you know whence this sort of fellow gets his sulk? not from life; for he's often too much of a recluse, or else too young to have seen anything of it. No, he gets it from some of those old plays he sees on the stage, or some of those old books he finds up

4. An adequate substitute; "any device, scheme, etc., which can be used temporarily to influence voters" (*Dictionary of Americanisms*). William Morgan (1774?–1826?) disappeared from Canandaigua, New York, while under arrest for petty theft. "It was freely charged that Masons had murdered him in order to prevent the publication of the book he was believed to be writing on Masonic secrets" (*DAB*). A body found in the Niagara River was inconclusively identified as Morgan's, but there was a rival identification. In 1827 the anti-Masonic Thurlow Weed answered a jest of an attorney for the Masons by calling the body "a good-enough Morgan for us until you bring back the one you carried off." The press quickly improved this into the boast that the body was a "good-enough Morgan until after the election." See Weed's *Autobiography* (1883), I, p. 319.

5. The sophomore has borrowed his dislike of gloomy souls from the Confidence Man himself, in his third disguise, as the man with the weed.

in garrets. Ten to one, he has lugged home from auction a musty old Seneca, and sets about stuffing himself with that stale old hay; and, thereupon, thinks it looks wise and antique to be a croaker, thinks it's taking a stand 'way above his kind."

"Just so," assented the youth. "I've lived some, and seen a good many such ravens at second hand. By the way, strange how that man with the weed, you were inquiring for, seemed to take me for some soft sentimentalist, only because I kept quiet, and thought, because I had a copy of Tacitus with me, that I was reading him for his gloom, instead of his gossip. But I let him talk. And, indeed, by my manner humored him."

"You shouldn't have done that, now. Unfortunate man, you must have made quite a fool of him."

"His own fault if I did. But I like prosperous fellows, comfortable fellows; fellows that talk comfortably and prosperously, like you. Such fellows are generally honest. And, I say now, I happen to have a superfluity in my pocket, and I'll just—"

"—Act the part of a brother to that unfortunate man?"

"Let the unfortunate man be his own brother. What are you dragging him in for all the time? One would think you didn't care to register any transfers, or dispose of any stock—mind running on something else. I say I will invest."

"Stay, stay, here come some uproarious fellows—this way, this way."

And with off-handed politeness the man with the book escorted his companion into a private little haven removed from the brawling swells without.

Business transacted, the two came forth, and walked the deck.

"Now tell me, sir," said he with the book, "how comes it that a young gentleman like you, a sedate student at the first appearance, should dabble in stocks and that sort of thing?"

"There are certain sophomorean errors in the world," drawled the sophomore, deliberately adjusting his shirt-collar, "not the least of which is the popular notion touching the nature of the modern scholar, and the nature of the modern scholastic sedateness."

"So it seems, so it seems. Really, this is quite a new leaf in my experience."

"Experience, sir," originally observed the sophomore, "is the only teacher."

"Hence am I your pupil; for it's only when experience speaks, that I can endure to listen to speculation."

"My speculations, sir," dryly drawing himself up, "have been chiefly governed by the maxim of Lord Bacon; I speculate in those philosophies which come home to my business and bosom—pray, do you know of any other good stocks?"

"You wouldn't like to be concerned in the New Jerusalem, would you?"

"New Jerusalem?"

"Yes, the new and thriving city, so called, in northern Minnesota. It was originally founded by certain fugitive Mormons. Hence the name. It stands on the Mississippi. Here, here is the map," producing a roll. "There—there, you see are the public buildings— here the landing—there the park—yonder the botanic gardens— and this, this little dot here, is a perpetual fountain, you understand. You observe there are twenty asterisks. Those are for the lyceums. They have lignum-vitæ rostrums."[6]

"And are all these buildings now standing?"

"All standing—bona fide."

"These marginal squares here, are they the water-lots?"

"Water-lots in the city of New Jerusalem? All terra firma—you don't seem to care about investing, though?"

"Hardly think I should read my title clear, as the law students say," yawned the collegian.[7]

"Prudent—you are prudent. Don't know that you are wholly out, either. At any rate, I would rather have one of your shares of coal stock than two of this other. Still, considering that the first settlement was by two fugitives, who had swum over naked from the opposite shore—it's a surprising place. It is, *bona fide.*—But dear me, I must go. Oh, if by possibility you should come across that unfortunate man—"

"— In that case," with drawling impatience, "I will send for the steward, and have him and his misfortunes consigned overboard."

"Ha ha!—now were some gloomy philosopher here, some theological bear, forever taking occasion to growl down the stock of human nature (with ulterior views, d'ye see, to a fat benefice in the gift of the worshipers of Arimanius[8]), he would pronounce that the sign of a hardening heart and a softening brain. Yes, that would be his sinister construction. But it's nothing more than the oddity of a genial humor—genial but dry. Confess it. Good-bye."

6. For Hawthorne in "The Celestial Railroad" just one lyceum is enough to allow citizens to "acquire an omnigenous erudition without the trouble of even learning to read." What he and Melville are satirizing is an American characteristic now revealed in the popularity of condensed books, college outline series, recorded highlights of musical masterpieces, on-the-hour capsule news reports on radio, and late-night television talk shows. For both men, there are no fast, easy ways to moral, spiritual, intellectual, or aesthetic perfection—no celestial railroads.

7. The sophomore is unwittingly alluding not to the words of law students but to a hymn by Isaac Watts: "When I can read my title clear / To mansions in the skies, / I'll bid farewell to ev'ry fear, / And wipe my weeping eyes." See the Norton Critical Edition of *Moby-Dick*, Chapter 22, p. 94, for another reference to Watts.

8. The spelling "Ariamius" in the original is a mistake for Arimanius, "the evil principle in Zoroastrianism" (Foster). The joke is that the speaker himself is the primal evil principle.

Chapter 10

IN THE CABIN

Stools, settees, sofas, divans, ottomans; occupying them are clusters of men, old and young, wise and simple: in their hands are cards spotted with diamonds, spades, clubs, hearts; the favorite games are whist, cribbage, and brag. Lounging in arm-chairs or sauntering among the marble-topped tables, amused with the scene, are the comparatively few, who, instead of having hands in the games, for the most part keep their hands in their pockets. These may be the philosophes. But here and there, with a curious expression, one is reading a small sort of handbill of anonymous poetry, rather wordily entitled:—

"ODE

ON THE INTIMATIONS

OF

DISTRUST IN MAN,

UNWILLINGLY INFERRED FROM REPEATED REPULSES,

IN DISINTERESTED ENDEAVORS

TO PROCURE HIS

CONFIDENCE."[1]

On the floor are many copies, looking as if fluttered down from a balloon. The way they came there was this: A somewhat elderly person, in the quaker dress, had quietly passed through the cabin, and, much in the manner of those railway book-peddlers who precede their proffers of sale by a distribution of puffs, direct or indirect, of the volumes to follow, had, without speaking, handed about the odes, which, for the most part, after a cursory glance, had been disrespectfully tossed aside, as no doubt, the moonstruck production of some wandering rhapsodist.

In due time, book under arm, in trips the ruddy man with the traveling-cap, who, lightly moving to and fro, looks animatedly about him, with a yearning sort of gratulatory affinity and longing, expressive of the very soul of sociality; as much as to say, "Oh, boys, would that I were personally acquainted with each mother's son of you, since what a sweet world, to make sweet acquaintance in, is ours, my brothers; yea, and what dear, happy dogs are we all!"

1. A play on the title of Wordsworth's "Immortality" ode. In Melville's roughly chronological survey of several varieties of eighteenth- and nineteenth-century optimistic philosophies, it is somewhat surprising that the English Romantics are so lightly skipped over.

And just as if he had really warbled it forth, he makes fraternally up to one lounging stranger or another, exchanging with him some pleasant remark.

"Pray, what have you there?" he asked of one newly accosted, a little, dried-up man, who looked as if he never dined.

"A little ode, rather queer, too," was the reply, "of the same sort you see strewn on the floor here."

"I did not observe them. Let me see;" picking one up and looking it over. "Well now, this is pretty; plaintive, especially the opening:—

'Alas for man, he hath small sense
Of genial trust and confidence.'

—If it be so, alas for him, indeed. Runs off very smoothly, sir. Beautiful pathos. But do you think the sentiment just?"

"As to that," said the little dried-up man, "I think it a kind of queer thing altogether, and yet I am almost ashamed to add, it really has set me to thinking; yes and to feeling. Just now, somehow, I feel as it were trustful and genial. I don't know that ever I felt so much so before. I am naturally numb in my sensibilities; but this ode, in its way, works on my numbness not unlike a sermon, which, by lamenting over my lying dead in trespasses and sins, thereby stirs me up to be all alive in well-doing."

"Glad to hear it, and hope you will do well, as the doctors say. But who snowed the odes about here?"

"I cannot say; I have not been here long."

"Wasn't an angel, was it? Come, you say you feel genial, let us do as the rest, and have cards."

"Thank you, I never play cards."

"A bottle of wine?"

"Thank you, I never drink wine."

"Cigars?"

"Thank you, I never smoke cigars."

"Tell stories?"

"To speak truly, I hardly think I know one worth telling."

"Seems to me, then, this geniality you say you feel waked in you, is a water-power in a land without mills. Come, you had better take a genial hand at the cards. To begin, we will play for as small a sum as you please; just enough to make it interesting."

"Indeed, you must excuse me. Somehow I distrust cards."

"What, distrust cards? Genial cards? Then for once I join with our sad Philomel here:—

'Alas for man, he hath small sense
Of genial trust and confidence.'

Good-bye!"

Sauntering and chatting here and there, again, he with the book at length seems fatigued, looks round for a seat, and spying a partly-vacant settee drawn up against the side, drops down there; soon, like his chance neighbor, who happens to be the good merchant, becoming not a little interested in the scene more immediately before him; a party at whist; two cream-faced, giddy, unpolished youths, the one in a red cravat, the other in a green, opposed to two bland, grave, handsome, self-possessed men of middle age, decorously dressed in a sort of professional black, and apparently doctors of some eminence in the civil law.

By-and-by, after a preliminary scanning of the new comer next him the good merchant, sideways leaning over, whispers behind a crumpled copy of the Ode which he holds: "Sir, I don't like the looks of those two, do you?"[2]

"Hardly," was the whispered reply; "those colored cravats are not in the best taste, at least not to mine; but my taste is no rule for all."

"You mistake; I mean the other two, and I don't refer to dress, but countenance. I confess I am not familiar with such gentry any further than reading about them in the papers—but those two are—are sharpers, aint they?"

"Far be from us the captious and fault-finding spirit, my dear sir."

"Indeed, sir, I would not find fault; I am little given that way; but certainly, to say the least, these two youths can hardly be adepts, while the opposed couple may be even more."

"You would not hint that the colored cravats would be so bungling as to lose, and the dark cravats so dextrous as to cheat?—Sour imaginations, my dear sir. Dismiss them. To little purpose have you read the Ode you have there. Years and experience, I trust, have not sophisticated you. A fresh and liberal construction would teach us to regard those four players—indeed, this whole cabin-full of players—as playing at games in which every player plays fair, and not a player but shall win."

"Now, you hardly mean that; because games in which all may win, such games remain as yet in this world uninvented, I think."

"Come, come," luxuriously laying himself back, and casting a free glance upon the players, "fares all paid; digestion sound; care, toil, penury, grief, unknown; lounging on this sofa, with waistband relaxed, why not be cheerfully resigned to one's fate, nor peevishly pick holes in the blessed fate of the world?"

Upon this, the good merchant, after staring long and hard, and then rubbing his forehead, fell into meditation, at first uneasy, but at last composed, and in the end, once more addressed his compan-

2. Like Mark Winsome in Chapter 36, the good merchant recognizes lesser evil but not the Devil himself.

ion: "Well, I see it's good to out with one's private thoughts now and then. Somehow, I don't know why, a certain misty suspiciousness seems inseparable from most of one's private notions about some men and some things; but once out with these misty notions, and their mere contact with other men's soon dissipates, or, at least, modifies them."

"You think I have done you good, then? may be, I have. But don't thank me, don't thank me. If by words, casually delivered in the social hour, I do any good to right or left, it is but involuntary influence—locust-tree sweetening the herbage under it; no merit at all; mere wholesome accident, of a wholesome nature.—Don't you see?"

Another stare from the good merchant, and both were silent again.

Finding his book, hitherto resting on his lap, rather irksome there, the owner now places it edgewise on the settee, between himself and neighbor; in so doing, chancing to expose the lettering on the back—*"Black Rapids Coal Company"*—which the good merchant, scrupulously honorable, had much ado to avoid reading, so directly would it have fallen under his eye, had he not conscientiously averted it. On a sudden, as if just reminded of something, the stranger starts up, and moves away in his haste leaving his book; which the merchant observing, without delay takes it up, and, hurrying after, civilly returns it; in which act he could not avoid catching sight by an involuntary glance of part of the lettering.

"Thank you, thank you, my good sir," said the other, receiving the volume, and was resuming his retreat, when the merchant spoke: "Excuse me, but are you not in some way connected with the—the Coal Company I have heard of?"

"There is more than one Coal Company that may be heard of, my good sir," smiled the other, pausing with an expression of painful impatience, disinterestedly mastered.

"But you are connected with one in particular.—The 'Black Rapids,' are you not?"

"How did you find that out?"

"Well, sir, I have heard rather tempting information of your Company."

"Who is your informant, pray?" somewhat coldly.

"A—a person by the name of Ringman."

"Don't know him. But, doubtless, there are plenty who know our Company, whom our Company does not know; in the same way that one may know an individual, yet be unknown to him.— Known this Ringman long? Old friend, I suppose.—But pardon, I must leave you."

"Stay, sir, that—that stock."

"Stock?"

"Yes, it's a little irregular, perhaps, but—"

"Dear me, you don't think of doing any business with me, do you? In my official capacity I have not been authenticated to you. This transfer-book, now," holding it up so as to bring the lettering in sight, "how do you know that it may not be a bogus one? And I, being personally a stranger to you, how can you have confidence in me?"

"Because," knowingly smiled the good merchant, "if you were other than I have confidence that you are, hardly would you challenge distrust that way."

"But you have not examined my book."

"What need to, if already I believe that it is what it is lettered to be?"

"But you had better. It might suggest doubts."

"Doubts, may be, it might suggest, but not knowledge; for how, by examining the book, should I think I knew any more than I now think I do; since, if it be the true book, I think it so already; and since if it be otherwise, then I have never seen the true one,[3] and don't know what that ought to look like."

"Your logic I will not criticize, but your confidence I admire, and earnestly, too, jocose as was the method I took to draw it out. Enough, we will go to yonder table, and if there be any business which, either in my private or official capacity, I can help you do, pray command me."

Chapter 11

ONLY A PAGE OR SO

The transaction concluded, the two still remained seated, falling into familiar conversation, by degrees verging into that confidential sort of sympathetic silence, the last refinement and luxury of unaffected good feeling. A kind of social superstition, to suppose that to be truly friendly one must be saying friendly words all the time, any more than be doing friendly deeds continually. True friendliness, like true religion, being in a sort independent of works.[1]

At length, the good merchant, whose eyes were pensively resting upon the gay tables in the distance, broke the spell by saying that, from the spectacle before them, one would little divine what other

<hr />

3. The merchant is unaware of the cosmic implications, but Melville is contrasting the Bible, "the true book," with the "transfer-book" in which the Devil records his transactions in human souls.

1. Since Jesus declares that one can know his followers by their works ("by their fruits ye shall know them"—Matthew 7:20), this is blasphemy, however modest and muffled.

quarters of the boat might reveal. He cited the case, accidentally encountered but an hour or two previous, of a shrunken old miser, clad in shrunken old moleskin, stretched out, an invalid, on a bare plank in the emigrants' quarters, eagerly clinging to life and lucre, though the one was gasping for outlet, and about the other he was in torment lest death, or some other unprincipled cut-purse, should be the means of his losing it; by like feeble tenure holding lungs and pouch, and yet knowing and desiring nothing beyond them; for his mind, never raised above mould, was now all but mouldered away. To such a degree, indeed, that he had no trust in anything, not even in his parchment bonds, which, the better to preserve from the tooth of time, he had packed down and sealed up, like brandy peaches, in a tin case of spirits.

The worthy man proceeded at some length with these dispiriting particulars. Nor would his cheery companion wholly deny that there might be a point of view from which such a case of extreme want of confidence might, to the humane mind, present features not altogether welcome as wine and olives after dinner. Still, he was not without compensatory considerations, and, upon the whole, took his companion to task for evincing what, in a good-natured, round-about way, he hinted to be a somewhat jaundiced sentimentality. Nature, he added, in Shakespeare's words, had meal and bran; and, rightly regarded, the bran in its way was not to be condemned.[2]

The other was not disposed to question the justice of Shakespeare's thought, but would hardly admit the propriety of the application in this instance, much less of the comment. So, after some further temperate discussion of the pitiable miser, finding that they could not entirely harmonize, the merchant cited another case, that of the negro cripple. But his companion suggested whether the alleged hardships of that alleged unfortunate might not exist more in the pity of the observer than the experience of the observed. He knew nothing about the cripple, nor had seen him, but ventured to surmise that, could one but get at the real state of his heart, he would be found about as happy as most men, if not, in fact, full as happy as the speaker himself. He added that negroes were by nature a singularly cheerful race; no one ever heard of a native-born African Zimmermann or Torquemada;[3] that even from religion they dismissed all gloom; in their hilarious rituals they danced, so to speak, and, as it were, cut pigeon-wings. It was improbable, therefore, that a negro, however reduced to his stumps by fortune, could be ever thrown off the legs of a laughing philosophy.

2. *Cymbeline*, IV, ii, 26–27: "Cowards father cowards, and base things sire base; Nature hath meal, and bran; contempt, and grace." *Cymbeline* may have supplied the name of Melville's steamboat, since Imogen in her disguise calls herself Fidele.

3. Zimmermann (1728–1795) wrote *On Solitude*. Melville knew Torquemada (1420–1498) as a Spanish inquisitor general (*White-Jacket*, Chapter 70).

Foiled again, the good merchant would not desist, but ventured still a third case, that of the man with the weed, whose story, as narrated by himself, and confirmed and filled out by the testimony of a certain man in a gray coat, whom the merchant had afterwards met, he now proceeded to give; and that, without holding back those particulars disclosed by the second informant, but which delicacy had prevented the unfortunate man himself from touching upon.

But as the good merchant could, perhaps, do better justice to the man than the story, we shall venture to tell it in other words than his, though not to any other effect.

Chapter 12

STORY OF THE UNFORTUNATE MAN, FROM WHICH MAY BE GATHERED WHETHER OR NOT HE HAS BEEN JUSTLY SO ENTITLED

It appeared that the unfortunate man had had for a wife one of those natures, anomalously vicious, which would almost tempt a metaphysical lover of our species to doubt whether the human form be, in all cases, conclusive evidence of humanity, whether, sometimes, it may not be a kind of unpledged and indifferent tabernacle, and whether, once for all to crush the saying of Thrasea, (an unaccountable one, considering that he himself was so good a man) that "he who hates vice, hates humanity," it should not, in self-defense, be held for a reasonable maxim, that none but the good are human.

Goneril[1] was young, in person lithe and straight, too straight, indeed, for a woman, a complexion naturally rosy, and which would have been charmingly so, but for a certain hardness and bakedness, like that of the glazed colors on stone-ware. Her hair was of a deep, rich chestnut, but worn in close, short curls all round her head. Her Indian figure was not without its impairing effect on her bust, while her mouth would have been pretty but for a trace of moustache. Upon the whole, aided by the resources of the toilet, her appearance at distance was such, that some might have thought

1. Egbert S. Oliver (1945) showed that Goneril is based in part on Fanny Kemble Butler, the actress, who was Melville's neighbor in the Berkshires. Melville had read this passage (not cited by Oliver) in *Taghconic; or Letters and Legends about Our Summer Home* (Boston, 1852), p. 107: "It was not to be supposed that many of the graver people would look with much complacency on the *port* and demeanor of so singularly spirited a lady, much less on her man-like propensities to driving, hunting, and fishing, and less than all on her man-like attire, while engaged in them. There are many who did not know her, save as a splendid, imperious, passionate woman; they could not love her who knew not also how ardent and generous a nature was hers." The chapter is more a fantasy suggested by Mrs. Butler (and by Shakespeare's Goneril, the daughter of King Lear) than a savage personal caricature of her.

her, if anything, rather beautiful, though of a style of beauty rather peculiar and cactus-like.

It was happy for Goneril that her more striking peculiarities were less of the person than of temper and taste. One hardly knows how to reveal, that, while having a natural antipathy to such things as the breast of chicken, or custard, or peach, or grape, Goneril could yet in private make a satisfactory lunch on hard crackers and brawn of ham. She liked lemons, and the only kind of candy she loved were little dried sticks of blue clay, secretly carried in her pocket. Withal she had hard, steady health like a squaw's, with as firm a spirit and resolution. Some other points about her were likewise such as pertain to the women of savage life. Lithe though she was, she loved supineness, but upon occasion could endure like a stoic. She was taciturn, too. From early morning till about three o'clock in the afternoon she would seldom speak—it taking that time to thaw her, by all accounts, into but talking terms with humanity. During the interval she did little but look, and keep looking out of her large, metallic eyes, which her enemies called cold as a cuttle-fish's, but which by her were esteemed gazelle-like; for Goneril was not without vanity. Those who thought they best knew her, often wondered what happiness such a being could take in life, not considering the happiness which is to be had by some natures in the very easy way of simply causing pain to those around them. Those who suffered from Goneril's strange nature, might, with one of those hyperboles to which the resentful incline, have pronounced her some kind of toad; but her worst slanderers could never, with any show of justice, have accused her of being a toady. In a large sense she possessed the virtue of independence of mind. Goneril held it flattery to hint praise even of the absent, and even if merited; but honesty, to fling people's imputed faults into their faces. This was thought malice, but it certainly was not passion. Passion is human. Like an icicle-dagger, Goneril at once stabbed and froze; so at least they said; and when she saw frankness and innocence tyrannized into sad nervousness under her spell, according to the same authority, inly she chewed her blue clay, and you could mark that she chuckled. These peculiarities were strange and unpleasing; but another was alleged, one really incomprehensible. In company she had a strange way of touching, as by accident, the arm or hand of comely young men, and seemed to reap a secret delight from it, but whether from the humane satisfaction of having given the evil-touch, as it is called, or whether it was something else in her, not equally wonderful, but quite as deplorable, remained an enigma.

Needless to say what distress was the unfortunate man's, when, engaged in conversation with company, he would suddenly perceive his Goneril bestowing her mysterious touches, especially in such cases where the strangeness of the thing seemed to strike upon the touched person, notwithstanding good-breeding forbade his proposing the mystery, on the spot, as a subject of discussion for the company. In these cases, too, the unfortunate man could never endure so much as to look upon the touched young gentleman afterwards, fearful of the mortification of meeting in his countenance some kind of more or less quizzingly-knowing expression. He would shudderingly shun the young gentleman. So that here, to the husband, Goneril's touch had the dread operation of the heathen taboo. Now Goneril brooked no chiding. So, at favorable times, he, in a wary manner, and not indelicately, would venture in private interviews gently to make distant allusions to this questionable propensity. She divined him. But, in her cold loveless way, said it was witless to be telling one's dreams, especially foolish ones; but if the unfortunate man liked connubially to rejoice his soul with such chimeras, much connubial joy might they give him. All this was sad—a touching case—but all might, perhaps, have been borne by the unfortunate man—conscientiously mindful of his vow—for better or for worse—to love and cherish his dear Goneril so long as kind heaven might spare her to him—but when, after all that had happened, the devil of jealousy entered her, a calm, clayey, cakey devil, for none other could possess her, and the object of that deranged jealousy, her own child, a little girl of seven, her father's consolation and pet; when he saw Goneril artfully torment the little innocent, and then play the maternal hypocrite with it, the unfortunate man's patient long-suffering gave way. Knowing that she would neither confess nor amend, and might, possibly, become even worse than she was, he thought it but duty as a father, to withdraw the child from her; but, loving it as he did, he could not do so without accompanying it into domestic exile himself. Which, hard though it was, he did. Whereupon the whole female neighborhood, who till now had little enough admired dame Goneril, broke out in indignation against a husband, who, without assigning a cause, could deliberately abandon the wife of his bosom, and sharpen the sting to her, too, by depriving her of the solace of retaining her offspring. To all this, self-respect, with Christian charity towards Goneril, long kept the unfortunate man dumb. And well had it been had he continued so; for when, driven to desperation, he hinted something of the truth of the case, not a soul would credit it; while for Goneril, she pronounced all he said to be a malicious invention. Ere long, at the suggestion of some woman's-rights women, the injured wife began a suit, and, thanks to able counsel and accommodating testimony, succeeded in such a way, as not only to recover custody of the child, but to get such a settlement awarded upon a separation, as to make penniless the unfortunate man (so he averred), besides, through the legal sympathy she enlisted, effecting a judicial blasting of his private reputation. What made it yet more lamentable was, that the unfortunate man, thinking that, before the court, his wisest plan, as well as the most Christian besides, being, as he deemed, not at variance with the truth of the matter, would be to put forth the plea of the mental derangement of Goneril, which done, he could, with less of mortification to himself, and odium to her, reveal in self-defense those eccentricities which had led to his retirement from the joys of wedlock, had much ado in the end to prevent this charge of derangement from fatally recoiling upon himself—especially, when, among other things, he alleged her mysterious touchings. In vain did his counsel, striving to make out the derangement to be where, in fact, if anywhere, it was, urge that, to hold otherwise, to hold that such a being as Goneril was sane, this was constructively a libel upon womankind. Libel be it. And all ended by the unfortunate man's subsequently getting wind of Goneril's intention to procure him to be permanently committed for a lunatic. Upon which he fled, and was now an innocent outcast, wandering forlorn in the great valley of the Mississippi, with a weed on his hat for the loss of his Goneril; for he had lately seen by the papers that she was dead, and thought it but proper to comply with the prescribed form of mourning in such cases. For some days past he had been trying to get money enough to return to his child, and was but now started with inadequate funds.

Now all of this, from the beginning, the good merchant could not but consider rather hard for the unfortunate man.

Chapter 13

THE MAN WITH THE TRAVELING-CAP EVINCES MUCH HUMANITY, AND IN A WAY WHICH WOULD SEEM TO SHOW HIM TO BE ONE OF THE MOST LOGICAL OF OPTIMISTS[1]

Years ago, a grave American savan, being in London, observed at an evening party there, a certain coxcombical fellow, as he thought,

1. More than any other chapter, this illustrates Melville's consummate skill in sustaining an indirect, bland, infinitely unassertive style that allows him to blaspheme with impunity in mid-nineteenth-century America. The chapter is also the culmination of Melville's jokes which depend on the fact that the Devil appears in many disguises. The story about the man with the weed and Goneril (made up by the man with the weed and substantiated and elaborated by the man in gray) is told (though not in the words used in Chapter 12) by Mr. Roberts to the man with the book (Truman) in order to convince him of the occasional existence of hardship in the world. The joke is capped when the man with the book—who originated the story in an earlier disguise—mildly doubts that the "alleged experience" happened, at least as told by Mr. Roberts.

an absurd ribbon in his lapel, and full of smart persiflage, whisking about to the admiration of as many as were disposed to admire. Great was the savan's disdain; but, chancing ere long to find himself in a corner with the jackanapes, got into conversation with him, when he was somewhat ill-prepared for the good sense of the jackanapes, but was altogether thrown aback, upon subsequently being whispered by a friend that the jackanapes was almost as great a savan as himself, being no less a personage than Sir Humphrey Davy.

The above anecdote is given just here by way of an anticipative reminder to such readers as, from the kind of jaunty levity, or what may have passed for such, hitherto for the most part appearing in the man with the traveling-cap, may have been tempted into a more or less hasty estimate of him; that such readers, when they find the same person, as they presently will, capable of philosophic and humanitarian discourse—no mere casual sentence or two as heretofore at times, but solidly sustained throughout an almost entire sitting; that they may not, like the American savan, be thereupon betrayed into any surprise incompatible with their own good opinion of their previous penetration.

The merchant's narration being ended, the other would not deny but that it did in some degree affect him. He hoped he was not without proper feeling for the unfortunate man. But he begged to know in what spirit he bore his alleged calamities. Did he despond or have confidence?

The merchant did not, perhaps, take the exact import of the last member of the question; but answered, that, if whether the unfortunate man was becomingly resigned under his affliction or no, was the point, he could say for him that resigned he was, and to an exemplary degree: for not only, so far as known, did he refrain from any one-sided reflections upon human goodness and human justice, but there was observable in him an air of chastened reliance, and at times tempered cheerfulness.

Upon which the other observed, that since the unfortunate man's alleged experience could not be deemed very conciliatory towards a view of human nature better than human nature was, it largely redounded to his fair-mindedness, as well as piety, that under the alleged dissuasives, apparently so, from philanthropy, he had not, in a moment of excitement, been warped over to the ranks of the misanthropes. He doubted not, also, that with such a man his experience would, in the end, act by a complete and beneficent inversion, and so far from shaking his confidence in his kind, confirm it, and rivet it. Which would the more surely be the case, did he (the unfortunate man) at last become satisfied (as sooner or later he probably would be) that in the distraction of his mind his Goneril had not in all respects had fair play. At all events, the description of the lady, charity could not but regard as more or less exaggerated, and so far unjust. The truth probably was that she was a wife with some blemishes mixed with some beauties. But when the blemishes were displayed, her husband, no adept in the female nature, had tried to use reason with her, instead of something far more persuasive. Hence his failure to convince and convert. The act of withdrawing from her, seemed, under the circumstances, abrupt. In brief, there were probably small faults on both sides, more than balanced by large virtues; and one should not be hasty in judging.

When the merchant, strange to say, opposed views so calm and impartial, and again, with some warmth, deplored the case of the unfortunate man, his companion, not without seriousness, checked him, saying, that this would never do; that, though but in the most exceptional case, to admit the existence of unmerited misery, more particularly if alleged to have been brought about by unhindered arts of the wicked, such an admission was, to say the least, not prudent; since, with some, it might unfavorably bias their most important persuasions. Not that those persuasions were legitimately servile to such influences. Because, since the common occurrences of life could never, in the nature of things, steadily look one way and tell one story, as flags in the trade-wind; hence, if the conviction of a Providence, for instance, were in any way made dependent upon such variabilities as everyday events, the degree of that conviction would, in thinking minds, be subject to fluctuations akin to those of the stock-exchange during a long and uncertain war. Here he glanced aside at his transfer-book, and after a moment's pause continued. It was of the essence of a right conviction of the divine nature, as with a right conviction of the human, that, based less on experience than intuition, it rose above the zones of weather.

When now the merchant, with all his heart, coincided with this (as being a sensible, as well as religious person, he could not but do), his companion expressed satisfaction, that, in an age of some distrust on such subjects, he could yet meet with one who shared with him, almost to the full, so sound and sublime a confidence.

Still, he was far from the illiberality of denying that philosophy duly bounded was permissible. Only he deemed it at least desirable that, when such a case as that alleged of the unfortunate man was made the subject of philosophic discussion, it should be so philosophized upon, as not to afford handles to those unblessed with the true light. For, but to grant that there was so much as a mystery about such a case, might by those persons be held for a tacit surrender of the question. And as for the apparent license temporarily permitted sometimes, to the bad over the good (as was by implication alleged with regard to Goneril and the unfortunate man), it might be injudicious there to lay too much polemic stress upon the doctrine of future retribution as the vindication of present impunity. For though, indeed, to the right-minded that doctrine was true, and of sufficient solace, yet with the perverse the polemic mention of it might but provoke the shallow, though mischievous conceit, that such a doctrine was but tantamount to the one which should affirm that Providence was not now, but was going to be. In short, with all sorts of cavilers, it was best, both for them and everybody, that whoever had the true light should stick behind the secure Malakoff[2] of confidence, nor be tempted forth to hazardous skirmishes on the open ground of reason. Therefore, he deemed it unadvisable in the good man, even in the privacy of his own mind, or in communion with a congenial one, to indulge in too much latitude of philosophizing, or, indeed, of compassionating, since this might beget an indiscreet habit of thinking and feeling which might unexpectedly betray him upon unsuitable occasions. Indeed, whether in private or public, there was nothing which a good man was more bound to guard himself against than, on some topics, the emotional unreserve of his natural heart; for, that the natural heart, in certain points, was not what it might be, men had been authoritatively admonished.

But he thought he might be getting dry.

The merchant, in his good-nature, thought otherwise, and said that he would be glad to refresh himself with such fruit all day. It was sitting under a ripe pulpit, and better such a seat than under a ripe peach-tree.

The other was pleased to find that he had not, as he feared, been prosing; but would rather not be considered in the formal light of a preacher; he preferred being still received in that of the equal and genial companion. To which end, throwing still more of sociability into his manner, he again reverted to the unfortunate man. Take the very worst view of that case; admit that his Goneril was, indeed, a Goneril; how fortunate to be at last rid of this Goneril, both by nature and by law! If he were acquainted with the unfortunate man, instead of condoling with him, he would congratulate him. Great good fortune had this unfortunate man. Lucky dog, he dared say, after all.

To which the merchant replied, that he earnestly hoped it might

---

2. A fort defended by the Russians in the Crimean War. The reference helps to date the composition of this passage, since Malakoff fell to the French on September 8, 1855. "The *Berkshire County Eagle* carried news of the siege of 'impregnable Malakoff' throughout the summer of 1855, and did not announce its fall until October 5, 1855" (Foster). The involuted irony of this section is such that the reference need not have been written before the fall of Malakoff.

be so, and at any rate he tried his best to comfort himself with the
persuasion that, if the unfortunate man was not happy in this
world, he would, at least, be so in another.

His companion made no question of the unfortunate man's happiness in both worlds; and, presently calling for some champagne,
invited the merchant to partake, upon the playful plea that, whatever notions other than felicitous ones he might associate with the
unfortunate man, a little champagne would readily bubble away.

At intervals they slowly quaffed several glasses in silence and
thoughtfulness. At last the merchant's expressive face flushed, his
eye moistly beamed, his lips trembled with an imaginative and fem-
inine sensibility. Without sending a single fume to his head, the
wine seemed to shoot to his heart, and begin soothsaying there.
"Ah," he cried, pushing his glass from him, "Ah, wine is good, and
confidence is good; but can wine or confidence percolate down
through all the stony strata of hard considerations, and drop
warmly and ruddily into the cold cave of truth? Truth will *not* be
comforted. Led by dear charity, lured by sweet hope, fond fancy
essays this feat; but in vain; mere dreams and ideals, they explode
in your hand, leaving naught but the scorching behind!"

"Why, why, why!" in amaze, at the burst; "bless me, if *In vino
veritas* be a true saying, then, for all the fine confidence you professed with me, just now, distrust, deep distrust, underlies it; and
ten thousand strong, like the Irish Rebellion, breaks out in you
now. That wine, good wine, should do it! Upon my soul," half seriously, half humorously, securing the bottle, "you shall drink no
more of it. Wine was meant to gladden the heart, not grieve it;
to heighten confidence, not depress it."

Sobered, shamed, all but confounded, by this raillery, the most
telling rebuke under such circumstances, the merchant stared about
him, and then, with altered mien, stammeringly confessed, that he
was almost as much surprised as his companion, at what had
escaped him. He did not understand it; was quite at a loss to
account for such a rhapsody popping out of him unbidden. It could
hardly be the champagne; he felt his brain unaffected; in fact, if
anything, the wine had acted upon it something like white of egg
in coffee, clarifying and brightening.

"Brightening? brightening it may be, but less like the white of
egg in coffee, than like stove-lustre on a stove—black, brightening.
Seriously, I repent calling for the champagne. To a temperament
like yours, champagne is not to be recommended. Pray, my dear sir,
do you feel quite yourself again? Confidence restored?"

"I hope so; I think I may say it is so. But we have had a long
talk, and I think I must retire now."

So saying, the merchant rose, and making his adieus, left the table with the air of one, mortified at having been tempted by his own honest goodness, accidentally stimulated into making mad disclosures—to himself as to another—of the queer, unaccountable caprices of his natural heart.

Chapter 14

WORTH THE CONSIDERATION OF THOSE TO WHOM
IT MAY PROVE WORTH CONSIDERING

As the last chapter was begun with a reminder looking forwards, so the present must consist of one glancing backwards.

To some, it may raise a degree of surprise that one so full of confidence, as the merchant has throughout shown himself, up to the moment of his late sudden impulsiveness, should, in that instance, have betrayed such a depth of discontent. He may be thought inconsistent, and even so he is. But for this, is the author to be blamed? True, it may be urged that there is nothing a writer of fiction should more carefully see to, as there is nothing a sensible reader will more carefully look for, than that, in the depiction of any character, its consistency should be preserved. But this, though at first blush, seeming reasonable enough, may, upon a closer view, prove not so much so. For how does it couple with another requirement—equally insisted upon, perhaps—that, while to all fiction is allowed some play of invention, yet, fiction based on fact should never be contradictory to it; and is it not a fact, that, in real life, a consistent character is a *rara avis*? Which being so, the distaste of readers to the contrary sort in books, can hardly arise from any sense of their untrueness. It may rather be from perplexity as to understanding them. But if the acutest sage be often at his wits' ends to understand living character, shall those who are not sages expect to run and read[1] character in those mere phantoms which flit along a page, like shadows along a wall? That fiction, where every character can, by reason of its consistency, be comprehended at a glance, either exhibits but sections of character, making them appear for wholes, or else is very untrue to reality; while, on the other hand, that author who draws a character, even though to common view incongruous in its parts, as the flying-squirrel, and, at different periods, as much at variance with itself as the caterpillar is with the butterfly into which it changes, may yet, in so doing, be not false but faithful to facts.

1. Habakkuk 2:2: "And the Lord answered me, and said, Write the vision, and make it plain upon tables, that he may run that readeth it."

If reason be judge, no writer has produced such inconsistent characters as nature herself has. It must call for no small sagacity in a reader unerringly to discriminate in a novel between the inconsistencies of conception and those of life. As elsewhere, experience is the only guide here; but as no one man can be coextensive with *what is*, it may be unwise in every case to rest upon it. When the duck-billed beaver of Australia was first brought stuffed to England, the naturalists, appealing to their classifications, maintained that there was, in reality, no such creature; the bill in the specimen must needs be, in some way, artificially stuck on.

But let nature, to the perplexity of the naturalists, produce her duck-billed beavers as she may, lesser authors, some may hold, have no business to be perplexing readers with duck-billed characters. Always, they should represent human nature not in obscurity, but transparency, which, indeed, is the practice with most novelists, and is, perhaps, in certain cases, someway felt to be a kind of honor rendered by them to their kind. But whether it involve honor or otherwise might be mooted, considering that, if these waters of human nature can be so readily seen through, it may be either that they are very pure or very shallow. Upon the whole, it might rather be thought, that he, who, in view of its inconsistencies, says of human nature the same that, in view of its contrasts, is said of the divine nature, that it is past finding out, thereby evinces a better appreciation of it than he who, by always representing it in a clear light, leaves it to be inferred that he clearly knows all about it.

But though there is a prejudice against inconsistent characters in books, yet the prejudice bears the other way, when what seemed at first their inconsistency, afterwards, by the skill of the writer, turns out to be their good keeping. The great masters excel in nothing so much as in this very particular. They challenge astonishment at the tangled web of some character, and then raise admiration still greater at their satisfactory unraveling of it; in this way throwing open, sometimes to the understanding even of school misses, the last complications of that spirit which is affirmed by its Creator to be fearfully and wonderfully made.[2]

At least, something like this is claimed for certain psychological novelists; nor will the claim be here disputed. Yet, as touching this point, it may prove suggestive, that all those sallies of ingenuity, having for their end the revelation of human nature on fixed principles, have, by the best judges, been excluded with contempt from the ranks of the sciences—palmistry, physiognomy, phrenology, psychology. Likewise, the fact, that in all ages such conflicting views have, by the most eminent minds, been taken of mankind, would, as with other topics, seem some presumption of a pretty

2. Psalms 139:14.

general and pretty thorough ignorance of it. Which may appear the
less improbable if it be considered that, after poring over the best
novels professing to portray human nature, the studious youth will
still run risk of being too often at fault upon actually entering the
world; whereas, had he been furnished with a true delineation, it
ought to fare with him something as with a stranger entering, map
in hand, Boston town; the streets may be very crooked, he may
often pause; but, thanks to his true map, he does not hopelessly
lose his way. Nor, to this comparison, can it be an adequate
objection, that the twistings of the town are always the same, and
those of human nature subject to variation. The grand points of
human nature are the same to-day they were a thousand years ago.
The only variability in them is in expression, not in feature.

But as, in spite of seeming discouragement, some mathemati-
cians are yet in hopes of hitting upon an exact method of determin-
ing the longitude, the more earnest psychologists may, in the face
of previous failures, still cherish expectations with regard to some
mode of infallibly discovering the heart of man.

But enough has been said by way of apology for whatever may
have seemed amiss or obscure in the character of the merchant; so
nothing remains but to turn to our comedy, or, rather, to pass from
the comedy of thought to that of action.

Chapter 15

AN OLD MISER, UPON SUITABLE REPRESENTATIONS,
IS PREVAILED UPON TO VENTURE AN INVESTMENT

The merchant having withdrawn, the other remained seated
alone for a time, with the air of one who, after having conversed
with some excellent man, carefully ponders what fell from him,
however intellectually inferior it may be, that none of the profit
may be lost; happy if from any honest word he has heard he can
derive some hint, which, besides confirming him in the theory of
virtue, may, likewise, serve for a finger-post to virtuous action.

Ere long his eye brightened, as if some such hint was now
caught. He rises, book in hand, quits the cabin, and enters upon a
sort of corridor, narrow and dim, a by-way to a retreat less ornate
and cheery than the former; in short, the emigrants' quarters; but
which, owing to the present trip being a down-river one, will doubtless be found comparatively tenantless. Owing to obstructions
against the side windows, the whole place is dim and dusky; very
much so, for the most part; yet, by starts, haggardly lit here and
there by narrow, capricious sky-lights in the cornices. But there

would seem no special need for light, the place being designed more to pass the night in, than the day; in brief, a pine barrens dormitory, of knotty pine bunks, without bedding. As with the nests in the geometrical towns of the associate penguin and pelican, these bunks were disposed with Philadelphian regularity, but, like the cradle of the oriole, they were pendulous, and, moreover, were, so to speak, three-story cradles; the description of one of which will suffice for all.

Four ropes, secured to the ceiling, passed downwards through auger-holes bored in the corners of three rough planks, which at equal distances rested on knots vertically tied in the ropes, the lowermost plank but an inch or two from the floor, the whole affair resembling, on a large scale, rope book-shelves; only, instead of hanging firmly against a wall, they swayed to and fro at the least suggestion of motion, but were more especially lively upon the provocation of a green emigrant sprawling into one, and trying to lay himself out there, when the cradling would be such as almost to toss him back whence he came. In consequence, one less inexperienced, essaying repose on the uppermost shelf, was liable to serious disturbance, should a raw beginner select a shelf beneath. Sometimes a throng of poor emigrants, coming at night in a sudden rain to occupy these oriole nests, would—through ignorance of their peculiarity—bring about such a rocking uproar of carpentry, joining to it such an uproar of exclamations, that it seemed as if some luckless ship, with all its crew, was being dashed to pieces among the rocks. They were beds devised by some sardonic foe of poor travelers, to deprive them of that tranquillity which should precede, as well as accompany, slumber. Procrustean beds, on whose hard grain humble worth and honesty writhed, still invoking repose, while but torment responded.[1] Ah, did any one make such a bunk for himself, instead of having it made for him, it might be just, but how cruel, to say, You must lie on it!

But, purgatory as the place would appear, the stranger advances into it; and, like Orpheus in his gay descent to Tartarus, lightly hums to himself an opera snatch.

Suddenly there is a rustling, then a creaking, one of the cradles swings out from a murky nook, a sort of wasted penguin-flipper is supplicatingly put forth, while a wail like that of Dives is heard:—"Water, water!"

It was the miser of whom the merchant had spoken.

Swift as a sister-of-charity, the stranger hovers over him:—

"My poor, poor sir, what can I do for you?"

"Ugh, ugh—water!"

Darting out, he procures a glass, returns, and holding it to the

1. Procrustes was the legendary Greek robber who made all his victims fit his bed by either stretching or cutting off their legs.

sufferer's lips, supports his head while he drinks: "And did they let you lie here, my poor sir, racked with this parching thirst?"

The miser, a lean old man, whose flesh seemed salted cod-fish, dry as combustibles; head, like one whittled by an idiot out of a knot; flat, bony mouth, nipped between buzzard nose and chin; expression, flitting between hunks and imbecile—now one, now the other—he made no response. His eyes were closed, his cheek lay upon an old white moleskin coat, rolled under his head, like a wizened apple upon a grimy snow-bank.

Revived at last, he inclined towards his ministrant, and, in a voice disastrous with a cough, said:—"I am old and miserable, a poor beggar, not worth a shoe-string—how can I repay you?"

"By giving me your confidence."

"Confidence!" he squeaked, with changed manner, while the pallet swung, "little left at my age, but take the stale remains, and welcome."

"Such as it is, though, you give it. Very good. Now give a hundred dollars."

Upon this the miser was all panic. His hands groped towards his waist, then suddenly flew upward beneath his moleskin pillow, and there lay clutching something out of sight. Meantime, to himself he incoherently mumbled:—"Confidence? Cant, gammon! Confidence? hum, bubble!—Confidence? fetch, gouge!—Hundred dollars?—hundred devils!"[2]

Half spent, he lay mute awhile, then feebly raising himself, in a voice for the moment made strong by the sarcasm, said, "A hundred dollars? rather high price to put on confidence. But don't you see I am a poor, old rat here, dying in the wainscot? You have served me; but, wretch that I am, I can but cough you my thanks,—ugh, ugh, ugh!"

This time his cough was so violent that its convulsions were imparted to the plank, which swung him about like a stone in a sling preparatory to its being hurled.

"Ugh, ugh, ugh!"

"What a shocking cough. I wish my friend, the herb-doctor, was here now; a box of his Omni-Balsamic Reinvigorator would do you good."

"Ugh, ugh, ugh!"

"I've a good mind to go find him. He's aboard somewhere. I saw his long, snuff-colored surtout. Trust me, his medicines are the best in the world."

2. The old miser is speaking the secret language of the underworld. Cant is the secret language or jargon of gipsies, thieves, and professional beggars; a gammon is the accomplice of a pick-pocket (*A Dictionary of the Underworld*); a bubble is a dupe, a person cheated (*A Dictionary of the Underworld*); to fetch is to steal (*OED*): and to gouge is to swindle.

"Ugh, ugh, ugh!"

"Oh, how sorry I am."

"No doubt of it," squeaked the other again, "but go, get your charity out on deck. There parade the pursy peacocks; they don't cough down here in desertion and darkness, like poor old me. Look how scaly a pauper I am, clove with this churchyard cough. Ugh, ugh, ugh!"

"Again, how sorry I feel, not only for your cough, but your poverty. Such a rare chance made unavailable. Did you have but the sum named, how I could invest it for you. Treble profits. But confidence—I fear that, even had you the precious cash, you would not have the more precious confidence I speak of."

"Ugh, ugh, ugh!" flightily raising himself. "What's that? How, how? Then you don't want the money for yourself?"

"My dear, *dear* sir, how could you impute to me such preposterous self-seeking? To solicit out of hand, for my private behoof, an hundred dollars from a perfect stranger? I am not mad, my dear sir."

"How, how?" still more bewildered, "do you, then, go about the world, gratis, seeking to invest people's money for them?"

"My humble profession, sir. I live not for myself; but the world will not have confidence in me, and yet confidence in me were great gain."[3]

"But, but," in a kind of vertigo, "what do—do you do—do with people's money? Ugh, ugh! How is the gain made?"

"To tell that would ruin me. That known, every one would be going into the business, and it would be overdone. A secret, a mystery—all I have to do with you is to receive your confidence, and all you have to do with me is, in due time, to receive it back, thrice paid in trebling profits."

"What, what?" imbecility in the ascendant once more; "but the vouchers, the vouchers," suddenly hunkish again.

"Honesty's best voucher is honesty's face."

"Can't see yours, though," peering through the obscurity.

From this last alternating flicker of rationality, the miser fell back, sputtering, into his previous gibberish, but it took now an arithmetical turn. Eyes closed, he lay muttering to himself—

"One hundred, one hundred—two hundred, two hundred—three hundred, three hundred."

He opened his eyes, feebly stared, and still more feebly said—

"It's a little dim here, ain't it? Ugh, ugh! But, as well as my poor old eyes can see, you look honest."

"I am glad to hear that."

3. A blasphemous melange. One close Biblical parallel is I Timothy 6:6: "But godliness with contentment is great gain."

"If—if, now, I should put"—trying to raise himself, but vainly, excitement having all but exhausted him—"if, if now, I should put, put—"

"No ifs. Downright confidence, or none. So help me heaven, I will have no half-confidences."

He said it with an indifferent and superior air, and seemed moving to go.

"Don't, don't leave me, friend; bear with me; age can't help some distrust; it can't, friend, it can't. Ugh, ugh, ugh! Oh, I am so old and miserable. I ought to have a guardeean. Tell me, if —"

"If? No more!"

"Stay! how soon—ugh, ugh!—would my money be trebled? How soon, friend?"

"You won't confide. Good-bye!"

"Stay, stay," falling back now like an infant, "I confide, I confide; help, friend, my distrust!"[4]

From an old buckskin pouch, tremulously dragged forth, ten hoarded eagles, tarnished into the appearance of ten old horn-buttons, were taken, and half-eagerly, half-reluctantly, offered.

"I know not whether I should accept this slack confidence," said the other coldly, receiving the gold, "but an eleventh-hour confidence, a sick-bed confidence, a distempered, death-bed confidence, after all. Give me the healthy confidence of healthy men, with their healthy wits about them. But let that pass. All right. Good-bye!"

"Nay, back, back—receipt, my receipt! Ugh, ugh, ugh! Who are you? What have I done? Where go you? My gold, my gold! Ugh, ugh, ugh!"

But, unluckily for this final flicker of reason, the stranger was now beyond ear-shot, nor was any one else within hearing of so feeble a call.

Chapter 16

A SICK MAN, AFTER SOME IMPATIENCE, IS INDUCED TO BECOME A PATIENT

The sky slides into blue, the bluffs into bloom; the rapid Mississippi expands; runs sparkling and gurgling, all over in eddies; one magnified wake of a seventy-four.[1] The sun comes out, a golden

---

4. A parody of Mark 9:24: "And straightway the father of the child cried out, and said with tears, Lord, I believe; help thou mine unbelief." The word "confide" as used here means "to trust," not "to tell secrets."

1. Despite the drinking already described, this is still the early morning of the first of April. Ante meridiem drinking was a custom among American travelers even in the nineteenth century.

huzzar, from his tent, flashing his helm on the world. All things, warmed in the landscape, leap. Speeds the dædal[2] boat as a dream.

But, withdrawn in a corner, wrapped about in a shawl, sits an unparticipating man, visited, but not warmed, by the sun—a plant whose hour seems over, while buds are blowing and seeds are astir. On a stool at his left sits a stranger in a snuff-colored surtout, the collar thrown back; his hand waving in persuasive gesture, his eye beaming with hope. But not easily may hope be awakened in one long tranced into hopelessness by a chronic complaint.

To some remark the sick man, by word or look, seemed to have just made an impatiently querulous answer, when, with a deprecatory air, the other resumed:

"Nay, think not I seek to cry up my treatment by crying down that of others. And yet, when one is confident he has truth on his side, and that it is not on the other, it is no very easy thing to be charitable; not that temper is the bar, but conscience; for charity would beget toleration, you know, which is a kind of implied permitting, and in effect a kind of countenancing; and that which is countenanced is so far furthered. But should untruth be furthered? Still, while for the world's good I refuse to further the cause of these mineral doctors, I would fain regard them, not as willful wrong-doers, but good Samaritans erring.[3] And is this—I put it to you, sir—is this the view of an arrogant rival and pretender?"

His physical power all dribbled and gone, the sick man replied not by voice or by gesture; but, with feeble dumb-show of his face, seemed to be saying, "Pray leave me; who was ever cured by talk?"

But the other, as if not unused to make allowances for such despondency, proceeded; and kindly, yet firmly:

"You tell me, that by advice of an eminent physiologist in Louisville, you took tincture of iron. For what? To restore your lost energy. And how? Why, in healthy subjects iron is naturally found in the blood, and iron in the bar is strong; ergo, iron is the source of animal invigoration. But you being deficient in vigor, it follows that the cause is deficiency of iron. Iron, then, must be put into you; and so your tincture. Now as to the theory here, I am mute. But in modesty assuming its truth, and then, as a plain man viewing that theory in practice, I would respectfully question your eminent physiologist: 'Sir,' I would say, 'though by natural processes, lifeless natures taken as nutriment become vitalized, yet is a lifeless nature, under any circumstances, capable of a living transmission, with all its qualities as a lifeless nature unchanged? If, sir, nothing can be incorporated with the living body but by assimilation, and if that implies the conversion of one thing to a different thing (as, in a lamp, oil is assimilated into flame), is it, in this view, likely, that

2. Cunningly fashioned, ingenious.　　3. See Luke 10:30–37.

by banqueting on fat, Calvin Edson will fatten?[4] That is, will what is fat on the board prove fat on the bones? If it will, then, sir, what is iron in the vial will prove iron in the vein.' Seems that conclusion too confident?"

But the sick man again turned his dumb-show look, as much as to say, "Pray leave me. Why, with painful words, hint the vanity of that which the pains of this body have too painfully proved?"

But the other, as if unobservant of that querulous look, went on: "But this notion, that science can play farmer to the flesh, making there what living soil it pleases, seems not so strange as that other conceit—that science is now-a-days so expert that, in consumptive cases, as yours, it can, by prescription of the inhalation of certain vapors, achieve the sublimest act of omnipotence, breathing into all but lifeless dust the breath of life. For did you not tell me, my poor sir, that by order of the great chemist in Baltimore, for three weeks you were never driven out without a respirator, and for a given time of every day sat bolstered up in a sort of gasometer, inspiring vapors generated by the burning of drugs? as if this concocted atmosphere of man were an antidote to the poison of God's natural air. Oh, who can wonder at that old reproach against science, that it is atheistical? And here is my prime reason for opposing these chemical practitioners, who have sought out so many inventions. For what do their inventions indicate, unless it be that kind and degree of pride in human skill, which seems scarce compatible with reverential dependence upon the power above? Try to rid my mind of it as I may, yet still these chemical practitioners with their tinctures, and fumes, and braziers, and occult incantations, seem to me like Pharaoh's vain sorcerers, trying to beat down the will of heaven.[5] Day and night, in all charity, I intercede for them, that heaven may not, in its own language, be provoked to anger with their inventions; may not take vengeance of their inventions. A thousand pities that you should ever have been in the hands of these Egyptians."

But again came nothing but the dumb-show look, as much as to say, "Pray leave me; quacks, and indignation against quacks, both are vain."

But, once more, the other went on: "How different we herb-doctors! who claim nothing, invent nothing; but staff in hand, in glades, and upon hillsides, go about in nature, humbly seeking her cures. True Indian doctors,[6] though not learned in names, we are not unfamiliar with essences—successors of Solomon the Wise,

4. A "living skeleton" displayed by P. T. Barnum at his American Museum in New York City.
5. Pharaoh's vain sorcerers are in Exo-
dus 7–9. See Psalms 106:29.
6. White men could be Indian doctors; one of the links between Indians and devils.

who knew all vegetables, from the cedar of Lebanon, to the hyssop on the wall.[7] Yes, Solomon was the first of herb-doctors. Nor were the virtues of herbs unhonored by yet older ages. Is it not writ, that on a moonlight night,

> 'Medea gathered the enchanted herbs
> That did renew old Æson?'[8]

Ah, would you but have confidence, you should be the new Æson, and I your Medea. A few vials of my Omni-Balsamic Reinvigorator would, I am certain, give you some strength."

Upon this, indignation and abhorrence seemed to work by their excess the effect promised of the balsam. Roused from that long apathy of impotence, the cadaverous man started, and, in a voice that was as the sound of obstructed air gurgling through a maze of broken honey-combs, cried: "Begone! You are all alike. The name of doctor, the dream of helper, condemns you. For years I have been but a gallipot for you experimentizers to rinse your experiments into, and now, in this livid skin, partake of the nature of my contents. Begone! I hate ye."

"I were inhuman, could I take affront at a want of confidence, born of too bitter an experience of betrayers. Yet, permit one who is not without feeling—"

"Begone! Just in that voice talked to me, not six months ago, the German doctor at the water cure, from which I now return, six months and sixty pangs nigher my grave."

"The water-cure? Oh, fatal delusion of the well-meaning Preissnitz!—Sir, trust me—"[9]

"Begone!"

"Nay, an invalid should not always have his own way. Ah, sir, reflect how untimely this distrust in one like you. How weak you are; and weakness, is it not the time for confidence? Yes, when through weakness everything bids despair, then is the time to get strength by confidence."[1]

Relenting in his air, the sick man cast upon him a long glance of beseeching, as if saying, "With confidence must come hope; and how can hope be?"

The herb-doctor took a sealed paper box from his surtout pocket, and holding it towards him, said solemnly, "Turn not away. This may be the last time of health's asking. Work upon yourself; invoke

7. I Kings 4:33.
8. *The Merchant of Venice*, V, i, 12–14.
9. "Vincenz Preissnitz (1799–1851), a Silesian, author of a book on hydrotherapy and operator of a hydrotherapeutic establishment" (Foster); Frank-

lin cites *Nature in Disease* (referred to below) for the fact that Preissnitz died "in the midst of his own water-cure." Water cures were a great fad in the 1840's and 1850's.
1. "In quietness and in confidence shall be your strength" (Isaiah 30:15).

confidence, though from ashes; rouse it; for your life, rouse it, and invoke it, I say."

The other trembled, was silent; and then, a little commanding himself, asked the ingredients of the medicine.

"Herbs."

"What herbs? And the nature of them? And the reason for giving them?"

"It cannot be made known."

"Then I will none of you."

Sedately observant of the juiceless, joyless form before him, the herb-doctor was mute a moment, then said:—"I give up."

"How?"

"You are sick, and a philosopher."

"No, no;—not the last."

"But, to demand the ingredient, with the reason for giving, is the mark of a philosopher; just as the consequence is the penalty of a fool. A sick philosopher is incurable."

"Why?"

"Because he has no confidence."

"How does that make him incurable?"

"Because either he spurns his powder, or, if he take it, it proves a blank cartridge, though the same given to a rustic in like extremity, would act like a charm. I am no materialist; but the mind so acts upon the body, that if the one have no confidence, neither has the other."

Again, the sick man appeared not unmoved. He seemed to be thinking what in candid truth could be said to all this. At length, "You talk of confidence. How comes it that when brought low himself, the herb-doctor, who was most confident to prescribe in other cases, proves least confident to prescribe in his own; having small confidence in himself for himself?"

"But he has confidence in the brother he calls in. And that he does so, is no reproach to him, since he knows that when the body is prostrated, the mind is not erect. Yes, in this hour the herb-doctor does distrust himself, but not his art."

The sick man's knowledge did not warrant him to gainsay this. But he seemed not grieved at it; glad to be confuted in a way tending towards his wish.

"Then you give me hope?" his sunken eye turned up.

"Hope is proportioned to confidence. How much confidence you give me, so much hope do I give you. For this," lifting the box, "if all depended upon this, I should rest. It is nature's own."

"Nature!"

"Why do you start?"

"I know not," with a sort of shudder, "but I have heard of a book entitled 'Nature in Disease.' "[2]

"A title I cannot approve; it is suspiciously scientific. 'Nature in Disease?' As if nature, divine nature, were aught but health; as if through nature disease is decreed! But did I not before hint of the tendency of science, that forbidden tree? Sir, if despondency is yours from recalling that title, dismiss it. Trust me, nature is health;[3] for health is good, and nature cannot work ill. As little can she work error. Get nature, and you get well. Now, I repeat, this medicine is nature's own."

Again the sick man could not, according to his light, conscientiously disprove what was said. Neither, as before, did he seem over-anxious to do so; the less, as in his sensitiveness it seemed to him, that hardly could he offer so to do without something like the appearance of a kind of implied irreligion; nor in his heart was he ungrateful, that since a spirit opposite to that pervaded all the herb-doctor's hopeful words, therefore, for hopefulness, he (the sick man) had not alone medical warrant, but also doctrinal.

"Then you do really think," hectically, "that if I take this medicine," mechanically reaching out for it, "I shall regain my health?"

"I will not encourage false hopes," relinquishing to him the box, "I will be frank with you. Though frankness is not always the weakness of the mineral practitioner, yet the herb doctor must be frank, or nothing. Now then, sir, in your case, a radical cure—such a cure, understand, as should make you robust—such a cure, sir, I do not and cannot promise."

"Oh, you need not! only restore me the power of being something else to others than a burdensome care, and to myself a droning grief. Only cure me of this misery of weakness; only make me so that I can walk about in the sun and not draw the flies to me, as lured by the coming of decay. Only do that—but that."

"You ask not much; you are wise; not in vain have you suffered. That little you ask, I think, can be granted. But remember, not in a day, nor a week, nor perhaps a month, but sooner or later; I say not exactly when, for I am neither prophet nor charlatan. Still, if, according to the directions in your box there, you take my medicine steadily, without assigning an especial day, near or remote, to discontinue it, then may you calmly look for some eventual result

2. "Jacob Bigelow, M.D., *Nature in Disease* (Boston, 1854), a collection of essays on various diseases and medical subjects including quackery, homeopathy, and the history of medicine. The title refers to a thesis in a number of the essays that some diseases cure themselves and should not be treated" (Franklin). On the same page as the review of *Pierre* in *Littell's Living Age* (September 4, 1852) was a review of an American edition of *God in Disease; or the Manifestation of Design in Morbid Phenomena*, by James F. Duncan, M.D.
3. A plausible statement of a pre-Romantic and Romantic doctrine.

of good. But again I say, you must have confidence."

Feverishly he replied that he now trusted he had, and hourly should pray for its increase. When suddenly relapsing into one of those strange caprices peculiar to some invalids, he added: "But to one like me, it is so hard, so hard. The most confident hopes so often have failed me, and as often have I vowed never, no, never, to trust them again. Oh," feebly wringing his hands, "you do not know, you do not know."

"I know this, that never did a right confidence come to naught. But time is short; you hold your cure, to retain or reject."

"I retain," with a clinch, "and now how much?"

"As much as you can evoke from your heart and heaven."

"How?—the price of this medicine?"

"I thought it was confidence you meant; how much confidence you should have. The medicine,—that is half a dollar a vial. Your box holds six."

The money was paid.

"Now, sir," said the herb-doctor, "my business calls me away, and it may so be that I shall never see you again; if then—"

He paused, for the sick man's countenance fell blank.

"Forgive me," cried the other, "forgive that imprudent phrase 'never see you again.' Though I solely intended it with reference to myself, yet I had forgotten what your sensitiveness might be. I repeat, then, that it may be that we shall not soon have a second interview, so that hereafter, should another of my boxes be needed, you may not be able to replace it except by purchase at the shops; and, in so doing, you may run more or less risk of taking some not salutary mixture. For such is the popularity of the Omni-Balsamic Reinvigorator—thriving not by the credulity of the simple, but the trust of the wise—that certain contrivers have not been idle, though I would not, indeed, hastily affirm of them that they are aware of the sad consequences to the public. Homicides and murderers, some call those contrivers; but I do not; for murder (if such a crime be possible) comes from the heart, and these men's motives come from the purse. Were they not in poverty, I think they would hardly do what they do. Still, the public interests forbid that I should let their needy device for a living succeed. In short, I have adopted precautions. Take the wrapper from any of my vials and hold it to the light, you will see water-marked in capitals the word '*confidence*,' which is the countersign of the medicine, as I wish it was of the world. The wrapper bears that mark or else the medicine is counterfeit. But if still any lurking doubt should remain, pray enclose the wrapper to this address," handing a card, "and by return mail I will answer."

At first the sick man listened, with the air of vivid interest, but gradually, while the other was still talking, another strange caprice came over him, and he presented the aspect of the most calamitous dejection.

"How now?" said the herb-doctor.

"You told me to have confidence, said that confidence was indispensable, and here you preach to me distrust. Ah, truth will out!"

"I told you, you must have confidence, unquestioning confidence, I meant confidence in the genuine medicine, and the genuine *me*."

"But in your absence, buying vials purporting to be yours, it seems I cannot have unquestioning confidence."

"Prove all the vials; trust those which are true."[4]

"But to doubt, to suspect, to prove—to have all this wearing work to be doing continually—how opposed to confidence. It is evil!"

"From evil comes good. Distrust is a stage to confidence. How has it proved in our interview? But your voice is husky; I have let you talk too much. You hold your cure; I leave you. But stay—when I hear that health is yours, I will not, like some I know, vainly make boasts; but, giving glory where all glory is due, say, with the devout herb-doctor, Japus in Virgil, when, in the unseen but efficacious presence of Venus, he with simples healed the wound of Æneas:—

'This is no mortal work, no cure of mine,
Nor art's effect, but done by power divine.' "

Chapter 17

TOWARDS THE END OF WHICH THE HERB-DOCTOR
PROVES HIMSELF A FORGIVER OF INJURIES

In a kind of ante-cabin, a number of respectable looking people, male and female, way-passengers, recently come on board, are listlessly sitting in a mutually shy sort of silence.

Holding up a small, square bottle, ovally labeled with the engraving of a countenance full of soft pity as that of the Romish-painted Madonna, the herb-doctor passes slowly among them, benignly urbane, turning this way and that, saying:—

"Ladies and gentlemen, I hold in my hand here the Samaritan Pain Dissuader, thrice-blessed discovery of that disinterested friend of humanity whose portrait you see. Pure vegetable extract. Warranted to remove the acutest pain within less than ten minutes.

4. "Prove all things; hold fast that   ("Prove" means "test.")
which is good" (I Thessalonians 5:21).

Five hundred dollars to be forfeited on failure. Especially efficacious in heart disease and tic-douloureux. Observe the expression of
this pledged friend of humanity.—Price only fifty cents."

In vain. After the first idle stare, his auditors—in pretty good
health, it seemed—instead of encouraging his politeness, appeared,
if anything, impatient of it; and, perhaps, only diffidence, or some
small regard for his feelings, prevented them from telling him so.
But, insensible to their coldness, or charitably overlooking it, he
more wooingly than ever resumed: "May I venture upon a small
supposition? Have I your kind leave, ladies and gentlemen?"

To which modest appeal, no one had the kindness to answer a
syllable.

"Well," said he, resignedly, "silence is at least not denial, and
may be consent. My supposition is this: possibly some lady, here
present, has a dear friend at home, a bed-ridden sufferer from
spinal complaint. If so, what gift more appropriate to that sufferer
than this tasteful little bottle of Pain Dissuader?"

Again he glanced about him, but met much the same reception
as before. Those faces, alien alike to sympathy or surprise, seemed
patiently to say, "We are travelers; and, as such, must expect to
meet, and quietly put up with, many antic fools, and more antic
quacks."

"Ladies and gentlemen," (deferentially fixing his eyes upon their
now self-complacent faces) "ladies and gentlemen, might I, by your
kind leave, venture upon one other small supposition? It is this: that
there is scarce a sufferer, this noonday, writhing on his bed, but in
his hour he sat satisfactorily healthy and happy; that the Samaritan
Pain Dissuader is the one only balm for that to which each living
creature—who knows?—may be a draughted victim, present or prospective. In short:—Oh, Happiness on my right hand, and oh, Security on my left, can ye wisely adore a Providence, and not think it
wisdom to provide?—Provide!" (Uplifting the bottle.)

What immediate effect, if any, this appeal might have had, is
uncertain. For just then the boat touched at a houseless landing,
scooped, as by a land-slide, out of sombre forests; back through
which led a road, the sole one, which from its narrowness, and its
being walled up with story on story of dusk, matted foliage, presented the vista of some cavernous old gorge in a city, like haunted
Cock Lane in London. Issuing from that road, and crossing that
landing, there stooped his shaggy form in the door-way, and
entered the ante-cabin, with a step so burdensome that shot seemed
in his pockets, a kind of invalid Titan in homespun; his beard
blackly pendant, like the Carolina-moss, and dank with cypress
dew; his countenance tawny and shadowy as an iron-ore country in
a clouded day. In one hand he carried a heavy walking-stick of
swamp-oak; with the other, led a puny girl, walking in moccasins,

not improbably his child, but evidently of alien maternity, perhaps Creole, or even Camanche.[1] Her eye would have been large for a woman, and was inky as the pools of falls among mountain-pines. An Indian blanket, orange-hued, and fringed with lead tassel-work, appeared that morning to have shielded the child from heavy showers. Her limbs were tremulous; she seemed a little Cassandra, in nervousness.

No sooner was the pair spied by the herb-doctor, than with a cheerful air, both arms extended like a host's, he advanced, and taking the child's reluctant hand, said, trippingly: "On your travels, ah, my little May Queen? Glad to see you. What pretty moccasins. Nice to dance in." Then with a half caper sang—

" 'Hey diddle, diddle, the cat and the fiddle;
The cow jumped over the moon.'

Come, chirrup, chirrup, my little robin!"

Which playful welcome drew no responsive playfulness from the child, nor appeared to gladden or conciliate the father; but rather, if anything, to dash the dead weight of his heavy-hearted expression with a smile hypochondriacally scornful.

Sobering down now, the herb-doctor addressed the stranger in a manly, business-like way—a transition which, though it might seem a little abrupt, did not appear constrained, and, indeed, served to show that his recent levity was less the habit of a frivolous nature, than the frolic condescension of a kindly heart.

"Excuse me," said he, "but, if I err not, I was speaking to you the other day;—on a Kentucky boat, wasn't it?"

"Never to me," was the reply; the voice deep and lonesome enough to have come from the bottom of an abandoned coal-shaft.

"Ah!—But am I again mistaken, (his eye falling on the swamp-oak stick,) or don't you go a little lame, sir?"

"Never was lame in my life."

"Indeed? I fancied I had perceived not a limp, but a hitch, a slight hitch;—some experience in these things—divined some hidden cause of the hitch—buried bullet, may be—some dragoons in the Mexican war discharged with such, you know.—Hard fate!" he sighed, "little pity for it, for who sees it?—have you dropped anything?"

Why, there is no telling, but the stranger was bowed over, and might have seemed bowing for the purpose of picking up something, were it not that, as arrested in the imperfect posture, he for the moment so remained; slanting his tall stature like a mainmast yielding to the gale, or Adam to the thunder.

The little child pulled him. With a kind of a surge he righted

1. The single violation of the Indian-Devil pattern, unless one assumes that any man so heroic as this invalid Titan has at some time mated with diabolic forces, and that this daughter is the consequence.

himself, for an instant looked toward the herb-doctor; but, either from emotion or aversion, or both together, withdrew his eyes, saying nothing. Presently, still stooping, he seated himself, drawing his child between his knees, his massy hands tremulous, and still averting his face, while up into the compassionate one of the herb-doctor the child turned a fixed, melancholy glance of repugnance.

The herb-doctor stood observant a moment, then said:

"Surely you have pain, strong pain, somewhere; in strong frames pain is strongest. Try, now, my specific," (holding it up). "Do but look at the expression of this friend of humanity. Trust me, certain cure for any pain in the world. Won't you look?"

"No," choked the other.

"Very good. Merry time to you, little May Queen."

And so, as if he would intrude his cure upon no one, moved pleasantly off, again crying his wares, nor now at last without result. A new-comer, not from the shore, but another part of the boat, a sickly young man, after some questions, purchased a bottle. Upon this, others of the company began a little to wake up as it were; the scales of indifference or prejudice fell from their eyes;[2] now, at last, they seemed to have an inkling that here was something not undesirable which might be had for the buying.

But while, ten times more briskly bland than ever, the herb-doctor was driving his benevolent trade, accompanying each sale with added praises of the thing traded, all at once the dusk giant, seated at some distance, unexpectedly raised his voice with—

"What was that you last said?"

The question was put distinctly, yet resonantly, as when a great clock-bell—stunning admonisher—strikes one; and the stroke, though single, comes bedded in the belfry clamor.

All proceedings were suspended. Hands held forth for the specific were withdrawn, while every eye turned towards the direction whence the question came. But, no way abashed, the herb-doctoi, elevating his voice with even more than wonted self-possession, replied—

"I was saying what, since you wish it, I cheerfully repeat, that the Samaritan Pain Dissuader, which I here hold in my hand, will either cure or ease any pain you please, within ten minutes after its application."

"Does it produce insensibility?"

"By no means. Not the least of its merits is, that it is not an opiate. It kills pain without killing feeling."

"You lie! Some pains cannot be eased but by producing insensibility, and cannot be cured but by producing death."

2. See Acts 9:18. What the herb-doctor hawks is a travesty of the Great Salve— Christian salvation.

Beyond this the dusk giant said nothing; neither, for impairing the other's market, did there appear much need to. After eying the rude speaker a moment with an expression of mingled admiration and consternation, the company silently exchanged glances of mutual sympathy under unwelcome conviction. Those who had purchased looked sheepish or ashamed; and a cynical-looking little man, with a thin flaggy beard, and a countenance ever wearing the rudiments of a grin, seated alone in a corner commanding a good view of the scene, held a rusty hat before his face.

But, again, the herb-doctor, without noticing the retort, over-bearing though it was, began his panegyrics anew, and in a tone more assured than before, going so far now as to say that his specific was sometimes almost as effective in cases of mental suffering as in cases of physical; or rather, to be more precise, in cases when, through sympathy, the two sorts of pain coöperated into a climax of both—in such cases, he said, the specific had done very well. He cited an example: Only three bottles, faithfully taken, cured a Louisiana widow (for three weeks sleepless in a darkened chamber) of neuralgic sorrow for the loss of husband and child, swept off in one night by the last epidemic. For the truth of this, a printed voucher was produced, duly signed.

While he was reading it aloud, a sudden side-blow all but felled him.

It was the giant, who, with a countenance lividly epileptic with hypochondriac mania, exclaimed—

"Profane fiddler on heart-strings! Snake!"

More he would have added, but, convulsed, could not; so, without another word, taking up the child, who had followed him, went with a rocking pace out of the cabin.

"Regardless of decency, and lost to humanity!" exclaimed the herb-doctor, with much ado recovering himself. Then, after a pause, during which he examined his bruise, not omitting to apply externally a little of his specific, and with some success, as it would seem, plained to himself:

"No, no, I don't seek redress; innocence is my redress. But," turning upon them all, "if that man's wrathful blow provokes me to no wrath, should his evil distrust arouse you to distrust? I do devoutly hope," proudly raising voice and arm, "for the honor of humanity—hope that, despite this coward assault, the Samaritan Pain Dissuader stands unshaken in the confidence of all who hear me!"

But, injured as he was, and patient under it, too, somehow his case excited as little compassion as his oratory now did enthusiasm. Still, pathetic to the last, he continued his appeals, notwithstanding the frigid regard of the company, till, suddenly interrupting himself, as if in reply to a quick summons from without, he said hurriedly, "I come, I come," and so, with every token of precipitate dispatch, out of the cabin the herb-doctor went.

Chapter 18

INQUEST INTO THE TRUE CHARACTER OF THE HERB-DOCTOR

"Sha'n't see that fellow again in a hurry," remarked an auburn-haired gentleman, to his neighbor with a hook-nose. "Never knew an operator so completely unmasked."

"But do you think it the fair thing to unmask an operator that way?"

"Fair? It is right."

"Supposing that at high 'change on the Paris Bourse, Asmodeus[1] should lounge in, distributing hand-bills, revealing the true thoughts and designs of all the operators present—would that be the fair thing in Asmodeus? Or, as Hamlet says, were it 'to consider the thing too curiously?' "

"We won't go into that. But since you admit the fellow to be a knave—"

"I don't admit it. Or, if I did, I take it back. Shouldn't wonder if, after all, he is no knave at all, or, but little of one. What can you prove against him?"

"I can prove that he makes dupes."

"Many held in honor do the same; and many, not wholly knaves, do it too."

"How about that last?"

"He is not wholly at heart a knave, I fancy, among whose dupes is himself. Did you not see our quack friend apply to himself his own quackery? A fanatic quack; essentially a fool, though effectively a knave."

Bending over, and looking down between his knees on the floor, the auburn-haired gentleman meditatively scribbled there awhile with his cane, then, glancing up, said:

"I can't conceive how you, in any way, can hold him a fool. How he talked—so glib, so pat, so well."

"A smart fool always talks well; takes a smart fool to be tonguey."

In much the same strain the discussion continued—the hook-

---

1. A "demon in *Le Diable Boiteux* by Alain René Le Sage (1668–1747), who lifts the roofs off houses to show his benefactor what is passing within" (Foster); also the name of the demon in Tobit (see the use of the Apocrypha in the last chapters of *The Confidence-Man*).

nosed gentleman talking at large and excellently, with a view of demonstrating that a smart fool always talks just so. Ere long he talked to such purpose as almost to convince.

Presently, back came the person of whom the auburn-haired gentleman had predicted that he would not return. Conspicuous in the door-way he stood, saying, in a clear voice, "Is the agent of the Seminole Widow and Orphan Asylum within here?"

No one replied.

"Is there within here any agent or any member of any charitable institution whatever?"

No one seemed competent to answer, or, no one thought it worth while to.

"If there be within here any such person, I have in my hand two dollars for him."

Some interest was manifested.

"I was called away so hurriedly, I forgot this part of my duty. With the proprietor of the Samaritan Pain Dissuader it is a rule, to devote, on the spot, to some benevolent purpose, the half of the proceeds of sales. Eight bottles were disposed of among this company. Hence, four half-dollars remain to charity. Who, as steward, takes the money?"

One or two pair of feet moved upon the floor, as with a sort of itching; but nobody rose.

"Does diffidence prevail over duty? If, I say, there be any gentleman, or any lady, either, here present, who is in any connection with any charitable institution whatever, let him or her come forward. He or she happening to have at hand no certificate of such connection, makes no difference. Not of a suspicious temper, thank God, I shall have confidence in whoever offers to take the money."

A demure-looking woman, in a dress rather tawdry and rumpled, here drew her veil well down and rose; but, marking every eye upon her, thought it advisable, upon the whole, to sit down again.

"Is it to be believed that, in this Christian company, there is no one charitable person? I mean, no one connected with any charity? Well, then, is there no object of charity here?"

Upon this, an unhappy-looking woman, in a sort of mourning, neat, but sadly worn, hid her face behind a meagre bundle, and was heard to sob. Meantime, as not seeing or hearing her, the herb-doctor again spoke, and this time not unpathetically:

"Are there none here who feel in need of help, and who, in accepting such help, would feel that they, in their time, have given or done more than may ever be given or done to them? Man or woman, is there none such here?"

The sobs of the woman were more audible, though she strove to repress them. While nearly every one's attention was bent upon her, a man of the appearance of a day-laborer, with a white bandage across his face, concealing the side of the nose, and who, for coolness' sake, had been sitting in his red-flannel shirt-sleeves, his coat thrown across one shoulder, the darned cuffs drooping behind—this man shufflingly rose, and, with a pace that seemed the lingering memento of the lock-step of convicts, went up for a duly-qualified claimant.

"Poor wounded huzzar!" sighed the herb-doctor, and dropping the money into the man's clam-shell of a hand turned and departed.

The recipient of the alms was about moving after, when the auburn-haired gentleman staid him: "Don't be frightened, you; but I want to see those coins. Yes, yes; good silver, good silver. There, take them again, and while you are about it, go bandage the rest of yourself behind something. D'ye hear? Consider yourself, wholly, the scar of a nose, and be off with yourself."

Being of a forgiving nature, or else from emotion not daring to trust his voice, the man silently, but not without some precipitancy, withdrew.

"Strange," said the auburn-haired gentleman, returning to his friend, "the money was good money."

"Aye, and where your fine knavery now? Knavery to devote the half of one's receipts to charity? He's a fool I say again."

"Others might call him an original genius."

"Yes, being original in his folly. Genius? His genius is a cracked pate, and, as this age goes, not much originality about that."

"May he not be knave, fool, and genius all together?"

"I beg pardon," here said a third person with a gossiping expression who had been listening, "but you are somewhat puzzled by this man, and well you may be."

"Do you know anything about him?" asked the hooked-nosed gentleman.

"No, but I suspect him for something."

"Suspicion. We want knowledge."

"Well, suspect first and know next. True knowledge comes but by suspicion or revelation. That's my maxim."

"And yet," said the auburn-haired gentleman, "since a wise man will keep even some certainties to himself, much more some suspicions, at least he will at all events so do till they ripen into knowledge."

"Do you hear that about the wise man?" said the hook-nosed gentleman, turning upon the new comer. "Now what is it you suspect of this fellow?"

"I shrewdly suspect him," was the eager response, "for one of those Jesuit emissaries prowling all over our country.[2] The better to accomplish their secret designs, they assume, at times, I am told, the most singular masques; sometimes, in appearance, the absurdest."

This, though indeed for some reason causing a droll smile upon the face of the hook-nosed gentleman, added a third angle to the discussion, which now became a sort of triangular duel, and ended, at last, with but a triangular result.

Chapter 19

A SOLDIER OF FORTUNE

"Mexico? Molino del Rey? Resaca de la Palma?"

"Resaca de la *Tombs!*"[1]

Leaving his reputation to take care of itself, since, as is not seldom the case, he knew nothing of its being in debate, the herb-doctor, wandering towards the forward part of the boat, had there espied a singular character in a grimy old regimental coat, a countenance at once grim and wizened, interwoven paralyzed legs, stiff as icicles, suspended between rude crutches, while the whole rigid body, like a ship's long barometer on gimbals, swung to and fro, mechanically faithful to the motion of the boat. Looking downward while he swung, the cripple seemed in a brown study.

As moved by the sight, and conjecturing that here was some battered hero from the Mexican battle-fields, the herb-doctor had sympathetically accosted him as above, and received the above rather dubious reply. As, with a half moody, half surly sort of air that reply was given, the cripple, by a voluntary jerk, nervously increased his swing (his custom when seized by emotion), so that one would have thought some squall had suddenly rolled the boat and with it the barometer.

"Tombs? my friend," exclaimed the herb-doctor in mild surprise. "You have not descended to the dead, have you? I had

2. "It is an ascertained fact, that Jesuits are prowling about all parts of the United States in every possible disguise, expressly to ascertain the most advantageous situations and modes to disseminate popery. A minister of the gospel from Ohio, has informed us, that he discovered one carrying on his devices in his congregation; and he says, that the western country swarms with them under the names of puppet show-men, dancing masters, music teachers, pedlars of images and ornaments, barrel organ players, and similar practitioners. . . . Beware of the Jesuits!" (*American Protestant Vindicator*, December 24, 1834). For this lurid quotation I am indebted to Michael Williams, S.J., and Donald F. Crosby, S.J. Among other things, Melville is satirizing the current paranoia of the ultra-American Know-Nothings.

1. The speaker is brusquely crediting his condition not to one glorious Mexican battlefield or another but to the jail cells in the Halls of Justice (the Tombs) in lower Manhattan.

imagined you a scarred campaigner, one of the noble children of war, for your dear country a glorious sufferer. But you are Lazarus, it seems."

"Yes, he who had sores."

"Ah, the *other* Lazarus.[2] But I never knew that either of them was in the army," glancing at the dilapidated regimentals.

"That will do now. Jokes enough."

"Friend," said the other reproachfully, "you think amiss. On principle, I greet unfortunates with some pleasant remark, the better to call off their thoughts from their troubles. The physician who is at once wise and humane seldom unreservedly sympathizes with his patient. But come, I am a herb-doctor, and also a natural bone-setter. I may be sanguine, but I think I can do something for you. You look up now. Give me your story. Ere I undertake a cure, I require a full account of the case."

"You can't help me," returned the cripple gruffly. "Go away."

"You seem sadly destitute of—"

"No I ain't destitute; to-day, at least, I can pay my way."

"The Natural Bone-setter is happy, indeed, to hear that. But you were premature. I was deploring your destitution, not of cash, but of confidence. You think the Natural Bone-setter can't help you. Well, suppose he can't, have you any objection to telling him your story? You, my friend, have, in a signal way, experienced adversity. Tell me, then, for my private good, how, without aid from the noble cripple, Epictetus,[3] you have arrived at his heroic sang-froid in misfortune."

At these words the cripple fixed upon the speaker the hard ironic eye of one toughened and defiant in misery, and, in the end, grinned upon him with his unshaven face like an ogre.

"Come, come, be sociable—be human, my friend. Don't make that face; it distresses me."

"I suppose," with a sneer, "you are the man I've long heard of—The Happy Man."

"Happy? my friend. Yes, at least I ought to be. My conscience is peaceful. I have confidence in everybody. I have confidence that, in my humble profession, I do some little good to the world. Yes, I think that, without presumption, I may venture to assent to the proposition that I am the Happy Man—the Happy Bone-setter."

"Then you shall hear my story. Many a month I have longed to get hold of the Happy Man, drill him, drop the powder, and leave him to explode at his leisure."

"What a demoniac unfortunate," exclaimed the herb-doctor

2. For the Lazarus who had sores see Luke 16:19–31, and for the other Lazarus see John 11–12.
3. "Epictetus of Hieropolis (c. 60–140) eminent Stoic philosopher, born a slave and lame from early youth, gave as a formula for the good life, 'Endure and renounce' " (Foster).

retreating. "Regular infernal machine!"

"Look ye," cried the other, stumping after him, and with his horny hand catching him by a horn button, "my name is Thomas Fry. Until my—"

—"Any relation to Mrs. Fry?" interrupted the other. "I still correspond with that excellent lady on the subject of prisons. Tell me, are you anyway connected with *my* Mrs. Fry?"[4]

"Blister Mrs. Fry! What do them sentimental souls know of prisons or any other black fact? I'll tell ye a story of prisons. Ha, ha!"

The herb-doctor shrank, and with reason, the laugh being strangely startling.

"Positively, my friend," said he, "you must stop that; I can't stand that; no more of that. I hope I have the milk of kindness, but your thunder will soon turn it."

"Hold, I haven't come to the milk-turning part yet. My name is Thomas Fry. Until my twenty-third year I went by the nickname of Happy Tom—happy—ha, ha! They called me Happy Tom, d'ye see? because I was so good-natured and laughing all the time, just as I am now—ha, ha!"

Upon this the herb-doctor would, perhaps, have run, but once more the hyæna clawed him. Presently, sobering down, he continued:

"Well, I was born in New York, and there I lived a steady, hard-working man, a cooper by trade. One evening I went to a political meeting in the Park[5]—for you must know, I was in those days a great patriot. As bad luck would have it, there was trouble near, between a gentleman who had been drinking wine, and a pavior[6] who was sober. The pavior chewed tobacco, and the gentleman said it was beastly in him, and pushed him, wanting to have his place. The pavior chewed on and pushed back. Well, the gentleman carried a sword-cane, and presently the pavior was down—skewered."

"How was that?"

"Why you see the pavior undertook something above his strength."

"The other must have been a Samson then. 'Strong as a pavior,' is a proverb."

"So it is, and the gentleman was in body a rather weakly man, but, for all that, I say again, the pavior undertook something above his strength."

"What are you talking about? He tried to maintain his rights, didn't he?"

---

4. Elizabeth Gurney Fry (1780–1845), English Quakeress and philanthropist, best known for her reform of conditions in Newgate and other prisons.
5. City Hall Park. Melville's brother Gansevoort had hours of imperialistic glory there in 1844, proclaiming a war cry for his party: "*Up, Democrats, and at them.*"
6. A street-paver.

"Yes; but, for all that, I say again, he undertook something above his strength."

"I don't understand you. But go on."

"Along with the gentleman, I, with other witnesses, was taken to the Tombs. There was an examination, and, to appear at the trial, the gentleman and witnesses all gave bail—I mean all but me."

"And why didn't you?"

"Couldn't get it."

"Steady, hard-working cooper like you; what was the reason you couldn't get bail?"

"Steady, hard-working cooper hadn't no friends. Well, souse I went into a wet cell, like a canal-boat splashing into the lock; locked up in pickle, d'ye see? against the time of the trial."

"But what had you done?"

"Why, I hadn't got any friends, I tell ye. A worse crime than murder, as ye'll see afore long."

"Murder? Did the wounded man die?"

"Died the third night."

"Then the gentleman's bail didn't help him. Imprisoned now, wasn't he?"

"Had too many friends. No, it was *I* that was imprisoned.—But I was going on: They let me walk about the corridor by day; but at night I must into lock. There the wet and the damp struck into my bones. They doctored me, but no use. When the trial came, I was boosted up and said my say."

"And what was that?"

"My say was that I saw the steel go in, and saw it sticking in."

"And that hung the gentleman."

"Hung him with a gold chain! His friends called a meeting in the Park, and presented him with a gold watch and chain upon his acquittal."

"Acquittal?"

"Didn't I say he had friends?"

There was a pause, broken at last by the herb-doctor's saying: "Well, there is a bright side to everything. If this speak prosaically for justice, it speaks romantically for friendship! But go on, my fine fellow."

"My say being said, they told me I might go. I said I could not without help. So the constables helped me, asking *where* would I go? I told them back to the 'Tombs.' I knew no other place. 'But where are your friends?' said they. 'I have none.' So they put me into a hand-barrow with an awning to it, and wheeled me down to the dock and on board a boat, and away to Blackwell's Island to the Corporation Hospital. There I got worse—got pretty much as you see me now. Couldn't cure me. After three years, I grew sick of lying in a grated iron bed alongside of groaning thieves and mould-ering burglars. They gave me five silver dollars, and these crutches, and I hobbled off. I had an only brother who went to Indiana, years ago. I begged about, to make up a sum to go to him; got to Indiana at last, and they directed me to his grave. It was on a great plain, in a log-church yard with a stump fence, the old gray roots sticking all ways like moose-antlers. The bier, set over the grave, it being the last dug, was of green hickory; bark on, and green twigs sprouting from it. Some one had planted a bunch of violets on the mound, but it was a poor soil (always choose the poorest soils for grave-yards), and they were all dried to tinder. I was going to sit and rest myself on the bier and think about my brother in heaven, but the bier broke down, the legs being only tacked on. So, after driving some hogs out of the yard that were rooting there, I came away, and, not to make too long a story of it, here I am, drifting down stream like any other bit of wreck."

The herb-doctor was silent for a time, buried in thought. At last, raising his head, he said: "I have considered your whole story, my friend, and strove to consider it in the light of a commentary on what I believe to be the system of things; but it so jars with all, is so incompatible with all, that you must pardon me, if I honestly tell you, I cannot believe it."

"That don't surprise me."

"How?"

"Hardly anybody believes my story, and so to most I tell a differ-ent one."

"How, again?"

"Wait here a bit and I'll show ye."

With that, taking off his rag of a cap, and arranging his tattered regimentals the best he could, off he went stumping among the passengers in an adjoining part of the deck, saying with a jovial kind of air: "Sir, a shilling for Happy Tom, who fought at Buena Vista. Lady, something for General Scott's soldier, crippled in both pins at glorious Contreras."

Now, it so chanced that, unbeknown to the cripple, a prim-looking stranger had overheard part of his story. Beholding him, then, on his present begging adventure, this person, turning to the herb-doctor, indignantly said: "Is it not too bad, sir, that yonder rascal should lie so?"

"Charity never faileth, my good sir," was the reply. "The vice of this unfortunate is pardonable. Consider, he lies not out of wanton-ness."

"Not out of wantonness. I never heard more wanton lies. In one breath to tell you what would appear to be his true story, and, in the next, away and falsify it."

"For all that, I repeat he lies not out of wantonness. A ripe philosopher, turned out of the great Sorbonne of hard times, he thinks that woes, when told to strangers for money, are best sugared. Though the inglorious lock-jaw of his knee-pans in a wet dungeon is a far more pitiable ill than to have been crippled at glorious Contreras, yet he is of opinion that this lighter and false ill shall attract, while the heavier and real one might repel."

"Nonsense: he belongs to the Devil's regiment;[7] and I have a great mind to expose him."

"Shame upon you. Dare to expose that poor unfortunate, and by heaven—don't you do it, sir."

Noting something in his manner, the other thought it more prudent to retire than retort. By-and-by, the cripple came back, and with glee, having reaped a pretty good harvest.

"There," he laughed, "you know now what sort of soldier I am."

"Aye, one that fights not the stupid Mexican, but a foe worthy your tactics—Fortune!"

"Hi, hi!" clamored the cripple, like a fellow in the pit of a sixpenny theatre, then said, "don't know much what you meant, but it went off well."

This over, his countenance capriciously put on a morose ogreness. To kindly questions he gave no kindly answers. Unhandsome notions were thrown out about "free Ameriky," as he sarcastically called his country. These seemed to disturb and pain the herbdoctor, who, after an interval of thoughtfulness, gravely addressed him in these words:

"You, my worthy friend, to my concern, have reflected upon the government under which you live and suffer. Where is your patriotism? Where your gratitude? True, the charitable may find something in your case, as you put it, partly to account for such reflections as coming from you. Still, be the facts how they may, your reflections are none the less unwarrantable. Grant, for the moment, that your experiences are as you give them; in which case I would admit that government might be thought to have more or less to do with what seems undesirable in them. But it is never to be forgotten that human government, being subordinate to the divine, must needs, therefore, in its degree, partake of the characteristics of the divine. That is, while in general efficacious to happiness, the world's law may yet, in some cases, have, to the eye of reason, an unequal operation, just as, in the same imperfect view, some inequalities may appear in the operations of heaven's law; nevertheless, to one who has a right confidence, final benignity is, in every instance, as sure with the one law as the other. I expound the point at some length, because these are the considerations, my poor

7. An unresolved critical problem is whether only the Devil is at large on the *Fidèle* or whether his legions are at hand.

fellow, which, weighed as they merit, will enable you to sustain with unimpaired trust the apparent calamities which are yours."

"What do you talk your hog-latin to me for?" cried the cripple, who, throughout the address, betrayed the most illiterate obduracy; and, with an incensed look, anew he swung himself.

Glancing another way till the spasm passed, the other continued: "Charity marvels not that you should be somewhat hard of conviction, my friend, since you, doubtless, believe yourself hardly dealt by; but forget not that those who are loved are chastened."[8]

"Mustn't chasten them too much, though, and too long, because their skin and heart get hard, and feel neither pain nor tickle."

"To mere reason, your case looks something piteous, I grant. But never despond; many things—the choicest—yet remain. You breathe this bounteous air, are warmed by this gracious sun, and, though poor and friendless, indeed, nor so agile as in your youth, yet, how sweet to roam, day by day, through the groves, plucking the bright mosses and flowers, till forlornness itself becomes a hilarity, and, in your innocent independence, you skip for joy."[9]

"Fine skipping with these 'ere horse-posts—ha ha!"

"Pardon; I forgot the crutches. My mind, figuring you after receiving the benefit of my art, overlooked you as you stand before me."

"Your art? You call yourself a bone-setter—a natural bone-setter, do ye? Go, bone-set the crooked world, and then come bone-set crooked me."

"Truly, my honest friend, I thank you for again recalling me to my original object. Let me examine you," bending down; "ah, I see, I see; much such a case as the negro's. Did you see him? Oh no, you came aboard since. Well, his case was a little something like yours. I prescribed for him, and I shouldn't wonder at all if, in a very short time, he were able to walk almost as well as myself. Now, have you no confidence in my art?"

"Ha, ha!"

The herb-doctor averted himself; but, the wild laugh dying away, resumed:

"I will not force confidence on you. Still, I would fain do the friendly thing by you. Here, take this box; just rub that liniment on the joints night and morning. Take it. Nothing to pay. God bless you. Good-bye."

"Stay," pausing in his swing, not untouched by so unexpected an

8. Hebrews 12:6 ("For whom the Lord loveth he chasteneth") is the closest Biblical text.
9. A not-unwarranted travesty of Romantic inanities. Compare James Russell Lowell's "To The Dandelion" (1848): "How like a prodigal doth nature seem, / When thou, for all thy gold, so common art! / Thou teachest me to deem / More sacredly of every human heart, / Since each reflects in joy its scanty gleam / Of heaven, and could some wondrous secret show, / Did we but pay the love we owe, / And with a child's undoubting wisdom look / On all these living pages of God's book."

act; "stay—thank'ee—but will this really do me good? Honor bright, now; will it? Don't deceive a poor fellow," with changed mien and glistening eye.

"Try it. Good-bye."

"Stay, stay! *Sure* it will do me good?"

"Possibly, possibly; no harm in trying. Good-bye."

"Stay, stay; give me three more boxes, and here's the money."

"My friend," returning towards him with a sadly pleased sort of air, "I rejoice in the birth of your confidence and hopefulness. Believe me that, like your crutches, confidence and hopefulness will long support a man when his own legs will not. Stick to confidence and hopefulness, then, since how mad for the cripple to throw his crutches away. You ask for three more boxes of my liniment. Luckily, I have just that number remaining. Here they are. I sell them at half-a-dollar apiece. But I shall take nothing from you. There; God bless you again; good-bye."

"Stay," in a convulsed voice, and rocking himself, "stay, stay! You have made a better man of me. You have borne with me like a good Christian, and talked to me like one, and all that is enough without making me a present of these boxes. Here is the money. I won't take nay. There, there; and may Almighty goodness go with you."

As the herb-doctor withdrew, the cripple gradually subsided from his hard rocking into a gentle oscillation. It expressed, perhaps, the soothed mood of his reverie.

Chapter 20

REAPPEARANCE OF ONE WHO MAY BE REMEMBERED

The herb-doctor had not moved far away, when, in advance of him, this spectacle met his eye. A dried-up old man, with the stature of a boy of twelve, was tottering about like one out of his mind, in rumpled clothes of old moleskin, showing recent contact with bedding, his ferret eyes, blinking in the sunlight of the snowy boat, as imbecilely eager, and, at intervals, coughing, he peered hither and thither as if in alarmed search for his nurse. He presented the aspect of one who, bed-rid, has, through overruling excitement, like that of a fire, been stimulated to his feet.

"You seek some one," said the herb-doctor, accosting him. "Can I assist you?"

"Do do; I am so old and miserable," coughed the old man. "Where is he? This long time I've been trying to get up and find him. But I haven't any friends, and couldn't get up till now. Where is he?"

"Who do you mean?" drawing closer, to stay the further wanderings of one so weakly.

"Why, why, why," now marking the other's dress, "why you, yes you—you, you—ugh, ugh, ugh!"

"I?"

"Ugh, ugh, ugh!—you are the man he spoke of. Who is he?"

"Faith, that is just what I want to know."

"Mercy, mercy!" coughed the old man, bewildered, "ever since seeing him, my head spins round so. I ought to have a guardeean. Is this a snuff-colored surtout of yours, or ain't it? Somehow, can't trust my senses any more, since trusting him—ugh, ugh, ugh!"

"Oh, you have trusted somebody? Glad to hear it. Glad to hear of any instance of that sort. Reflects well upon all men. But you inquire whether this is a snuff-colored surtout. I answer it is; and will add that a herb-doctor wears it."

Upon this the old man, in his broken way, replied that then he (the herb-doctor) was the person he sought—the person spoken of by the other person as yet unknown. He then, with flighty eagerness, wanted to know who this last person was, and where he was, and whether he could be trusted with money to treble it.

"Aye, now, I begin to understand; ten to one you mean my worthy friend, who, in pure goodness of heart, makes people's fortunes for them—their everlasting fortunes, as the phrase goes— only charging his one small commission of confidence. Aye, aye; before intrusting funds with my friend, you want to know about him. Very proper—and, I am glad to assure you, you need have no hesitation; none, none, just none in the world; bona fide, nonc. Turned me in a trice a hundred dollars the other day into as many eagles."

"Did he? did he? But where is he? Take me to him."

"Pray, take my arm! The boat is large! We may have something of a hunt! Come on! Ah, is that he?"

"Where? where?"

"O, no; I took yonder coat-skirts for his. But no, my honest friend would never turn tail that way. Ah!—"

"Where? where?"

"Another mistake. Surprising resemblance. I took yonder clergyman for him. Come on!"

Having searched that part of the boat without success, they went to another part, and, while exploring that, the boat sided up to a landing, when, as the two were passing by the open guard, the herb-doctor suddenly rushed towards the disembarking throng, crying out: "Mr. Truman, Mr. Truman! There he goes—that's he.

Mr. Truman, Mr. Truman!—Confound that steam-pipe. Mr. Truman! for God's sake, Mr. Truman!—No, no.—There, plank's in—too late—we're off."

With that, the huge boat, with a mighty, walrus wallow, rolled away from the shore, resuming her course.

"How vexatious!" exclaimed the herb-doctor, returning. "Had we been but one single moment sooner.—There he goes, now, towards yon hotel, his portmanteau following. You see him, don't you?"

"Where? where?"

"Can't see him any more. Wheel-house shot between. I am very sorry. I should have so liked you to have let him have a hundred or so of your money. You would have been pleased with the investment, believe me."

"Oh, I *have* let him have some of my money," groaned the old man.

"You have? My dear sir," seizing both the miser's hands in both his own and heartily shaking them. "My dear sir, how I congratulate you. You don't know."

"Ugh, ugh! I fear I don't," with another groan. "His name is Truman, is it?"

"John Truman."

"Where does he live?"

"In St. Louis."

"Where's his office?"

"Let me see. Jones street, number one hundred and—no, no—anyway, it's somewhere or other up-stairs in Jones street."

"Can't you remember the number? Try, now."

"One hundred—two hundred—three hundred—"

"Oh, my hundred dollars! I wonder whether it will be one hundred, two hundred, three hundred, with them! Ugh, ugh! Can't remember the number?"

"Positively, though I once knew, I have forgotten, quite forgotten it. Strange. But never mind. You will easily learn in St. Louis. He is well known there."

"But I have no receipt—ugh, ugh! Nothing to show—don't know where I stand—ought to have a guardeean—ugh, ugh! Don't know anything. Ugh, ugh!"

"Why, you know that you gave him your confidence, don't you?"

"Oh, yes."

"Well, then?"

"But what, what—how, how—ugh, ugh!"

"Why, didn't he tell you?"

"No."

"What! Didn't he tell you that it was a secret, a mystery?"

"Oh—yes."

"Well, then?"

"But I have no bond.'

"Don't need any with Mr. Truman. Mr. Truman's word is his bond."

"But how am I to get my profits—ugh, ugh!—and my money back? Don't know anything. Ugh, ugh!"

"Oh, you must have confidence."

"Don't say that word again. Makes my head spin so. Oh, I'm so old and miserable, nobody caring for me, everybody fleecing me, and my head spins so—ugh, ugh!—and this cough racks me so. I say again, I ought to have a guardeean."

"So you ought; and Mr. Truman is your guardian to the extent you invested with him. Sorry we missed him just now. But you'l hear from him. All right. It's imprudent, though, to expose yours at this way. Let me take you to your berth."

Forlornly enough the old miser moved slowly away with him. But, while descending a stairway, he was seized with such coughing that he was fain to pause.

"That is a very bad cough."

"Church-yard—ugh, ugh!—church-yard cough.—Ugh!"

"Have you tried anything for it?"

"Tired of trying. Nothing does me any good—ugh! ugh! Not even the Mammoth Cave.[1] Ugh! ugh! Denned there six months, but coughed so bad the rest of the coughers—ugh! ugh!—black-balled me out. Ugh, ugh! Nothing does me good."

"But have you tried the Omni-Balsamic Reinvigorator, sir?"

"That's what that Truman—ugh, ugh!—said I ought to take. Yarb-medicine; you are that yarb-doctor, too?"

"The same. Suppose you try one of my boxes now. Trust me, from what I know of Mr. Truman, he is not the gentleman to recommend, even in behalf of a friend, anything of whose excellence he is not conscientiously satisfied."

"Ugh!—how much?"

"Only two dollars a box."

"Two dollars? Why don't you say two millions? ugh, ugh! Two dollars, that's two hundred cents; that's eight hundred farthings; that's two thousand mills; and all for one little box of yarb-medicine. My head, my head!—oh, I ought to have a guardeean for my head. Ugh, ugh, ugh, ugh!"

"Well, if two dollars a box seems too much, take a dozen boxes at twenty dollars; and that will be getting four boxes for nothing,

1. The famous Kentucky cave had in fact been occupied by consumptives who thought its uniform temperature might be curative.

and you need use none but those four, the rest you can retail out at a premium, and so cure your cough, and make money by it.[2] Come, you had better do it. Cash down. Can fill an order in a day or two. Here, now," producing a box; "pure herbs."

At that moment, seized with another spasm, the miser snatched each interval to fix his half distrustful, half hopeful eye upon the medicine, held alluringly up. "Sure—ugh! Sure it's all nat'ral? Nothing but yarbs? If I only thought it was a purely nat'ral medicine now—all yarbs—ugh, ugh!—oh this cough, this cough—ugh, ugh!—shatters my whole body. Ugh, ugh, ugh!"

"For heaven's sake try my medicine, if but a single box. That it is pure nature you may be confident. Refer you to Mr. Truman."

"Don't know his number—ugh, ugh, ugh, ugh! Oh this cough. He did speak well of this medicine though; said solemnly it would cure me—ugh, ugh, ugh, ugh!—take off a dollar and I'll have a box."

"Can't sir, can't."

"Say a dollar-and-half. Ugh!"

"Can't. Am pledged to the one-price system, only honorable one."

"Take off a shilling—ugh, ugh!"

"Can't."

"Ugh, ugh, ugh—I'll take it.—There."

Grudgingly he handed eight silver coins, but while still in his hand, his cough took him, and they were shaken upon the deck.

One by one, the herb-doctor picked them up, and, examining them said: "These are not quarters, these are pistareens; and clipped, and sweated, at that."

"Oh don't be so miserly—ugh, ugh!—better a beast than a miser—ugh, ugh!"

"Well, let it go. Anything rather than the idea of your not being cured of such a cough. And I hope, for the credit of humanity, you have not made it appear worse than it is, merely with a view to working upon the weak point of my pity, and so getting my medicine the cheaper. Now, mind, don't take it till night. Just before retiring is the time. There, you can get along now, can't you? I would attend you further, but I land presently, and must go hunt up my luggage."

2. The herb-doctor's arithmetic may be deliberately shaky, but several such errors appear in Melville's books, and his brother Allan and later his wife kept track of his own financial matters. Daniel G. Hoffman (1961) pointed out the error.

Chapter 21

A HARD CASE

"Yarbs, yarbs; natur, natur; you foolish old file you! He diddled you with that hocus-pocus, did he? Yarbs and natur will cure your incurable cough, you think."

It was a rather eccentric-looking person who spoke; somewhat ursine in aspect; sporting a shaggy spencer[1] of the cloth called bear's-skin; a high-peaked cap of raccoon-skin, the long bushy tail switching over behind; raw-hide leggings; grim stubble chin; and to end, a double-barreled gun in hand—a Missouri bachelor, a Hoosier gentleman, of Spartan leisure and fortune, and equally Spartan manners and sentiments; and, as the sequel may show, not less acquainted, in a Spartan way of his own, with philosophy and books, than with wood-craft and rifles.

He must have overheard some of the talk between the miser and the herb-doctor; for, just after the withdrawal of the one, he made up to the other—now at the foot of the stairs leaning against the baluster there—with the greeting above.

"Think it will cure me?" coughed the miser in echo; "why shouldn't it? The medicine is nat'ral yarbs, pure yarbs; yarbs must cure me."

"Because a thing is nat'ral, as you call it, you think it must be good. But who gave you that cough? Was it, or was it not, nature?"

"Sure, you don't think that natur, Dame Natur, will hurt a body, do you?"

"Natur is good Queen Bess; but who's responsible for the cholera?"

"But yarbs, yarbs; yarbs are good?"

"What's deadly-nightshade? Yarb, ain't it?"

"Oh, that a Christian man should speak agin natur and yarbs—ugh, ugh, ugh!—ain't sick men sent out into the country; sent out to natur and grass?"

"Aye, and poets send out the sick spirit to green pastures, like lame horses turned out unshod to the turf to renew their hoofs. A sort of yarb-doctors in their way, poets have it that for sore hearts, as for sore lungs, nature is the grand cure. But who froze to death

1. A waist-length jacket.

my teamster on the prairie? And who made an idiot of Peter the Wild Boy?"[2]

"Then you don't believe in these 'ere yarb-doctors?"

"Yarb-doctors? I remember the lank yarb-doctor I saw once on a hospital-cot in Mobile. One of the faculty passing round and seeing who lay there, said with professional triumph, 'Ah, Dr. Green, your yarbs don't help ye now, Dr. Green. Have to come to us and the mercury now, Dr. Green.'—Natur! Y-a-r-b-s!"

"Did I hear something about herbs and herb-doctors?" here said a flute-like voice, advancing.

It was the herb-doctor in person. Carpet-bag in hand, he happened to be strolling back that way.

"Pardon me," addressing the Missourian, "but if I caught your words aright, you would seem to have little confidence in nature; which, really, in my way of thinking, looks like carrying the spirit of distrust pretty far."

"And who of my sublime species may you be?" turning short round upon him, clicking his rifle-lock, with an air which would have seemed half cynic, half wild-cat, were it not for the grotesque excess of the expression, which made its sincerity appear more or less dubious.

"One who has confidence in nature, and confidence in man, with some little modest confidence in himself."

"That's your Confession of Faith, is it? Confidence in man, eh? Pray, which do you think are most, knaves or fools?"

"Having met with few or none of either, I hardly think I am competent to answer."

"I will answer for you. Fools are most."

"Why do you think so?"

"For the same reason that I think oats are numerically more than horses. Don't knaves munch up fools just as horses do oats?"

"A droll, sir; you are a droll. I can appreciate drollery—ha, ha, ha!"

"But I'm in earnest."

"That's the drollery, to deliver droll extravagance with an earnest air—knaves munching up fools as horses oats.—Faith, very droll, indeed, ha, ha, ha! Yes, I think I understand you now, sir. How silly I was to have taken you seriously, in your droll conceits, too, about having no confidence in nature. In reality you have just as much as I have."

2. Peter the Wild Boy (1712–1785) was found in 1725 in the woods near Hamelin, walking on his hands and feet, climbing trees like an animal, and eating grass and moss. His Hanoverian ruler, George I of England, brought him to London in 1726 and put him under the care of Dr. Arbuthnot, amid speculation on what wild creature had suckled him. Swift and Defoe were among the many who wrote about him. Foster points out that he became a center of the controversy about the existence of innate ideas.

"*I* have confidence in nature? *I*? I say again there is nothing I am more suspicious of. I once lost ten thousand dollars by nature. Nature embezzled that amount from me; absconded with ten thousand dollars' worth of my property; a plantation on this stream, swept clean away by one of those sudden shiftings of the banks in a freshet; ten thousand dollars' worth of alluvion thrown broad off upon the waters."

"But have you no confidence that by a reverse shifting that soil will come back after many days[3]—ah, here is my venerable friend," observing the old miser, "not in your berth yet? Pray, if you *will* keep afoot, don't lean against that baluster; take my arm."

It was taken; and the two stood together; the old miser leaning against the herb-doctor with something of that air of trustful fraternity with which, when standing, the less strong of the Siamese twins habitually leans against the other.[4]

The Missourian eyed them in silence, which was broken by the herb-doctor.

"You look surprised, sir. Is it because I publicly take under my protection a figure like this? But I am never ashamed of honesty, whatever his coat."

"Look you," said the Missourian, after a scrutinizing pause, "you are a queer sort of chap. Don't know exactly what to make of you. Upon the whole though, you somewhat remind me of the last boy I had on my place."

"Good, trustworthy boy, I hope?"

"Oh, very! I am now started to get me made some kind of machine to do the sort of work which boys are supposed to be fitted for."

"Then you have passed a veto upon boys?"

"And men, too."

"But, my dear sir, does not that again imply more or less lack of confidence?—(Stand up a little, just a very little, my venerable friend; you lean rather hard.)—No confidence in boys, no confidence in men, no confidence in nature. Pray, sir, who or what may you have confidence in?"

"I have confidence in distrust; more particularly as applied to you and your herbs."

"Well," with a forbearing smile, "that is frank. But pray, don't forget that when you suspect my herbs you suspect nature."

"Didn't I say that before?"

"Very good. For the argument's sake I will suppose you are in earnest. Now, can you, who suspect nature, deny, that this same

---

3. "Cast thy bread upon the waters: for thou shalt find it after many days" (Ecclesiastes 11:1).

4. The famous Chang and Eng were displayed at Barnum's American Museum and taken on various tours.

nature not only kindly brought you into being, but has faithfully nursed you to your present vigorous and independent condition? Is it not to nature that you are indebted for that robustness of mind which you so unhandsomely use to her scandal? Pray, is it not to nature that you owe the very eyes by which you criticise her?"

"No! for the privilege of vision I am indebted to an oculist, who in my tenth year operated upon me in Philadelphia. Nature made me blind and would have kept me so. My oculist counterplotted her."

"And yet, sir, by your complexion, I judge you live an out-of-door life; without knowing it, you are partial to nature; you fly to nature, the universal mother."

"Very motherly! Sir, in the passion-fits of nature, I've known birds fly from nature to me, rough as I look; yes, sir, in a tempest, refuge here," smiting the folds of his bearskin. "Fact, sir, fact. Come, come, Mr. Palaverer, for all your palavering, did you yourself never shut out nature of a cold, wet night? Bar her out? Bolt her out? Lint her out?"

"As to that," said the herb-doctor calmly, "much may be said."

"Say it, then," ruffling all his hairs. "You can't, sir, can't." Then, as in apostrophe: "Look you, nature! I don't deny but your clover is sweet, and your dandelions don't roar; but whose hailstones smashed my windows?"

"Sir," with unimpaired affability, producing one of his boxes, "I am pained to meet with one who holds nature a dangerous character. Though your manner is refined your voice is rough; in short, you seem to have a sore throat. In the calumniated name of nature, I present you with this box; my venerable friend here has a similar one; but to you, a free gift, sir. Through her regularly-authorized agents, of whom I happen to be one, Nature delights in benefiting those who most abuse her. Pray, take it."

"Away with it! Don't hold it so near. Ten to one there is a torpedo in it. Such things have been. Editors been killed that way. Take it further off, I say."

"Good heavens! my dear sir—"

"I tell you I want none of your boxes," snapping his rifle.

"Oh, take it—ugh, ugh! do take it," chimed in the old miser; "I wish he would give me one for nothing."

"You find it lonely, eh," turning short round; "gulled yourself, you would have a companion."

"How can he find it lonely," returned the herb-doctor, "or how desire a companion, when here I stand by him; I, even I, in whom he has trust? For the gulling, tell me, is it humane to talk so to this poor old man? Granting that his dependence on my medicine is vain, is it kind to deprive him of what, in mere imagination, if nothing more, may help eke out, with hope, his disease? For you, if you have no confidence, and, thanks to your native health, can get along without it, so far, at least, as trusting in my medicine goes; yet, how cruel an argument to use, with this afflicted one here. Is it not for all the world as if some brawny pugilist, aglow in December, should rush in and put out a hospital-fire, because, forsooth, he feeling no need of artificial heat, the shivering patients shall have none? Put it to your conscience, sir, and you will admit, that, whatever be the nature of this afflicted one's trust, you, in opposing it, evince either an erring head or a heart amiss. Come, own, are you not pitiless?"

"Yes, poor soul," said the Missourian, gravely eying the old man—"yes, it *is* pitiless in one like me to speak too honestly to one like you. You are a late sitter-up in this life; past man's usual bedtime; and truth, though with some it makes a wholesome breakfast, proves to all a supper too hearty. Hearty food, taken late, gives bad dreams."

"What, in wonder's name—ugh, ugh!—is he talking about?" asked the old miser, looking up to the herb-doctor.

"Heaven be praised for that!" cried the Missourian.

"Out of his mind, ain't he?" again appealed the old miser.

"Pray, sir," said the herb-doctor to the Missourian, "for what were you giving thanks just now?"

"For this: that, with some minds, truth is, in effect, not so cruel a thing after all, seeing that, like a loaded pistol found by poor devils of savages, it raises more wonder than terror—its peculiar virtue being unguessed, unless, indeed, by indiscreet handling, it should happen to go off of itself."[5]

"I pretend not to divine your meaning there," said the herb-doctor, after a pause, during which he eyed the Missourian with a kind of pinched expression, mixed of pain and curiosity, as if he grieved at his state of mind, and, at the same time, wondered what had brought him to it, "but this much I know," he added, "that the general cast of your thoughts is, to say the least, unfortunate. There is strength in them, but a strength, whose source, being physical, must wither. You will yet recant."

"Recant?"

"Yes, when, as with this old man, your evil days of decay come on, when a hoary captive in your chamber, then will you, something like the dungeoned Italian[6] we read of, gladly seek the breast of that confidence begot in the tender time of your youth, blessed beyond telling if it return to you in age."

5. Possibly a private joke about the reception Melville's potentially explosive book was apt to receive from mid-century American readers.

6. "Perhaps the Abbé Faria in *The Count of Monte Cristo*, by Alexandre Dumas, which had been translated into English in 1846" (Foster).

"Go back to nurse again, eh? Second childhood, indeed. You are soft."

"Mercy, mercy!" cried the old miser, "what is all this!—ugh, ugh! Do talk sense, my good friends. Ain't you," to the Missourian, "going to buy some of that medicine?"

"Pray, my venerable friend," said the herb-doctor, now trying to straighten himself, "Don't lean *quite* so hard; my arm grows numb; abate a little, just a very little."

"Go," said the Missourian, "go lay down in your grave, old man, if you can't stand of yourself. It's a hard world for a leaner."

"As to his grave," said the herb-doctor, "that is far enough off, so he but faithfully take my medicine."

"Ugh, ugh, ugh!—He says true. No, I ain't—ugh! a going to die yet—ugh, ugh, ugh! Many years to live yet, ugh, ugh, ugh!"

"I approve your confidence," said the herb-doctor; "but your coughing distresses me, besides being injurious to you. Pray, let me conduct you to your berth. You are best there. Our friend here will wait till my return, I know."

With which he led the old miser away, and then, coming back, the talk with the Missourian was resumed.

"Sir," said the herb-doctor, with some dignity and more feeling, "now that our infirm friend is withdrawn, allow me, to the full, to express my concern at the words you allowed to escape you in his hearing. Some of those words, if I err not, besides being calculated to beget deplorable distrust in the patient, seemed fitted to convey unpleasant imputations against me, his physician."

"Suppose they did?" with a menacing air.

"Why, then—then, indeed," respectfully retreating, "I fall back upon my previous theory of your general facetiousness. I have the fortune to be in company with a humorist—a wag."

"Fall back you had better, and wag it is," cried the Missourian, following him up, and wagging his raccoon tail almost into the herb-doctor's face, "look you!"

"At what?"

"At this coon. Can you, the fox, catch him?"

"If you mean," returned the other, not unselfpossessed, "whether I flatter myself that I can in any way dupe you, or impose upon you, or pass myself off upon you for what I am not, I, as an honest man, answer that I have neither the inclination nor the power to do aught of the kind."

"Honest man? Seems to me you talk more like a craven."

"You in vain seek to pick a quarrel with me, or put any affront upon me. The innocence in me heals me."

"A healing like your own nostrums. But you are a queer man—a very queer and dubious man; upon the whole, about the most so I ever met."

The scrutiny accompanying this seemed unwelcome to the diffidence of the herb-doctor. As if at once to attest the absence of resentment, as well as to change the subject, he threw a kind of familiar cordiality into his air, and said: "So you are going to get some machine made to do your work? Philanthropic scruples, doubtless, forbid you going as far as New Orleans for slaves?"

"Slaves?" morose again in a twinkling, "won't have 'em! Bad enough to see whites ducking and grinning round for a favor, without having those poor devils of niggers congeeing round for their corn. Though, to me, the niggers are the freer of the two. You are an abolitionist, ain't you?" he added, squaring himself with both hands on his rifle, used for a staff, and gazing in the herb-doctor's face with no more reverence than if it were a target. "You are an abolitionist, ain't you?"

"As to that, I cannot so readily answer. If by abolitionist you mean a zealot, I am none; but if you mean a man, who, being a man, feels for all men, slaves included, and by any lawful act, opposed to nobody's interest, and therefore, rousing nobody's enmity, would willingly abolish suffering (supposing it, in its degree, to exist) from among mankind, irrespective of color, then am I what you say."[7]

"Picked and prudent sentiments. You are the moderate man, the invaluable understrapper of the wicked man. You, the moderate man, may be used for wrong, but are useless for right."

"From all this," said the herb-doctor, still forgivingly, "I infer, that you, a Missourian, though living in a slave-state, are without slave sentiments."

"Aye, but are you? Is not that air of yours, so spiritlessly enduring and yielding, the very air of a slave? Who is your master, pray; or are you owned by a company?"

"My master?"

"Aye, for come from Maine or Georgia, you come from a slave-state, and a slave-pen, where the best breeds are to be bought up at any price from a livelihood to the Presidency. Abolitionism, ye gods, but expresses the fellow-feeling of slave for slave."

"The back-woods would seem to have given you rather eccentric notions," now with polite superiority smiled the herb-doctor, still with manly intrepidity forbearing each unmanly thrust, "but to return; since, for your purpose, you will have neither man nor boy, bond nor free, truly, then some sort of machine for you is all there is left. My desires for your success attend you, sir.—Ah!" glancing shoreward, "here is Cape Girardeau; I must leave you."

---

7. For this fatuous shilly-shallying, the judgment of Jesus is relevant: "So then because thou art lukewarm, and neither cold nor hot, I will spue thee out of my mouth" (Revelation 3:16). Ironically, it has been cited as Melville's own considered judgment on abolitionism.

Chapter 22

IN THE POLITE SPIRIT OF THE TUSCULAN DISPUTATIONS

—" 'Philosophical Intelligence Office[1]—novel idea! But how did you come to dream that I wanted anything in your absurd line, eh?"

About twenty minutes after leaving Cape Girardeau, the above was growled out over his shoulder by the Missourian to a chance stranger who had just accosted him; a round-backed, baker-kneed man,[2] in a mean five-dollar suit, wearing, collar-wise by a chain, a small brass plate, inscribed P. I. O., and who, with a sort of canine deprecation, slunk obliquely behind.

"How did you come to dream that I wanted anything in your line, eh?"

"Oh, respected sir," whined the other, crouching a pace nearer, and, in his obsequiousness, seeming to wag his very coat-tails behind him, shabby though they were, "oh, sir, from long experience, one glance tells me the gentleman who is in need of our humble services."

"But suppose I did want a boy—what they jocosely call a good boy—how could your absurd office help me?—Philosophical Intelligence Office?"

"Yes, respected sir, an office founded on strictly philosophical and physio—"

"Look you—come up here—how, by philosophy or physiology either, make good boys to order? Come up here. Don't give me a crick in the neck. Come up here, come, sir, come," calling as if to his pointer. "Tell me, how put the requisite assortment of good qualities into a boy, as the assorted mince into the pie?"

"Respected sir, our office—"

"You talk much of that office. Where is it? On board this boat?"

"Oh no, sir, I just came aboard. Our office—"

"Came aboard at that last landing, eh? Pray, do you know a herb-doctor there? Smooth scamp in a snuff-colored surtout?"

"Oh, sir, I was but a sojourner at Cape Girardeau. Though, now that you mention a snuff-colored surtout, I think I met such a man as you speak of stepping ashore as I stepped aboard, and 'pears to me I have seen him somewhat before. Looks like a very mild Chris-

1. Employment agency. Melville had read Hawthorne's story "The Intelligence Office."
2. The *OED* quotes from *Figure Training* (1871): "An inclining in-wards of the right knee-joint until it closely resembles the right side of a letter K, is the almost certain penalty of habitually bearing any burden of bulk in the right hand."

tian sort of person, I should say. Do you know him, respected sir?"
"Not much, but better than you seem to. Proceed with your business."

With a low, shabby bow, as grateful for the permission, the other began: "Our office—"

"Look you," broke in the bachelor with ire, "have you the spinal complaint? What are you ducking and groveling about? Keep still. Where's your office?"

"The branch one which I represent, is at Alton, sir, in the free state we now pass," (pointing somewhat proudly ashore).

"Free, eh? You are a freeman, you flatter yourself? With those coat-tails and that spinal complaint of servility? Free? Just cast up in your private mind who is your master, will you?"

"Oh, oh, oh! I don't understand—indeed—indeed. But, respected sir, as before said, our office, founded on principles wholly new—"

"To the devil with your principles! Bad sign when a man begins to talk of his principles. Hold, come back, sir; back here, back, sir, back! I tell you no more boys for me. Nay, I'm a Mede and Persian. In my old home in the woods I'm pestered enough with squirrels, weasels, chipmunks, skunks. I want no more wild vermin to spoil my temper and waste my substance. Don't talk of boys; enough of your boys; a plague of your boys; chilblains on your boys! As for Intelligence Offices, I've lived in the East, and know 'em. Swindling concerns kept by low-born cynics, under a fawning exterior wreaking their cynic malice upon mankind. You are a fair specimen of 'em."

"Oh dear, dear, dear!"

"Dear? Yes, a thrice dear purchase one of your boys would be to me. A rot on your boys!"

"But, respected sir, if you will not have boys, might we not, in our small way, accommodate you with a man?"

"Accommodate?[3] Pray, no doubt you could accommodate me with a bosom-friend too, couldn't you? Accommodate! Obliging word accommodate: there's accommodation notes now, where one accommodates another with a loan, and if he don't pay it pretty quickly, accommodates him with a chain to his foot. Accommodate! God forbid that I should ever be accommodated. No, no. Look you, as I told that cousin-german of yours, the herb-doctor, I'm now on the road to get me made some sort of machine to do my work. Machines for me. My cider-mill—does that ever steal my cider? My mowing-machine—does that ever lay a-bed mornings? My corn-husker—does that ever give me insolence? No: cider-mill,

3. Bardolph and Shallow mouth back and forth the "good phrase" "accom-modated" in *Henry IV*, Part Two, III, ii.

mowing-machine, corn-husker—all faithfully attend to their business. Disinterested, too; no board, no wages; yet doing good all their lives long; shining examples that virtue is its own reward—the only practical Christians I know."

"Oh dear, dear, dear, dear!"

"Yes, sir:—boys? Start my soul-bolts, what a difference, in a moral point of view, between a corn-husker and a boy! Sir, a corn-husker, for its patient continuance in well-doing,[4] might not unfitly go to heaven. Do you suppose a boy will?"

"A corn-husker in heaven! (turning up the whites of his eyes). Respected sir, this way of talking as if heaven were a kind of Washington patent-office museum—oh, oh, oh!—as if mere machine-work and puppet-work went to heaven—oh, oh, oh! Things incapable of free agency, to receive the eternal reward of well-doing—oh, oh, oh!"

"You Praise-God-Barebones[5] you, what are you groaning about? Did I say anything of that sort? Seems to me, though you talk so good, you are mighty quick at a hint the other way, or else you want to pick a polemic quarrel with me."

"It may be so or not, respected sir," was now the demure reply; "but if it be, it is only because as a soldier out of honor is quick in taking affront, so a Christian out of religion is quick, sometimes perhaps a little too much so, in spying heresy."

"Well," after an astonished pause, "for an unaccountable pair you and the herb-doctor ought to yoke together."

So saying, the bachelor was eying him rather sharply, when he with the brass plate recalled him to the discussion by a hint, not unflattering, that he (the man with the brass plate) was all anxiety to hear him further on the subject of servants.

"About that matter," exclaimed the impulsive bachelor, going off at the hint like a rocket, "all thinking minds are, now-a-days, coming to the conclusion—one derived from an immense hereditary experience—see what Horace and others of the ancients say of servants—coming to the conclusion, I say, that boy or man, the human animal is, for most work-purposes, a losing animal. Can't be trusted; less trustworthy than oxen; for conscientiousness a turn-spit dog excels him. Hence these thousand new inventions—carding machines, horse-shoe machines, tunnel-boring machines, reaping machines, apple-paring machines, boot-blacking machines, sewing machines, shaving machines, run-of-errand machines, dumb-waiter machines, and the Lord-only-knows-what machines; all of which announce the era when that refractory animal, the working or serv-

4. Romans 2:7.
5. Also spelled Praisegod Barbon (1596?–1679), London Anabaptist leather-seller, under Oliver Cromwell in 1653 a member of the Parliament which was called by its enemies "Barebone's Parliament" or the "Little Parliament." He was a fervid opponent of the restoration of Charles II.

ing man, shall be a buried by-gone, a superseded fossil. Shortly
prior to which glorious time, I doubt not that a price will be put
upon their peltries as upon the knavish 'possums, especially the
boys. Yes, sir (ringing his rifle down on the deck), I rejoice to
think that the day is at hand, when, prompted to it by law, I shall
shoulder this gun and go out a boy-shooting."

"Oh, now! Lord, Lord, Lord!—But *our* office, respected sir, conducted as I ventured to observe—"

"No, sir," bristlingly settling his stubble chin in his coon-skins.
"Don't try to oil me; the herb-doctor tried that. My experience,
carried now through a course—worse than salivation—a course of
five and thirty boys, proves to me that boyhood is a natural state of
rascality."

"Save us, save us!"

"Yes, sir, yes. My name is Pitch; I stick to what I say. I speak
from fifteen years' experience; five and thirty boys; American, Irish,
English, German, African, Mulatto; not to speak of that China boy
sent me by one who well knew my perplexities, from California;
and that Lascar boy from Bombay. Thug! I found him sucking the
embryo life from my spring eggs. All rascals, sir, every soul of
them; Caucasian or Mongol. Amazing the endless variety of rascality in human nature of the juvenile sort. I remember that, having
discharged, one after another, twenty-nine boys—each, too, for
some wholly unforeseen species of viciousness peculiar to that one
peculiar boy—I remember saying to myself: Now, then, surely, I
have got to the end of the list, wholly exhausted it; I have only
now to get me a boy, any boy different from those twenty-nine
preceding boys, and he infallibly shall be that virtuous boy I have
so long been seeking. But, bless me! this thirtieth boy—by the way,
having at the time long forsworn your intelligence offices, I had
him sent to me from the Commissioners of Emigration, all the way
from New York, culled out carefully, in fine, at my particular
request, from a standing army of eight hundred boys, the flowers of
all nations, so they wrote me, temporarily in barracks on an East
River island—I say, this thirtieth boy was in person not ungraceful;
his deceased mother a lady's maid, or something of that sort; and
in manner, why, in a plebeian way, a perfect Chesterfield;[6] very
intelligent, too—quick as a flash. But, such suavity! 'Please sir!
please sir!' always bowing and saying, 'Please sir.' In the strangest
way, too, combining a filial affection with a menial respect. Took
such warm, singular interest in my affairs. Wanted to be considered
one of the family—sort of adopted son of mine, I suppose. Of a
morning, when I would go out to my stable, with what childlike

6. In Melville's absolute scale, Chesterfield the gentleman figures as an opposite of Jesus, an embodiment of
terrestrial rather than celestial values.
See paragraph 8 in Chapter 24.

good nature he would trot out my nag, 'Please sir, I think he's getting fatter and fatter.' 'But, he don't look very clean, does he?' unwilling to be downright harsh with so affectionate a lad; 'and he seems a little hollow inside the haunch there, don't he? or no, perhaps I don't see plain this morning.' 'Oh, please sir, it's just there I think he's gaining so, please.' Polite scamp. I soon found he never gave that wretched nag his oats of nights; didn't bed him either. Was above that sort of chambermaid work. No end to his willful neglects. But the more he abused my service, the more polite he grew."

"Oh, sir, some way you mistook him."

"Not a bit of it. Besides, sir, he was a boy who under a Chesterfieldian exterior hid strong destructive propensities. He cut up my horse-blanket for the bits of leather, for hinges to his chest. Denied it point-blank. After he was gone, found the shreds under his mattress. Would slyly break his hoe-handle, too, on purpose to get rid of hoeing. Then be so gracefully penitent for his fatal excess of industrious strength. Offer to mend all by taking a nice stroll to the nighest settlement—cherry-trees in full bearing all the way—to get the broken thing cobbled. Very politely stole my pears, odd pennies, shillings, dollars, and nuts; regular squirrel at it. But I could prove nothing. Expressed to him my suspicions. Said I, moderately enough, 'A little less politeness, and a little more honesty would suit me better.' He fired up; threatened to sue for libel. I won't say anything about his afterwards, in Ohio, being found in the act of gracefully putting a bar across a rail-road track, for the reason that a stoker called him the rogue that he was. But enough: polite boys or saucy boys, white boys or black boys, smart boys or lazy boys, Caucasian boys or Mongol boys—all are rascals."

"Shocking, shocking!" nervously tucking his frayed cravat-end out of sight. "Surely, respected sir, you labor under a deplorable hallucination. Why, pardon again, you seem to have not the slightest confidence in boys. I admit, indeed, that boys, some of them at least, are but too prone to one little foolish foible or other. But, what then, respected sir, when, by natural laws, they finally outgrow such things, and wholly?"

Having until now vented himself mostly in plaintive dissent of canine whines and groans, the man with the brass-plate seemed beginning to summon courage to a less timid encounter. But, upon his maiden essay, was not very encouragingly handled, since the dialogue immediately continued as follows:

"Boys outgrow what is amiss in them? From bad boys spring good men? Sir, 'the child is father of the man;' hence, as all boys are rascals, so are all men. But, God bless me, you must know these things better than I; keeping an intelligence office as you do; a business which must furnish peculiar facilities for studying mankind. Come, come up here, sir; confess you know these things pretty well, after all. Do you not know that all men are rascals, and all boys, too?"

"Sir," replied the other, spite of his shocked feelings seeming to pluck up some spirit, but not to an indiscreet degree, "Sir, heaven be praised, I am far, very far from knowing what you say. True," he thoughtfully continued, "with my associates, I keep an intelligence office, and for ten years, come October, have, one way or other, been concerned in that line; for no small period in the great city of Cincinnati, too; and though, as you hint, within that long interval, I must have had more or less favorable opportunity for studying mankind—in a business way, scanning not only the faces, but ransacking the lives of several thousands of human beings, male and female, of various nations, both employers and employed, genteel and ungenteel, educated and uneducated; yet—of course, I candidly admit, with some random exceptions, I have, so far as my small observation goes, found that mankind thus domestically viewed, confidentially viewed, I may say; they, upon the whole— making some reasonable allowances for human imperfection— present as pure a moral spectacle as the purest angel could wish. I say it, respected sir, with confidence."

"Gammon! You don't mean what you say. Else you are like a landsman at sea: don't know the ropes, the very things everlastingly pulled before your eyes. Serpent-like, they glide about, traveling blocks too subtle for you. In short, the entire ship is a riddle. Why, you green ones wouldn't know if she were unseaworthy; but still, with thumbs stuck back into your arm-holes, pace the rotten planks, singing, like a fool, words put into your green mouth by the cunning owner, the man who, heavily insuring it, sends his ship to be wrecked—

'A wet sheet and a flowing sea!'—

and, sir, now that it occurs to me, your talk, the whole of it, is but a wet sheet and a flowing sea, and an idle wind that follows fast, offering a striking contrast to my own discourse."

"Sir," exclaimed the man with the brass-plate, his patience now more or less tasked, "permit me with deference to hint that some of your remarks are injudiciously worded. And thus we say to our patrons, when they enter our office full of abuse of us because of some worthy boy we may have sent them—some boy wholly misjudged for the time. Yes, sir, permit me to remark that you do not sufficiently consider that, though a small man, I may have my small share of feelings."

"Well, well, I didn't mean to wound your feelings at all. And that they are small, very small, I take your word for it. Sorry, sorry. But truth is like a thrashing-machine; tender sensibilities must keep out of the way. Hope you understand me. Don't want to hurt you. All I say is, what I said in the first place, only now I swear it, that all boys are rascals."

"Sir," lowly replied the other, still forbearing like an old lawyer badgered in court, or else like a good-hearted simpleton, the butt of mischievous wags, "Sir, since you come back to the point, will you allow me, in my small, quiet way, to submit to you certain small, quiet views of the subject in hand?"

"Oh, yes!" with insulting indifference, rubbing his chin and looking the other way. "Oh, yes; go on."

"Well, then, respected sir," continued the other, now assuming as genteel an attitude as the irritating set of his pinched five-dollar suit would permit; "well, then, sir, the peculiar principles, the strictly philosophical principles, I may say," guardedly rising in dignity, as he guardedly rose on his toes, "upon which our office is founded, have led me and my associates, in our small, quiet way, to a careful analytical study of man, conducted, too, on a quiet theory, and with an unobtrusive aim wholly our own. That theory I will not now at large set forth. But some of the discoveries resulting from it, I will, by your permission, very briefly mention; such of them, I mean, as refer to the state of boyhood scientifically viewed."

"Then you have studied the thing? expressly studied boys, eh? Why didn't you out with that before?"

"Sir, in my small business way, I have not conversed with so many masters, gentlemen masters, for nothing. I have been taught that in this world there is a precedence of opinions as well as of persons. You have kindly given me your views, I am now, with modesty, about to give you mine."

"Stop flunkying—go on."

"In the first place, sir, our theory teaches us to proceed by analogy from the physical to the moral. Are we right there, sir? Now, sir, take a young boy, a young male infant rather, a man-child in short—what sir, I respectfully ask, do you in the first place remark?"

"A rascal, sir! present and prospective, a rascal!"

"Sir, if passion is to invade, surely science must evacuate. May I proceed? Well, then, what, in the first place, in a general view, do you remark, respected sir, in that male baby or man-child?"

The bachelor privily growled, but this time, upon the whole, better governed himself than before, though not, indeed, to the degree of thinking it prudent to risk an articulate response.

"What do you remark? I respectfully repeat." But, as no answer came, only the low, half-suppressed growl, as of Bruin in a hollow trunk, the questioner continued: "Well, sir, if you will permit me, in my small way, to speak for you, you remark, respected sir, an incipient creation; loose sort of sketchy thing; a little preliminary rag-paper study, or careless cartoon, so to speak, of a man. The idea, you see, respected sir, is there; but, as yet, wants filling out. In a word, respected sir, the man-child is at present but little, every way; I don't pretend to deny it; but, then, he *promises* well, does he not? Yes, promises very well indeed, I may say. (So, too, we say to our patrons in reference to some noble little youngster objected to for being a *dwarf*.) But, to advance one step further," extending his thread-bare leg, as he drew a pace nearer, "we must now drop the figure of the rag-paper cartoon, and borrow one—to use presently, when wanted—from the horticultural kingdom. Some bud, lily-bud, if you please. Now, such points as the new-born man-child has—as yet not all that could be desired, I am free to confess— still, such as they are, there they are, and palpable as those of an adult. But we stop not here," taking another step. "The man-child not only possesses these present points, small though they are, but, likewise—now our horticultural image comes into play—like the bud of the lily, he contains concealed rudiments of others: that is, points at present invisible, with beauties at present dormant."

"Come, come, this talk is getting too horticultural and beautiful altogether. Cut it short, cut it short!"

"Respected sir," with a rustily martial sort of gesture, like a decayed corporal's, "when deploying into the field of discourse the vanguard of an important argument, much more in evolving the grand central forces of a new philosophy of boys, as I may say, surely you will kindly allow scope adequate to the movement in hand, small and humble in its way as that movement may be. Is it worth my while to go on, respected sir?"

"Yes, stop flunkying and go on."

Thus encouraged, again the philosopher with the brass-plate proceeded:

"Supposing, sir, that worthy gentleman (in such terms, to an applicant for service, we allude to some patron we chance to have in our eye), supposing, respected sir, that worthy gentleman, Adam, to have been dropped overnight in Eden, as a calf in the pasture; supposing that, sir—then how could even the learned serpent himself have foreknown that such a downy-chinned little innocent would eventually rival the goat in a beard? Sir, wise as the serpent was, that eventuality would have been entirely hidden from his wisdom."

"I don't know about that. The devil is very sagacious. To judge by the event, he appears to have understood man better even than the Being who made him."

"For God's sake, don't say that, sir! To the point. Can it now with fairness be denied that, in his beard, the man-child prospectively possesses an appendix, not less imposing than patriarchal; and for this goodly beard, should we not by generous anticipation give the man-child, even in his cradle, credit? Should we not now sir? respectfully I put it."

"Yes, if like pig-weed he mows it down soon as it shoots," porcinely rubbing his stubble-chin against his coon-skins.

"I have hinted at the analogy," continued the other, calmly disregardful of the digression; "now to apply it. Suppose a boy evince no noble quality. Then generously give him credit for his prospective one. Don't you see? So we say to our patrons when they would fain return a boy upon us as unworthy; 'Madam, or sir, (as the case may be) has this boy a beard?' 'No.' 'Has he, we respectfully ask, as yet, evinced any noble quality?' 'No, indeed.' 'Then, madam, or sir, take him back, we humbly beseech; and keep him till that same noble quality sprouts; for, have confidence, it, like the beard, is in him.' "

"Very fine theory," scornfully exclaimed the bachelor, yet in secret, perhaps, not entirely undisturbed by these strange new views of the matter; "but what trust is to be placed in it?"

"The trust of perfect confidence, sir. To proceed. Once more, if you please, regard the man-child."

"Hold!" paw-like thrusting out his bearskin arm, "don't intrude that man-child upon me too often. He who loves not bread, dotes not on dough. As little of your man-child as your logical arrangements will admit."

"Anew regard the man-child," with inspired intrepidity repeated he with the brass-plate, "in the perspective of his developments, I mean. At first the man-child has no teeth, but about the sixth month—am I right, sir?"

"Don't know anything about it."

"To proceed then: though at first deficient in teeth, about the sixth month the man-child begins to put forth in that particular. And sweet those tender little puttings-forth are."

"Very, but blown out of his mouth directly, worthless enough."

"Admitted. And, therefore, we say to our patrons returning with a boy alleged not only to be deficient in goodness, but redundant in ill: 'The lad, madam or sir, evinces very corrupt qualities, does he?' 'No end to them.' 'But, have confidence, there will be; for pray, madam, in this lad's early childhood, were not those frail first teeth, then his, followed by his present sound, even, beautiful and permanent set? And the more objectionable those first teeth became, was not that, madam, we respectfully submit, so much the more reason to look for their speedy substitution by the present sound, even, beautiful and permanent ones?' 'True, true, can't deny that.' 'Then, madam, take him back, we respectfully beg, and wait till, in the now swift course of nature, dropping those transient moral blemishes you complain of, he replacingly buds forth in the sound, even, beautiful and permanent virtues.' "

"Very philosophical again," was the contemptuous reply—the outward contempt, perhaps, proportioned to the inward misgiving. "Vastly philosophical, indeed, but tell me—to continue your analogy—since the second teeth followed—in fact, came from—the first, is there no chance the blemish may be transmitted?"

"Not at all." Abating in humility as he gained in the argument. "The second teeth follow, but do not come from, the first; successors, not sons. The first teeth are not like the germ blossom of the apple, at once the father of, and incorporated into, the growth it foreruns; but they are thrust from their place by the independent undergrowth of the succeeding set—an illustration, by the way, which shows more for me than I meant, though not more than I wish."

"What does it show?" Surly-looking as a thunder-cloud with the inkept unrest of unacknowledged conviction.

"It shows this, respected sir, that in the case of any boy, especially an ill one, to apply unconditionally the saying, that the 'child is father of the man', is, besides implying an uncharitable aspersion of the race, affirming a thing very wide of—"

"—Your analogy," like a snapping turtle.

"Yes, respected sir."

"But is analogy argument? You are a punster."

"Punster, respected sir?" with a look of being aggrieved.

"Yes, you pun with ideas as another man may with words."

"Oh well, sir, whoever talks in that strain, whoever has no confidence in human reason, whoever despises human reason, in vain to reason with him. Still, respected sir," altering his air, "permit me to hint that, had not the force of analogy moved you somewhat, you would hardly have offered to contemn it."

"Talk away," disdainfully; "but pray tell me what has that last analogy of yours to do with your intelligence office business?"

"Everything to do with it, respected sir. From that analogy we derive the reply made to such a patron as, shortly after being supplied by us with an adult servant, proposes to return him upon our hands; not that, while with the patron, said adult has given any cause of dissatisfaction, but the patron has just chanced to hear something unfavorable concerning him from some gentleman who employed said adult long before, while a boy. To which too fastidious patron, we, taking said adult by the hand, and graciously reintroducing him to the patron, say: 'Far be it from you, madam, or sir, to proceed in your censure against this adult, in anything of the spirit of an ex-post-facto law. Madam, or sir, would you visit upon the butterfly the sins of the caterpillar? In the natural advance of all creatures, do they not bury themselves over and over again in the endless resurrection of better and better? Madam, or sir, take back this adult; he may have been a caterpillar, but is now a butterfly.' "

"Pun away; but even accepting your analogical pun, what does it amount to? Was the caterpillar one creature, and is the butterfly another? The butterfly is the caterpillar in a gaudy cloak; stripped of which, there lies the impostor's long spindle of a body, pretty much worm-shaped as before."

"You reject the analogy. To the facts then. You deny that a youth of one character can be transformed into a man of an opposite character. Now then—yes, I have it. There's the founder of La Trappe, and Ignatius Loyola; in boyhood, and someway into manhood, both devil-may-care bloods, and yet, in the end, the wonders of the world for anchoritish self-command.[7] These two examples, by-the-way, we cite to such patrons as would hastily return rakish young waiters upon us. 'Madam, or sir—patience; patience,' we say; 'good madam, or sir, would you discharge forth your cask of good wine, because, while working, it riles more or less? Then discharge not forth this young waiter; the good in him is working.' 'But he is a sad rake.' 'Therein is his promise; the rake being crude material for the saint.' "

"Ah, you are a talking man—what I call a wordy man. You talk, talk."

"And with submission, sir, what is the greatest judge, bishop or prophet, but a talking man? He talks, talks. It is the peculiar vocation of a teacher to talk. What's wisdom itself but table-talk? The best wisdom in this world, and the last spoken by its teacher, did it not literally and truly come in the form of table-talk?"[8]

"You, you you!" rattling down his rifle.

"To shift the subject, since we cannot agree. Pray, what is your opinion, respected sir, of St. Augustine?"

"St. Augustine? What should I, or you either, know of him? Seems to me, for one in such a business, to say nothing of such a coat, that though you don't know a great deal, indeed, yet you know a good deal more than you ought to know, or than you have a right to know, or than it is safe or expedient for you to know, or than, in the fair course of life, you could have honestly come to

---

7. "Probably Melville means Abbot de Rancé (1626–1700), who reformed the Cistercian abbey of La Trappe" (Foster). Praise of Loyola (1491–1556) is ironic, for Melville associated him with the horrors of the Spanish Inquisition, as in *White-Jacket*, Chapter 70: "Your honors of the Spanish Inquisition, Loyola and Torquemada! produce, reverend gentlemen, your most secret code, and match these Articles of War, if you can."
8. A reference to the Last Supper (John 13–17).

know. I am of opinion you should be served like a Jew in the middle ages with his gold; this knowledge of yours, which you haven't enough knowledge to know how to make a right use of, it should be taken from you. And so I have been thinking all along."

"You are merry, sir. But you have a little looked into St. Augustine I suppose?"

"St. Augustine on Original Sin is my text book. But you, I ask again, where do you find time or inclination for these out-of-the-way speculations? In fact, your whole talk, the more I think of it, is altogether unexampled and extraordinary."

"Respected sir, have I not already informed you that the quite new method, the strictly philosophical one, on which our office is founded, has led me and my associates to an enlarged study of mankind. It was my fault, if I did not, likewise, hint, that these studies directed always to the scientific procuring of good servants of all sorts, boys included, for the kind gentlemen, our patrons— that these studies, I say, have been conducted equally among all books of all libraries, as among all men of all nations. Then, you rather like St. Augustine, sir?"

"Excellent genius!"

"In some points he was; yet, how comes it that under his own hand, St. Augustine confesses that, until his thirtieth year, he was a very sad dog?"

"A saint a sad dog?"

"Not the saint, but the saint's irresponsible little forerunner—the boy."

"All boys are rascals, and so are all men," again flying off at his tangent; "my name is Pitch; I stick to what I say."

"Ah, sir, permit me—when I behold you on this mild summer's eve, thus eccentrically clothed in the skins of wild beasts, I cannot but conclude that the equally grim and unsuitable habit of your mind is likewise but an eccentric assumption, having no basis in your genuine soul, no more than in nature herself."

"Well, really, now—really," fidgeted the bachelor, not unaffected in his conscience by these benign personalities, "really, really, now, I don't know but that I may have been a little bit too hard upon those five and thirty boys of mine."

"Glad to find you a little softening, sir. Who knows now, but that flexile gracefulness, however questionable at the time of that thirtieth boy of yours, might have been the silky husk of the most solid qualities of maturity. It might have been with him as with the ear of the Indian corn."

"Yes, yes, yes," excitedly cried the bachelor, as the light of this new illustration broke in, "yes, yes; and now that I think of it, how often I've sadly watched my Indian corn in May, wondering whether such sickly, half-eaten sprouts, could ever thrive up into the stiff, stately spear of August."

"A most admirable reflection, sir, and you have only, according to the analogical theory first started by our office, to apply it to that thirtieth boy in question, and see the result. Had you but kept that thirtieth boy—been patient with his sickly virtues, cultivated them, hoed round them, why what a glorious guerdon would have been yours, when at last you should have had a St. Augustine for an ostler."

"Really, really—well, I am glad I didn't send him to jail, as at first I intended."

"Oh that would have been too bad. Grant he was vicious. The petty vices of boys are like the innocent kicks of colts, as yet imperfectly broken. Some boys know not virtue only for the same reason they know not French; it was never taught them. Established upon the basis of parental charity, juvenile asylums exist by law for the benefit of lads convicted of acts which, in adults, would have received other requital. Why? Because, do what they will, society, like our office, at bottom has a Christian confidence in boys. And all this we say to our patrons."

"Your patrons, sir, seem your marines to whom you may say anything," said the other, relapsing. "Why do knowing employers shun youths from asylums, though offered them at the smallest wages? I'll none of your reformado boys."

"Such a boy, respected sir, I would not get for you, but a boy that never needed reform. Do not smile, for as whooping-cough and measles are juvenile diseases, and yet some juveniles never have them, so are there boys equally free from juvenile vices. True, for the best of boys, measles may be contagious, and evil communications corrupt good manners; but a boy with a sound mind in a sound body—such is the boy I would get you. If hitherto, sir, you have struck upon a peculiarly bad vein of boys, so much the more hope now of your hitting a good one."

"That sounds a kind of reasonable, as it were—a little so, really. In fact, though you have said a great many foolish things, very foolish and absurd things, yet, upon the whole, your conversation has been such as might almost lead one less distrustful than I to repose a certain conditional confidence in you, I had almost added in your office, also. Now, for the humor of it, supposing that even I, I myself, really had this sort of conditional confidence, though but a grain, what sort of a boy, in sober fact, could you send me? And what would be your fee?"

"Conducted," replied the other somewhat loftily, rising now in eloquence as his proselyte, for all his pretenses, sunk in conviction, "conducted upon principles involving care, learning, and labor, exceeding what is usual in kindred institutions, the Philosophical Intelligence Office is forced to charges somewhat higher than customary. Briefly, our fee is three dollars in advance. As for the boy, by a lucky chance, I have a very promising little fellow now in my eye—a very likely little fellow, indeed."

"Honest?"

"As the day is long. Might trust him with untold millions. Such, at least, were the marginal observations on the phrenological chart of his head, submitted to me by the mother."

"How old?"

"Just fifteen."

"Tall? Stout?"

"Uncommonly so, for his age, his mother remarked."

"Industrious?"

"The busy bee."

The bachelor fell into a troubled reverie. At last, with much hesitancy, he spoke:

"Do you think now, candidly, that—I say candidly—candidly— could I have some small, limited—some faint, conditional degree of confidence in that boy? Candidly, now?"

"Candidly, you could."

"A sound boy? A good boy?"

"Never knew one more so."

The bachelor fell into another irresolute reverie; then said: "Well, now, you have suggested some rather new views of boys, and men, too. Upon those views in the concrete I at present decline to determine. Nevertheless, for the sake purely of a scientific experiment, I will try that boy. I don't think him an angel, mind. No, no. But I'll try him. There are my three dollars, and here is my address. Send him along this day two weeks. Hold, you will be wanting the money for his passage. There," handing it somewhat reluctantly.

"Ah, thank you. I had forgotten his passage;" then, altering in manner, and gravely holding the bills, continued: "Respected sir, never willingly do I handle money not with perfect willingness, nay, with a certain alacrity, paid. Either tell me that you have a perfect and unquestioning confidence in me (never mind the boy now) or permit me respectfully to return these bills."

"Put 'em up, put 'em up!"

"Thank you. Confidence is the indispensable basis of all sorts of business transactions. Without it, commerce between man and man, as between country and country, would, like a watch, run down and stop. And now, supposing that against present expectation the lad should, after all, evince some little undesirable trait, do not, respected sir, rashly dismiss him. Have but patience, have but confidence. Those transient vices will, ere long, fall out, and be replaced by the sound, firm, even and permanent virtues. Ah," glancing shoreward, towards a grotesquely-shaped bluff, "there's the Devil's Joke, as they call it; the bell for landing will shortly ring. I must go look up the cook I brought for the inn-keeper at Cairo."

Chapter 23

IN WHICH THE POWERFUL EFFECT OF NATURAL SCENERY IS EVINCED IN THE CASE OF THE MISSOURIAN, WHO, IN VIEW OF THE REGION ROUND-ABOUT CAIRO, HAS A RETURN OF HIS CHILLY FIT

At Cairo, the old established firm of Fever & Ague is still settling up its unfinished business; that Creole grave-digger, Yellow Jack—his hand at the mattock and spade has not lost its cunning;[1] while Don Saturninus Typhus taking his constitutional with Death, Calvin Edson and three undertakers, in the morass, snuffs up the mephitic breeze with zest.

In the dank twilight, fanned with mosquitoes, and sparkling with fire-flies, the boat now lies before Cairo. She has landed certain passengers, and tarries for the coming of expected ones. Leaning over the rail on the inshore side, the Missourian eyes through the dubious medium that swampy and squalid domain; and over it audibly mumbles his cynical mind to himself, as Apemantus' dog may have mumbled his bone.[2] He bethinks him that the man with the brass-plate was to land on this villainous bank, and for that cause, if no other, begins to suspect him. Like one beginning to rouse himself from a dose of chloroform treacherously given, he half divines, too, that he, the philosopher, had unwittingly been betrayed into being an unphilosophical dupe. To what vicissitudes of light and shade is man subject! He ponders the mystery of human subjectivity in general. He thinks he perceives with Cross-bones, his favorite author, that, as one may wake up well in the morning, very well, indeed, and brisk as a buck, I thank you, but ere bed-time get under the weather, there is no telling how—so one may wake up wise, and slow of assent, very wise and very slow, I assure you, and for all that, before night, by like trick in the atmosphere, be left in the lurch a ninny. Health and wisdom equally precious, and equally little as unfluctuating possessions to be relied on.

But where was slipped in the entering wedge? Philosophy, knowl-

1. "If I forget thee, O Jerusalem, let my right hand forget her cunning" (Psalms 137:5).
2. Apemantus is the churlish philoso-pher of *Timon of Athens*. Here and elsewhere Melville is punning on the Latin sense of cynic ("doglike").

edge, experience—were those trusty knights of the castle recreant? No, but unbeknown to them, the enemy stole on the castle's south side, its genial one, where Suspicion, the warder, parleyed. In fine, his too indulgent, too artless and companionable nature betrayed him. Admonished by which, he thinks he must be a little splenetic in his intercourse henceforth.

He revolves the crafty process of sociable chat, by which, as he fancies, the man with the brass-plate wormed into him, and made such a fool of him as insensibly to persuade him to waive, in his exceptional case, that general law of distrust systematically applied to the race. He revolves, but cannot comprehend, the operation, still less the operator. Was the man a trickster, it must be more for the love than the lucre. Two or three dirty dollars the motive to so many nice wiles? And yet how full of mean needs his seeming. Before his mental vision the person of that threadbare Talleyrand, that impoverished Machiavelli, that seedy Rosicrucian —for something of all these he vaguely deems him—passes now in puzzled review. Fain, in his disfavor, would he make out a logical case. The doctrine of analogies recurs. Fallacious enough doctrine when wielded against one's prejudices, but in corroboration of cherished suspicions not without likelihood. Analogically, he couples the slanting cut of the equivocator's coat-tails with the sinister cast in his eye; he weighs slyboot's sleek speech in the light imparted by the oblique import of the smooth slope of his worn boot-heels; the insinuator's undulating flunkyisms dovetail into those of the flunky beast that windeth his way on his belly.[3]

From these uncordial reveries he is roused by a cordial slap on the shoulder, accompanied by a spicy volume of tobacco-smoke, out of which came a voice, sweet as a seraph's:

"A penny for your thoughts, my fine fellow."

Chapter 24

A PHILANTHROPIST UNDERTAKES TO CONVERT A MISANTHROPE, BUT DOES NOT GET BEYOND CONFUTING HIM

"Hands off!" cried the bachelor, involuntarily covering dejection with moroseness.

"Hands off? that sort of label won't do in our Fair. Whoever

3. See Genesis 3:14. Pitch is the loser by three dollars plus passage money for the boy, but among the passengers of the *Fidèle* he is the most admirable opponent of the Devil's false, delusive optimism, and at this moment he becomes the only one—except perhaps the invalid Titan—to penetrate the masquerade.

in our Fair has fine feelings loves to feel the nap of fine cloth, especially when a fine fellow wears it."

"And who of my fine-fellow species may you be? From the Brazils, ain't you? Toucan fowl. Fine feathers on foul meat."

This ungentle mention of the toucan was not improbably suggested by the parti-hued, and rather plumagy aspect of the stranger, no bigot it would seem, but a liberalist, in dress, and whose wardrobe, almost anywhere than on the liberal Mississippi, used to all sorts of fantastic informalities, might, even to observers less critical than the bachelor, have looked, if anything, a little out of the common; but not more so perhaps, than, considering the bear and raccoon costume, the bachelor's own appearance. In short, the stranger sported a vesture barred with various hues, that of the cochineal predominating, in style participating of a Highland plaid, Emir's robe, and French blouse; from its plaited sort of front peeped glimpses of a flowered regatta-shirt, while, for the rest, white trowsers of ample duck flowed over maroon-colored slippers, and a jaunty smoking-cap of regal purple crowned him off at top; king of traveled good-fellows, evidently. Grotesque as all was, nothing looked stiff or unused; all showed signs of easy service, the least wonted thing setting like a wonted glove. That genial hand, which had just been laid on the ungenial shoulder, was now carelessly thrust down before him, sailor-fashion, into a sort of Indian belt, confining the redundant vesture; the other held, by its long bright cherry-stem, a Nuremburgh pipe in blast, its great porcelain bowl painted in miniature with linked crests and arms of interlinked nations—a florid show. As by subtle saturations of its mellowing essence the tobacco had ripened the bowl, so it looked as if something similar of the interior spirit came rosily out on the cheek. But rosy pipe-bowl, or rosy countenance, all was lost on that unrosy man, the bachelor, who, waiting a moment till the commotion, caused by the boat's renewed progress, had a little abated, thus continued:

"Hark ye," jeeringly eying the cap and belt, "did you ever see Signor Marzetti in the African pantomime?"[1]

"No;—good performer?"

"Excellent; plays the intelligent ape till he seems it. With such naturalness can a being endowed with an immortal spirit enter into that of a monkey. But where's your tail? In the pantomime, Marzetti, no hypocrite in his monkery, prides himself on that."

The stranger, now at rest, sideways and genially, on one hip, his right leg cavalierly crossed before the other, the toe of his vertical slipper pointed easily down on the deck, whiffed out a long, lei-

---

1. Melville may have seen Joseph Marzetti pantomime the role of an ape in more than one New York theater; for instance, he played in *The Brazilian Ape* at Burton's in 1848 and in *Jocko* at Niblo's Garden in 1849.

surely sort of indifferent and charitable puff, betokening him more
or less of the mature man of the world, a character which, like its
opposite, the sincere Christian's, is not always swift to take offense;
and then, drawing near, still smoking, again laid his hand, this
time with mild impressiveness, on the ursine shoulder, and not una-
miably said: "That in your address there is a sufficiency of the *fortiter in re* few unbiased observers will question; but that this is duly
attempered with the *suaviter in modo* may admit, I think, of an
honest doubt.[2] My dear fellow," beaming his eyes full upon him,
"what injury have I done you, that you should receive my greeting
with a curtailed civility?"

"Off hands;" once more shaking the friendly member from him.
"Who in the name of the great chimpanzee, in whose likeness,
you, Marzetti, and the other chatterers are made, who in thunder
are you?"

"A cosmopolitan, a catholic man; who, being such, ties himself
to no narrow tailor or teacher, but federates, in heart as in costume,
something of the various gallantries of men under various suns. Oh,
one roams not over the gallant globe in vain. Bred by it, is a fraternal and fusing feeling. No man is a stranger. You accost anybody.
Warm and confiding, you wait not for measured advances. And
though, indeed, mine, in this instance, have met with no very hilarious encouragement, yet the principle of a true citizen of the
world is still to return good for ill.—My dear fellow, tell me how
I can serve you."

"By dispatching yourself, Mr. Popinjay-of-the-world, into the
heart of the Lunar Mountains. You are another of them. Out of
my sight!"

"Is the sight of humanity so very disagreeable to you then? Ah, I
may be foolish, but for my part, in all its aspects, I love it. Served
up à la Pole, or à la Moor, à la Ladrone, or à la Yankee, that good
dish, man, still delights me; or rather is man a wine I never weary
of comparing and sipping; wherefore am I a pledged cosmopolitan,
a sort of London-Dock-Vault connoisseur, going about from Te-
heran to Natchitoches, a taster of races; in all his vintages, smacking
my lips over this racy creature, man, continually. But as there are
teetotal palates which have a distaste even for Amontillado, so I suppose there may be teetotal souls which relish not even the very best
brands of humanity. Excuse me, but it just occurs to me that you,
my dear fellow, possibly lead a solitary life."

"Solitary?" starting as at a touch of divination.

"Yes: in a solitary life one insensibly contracts oddities,—talking
to one's self now."

"Been eaves-dropping, eh?"

2. *Fortiter in re, suaviter in modo:* strongly in deed, gently in manner.

"Why, a soliloquist in a crowd can hardly but be overheard, and without much reproach to the hearer."

"You are an eaves-dropper."

"Well. Be it so."

"Confess yourself an eaves-dropper?"

"I confess that when you were muttering here I, passing by, caught a word or two, and, by like chance, something previous of your chat with the Intelligence-office man;—a rather sensible fellow, by the way; much of my style of thinking; would, for his own sake, he were of my style of dress. Grief to good minds, to see a man of superior sense forced to hide his light under the bushel[3] of an inferior coat.—Well, from what little I heard, I said to myself, Here now is one with the unprofitable philosophy of disesteem for man. Which disease, in the main, I have observed—excuse me—to spring from a certain lowness, if not sourness, of spirits inseparable from sequestration. Trust me, one had better mix in, and do like others. Sad business, this holding out against having a good time. Life is a pic-nic *en costume*; one must take a part, assume a character, stand ready in a sensible way to play the fool. To come in plain clothes, with a long face, as a wiseacre, only makes one a discomfort to himself, and a blot upon the scene. Like your jug of cold water among the wine-flasks, it leaves you unelated among the elated ones. No, no. This austerity won't do. Let me tell you too—*en confiance*—that while revelry may not always merge into ebriety, soberness, in too deep potations, may become a sort of sottishness. Which sober sottishness, in my way of thinking, is only to be cured by beginning at the other end of the horn, to tipple a little."

"Pray, what society of vintners and old topers are you hired to lecture for?"

"I fear I did not give my meaning clearly. A little story may help. The story of the worthy old woman of Goshen, a very moral old woman, who wouldn't let her shoats eat fattening apples in fall, for fear the fruit might ferment upon their brains, and so make them swinish. Now, during a green Christmas, inauspicious to the old, this worthy old woman fell into a moping decline, took to her bed, no appetite, and refused to see her best friends. In much concern her good man sent for the doctor, who, after seeing the patient and putting a question or two, beckoned the husband out, and said: 'Deacon, do you want her cured?' 'Indeed I do.' 'Go directly, then, and buy a jug of Santa Cruz.' 'Santa Cruz? my wife drink Santa Cruz?' 'Either that or die.' 'But how much?' 'As much as she can get down.' 'But she'll get drunk!' 'That's the cure.' Wise men, like doctors, must be obeyed. Much against the grain, the sober deacon got the unsober medicine, and, equally against

3. Matthew 5:15.

her conscience, the poor old woman took it; but, by so doing, ere long recovered health and spirits, famous appetite, and glad again to see her friends; and having by this experience broken the ice of arid abstinence, never afterwards kept herself a cup too low."

This story had the effect of surprising the bachelor into interest, though hardly into approval.

"If I take your parable right," said he, sinking no little of his former churlishness, "the meaning is, that one cannot enjoy life with gusto unless he renounce the too-sober view of life. But since the too-sober view is, doubtless, nearer true than the too-drunken; I, who rate truth, though cold water, above untruth, though Tokay, will stick to my earthen jug."

"I see," slowly spirting upward a spiral staircase of lazy smoke, "I see; you go in for the lofty."

"How?"

"Oh, nothing! but if I wasn't afraid of prosing, I might tell another story about an old boot in a pieman's loft, contracting there between sun and oven an unseemly, dry-seasoned curl and warp. You've seen such leathery old garretteers, haven't you? Very high, sober, solitary, philosophic, grand, old boots, indeed; but I, for my part, would rather be the pieman's trodden slipper on the ground. Talking of piemen, humble-pie before proud-cake for me. This notion of being lone and lofty is a sad mistake. Men I hold in this respect to be like roosters; the one that betakes himself to a lone and lofty perch is the hen-pecked one, or the one that has the pip."

"You are abusive!" cried the bachelor, evidently touched.

"Who is abused? You, or the race? You won't stand by and see the human race abused? Oh, then, you have some respect for the human race."

"I have some respect for *myself*," with a lip not so firm as before.

"And what race may *you* belong to? now don't you see, my dear fellow, in what inconsistencies one involves himself by affecting disesteem for men? To a charm, my little stratagem succeeded. Come, come, think better of it, and, as a first step to a new mind, give up solitude. I fear, by the way, you have at some time been reading Zimmermann, that old Mr. Megrims of a Zimmermann, whose book on Solitude is as vain as Hume's on Suicide, as Bacon's on Knowledge; and, like these, will betray him who seeks to steer soul and body by it, like a false religion. All they, be they what boasted ones you please, who, to the yearning of our kind after a founded rule of content, offer aught not in the spirit of fellowly gladness based on due confidence in what is above, away with them for poor dupes, or still poorer impostors."

His manner here was so earnest that scarcely any auditor, perhaps, but would have been more or less impressed by it, while, possibly, nervous opponents might have a little quailed under it. Thinking within himself a moment, the bachelor replied: "Had you experience, you would know that your tippling theory, take it in what sense you will, is poor as any other. And Rabelais's pro-wine Koran no more trustworthy than Mahomet's anti-wine one."

"Enough," for a finality knocking the ashes from his pipe, "we talk and keep talking, and still stand where we did. What do you say for a walk? My arm, and let's a turn. They are to have dancing on the hurricane-deck to-night. I shall fling them off a Scotch jig, while, to save the pieces, you hold my loose change; and following that, I propose that you, my dear fellow, stack your gun, and throw your bearskins in a sailor's hornpipe—I holding your watch. What do you say?"

At this proposition the other was himself again, all raccoon.

"Look you," thumping down his rifle, "are you Jeremy Diddler No. 3?"

"Jeremy Diddler? I have heard of Jeremy the prophet, and Jeremy Taylor the divine, but your other Jeremy is a gentleman I am unacquainted with."

"You are his confidential clerk, ain't you?"

"*Whose*, pray? Not that I think myself unworthy of being confided in, but I don't understand."

"You are another of them. Somehow I meet with the most extraordinary metaphysical scamps to-day. Sort of visitation of them. And yet that herb-doctor Diddler somehow takes off the raw edge of the Diddlers that come after him."

"Herb-doctor? who is he?"

"Like you—another of them."

"*Who?*" Then drawing near, as if for a good long explanatory chat, his left hand spread, and his pipe-stem coming crosswise down upon it like a ferule, "You think amiss of me. Now to undeceive you, I will just enter into a little argument and—"

"No you don't. No more little arguments for me. Had too many little arguments to-day."

"But put a case. Can you deny—I dare you to deny—that the man leading a solitary life is peculiarly exposed to the sorriest misconceptions touching strangers?"

"Yes, I *do* deny it," again, in his impulsiveness, snapping at the controversial bait, "and I will confute you there in a trice. Look, you—"

"Now, now, now, my dear fellow," thrusting out both vertical palms for double shields, "you crowd me too hard. You don't give one a chance. Say what you will, to shun a social proposition like

mine, to shun society in any way, evinces a churlish nature—cold,
loveless; as, to embrace it, shows one warm and friendly, in fact,
sunshiny."

Here the other, all agog again, in his perverse way, launched
forth into the unkindest references to deaf old worldlings keeping
in the deafening world; and gouty gluttons limping to their gouty
gormandizings; and corseted coquets clasping their corseted cava-
liers in the waltz, all for disinterested society's sake; and thousands,
bankrupt through lavishness, ruining themselves out of pure love
of the sweet company of man—no envies, rivalries, or other unhandsome motive to it.

"Ah, now," deprecating with his pipe, "irony is so unjust; never
could abide irony; something Satanic about irony. God defend me
from Irony, and Satire, his bosom friend."

"A right knave's prayer, and a right fool's, too," snapping his
rifle-lock.

"Now be frank. Own that was a little gratuitous. But, no, no,
you didn't mean it; any way, I can make allowances. Ah, did you
but know it, how much pleasanter to puff at this philanthropic pipe,
than still to keep fumbling at that misanthropic rifle. As for your
worldling, glutton, and coquette, though, doubtless, being such,
they may have their little foibles—as who has not?—yet not one of
the three can be reproached with that awful sin of shunning society;
awful I call it, for not seldom it presupposes a still darker thing
than itself—remorse."

"Remorse drives man away from man? How came your fellow-
creature, Cain, after the first murder, to go and build the first city?
And why is it that the modern Cain dreads nothing so much as solitary confinement?"

"My dear fellow, you get excited. Say what you will, I for one
must have my fellow-creatures round me. Thick, too—I must have
them thick."

"The pick-pocket, too, loves to have his fellow-creatures round
him. Tut, man! no one goes into the crowd but for his end; and
the end of too many is the same as the pick-pocket's—a purse."

"Now, my dear fellow, how can you have the conscience to say
that, when it is as much according to natural law that men are
social as sheep gregarious. But grant that, in being social, each man
has his end, do you, upon the strength of that, do you yourself, I
say, mix with man, now, immediately, and be your end a more
genial philosophy. Come, let's take a turn."

Again he offered his fraternal arm; but the bachelor once more
flung it off, and, raising his rifle in energetic invocation, cried:
"Now the high-constable catch and confound all knaves in towns

and rats in grain-bins, and if in this boat, which is a human grain-bin for the time, any sly, smooth, philandering rat be dodging now, pin him, thou high rat-catcher, against this rail."

"A noble burst! shows you at heart a trump. And when a card's that, little matters it whether it be spade or diamond. You are good wine that, to be still better, only needs a shaking up. Come, let's agree that we'll to New Orleans, and there embark for London—I staying with my friends nigh Primrose-hill, and you putting up at the Piazza, Covent Garden—Piazza, Covent Garden; for tell me—since you will not be a disciple to the full—tell me, was not that humor, of Diogenes, which led him to live, a merry-andrew, in the flower-market, better than that of the less wise Athenian, which made him a skulking scare-crow in pine-barrens? An injudicious gentleman, Lord Timon."

"Your hand!" seizing it.

"Bless me, how cordial a squeeze. It is agreed we shall be brothers, then?"

"As much so as a brace of misanthropes can be," with another and terrific squeeze. "I had thought that the moderns had degenerated beneath the capacity of misanthropy. Rejoiced, though but in one instance, and that disguised, to be undeceived."

The other stared in blank amaze.

"Won't do. You are Diogenes, Diogenes in disguise. I say—Diogenes masquerading as a cosmopolitan."

With ruefully altered mien, the stranger still stood mute awhile. At length, in a pained tone, spoke: "How hard the lot of that pleader who, in his zeal conceding too much, is taken to belong to a side which he but labors, however ineffectually, to convert!" Then with another change of air: "To you, an Ishmael, disguising in sportiveness my intent, I came ambassador from the human race, charged with the assurance that for your mislike they bore no answering grudge, but sought to conciliate accord between you and them. Yet you take me not for the honest envoy, but I know not what sort of unheard-of spy. Sir," he less lowly added, "this mistaking of your man should teach you how you may mistake all men. For God's sake," laying both hands upon him, "get you confidence. See how distrust has duped you. I, Diogenes? I he who, going a step beyond misanthropy, was less a man-hater than a man-hooter? Better were I stark and stiff!"

With which the philanthropist moved away less lightsome than he had come, leaving the discomfited misanthrope to the solitude he held so sapient.

Chapter 25

THE COSMOPOLITAN MAKES AN ACQUAINTANCE

In the act of retiring, the cosmopolitan was met by a passenger, who, with the bluff *abord* of the West, thus addressed him, though a stranger.

"Queer 'coon, your friend. Had a little skrimmage with him myself. Rather entertaining old 'coon, if he wasn't so deuced analytical. Reminded me somehow of what I've heard about Colonel John Moredock, of Illinois, only your friend ain't quite so good a fellow at bottom, I should think."

It was in the semicircular porch of a cabin, opening a recess from the deck, lit by a zoned lamp swung overhead, and sending its light vertically down, like the sun at noon. Beneath the lamp stood the speaker, affording to any one disposed to it no unfavorable chance for scrutiny; but the glance now resting on him betrayed no such rudeness.

A man neither tall nor stout, neither short nor gaunt; but with a body fitted, as by measure, to the service of his mind. For the rest, one less favored perhaps in his features than his clothes; and of these the beauty may have been less in the fit than the cut; to say nothing of the fineness of the nap, seeming out of keeping with something the reverse of fine in the skin; and the unsuitableness of a violet vest, sending up sunset hues to a countenance betokening a kind of bilious habit.

But, upon the whole, it could not be fairly said that his appearance was unprepossessing; indeed, to the congenial, it would have been doubtless not uncongenial; while to others, it could not fail to be at least curiously interesting, from the warm air of florid cordiality, contrasting itself with one knows not what kind of aguish sallowness of saving discretion lurking behind it. Ungracious critics might have thought that the manner flushed the man, something in the same fictitious way that the vest flushed the cheek. And though his teeth were singularly good, those same ungracious ones might have hinted that they were too good to be true; or rather, were not so good as they might be; since the best false teeth are those made with at least two or three blemishes, the more to look like life. But fortunately for better constructions, no such critics had the stranger now in eye; only the cosmopolitan, who, after, in the first place, acknowledging his advances with a mute salute—in which acknowledgment, if there seemed less of spirit than in his way of accosting the Missourian, it was probably because of the saddening sequel of that late interview—thus now replied: "Colonel John Moredock," repeating the words abstractedly; "that surname recalls reminiscences. Pray," with enlivened air, "was he anyway connected with the Moredocks of Moredock Hall, Northamptonshire, England?"

"I know no more of the Moredocks of Moredock Hall than of the Burdocks of Burdock Hut," returned the other, with the air somehow of one whose fortunes had been of his own making; "all I know is, that the late Colonel John Moredock was a famous one in his time; eye like Lochiel's;[1] finger like a trigger; nerve like a catamount's; and with but two little oddities—seldom stirred without his rifle, and hated Indians like snakes."

"Your Moredock, then, would seem a Moredock of Misanthrope Hall—the Woods. No very sleek creature, the colonel, I fancy."

"Sleek or not, he was no uncombed one, but silky bearded ana curly headed, and to all but Indians juicy as a peach. But Indians—how the late Colonel John Moredock, Indian-hater of Illinois, did hate Indians, to be sure!"

"Never heard of such a thing. Hate Indians? Why should he or anybody else hate Indians? *I* admire Indians. Indians I have always heard to be one of the finest of the primitive races, possessed of many heroic virtues. Some noble women, too. When I think of Pocahontas, I am ready to love Indians. Then there's Massasoit, and Philip of Mount Hope, and Tecumseh, and Red-Jacket, and Logan—all heroes; and there's the Five Nations, and Araucanians—federations and communities of heroes. God bless me; hate Indians? Surely, the late Colonel John Moredock must have wandered in his mind."

"Wandered in the woods considerably, but never wandered elsewhere, that I ever heard."

"Are you in earnest? Was there ever one who so made it his particular mission to hate Indians that, to designate him, a special word has been coined—Indian-hater?"

"Even so."

"Dear me, you take it very calmly.—But really, I would like to know something about this Indian-hating. I can hardly believe such a thing to be. Could you favor me with a little history of the extraordinary man you mentioned?"

"With all my heart," and immediately stepping from the porch, gestured the cosmopolitan to a settee near by, on deck. "There, sir, sit you there, and I will sit here beside you—you desire to hear of Colonel John Moredock. Well, a day in my boyhood is marked

1. Sir Ewan Cameron of Lochiel (1629–1719). Foster quotes from Macaulay's *History of England*: "In agility and skill at his weapons he had few equals among the inhabitants of the hills. He had repeatedly been victo-rious in single combat. He was a hunter of great fame. He made vigorous war on the wolves . . . ; and by his hand perished the last of the ferocious breed which is known to have wandered at large in our island."

with a white stone[2]—the day I saw the colonel's rifle, powder-horn attached, hanging in a cabin on the West bank of the Wabash river. I was going westward a long journey through the wilderness with my father. It was nigh noon, and we had stopped at the cabin to unsaddle and bait. The man at the cabin pointed out the rifle, and told whose it was, adding that the colonel was that moment sleeping on wolf-skins in the corn-loft above, so we must not talk very loud, for the colonel had been out all night hunting (Indians, mind), and it would be cruel to disturb his sleep. Curious to see one so famous, we waited two hours over, in hopes he would come forth; but he did not. So, it being necessary to get to the next cabin before nightfall, we had at last to ride off without the wished-for satisfaction. Though, to tell the truth, I, for one, did not go away entirely ungratified, for, while my father was watering the horses, I slipped back into the cabin, and stepping a round or two up the ladder, pushed my head through the trap, and peered about. Not much light in the loft; but off, in the further corner, I saw what I took to be the wolf-skins, and on them a bundle of something, like a drift of leaves; and at one end, what seemed a moss-ball; and over it, deer-antlers branched; and close by, a small squirrel sprang out from a maple-bowl of nuts, brushed the moss-ball with his tail, through a hole, and vanished, squeaking. That bit of woodland scene was all I saw. No Colonel Moredock there, unless that moss-ball was his curly head, seen in the back view. I would have gone clear up, but the man below had warned me, that though, from his camping habits, the colonel could sleep through thunder, he was for the same cause amazing quick to waken at the sound of footsteps, however soft, and especially if human."

"Excuse me," said the other, softly laying his hand on the narrator's wrist, "but I fear the colonel was of a distrustful nature—little or no confidence. He *was* a little suspicious-minded, wasn't he?"

"Not a bit. Knew too much. Suspected nobody, but was not ignorant of Indians. Well: though, as you may gather, I never fully saw the man, yet, have I, one way and another, heard about as much of him as any other; in particular, have I heard his history again and again from my father's friend, James Hall, the judge, you know. In every company being called upon to give this history, which none could better do, the judge at last fell into a style so methodic, you would have thought he spoke less to mere auditors than to an invisible amanuensis; seemed talking for the press; very impressive way with him indeed. And I, having an equally impressible memory, think that, upon a pinch, I can render you the judge upon the colonel almost word for word."

"Do so, by all means," said the cosmopolitan, well pleased.

2. The meaning is simply that the day was memorable, since the ancients used a white stone "as a memorial of a fortunate event" (*OED*), but Melville may have in mind Revelation 2:17.

"Shall I give you the judge's philosophy, and all?"

"As to that," rejoined the other gravely, pausing over the pipe-bowl he was filling, "the desirableness, to a man of a certain mind, of having another man's philosophy given, depends considerably upon what school of philosophy that other man belongs to. Of what school or system was the judge, pray?"

"Why, though he knew how to read and write, the judge never had much schooling. But, I should say he belonged, if anything, to the free-school system. Yes, a true patriot, the judge went in strong for free-schools."

"In philosophy? The man of a certain mind, then, while respecting the judge's patriotism, and not blind to the judge's capacity for narrative, such as he may prove to have, might, perhaps, with prudence, waive an opinion of the judge's probable philosophy. But I am no rigorist; proceed, I beg; his philosophy or not, as you please."

"Well, I would mostly skip that part, only, to begin, some reconnoitering of the ground in a philosophical way the judge always deemed indispensable with strangers. For you must know that Indian-hating was no monopoly of Colonel Moredock's; but a passion, in one form or other, and to a degree, greater or less, largely shared among the class to which he belonged. And Indian-hating still exists; and, no doubt, will continue to exist, so long as Indians do. Indian-hating, then, shall be my first theme, and Colonel Moredock, the Indian-hater, my next and last."

With which the stranger, settling himself in his seat, commenced—the hearer paying marked regard, slowly smoking, his glance, meanwhile, steadfastly abstracted towards the deck, but his right ear so disposed towards the speaker that each word came through as little atmospheric intervention as possible. To intensify the sense of hearing, he seemed to sink the sense of sight. No complaisance of mere speech could have been so flattering, or expressed such striking politeness as this mute eloquence of thoroughly digesting attention.

Chapter 26

CONTAINING THE METAPHYSICS OF INDIAN-HATING, ACCORDING
TO THE VIEWS OF ONE EVIDENTLY NOT SO PREPOSSESSED AS
ROUSSEAU IN FAVOR OF SAVAGES

"The judge always began in these words: 'The backwoodsman's hatred of the Indian has been a topic for some remark. In the earlier times of the frontier the passion was thought to be readily accounted for. But Indian rapine having mostly ceased through regions where it once prevailed, the philanthropist is surprised that Indian-hating has not in like degree ceased with it. He wonders why the backwoodsman still regards the red man in much the same spirit that a jury does a murderer, or a trapper a wild cat—a creature, in whose behalf mercy were not wisdom; truce is vain; he must be executed.

"'A curious point,' the judge would continue, 'which perhaps not everybody, even upon explanation, may fully understand; while, in order for any one to approach to an understanding, it is necessary for him to learn, or if he already know, to bear in mind, what manner of man the backwoodsman is; as for what manner of man the Indian is, many know, either from history or experience.

"'The backwoodsman is a lonely man. He is a thoughtful man. He is a man strong and unsophisticated. Impulsive, he is what some might call unprincipled. At any rate, he is self-willed; being one who less hearkens to what others may say about things, than looks for himself, to see what are things themselves. If in straits, there are few to help; he must depend upon himself; he must continually look to himself. Hence self-reliance, to the degree of standing by his own judgment, though it stand alone. Not that he deems himself infallible; too many mistakes in following trails prove the contrary; but he thinks that nature destines such sagacity as she has given him, as she destines it to the 'possum. To these fellow-beings of the wilds their untutored sagacity is their best dependence. If with either it prove faulty, if the 'possum's betray it to the trap, or the backwoodsman's mislead him into ambuscade, there are consequences to be undergone, but no self-blame. As with the 'possum, instincts prevail with the backwoodsman over precepts. Like the 'possum, the backwoodsman presents the spectacle of a creature dwelling exclusively among the works of God, yet these, truth must confess, breed little in him of a godly mind. Small bowing and scraping is his, further than when with bent knee he points his rifle, or picks its flint. With few companions, solitude by necessity his lengthened lot, he stands the trial—no slight one, since, next to dying, solitude, rightly borne, is perhaps of fortitude the most rigorous test. But not merely is the backwoodsman content to be alone, but in no few cases is anxious to be so. The sight of smoke ten miles off is provocation to one more remove from man, one step deeper into nature. Is it that he feels that whatever man may be, man is not the universe? that glory, beauty, kindness, are not all engrossed by him? that as the presence of man frights birds away, so, many bird-like thoughts? Be that how it will, the backwoodsman is not without some fineness to his nature. Hairy

Orson[1] as he looks, it may be with him as with the Shetland seal—beneath the bristles lurks the fur.

" 'Though held in a sort a barbarian, the backwoodsman would seem to America what Alexander was to Asia—captain in the vanguard of conquering civilization. Whatever the nation's growing opulence or power, does it not lackey his heels? Pathfinder, provider of security to those who come after him, for himself he asks nothing but hardship. Worthy to be compared with Moses in the Exodus, or the Emperor Julian in Gaul, who on foot, and barebrowed, at the head of covered or mounted legions, marched so through the elements, day after day. The tide of emigration, let it roll as it will, never overwhelms the backwoodsman into itself; he rides upon advance, as the Polynesian upon the comb of the surf.

" 'Thus, though he keep moving on through life, he maintains with respect to nature much the same unaltered relation throughout; with her creatures, too, including panthers and Indians. Hence, it is not unlikely that, accurate as the theory of the Peace Congress may be with respect to those two varieties of beings, among others, yet the backwoodsman might be qualified to throw out some practical suggestions.

" 'As the child born to a backwoodsman must in turn lead his father's life—a life which, as related to humanity, is related mainly to Indians—it is thought best not to mince matters, out of delicacy; but to tell the boy pretty plainly what an Indian is, and what he must expect from him. For however charitable it may be to view Indians as members of the Society of Friends,[2] yet to affirm them such to one ignorant of Indians, whose lonely path lies a long way through their lands, this, in the event, might prove not only injudicious but cruel. At least something of this kind would seem the maxim upon which backwoods' education is based. Accordingly, if in youth the backwoodsman incline to knowledge, as is generally the case, he hears little from his schoolmasters, the old chroniclers of the forest, but histories of Indian lying, Indian theft, Indian double-dealing, Indian fraud and perfidy, Indian want of conscience, Indian blood-thirstiness, Indian diabolism—histories which, though of wild woods, are almost as full of things unangelic

---

1. Character in a medieval French romance who is stolen by a bear and grows up as a wild man. Another reminder that the human form may be occupied by sub-human or extra-human creatures.
2. Submerged in this sentence is Melville's memory of a story he once planned about the Devil's bargaining for a man's soul. He made these notes for it in a volume of his set of Shakespeare, under the heading "(Devil as a a Quaker)": A formal compact— —Imprimis—First—Second. The aforesaid soul. said soul &c—Duplicates— "How was it about the temptation on the hill?" &c Conversation upon Gabriel, Michael & Raphael—gentlemanly &c—D begs the hero to form one of a "*Society of D's*"—his name would be mighty &c—Leaves a letter to the D— "My Dear D"— . . . Receives visits from the principal d's—"Gentlemen" &c *arguments* to persuade—"Would you not rather be below with kings than above with fools?"

as the Newgate Calendar or the Annals of Europe. In these Indian narratives and traditions the lad is thoroughly grounded. "As the twig is bent the tree's inclined." The instinct of antipathy against an Indian grows in the backwoodsman with the sense of good and bad, right and wrong. In one breath he learns that a brother is to be loved, and an Indian to be hated.

" 'Such are the facts,' the judge would say, 'upon which, if one seek to moralize, he must do so with an eye to them. It is terrible that one creature should so regard another, should make it conscience to abhor an entire race. It is terrible; but is it surprising? Surprising, that one should hate a race which he believes to be red from a cause akin to that which makes some tribes of garden insects green? A race whose name is upon the frontier a *memento mori*; painted to him in every evil light; now a horse-thief like those in Moyamensing; now an assassin like a New York rowdy; now a treaty-breaker like an Austrian; now a Palmer with poisoned arrows; now a judicial murderer and Jeffries, after a fierce farce of trial condemning his victim to bloody death;[3] or a Jew with hospitable speeches cozening some fainting stranger into ambuscade, there to burke him, and account it a deed grateful to Manitou, his god.

" 'Still, all this is less advanced as truths of the Indians than as examples of the backwoodsman's impression of them—in which the charitable may think he does them some injustice. Certain it is, the Indians themselves think so; quite unanimously, too. The Indians, indeed, protest against the backwoodsman's view of them; and some think that one cause of their returning his antipathy so sincerely as they do, is their moral indignation at being so libeled by him, as they really believe and say. But whether, on this or any point, the Indians should be permitted to testify for themselves, to the exclusion of other testimony, is a question that may be left to the Supreme Court. At any rate, it has been observed that when an Indian becomes a genuine proselyte to Christianity (such cases, however, not being very many; though, indeed, entire tribes are sometimes nominally brought to the true light,) he will not in that case conceal his enlightened conviction, that his race's portion by nature is total depravity; and, in that way, as much as admits that the backwoodsman's worst idea of it is not very far from true; while, on the other hand, those red men who are the greatest sticklers for the theory of Indian virtue, and Indian loving-kindness, are

3. Moyamensing is not the section in southern Philadelphia County, but the Philadelphia County Prison of the same name (*History of Philadelphia, 1609–1884.*) Palmer is Dr. William Palmer (1824–1856), a notorious British poisoner who was arrested December 15, 1855, tried at Old Bailey on May 14, 1856, and hanged June 14, 1856. The reference provides one of the few clues to the date a section of the book may have been composed. George Jeffries (1648–1689) is the brutal judge under Charles II and James II. He presided at the trial of Algernon Sidney for treason in 1683 and at the trial of Titus Oates in 1685.

sometimes the arrantest horse-thieves and tomahawkers among them. So, at least, avers the backwoodsman. And though, knowing the Indian nature, as he thinks he does, he fancies he is not ignorant that an Indian may in some points deceive himself almost as effectually as in bush-tactics he can another, yet his theory and his practice as above contrasted seem to involve an inconsistency so extreme, that the backwoodsman only accounts for it on the supposition that when a tomahawking red-man advances the notion of the benignity of the red race, it is but part and parcel with that subtle strategy which he finds so useful in war, in hunting, and the general conduct of life.'

"In further explanation of that deep abhorrence with which the backwoodsman regards the savage, the judge used to think it might perhaps a little help, to consider what kind of stimulus to it is furnished in those forest histories and traditions before spoken of. In which behalf, he would tell the story of the little colony of Wrights and Weavers, originally seven cousins from Virginia, who, after successive removals with their families, at last established themselves near the southern frontier of the Bloody Ground, Kentucky: 'They were strong, brave men; but, unlike many of the pioneers in those days, theirs was no love of conflict for conflict's sake. Step by step they had been lured to their lonely resting-place by the ever-beckoning seductions of a fertile and virgin land, with a singular exemption, during the march, from Indian molestation. But clearings made and houses built, the bright shield was soon to turn its other side. After repeated persecutions and eventual hostilities, forced on them by a dwindled tribe in their neighborhood—persecutions resulting in loss of crops and cattle; hostilities in which they lost two of their number, illy to be spared, besides others getting painful wounds—the five remaining cousins made, with some serious concessions, a kind of treaty with Mocmohoc, the chief—being to this induced by the harryings of the enemy, leaving them no peace. But they were further prompted, indeed, first incited, by the suddenly changed ways of Mocmohoc, who, though hitherto deemed a savage almost perfidious as Cæsar Borgia, yet now put on a seeming the reverse of this, engaging to bury the hatchet, smoke the pipe, and be friends forever; not friends in the mere sense of renouncing enmity, but in the sense of kindliness, active and familiar.

" 'But what the chief now seemed, did not wholly blind them to what the chief had been; so that, though in no small degree influenced by his change of bearing, they still distrusted him enough to covenant with him, among other articles on their side, that though friendly visits should be exchanged between the wigwams and the cabins, yet the five cousins should never, on any account, be expected to enter the chief's lodge together. The intention was, though they reserved it, that if ever, under the guise of amity, the chief should mean them mischief, and effect it, it should be but partially; so that some of the five might survive, not only for their families' sake, but also for retribution's. Nevertheless, Mocmohoc did, upon a time, with such fine art and pleasing carriage win their confidence, that he brought them all together to a feast of bear's meat, and there, by stratagem, ended them. Years after, over their calcined bones and those of all their families, the chief, reproached for his treachery by a proud hunter whom he had made captive, jeered out, "Treachery? pale face! 'Twas they who broke their covenant first, in coming all together; they that broke it first, in trusting Mocmohoc." '

"At this point the judge would pause, and lifting his hand, and rolling his eyes, exclaim in a solemn enough voice, 'Circling wiles and bloody lusts. The acuteness and genius of the chief but make him the more atrocious.'

"After another pause, he would begin an imaginary kind of dialogue between a backwoodsman and a questioner:

" 'But are all Indians like Mocmohoc?—Not all have proved such; but in the least harmful may lie his germ. There is an Indian nature. "Indian blood is in me," is the half-breed's threat.—But are not some Indians kind?—Yes, but kind Indians are mostly lazy, and reputed simple—at all events, are seldom chiefs; chiefs among the red man being taken from the active, and those accounted wise. Hence, with small promotion, kind Indians have but proportionate influence. And kind Indians may be forced to do unkind biddings. So "beware the Indian, kind or unkind," said Daniel Boone, who lost his sons by them.—But, have all you backwoodsmen been some way victimized by Indians?—No.— Well, and in certain cases may not at least some few of you be favored by them?—Yes, but scarce one among us so self-important, or so selfish-minded, as to hold his personal exemption from Indian outrage such a set-off against the contrary experience of so many others, as that he must needs, in a general way, think well of Indians; or, if he do, an arrow in his flank might suggest a pertinent doubt.

" 'In short,' according to the judge, 'if we at all credit the backwoodsman, his feeling against Indians, to be taken aright, must be considered as being not so much on his own account as on others', or jointly on both accounts. True it is, scarce a family he knows but some member of it, or connection, has been by Indians maimed or scalped. What avails, then, that some one Indian, or some two or three, treat a backwoodsman friendly-like? He fears me, he thinks. Take my rifle from me, give him motive, and what will come? Or if not so, how know I what involuntary preparations may be going on in him for things as unbeknown in present time to him as me—a sort of chemical preparation in the soul for malice, as chemical preparation in the body for malady.'

"Not that the backwoodsman ever used those words, you see, but the judge found him expression for his meaning. And this point he would conclude with saying, that, 'what is called a "friendly Indian" is a very rare sort of creature; and well it was so, for no ruthlessness exceeds that of a "friendly Indian" turned enemy. A coward friend, he makes a valiant foe.

" 'But, thus far the passion in question has been viewed in a general way as that of a community. When to his due share of this the backwoodsman adds his private passion, we have then the stock out of which is formed, if formed at all, the Indian-hater *par excellence.*'

"The Indian-hater *par excellence* the judge defined to be one 'who, having with his mother's milk drank in small love for red men, in youth or early manhood, ere the sensibilities become osseous, receives at their hand some signal outrage, or, which in effect is much the same, some of his kin have, or some friend. Now, nature all around him by her solitudes wooing or bidding him muse upon this matter, he accordingly does so, till the thought develops such attraction, that much as straggling vapors troop from all sides to a storm-cloud, so straggling thoughts of other outrages troop to the nucleus thought, assimilate with it, and swell it. At last, taking counsel with the elements, he comes to his resolution. An intenser Hannibal, he makes a vow, the hate of which is a vortex from whose suction scarce the remotest chip of the guilty race may reasonably feel secure. Next, he declares himself and settles his temporal affairs. With the solemnity of a Spaniard turned monk, he takes leave of his kin; or rather, these leave-takings have something of the still more impressive finality of death-bed adieus. Last, he commits himself to the forest primeval; there, so long as life shall be his, to act upon a calm, cloistered scheme of strategical, implacable, and lonesome vengeance. Ever on the noiseless trail; cool, collected, patient; less seen than felt; snuffing, smelling—a Leather-stocking Nemesis. In the settlements he will not be seen again; in eyes of old companions tears may start at some chance thing that speaks of him; but they never look for him, nor call; they know he will not come. Suns and seasons fleet; the tiger-lily blows and falls; babes are born and leap in their mothers' arms; but, the Indian-hater is good as gone to his long home,[4] and

4. "Also, when they shall be afraid of that which is high, and fears shall be in the way, and the almond tree shall flourish, and the grasshopper shall be a burden, and desire shall fail: because man goeth to his long home, and the mourners go about the streets" (Ecclesiastes 12:5).

"Terror" is his epitaph.'

"Here the judge, not unaffected, would pause again, but presently resume: 'How evident that in strict speech there can be no biography of an Indian-hater *par excellence*, any more than one of a sword-fish, or other deep-sea denizen; or, which is still less imaginable, one of a dead man. The career of the Indian-hater *par excellence* has the impenetrability of the fate of a lost steamer. Doubtless, events, terrible ones, have happened, must have happened; but the powers that be in nature have taken order that they shall never become news.

"'But, luckily for the curious, there is a species of diluted Indian-hater, one whose heart proves not so steely as his brain. Soft enticements of domestic life too often draw him from the ascetic trail; a monk who apostatizes to the world at times. Like a mariner, too, though much abroad, he may have a wife and family in some green harbor which he does not forget. It is with him as with the Papist converts in Senegal; fasting and mortification prove hard to bear.'[5]

"The judge, with his usual judgment, always thought that the intense solitude to which the Indian-hater consigns himself, has, by its overawing influence, no little to do with relaxing his vow. He would relate instances where, after some months' lonely scoutings, the Indian-hater is suddenly seized with a sort of calenture; hurries openly towards the first smoke, though he knows it is an Indian's, announces himself as a lost hunter, gives the savage his rifle, throws himself upon his charity, embraces him with much affection, imploring the privilege of living a while in his sweet companionship. What is too often the sequel of so distempered a procedure may be best known by those who best know the Indian. Upon the whole, the judge, by two and thirty good and sufficient reasons, would maintain that there was no known vocation whose consistent following calls for such self-containings as that of the Indian-hater *par excellence*. In the highest view, he considered such a soul one peeping out but once an age.

"For the diluted Indian-hater, although the vacations he permits himself impair the keeping of the character, yet, it should not be overlooked that this is the man who, by his very infirmity, enables us to form surmises, however inadequate, of what Indian-hating in its perfection is."

"One moment," gently interrupted the cosmopolitan here, "and let me refill my calumet."

Which being done, the other proceeded:—

5. In "Benito Cereno," written before this book, Melville used Senegal as the symbolic home of a kind of primitive evil.

Chapter 27

SOME ACCOUNT OF A MAN OF QUESTIONABLE MORALITY, BUT
WHO, NEVERTHELESS, WOULD SEEM ENTITLED TO THE ESTEEM
OF THAT EMINENT ENGLISH MORALIST WHO SAID HE LIKED
A GOOD HATER

"Coming to mention the man to whose story all thus far said was but the introduction, the judge, who, like you, was a great smoker, would insist upon all the company taking cigars, and then lighting a fresh one himself, rise in his place, and, with the solemnest voice, say—'Gentlemen, let us smoke to the memory of Colonel John Moredock;' when, after several whiffs taken standing in deep silence and deeper reverie, he would resume his seat and his discourse, something in these words:

" 'Though Colonel John Moredock was not an Indian-hater *par excellence,* he yet cherished a kind of sentiment towards the red man, and in that degree, and so acted out his sentiment as sufficiently to merit the tribute just rendered to his memory.

" 'John Moredock was the son of a woman married thrice, and thrice widowed by a tomahawk. The three successive husbands of this woman had been pioneers, and with them she had wandered from wilderness to wilderness, always on the frontier. With nine children, she at last found herself at a little clearing, afterwards Vincennes. There she joined a company about to remove to the new country of Illinois. On the eastern side of Illinois there were then no settlements; but on the west side, the shore of the Mississippi, there were, near the mouth of the Kaskaskia, some old hamlets of the French. To the vicinity of those hamlets, very innocent and pleasant places, a new Arcadia, Mrs. Moredock's party was destined; for thereabouts, among the vines, they meant to settle. They embarked upon the Wabash in boats, proposing descending that stream into the Ohio, and the Ohio into the Mississippi, and so, northwards, towards the point to be reached. All went well till they made the rock of the Grand Tower on the Mississippi, where they had to land and drag their boats round a point swept by a strong current. Here a party of Indians, lying in wait, rushed out and murdered nearly all of them. The widow was among the victims with her children, John excepted, who, some fifty miles distant, was following with a second party.

" 'He was just entering upon manhood, when thus left in nature sole survivor of his race. Other youngsters might have turned mourners; he turned avenger. His nerves were electric wires—sensitive, but steel. He was one who, from self-possession, could be made neither to flush nor pale. It is said that when the tidings were brought him, he was ashore sitting beneath a hemlock eating his dinner of venison—and as the tidings were told him, after the first start he kept on eating, but slowly and deliberately, chewing the wild news with the wild meat, as if both together, turned to chyle, together should sinew him to his intent. From that meal he rose an Indian-hater. He rose; got his arms, prevailed upon some comrades to join him, and without delay started to discover who were the actual transgressors. They proved to belong to a band of twenty renegades from various tribes, outlaws even among Indians, and who had formed themselves into a marauding crew. No opportunity for action being at the time presented, he dismissed his friends; told them to go on, thanking them, and saying he would ask their aid at some future day. For upwards of a year, alone in the wilds, he watched the crew. Once, what he thought a favorable chance having occurred—it being midwinter, and the savages encamped, apparently to remain so—he anew mustered his friends, and marched against them; but, getting wind of his coming, the enemy fled, and in such panic that everything was left behind but their weapons. During the winter, much the same thing happened upon two subsequent occasions. The next year he sought them at the head of a party pledged to serve him for forty days. At last the hour came. It was on the shore of the Mississippi. From their covert, Moredock and his men dimly descried the gang of Cains in the red dusk of evening, paddling over to a jungled island in midstream, there the more securely to lodge; for Moredock's retributive spirit in the wilderness spoke ever to their trepidations now, like the voice calling through the garden. Waiting until dead of night, the whites swam the river, towing after them a raft laden with their arms. On landing, Moredock cut the fastenings of the enemy's canoes, and turned them, with his own raft, adrift; resolved that there should be neither escape for the Indians, nor safety, except in victory, for the whites. Victorious the whites were; but three of the Indians saved themselves by taking to the stream. Moredock's band lost not a man.

" 'Three of the murderers survived. He knew their names and persons. In the course of three years each successively fell by his own hand. All were now dead. But this did not suffice. He made no avowal, but to kill Indians had become his passion. As an athlete, he had few equals; as a shot, none; in single combat, not to be beaten. Master of that woodland-cunning enabling the adept to subsist where the tyro would perish, and expert in all those arts by which an enemy is pursued for weeks, perhaps months, without once suspecting it, he kept to the forest. The solitary Indian that met him, died. When a number[1] was descried, he would either secretly pursue their track for some chance to strike at least one blow; or if, while thus engaged, he himself was discovered, he would elude them by superior skill.

" 'Many years he spent thus; and though after a time he was, in a degree, restored to the ordinary life of the region and period, yet it is believed that John Moredock never let pass an opportunity of quenching an Indian. Sins of commission in that kind may have been his, but none of omission.

" 'It were to err to suppose,' the judge would say, 'that this gentleman was naturally ferocious, or peculiarly possessed of those qualities, which, unhelped by provocation of events, tend to withdraw man from social life. On the contrary, Moredock was an example of something apparently self-contradicting, certainly curious, but, at the same time, undeniable: namely, that nearly all Indian-haters have at bottom loving hearts; at any rate, hearts, if anything, more generous than the average. Certain it is, that, to the degree in which he mingled in the life of the settlements, Moredock showed himself not without humane feelings. No cold husband or colder father, he; and, though often and long away from his household, bore its needs in mind, and provided for them. He could be very convivial; told a good story (though never of his more private exploits), and sung a capital song. Hospitable, not backward to help a neighbor; by report, benevolent, as retributive, in secret; while, in a general manner, though sometimes grave—as is not unusual with men of his complexion, a sultry and tragical brown—yet with nobody, Indians excepted, otherwise than courteous in a manly fashion; a moccasined gentleman, admired and loved. In fact, no one more popular, as an incident to follow may prove.

" 'His bravery, whether in Indian fight or any other, was unquestionable. An officer in the ranging service during the war of 1812, he acquitted himself with more than credit. Of his soldierly character, this anecdote is told: Not long after Hull's dubious surrender at Detroit, Moredock with some of his rangers rode up at night to a log-house, there to rest till morning. The horses being attended to, supper over, and sleeping-places assigned the troop, the host showed the colonel his best bed, not on the ground like the rest, but a bed that stood on legs. But out of delicacy, the guest declined to monopolize it, or, indeed, to occupy it at all; when, to increase the inducement, as the host thought, he was told that a general officer had once slept in that bed. "Who pray?" asked the colonel. "General Hull." "Then you must not take offense," said the colonel, buttoning up his coat, "but, really, no coward's bed,

1. My conjecture (1963) for the original's "murder," first introduced into the text in Franklin (1967). The corresponding word in Hall is "party" (see Backgrounds and Sources).

for me, however comfortable." Accordingly he took up with valor's bed—a cold one on the ground.

" 'At one time the colonel was a member of the territorial council of Illinois, and at the formation of the state government, was pressed to become candidate for governor, but begged to be excused. And, though he declined to give his reasons for declining, yet by those who best knew him the cause was not wholly unsurmised. In his official capacity he might be called upon to enter into friendly treaties with Indian tribes, a thing not to be thought of. And even did no such contingency arise, yet he felt there would be an impropriety in the Governor of Illinois stealing out now and then, during a recess of the legislative bodies, for a few days' shooting at human beings, within the limits of his paternal chief-magistracy. If the governorship offered large honors, from Moredock it demanded larger sacrifices. These were incompatibles. In short, he was not unaware that to be a consistent Indian-hater involves the renunciation of ambition, with its objects—the pomps and glories of the world; and since religion, pronouncing such things vanities, accounts it merit to renounce them, therefore, so far as this goes, Indian-hating, whatever may be thought of it in other respects, may be regarded as not wholly without the efficacy of a devout sentiment.' "

Here the narrator paused. Then, after his long and irksome sitting, started to his feet, and regulating his disordered shirt-frill, and at the same time adjustingly shaking his legs down in his rumpled pantaloons, concluded: "There, I have done; having given you, not my story, mind, or my thoughts, but another's. And now, for your friend Coonskins, I doubt not, that, if the judge were here, he would pronounce him a sort of comprehensive Colonel Moredock, who, too much spreading his passion, shallows it."

Chapter 28

MOOT POINTS TOUCHING THE LATE COLONEL JOHN MOREDOCK

"Charity, charity!" exclaimed the cosmopolitan, "never a sound judgment without charity. When man judges man, charity is less a bounty from our mercy than just allowance for the insensible lee-way of human fallibility. God forbid that my eccentric friend should be what you hint. You do not know him, or but imperfectly. His outside deceived you; at first it came near deceiving even me. But I seized a chance, when, owing to indignation against some wrong, he laid himself a little open; I seized that lucky chance, I say, to inspect his heart, and found it an inviting oyster in a forbidding shell. His outside is but put on. Ashamed of his own goodness, he treats mankind as those strange old uncles in romances do their nephews—snapping at them all the time and yet loving them as the apple of their eye."

"Well, my words with him were few. Perhaps he is not what I took him for. Yes, for aught I know, you may be right."

"Glad to hear it. Charity, like poetry, should be cultivated, if only for its being graceful. And now, since you have renounced your notion, I should be happy would you, so to speak, renounce your story, too. That story strikes me with even more incredulity than wonder. To me some parts don't hang together. If the man of hate, how could John Moredock be also the man of love? Either his lone campaigns are fabulous as Hercules'; or else, those being true, what was thrown in about his geniality is but garnish. In short, if ever there was such a man as Moredock, he, in my way of thinking, was either misanthrope or nothing; and his misanthropy the more intense from being focused on one race of men. Though, like suicide, man-hatred would seem peculiarly a Roman and a Grecian passion—that is, Pagan; yet, the annals of neither Rome nor Greece can produce the equal in man-hatred of Colonel Moredock, as the judge and you have painted him. As for this Indian-hating in general, I can only say of it what Dr. Johnson said of the alleged Lisbon earthquake: 'Sir, I don't believe it.' "

"Didn't believe it? Why not? Clashed with any little prejudice of his?"

"Doctor Johnson had no prejudice; but, like a certain other person," with an ingenuous smile, "he had sensibilities, and those were pained."

"Dr. Johnson was a good Christian, wasn't he?"

"He was."

"Suppose he had been something else."

"Then small incredulity as to the alleged earthquake."

"Suppose he had been also a misanthrope?"

"Then small incredulity as to the robberies and murders alleged to have been perpetrated under the pall of smoke and ashes. The infidels of the time were quick to credit those reports and worse. So true is it that, while religion, contrary to the common notion, implies, in certain cases, a spirit of slow reserve as to assent, infidelity, which claims to despise credulity, is sometimes swift to it."

"You rather jumble together misanthropy and infidelity."

"I do not jumble them; they are coordinates. For misanthropy, springing from the same root with disbelief of religion, is twin with that. It springs from the same root, I say; for, set aside materialism, and what is an atheist, but one who does not, or will not, see in the universe a ruling principle of love; and what a misanthrope, but one who does not, or will not, see in man a ruling principle of kindness? Don't you see? In either case the vice consists in a want of confidence."

"What sort of a sensation is misanthropy?"

"Might as well ask me what sort of sensation is hydrophobia. Don't know; never had it. But I have often wondered what it can be like. Can a misanthrope feel warm, I ask myself; take ease? be companionable with himself? Can a misanthrope smoke a cigar and muse? How fares he in solitude? Has the misanthrope such a thing as an appetite? Shall a peach refresh him? The effervescence of champagne, with what eye does he behold it? Is summer good to him? Of long winters how much can he sleep? What are his dreams? How feels he, and what does he, when suddenly awakened, alone, at dead of night, by fusilades of thunder?"

"Like you," said the stranger, "I can't understand the misanthrope. So far as my experience goes, either mankind is worthy one's best love, or else I have been lucky. Never has it been my lot to have been wronged, though but in the smallest degree. Cheating, backbiting, superciliousness, disdain, hard-heartedness, and all that brood, I know but by report. Cold regards tossed over the sinister shoulder of a former friend, ingratitude in a beneficiary, treachery in a confidant—such things may be; but I must take somebody's word for it.[1] Now the bridge that has carried me so well over, shall I not praise it?"

"Ingratitude to the worthy bridge not to do so. Man is a noble fellow, and in an age of satirists, I am not displeased to find one who has confidence in him, and bravely stands up for him."

"Yes, I always speak a good word for man; and what is more, am always ready to do a good deed for him."

"You are a man after my own heart," responded the cosmopolitan, with a candor which lost nothing by its calmness. "Indeed," he added, "our sentiments agree so, that were they written in a book, whose was whose, few but the nicest critics might determine."

"Since we are thus joined in mind," said the stranger, "why not be joined in hand?"

"My hand is always at the service of virtue," frankly extending it to him as to virtue personified.

1. Melville may be wryly altering some words in Amasa Delano's *Voyages* (Boston, 1817), p. 328: "After our arrival at Conception, I was mortified and very much hurt at the treatment which I received from Don Bonito Sereno [sic]; but had this been the only time that I ever was treated with ingratitude, injustice, or want of compassion, I would not complain." See also p. 330: "When I take a retrospective view of my life, I cannot find in my soul, that I ever have done anything to deserve such misery and ingratitude as I have suffered at different periods, and in general, from the very persons to whom I have rendered the greatest services."

"And now," said the stranger, cordially retaining his hand, "you know our fashion here at the West. It may be a little low, but it is kind. Briefly, we being newly-made friends must drink together. What say you?"

"Thank you; but indeed, you must excuse me."

"Why?"

"Because, to tell the truth, I have to-day met so many old friends, all free-hearted, convivial gentlemen, that really, really, though for the present I succeed in mastering it, I am at bottom almost in the condition of a sailor who, stepping ashore after a long voyage, ere night reels with loving welcomes, his head of less capacity than his heart."

At the allusion to old friends, the stranger's countenance a little fell, as a jealous lover's might at hearing from his sweetheart of former ones. But rallying, he said: "No doubt they treated you to something strong; but wine—surely, that gentle creature, wine; come, let us have a little gentle wine at one of these little tables here. Come, come." Then essaying to roll about like a full pipe in the sea, sang in a voice which had had more of good-fellowship, had there been less of a latent squeak to it:

> "Let us drink of the wine of the vine benign,
> That sparkles warm in Zansovine."[2]

The cosmopolitan, with longing eye upon him, stood as sorely tempted and wavering a moment; then, abruptly stepping towards him, with a look of dissolved surrender, said: "When mermaid songs move figure-heads, then may glory, gold, and women try their blandishments on me. But a good fellow, singing a good song, he woos forth my every spike, so that my whole hull, like a ship's, sailing by a magnetic rock, caves in with acquiescence. Enough: when one has a heart of a certain sort, it is in vain trying to be resolute."

Chapter 29

THE BOON COMPANIONS

The wine, port, being called for, and the two seated at the little table, a natural pause of convivial expectancy ensued; the stranger's eye turned towards the bar near by, watching the red-cheeked, white-aproned man there, blithely dusting the bottle, and invitingly arranging the salver and glasses; when, with a sudden impulse turning round his head towards his companion, he said, "Ours is friendship at first sight, ain't it?"

2. Slightly misquoted from Leigh Hunt's *Bacchus in Tuscany.*

"It is," was the placidly pleased reply: "and the same may be said of friendship at first sight as of love at first sight: it is the only true one, the only noble one. It bespeaks confidence. Who would go sounding his way into love or friendship, like a strange ship by night, into an enemy's harbor?"

"Right. Boldly in before the wind. Agreeable, how we always agree. By-the-way, though but a formality, friends should know each other's names. What is yours, pray?"

"Francis Goodman. But those who love me, call me Frank. And yours?"

"Charles Arnold Noble. But do you call me Charlie."

"I will, Charlie; nothing like preserving in manhood the fraternal familiarities of youth. It proves the heart a rosy boy to the last."

"My sentiments again. Ah!"

It was a smiling waiter, with the smiling bottle, the cork drawn; a common quart bottle, but for the occasion fitted at bottom into a little bark basket, braided with porcupine quills, gayly tinted in the Indian fashion. This being set before the entertainer, he regarded it with affectionate interest, but seemed not to understand, or else to pretend not to, a handsome red label pasted on the bottle, bearing the capital letters, P. W.

"P. W.," said he at last, perplexedly eying the pleasing poser, "now what does P. W. mean?"

"Shouldn't wonder," said the cosmopolitan gravely, "if it stood for port wine. You called for port wine, didn't you?"

"Why so it is, so it is!"

"I find some little mysteries not very hard to clear up," said the other, quietly crossing his legs.

This commonplace seemed to escape the stranger's hearing, for, full of his bottle, he now rubbed his somewhat sallow hands over it, and with a strange kind of cackle, meant to be a chirrup, cried: "Good wine, good wine; is it not the peculiar bond of good feeling?" Then brimming both glasses, pushed one over, saying, with what seemed intended for an air of fine disdain: "Ill betide those gloomy skeptics who maintain that now-a-days pure wine is unpurchasable; that almost every variety on sale is less the vintage of vineyards than laboratories; that most bar-keepers are but a set of male Brinvillierses,[1] with complaisant arts practicing against the lives of their best friends, their customers."

A shade passed over the cosmopolitan. After a few minutes' down-cast musing, he lifted his eyes and said: "I have long thought, my dear Charlie, that the spirit in which wine is regarded

1. That is, poisoners, from the notorious Marquise de Brinvilliers (1630–1676), who murdered at least her father and two brothers. The *Britannica* has this comment: "Having admitted her crimes under torture and expressed her repentence, she received the consolations of the church and was executed. . . ."

by too many in these days is one of the most painful examples of want of confidence. Look at these glasses. He who could mistrust poison in this wine would mistrust consumption in Hebe's cheek. While, as for suspicions against the dealers in wine and sellers of it, those who cherish such suspicions can have but limited trust in the human heart. Each human heart they must think to be much like each bottle of port, not such port as this, but such port as they hold to. Strange traducers, who see good faith in nothing, however sacred. Not medicines, not the wine in sacraments, has escaped them. The doctor with his phial, and the priest with his chalice, they deem equally the unconscious dispensers of bogus cordials to the dying."

"Dreadful!"

"Dreadful indeed," said the cosmopolitan solemnly. "These distrusters stab at the very soul of confidence. If this wine," impressively holding up his full glass, "if this wine with its bright promise be not true, how shall man be, whose promise can be no brighter? But if wine be false, while men are true, whither shall fly convivial geniality? To think of sincerely-genial souls drinking each other's health at unawares in perfidious and murderous drugs!"

"Horrible!"

"Much too much so to be true, Charlie. Let us forget it. Come, you are my entertainer on this occasion, and yet you don't pledge me. I have been waiting for it."

"Pardon, pardon," half confusedly and half ostentatiously lifting his glass. "I pledge you, Frank, with my whole heart, believe me," taking a draught too decorous to be large, but which, small though it was, was followed by a slight involuntary wryness to the mouth.

"And I return you the pledge, Charlie, heart-warm as it came to me, and honest as this wine I drink it in," reciprocated the cosmopolitan with princely kindliness in his gesture, taking a generous swallow, concluding in a smack, which, though audible, was not so much so as to be unpleasing.

"Talking of alleged spuriousness of wines," said he, tranquilly setting down his glass, and then sloping back his head and with friendly fixedness eying the wine, "perhaps the strangest part of those allegings is, that there is, as claimed, a kind of man who, while convinced that on this continent most wines are shams, yet still drinks away at them; accounting wine so fine a thing, that even the sham article is better than none at all. And if the temperance people urge that, by this course, he will sooner or later be undermined in health, he answers, 'And do you think I don't know that? But health without cheer I hold a bore; and cheer, even of the spurious sort, has its price, which I am willing to pay.'"

"Such a man, Frank, must have a disposition ungovernably bacchanalian."

"Yes, if such a man there be, which I don't credit. It is a fable, but a fable from which I once heard a person of less genius than grotesqueness draw a moral even more extravagant than the fable itself. He said that it illustrated, as in a parable, how that a man of a disposition ungovernably good-natured might still familiarly associate with men, though, at the same time, he believed the greater part of men false-hearted—accounting society so sweet a thing that even the spurious sort was better than none at all. And if the Rochefoucaultites urge that, by this course, he will sooner or later be undermined in security, he answers, 'And do you think I don't know that? But security without society I hold a bore; and society, even of the spurious sort, has its price, which I am willing to pay.' "

"A most singular theory," said the stranger with a slight fidget, eying his companion with some inquisitiveness, "indeed, Frank, a most slanderous thought," he exclaimed in sudden heat and with an involuntary look almost of being personally aggrieved.

"In one sense it merits all you say, and more," replied the other with wonted mildness, "but for a kind of drollery in it, charity might, perhaps, overlook something of the wickedness. Humor is, in fact, so blessed a thing, that even in the least virtuous product of the human mind, if there can be found but nine good jokes, some philosophers are clement enough to affirm that those nine good jokes should redeem all the wicked thoughts, though plenty as the populace of Sodom.[2] At any rate, this same humor has something, there is no telling what, of beneficence in it, it is such a catholicon and charm—nearly all men agreeing in relishing it, though they may agree in little else—and in its way it undeniably does such a deal of familiar good in the world, that no wonder it is almost a proverb, that a man of humor, a man capable of a good loud laugh—seem how he may in other things—can hardly be a heartless scamp."

"Ha, ha, ha!" laughed the other, pointing to the figure of a pale pauper-boy on the deck below, whose pitiableness was touched, as it were, with ludicrousness by a pair of monstrous boots, apparently some mason's discarded ones, cracked with drouth, half eaten by lime, and curled up about the tie like a bassoon. "Look—ha, ha, ha!"

"I see," said the other, with what seemed quiet appreciation, but of a kind expressing an eye to the grotesque, without blindness to what in this case accompanied it, "I see; and the way in which it moves you, Charlie, comes in very apropos to point the proverb I was speaking of. Indeed, had you intended this effect, it could not have been more so. For who that heard that laugh, but would as naturally argue from it a sound heart as sound lungs? True, it is

2. See Genesis 18:23–32

said that a man may smile, and smile, and smile, and be a villain; but it is not said that a man may laugh, and laugh, and laugh, and be one, is it, Charlie?"

"Ha, ha, ha!—no no, no no."

"Why Charlie, your explosions illustrate my remarks almost as aptly as the chemist's imitation volcano did his lectures. But even if experience did not sanction the proverb, that a good laugher cannot be a bad man, I should yet feel bound in confidence to believe it, since it is a saying current among the people, and I doubt not originated among them, and hence *must* be true; for the voice of the people is the voice of truth. Don't you think so?"

"Of course I do. If Truth don't speak through the people, it never speaks at all; so I heard one say."

"A true saying. But we stray. The popular notion of humor, considered as index to the heart, would seem curiously confirmed by Aristotle—I think, in his 'Politics,' (a work, by-the-by, which, however it may be viewed upon the whole, yet, from the tenor of certain sections, should not, without precaution, be placed in the hands of youth)—who remarks that the least lovable men in history seem to have had for humor not only a disrelish, but a hatred; and this, in some cases, along with an extraordinary dry taste for practical punning. I remember it is related of Phalaris, the capricious tyrant of Sicily, that he once caused a poor fellow to be beheaded on a horse-block, for no other cause than having a horse-laugh."

"Funny Phalaris!"

"Cruel Phalaris!"

As after fire-crackers, there was a pause, both looking downward on the table as if mutually struck by the contrast of exclamations, and pondering upon its significance, if any. So, at least, it seemed; but on one side it might have been otherwise: for presently glancing up, the cosmopolitan said: "In the instance of the moral, drolly cynic, drawn from the queer bacchanalian fellow we were speaking of, who had his reasons for still drinking spurious wine, though knowing it to-be such—there, I say, we have an example of what is certainly a wicked thought, but conceived in humor. I will now give you one of a wicked thought conceived in wickedness. You shall compare the two, and answer, whether in the one case the sting is not neutralized by the humor, and whether in the other the absence of humor does leave the sting free play. I once heard a wit, a mere wit, mind, an irreligious Parisian wit, say, with regard to the temperance movement, that none, to their personal benefit, joined it sooner than niggards and knaves; because, as he affirmed, the one by it saved money and the other made money, as in ship-owners cutting off the spirit ration without giving its equivalent, and gamblers and all sorts of subtle tricksters sticking to cold water, the better to keep a cool head for business."

"A wicked thought, indeed!" cried the stranger, feelingly.

"Yes," leaning over the table on his elbow and genially gesturing at him with his forefinger: "yes, and, as I said, you don't remark the sting of it?"

"I do, indeed. Most calumnious thought, Frank!"

"No humor in it?"

"Not a bit!"

"Well now, Charlie," eying him with moist regard, "let us drink. It appears to me you don't drink freely."

"Oh, oh—indeed, indeed—I am not backward there. I protest, a freer drinker than friend Charlie you will find nowhere," with feverish zeal snatching his glass, but only in the sequel to dally with it. "By-the-way, Frank," said he, perhaps, or perhaps not, to draw attention from himself, "by-the-way, I saw a good thing the other day; capital thing; a panegyric on the press. It pleased me so, I got it by heart at two readings. It is a kind of poetry, but in a form which stands in something the same relation to blank verse which that does to rhyme. A sort of free-and-easy chant with refrains to it. Shall I recite it?"

"Anything in praise of the press I shall be happy to hear," rejoined the cosmopolitan, "the more so," he gravely proceeded, "as of late I have observed in some quarters a disposition to disparage the press."

"Disparage the press?"

"Even so; some gloomy souls affirming that it is proving with that great invention as with brandy or eau-de-vie, which, upon its first discovery, was believed by the doctors to be, as its French name implies, a panacea—a notion which experience, it may be thought, has not fully verified."

"You surprise me, Frank. Are there really those who so decry the press? Tell me more. Their reasons."

"Reasons they have none, but affirmations they have many; among other things affirming that, while under dynastic despotisms, the press is to the people little but an improvisatore, under popular ones it is too apt to be their Jack Cade.[3] In fine, these sour sages regard the press in the light of a Colt's revolver, pledged to no cause but his in whose chance hands it may be; deeming the one invention an improvement upon the pen, much akin to what the other is upon the pistol; involving, along with the multiplication of the barrel, no consecration of the aim. The term 'freedom of the press' they consider on a par with *freedom of Colt's revolver.*

3. In Shakespeare's *Henry VI*, Part Two, Cade is portrayed as a cynical and arbitrary exploiter of mob fury— an archetypal rebel.

Hence, for truth and the right, they hold, to indulge hopes from the one is little more sensible than for Kossuth and Mazzini to indulge hopes from the other. Heart-breaking views enough, you think; but their refutation is in every true reformer's contempt. Is it not so?"

"Without doubt. But go on, go on. I like to hear you," flatteringly brimming up his glass for him.

"For one," continued the cosmopolitan, grandly swelling his chest, "I hold the press to be neither the people's improvisatore, nor Jack Cade; neither their paid fool, nor conceited drudge. I think interest never prevails with it over duty. The press still speaks for truth though impaled, in the teeth of lies though intrenched. Disdaining for it the poor name of cheap diffuser of news, I claim for it the independent apostleship of Advancer of Knowledge:—the iron Paul! Paul, I say; for not only does the press advance knowledge, but righteousness. In the press, as in the sun, resides, my dear Charlie, a dedicated principle of beneficent force and light. For the Satanic press, by its coappearance with the apostolic, it is no more an aspersion to that, than to the true sun is the coappearance of the mock one. For all the baleful-looking parhelion, god Apollo dispenses the day. In a word, Charlie, what the sovereign of England is titularly, I hold the press to be actually—Defender of the Faith!—defender of the faith in the final triumph of truth over error, metaphysics over superstition, theory over falsehood, machinery over nature, and the good man over the bad. Such are my views, which, if stated at some length, you, Charlie, must pardon, for it is a theme upon which I cannot speak with cold brevity. And now I am impatient for your panegyric, which, I doubt not, will put mine to the blush."

"It is rather in the blush-giving vein," smiled the other; "but such as it is, Frank, you shall have it."

"Tell me when you are about to begin," said the cosmopolitan, "for, when at public dinners the press is toasted, I always drink the toast standing, and shall stand while you pronounce the panegyric."

"Very good, Frank; you may stand up now."

He accordingly did so, when the stranger likewise rose, and uplifting the ruby wine-flask, began.

Chapter 30

OPENING WITH A POETICAL EULOGY OF THE PRESS AND CONTINUING WITH TALK INSPIRED BY THE SAME

" 'Praise be unto the press, not Faust's, but Noah's; let us extol and magnify the press, the true press of Noah, from which break-

eth the true morning.[1] Praise be unto the press, not the black press
but the red; let us extol and magnify the press, the red press of
Noah, from which cometh inspiration. Ye pressmen of the Rhine-
land and the Rhine, join in with all ye who tread out the glad tidings on isle Madeira or Mitylene.—Who giveth redness of eyes by
making men long to tarry at the fine print?—Praise be unto the
press, the rosy press of Noah, which giveth rosiness of hearts, by
making men long to tarry at the rosy wine.—Who hath babblings
and contentions? Who, without cause, inflicteth wounds? Praise be
unto the press, the kindly press of Noah, which knitteth friends,
which fuseth foes.—Who may be bribed?—Who may be
bound?—Praise be unto the press, the free press of Noah, which
will not lie for tyrants, but make tyrants speak the truth.—Then
praise be unto the press, the frank old press of Noah; then let us
extol and magnify the press, the brave old press of Noah; then let
us with roses garland and enwreath the press, the grand old press of
Noah, from which flow streams of knowledge which give man a
bliss no more unreal than his pain.' "

"You deceived me," smiled the cosmopolitan, as both now
resumed their seats; "you roguishly took advantage of my simplicity; you archly played upon my enthusiasm. But never mind; the
offense, if any, was so charming, I almost wish you would offend
again. As for certain poetic left-handers in your panegyric, those I
cheerfully concede to the indefinite privileges of the poet. Upon
the whole, it was quite in the lyric style—a style I always admire on
account of that spirit of Sibyllic confidence and assurance which is,
perhaps, its prime ingredient. But come," glancing at his companion's glass, "for a lyrist, you let the bottle stay with you too long."

"The lyre and the vine forever!" cried the other in his rapture, or
what seemed such, heedless of the hint, "the vine, the vine! is it
not the most graceful and bounteous of all growths? And, by its
being such, is not something meant—divinely meant? As I live, a
vine, a Catawba vine, shall be planted on my grave!"

"A genial thought; but your glass there."

"Oh, oh," taking a moderate sip, "but you, why don't you
drink?"

"You have forgotten, my dear Charlie, what I told you of my
previous convivialities to-day."

"Oh," cried the other, now in manner quite abandoned to the
lyric mood, not without contrast to the easy sociability of his companion. "Oh, one can't drink too much of good old wine—the gen-

1. This paragraph is an imitation of
Biblical formulas, as Nathalia Wright
pointed out (1949). See Proverbs
23:29–32: "Who hath woe? who hath
sorrow? who hath contentions? who
hath babbling? who hath wounds without cause? who hath redness of eyes?

They that tarry long at the wine; they
that go to seek mixed wine. Look not
thou upon the wine when it is red,
when it giveth his color in the cup,
when it moveth itself aright. At the
last it biteth like a serpent, and sting-
eth like an adder."

uine, mellow old port. Pooh, pooh! drink away."

"Then keep me company."

"Of course," with a flourish, taking another sip—"suppose we have cigars. Never mind your pipe there; a pipe is best when alone. I say, waiter, bring some cigars—your best."[2]

They were brought in a pretty little bit of western pottery, representing some kind of Indian utensil, mummy-colored, set down in a mass of tobacco leaves, whose long, green fans, fancifully grouped, formed with peeps of red the sides of the receptacle.

Accompanying it were two accessories, also bits of pottery, but smaller, both globes; one in guise of an apple flushed with red and gold to the life, and, through a cleft at top, you saw it was hollow. This was for the ashes. The other, gray, with wrinkled surface, in the likeness of a wasp's nest, was the match-box.

"There," said the stranger, pushing over the cigar-stand, "help yourself, and I will touch you off," taking a match. "Nothing like tobacco," he added, when the fumes of the cigar began to wreathe, glancing from the smoker to the pottery, "I will have a Virginia tobacco-plant set over my grave beside the Catawba vine."

"Improvement upon your first idea, which by itself was good—but you don't smoke."

"Presently, presently—let me fill your glass again. You don't drink."

"Thank you; but no more just now. Fill *your* glass."

"Presently, presently; do you drink on. Never mind me. Now that it strikes me, let me say, that he who, out of superfine gentility or fanatic morality, denies himself tobacco, suffers a more serious abatement in the cheap pleasures of life than the dandy in his iron boot, or the celibate on his iron cot. While for him who would fain revel in tobacco, but cannot, it is a thing at which philanthropists must weep, to see such an one, again and again, madly returning to the cigar, which, for his incompetent stomach, he cannot enjoy, while still, after each shameful repulse, the sweet dream of the impossible good goads him on to his fierce misery once more—poor eunuch!"

"I agree with you," said the cosmopolitan, still gravely social, "but you don't smoke."

"Presently, presently, do you smoke on. As I was saying about—"

"But *why* don't you smoke—come. You don't think that tobacco, when in league with wine, too much enhances the latter's

2. "Now a bunch of cigars, all banded together, is a type and a symbol of the brotherly love between smokers. Likewise, for the time, in a community of pipes is a community of hearts. Nor was it an ill thing for the Indian Sach-ems to circulate their calumet tobacco-bowl—even as our fore-fathers circulated their punch-bowl—in token of peace, charity, and good-will, friendly feelings, and sympathizing souls" (*White-Jacket*, Chapter 91).

vinous quality—in short, with certain constitutions tends to impair self-possession, do you?"

"To think that, were treason to good fellowship," was the warm disclaimer. "No, no. But the fact is, there is an unpropitious flavor in my mouth just now. Ate of a diabolical ragout at dinner, so I shan't smoke till I have washed away the lingering memento of it with wine. But smoke away, you, and pray, don't forget to drink. By-the-way, while we sit here so companionably, giving loose to any companionable nothing, your uncompanionable friend, Coonskins, is, by pure contrast, brought to recollection. If he were but here now, he would see how much of real heart-joy he denies himself by not hob-a-nobbing with his kind."

"Why," with loitering emphasis, slowly withdrawing his cigar, "I thought I had undeceived you there. I thought you had come to a better understanding of my eccentric friend."

"Well, I thought so, too; but first impressions will return, you know. In truth, now that I think of it, I am led to conjecture from chance things which dropped from Coonskins, during the little interview I had with him, that he is not a Missourian by birth, but years ago came West here, a young misanthrope from the other side of the Alleghanies, less to make his fortune, than to flee man. Now, since they say trifles sometimes effect great results, I shouldn't wonder, if his history were probed, it would be found that what first indirectly gave his sad bias to Coonskins was his disgust at reading in boyhood the advice of Polonius to Laertes— advice which, in the selfishness it inculcates, is almost on a par with a sort of ballad upon the economies of money-making, to be occasionally seen pasted against the desk of small retail traders in New England."[3]

"I do hope now, my dear fellow," said the cosmopolitan with an air of bland protest, "that, in my presence at least, you will throw out nothing to the prejudice of the sons of the Puritans."

"Hey-day and high times indeed," exclaimed the other, nettled, "sons of the Puritans forsooth! And who be Puritans, that I, an Alabamaian, must do them reverence? A set of sourly conceited old Malvolios,[4] whom Shakespeare laughs his fill at in his comedies."

"Pray, what were you about to suggest with regard to Polonius," observed the cosmopolitan with quiet forbearance, expressive of the patience of a superior mind at the petulance of an inferior one; "how do you characterize his advice to Laertes?"

3. For Melville, Polonius is a type of expedient, worldly morality to be judged by the other-worldly standards of Jesus. See especially Polonius' set speech of paternal advice to Laertes (*Hamlet*, I, iii). Kindred figures in Melville's mind are historical people like Bacon and Chesterfield and his own characters like Falsgrave and Plinlimmon in *Pierre*.
4. Charlie makes Malvolio, in *Twelfth Night*, a type name; another character in the "set" would be Jaques, in *As You Like It*.

"As false, fatal, and calumnious," exclaimed the other, with a degree of ardor befitting one resenting a stigma upon the family escutcheon, "and for a father to give his son—monstrous. The case you see is this: The son is going abroad, and for the first. What does the father? Invoke God's blessing upon him? Put the blessed Bible in his trunk? No. Crams him with maxims smacking of my Lord Chesterfield, with maxims of France, with maxims of Italy."

"No, no, be charitable, not that. Why, does he not among other things say:—

> 'The friends thou hast, and their adoption tried,
> Grapple them to thy soul with hooks of steel'?

Is that compatible with maxims of Italy?"

"Yes it is, Frank. Don't you see? Laertes is to take the best care of his friends—his proved friends, on the same principle that a wine-corker takes the best of care of his proved bottles. When a bottle gets a sharp knock and don't break, he says, 'Ah, I'll keep that bottle.' Why? Because he loves it? No, he has particular use for it."

"Dear, dear!" appealingly turning in distress, "that—that kind of criticism is—is—in fact—it won't do."

"Won't truth do, Frank? You are so charitable with everybody, do but consider the tone of the speech. Now I put it to you, Frank; is there anything in it hortatory to high, heroic, disinterested effort? Anything like 'sell all thou hast and give to the poor?'[5] And, in other points, what desire seems most in the father's mind, that his son should cherish nobleness for himself, or be on his guard against the contrary thing in others? An irreligious warner, Frank—no devout counselor, is Polonius. I hate him. Nor can I bear to hear your veterans of the world affirm, that he who steers through life by advice of old Polonius will not steer among the breakers."

"No, no—I hope nobody affirms that," rejoined the cosmopolitan, with tranquil abandonment; sideways reposing his arm at full length upon the table. "I hope nobody affirms that; because, if Polonius' advice be taken in your sense, then the recommendation of it by men of experience would appear to involve more or less of an unhandsome sort of reflection upon human nature. And yet," with a perplexed air, "your suggestions have put things in such a strange light to me as in fact a little to disturb my previous notions of Polonius and what he says. To be frank, by your ingenuity you have unsettled me there, to that degree that were it not for our coincidence of opinion in general, I should almost think I was now

5. The words of Jesus to the rich young man: "If thou wilt be perfect, go and sell that thou hast, and give to the poor, and thou shalt have treasure in heaven: and come and follow me" (Matthew 19:21). The young man went away sorrowful, "for he had great possessions."

at length beginning to feel the ill effect of an immature mind, too much consorting with a mature one, except on the ground of first principles in common."

"Really and truly," cried the other with a kind of tickled modesty and pleased concern, "mine is an understanding too weak to throw out grapnels and hug another to it. I have indeed heard of some great scholars in these days, whose boast is less that they have made disciples than victims. But for me, had I the power to do such things, I have not the heart to desire."

"I believe you, my dear Charlie. And yet, I repeat, by your commentaries on Polonius you have, I know not how, unsettled me; so that now I don't exactly see how Shakespeare meant the words he puts in Polonius' mouth."

"Some say that he meant them to open people's eyes; but I don't think so."

"Open their eyes?" echoed the cosmopolitan, slowly expanding his; "what is there in this world for one to open his eyes to? I mean in the sort of invidious sense you cite?"

"Well, others say he meant to corrupt people's morals; and still others, that he had no express intention at all, but in effect opens their eyes and corrupts their morals in one operation. All of which I reject."

"Of course you reject so crude an hypothesis; and yet, to confess, in reading Shakespeare in my closet, struck by some passage, I have laid down the volume, and said: 'This Shakespeare is a queer man.' At times seeming irresponsible, he does not always seem reliable. There appears to be a certain—what shall I call it?—hidden sun, say, about him, at once enlightening and mystifying. Now, I should be afraid to say what I have sometimes thought that hidden sun might be."

"Do you think it was the true light?" with clandestine geniality again filling the other's glass.

"I would prefer to decline answering a categorical question there. Shakespeare has got to be a kind of deity. Prudent minds, having certain latent thoughts concerning him, will reserve them in a condition of lasting probation. Still, as touching avowable speculations, we are permitted a tether. Shakespeare himself is to be adored, not arraigned; but, so we do it with humility, we may a little canvass his characters. There's his Autolycus[6] now, a fellow that always puzzled me. How is one to take Autolycus? A rogue so happy, so lucky, so triumphant, of so almost captivatingly vicious a career that a virtuous man reduced to the poor-house (were such a contingency conceivable), might almost long to change sides with him. And yet, see the words put into his mouth: 'Oh,' cries Autol-

6. The rogue in *The Winter's Tale.*

ycus, as he comes galloping, gay as a buck, upon the stage, 'oh,'
he laughs, 'oh what a fool is Honesty, and Trust, his sworn brother,
a very simple gentleman.' Think of that. Trust, that is, confidence
—that is, the thing in this universe the sacredest—is rattlingly
pronounced just the simplest. And the scenes in which the rogue
figures seem purposely devised for verification of his principles.
Mind, Charlie, I do not say it *is* so, far from it; but I *do* say it
seems so. Yes, Autolycus would seem a needy varlet acting upon
the persuasion that less is to be got by invoking pockets than
picking them, more to be made by an expert knave than a bungling
beggar; and for this reason, as he thinks, that the soft heads out-
number the soft hearts. The devil's drilled recruit, Autolycus is
joyous as if he wore the livery of heaven. When disturbed by the
character and career of one thus wicked and thus happy, my sole
consolation is in the fact that no such creature ever existed, except
in the powerful imagination which evoked him. And yet, a creature, a living creature, he is, though only a poet was his maker. It
may be, that in that paper-and-ink investiture of his, Autolycus acts
more effectively upon mankind than he would in a flesh-and-blood
one. Can his influence be salutary? True, in Autolycus there is
humor; but though, according to my principle, humor is in general to be held a saving quality, yet the case of Autolycus is an
exception; because it is his humor which, so to speak, oils his mischievousness. The bravadoing mischievousness of Autolycus is slid
into the world on humor, as a pirate schooner, with colors flying,
is launched into the sea on greased ways."

"I approve of Autolycus as little as you," said the stranger, who,
during his companion's commonplaces, had seemed less attentive to
them than to maturing within his own mind the original conceptions destined to eclipse them. "But I cannot believe that Autolycus, mischievous as he must prove upon the stage, can be near so
much so as such a character as Polonius."

"I don't know about that," bluntly, and yet not impolitely,
returned the cosmopolitan; "to be sure, accepting your view of the
old courtier, then if between him and Autolycus you raise the question of unprepossessingness, I grant you the latter comes off best.
For a moist rogue may tickle the midriff, while a dry worldling may
but wrinkle the spleen."

"But Polonius is not dry," said the other excitedly; "he drules.
One sees the fly-blown old fop drule and look wise. His vile wisdom
is made the viler by his vile rheuminess. The bowing and cring-
ing, time-serving old sinner—is such an one to give manly precepts
to youth? The discreet, decorous, old dotard-of-state; senile prudence; fatuous soullessness! The ribanded old dog is paralytic all
down one side, and that the side of nobleness. His soul is gone
out. Only nature's automatonism keeps him on his legs. As with

some old trees, the bark survives the pith, and will stand stiffly up, though but to rim round punk, so the body of old Polonius has outlived his soul."

"Come, come," said the cosmopolitan with serious air, almost displeased; "though I yield to none in admiration of earnestness, yet, I think, even earnestness may have limits. To humane minds, strong language is always more or less distressing. Besides, Polonius is an old man—as I remember him upon the stage—with snowy locks. Now charity requires that such a figure—think of it how you will—should at least be treated with civility. Moreover, old age is ripeness, and I once heard say, 'Better ripe than raw.' "

"But not better rotten than raw!" bringing down his hand with energy on the table.

"Why, bless me," in mild surprise contemplating his heated comrade, "how you fly out against this unfortunate Polonius—a being that never was, nor will be. And yet, viewed in a Christian light," he added pensively, "I don't know that anger against this man of straw is a whit less wise than anger against a man of flesh. Madness, to be mad with anything."

"That may be, or may not be," returned the other, a little testily, perhaps; "but I stick to what I said, that it is better to be raw than rotten. And what is to be feared on that head, may be known from this: that it is with the best of hearts as with the best of pears—a dangerous experiment to linger too long upon the scene. This did Polonius. Thank fortune, Frank, I am young, every tooth sound in my head, and if good wine can keep me where I am, long shall I remain so."

"True," with a smile. "But wine, to do good, must be drunk. You have talked much and well, Charlie; but drunk little and indifferently—fill up."

"Presently, presently," with a hasty and preoccupied air. "If I remember right, Polonius hints as much as that one should under no circumstances, commit the indiscretion of aiding in a pecuniary way an unfortunate friend. He drules out some stale stuff about 'loan losing both itself and friend,' don't he? But our bottle; is it glued fast? Keep it moving, my dear Frank. Good wine, and upon my soul I begin to feel it, and through me old Polonius—yes, this wine, I fear, is what excites me so against that detestable old dog without a tooth."

Upon this, the cosmopolitan, cigar in mouth, slowly raised the bottle, and brought it slowly to the light, looking at it steadfastly, as one might at a thermometer in August, to see not how low it was, but how high. Then whiffing out a puff, set it down, and said: "Well, Charlie, if what wine you have drunk came out of this bottle, in that case I should say that if—supposing a case—that if one fellow had an object in getting another fellow fuddled, and this fellow to be fuddled was of your capacity, the operation would be comparatively inexpensive. What do you think, Charlie?"

"Why, I think I don't much admire the supposition," said Charlie, with a look of resentment; "it ain't safe, depend upon it, Frank, to venture upon too jocose suppositions with one's friends."

"Why, bless you, Charlie,[7] my supposition wasn't personal, but general. You mustn't be so touchy."

"If I am touchy it is the wine. Sometimes, when I freely drink it, it has a touchy effect on me, I have observed."

"Freely drink? you haven't drunk the perfect measure of one glass, yet. While for me, this must be my fourth or fifth, thanks to your importunity; not to speak of all I drank this morning, for old acquaintance' sake. Drink, drink; you must drink."

"Oh, I drink while you are talking," laughed the other; "you have not noticed it, but I have drunk my share. Have a queer way I learned from a sedate old uncle, who used to tip off his glass unperceived. Do you fill up, and my glass, too. There! Now away with that stump, and have a new cigar. Good fellowship forever!" again in the lyric mood. "Say, Frank, are we not men? I say are we not human? Tell me, were they not human who engendered us, as before heaven I believe they shall be whom we shall engender? Fill up, up, up, my friend. Let the ruby tide aspire, and all ruby aspirations with it! Up, fill up! Be we convivial. And conviviality, what is it? The word, I mean; what expresses it? A living together. But bats live together, and did you ever hear of convivial bats?"

"If I ever did," observed the cosmopolitan, " it has quite slipped my recollection."

"But why did you never hear of convivial bats, nor anybody else? Because bats, though they live together, live not together genially. Bats are not genial souls. But men are; and how delightful to think that the word which among men signifies the highest pitch of geniality, implies, as indispensable auxiliary, the cheery benediction of the bottle. Yes, Frank, to live together in the finest sense, we must drink together. And so, what wonder that he who loves not wine, that sober wretch has a lean heart—a heart like a wrung-out old bluing-bag, and loves not his kind? Out upon him, to the rag-house with him, hang him—the ungenial soul!"

"Oh, now, now, can't you be convivial without being censorious? I like easy, unexcited conviviality. For the sober man, really, though for my part I naturally love a cheerful glass, I will not prescribe my nature as the law to other natures. So don't abuse the sober man. Conviviality is one good thing, and sobriety is another good thing. So don't be one-sided."

"Well, if I am one-sided, it is the wine. Indeed, indeed, I have indulged too genially. My excitement upon slight provocation

7. The original reads "Frank"; Leon Howard (1951) pointed out the error.

shows it. But yours is a stronger head; drink you. By the way, talking of geniality, it is much on the increase in these days, ain't it?" "It is, and I hail the fact. Nothing better attests the advance of the humanitarian spirit. In former and less humanitarian ages— the ages of amphitheatres and gladiators—geniality was mostly confined to the fireside and table. But in our age—the age of joint-stock companies and free-and-easies—it is with this precious quality as with precious gold in old Peru, which Pizarro found making up the scullion's sauce-pot as the Inca's crown. Yes, we golden boys, the moderns, have geniality everywhere—a bounty broadcast like noonlight."

"True, true; my sentiments again. Geniality has invaded each department and profession. We have genial senators, genial authors, genial lecturers, genial doctors, genial clergymen, genial surgeons, and the next thing we shall have genial hangmen."

"As to the last-named sort of person," said the cosmopolitan, I trust that the advancing spirit of geniality will at last enable us to dispense with him. No murderers—no hangmen. And surely, when the whole world shall have been genialized, it will be as out of place to talk of murderers, as in a Christianized world to talk of sinners."

"To pursue the thought," said the other, "every blessing is attended with some evil, and—"

"Stay," said the cosmopolitan, "that may be better let pass for a loose saying, than for hopeful doctrine."

"Well, assuming the saying's truth, it would apply to the future supremacy of the genial spirit, since then it will fare with the hangman as it did with the weaver when the spinning-jenny whizzed into the ascendant. Thrown out of employment, what could Jack Ketch[8] turn his hand to? Butchering?"

"That he could turn his hand to it seems probable; but that, under the circumstances, it would be appropriate, might in some minds admit of a question. For one, I am inclined to think—and I trust it will not be held fastidiousness—that it would hardly be suitable to the dignity of our nature, that an individual, once employed in attending the last hours of human unfortunates, should, that office being extinct, transfer himself to the business of attending the last hours of unfortunate cattle. I would suggest that the individual turn valet—a vocation to which he would, perhaps, appear not wholly inadapted by his familiar dexterity about the person. In particular, for giving a finishing tie to a gentleman's cravat, I know few who would, in all likelihood, be, from previous occupation, better fitted than the professional person in question."

"Are you in earnest?" regarding the serene speaker with

8. Notorious hangman under Charles II, remembered for bungling the decap-itations of Lord Russell (1683) and the Duke of Monmouth (1685).

unaffected curiosity; "are you really in earnest?"

"I trust I am never otherwise," was the mildly earnest reply; "but talking of the advance of geniality, I am not without hopes that it will eventually exert its influence even upon so difficult a subject as the misanthrope."

"A genial misanthrope! I thought I had stretched the rope pretty hard in talking of genial hangmen. A genial misanthrope is no more conceivable than a surly philanthropist."

"True," lightly depositing in an unbroken little cylinder the ashes of his cigar, "true, the two you name are well opposed."

"Why, you talk as if there *was* such a being as a surly philanthropist."

"I do. My eccentric friend, whom you call Coonskins, is an example. Does he not, as I explained to you, hide under a surly air a philanthropic heart? Now, the genial misanthrope, when, in the process of eras, he shall turn up, will be the converse of this; under an affable air, he will hide a misanthropical heart. In short, the genial misanthrope will be a new kind of monster, but still no small improvement upon the original one, since, instead of making faces and throwing stones at people, like that poor old crazy man, Timon, he will take steps, fiddle in hand, and set the tickled world a' dancing. In a word, as the progress of Christianization mellows those in manner whom it cannot mend in mind, much the same will it prove with the progress of genialization. And so, thanks to geniality, the misanthrope, reclaimed from his boorish address, will take on refinement and softness—to so genial a degree, indeed, that it may possibly fall out that the misanthrope of the coming century will be almost as popular as, I am sincerely sorry to say, some philanthropists of the present time would seem not to be, as witness my eccentric friend named before."

"Well," cried the other, a little weary, perhaps, of a speculation so abstract, "well, however it may be with the century to come, certainly in the century which is, whatever else one may be, he must be genial or he is nothing. So fill up, fill up, and be genial!"

"I am trying my best," said the cosmopolitan, still calmly companionable. "A moment since, we talked of Pizarro, gold, and Peru; no doubt, now, you remember that when the Spaniard first entered Atahalpa's treasure-chamber, and saw such profusion of plate stacked up, right and left, with the wantonness of old barrels in a brewer's yard, the needy fellow felt a twinge of misgiving, of want of confidence, as to the genuineness of an opulence so profuse. He went about rapping the shining vases with his knuckles. But it was all gold, pure gold, good gold, sterling gold, which how cheerfully would have been stamped such at Goldsmiths' Hall. And just so those needy minds, which, through their own insincerity, having no confidence in mankind, doubt lest the liberal geniality of this age be spurious. They are small Pizarros in their way—by the very princeliness of men's geniality stunned into distrust of it."

"Far be such distrust from you and me, my genial friend," cried the other fervently; "fill up, fill up!"

"Well, this all along seems a division of labor," smiled the cosmopolitan. "I do about all the drinking, and you do about all—the genial. But yours is a nature competent to do that to a large population. And now, my friend," with a peculiarly grave air, evidently foreshadowing something not unimportant, and very likely of close personal interest; "wine, you know, opens the heart, and—"

"Opens it!" with exultation, "it thaws it right out. Every heart is ice-bound till wine melt it, and reveal the tender grass and sweet herbage budding below, with every dear secret, hidden before like a dropped jewel in a snow-bank, lying there unsuspected through winter till spring."

"And just in that way, my dear Charlie, is one of my little secrets now to be shown forth."

"Ah!" eagerly moving round his chair, "what is it?"

"Be not so impetuous, my dear Charlie. Let me explain. You see, naturally, I am a man not overgifted with assurance; in general, I am, if anything, diffidently reserved; so, if I shall presently seem otherwise, the reason is, that you, by the geniality you have evinced in all your talk, and especially the noble way in which, while affirming your good opinion of men, you intimated that you never could prove false to any man, but most by your indignation at a particularly illiberal passage in Polonius' advice—in short, in short," with extreme embarrassment, "how shall I express what I mean, unless I add that by your whole character you impel me to throw myself upon your nobleness; in one word, put confidence in you, a generous confidence?"

"I see, I see," with heightened interest, "something of moment you wish to confide. Now, what is it, Frank? Love affair?"

"No, not that."

"What, then, my *dear* Frank? Speak—depend upon me to the last. Out with it."

"Out it shall come, then," said the cosmopolitan. "I am in want, urgent want, of money."

Chapter 31

A METAMORPHOSIS MORE SURPRISING THAN ANY IN OVID

"In want of money!" pushing back his chair as from a suddenly-disclosed man-trap or crater.

"Yes," naïvely assented the cosmopolitan, "and you are going to loan me fifty dollars. I could almost wish I was in need of more, only for your sake. Yes, my dear Charlie, for your sake; that you might the better prove your noble kindliness, my dear Charlie."

"None of your dear Charlies," cried the other, springing to his feet, and buttoning up his coat, as if hastily to depart upon a long journey.

"Why, why, why?" painfully looking up.

"None of your why, why, whys!" tossing out a foot, "go to the devil, sir! Beggar, impostor!—never so deceived in a man in my life."

Chapter 32

SHOWING THAT THE AGE OF MAGIC AND MAGICIANS IS NOT YET OVER

While speaking or rather hissing those words, the boon companion underwent much such a change as one reads of in fairy-books. Out of old materials sprang a new creature. Cadmus glided into the snake.

The cosmopolitan rose, the traces of previous feeling vanished; looked steadfastly at his transformed friend a moment, then, taking ten half-eagles from his pocket, stooped down, and laid them, one by one, in a circle round him; and, retiring a pace, waved his long tasseled pipe with the air of a necromancer, an air heightened by his costume, accompanying each wave with a solemn murmur of cabalistical words.

Meantime, he within the magic-ring stood suddenly rapt, exhibiting every symptom of a successful charm—a turned cheek, a fixed attitude, a frozen eye; spellbound, not more by the waving wand than by the ten invincible talismans on the floor.

"Reappear, reappear, reappear, oh, my former friend! Replace this hideous apparition with thy blest shape, and be the token of thy return the words, 'My dear Frank.'"

"My dear Frank," now cried the restored friend, cordially stepping out of the ring, with regained self-possession regaining lost identity, "My dear Frank, what a funny man you are; full of fun as an egg of meat. How could you tell me that absurd story of your being in need? But I relish a good joke too well to spoil it by letting on. Of course, I humored the thing; and, on my side, put on all the cruel airs you would have me. Come, this little episode of fictitious estrangement will but enhance the delightful reality. Let us sit down again, and finish our bottle."

"With all my heart," said the cosmopolitan, dropping the necromancer with the same facility with which he had assumed it. "Yes," he added, soberly picking up the gold pieces, and returning them with a chink to his pocket, "yes, I am something of a funny man now and then; while for you, Charlie," eying him in tenderness, "what you say about your humoring the thing is true enough; never did man second a joke better than you did just now. You played your part better than I did mine; you played it, Charlie, to the life."

"You see, I once belonged to an amateur play company; that accounts for it. But come, fill up, and let's talk of something else."

"Well," acquiesced the cosmopolitan, seating himself, and quietly brimming his glass, "what shall we talk about?"

"Oh, anything you please," a sort of nervously accommodating.

"Well, suppose we talk about Charlemont?"

"Charlemont? What's Charlemont? Who's Charlemont?"

"You shall hear, my dear Charlie," answered the cosmopolitan. "I will tell you the story of Charlemont, the gentleman-madman."

Chapter 33

WHICH MAY PASS FOR WHATEVER IT MAY PROVE TO BE WORTH

But ere be given the rather grave story of Charlemont, a reply must in civility be made to a certain voice which methinks I hear, that, in view of past chapters, and more particularly the last, where certain antics appear, exclaims: How unreal all this is! Who did ever dress or act like your cosmopolitan? And who, it might be returned, did ever dress or act like harlequin?

Strange, that in a work of amusement, this severe fidelity to real life should be exacted by any one, who, by taking up such a work, sufficiently shows that he is not unwilling to drop real life, and turn, for a time, to something different. Yes, it is, indeed, strange that any one should clamor for the thing he is weary of; that any one, who, for any cause, finds real life dull, should yet demand of him who is to divert his attention from it, that he should be true to that dullness.

There is another class, and with this class we side, who sit down to a work of amusement tolerantly as they sit at a play, and with much the same expectations and feelings. They look that fancy shall evoke scenes different from those of the same old crowd round the custom-house counter, and same old dishes on the boarding-house table, with characters unlike those of the same old acquaintances they meet in the same old way every day in the same old street. And as, in real life, the proprieties will not allow people to act out themselves with that unreserve permitted to the stage; so, in books of fiction, they look not only for more entertainment, but, at bottom, even for more reality, than real life itself can show Thus, though they want novelty, they want nature, too; but nature unfettered, exhilarated, in effect transformed. In this way of thinking, the people in a fiction, like the people in a play, must dress as nobody exactly dresses, talk as nobody exactly talks, act as nobody exactly acts. It is with fiction as with religion: it should present another world, and yet one to which we feel the tie.

If, then, something is to be pardoned to well-meant endeavor, surely a little is to be allowed to that writer who, in all his scenes, does but seek to minister to what, as he understands it, is the implied wish of the more indulgent lovers of entertainment, before whom harlequin can never appear in a coat too parti-colored, or cut capers too fantastic.

One word more. Though every one knows how bootless it is to be in all cases vindicating one's self, never mind how convinced one may be that he is never in the wrong; yet, so precious to man is the approbation of his kind, that to rest, though but under an imaginary censure applied to but a work of imagination, is no easy thing.[1] The mention of this weakness will explain why all such readers as may think they perceive something inharmonious between the boisterous hilarity of the cosmopolitan with the bristling cynic, and his restrained good-nature with the booncompanion, are now referred to that chapter where some similar apparent inconsistency in another character is, on general principles, modestly endeavored to be apologized for.

Chapter 34

IN WHICH THE COSMOPOLITAN TELLS THE STORY OF THE GENTLEMAN-MADMAN

"Charlemont was a young merchant of French descent, living in St. Louis—a man not deficient in mind, and possessed of that sterling and captivating kindliness, seldom in perfection seen but in youthful bachelors, united at times to a remarkable sort of gracefully devil-may-care and witty good-humor. Of course, he was admired by everybody, and loved, as only mankind can love, by not a few. But in his twenty-ninth year a change came over him. Like

---

1. An oblique comment on the critical reception of some of Melville's earlier books, especially *Pierre* (1852), the censure of which was anything but imaginary.

one whose hair turns gray in a night, so in a day Charlemont turned from affable to morose. His acquaintances were passed without greeting; while, as for his confidential friends, them he pointedly, unscrupulously, and with a kind of fierceness, cut dead.

"One, provoked by such conduct, would fain have resented it with words as disdainful; while another, shocked by the change, and, in concern for a friend, magnanimously overlooking affronts, implored to know what sudden, secret grief had distempered him. But from resentment and from tenderness Charlemont alike turned away.

"Ere long, to the general surprise, the merchant Charlemont was gazetted,[1] and the same day it was reported that he had withdrawn from town, but not before placing his entire property in the hands of responsible assignees for the benefit of creditors.

"Whither he had vanished, none could guess. At length, nothing being heard, it was surmised that he must have made away with himself—a surmise, doubtless, originating in the remembrance of the change some months previous to his bankruptcy—a change of a sort only to be ascribed to a mind suddenly thrown from its balance.

"Years passed. It was spring-time, and lo, one bright morning, Charlemont lounged into the St. Louis coffee-houses—gay, polite, humane, companionable, and dressed in the height of costly elegance. Not only was he alive, but he was himself again. Upon meeting with old acquaintances, he made the first advances, and in such a manner that it was impossible not to meet him half-way. Upon other old friends, whom he did not chance casually to meet, he either personally called, or left his card and compliments for them; and to several, sent presents of game or hampers of wine.

"They say the world is sometimes harshly unforgiving, but it was not so to Charlemont. The world feels a return of love for one who returns to it as he did. Expressive of its renewed interest was a whisper, an inquiring whisper, how now, exactly, so long after his bankruptcy, it fared with Charlemont's purse. Rumor, seldom at a loss for answers, replied that he had spent nine years in Marseilles in France, and there acquiring a second fortune, had returned with it, a man devoted henceforth to genial friendships.

"Added years went by, and the restored wanderer still the same; or rather, by his noble qualities, grew up like golden maize in the encouraging sun of good opinions. But still the latent wonder was, what had caused that change in him at a period when, pretty much as now, he was, to all appearance, in the possession of the same fortune, the same friends, the same popularity. But nobody thought it would be the thing to question him here.

1. Listed in the newspaper notices of bankruptcy.

"At last, at a dinner at his house, when all the guests but one had successively departed; this remaining guest, an old acquaintance, being just enough under the influence of wine to set aside the fear of touching upon a delicate point, ventured, in a way which perhaps spoke more favorably for his heart than his tact, to beg of his host to explain the one enigma of his life. Deep melancholy overspread the before cheery face of Charlemont; he sat for some moments tremulously silent; then pushing a full decanter towards the guest, in a choked voice, said: 'No, no! when by art, and care, and time, flowers are made to bloom over a grave, who would seek to dig all up again only to know the mystery?—The wine.' When both glasses were filled, Charlemont took his, and lifting it, added slowly: 'If ever, in days to come, you shall see ruin at hand, and, thinking you understand mankind, shall tremble for your friendships, and tremble for your pride; and, partly through love for the one and fear for the other, shall resolve to be beforehand with the world, and save it from a sin by prospectively taking that sin to yourself, then will you do as one I now dream of once did, and like him will you suffer; but how fortunate and how grateful should you be, if like him, after all that had happened, you could be a little happy again.'

"When the guest went away, it was with the persuasion, that though outwardly restored in mind as in fortune, yet, some taint of Charlemont's old malady survived, and that it was not well for friends to touch one dangerous string."

Chapter 35

IN WHICH THE COSMOPOLITAN STRIKINGLY EVINCES THE ARTLESSNESS OF HIS NATURE

"Well, what do you think of the story of Charlemont?" mildly asked he who had told it.

"A very strange one," answered the auditor, who had been such not with perfect ease, "but is it true?"

"Of course not; it is a story which I told with the purpose of every story-teller—to amuse. Hence, if it seem strange to you, that strangeness is the romance; it is what contrasts it with real life; it is the invention, in brief, the fiction as opposed to the fact. For do but ask yourself, my dear Charlie," lovingly leaning over towards him, "I rest it with your own heart now, whether such a forereaching motive as Charlemont hinted he had acted on in his change—whether such a motive, I say, were a sort of one at all justified by the nature of human society? Would you, for one, turn

the cold shoulder to a friend—a convivial one, say, whose penniless-
ness should be suddenly revealed to you?"

"How can you ask me, my dear Frank? You know I would scorn
such meanness." But rising somewhat disconcerted—"really, early
as it is, I think I must retire; my head," putting up his hand to it,
"feels unpleasantly; this confounded elixir of logwood, little as I
drank of it, has played the deuce with me."

"Little as you drank of this elixir of logwood? Why, Charlie, you
are losing your mind. To talk so of the genuine, mellow old port.
Yes, I think that by all means you had better away, and sleep it off.
There—don't apologize—don't explain—go, go—I understand you
exactly. I will see you to-morrow."

Chapter 36

IN WHICH THE COSMOPOLITAN IS ACCOSTED BY A MYSTIC,
WHEREUPON ENSUES PRETTY MUCH SUCH TALK
AS MIGHT BE EXPECTED

As, not without some haste, the boon companion withdrew, a
stranger advanced, and touching the cosmopolitan, said: "I think I
heard you say you would see that man again. Be warned; don't you
do so."

He turned, surveying the speaker; a blue-eyed man, sandy-
haired, and Saxon-looking; perhaps five and forty; tall, and, but for
a certain angularity, well made; little touch of the drawing-room
about him, but a look of plain propriety of a Puritan sort, with a
kind of farmer dignity.[1] His age seemed betokened more by his
brow, placidly thoughtful, than by his general aspect, which had
that look of youthfulness in maturity, peculiar sometimes to habitual health of body, the original gift of nature, or in part the effect
or reward of steady temperance of the passions, kept so, perhaps,
by constitution as much as morality. A neat, comely, almost ruddy
cheek, coolly fresh, like a red clover-blossom at coolish dawn—the
color of warmth preserved by the virtue of chill. Toning the whole
man, was one-knows-not-what of shrewdness and mythiness,[2]

1. As Egbert S. Oliver demonstrated
(1946), Mark Winsome is modeled
physically and philosophically on
Ralph Waldo Emerson. The effective-
ness of the portrait—or caricature—
depends upon its being savagely one-
sided; in other moods, Melville found
much in Emerson to admire.
2. Branch's conjecture that this is an
error for "mysticness" is paleographi-
cally possible and makes the sense
clearer. However, in a letter to Evert

A. Duyckinck (March 3, 1849) Melville said he had expected to find
Emerson "full of transcendentalisms,
myths & oracular gibberish." In the
Literary World for October 16, 1847,
the Duyckincks wrote: "Ingenuity and
Yankee shrewdness is the forte of Mr.
Emerson, obscured or enlightened as
the case may be, by his Platonic and
Transcendental doctrine or modes of
expression."

strangely jumbled; in that way, he seemed a kind of cross between a Yankee peddler and a Tartar priest, though it seemed as if, at a pinch, the first would not in all probability play second fiddle to the last.

"Sir," said the cosmopolitan, rising and bowing with slow dignity, "if I cannot with unmixed satisfaction hail a hint pointed at one who has just been clinking the social glass with me, on the other hand, I am not disposed to underrate the motive which, in the present case, could alone have prompted such an intimation. My friend, whose seat is still warm, has retired for the night, leaving more or less in his bottle here. Pray, sit down in his seat, and partake with me; and then, if you choose to hint aught further unfavorable to the man, the genial warmth of whose person in part passes into yours, and whose genial hospitality meanders through you—be it so."

"Quite beautiful conceits," said the stranger, now scholastically and artistically eying the picturesque speaker, as if he were a statue in the Pitti Palace; "very beautiful:" then with the gravest interest, "yours, sir, if I mistake not, must be a beautiful soul—one full of all love and truth; for where beauty is, there must those be."

"A pleasing belief," rejoined the cosmopolitan, beginning with an even air, "and to confess, long ago it pleased me. Yes, with you and Schiller, I am pleased to believe that beauty is at bottom incompatible with ill, and therefore am so eccentric as to have confidence in the latent benignity of that beautiful creature, the rattle-snake, whose lithe neck and burnished maze of tawny gold, as he sleekly curls aloft in the sun, who on the prairie can behold without wonder?"

As he breathed these words, he seemed so to enter into their spirit—as some earnest descriptive speakers will—as unconsciously to wreathe his form and sidelong crest his head, till he all but seemed the creature described. Meantime, the stranger regarded him with little surprise, apparently, though with much contemplativeness of a mystical sort, and presently said: "When charmed by the beauty of that viper, did it never occur to you to change personalities with him? to feel what it was to be a snake? to glide unsuspected in grass? to sting, to kill at a touch; your whole beautiful body one iridescent scabbard of death? In short, did the wish never occur to you to feel yourself exempt from knowledge, and conscience, and revel for a while in the care-free, joyous life of a perfectly instinctive, unscrupulous, and irresponsible creature?"

"Such a wish," replied the other, not perceptibly disturbed, "I must confess, never consciously was mine. Such a wish, indeed, could hardly occur to ordinary imaginations, and mine I cannot think much above the average."

"But now that the idea is suggested," said the stranger, with infantile intellectuality, "does it not raise the desire?"

"Hardly. For though I do not think I have any uncharitable prejudice against the rattle-snake, still, I should not like to be one. If I were a rattle-snake now, there would be no such thing as being genial with men—men would be afraid of me, and then I should be a very lonesome and miserable rattle-snake."

"True, men would be afraid of you. And why? Because of your rattle, your hollow rattle—a sound, as I have been told, like the shaking together of small, dry skulls in a tune of the Waltz of Death. And here we have another beautiful truth. When any creature is by its make inimical to other creatures, nature in effect labels that creature, much as an apothecary does a poison. So that whoever is destroyed by a rattle-snake, or other harmful agent, it is his own fault. He should have respected the label. Hence that significant passage in Scripture, 'Who will pity the charmer that is bitten with a serpent?' "[3]

"*I* would pity him," said the cosmopolitan, a little bluntly, perhaps.

"But don't you think," rejoined the other, still maintaining his passionless air, "don't you think, that for a man to pity where nature is pitiless, is a little presuming?"

"Let casuists decide the casuistry, but the compassion the heart decides for itself. But, sir," deepening in seriousness, "as I now for the first realize, you but a moment since introduced the word irresponsible in a way I am not used to. Now, sir, though, out of a tolerant spirit, as I hope, I try my best never to be frightened at any speculation, so long as it is pursued in honesty, yet, for once, I must acknowledge that you do really, in the point cited, cause me uneasiness; because a proper view of the universe, that view which is suited to breed a proper confidence, teaches, if I err not, that since all things are justly presided over, not very many living agents but must be some way accountable."

"Is a rattle-snake accountable?" asked the stranger with such a preternaturally cold, gemmy glance out of his pellucid blue eye, that he seemed more a metaphysical merman than a feeling man; "is a rattle-snake accountable?"

"If I will not affirm that it is," returned the other, with the caution of no inexperienced thinker, "neither will I deny it. But if we suppose it so, I need not say that such accountability is neither to you, nor me, nor the Court of Common Pleas, but to something superior."

He was proceeding, when the stranger would have interrupted him; but as reading his argument in his eye, the cosmopolitan,

3. Ecclesiasticus 12:13.

without waiting for it to be put into words, at once spoke to it: "You object to my supposition, for but such it is, that the rattle-snake's accountability is not by nature manifest; but might not much the same thing be urged against man's? A *reductio ad absurdum*, proving the objection vain. But if now," he continued, " you consider what capacity for mischief there is in a rattle-snake (observe, I do not charge it with being mischievous, I but say it has the capacity), could you well avoid admitting that that would be no symmetrical view of the universe which should maintain that, while to man it is forbidden to kill, without judicial cause, his fellow, yet the rattle-snake has an implied permit of unaccountability to murder any creature it takes capricious umbrage at—man included?—But," with a wearied air, "this is no genial talk; at least it is not so to me. Zeal at unawares embarked me in it. I regret it. Pray, sit down, and take some of this wine."

"Your suggestions are new to me," said the other, with a kind of condescending appreciativeness, as of one who, out of devotion to knowledge, disdains not to appropriate the least crumb of it, even from a pauper's board; "and, as I am a very Athenian in hailing a new thought, I cannot consent to let it drop so abruptly. Now, the rattle-snake—"

"Nothing more about rattle-snakes, I beseech," in distress; "I must positively decline to reënter upon that subject. Sit down, sir, I beg, and take some of this wine."

"To invite me to sit down with you is hospitable," collectedly acquiescing now in the change of topics; "and hospitality being fabled to be of oriental origin, and forming, as it does, the subject of a pleasing Arabian romance, as well as being a very romantic thing in itself—hence I always hear the expressions of hospitality with pleasure. But, as for the wine, my regard for that beverage is so extreme, and I am so fearful of letting it sate me, that I keep my love for it in the lasting condition of an untried abstraction. Briefly, I quaff immense draughts of wine from the page of Hafiz, but wine from a cup I seldom as much as sip."[4]

The cosmopolitan turned a mild glance upon the speaker, who, now occupying the chair opposite him, sat there purely and coldly radiant as a prism. It seemed as if one could almost hear him vitreously chime and ring. That moment a waiter passed, whom, arresting with a sign, the cosmopolitan bid go bring a goblet of

4. In "The Poet" Emerson explains "why bards love wine, mead, narcotics, coffee, tea, opium, the fumes of sandalwood and tobacco" and all other "coarser or finer *quasi*-mechanical substitutes for the true nectar, which is the ravishment of the intellect by coming nearer to the fact." Never, he says, "can any advantage be taken of nature by a trick." He concludes that "the poet's habit of living should be set on a key so low that the common influences should delight him. His cheerfulness should be the gift of the sunlight; the air should suffice for his inspiration, and he should be tipsy with water."

ice-water. "Ice it well, waiter," said he; "and now," turning to the stranger, "will you, if you please, give me your reason for the warning words you first addressed to me?"

"I hope they were not such warnings as most warnings are," said the stranger; "warnings which do not forewarn, but in mockery come after the fact. And yet something in you bids me think now, that whatever latent design your impostor friend might have had upon you, it as yet remains unaccomplished. You read his label."

"And what did it say? 'This is a genial soul.' So you see you must either give up your doctrine of labels, or else your prejudice against my friend. But tell me," with renewed earnestness, "what do you take him for? What is he?"

"What are you? What am I? Nobody knows who anybody is. The data which life furnishes, toward forming a true estimate of any being, are as insufficient to that end as in geometry one side given would be to determine the triangle."

"But is not this doctrine of triangles someway inconsistent with your doctrine of labels?"

"Yes; but what of that? I seldom care to be consistent.[5] In a philosophical view, consistency is a certain level at all times, maintained in all the thoughts of one's mind. But, since nature is nearly all hill and dale, how can one keep naturally advancing in knowledge without submitting to the natural inequalities in the progress? Advance into knowledge is just like advance upon the grand Erie canal, where, from the character of the country, change of level is inevitable; you are locked up and locked down with perpetual inconsistencies, and yet all the time you get on; while the dullest part of the whole route is what the boatmen call the 'long level'—a consistently-flat surface of sixty miles through stagnant swamps."

"In one particular," rejoined the cosmopolitan, "your simile is, perhaps, unfortunate. For, after all these weary lockings-up and lockings-down, upon how much of a higher plain do you finally stand? Enough to make it an object? Having from youth been taught reverence for knowledge, you must pardon me if, on but this one account, I reject your analogy. But really you someway bewitch me with your tempting discourse, so that I keep straying from my point unawares. You tell me you cannot certainly know who or what my friend is; pray, what do you conjecture him to be?"

"I conjecture him to be what, among the ancient Egyptians, was called a ——" using some unknown word.[6]

"A ——! And what is that?"

5. An echo of a notoriously misunderstood passage in Emerson's "Self-Reliance": "A foolish consistency is the hobgoblin of little minds, adored by little statesmen and philosophers and divines. With consistency a great soul has simply nothing to do."
6. A standard jibe was that the Transcendentalists were unintelligible.

"A —— is what Proclus, in a little note to his third book on the theology of Plato, defines as —— ——" coming out with a sentence of Greek.

Holding up his glass, and steadily looking through its transparency, the cosmopolitan rejoined: "That, in so defining the thing, Proclus set it to modern understandings in the most crystal light it was susceptible of, I will not rashly deny; still, if you could put the definition in words suited to perceptions like mine, I should take it for a favor."

"A favor!" slightly lifting his cool eyebrows; "a bridal favor I understand, a knot of white ribands, a very beautiful type of the purity of true marriage; but of other favors I am yet to learn; and still, in a vague way, the word, as you employ it, strikes me as unpleasingly significant in general of some poor, unheroic submission to being done good to."

Here the goblet of iced-water was brought, and, in compliance with a sign from the cosmopolitan, was placed before the stranger, who, not before expressing acknowledgments, took a draught, apparently refreshing—its very coldness, as with some is the case, proving not entirely uncongenial.

At last, setting down the goblet, and gently wiping from his lips the beads of water freshly clinging there as to the valve of a coral-shell upon a reef, he turned upon the cosmopolitan, and, in a manner the most cool, self-possessed, and matter-of-fact possible, said: "I hold to the metempsychosis; and whoever I may be now, I feel that I was once the stoic Arrian, and have inklings of having been equally puzzled by a word in the current language of that former time, very probably answering to your word *favor*."

"Would you favor me by explaining?" said the cosmopolitan, blandly.

"Sir," responded the stranger, with a very slight degree of severity, "I like lucidity, of all things, and am afraid I shall hardly be able to converse satisfactorily with you, unless you bear it in mind."

The cosmopolitan ruminatingly eyed him awhile, then said: "The best way, as I have heard, to get out of a labyrinth, is to retrace one's steps. I will accordingly retrace mine, and beg you will accompany me. In short, once again to return to the point: for what reason did you warn me against my friend?"

"Briefly, then, and clearly, because, as before said, I conjecture him to be what, among the ancient Egyptians—"

"Pray, now," earnestly deprecated the cosmopolitan, "pray, now, why disturb the repose of those ancient Egyptians? What to us are their words or their thoughts? Are we pauper Arabs, without a house of our own, that, with the mummies, we must turn squatters among the dust of the Catacombs?"

"Pharaoh's poorest brick-maker lies proudlier in his rags than the Emperor of all the Russias in his hollands," oracularly said the stranger; "for death, though in a worm, is majestic; while life, though in a king, is contemptible. So talk not against mummies. It is a part of my mission to teach mankind a due reverence for mummies."

Fortunately, to arrest these incoherencies, or rather, to vary them, a haggard, inspired-looking man now approached—a crazy beggar, asking alms under the form of peddling a rhapsodical tract, composed by himself, and setting forth his claims to some rhapsodical apostleship.[7] Though ragged and dirty, there was about him no touch of vulgarity; for, by nature, his manner was not unrefined, his frame slender, and appeared the more so from the broad, untanned frontlet of his brow, tangled over with a disheveled mass of raven curls, throwing a still deeper tinge upon a complexion like that of a shriveled berry. Nothing could exceed his look of picturesque Italian ruin and dethronement, heightened by what seemed just one glimmering peep of reason, insufficient to do him any lasting good, but enough, perhaps, to suggest a torment of latent doubts at times, whether his addled dream of glory were true.

Accepting the tract offered him, the cosmopolitan glanced over it, and, seeming to see just what it was, closed it, put it in his pocket, eyed the man a moment, then, leaning over and presenting him with a shilling, said to him, in tones kind and considerate: "I am sorry, my friend, that I happen to be engaged just now; but, having purchased your work, I promise myself much satisfaction in its perusal at my earliest leisure."

In his tattered, single-breasted frock-coat, buttoned meagerly up to his chin, the shatter-brain made him a bow, which, for courtesy, would not have misbecome a viscount, then turned with silent appeal to the stranger. But the stranger sat more like a cold prism than ever, while an expression of keen Yankee cuteness, now replacing his former mystical one, lent added icicles to his aspect. His whole air said: "Nothing from me." The repulsed petitioner threw a look full of resentful pride and cracked disdain upon him, and went his way.

"Come, now," said the cosmopolitan, a little reproachfully, "you ought to have sympathized with that man; tell me, did you feel no fellow-feeling? Look at his tract here, quite in the transcendental vein."

"Excuse me," said the stranger, declining the tract, "I never patronize scoundrels."

"Scoundrels?"

7. Harrison Hayford (1959) assembled evidence that this crazy beggar was based on Edgar Allan Poe.

"I detected in him, sir, a damning peep of sense—damning, I say; for sense in a seeming madman is scoundrelism. I take him for a cunning vagabond, who picks up a vagabond living by adroitly playing the madman. Did you not remark how he flinched under my eye?"

"Really," drawing a long, astonished breath, "I could hardly have divined in you a temper so subtlely distrustful. Flinched? to be sure he did, poor fellow; you received him with so lame a welcome. As for his adroitly playing the madman, invidious critics might object the same to some one or two strolling magi of these days.[8] But that is a matter I know nothing about. But, once more, and for the last time, to return to the point: why sir, did you warn me against my friend? I shall rejoice, if, as I think it will prove, your want of confidence in my friend rests upon a basis equally slender with your distrust of the lunatic. Come, why did you warn me? Put it, I beseech, in few words, and those English."

"I warned you against him because he is suspected for what on these boats is known—so they tell me—as a Mississippi operator."

"An operator, ah? he operates, does he? My friend, then, is something like what the Indians call a Great Medicine, is he? He operates, he purges, he drains off the repletions."

"I perceive, sir," said the stranger, constitutionally obtuse to the pleasant drollery, "that your notion, of what is called a Great Medicine, needs correction. The Great Medicine among the Indians is less a bolus than a man in grave esteem for his politic sagacity."

"And is not my friend politic? Is not my friend sagacious? By your own definition, is not my friend a Great Medicine?"

"No, he is an operator, a Mississippi operator; an equivocal character. That he is such, I little doubt, having had him pointed out to me as such by one desirous of initiating me into any little novelty of this western region, where I never before traveled. And, sir, if I am not mistaken, you also are a stranger here (but, indeed, where in this strange universe is not one a stranger?) and that is a reason why I felt moved to warn you against a companion who could not be otherwise than perilous to one of a free and trustful disposition. But I repeat the hope, that, thus far at least, he has not succeeded with you, and trust that, for the future, he will not."[9]

"Thank you for your concern; but hardly can I equally thank you for so steadily maintaining the hypothesis of my friend's objectionableness. True, I but made his acquaintance for the first to-day, and know little of his antecedents; but that would seem no just

8. Possibly a jibe at Emerson's success on the American lecture circuit: Melville may also have known of Thoreau's lectures and have thought them more successful than they were.
9. The butt of this long joke is the Transcendental refusal to acknowledge evil. Winsome can unmask the ordinary Mississippi con man Charlie Noble, but without knowing it he talks at length with the Devil.

reason why a nature like his should not of itself inspire confidence. And since your own knowledge of the gentleman is not, by your account, so exact as it might be, you will pardon me if I decline to welcome any further suggestions unflattering to him. Indeed, sir," with friendly decision, "let us change the subject."

Chapter 37

THE MYSTICAL MASTER INTRODUCES THE PRACTICAL DISCIPLE

"Both, the subject and the interlocutor," replied the stranger rising, and waiting the return towards him of a promenader, that moment turning at the further end of his walk.

"Egbert!" said he, calling.

Egbert, a well-dressed, commercial-looking gentleman of about thirty, responded in a way strikingly deferential, and in a moment stood near, in the attitude less of an equal companion apparently than a confidential follower.

"This," said the stranger, taking Egbert by the hand and leading him to the cosmopolitan, "this is Egbert, a disciple. I wish you to know Egbert. Egbert was the first among mankind to reduce to practice the principles of Mark Winsome—principles previously accounted as less adapted to life than the closet.[1] Egbert," turning to the disciple, who, with seeming modesty, a little shrank under these compliments, "Egbert, this," with a salute towards the cosmopolitan, "is, like all of us, a stranger. I wish you, Egbert, to know this brother stranger; be communicative with him. Particularly if, by anything hitherto dropped, his curiosity has been roused as to the precise nature of my philosophy, I trust you will not leave such curiosity ungratified. You, Egbert, by simply setting forth your practice, can do more to enlighten one as to my theory, than I myself can by mere speech. Indeed, it is by you that I myself best understand myself. For to every philosophy are certain rear parts, very important parts, and these, like the rear of one's head, are best seen by reflection. Now, as in a glass, you, Egbert, in your life, reflect to me the more important part of my system. He, who approves you, approves the philosophy of Mark Winsome."

Though portions of this harangue may, perhaps, in the phraseology seem self-complaisant, yet no trace of self-complacency was perceptible in the speaker's manner, which throughout was plain, unassuming, dignified, and manly; the teacher and prophet seemed

1. Egbert S. Oliver (1946), assembled convincing evidence that Egbert is modeled upon Thoreau, known even in the 1850's for his application of Emerson's principles.

to lurk more in the idea, so to speak, than in the mere bearing of him who was the vehicle of it.

"Sir," said the cosmopolitan, who seemed not a little interested in this new aspect of matters, "you speak of a certain philosophy, and a more or less occult one it may be, and hint of its bearing upon practical life; pray, tell me, if the study of this philosophy tends to the same formation of character with the experiences of the world?"

"It does; and that is the test of its truth; for any philosophy that, being in operation contradictory to the ways of the world, tends to produce a character at odds with it, such a philosophy must necessarily be but a cheat and a dream."

"You a little surprise me," answered the cosmopolitan; "for, from an occasional profundity in you, and also from your allusions to a profound work on the theology of Plato, it would seem but natural to surmise that, if you are the originator of any philosophy, it must needs so partake of the abstruse, as to exalt it above the comparatively vile uses of life."

"No uncommon mistake with regard to me," rejoined the other. Then meekly standing like a Raphael: "If still in golden accents old Memnon murmurs his riddle, none the less does the balance-sheet of every man's ledger unriddle the profit or loss of life. Sir," with calm energy, "man came into this world, not to sit down and muse, not to befog himself with vain subtleties, but to gird up his loins and to work. Mystery is in the morning, and mystery in the night, and the beauty of mystery is everywhere; but still the plain truth remains, that mouth and purse must be filled. If, hitherto, you have supposed me a visionary, be undeceived. I am no one-ideaed one, either; no more than the seers before me. Was not Seneca a usurer? Bacon a courtier? and Swedenborg, though with one eye on the invisible, did he not keep the other on the main chance? Along with whatever else it may be given me to be, I am a man of serviceable knowledge, and a man of the world. Know me for such. And as for my disciple here," turning towards him, "if you look to find any soft Utopianisms and last year's sunsets in him, I smile to think how he will set you right. The doctrines I have taught him will, I trust, lead him neither to the mad-house nor the poor-house, as so many other doctrines have served credulous sticklers. Furthermore," glancing upon him paternally, "Egbert is both my disciple and my poet. For poetry is not a thing of ink and rhyme, but of thought and act, and, in the latter way, is by any one to be found anywhere, when in useful action sought. In a word, my disciple here is a thriving young merchant, a practical poet in the West India trade.[2] There," presenting Egbert's hand to the cos-

2. Presumably a recollection of Thoreau's comment on "the West Indian provinces of the fancy and imagina-tion" in *Walden*, Chapter 1, paragraph 8.

mopolitan, "I join you, and leave you." With which words, and without bowing, the master withdrew.

Chapter 38

THE DISCIPLE UNBENDS, AND CONSENTS TO ACT A SOCIAL PART

In the master's presence the disciple had stood as one not ignorant of his place; modesty was in his expression, with a sort of reverential depression. But the presence of the superior withdrawn, he seemed lithely to shoot up erect from beneath it, like one of those wire men from a toy snuff-box.

He was, as before said, a young man of about thirty. His countenance of that neuter sort, which, in repose, is neither prepossessing nor disagreeable; so that it seemed quite uncertain how he would turn out. His dress was neat, with just enough of the mode to save it from the reproach of originality; in which general respect, though with a readjustment of details, his costume seemed modeled upon his master's. But, upon the whole, he was, to all appearances, the last person in the world that one would take for the disciple of any transcendental philosophy; though, indeed, something about his sharp nose and shaved chin seemed to hint that if mysticism, as a lesson, ever came in his way, he might, with the characteristic knack of a true New-Englander, turn even so profitless a thing to some profitable account.

"Well," said he, now familiarly seating himself in the vacated chair, "what do you think of Mark? Sublime fellow, ain't he?"

"That each member of the human guild is worthy respect, my friend," rejoined the cosmopolitan, "is a fact which no admirer of that guild will question; but that, in view of higher natures, the word sublime, so frequently applied to them, can, without confusion, be also applied to man, is a point which man will decide for himself; though, indeed, if he decide it in the affirmative, it is not for me to object. But I am curious to know more of that philosophy of which, at present, I have but inklings. You, its first disciple among men, it seems, are peculiarly qualified to expound it. Have you any objections to begin now?"

"None at all," squaring himself to the table. "Where shall I begin? At first principles?"

"You remember that it was in a practical way that you were represented as being fitted for the clear exposition. Now, what you call first principles, I have, in some things, found to be more or less vague. Permit me, then, in a plain way, to suppose some common case in real life, and that done, I would like you to tell me how you, the practical disciple of the philosophy I wish to know about, would, in that case, conduct."

"A business-like view. Propose the case."

"Not only the case, but the persons. The case is this: There are two friends, friends from childhood, bosom-friends; one of whom, for the first time, being in need, for the first time seeks a loan from the other, who, so far as fortune goes, is more than competent to grant it. And the persons are to be you and I: you, the friend from whom the loan is sought—I, the friend who seeks it: you, the disciple of the philosophy in question—I, a common man with no more philosophy than to know that when I am comfortably warm I don't feel cold, and when I have the ague I shake. Mind, now, you must work up your imagination, and, as much as possible, talk and behave just as if the case supposed were a fact. For brevity, you shall call me Frank, and I will call you Charlie. Are you agreed?"

"Perfectly. You begin."

The cosmopolitan paused a moment, then, assuming a serious and care-worn air, suitable to the part to be enacted, addressed his hypothesized friend.

Chapter 39

THE HYPOTHETICAL FRIENDS

"Charlie, I am going to put confidence in you."[1]

"You always have, and with reason. What is it, Frank?"

"Charlie, I am in want—urgent want of money."

"That's not well."

"But it *will* be well, Charlie, if you loan me a hundred dollars. I would not ask this of you, only my need is sore, and you and I have so long shared hearts and minds together, however unequally on my side, that nothing remains to prove our friendship than, with the same inequality on my side, to share purses. You will do me the favor, won't you?"

"Favor? What do you mean, by asking me to do you a favor?"

"Why, Charlie, you never used to talk so."

"Because, Frank, you on your side, never used to talk so."

"But won't you loan me the money?"

"No, Frank."

1. In this chapter Melville is satirizing rarefied Transcendental notions about friendship. One or more of these was in his mind: a section of "Wednesday" in Thoreau's *Week* ("Nothing is so difficult as to help a Friend in matters which do not require the aid of Friend- ship, but only a cheap and trivial service"); or of "Visitors" in *Walden* ("Objects of charity are not guests"); or Emerson's "Friendship," which is pointedly alluded to just below. See Backgrounds and Sources.

"Why?"

"Because my rule forbids. I give away money, but never loan it; and of course the man who calls himself my friend is above receiving alms. The negotiation of a loan is a business transaction. And I will transact no business with a friend. What a friend is, he is socially and intellectually; and I rate social and intellectual friendship too high to degrade it on either side into a pecuniary make-shift. To be sure there are, and I have, what is called business friends; that is, commercial acquaintances, very convenient persons. But I draw a red-ink line between them and my friends in the true sense—my friends social and intellectual. In brief, a true friend has nothing to do with loans; he should have a soul above loans. Loans are such unfriendly accommodations as are to be had from the soulless corporation of a bank, by giving the regular security and paying the regular discount."

"An *unfriendly* accommodation? Do those words go together handsomely?"

"Like the poor farmer's team, of an old man and a cow—not handsomely, but to the purpose. Look, Frank, a loan of money on interest is a sale of money on credit. To sell a thing on credit may be an accommodation, but where is the friendliness? Few men in their senses, except operators, borrow money on interest, except upon a necessity akin to starvation. Well, now, where is the friendliness of my letting a starving man have, say, the money's worth of a barrel of flour upon the condition that, on a given day, he shall let me have the money's worth of a barrel and a half of flour; especially if I add this further proviso, that if he fail so to do, I shall then, to secure to myself the money's worth of my barrel and his half barrel, put his heart up at public auction, and, as it is cruel to part families, throw in his wife's and children's?"

"I understand," with a pathetic shudder; "but even did it come to that, such a step on the creditor's part, let us, for the honor of human nature, hope, were less the intention than the contingency."

"But, Frank, a contingency not unprovided for in the taking beforehand of due securities."

"Still, Charlie, was not the loan in the first place a friend's act?"

"And the auction in the last place an enemy's act. Don't you see? The enmity lies couched in the friendship, just as the ruin in the relief."

"I must be very stupid to-day, Charlie, but really, I can't understand this. Excuse me, my dear friend, but it strikes me that in going into the philosophy of the subject, you go somewhat out of your depth."

"So said the incautious wader-out to the ocean; but the ocean replied: 'It is just the other way, my wet friend,' and drowned him."

"That, Charlie, is a fable about as unjust to the ocean, as some of Æsop's are to the animals. The ocean is a magnanimous element, and would scorn to assassinate a poor fellow, let alone taunting him in the act. But I don't understand what you say about enmity couched in friendship, and ruin in relief."

"I will illustrate, Frank. The needy man is a train slipped off the rail. He who loans him money on interest is the one who, by way of accommodation, helps get the train back where it belongs; but then, by way of making all square, and a little more, telegraphs to an agent, thirty miles a-head by a precipice, to throw just there, on his account, a beam across the track. Your needy man's principal-and-interest friend is, I say again, a friend with an enmity in reserve. No, no, my dear friend, no interest for me. I scorn interest."

"Well, Charlie, none need you charge. Loan me without interest."

"That would be alms again."

"Alms, if the sum borrowed is returned?"

"Yes: an alms, not of the principal, but the interest."

"Well, I am in sore need, so I will not decline the alms. Seeing that it is you, Charlie, gratefully will I accept the alms of the interest. No humiliation between friends."

"Now, how in the refined view of friendship can you suffer yourself to talk so, my dear Frank? It pains me. For though I am not of the sour mind of Solomon, that, in the hour of need, a stranger is better than a brother;[2] yet I entirely agree with my sublime master, who, in his Essay on Friendship, says so nobly, that if he want a terrestrial convenience, not to his friend celestial (or friend social and intellectual) would he go; no: for his terrestrial convenience, to his friend terrestrial (or humbler business-friend) he goes. Very lucidly he adds the reason: Because, for the superior nature, which ɔn no account can ever descend to do good, to be annoyed with requests to do it, when the inferior one, which by no instruction can ever rise above that capacity, stands always inclined to it—this is unsuitable."

"Then I will not consider you as my friend celestial, but as the other."

2. Proverbs 18:24: "there is a friend that sticketh closer than a brother" and 27:10: "Thine own friend, and thy father's friend, forsake not; neither go into thy brother's house in the day of thy calamity; for better is a neighbour that is near than a brother far off." In the copy of "The Whale" which he gave his brother-in-law John C. Hoadley on January 6, 1854, Melville wrote: "John C Hoadley from his friend Herman Melville," then footnoted "friend" this way: "If my good brother John take exception to the use of the word *friend* here, thinking there is a *nearer* word; I beg him to remember that saying in the Good Book, which hints there is a *friend* that sticketh CLOSER than a *brother*."

"It racks me to come to that; but, to oblige you, I'll do it. We are business friends; business is business. You want to negotiate a loan. Very good. On what paper? Will you pay three per cent. a month? Where is your security?"

"Surely, you will not exact those formalities from your old schoolmate—him with whom you have so often sauntered down the groves of Academe, discoursing of the beauty of virtue, and the grace that is in kindliness—and all for so paltry a sum. Security? Our being fellow-academics, and friends from childhood up, is security."

"Pardon me, my dear Frank, our being fellow-academics is the worst of securities; while, our having been friends from childhood up is just no security at all. You forget we are now business friends."

"And you, on your side, forget, Charlie, that as your business friend I can give you no security; my need being so sore that I cannot get an indorser."

"No indorser, then, no business loan."

"Since then, Charlie, neither as the one nor the other sort of friend you have defined, can I prevail with you; how if, combining the two, I sue as both?"

"Are you a centaur?"

"When all is said then, what good have I of your friendship, regarded in what light you will?"

"The good which is in the philosophy of Mark Winsome, as reduced to practice by a practical disciple."

"And why don't you add, much good may the philosophy of Mark Winsome do me? Ah," turning invokingly, "what is friendship, if it be not the helping hand and the feeling heart, the good Samaritan pouring out at need the purse as the vial!"[3]

"Now, my dear Frank, don't be childish. Through tears never did man see his way in the dark. I should hold you unworthy that sincere friendship I bear you, could I think that friendship in the ideal is too lofty for you to conceive. And let me tell you, my dear Frank, that you would seriously shake the foundations of our love, if ever again you should repeat the present scene. The philosophy, which is mine in the strongest way, teaches plain-dealing. Let me, then, now, as at the most suitable time, candidly disclose certain circumstances you seem in ignorance of. Though our friendship began in boyhood, think not that, on my side at least, it began injudiciously. Boys are little men, it is said. You, I juvenilely picked out for my friend, for your favorable points at the time; not the least of which were your good manners, handsome dress, and your parents' rank and repute of wealth. In short, like any grown man,

3. See Luke 10:30–37.

boy though I was, I went into the market and chose me my mutton, not for its leanness, but its fatness. In other words, there seemed in you, the schoolboy who always had silver in his pocket, a reasonable probability that you would never stand in lean need of fat succor; and if my early impression has not been verified by the event, it is only because of the caprice of fortune producing a fallibility of human expectations, however discreet."

"Oh, that I should listen to this cold-blooded disclosure!"

"A little cold blood in your ardent veins, my dear Frank, wouldn't do you any harm, let me tell you. Cold-blooded? You say that, because my disclosure seems to involve a vile prudence on my side. But not so. My reason for choosing you in part for the points I have mentioned, was solely with a view of preserving inviolate the delicacy of the connection. For—do but think of it—what more distressing to delicate friendship, formed early, than your friend's eventually, in manhood, dropping in of a rainy night for his little loan of five dollars or so? Can delicate friendship stand that? And, on the other side, would delicate friendship, so long as it retained its delicacy, do that? Would you not instinctively say of your dripping friend in the entry, 'I have been deceived, fraudulently deceived, in this man; he is no true friend that, in platonic love to demand love-rites?' "

"And rites, doubly rights, they are, cruel Charlie!"

"Take it how you will, heed well how, by too importunately claiming those rights, as you call them, you shake those foundations I hinted of. For though, as it turns out, I, in my early friendship, built me a fair house on a poor site; yet such pains and cost have I lavished on that house, that, after all, it is dear to me. No, I would not lose the sweet boon of your friendship, Frank. But beware."

"And of what? Of being in need? Oh, Charlie! you talk not to a god, a being who in himself holds his own estate, but to a man who, being a man, is the sport of fate's wind and wave, and who mounts towards heaven or sinks towards hell, as the billows roll him in trough or on crest."

"Tut! Frank. Man is no such poor devil as that comes to—no poor drifting sea-weed of the universe. Man has a soul; which, if he will, puts him beyond fortune's finger and the future's spite. Don't whine like fortune's whipped dog, Frank, or by the heart of a true friend, I will cut ye."

"Cut me you have already, cruel Charlie, and to the quick. Call to mind the days we went nutting, the times we walked in the woods, arms wreathed about each other, showing trunks invined like the trees:—oh, Charlie!"

"Pish! we were boys."

"Then lucky the fate of the first-born of Egypt,[4] cold in the grave ere maturity struck them with a sharper frost.—Charlie?"

"Fie! you're a girl."

"Help, help, Charlie, I want help!"

"Help? to say nothing of the friend, there is something wrong about the man who wants help. There is somewhere a defect, a want, in brief, a need, a crying need, somewhere about that man."

"So there is, Charlie.—Help, Help!"

"How foolish a cry, when to implore help, is itself the proof of undesert of it."

"Oh, this, all along, is not you, Charlie, but some ventriloquist who usurps your larynx. It is Mark Winsome that speaks, not Charlie."

"If so, thank heaven, the voice of Mark Winsome is not alien but congenial to my larynx. If the philosophy of that illustrious teacher find little response among mankind at large, it is less that they do not possess teachable tempers, than because they are so unfortunate as not to have natures predisposed to accord with him."

"Welcome, that compliment to humanity," exclaimed Frank with energy, "the truer because unintended. And long in this respect may humanity remain what you affirm it. And long it will; since humanity, inwardly feeling how subject it is to straits, and hence how precious is help, will, for selfishness' sake, if no other, long postpone ratifying a philosophy that banishes help from the world. But Charlie, Charlie! speak as you used to; tell me you will help me. Were the case reversed, not less freely would I loan you the money than you would ask me to loan it."

"*I* ask? *I* ask a loan? Frank, by this hand, under no circumstances would I accept a loan, though without asking pressed on me. The experience of China Aster might warn me."

"And what was that?"

"Not very unlike the experience of the man that built himself a palace of moon-beams, and when the moon set was surprised that his palace vanished with it. I will tell you about China Aster. I wish I could do so in my own words, but unhappily the original story-teller here has so tyrannized over me, that it is quite impossible for me to repeat his incidents without sliding into his style. I forewarn you of this, that you may not think me so maudlin as, in some parts, the story would seem to make its narrator. It is too bad that any intellect, especially in so small a matter, should have such power to impose itself upon another, against its best exerted will, too. However, it is satisfaction to know that the main moral, to which all tends, I fully approve. But, to begin."

4. Exodus 12:29.

Chapter 40

IN WHICH THE STORY OF CHINA ASTER IS AT SECOND-HAND
TOLD BY ONE WHO, WHILE NOT DISAPPROVING THE MORAL,
DISCLAIMS THE SPIRIT OF THE STYLE

"China Aster was a young candle-maker of Marietta, at the mouth of the Muskingum—one whose trade would seem a kind of subordinate branch of that parent craft and mystery of the hosts of heaven, to be the means, effectively or otherwise, of shedding some light through the darkness of a planet benighted. But he made little money by the business. Much ado had poor China Aster and his family to li̇ve; he could, if he chose, light up from his stores a whole street, but not so easily could he light up with prosperity the hearts of his household.

"Now, China Aster, it so happened, had a friend, Orchis, a shoe-maker; one whose calling it is to defend the understandings of men from naked contact with the substance of things; a very useful vocation, and which, spite of all the wiseacres may prophesy, will hardly go out of fashion so long as rocks are hard and flints will gall. All at once, by a capital prize in a lottery, this useful shoe-maker was raised from a bench to a sofa. A small nabob was the shoemaker now, and the understandings of men, let them shift for themselves. Not that Orchis was, by prosperity, elated into heart-lessness. Not at all. Because, in his fine apparel, strolling one morn-ing into the candlery, and gayly switching about at the candle-boxes with his gold-headed cane—while poor China Aster, with his greasy paper cap and leather apron, was selling one candle for one penny to a poor orange-woman, who, with the patronizing coolness of a liberal customer, required it to be carefully rolled up and tied in a half sheet of paper—lively Orchis, the woman being gone, discontinued his gay switchings and said: 'This is poor business for you, friend China Aster; your capital is too small. You must drop this vile tallow and hold up pure spermaceti to the world. I tell you what it is, you shall have one thousand dollars to extend with. In fact, you must make money, China Aster. I don't like to see your little boy paddling about without shoes, as he does.'

" 'Heaven bless your goodness, friend Orchis,' replied the can-dle-maker, 'but don't take it illy if I call to mind the word of my uncle, the blacksmith, who, when a loan was offered him, declined it, saying: "To ply my own hammer, light though it be, I think best, rather than piece it out heavier by welding to it a bit off a neighbor's hammer, though that may have some weight to spare;

otherwise, were the borrowed bit suddenly wanted again, it might not split off at the welding, but too much to one side or the other." '

" 'Nonsense, friend China Aster, don't be so honest; your boy is barefoot. Besides, a rich man lose by a poor man? Or a friend be the worse by a friend? China Aster, I am afraid that, in leaning over into your vats here, this morning, you have spilled out your wisdom. Hush! I won't hear any more. Where's your desk? Oh, here.' With that, Orchis dashed off a check on his bank, and off-handedly presenting it, said: 'There, friend China Aster, is your one thousand dollars; when you make it ten thousand, as you soon enough will (for experience, the only true knowledge, teaches me that, for every one, good luck is in store), then, China Aster, why, then you can return me the money or not, just as you please. But, in any event, give yourself no concern, for I shall never demand payment.'[1]

"Now, as kind heaven will so have it that to a hungry man bread is a great temptation, and, therefore, he is not too harshly to be blamed, if, when freely offered, he take it, even though it be uncertain whether he shall ever be able to reciprocate; so, to a poor man, proffered money is equally enticing, and the worst that can be said of him, if he accept it, is just what can be said in the other case of the hungry man. In short, the poor candle-maker's scrupulous morality succumbed to his unscrupulous necessity, as is now and then apt to be the case. He took the check, and was about carefully putting it away for the present, when Orchis, switching about again with his gold-headed cane, said: 'By-the-way, China Aster, it don't mean anything, but suppose you make a little memorandum of this; won't do any harm, you know.' So China Aster gave Orchis his note for one thousand dollars on demand. Orchis took it, and looked at it a moment, 'Pooh, I told you, friend China Aster, I wasn't going ever to make any *demand*.' Then tearing up the note, and switching away again at the candle-boxes, said, carelessly; 'Put it at four years.' So China Aster gave Orchis his note for one thousand dollars at four years. 'You see I'll never trouble you about this,' said Orchis, slipping it in his pocket-book, 'give yourself no further thought, friend China Aster, than how best to invest your money. And don't forget my hint about spermaceti. Go into that, and I'll buy all my light of you,' with which encouraging words, he, with wonted, rattling kindness, took leave.

"China Aster remained standing just where Orchis had left him; when, suddenly, two elderly friends, having nothing better to do,

---

1. In the Franklinesque context of this story, one may hear an echo of the description in *The Autobiography* of young Franklin's "daily apprehensions of being called upon by Vernon" and of his listening to the blandishments of Governor Keith.

dropped in for a chat. The chat over, China Aster, in greasy cap and apron, ran after Orchis, and said: 'Friend Orchis, heaven will reward you for your good intentions, but here is your check, and now give my note.'

" 'Your honesty is a bore, China Aster,' said Orchis, not without displeasure. 'I won't take the check from you.'

" 'Then you must take it from the pavement, Orchis,' said China Aster; and, picking up a stone, he placed the check under it on the walk.

" 'China Aster,' said Orchis, inquisitively eying him, 'after my leaving the candlery just now, what asses dropped in there to advise with you, that now you hurry after me, and act so like a fool? Shouldn't wonder if it was those two old asses that the boys nickname Old Plain Talk and Old Prudence.'

" 'Yes, it was those two, Orchis, but don't call them names.'

" 'A brace of spavined old croakers. Old Plain Talk had a shrew for a wife, and that's made him shrewish; and Old Prudence, when a boy, broke down in an apple-stall, and that discouraged him for life. No better sport for a knowing spark like me than to hear Old Plain Talk wheeze out his sour old saws, while Old Prudence stands by, leaning on his staff, wagging his frosty old pow, and chiming in at every clause.'

" 'How can you speak so, friend Orchis, of those who were my father's friends?'

"Save me from my friends, if those old croakers were Old Honesty's friends. I call your father so, for every one used to. Why did they let him go in his old age on the town? Why, China Aster, I've often heard from my mother, the chronicler, that those two old fellows, with Old Conscience—as the boys called the crabbed old quaker, that's dead now—they three used to go to the poorhouse when your father was there, and get round his bed, and talk to him for all the world as Eliphaz, Bildad, and Zophar did to poor old pauper Job.[2] Yes, Job's comforters were Old Plain Talk, and Old Prudence, and Old Conscience, to your poor old father. Friends? I should like to know who you call foes? With their everlasting croaking and reproaching they tormented poor Old Honesty, your father, to death.'

"At these words, recalling the sad end of his worthy parent, China Aster could not restrain some tears. Upon which Orchis said: 'Why, China Aster, you are the dolefulest creature. Why don't you, China Aster, take a bright view of life? You will never get on in your business or anything else, if you don't take the bright view of life. It's the ruination of a man to take the dismal one.' Then, gayly poking at him with his gold-headed cane, 'Why

2. Job 2:11–25:6.

don't you then? Why don't you be bright and hopeful, like me? Why don't you have confidence, China Aster?'

"'I'm sure I don't know, friend Orchis,' soberly replied China Aster, 'but may be my not having drawn a lottery-prize, like you, may make some difference.'

"'Nonsense! before I knew anything about the prize I was gay as a lark, just as gay as I am now. In fact, it has always been a principle with me to hold to the bright view.'

"Upon this, China Aster looked a little hard at Orchis, because the truth was, that until the lucky prize came to him, Orchis had gone under the nickname of Doleful Dumps, he having been beforetimes of a hypochondriac turn, so much so as to save up and put by a few dollars of his scanty earnings against that rainy day he used to groan so much about.

"'I tell you what it is, now, friend China Aster,' said Orchis, pointing down to the check under the stone, and then slapping his pocket, 'the check shall lie there if you say so, but your note shan't keep it company. In fact, China Aster, I am too sincerely your friend to take advantage of a passing fit of the blues in you. You *shall* reap the benefit of my friendship.' With which, buttoning up his coat in a jiffy, away he ran, leaving the check behind.

"At first, China Aster was going to tear it up, but thinking that this ought not to be done except in the presence of the drawer of the check, he mused a while, and picking it up, trudged back to the candlery, fully resolved to call upon Orchis soon as his day's work was over, and destroy the check before his eyes. But it so happened that when China Aster called, Orchis was out, and, having waited for him a weary time in vain, China Aster went home, still with the check, but still resolved not to keep it another day. Bright and early next morning he would a second time go after Orchis, and would, no doubt, make a sure thing of it, by finding him in his bed; for since the lottery-prize came to him, Orchis, besides becoming more cheery, had also grown a little lazy. But as destiny would have it, that same night China Aster had a dream, in which a being in the guise of a smiling angel, and holding a kind of cornucopia in her hand, hovered over him, pouring down showers of small gold dollars, thick as kernels of corn. 'I am Bright Future, friend China Aster,' said the angel, 'and if you do what friend Orchis would have you do, just see what will come of it.' With which Bright Future, with another swing of her cornucopia, poured such another shower of small gold dollars upon him, that it seemed to bank him up all round, and he waded about in it like a maltster in malt.

"Now, dreams are wonderful things, as everybody knows—so wonderful, indeed, that some people stop not short of ascribing them directly to heaven; and China Aster, who was of a proper turn of mind in everything, thought that in consideration of the dream, it would be but well to wait a little, ere seeking Orchis again. During the day, China Aster's mind dwelling continually upon the dream, he was so full of it, that when Old Plain Talk dropped in to see him, just before dinner-time, as he often did, out of the interest he took in Old Honesty's son, China Aster told all about his vision, adding that he could not think that so radiant an angel could deceive; and, indeed, talked at such a rate that one would have thought he believed the angel some beautiful human philanthropist. Something in this sort Old Plain Talk understood him, and, accordingly, in his plain way, said: 'China Aster, you tell me that an angel appeared to you in a dream. Now, what does that amount to but this, that you dreamed an angel appeared to you? Go right away, China Aster, and return the check, as I advised you before. If friend Prudence were here, he would say just the same thing.' With which words Old Plain Talk went off to find friend Prudence, but not succeeding, was returning to the candlery himself, when, at distance mistaking him for a dun who had long annoyed him, China Aster in a panic barred all his doors, and ran to the back part of the candlery, where no knock could be heard.

"By this sad mistake, being left with no friend to argue the other side of the question, China Aster was so worked upon at last, by musing over his dream, that nothing would do but he must get the check cashed, and lay out the money the very same day in buying a good lot of spermaceti to make into candles, by which operation he counted upon turning a better penny than he ever had before in his life; in fact, this he believed would prove the foundation of that famous fortune which the angel had promised him.

"Now, in using the money, China Aster was resolved punctually to pay the interest every six months till the principal should be returned, howbeit not a word about such a thing had been breathed by Orchis; though, indeed, according to custom, as well as law, in such matters, interest would legitimately accrue on the loan, nothing to the contrary having been put in the bond. Whether Orchis at the time had this in mind or not, there is no sure telling; but, to all appearance, he never so much as cared to think about the matter, one way or other.

"Though the spermaceti venture rather disappointed China Aster's sanguine expectations, yet he made out to pay the first six months' interest, and though his next venture turned out still less prosperously, yet by pinching his family in the matter of fresh meat, and, what pained him still more, his boys' schooling, he contrived to pay the second six months' interest, sincerely grieved that integrity, as well as its opposite, though not in an equal degree, costs something, sometimes.

"Meanwhile, Orchis had gone on a trip to Europe by advice of a physician; it so happening that, since the lottery-prize came to him, it had been discovered to Orchis that his health was not very firm, though he had never complained of anything before but a slight ailing of the spleen, scarce worth talking about at the time. So Orchis, being abroad, could not help China Aster's paying his interest as he did, however much he might have been opposed to it; for China Aster paid it to Orchis's agent, who was of too business-like a turn to decline interest regularly paid in on a loan.

"But overmuch to trouble the agent on that score was not again to be the fate of China Aster; for, not being of that skeptical spirit which refuses to trust customers, his third venture resulted, through bad debts, in almost a total loss—a bad blow for the candle-maker. Neither did Old Plain Talk and Old Prudence neglect the opportunity to read him an uncheerful enough lesson upon the consequences of his disregarding their advice in the matter of having nothing to do with borrowed money. 'It's all just as I predicted,' said Old Plain Talk, blowing his old nose with his old bandana. 'Yea, indeed is it,' chimed in Old Prudence, rapping his staff on the floor, and then leaning upon it, looking with solemn forebodings upon China Aster. Low-spirited enough felt the poor candle-maker; till all at once who should come with a bright face to him but his bright friend, the angel, in another dream. Again the cornucopia poured out its treasure, and promised still more. Revived by the vision, he resolved not to be down-hearted, but up and at it once more—contrary to the advice of old Plain Talk, backed as usual by his crony, which was to the effect, that, under present circumstances, the best thing China Aster could do, would be to wind up his business, settle, if he could, all his liabilities, and then go to work as a journeyman, by which he could earn good wages, and give up, from that time henceforth, all thoughts of rising above being a paid subordinate to men more able than himself, for China Aster's career thus far plainly proved him the legitimate son of Old Honesty, who, as every one knew, had never shown much business-talent, so little, in fact, that many said of him that he had no business to be in business. And just this plain saying Plain Talk now plainly applied to China Aster, and Old Prudence never disagreed with him. But the angel in the dream did, and, maugre Plain Talk, put quite other notions into the candle-maker.

"He considered what he should do towards reëstablishing himself. Doubtless, had Orchis been in the country, he would have aided him in this strait. As it was, he applied to others; and as in the world, much as some may hint to the contrary, an honest man in misfortune still can find friends to stay by him and help him, even so it proved with China Aster, who at last succeeded in borrowing from a rich old farmer the sum of six hundred dollars, at the usual interest of money-lenders, upon the security of a secret bond signed by China Aster's wife and himself, to the effect that all such right and title to any property that should be left her by a well-to-do childless uncle, an invalid tanner, such property should, in the event of China Aster's failing to return the borrowed sum on the given day, be the lawful possession of the money-lender. True, it was just as much as China Aster could possibly do to induce his wife, a careful woman, to sign this bond; because she had always regarded her promised share in her uncle's estate as an anchor well to windward of the hard times in which China Aster had always been more or less involved, and from which, in her bosom, she never had seen much chance of his freeing himself. Some notion may be had of China Aster's standing in the heart and head of his wife, by a short sentence commonly used in reply to such persons as happened to sound her on the point. 'China Aster,' she would say, 'is a good husband, but a bad business man!' Indeed, she was a connection on the maternal side of Old Plain Talk's. But had not China Aster taken good care not to let Old Plain Talk and Old Prudence hear of his dealings with the old farmer, ten to one they would, in some way, have interfered with his success in that quarter.

"It has been hinted that the honesty of China Aster was what mainly induced the money-lender to befriend him in his misfortune, and this must be apparent; for, had China Aster been a different man, the money-lender might have dreaded lest, in the event of his failing to meet his note, he might some way prove slippery—more especially as, in the hour of distress, worked upon by remorse for so jeopardizing his wife's money, his heart might prove a traitor to his bond, not to hint that it was more than doubtful how such a secret security and claim, as in the last resort would be the old farmer's, would stand in a court of law. But though one inference from all this may be, that had China Aster been something else than what he was, he would not have been trusted, and, therefore, he would have been effectually shut out from running his own and wife's head into the usurer's noose; yet those who, when everything at last came out, maintained that, in this view and to this extent, the honesty of the candle-maker was no advantage to him, in so saying, such persons said what every good heart must deplore, and no prudent tongue will admit.

"It may be mentioned, that the old farmer made China Aster take part of his loan in three old dried-up cows and one lame horse, not improved by the glanders. These were thrown in at a pretty high figure, the old money-lender having a singular prejudice in regard to the high value of any sort of stock raised on his farm. With a great deal of difficulty, and at more loss, China Aster disposed of his cattle at public auction, no private purchaser being found who could be prevailed upon to invest. And now, raking and scraping in every way, and working early and late, China Aster at last started afresh, nor without again largely and confidently extending himself. However, he did not try his hand at the spermaceti again, but, admonished by experience, returned to tallow. But, having bought a good lot of it, by the time he got it into candles, tallow fell so low, and candles with it, that his candles per pound barely sold for what he had paid for the tallow. Meantime, a year's unpaid interest had accrued on Orchis' loan, but China Aster gave himself not so much concern about that as about the interest now due to the old farmer. But he was glad that the principal there had yet some time to run. However, the skinny old fellow gave him some trouble by coming after him every day or two on a scraggy old white horse, furnished with a musty old saddle, and goaded into his shambling old paces with a withered old raw hide. All the neighbors said that surely Death himself on the pale horse[3] was after poor China Aster now. And something so it proved; for, ere long, China Aster found himself involved in troubles mortal enough.

"At this juncture Orchis was heard of. Orchis, it seemed, had returned from his travels, and clandestinely married, and, in a kind of queer way, was living in Pennsylvania among his wife's relations, who, among other things, had induced him to join a church, or rather semi-religious school, of Come-Outers; and what was still more, Orchis, without coming to the spot himself, had sent word to his agent to dispose of some of his property in Marietta, and remit him the proceeds. Within a year after, China Aster received a letter from Orchis, commending him for his punctuality in paying the first year's interest, and regretting the necessity that he (Orchis) was now under of using all his dividends; so he relied upon China Aster's paying the next six months' interest, and of course with the back interest. Not more surprised than alarmed, China Aster thought of taking steamboat to go and see Orchis, but he was saved that expense by the unexpected arrival in Marietta of Orchis in person, suddenly called there by that strange kind of capriciousness lately characterizing him. No sooner did China Aster hear of his old friend's arrival than he hurried to call upon him. He found him curiously rusty in dress, sallow in cheek, and decidedly less gay and cordial in manner, which the more surprised China Aster, because, in former days, he had more than once heard

3. Revelation 6:8: "And I looked, and behold a pale horse: and his name that sat on him was Death, and Hell followed with him."

Orchis, in his light rattling way, declare that all he (Orchis) wanted to make him a perfectly happy, hilarious, and benignant man, was a voyage to Europe and a wife, with a free development of his inmost nature.

"Upon China Aster's stating his case, his rusted friend was silent for a time; then, in an odd way, said that he would not crowd China Aster, but still his (Orchis') necessities were urgent. Could not China Aster mortgage the candlery? He was honest, and must have moneyed friends; and could he not press his sales of candles? Could not the market be forced a little in that particular? The profits on candles must be very great. Seeing, now, that Orchis had the notion that the candle-making business was a very profitable one, and knowing sorely enough what an error was here, China Aster tried to undeceive him. But he could not drive the truth into Orchis—Orchis being very obtuse here, and, at the same time, strange to say, very melancholy. Finally, Orchis glanced off from so unpleasing a subject into the most unexpected reflections, taken from a religious point of view, upon the unstableness and deceitfulness of the human heart. But having, as he thought, experienced something of that sort of thing, China Aster did not take exception to his friend's observations, but still refrained from so doing, almost as much for the sake of sympathetic sociality as anything else. Presently, Orchis, without much ceremony, rose, and saying he must write a letter to his wife, bade his friend good-bye, but without warmly shaking him by the hand as of old.

"In much concern at the change, China Aster made earnest inquiries in suitable quarters, as to what things, as yet unheard of, had befallen Orchis, to bring about such a revolution; and learned at last that, besides traveling, and getting married, and joining the sect of Come-Outers, Orchis had somehow got a bad dyspepsia, and lost considerable property through a breach of trust on the part of a factor in New York. Telling these things to Old Plain Talk, that man of some knowledge of the world shook his old head, and told China Aster that, though he hoped it might prove otherwise, yet it seemed to him that all he had communicated about Orchis worked together for bad omens as to his future forbearance— especially, he added with a grim sort of smile, in view of his joining the sect of Come-Outers; for, if some men knew what was their inmost natures, instead of coming out with it, they would try their best to keep it in, which, indeed, was the way with the prudent sort. In all which sour notions Old Prudence, as usual, chimed in.

"When interest-day came again, China Aster, by the utmost exertions, could only pay Orchis' agent a small part of what was due, and a part of that was made up by his children's gift money (bright tenpenny pieces and new quarters, kept in their little money-boxes), and pawning his best clothes, with those of his wife and children, so that all were subjected to the hardship of staying away from church. And the old usurer, too, now beginning to be obstreperous, China Aster paid him his interest and some other pressing debts with money got by, at last, mortgaging the candlery.

"When next interest-day came round for Orchis, not a penny could be raised. With much grief of heart, China Aster so informed Orchis' agent. Meantime, the note to the old usurer fell due, and nothing from China Aster was ready to meet it; yet, as heaven sends its rain on the just and unjust alike, by a coincidence not unfavorable to the old farmer, the well-to-do uncle, the tanner, having died, the usurer entered upon possession of such part of his property left by will to the wife of China Aster. When still the next interest-day for Orchis came round, it found China Aster worse off than ever; for, besides his other troubles, he was now weak with sickness. Feebly dragging himself to Orchis' agent, he met him in the street, told him just how it was; upon which the agent, with a grave enough face, said that he had instructions from his employer not to crowd him about the interest at present, but to say to him that about the time the note would mature, Orchis would have heavy liabilities to meet, and therefore the note must at that time be certainly paid, and, of course, the back interest with it; and not only so, but, as Orchis had had to allow the interest for good part of the time, he hoped that, for the back interest, China Aster would, in reciprocation, have no objections to allowing interest on the interest annually. To be sure, this was not the law; but, between friends who accommodate each other, it was the custom.

"Just then, Old Plain Talk with Old Prudence turned the corner, coming plump upon China Aster as the agent left him; and whether it was a sun-stroke, or whether they accidentally ran against him, or whether it was his being so weak, or whether it was everything together, or how it was exactly, there is no telling, but poor China Aster fell to the earth, and, striking his head sharply, was picked up senseless. It was a day in July; such a light and heat as only the midsummer banks of the inland Ohio know. China Aster was taken home on a door; lingered a few days with a wandering mind, and kept wandering on, till at last, at dead of night, when nobody was aware, his spirit wandered away into the other world.

"Old Plain Talk and Old Prudence, neither of whom ever omitted attending any funeral, which, indeed, was their chief exercise—these two were among the sincerest mourners who followed the remains of the son of their ancient friend to the grave.

"It is needless to tell of the executions that followed; how that the candlery was sold by the mortgagee; how Orchis never got a penny for his loan; and how, in the case of the poor widow, chastisement was tempered with mercy; for, though she was left penniless, she was not left childless. Yet, unmindful of the alleviation, a spirit of complaint, at what she impatiently called the bitterness of her lot and the hardness of the world, so preyed upon her, as ere long to hurry her from the obscurity of indigence to the deeper shades of the tomb.

"But though the straits in which China Aster had left his family had, besides apparently dimming the world's regard, likewise seemed to dim its sense of the probity of its deceased head, and though this, as some thought, did not speak well for the world, yet it happened in this case, as in others, that, though the world may for a time seem insensible to that merit which lies under a cloud, yet, sooner or later, it always renders honor where honor is due; for, upon the death of the widow, the freemen of Marietta, as a tribute of respect for China Aster, and an expression of their conviction of his high moral worth, passed a resolution, that, until they attained maturity, his children should be considered the town's guests. No mere verbal compliment, like those of some public bodies; for, on the same day, the orphans were officially installed in that hospitable edifice where their worthy grandfather, the town's guest before them, had breathed his last breath.

"But sometimes honor may be paid to the memory of an honest man, and still his mound remain without a monument. Not so, however, with the candle-maker. At an early day, Plain Talk had procured a plain stone, and was digesting in his mind what pithy word or two to place upon it, when there was discovered, in China Aster's otherwise empty wallet, an epitaph, written, probably, in one of those disconsolate hours, attended with more or less mental aberration, perhaps, so frequent with him for some months prior to his end. A memorandum on the back expressed the wish that it might be placed over his grave. Though with the sentiment of the epitaph Plain Talk did not disagree, he himself being at times of a hypochondriac turn—at least, so many said—yet the language struck him as too much drawn out; so, after consultation with Old Prudence, he decided upon making use of the epitaph, yet not without verbal retrenchments. And though, when these were made, the thing still appeared wordy to him, nevertheless, thinking that, since a dead man was to be spoken about, it was but just to let him speak for himself, especially when he spoke sincerely, and when, by so doing, the more salutary lesson would be given, he had the retrenched inscription chiseled as follows upon the stone:

'HERE LIE

THE REMAINS OF

CHINA ASTER THE CANDLE-MAKER,

WHOSE CAREER

WAS AN EXAMPLE OF THE TRUTH OF SCRIPTURE, AS FOUND

IN THE

SOBER PHILOSOPHY

OF

SOLOMON THE WISE;

FOR HE WAS RUINED BY ALLOWING HIMSELF TO BE PERSUADED,

AGAINST HIS BETTER SENSE,

INTO THE FREE INDULGENCE OF CONFIDENCE,

AND

AN ARDENTLY BRIGHT VIEW OF LIFE,

TO THE EXCLUSION

OF

THAT COUNSEL WHICH COMES BY HEEDING

THE

OPPOSITE VIEW.'

"This inscription raised some talk in the town, and was rather severely criticised by the capitalist—one of a very cheerful turn—who had secured his loan to China Aster by the mortgage; and though it also proved obnoxious to the man who, in town-meeting, had first moved for the compliment to China Aster's memory, and, indeed, was deemed by him a sort of slur upon the candle-maker, to that degree that he refused to believe that the candle-maker himself had composed it, charging Old Plain Talk with the authorship, alleging that the internal evidence showed that none but that veteran old croaker could have penned such a jeremiade—yet, for all this, the stone stood. In everything, of course, Old Plain Talk was seconded by Old Prudence; who, one day going to the grave-yard, in great-coat and over-shoes—for, though it was a sunshiny morning, he thought that, owing to heavy dews, dampness might lurk in the ground—long stood before the stone, sharply leaning over on his staff, spectacles on nose, spelling out the epitaph word by word; and, afterwards meeting Old Plain Talk in the street, gave a great rap with his stick, and said: 'Friend Plain Talk, that epitaph will do very well. Nevertheless, one short sentence is wanting.' Upon which, Plain Talk said it was too late, the chiseled words being so arranged, after the usual manner of such inscriptions, that nothing could be interlined. 'Then,' said Old Prudence, 'I will put it in the shape of a postscript.' Accordingly, with the approbation of Old

Plain Talk, he had the following words chiseled at the left-hand corner of the stone, and pretty low down:

'The root of all was a friendly loan.' "

Chapter 41

ENDING WITH A RUPTURE OF THE HYPOTHESIS

"With what heart," cried Frank, still in character, "have you told me this story? A story I can no way approve; for its moral, if accepted, would drain me of all reliance upon my last stay, and, therefore, of my last courage in life. For, what was that bright view of China Aster but a cheerful trust that, if he but kept up a brave heart, worked hard, and ever hoped for the best, all at last would go well? If your purpose, Charlie, in telling me this story, was to pain me, and keenly, you have succeeded; but, if it was to destroy my last confidence, I praise God you have not."

"Confidence?" cried Charlie, who, on his side, seemed with his whole heart to enter into the spirit of the thing, "what has confidence to do with the matter? That moral of the story, which I am for commending to you, is this: the folly, on both sides, of a friend's helping a friend. For was not that loan of Orchis to China Aster the first step towards their estrangement? And did it not bring about what in effect was the enmity of Orchis? I tell you, Frank, true friendship, like other precious things, is not rashly to be meddled with. And what more meddlesome between friends than a loan? A regular marplot. For how can you help that the helper must turn out a creditor? A creditor and friend, can they ever be one? no, not in the most lenient case; since, out of lenity to forego one's claim, is less to be a friendly creditor than to cease to be a creditor at all. But it will not do to rely upon this lenity, no, not in the best man; for the best man, as the worst, is subject to all mortal contingencies. He may travel, he may marry, he may join the Come-Outers, or some equally untoward school or sect, not to speak of other things that more or less tend to new-cast the character. And were there nothing else, who shall answer for his digestion, upon which so much depends?"

"But Charlie, dear Charlie—"

"Nay, wait.—You have hearkened to my story in vain, if you do not see that, however indulgent and right-minded I may seem to you now, that is no guarantee for the future. And into the power of that uncertain personality which, through the mutability of my humanity, I may hereafter become, should not common sense dissuade you, my dear Frank, from putting yourself? Consider. Would you, in your present need, be willing to accept a loan from a friend, securing him by a mortgage on your homestead, and do so, knowing that you had no reason to feel satisfied that the mortgage might not eventually be transferred into the hands of a foe? Yet the difference between this man and that man is not so great as the difference between what the same man be to-day and what he may be in days to come. For there is no bent of heart or turn of thought which any man holds by virtue of an unalterable nature or will. Even those feelings and opinions deemed most identical with eternal right and truth, it is not impossible but that, as personal persuasions, they may in reality be but the result of some chance tip of Fate's elbow in throwing her dice. For, not to go into the first seeds of things, and passing by the accident of parentage predisposing to this or that habit of mind, descend below these, and tell me, if you change this man's experiences or that man's books, will wisdom go surety for his unchanged convictions? As particular food begets particular dreams, so particular experiences or books particular feelings or beliefs. I will hear nothing of that fine babble about development and its laws; there is no development in opinion and feeling but the developments of time and tide. You may deem all this talk idle, Frank; but conscience bids me show you how fundamental the reasons for treating you as I do."

"But Charlie, dear Charlie, what new notions are these? I thought that man was no poor drifting weed of the universe, as you phrased it; that, if so minded, he could have a will, a way, a thought, and a heart of his own. But now you have turned everything upside down again, with an inconsistency that amazes and shocks me."

"Inconsistency? Bah!"

"There speaks the ventriloquist again," sighed Frank, in bitterness.

Illy pleased, it may be, by this repetition of an allusion little flattering to his originality, however much so to his docility, the disciple sought to carry it off by exclaiming: "Yes, I turn over day and night, with indefatigable pains, the sublime pages of my master, and unfortunately for you, my dear friend, I find nothing *there* that leads me to think otherwise than I do. But enough: in this matter the experience of China Aster teaches a moral more to the point than anything Mark Winsome can offer, or I either."

"I cannot think so, Charlie; for neither am I China Aster, nor do I stand in his position. The loan to China Aster was to extend his business with; the loan I seek is to relieve my necessities."

"Your dress, my dear Frank, is respectable; your cheek is not gaunt. Why talk of necessities when nakedness and starvation beget the only real necessities?"

"But I need relief, Charlie; and so sorely, that I now conjure you to forget that I was ever your friend, while I apply to you only as a fellow-being, whom, surely, you will not turn away."

"That I will not. Take off your hat, bow over to the ground, and supplicate an alms of me in the way of London streets, and you shall not be a sturdy beggar in vain. But no man drops pennies into the hat of a friend, let me tell you. If you turn beggar, then, for the honor of noble friendship, I turn stranger."

"Enough," cried the other, rising, and with a toss of his shoulders seeming disdainfully to throw off the character he had assumed. "Enough. I have had my fill of the philosophy of Mark Winsome as put into action. And moonshiny as it in theory may be, yet a very practical philosophy it turns out in effect, as he himself engaged I should find. But, miserable for my race should I be, if I thought he spoke truth when he claimed, for proof of the soundness of his sytem, that the study of it tended to much the same formation of character with the experiences of the world.—Apt disciple! Why wrinkle the brow, and waste the oil both of life and the lamp, only to turn out a head kept cool by the under ice of the heart? What your illustrious magian has taught you, any poor, old, broken-down, heart-shrunken dandy might have lisped. Pray, leave me, and with you take the last dregs of your inhuman philosophy. And here, take this shilling, and at the first wood-landing buy yourself a few chips to warm the frozen natures of you and your philosopher by."

With these words and a grand scorn the cosmopolitan turned on his heel, leaving his companion at a loss to determine where exactly the fictitious character had been dropped, and the real one, if any, resumed. If any, because, with pointed meaning, there occurred to him, as he gazed after the cosmopolitan, these familiar lines:

> "All the world's a stage,
> And all the men and women merely players,
> Who have their exits and their entrances,
> And one man in his time plays many parts."[1]

Chapter 42

UPON THE HEEL OF THE LAST SCENE THE COSMOPOLITAN
ENTERS THE BARBER'S SHOP, A BENEDICTION ON HIS LIPS

"Bless you, barber!"

Now, owing to the lateness of the hour, the barber had been all alone until within the ten minutes last passed; when, finding him-

1. See *As You Like It*, II, vii, 139–142.

self rather dullish company to himself, he thought he would have a good time with Souter John and Tam O'Shanter, otherwise called Somnus and Morpheus, two very good fellows, though one was not very bright, and the other an arrant rattle-brain, who, though much listened to by some, no wise man would believe under oath.

In short, with back presented to the glare of his lamps, and so to the door, the honest barber was taking what are called cat-naps, and dreaming in his chair; so that, upon suddenly hearing the benediction above, pronounced in tones not unangelic, starting up, half awake, he stared before him, but saw nothing, for the stranger stood behind. What with cat-naps, dreams, and bewilderments, therefore, the voice seemed a sort of spiritual manifestation to him; so that, for the moment, he stood all agape, eyes fixed, and one arm in the air.

"Why, barber, are you reaching up to catch birds there with salt?"

"Ah!" turning round disenchanted, "it is only a man, then."

"*Only* a man? As if to be but man were nothing. But don't be too sure what I am. You call me *man*, just as the townsfolk called the angels who, in man's form, came to Lot's house; just as the Jew rustics called the devils who, in man's form, haunted the tombs.[1] You can conclude nothing absolute from the human form, barber."

"But I can conclude something from that sort of talk, with that sort of dress," shrewdly thought the barber, eying him with regained self-possession, and not without some latent touch of apprehension at being alone with him. What was passing in his mind seemed divined by the other, who now, more rationally and gravely, and as if he expected it should be attended to, said: "Whatever else you may conclude upon, it is my desire that you conclude to give me a good shave," at the same time loosening his neckcloth. "Are you competent to a good shave, barber?"

"No broker more so, sir," answered the barber, whom the business-like proposition instinctively made confine to business-ends his views of the visitor.

"Broker? What has a broker to do with lather? A broker I have always understood to be a worthy dealer in certain papers and metals."

"He, he!" taking him now for some dry sort of joker, whose jokes, he being a customer, it might be as well to appreciate, "he, he! You understand well enough, sir. Take this seat, sir," laying his hand on a great stuffed chair, high-backed and high-armed, crimson-covered, and raised on a sort of dais, and which seemed but to lack a canopy and quarterings, to make it in aspect quite a throne, "take this seat, sir."

1. See Genesis 19:5 and Matthew 8:28.

"Thank you," sitting down; "and now, pray, explain that about the broker. But look, look—what's this?" suddenly rising, and pointing, with his long pipe, towards a gilt notification swinging among colored fly-papers from the ceiling, like a tavern sign, "*No Trust?* No trust means distrust; distrust means no confidence. Barber," turning upon him excitedly, "what fell suspiciousness prompts this scandalous confession? My life!" stamping his foot, "if but to tell a dog that you have no confidence in him be matter for affront to the dog, what an insult to take that way the whole haughty race of man by the beard! By my heart, sir! but at least you are valiant; backing the spleen of Thersites with the pluck of Agamemnon."[2]

"Your sort of talk, sir, is not exactly in my line," said the barber, rather ruefully, being now again hopeless of his customer, and not without return of uneasiness; "not in my line, sir," he emphatically repeated.

"But the taking of mankind by the nose is; a habit, barber, which I sadly fear has insensibly bred in you a disrespect for man. For how, indeed, may respectful conceptions of him coexist with the perpetual habit of taking him by the nose? But, tell me, though I, too, clearly see the import of your notification, I do not, as yet, perceive the object. What is it?"

"Now you speak a little in my line, sir," said the barber, not unrelieved at this return to plain talk; "that notification I find very useful, sparing me much work which would not pay. Yes, I lost a good deal, off and on, before putting that up," gratefully glancing towards it.

"But what is its object? Surely, you don't mean to say, in so many words, that you have no confidence? For instance, now," flinging aside his neck-cloth, throwing back his blouse, and reseating himself on the tonsorial throne, at sight of which proceeding the barber mechanically filled a cup with hot water from a copper vessel over a spirit-lamp, "for instance now, suppose I say to you, 'Barber, my dear barber, unhappily I have no small change by me to-night, but shave me, and depend upon your money to-morrow'—suppose I should say that now, you would put trust in me, wouldn't you? You would have confidence?"

"Seeing that it is you, sir," with complaisance replied the barber, now mixing the lather, "seeing that it is *you*, sir, I won't answer that question. No need to."

"Of course, of course—in that view. But, as a supposition—you would have confidence in me, wouldn't you?"

"Why—yes, yes."

2. Probably familiar to Melville from Shakespeare's *Troilus and Cressida*. Like Timon and Apemantus, Thersites is one of the embittered, misanthropic characters who rail out unwelcome truths.

"Then why that sign?"

"Ah, sir, all people ain't like you," was the smooth reply, at the same time, as if smoothly to close the debate, beginning smoothly to apply the lather, which operation, however, was, by a motion, protested against by the subject, but only out of a desire to rejoin, which was done in these words:

"All people ain't like me. Then I must be either better or worse than most people. Worse, you could not mean; no, barber, you could not mean that; hardly that. It remains, then, that you think me better than most people. But that I ain't vain enough to believe; though, from vanity, I confess, I could never yet, by my best wrestlings, entirely free myself; nor, indeed, to be frank, am I at bottom over anxious to—this same vanity, barber, being so harmless, so useful, so comfortable, so pleasingly preposterous a passion."

"Very true, sir; and upon my honor, sir, you talk very well. But the lather is getting a little cold, sir."

"Better cold lather, barber, than a cold heart. Why that cold sign? Ah, I don't wonder you try to shirk the confession. You feel in your soul how ungenerous a hint is there. And yet, barber, now that I look into your eyes—which somehow speak to me of the mother that must have so often looked into them before me—I dare say, though you may not think it, that the spirit of that notification is not one with your nature. For look now, setting business views aside, regarding the thing in an abstract light; in short, supposing a case, barber; supposing, I say, you see a stranger, his face accidentally averted, but his visible part very respectable-looking; what now, barber—I put it to your conscience, to your charity—what would be your impression of that man, in a moral point of view? Being in a signal sense a stranger, would you, for that, signally set him down for a knave?"

"Certainly not, sir; by no means," cried the barber, humanely resentful.

"You would upon the face of him—"

"Hold, sir," said the barber, "nothing about the face; you remember, sir, that is out of sight."

"I forgot that. Well then, you would, upon the *back* of him, conclude him to be, not improbably, some worthy sort of person; in short, an honest man; wouldn't you?"

"Not unlikely I should, sir."

"Well now—don't be so impatient with your brush, barber—suppose that honest man meet you by night in some dark corner of the boat where his face would still remain unseen, asking you to trust him for a shave—how then?"

"Wouldn't trust him, sir."

"But is not an honest man to be trusted?'

"Why—why—yes sir."

"There! don't you see, now?"

"See what?" asked the disconcerted barber, rather vexedly.

"Why, you stand self-contradicted, barber; don't you?"

"No," doggedly.

"Barber," gravely, and after a pause of concern, "the enemies of our race have a saying that insincerity is the most universal and inveterate vice of man—the lasting bar to real amelioration, whether of individuals or of the world. Don't you now, barber, by your stubbornness on this occasion, give color to such a calumny?"

"Hity-tity!" cried the barber, losing patience, and with it respect; "stubbornness?" Then clattering round the brush in the cup, "Will you be shaved, or won't you?"

"Barber, I will be shaved, and with pleasure; but, pray, don't raise your voice that way. Why, now, if you go through life gritting your teeth in that fashion, what a comfortless time you will have."

"I take as much comfort in this world as you or any other man," cried the barber, whom the other's sweetness of temper seemed rather to exasperate than soothe.

"To resent the imputation of anything like unhappiness I have often observed to be peculiar to certain orders of men," said the other pensively, and half to himself, "just as to be indifferent to that imputation, from holding happiness but for a secondary good and inferior grace, I have observed to be equally peculiar to other kinds of men. Pray, barber," innocently looking up, "which think you is the superior creature?"

"All this sort of talk," cried the barber, still unmollified, "is, as I told you once before, not in my line. In a few minutes I shall shut up this shop. Will you be shaved?"

"Shave away, barber. What hinders?" turning up his face like a flower.

The shaving began, and proceeded in silence, till at length it became necessary to prepare to relather a little—affording an opportunity of resuming the subject, which, on one side, was not let slip.

"Barber," with a kind of cautious kindliness, feeling his way, "barber, now have a little patience with me; do; trust me, I wish not to offend. I have been thinking over that supposed case of the man with the averted face, and I cannot rid my mind of the impression that, by your opposite replies to my question at the time, you showed yourself much of a piece with a good many other men—that is, you have confidence, and then again, you have none. Now, what I would ask is, do you think it sensible standing for a sensible man, one foot on confidence and the other on suspicion? Don't you think, barber, that you ought to elect? Don't you think consistency requires that you should either say 'I have confidence in all men,' and take down your notification; or else say, 'I suspect all men,' and keep it up?"

This dispassionate, if not deferential, way of putting the case, did not fail to impress the barber, and proportionately conciliate him. Likewise, from its pointedness, it served to make him thoughtful; for, instead of going to the copper vessel for more water, as he had purposed, he halted half-way towards it, and, after a pause, cup in hand, said: "Sir, I hope you would not do me injustice. I don't say, and can't say, and wouldn't say, that I suspect all men; but I *do* say that strangers are not to be trusted, and so," pointing up to the sign, "no trust."

"But look, now, I beg, barber," rejoined the other deprecatingly, not presuming too much upon the barber's changed temper; "look, now; to say that strangers are not to be trusted, does not that imply something like saying that mankind is not to be trusted; for the mass of mankind, are they not necessarily strangers to each individual man? Come, come, my friend," winningly, "you are no Timon to hold the mass of mankind untrustworthy. Take down your notification; it is misanthropical; much the same sign that Timon traced with charcoal on the forehead of a skull stuck over his cave. Take it down, barber; take it down to-night. Trust men. Just try the experiment of trusting men for this one little trip. Come now, I'm a philanthropist, and will insure you against losing a cent."

The barber shook his head dryly, and answered, "Sir, you must excuse me. I have a family."[3]

Chapter 43

VERY CHARMING

"So you are a philanthropist, sir," added the barber with an illuminated look; "that accounts, then, for all. Very odd sort of man the philanthropist. You are the second one, sir, I have seen. Very odd sort of man, indeed, the philanthropist. Ah, sir," again meditatively stirring in the shaving-cup, "I sadly fear, lest you philanthropists know better what goodness is, than what men are." Then,

3. The barber, William Cream, a nominal Christian, explicitly rejects Jesus's words to the disciples after the rich young man has gone away: "And every one that hath forsaken houses, or brethren, or sisters, or father, or mother, or wife, or children, or lands, for my name's sake, shall receive an hundredfold, and shall inherit everlasting life" (Matthew 19:29; also told in Mark 10:29–30).

eying him as if he were some strange creature behind cage-bars, "So you are a philanthropist, sir."

"I am Philanthropos, and love mankind. And, what is more than you do, barber, I trust them."

Here the barber, casually recalled to his business, would have replenished his shaving-cup, but finding now that on his last visit to the water-vessel he had not replaced it over the lamp, he did so now; and, while waiting for it to heat again, became almost as sociable as if the heating water were meant for whisky-punch; and almost as pleasantly garrulous as the pleasant barbers in romances.

"Sir," said he, taking a throne beside his customer (for in a row there were three thrones on the dais, as for the three kings of Cologne, those patron saints of the barber), "sir, you say you trust men. Well, I suppose I might share some of your trust, were it not for this trade, that I follow, too much letting me in behind the scenes."

"I think I understand," with a saddened look; "and much the same thing I have heard from persons in pursuits different from yours—from the lawyer, from the congressman, from the editor, not to mention others, each, with a strange kind of melancholy vanity, claiming for his vocation the distinction of affording the surest inlets to the conviction that man is no better than he should be. All of which testimony, if reliable, would, by mutual corroboration, justify some disturbance in a good man's mind. But no, no; it is a mistake—all a mistake."

"True, sir, very true," assented the barber.

"Glad to hear that," brightening up.

"Not so fast, sir," said the barber; "I agree with you in thinking that the lawyer, and the congressman, and the editor, are in error, but only in so far as each claims peculiar facilities for the sort of knowledge in question; because, you see, sir, the truth is, that every trade or pursuit which brings one into contact with the facts, sir, such trade or pursuit is equally an avenue to those facts."

"*How* exactly is that?"

"Why, sir, in my opinion—and for the last twenty years I have, at odd times, turned the matter over some in my mind—he who comes to know man, will not remain in ignorance of man. I think I am not rash in saying that; am I, sir?"

"Barber, you talk like an oracle—obscurely, barber, obscurely."

"Well, sir," with some self-complacency, "the barber has always been held an oracle, but as for the obscurity, that I don't admit."

"But pray, now, by your account, what precisely may be this mysterious knowledge gained in your trade? I grant you, indeed, as before hinted, that your trade, imposing on you the necessity of functionally tweaking the noses of mankind, is, in that respect, unfortunate, very much so; nevertheless, a well-regulated imagination should be proof even to such a provocation to improper conceits. But what I want to learn from you, barber, is, how does the mere handling of the outside of men's heads lead you to distrust the inside of their hearts?"

"What, sir, to say nothing more, can one be forever dealing in macassar oil, hair dyes, cosmetics, false moustaches, wigs, and toupees, and still believe that men are wholly what they look to be? What think you, sir, are a thoughtful barber's reflections, when, behind a careful curtain, he shaves the thin, dead stubble off a head, and then dismisses it to the world, radiant in curling auburn? To contrast the shamefaced air behind the curtain, the fearful looking forward to being possibly discovered there by a prying acquaintance, with the cheerful assurance and challenging pride with which the same man steps forth again, a gay deception, into the street, while some honest, shock-headed fellow humbly gives him the wall. Ah, sir, they may talk of the courage of truth, but my trade teaches me that truth sometimes is sheepish. Lies, lies, sir, brave lies are the lions!"

"You twist the moral, barber; you sadly twist it. Look, now; take it this way: A modest man thrust out naked into the street, would he not be abashed? Take him in and clothe him; would not his confidence be restored? And in either case, is any reproach involved? Now, what is true of the whole, holds proportionably true of the part. The bald head is a nakedness which the wig is a coat to. To feel uneasy at the possibility of the exposure of one's nakedness at top, and to feel comforted by the consciousness of having it clothed—these feelings, instead of being dishonorable to a bald man, do, in fact, but attest a proper respect for himself and his fellows. And as for the deception, you may as well call the fine roof of a fine chateau a deception, since, like a fine wig, it also is an artificial cover to the head, and equally, in the common eye, decorates the wearer.—I have confuted you, my dear barber; I have confounded you."

"Pardon," said the barber, "but I do not see that you have. His coat and his roof no man pretends to palm off as a part of himself, but the bald man palms off hair, not his, for his own."

"Not *his*, barber? If he have fairly purchased his hair, the law will protect him in its ownership, even against the claims of the head on which it grew. But it cannot be that you believe what you say, barber; you talk merely for the humor. I could not think so of you as to suppose that you would contentedly deal in the impostures you condemn."

"Ah, sir, I must live."

"And can't you do that without sinning against your conscience, as you believe? Take up some other calling."

"Wouldn't mend the matter much, sir."

"Do you think, then, barber, that, in a certain point, all the trades and callings of men are much on a par? Fatal, indeed," raising his hand, "inexpressibly dreadful, the trade of the barber, if to such conclusions it necessarily leads. Barber," eying him not without emotion, "you appear to me not so much a misbeliever, as a man misled. Now, let me set you on the right track; let me restore you to trust in human nature, and by no other means than the very trade that has brought you to suspect it."

"You mean, sir, you would have me try the experiment of taking down that notification," again pointing to it with his brush; "but, dear me, while I sit chatting here, the water boils over."

With which words, and such a well-pleased, sly, snug, expression, as they say some men have when they think their little stratagem has succeeded, he hurried to the copper vessel, and soon had his cup foaming up with white bubbles, as if it were a mug of new ale.

Meantime, the other would have fain gone on with the discourse; but the cunning barber lathered him with so generous a brush, so piled up the foam on him, that his face looked like the yeasty crest of a billow, and vain to think of talking under it, as for a drowning priest in the sea to exhort his fellow-sinners on a raft. Nothing would do, but he must keep his mouth shut. Doubtless, the interval was not, in a meditative way, unimproved; for, upon the traces of the operation being at last removed, the cosmopolitan rose, and, for added refreshment, washed his face and hands; and having generally readjusted himself, began, at last, addressing the barber in a manner different, singularly so, from his previous one. Hard to say exactly what the manner was, any more than to hint it was a sort of magical; in a benign way, not wholly unlike the manner, fabled or otherwise, of certain creatures in nature, which have the power of persuasive fascination—the power of holding another creature by the button of the eye, as it were, despite the serious disinclination, and, indeed, earnest protest, of the victim. With this manner the conclusion of the matter was not out of keeping; for, in the end, all argument and expostulation proved vain, the barber being irresistibly persuaded to agree to try, for the remainder of the present trip, the experiment of trusting men, as both phrased it. True, to save his credit as a free agent, he was loud in averring that it was only for the novelty of the thing that he so agreed, and he required the other, as before volunteered, to go security to him against any loss that might ensue; but still the fact remained, that he engaged to trust men, a thing he had before said he would not do, at least not unreservedly. Still the more to save his credit, he now insisted upon it, as a last point, that the agreement should be put in black and white, especially the security part. The other made no demur;

pen, ink, and paper were provided, and grave as any notary the
cosmopolitan sat down, but, ere taking the pen, glanced up at the
notification, and said: "First down with that sign, barber—Timon's
sign, there; down with it." This, being in the agreement, was done—though a little reluctantly—with an eye to the future, the sign being carefully put away
in a drawer.

"Now, then, for the writing," said the cosmopolitan, squaring
himself. "Ah," with a sigh, "I shall make a poor lawyer, I fear.
Ain't used, you see, barber, to a business which, ignoring the principle of honor, holds no nail fast till clinched. Strange, barber,"
taking up the blank paper, "that such flimsy stuff as this should
make such strong hawsers; vile hawsers, too. Barber," starting up,
"I won't put it in black and white. It were a reflection upon our
joint honor. I will take your word, and you shall take mine."

"But your memory may be none of the best, sir. Well for you,
on your side, to have it in black and white, just for a memorandum
like, you know."

"That, indeed! Yes, and it would help *your* memory, too,
wouldn't it, barber? Yours, on your side, being a little weak, too, I
dare say. Ah, barber! how ingenious we human beings are; and how
kindly we reciprocate each other's little delicacies, don't we? What
better proof, now, that we are kind, considerate fellows, with
responsive fellow-feelings—eh, barber? But to business. Let me see.
What's your name, barber?"

"William Cream, sir."

Pondering a moment, he began to write; and, after some corrections, leaned back, and read aloud the following:

"AGREEMENT
"Between
"FRANK GOODMAN, Philanthropist, and Citizen of the World,
"and
"WILLIAM CREAM, Barber of the Mississippi steamer, Fidèle.

"The first hereby agrees to make good to the last any loss
that may come from his trusting mankind, in the way of
his vocation, for the residue of the present trip; PROVIDED
that William Cream keep out of sight, for the given
term, his notification of 'No TRUST,' and by no other
mode convey any, the least hint or intimation, tending to
discourage men from soliciting trust from him, in the way
of his vocation, for the time above specified; but, on the
contrary, he do, by all proper and reasonable words, gestures, manners, and looks, evince a perfect confidence in
all men, especially strangers; otherwise, this agreement to
be void.

"Done, in good faith, this 1st day of April, 18—, at a

quarter to twelve o'clock, P.M., in the shop of said William Cream, on board the said boat, Fidèle.'"

"There, barber; will that do?"

"That will do," said the barber, "only now put down your name."

Both signatures being affixed, the question was started by the barber, who should have custody of the instrument; which point, however, he settled for himself, by proposing that both should go together to the captain, and give the document into his hands—the barber hinting that this would be a safe proceeding, because the captain was necessarily a party disinterested, and, what was more, could not, from the nature of the present case, make anything by a breach of trust. All of which was listened to with some surprise and concern.

"Why, barber," said the cosmopolitan, "this don't show the right spirit; for me, I have confidence in the captain purely because he is a man; but he shall have nothing to do with our affair; for if you have no confidence in me, barber, I have in you. There, keep the paper yourself," handing it magnanimously.

"Very good," said the barber, "and now nothing remains but for me to receive the cash."

Though the mention of that word, or any of its singularly numerous equivalents, in serious neighborhood to a requisition upon one's purse, is attended with a more or less noteworthy effect upon the human countenance, producing in many an abrupt fall of it—in others, a writhing and screwing up of the features to a point not undistressing to behold, in some, attended with a blank pallor and fatal consternation—yet no trace of any of these symptoms was visible upon the countenance of the cosmopolitan, notwithstanding nothing could be more sudden and unexpected than the barber's demand.

"You speak of cash, barber; pray in what connection?"

"In a nearer one, sir," answered the barber, less blandly, "than I thought the man with the sweet voice stood, who wanted me to trust him once for a shave, on the score of being a sort of thirteenth cousin."

"Indeed, and what did you say to him?"

"I said, 'Thank you, sir, but I don't see the connection.' "

"How could you so unsweetly answer one with a sweet voice?"

"Because, I recalled what the son of Sirach says in the True Book: 'An enemy speaketh sweetly with his lips;' and so I did what the son of Sirach advises in such cases: 'I believed not his many words.' "[1]

"What, barber, do you say that such cynical sort of things are in

1. Ecclesiasticus 12:16 and 13:11.

the True Book, by which, of course, you mean the Bible?"

"Yes, and plenty more to the same effect. Read the Book of Proverbs."

"That's strange, now, barber; for I never happen to have met with those passages you cite. Before I go to bed this night, I'll inspect the Bible I saw on the cabin-table, to-day. But mind, you mustn't quote the True Book that way to people coming in here; it would be impliedly a violation of the contract. But you don't know how glad I feel that you have for one while signed off all that sort of thing."

"No, sir; not unless you down with the cash."

"Cash again! What do you mean?"

"Why, in this paper here, you engage, sir, to insure me against a certain loss, and—"

"Certain? Is it so *certain* you are going to lose?"

"Why, that way of taking the word may not be amiss, but I didn't mean it so. I meant a *certain* loss; you understand, a CERTAIN loss; that is to say, a certain loss. Now then, sir, what use your mere writing and saying you will insure me, unless beforehand you place in my hands a money-pledge, sufficient to that end?"

"I see; the material pledge."

"Yes, and I will put it low; say fifty dollars."

"Now what sort of beginning is this? You, barber, for a given time engage to trust man, to put confidence in men, and, for your first step, make a demand implying no confidence in the very man you engage with. But fifty dollars is nothing, and I would let you have it cheerfully, only I unfortunately happen to have but little change with me just now."

"But you have money in your trunk, though?"

"To be sure. But you see—in fact, barber, you must be consistent. No, I won't let you have the money now; I won't let you violate the inmost spirit of our contract, that way. So good-night, and I will see you again."

"Stay, sir"—humming and hawing—"you have forgotten something."

"Handkerchief?—gloves? No, forgotten nothing. Good-night."

"Stay, sir—the—the shaving."

"Ah, I *did* forget that. But now that it strikes me, I shan't pay you at present. Look at your agreement; you must trust. Tut! against loss you hold the guarantee. Good-night, my dear barber."

With which words he sauntered off, leaving the barber in a maze, staring after.

But it holding true in fascination as in natural philosophy, that nothing can act where it is not, so the barber was not long now in being restored to his self-possession and senses; the first evidence of which perhaps was, that, drawing forth his notification from the drawer, he put it back where it belonged; while, as for the agreement, that he tore up; which he felt the more free to do from the impression that in all human probability he would never again see the person who had drawn it. Whether that impression proved well-founded or not, does not appear. But in after days, telling the night's adventure to his friends, the worthy barber always spoke of his queer customer as the man-charmer—as certain East Indians are called snake-charmers—and all his friends united in thinking him QUITE AN ORIGINAL.

Chapter 44

IN WHICH THE LAST THREE WORDS OF THE LAST CHAPTER
ARE MADE THE TEXT OF DISCOURSE, WHICH WILL BE SURE OF
RECEIVING MORE OR LESS ATTENTION FROM THOSE READERS
WHO DO NOT SKIP IT

"QUITE AN ORIGINAL:" A phrase, we fancy, rather oftener used by the young, or the unlearned, or the untraveled, than by the old, or the well-read, or the man who has made the grand tour. Certainly, the sense of originality exists at its highest in an infant, and probably at its lowest in him who has completed the circle of the sciences.

As for original characters in fiction, a grateful reader will, on meeting with one, keep the anniversary of that day. True, we sometimes hear of an author who, at one creation, produces some two or three score such characters; it may be possible. But they can hardly be original in the sense that Hamlet is, or Don Quixote, or Milton's Satan. That is to say, they are not, in a thorough sense, original at all. They are novel, or singular, or striking, or captivating, or all four at once.

More likely, they are what are called odd characters; but for that, are no more original, than what is called an odd genius, in his way, is. But, if original, whence came they? Or where did the novelist pick them up?

Where does any novelist pick up any character? For the most part, in town, to be sure. Every great town is a kind of man-show, where the novelist goes for his stock, just as the agriculturist goes to the cattle-show for his. But in the one fair, new species of quadrupeds are hardly more rare, than in the other are new species of characters—that is, original ones. Their rarity may still the more appear from this, that, while characters, merely singular, imply but singular forms, so to speak, original ones, truly so, imply original instincts.

In short, a due conception of what is to be held for this sort of personage in fiction would make him almost as much of a prodigy there, as in real history is a new law-giver, a revolutionizing philosopher, or the founder of a new religion.

In nearly all the original characters, loosely accounted such in works of invention, there is discernible something prevailingly local, or of the age; which circumstance, of itself, would seem to invalidate the claim, judged by the principles here suggested.

Furthermore, if we consider, what is popularly held to entitle characters in fiction being deemed original, is but something personal—confined to itself. The character sheds not its characteristic on its surroundings, whereas, the original character, essentially such, is like a revolving Drummond light,[1] raying away from itself all round it—everything is lit by it, everything starts up to it (mark how it is with Hamlet), so that, in certain minds, there follows upon the adequate conception of such a character, an effect, in its way, akin to that which in Genesis attends upon the beginning of things.

For much the same reason that there is but one planet to one orbit, so can there be but one such original character to one work of invention. Two would conflict to chaos. In this view, to say that there are more than one to a book, is good presumption there is none at all. But for new, singular, striking, odd, eccentric, and all sorts of entertaining and instructive characters, a good fiction may be full of them. To produce such characters, an author, beside other things, must have seen much, and seen through much: to produce but one original character, he must have had much luck.

There would seem but one point in common between this sort of phenomenon in fiction and all other sorts: it cannot be born in the author's imagination—it being as true in literature as in zoology, that all life is from the egg.

In the endeavor to show, if possible, the impropriety of the phrase, *Quite an Original*, as applied by the barber's friends, we have, at unawares, been led into a dissertation bordering upon the prosy, perhaps upon the smoky. If so, the best use the smoke can be turned to, will be, by retiring under cover of it, in good trim as may be, to the story.

1. Another memory of P. T. Barnum in the 1840's. "Powerful Drummond lights were placed at the top of the Museum, which, in the darkest night, threw a flood of light up and down Broadway, from the Battery to Niblo's, that would enable one to read a newspaper in the street. These were the first Drummond lights ever seen in New York, and they made people talk, and so advertised my Museum" (Barnum in *Struggles and Triumphs: or Forty Years' Recollections* [Buffalo: The Courier Company, 1883], p. 61).

Chapter 45

THE COSMOPOLITAN INCREASES IN SERIOUSNESS

In the middle of the gentlemen's cabin burned a solar lamp, swung from the ceiling, and whose shade of ground glass was all round fancifully variegated, in transparency, with the image of a horned altar, from which flames rose, alternate with the figure of a robed man, his head encircled by a halo.[1] The light of this lamp, after dazzlingly striking on marble, snow-white and round—the slab of a centre-table beneath—on all sides went rippling off with ever-diminishing distinctness, till, like circles from a stone dropped in water, the rays died dimly away in the furthest nook of the place.

Here and there, true to their place, but not to their function, swung other lamps, barren planets, which had either gone out from exhaustion, or been extinguished by such occupants of berths as the light annoyed, or who wanted to sleep, not see.

By a perverse man, in a berth not remote, the remaining lamp would have been extinguished as well, had not a steward forbade, saying that the commands of the captain required it to be kept burning till the natural light of day should come to relieve it. This steward, who, like many in his vocation, was apt to be a little free-spoken at times, had been provoked by the man's pertinacity to remind him, not only of the sad consequences which might, upon occasion, ensue from the cabin being left in darkness, but, also, of the circumstance that, in a place full of strangers, to show one's self anxious to produce darkness there, such an anxiety was, to say the least, not becoming. So the lamp—last survivor of many— burned on, inwardly blessed by those in some berths, and inwardly execrated by those in others.

Keeping his lone vigils beneath his lone lamp, which lighted his book on the table, sat a clean, comely, old man, his head snowy as the marble, and a countenance like that which imagination ascribes to good Simeon, when, having at last beheld the Master of Faith, he blessed him and departed in peace.[2] From his hale look of greenness in winter, and his hands ingrained with the tan, less, apparently, of the present summer, than of accumulated ones past, the old man seemed a well-to-do farmer, happily dismissed, after a

1. Miss Foster explains the symbolism: "the light of the Old and New Testaments, to judge from its two transparencies, the horned altar and the robed man with a halo. On Mount Sinai the Lord gave Moses directions for making the altar, with 'the horns of it upon the four corners thereof' (Exodus 27:2)."
2. Luke 2:25–35.

thrifty life of activity, from the fields to the fireside—one of those who, at three-score-and-ten, are fresh-hearted as at fifteen; to whom seclusion gives a boon more blessed than knowledge, and at last sends them to heaven untainted by the world, because ignorant of it; just as a countryman putting up at a London inn, and never stirring out of it as a sight-seer, will leave London at last without once being lost in its fog, or soiled by its mud.

Redolent from the barber's shop, as any bridegroom tripping to the bridal chamber might come, and by his look of cheeriness seeming to dispense a sort of morning through the night, in came the cosmopolitan;[3] but marking the old man, and how he was occupied, he toned himself down, and trod softly, and took a seat on the other side of the table, and said nothing. Still, there was a kind of waiting expression about him.

"Sir," said the old man, after looking up puzzled at him a moment, "sir," said he, "one would think this was a coffee-house, and it was war-time, and I had a newspaper here with great news,[4] and the only copy to be had, you sit there looking at me so eager."

"And so you *have* good news there, sir—the very best of good news."

"Too good to be true," here came from one of the curtained berths.

"Hark!" said the cosmopolitan. "Some one talks in his sleep."

"Yes," said the old man, "and you—*you* seem to be talking in a dream. Why speak you, sir, of news, and all that, when you must see this is a book I have here—the Bible, not a newspaper?"

"I know that; and when you are through with it—but not a moment sooner—I will thank you for it. It belongs to the boat, I believe—a present from a society."

"Oh, take it, take it!"

"Nay, sir, I did not mean to touch you at all. I simply stated the fact in explanation of my waiting here—nothing more. Read on, sir, or you will distress me."

This courtesy was not without effect. Removing his spectacles, and saying he had about finished his chapter, the old man kindly presented the volume, which was received with thanks equally kind. After reading for some minutes, until his expression merged from attentiveness into seriousness, and from that into a kind of pain, the cosmopolitan slowly laid down the book, and turning to the old

3. Probably not an innocent comparison, since Jesus is more than once called the bridegroom (see Matthew 9:15 and the parable of the virgins in Matthew 25). The book begins with the conflict between the words of the New Testament on the slate of the mute (the Devil disguised in Christ-like apparel) and William Cream's two words on the sign "NO TRUST." It appropriately draws to a close with a repetition of that conflict in which the Devil again is associated with Jesus.
4. The old man puns unconsciously on the Anglo-Saxon roots of "Gospel."

man, who thus far had been watching him with benign curiosity, said: "Can you, my aged friend, resolve me a doubt—a disturbing doubt?"

"There are doubts, sir," replied the old man, with a changed countenance, "there are doubts, sir, which, if man have them, it is not man that can solve them."

"True; but look, now, what my doubt is. I am one who thinks well of man. I love man. I have confidence in man. But what was told me not a half-hour since? I was told that I would find it written—'Believe not his many words—an enemy speaketh sweetly with his lips'—and also I was told that I would find a good deal more to the same effect, and all in this book. I could not think it; and, coming here to look for myself, what do I read? Not only just what was quoted, but also, as was engaged, more to the same purpose, such as this: 'With much communication he will tempt thee; he will smile upon thee, and speak thee fair, and say What wantest thou? If thou be for his profit he will use thee; he will make thee bare, and will not be sorry for it. Observe and take good heed. When thou hearest these things, awake in thy sleep.' "⁵

"Who's that describing the confidence-man?" here came from the berth again.

"Awake in his sleep, sure enough, ain't he?" said the cosmopolitan, again looking off in surprise. "Same voice as before, ain't it? Strange sort of dreamy man, that. Which is his berth, pray?"

"Never mind *him*, sir," said the old man anxiously, "but tell me truly, did you, indeed, read from the book just now?"

"I did," with changed air, "and gall and wormwood it is to me, a truster in man; to me, a philanthropist."

"Why," moved, "you don't mean to say, that what you repeated is really down there? Man and boy, I have read the good book this seventy years, and don't remember seeing anything like that. Let me see it," rising earnestly, and going round to him.

"There it is; and there—and there"—turning over the leaves, and pointing to the sentences one by one; "there—all down in the 'Wisdom of Jesus, the Son of Sirach.' "

"Ah!" cried the old man, brightening up, "now I know. Look," turning the leaves forward and back, till all the Old Testament lay flat on one side, and all the New Testament flat on the other, while in his fingers he supported vertically the portion between, "look, sir, all this to the right is certain truth, and all this to the left is certain truth, but all I hold in my hand here is apocrypha."

"Apocrypha?"

5. In Ecclesiasticus 13 these passages occur in verses 11, 6, 4, 5, and 13. The first American edition's error of "bear" for "bare" in "he will make thee bare" probably stems from Melville's bad handwriting rather than a deliberate rewriting of the text. (Foster first noticed the error.)

"Yes; and there's the word in black and white," pointing to it. "And what says the word? It says as much as 'not warranted;' for what do college men say of anything of that sort? They say it is apocryphal. The word itself, I've heard from the pulpit, implies something of uncertain credit. So if your disturbance be raised from aught in this apocrypha," again taking up the pages, "in that case, think no more of it, for it's apocrypha."

"What's that about the Apocalypse?" here, a third time, came from the berth.

"He's seeing visions now, ain't he?" said the cosmopolitan, once more looking in the direction of the interruption. "But, sir," resuming, "I cannot tell you how thankful I am for your reminding me about the apocrypha here. For the moment, its being such escaped me. Fact is, when all is bound up together, it's sometimes confusing. The uncanonical part should be bound distinct. And, now that I think of it, how well did those learned doctors who rejected for us this whole book of Sirach. I never read anything so calculated to destroy man's confidence in man. This son of Sirach even says—I saw it but just now: 'Take heed of thy friends;'[6] not, observe, thy seeming friends, thy hypocitical friends, thy false friends, but thy *friends*, thy real friends—that is to say, not the truest friend in the world is to be implicitly trusted. Can Rochefoucault equal that? I should not wonder if his view of human nature, like Machiavelli's, was taken from this Son of Sirach. And to call it wisdom—the Wisdom of the Son of Sirach! Wisdom, indeed! What an ugly thing wisdom must be! Give me the folly that dimples the cheek, say I, rather than the wisdom that curdles the blood. But no, no; it ain't wisdom; it's apocrypha, as you say, sir. For how can that be trustworthy that teaches distrust?"

"I tell you what it is," here cried the same voice as before, only in less of mockery, "if you two don't know enough to sleep, don't be keeping wiser men awake. And if you want to know what wisdom is, go find it under your blankets."

"Wisdom?" cried another voice with a brogue; "arrah, and is't wisdom the two geese are gabbling about all this while? To bed with ye, ye divils, and don't be after burning your fingers with the likes of wisdom."

"We must talk lower," said the old man; "I fear we have annoyed these good people."

"I should be sorry if wisdom annoyed any one," said the other; "but we will lower our voices, as you say. To resume: taking the thing as I did, can you be surprised at my uneasiness in reading passages so charged with the spirit of distrust?"

"No, sir, I am not surprised," said the old man; then added:

6. Ecclesiasticus 6:13.

"From what you say, I see you are something of my way of think-ing—you think that to distrust the creature, is a kind of distrusting of the Creator. Well, my young friend, what is it? This is rather late for you to be about. What do you want of me?"

These questions were put to a boy in the fragment of an old linen coat, bedraggled and yellow, who, coming in from the deck barefooted on the soft carpet, had been unheard. All pointed and fluttering, the rags of the little fellow's red-flannel shirt, mixed with those of his yellow coat, flamed about him like the painted flames in the robes of a victim in *auto-da-fe*. His face, too, wore such a polish of seasoned grime, that his sloe-eyes sparkled from out it like lustrous sparks in fresh coal. He was a juvenile peddler, or *mar-chand*, as the polite French might have called him, of travelers' conveniences; and, having no allotted sleeping-place, had, in his wanderings about the boat, spied, through glass doors, the two in the cabin; and, late though it was, thought it might never be too much so for turning a penny.

Among other things, he carried a curious affair—a miniature mahogany door, hinged to its frame, and suitably furnished in all respects but one, which will shortly appear. This little door he now meaningly held before the old man, who, after staring at it a while, said: "Go thy ways with thy toys, child."

"Now, may I never get so old and wise as that comes to," laughed the boy through his grime; and, by so doing, disclosing leopard-like teeth, like those of Murillo's wild beggar-boy's.

"The divils are laughing now, are they?" here came the brogue from the berth. "What do the divils find to laugh about in wisdom, begorrah? To bed with ye, ye divils, and no more of ye."

"You see, child, you have disturbed that person," said the old man; "you mustn't laugh any more."

"Ah, now," said the cosmopolitan, "don't, pray, say that; don't let him think that poor Laughter is persecuted for a fool in this world."

"Well," said the old man to the boy, "you must, at any rate, speak very low."

"Yes, that wouldn't be amiss, perhaps," said the cosmopolitan; "but, my fine fellow, you were about saying something to my aged friend here; what was it?"

"Oh," with a lowered voice, coolly opening and shutting his little door, "only this: when I kept a toy-stand at the fair in Cincinnati last month, I sold more than one old man a child's rattle."

"No doubt of it," said the old man. "I myself often buy such things for my little grandchildren."

"But these old men I talk of were old bachelors."

The old man stared at him a moment; then, whispering to the

cosmopolitan: "Strange boy, this; sort of simple, ain't he? Don't know much, hey?"

"Not much," said the boy, "or I wouldn't be so ragged."

"Why, child, what sharp ears you have!" exclaimed the old man.

"If they were duller, I would hear less ill of myself," said the boy.

"You seem pretty wise, my lad," said the cosmopolitan; "why don't you sell your wisdom, and buy a coat?"

"Faith," said the boy, "that's what I did to-day, and this is the coat that the price of my wisdom bought. But won't you trade? See, now, it is not the door I want to sell; I only carry the door round for a specimen, like. Look now, sir," standing the thing up on the table, "supposing this little door is your state-room door; well," opening it, "you go in for the night; you close your door behind you—thus. Now, is all safe?"

"I suppose so, child," said the old man.

"Of course it is, my fine fellow," said the cosmopolitan.

"All safe. Well. Now, about two o'clock in the morning, say, a soft-handed gentleman comes softly and tries the knob here—thus; in creeps my soft-handed gentleman; and hey, presto! how comes on the soft cash?"

"I see, I see, child," said the old man; "your fine gentleman is a fine thief, and there's no lock to your little door to keep him out;" with which words he peered at it more closely than before.

"Well, now," again showing his white teeth, "well, now, some of you old folks are knowing 'uns, sure enough; but now comes the great invention," producing a small steel contrivance, very simple but ingenious, and which, being clapped on the inside of the little door, secured it as with a bolt. "There now," admiringly holding it off at arm's-length, "there now, let that soft-handed gentleman come now a' softly trying this little knob here, and let him keep a' trying till he finds his head as soft as his hand. Buy the traveler's patent lock, sir, only twenty-five cents."

"Dear me," cried the old man, "this beats printing. Yes, child, I will have one, and use it this very night."

With the phlegm of an old banker pouching the change, the boy now turned to the other: "Sell you one, sir?"

"Excuse me, my fine fellow, but I never use such blacksmiths' things."

"Those who give the blacksmith most work seldom do," said the boy, tipping him a wink expressive of a degree of indefinite knowingness, not uninteresting to consider in one of his years. But the wink was not marked by the old man, nor, to all appearances, by him for whom it was intended.

"Now, then," said the boy, again addressing the old man. "With your traveler's lock on your door to-night, you will think yourself all safe, won't you?"

"I think I will, child."

"But how about the window?"

"Dear me, the window, child. I never thought of that. I must see to that."

"Never you mind about the window," said the boy, "nor, to be honor bright, about the traveler's lock either, (though I ain't sorry for selling one), do you just buy one of these little jokers," producing a number of suspender-like objects, which he dangled before the old man; "money-belts, sir; only fifty cents."

"Money-belt? never heard of such a thing."

"A sort of pocket-book," said the boy, "only a safer sort. Very good for travelers."

"Oh, a pocket-book. Queer looking pocket-books though, seems to me. Ain't they rather long and narrow for pocket-books?"

"They go round the waist, sir, inside," said the boy; "door open or locked, wide awake on your feet or fast asleep in your chair, impossible to be robbed with a money-belt."

"I see, I see. It *would* be hard to rob one's money-belt. And I was told to-day the Mississippi is a bad river for pick-pockets. How much are they?"

"Only fifty cents, sir."

"I'll take one. There!"

"Thank-ee. And now there's a present for ye," with which, drawing from his breast a batch of little papers, he threw one before the old man, who, looking at it, read "*Counterfeit Detector.*"

"Very good thing," said the boy, "I give it to all my customers who trade seventy-five cents' worth; best present can be made them. Sell you a money-belt, sir?" turning to the cosmopolitan.

"Excuse me, my fine fellow, but I never use that sort of thing; my money I carry loose."

"Loose bait ain't bad," said the boy, "look a lie and find the truth; don't care about a Counterfeit Detector, do ye? or is the wind East, d'ye think?"

"Child," said the old man in some concern, "you mustn't sit up any longer, it affects your mind; there, go away, go to bed."

"If I had some people's brains to lie on, I would," said the boy, "but planks is hard, you know."

"Go, child—go, go!"

"Yes, child,—yes, yes," said the boy, with which roguish parody, by way of congé, he scraped back his hard foot on the woven flowers of the carpet, much as a mischievous steer in May scrapes back his horny hoof in the pasture; and then with a flourish of his hat—which, like the rest of his tatters, was, thanks to hard times, a belonging beyond his years, though not beyond his experience, being a grown man's cast-off beaver—turned, and with the air of a young Caffre, quitted the place.

"That's a strange boy," said the old man, looking after him. "I wonder who's his mother; and whether she knows what late hours he keeps?"

"The probability is," observed the other, "that his mother does not know. But if you remember, sir, you were saying something, when the boy interrupted you with his door."

"So I was.—Let me see," unmindful of his purchases for the moment, "what, now, was it? What was that I was saying? Do *you* remember?"

"Not perfectly, sir; but, if I am not mistaken, it was something like this; you hoped you did not distrust the creature; for that would imply distrust of the Creator."

"Yes, that was something like it," mechanically and unintelligently letting his eye fall now on his purchases.

"Pray, will you put your money in your belt tonight?"

"It's best, ain't it?" with a slight start. "Never too late to be cautious. 'Beware of pick-pockets' is all over the boat."

"Yes, and it must have been the Son of Sirach, or some other morbid cynic, who put them there. But that's not to the purpose. Since you are minded to it, pray, sir, let me help you about the belt. I think that, between us, we can make a secure thing of it."

"Oh no, no, no!" said the old man, not unperturbed, "no, no, I wouldn't trouble you for the world," then, nervously folding up the belt, "and I won't be so impolite as to do it for myself, before you, either. But, now that I think of it," after a pause, carefully taking a little wad from a remote corner of his vest pocket, "here are two bills they gave me at St. Louis, yesterday. No doubt they are all right; but just to pass time, I'll compare them with the Detector here. Blessed boy to make me such a present. Public benefactor, that little boy!"

Laying the Detector square before him on the table, he then, with something of the air of an officer bringing by the collar a brace of culprits to the bar, placed the two bills opposite the Detector, upon which, the examination began, lasting some time, prosecuted with no small research and vigilance, the forefinger of the right hand proving of lawyer-like efficacy in tracing out and pointing the evidence, whichever way it might go.

After watching him a while, the cosmopolitan said in a formal voice, "Well, what say you, Mr. Foreman; guilty, or not guilty? —Not guilty, ain't it?"

"I don't know, I don't know," returned the old man, perplexed, "there's so many marks of all sorts to go by, it makes it a kind of uncertain. Here, now, is this bill," touching one, "it looks to be a three dollar bill on the Vicksburgh Trust and Insurance Banking Company. Well, the Detector says—"

"But why, in this case, care what it says? Trust and Insurance! What more would you have?"

"No; but the Detector says, among fifty other things, that, if a good bill, it must have, thickened here and there into the substance of the paper, little wavy spots of red; and it says they must have a kind of silky feel, being made by the lint of a red silk handkerchief stirred up in the paper-maker's vat—the paper being made to order for the company."

"Well, and is—"

"Stay. But then it adds, that sign is not always to be relied on; for some good bills get so worn, the red marks get rubbed out. And that's the case with my bill here—see how old it is—or else it's a counterfeit, or else—I don't see right—or else—dear, dear me—I don't know what else to think."

"What a peck of trouble that Detector makes for you now; believe me, the bill is good; don't be so distrustful. Proves what I've always thought, that much of the want of confidence, in these days, is owing to these Counterfeit Detectors you see on every desk and counter. Puts people up to suspecting good bills. Throw it away, I beg, if only because of the trouble it breeds you."

"No; it's troublesome, but I think I'll keep it.—Stay, now, here's another sign. It says that, if the bill is good, it must have in one corner, mixed in with the vignette, the figure of a goose, very small, indeed, all but microscopic; and, for added precaution, like the figure of Napoleon outlined by the tree, not observable, even if magnified, unless the attention is directed to it. Now, pore over it as I will, I can't see this goose."

"Can't see the goose? why, I can; and a famous goose it is. There" (reaching over and pointing to a spot in the vignette).

"I don't see it—dear me—I don't see the goose. Is it a real goose?"

"A perfect goose; beautiful goose."

"Dear, dear, I don't see it."

"Then throw that Detector away, I say again; it only makes you purblind; don't you see what a wild-goose chase it has led you? The bill is good. Throw the Detector away."

"No; it ain't so satisfactory as I thought for, but I must examine this other bill."

"As you please, but I can't in conscience assist you any more; pray, then, excuse me."

So, while the old man with much painstakings resumed his work, the cosmopolitan, to allow him every facility, resumed his reading.

At length, seeing that he had given up his undertaking as hopeless, and was at leisure again, the cosmopolitan addressed some gravely interesting remarks to him about the book before him, and, presently, becoming more and more grave, said, as he turned the large volume slowly over on the table, and with much difficulty traced the faded remains of the gilt inscription giving the name of the society who had presented it to the boat, "Ah, sir, though every one must be pleased at the thought of the presence in public places of such a book, yet there is something that abates the satisfaction. Look at this volume; on the outside, battered as any old valise in the baggage-room; and inside, white and virgin as the hearts of lilies in bud."

"So it is, so it is," said the old man sadly, his attention for the first directed to the circumstance.

"Nor is this the only time," continued the other, "that I have observed these public Bibles in boats and hotels. All much like this—old without, and new within. True, this aptly typifies that internal freshness, the best mark of truth, however ancient; but then, it speaks not so well as could be wished for the good book's esteem in the minds of the traveling public. I may err, but it seems to me that if more confidence was put in it by the traveling public, it would hardly be so."

With an expression very unlike that with which he had bent over the Detector, the old man sat meditating upon his companion's remarks a while; and, at last, with a rapt look, said: "And yet, of all people, the traveling public most need to put trust in that guardianship which is made known in this book."

"True, true," thoughtfully assented the other.

"And one would think they would want to, and be glad to," continued the old man kindling; "for, in all our wanderings through this vale, how pleasant, not less than obligatory, to feel that we need start at no wild alarms, provide for no wild perils; trusting in that Power which is alike able and willing to protect us when we cannot ourselves."

His manner produced something answering to it in the cosmopolitan, who, leaning over towards him, said sadly: 'Though this is a theme on which travelers seldom talk to each other, yet, to you, sir, I will say, that I share something of your sense of security. I have moved much about the world, and still keep at it; nevertheless, though in this land, and especially in these parts of it, some stories are told about steamboats and railroads fitted to make one a little apprehensive, yet, I may say that, neither by land nor by water, am I ever seriously disquieted, however, at times, transiently uneasy; since, with you, sir, I believe in a Committee of Safety,[7]

7. God's guardian angels, not conspicuously active in Melville's time.

holding silent sessions over all, in an invisible patrol, most alert when we soundest sleep, and whose beat lies as much through forests as towns, along rivers as streets. In short, I never forget that passage of Scripture which says, 'Jehovah shall be thy confidence.'[8] The traveler who has not this trust, what miserable misgivings must be his; or, what vain, short-sighted care must he take of himself."

"Even so," said the old man, lowly.

"There is a chapter," continued the other, again taking the book, "which, as not amiss, I must read you. But this lamp, solar-lamp as it is, begins to burn dimly."

"So it does, so it does," said the old man with changed air, "dear me, it must be very late. I must to bed, to bed! Let me see," rising and looking wistfully all round, first on the stools and settees, and then on the carpet, "let me see, let me see;—is there anything I have forgot,—forgot? Something I a sort of dimly remember. Something, my son—careful man—told me at starting this morning, this very morning. Something about seeing to—something before I got into my berth. What could it be? Something for safety. Oh, my poor old memory!"

"Let me give a little guess, sir. Life-preserver?"

"So it was. He told me not to omit seeing I had a life-preserver in my state-room; said the boat supplied them, too. But where are they? I don't see any. What are they like?"

"They are something like this, sir, I believe," lifting a brown stool with a curved tin compartment underneath; "yes, this, I think, is a life-preserver, sir; and a very good one, I should say, though I don't pretend to know much about such things, never using them myself."[9]

"Why, indeed, now! Who would have thought it? *that* a life-preserver? That's the very stool I was sitting on, ain't it?"

"It is. And that shows that one's life is looked out for, when he ain't looking out for it himself. In fact, any of these stools here will float you, sir, should the boat hit a snag, and go down in the dark. But, since you want one in your room, pray take this one," handing it to him. "I think I can recommend this one; the tin part," rapping it with his knuckles, "seems so perfect—sounds so very hollow."

"Sure it's *quite* perfect, though?" Then, anxiously putting on his spectacles, he scrutinized it pretty closely—"well soldered? quite tight?"

"I should say so, sir; though, indeed, as I said, I never use this sort of thing, myself. Still, I think that in case of a wreck, barring

---

8. Proverbs 3:26.
9. The vulgar point is that in this ship of fools the best life preserver one can expect is a stool that doubles as a chamberpot. William Braswell (1943) first explained the passage.

sharp-pointed timbers, you could have confidence in that stool for a special providence."

"Then, good-night, good-night; and Providence have both of us in its good keeping."

"Be sure it will," eying the old man with sympathy, as for the moment he stood, money-belt in hand, and life-preserver under arm, "be sure it will, sir, since in Providence, as in man, you and I equally put trust. But, bless me, we are being left in the dark here. Pah! what a smell, too."

"Ah, my way now," cried the old man, peering before him, "where lies my way to my state-room?"

"I have indifferent eyes, and will show you; but, first, for the good of all lungs, let me extinguish this lamp."[1]

The next moment, the waning light expired, and with it the waning flames of the horned altar, and the waning halo round the robed man's brow; while in the darkness which ensued, the cosmopolitan kindly led the old man away. Something further may follow of this Masquerade.

1. When the cosmopolitan extinguishes this lamp, he is—on the basis of his long day's experiences with nominal Christians—relegating Christianity to the number of "barren planets" of lamps, or religions already dead.

Textual Appendix

A NOTE ON THE TEXT

Until recently the text of *The Confidence-Man* received little attention. The first to study it was Elizabeth S. Foster, who in 1954 reported the results of her collation of the American and English editions of 1857. The only two variants of any length are both footnotes apparently inserted in the English edition to define Yankeeisms: a footnote on "weed" at 10.13 ("Crape on his hat.") and another on "sophomore" at 21.16 ("A student in his second year."). Miss Foster overlooked some third of the substantive variants, but even the full list printed in the Northwestern-Newberry Edition is of little significance, since it reveals no revisions or corrections by Melville and no expurgations by the English publisher. About the only deliberate revisions in the English edition, aside from the two added footnotes, seem to be someone's attempt to change occurrences of "nigh" into "near" and of "illy" into "ill." Almost all of the variant English readings, in short, are routine memorial substitutions or corrections of obvious errors.

Several manuscript fragments survive, rescued from the attic at Arrowhead by one of Melville's grandnieces. These are mainly drafts of portions of Chapter 14 and a draft of "The River," which is not strictly a part of *The Confidence-Man* but may have been written as part of it. Miss Foster's analysis of the effects of Melville's revisions in the drafts of Chapter 14 is reprinted below (pp. 321–323), and Robert R. Allen's transcription of "The River" follows this Note on the Text. All the surviving manuscript fragments are fully presented in the Northwestern-Newberry Edition.

Like several of Melville's other books which underwent no authorial corrections or revisions from printing to printing or from edition to edition, *The Confidence-Man* does not benefit textually from Hinman Machine collations of the same editions (except for revealing a comma dropped at 205.2 in some copies of the American edition) or from sight collations of the two early editions (except for revealing some routine corrections in the English edition), but it does benefit from close attention to the meaning of the words. Not even Melville's copyist for *The Confidence-Man*, his sister Augusta, was able to copy his handwriting infallibly, and a good many corruptions worked their way into the printed book. Footnotes in the text identify the more important corrections that scholars have suggested; errors must still lurk in the pages of the book. In the following complete list of emendations made in this edition, N stands for the reading of the Norton Critical Edition and A for the reading of the first American edition. A slash (/) indicates where a word was broken at the end of a line, when that break seems to have led to an error.

xvi.5   N evidently not   A evidently
xvi.17 N magic   A music
5.36   N Corcovado   A Cocovarde
8.44   N men,   A men
10.30   N clergyman   A clergymen
12.26   N ye: A ye
14.28   N Acquaintance   A ACQUANT-
ANCE
15.45   N "don't   A don't
26.24   N scoffer?   A scoffer,
26.26   N falsehood?   A falsehood.
27.3   N negro?   A negro.
30.9   N prevalent   A prevailent
30.34   N prejudice   A prejudices
31.8   N thereby   A there by
35.13   N World's   A world's
35.13   N Charity   A charity
36.6   N World's   A world's
36.6   N Charity   A charity
36.13   N World's   A world's
36.13   N Charity   A charity
38.33   N hesitate?   A hesitate.
40.17   N unfortunate   A uufortunate
40.24   N company?   A company.
40.40   N added,   A added
42.4   N stand 'way   A stand-/way
43.30   N the   A the the
43.41   N Arimanius   A Ariamius
47.39   N pray?   A pray,
51.25   N hyperboles   A hyberboles
55.38   N permissible   A not permissible
56.2   N unfortunate   A unfortnnate
56.36   N law!   A law?
57.37   N brightening.   A brightening."
57.39   N brightening.   A brightening
57.40   N Seriously   A seriously
58.36   N caterpillar   A butterfly
58.37   N butterfly   A caterpillar
59.4   N life. As elsewhere, experience
A life as elsewhere. Experience
62.8   N head,   A head
62.35   N wish   A wish,
62.35   N herb-doctor,   A herb-doctor
65.26   N saying,   A saying
67.5   N 'Medea   A "Medea
67.6   N Aeson?'   A Aeson?"
67.25   N Preissnitz   A Preisnitz
68.17   N incurable.   A incurable?
72.24   N "ladies   A ladies
78.28   N all together   A altogether
78.38   N "since   A since
80.23   N story?   A story.
86.7   N money."   A money.
88.20   N "His   A His
92.6   N 'Ah   A "Ah
92.8   N Green.'   A Green.
94.43   N trust?   A trust.
97.42   N Girardeau   A Giradeau
98.6   N Girardeau   A Giradeau
98.34   N Girardeau   A Giradeau
101.3   N 'possums,   A 'possums,'
104.18 N have   A has
106.42 N set?   A set.
106.45 N ones?   A ones.
108.6   N butterfly.' "   A butterfly."
109.6   N suppose?"   A suppose.
110.29 N boys,   A boys'
116.40 N cured?'   A cured?
117.35 N men?   A men.

118.18 N have   A have have
119.15 N snapping   A snap-/ing
119.18 N mean   A mean;
119.18 N it;   A it
119.21 N worlding, glutton   A world-/
lingg, lutton
119.29 N confinement?"   A confinement?
126.30 N backwoods'   A backswoods'
127.20 N burke   A burk
127.25 N indeed   A in /deed
128.9   N is   A it
132.27 N of the   A of
133.12 N marauding   A maurauding
134.1   N number   A murder
135.4   N and   A ands
139.38 N Brinvillierses   A Brinvil-
liarses
142.16 N 'Politics,'   A "Politics,"
145.33 N grave!"   A grave!
147.30 N fellow   A fellew
148.14 N principle   A principal
151.6   N humane   A human
152.6   N Charlie   A Frank
152.8   N drink   A drink,
152.8   N it,   A it
153.10 N everywhere   A everwhere
155.36 N cosmopolitan.   A cosmopolitan
166.8   N definition   A defi-/tion
166.9   N favor."   A favor.
168.5   N eye?"   A eye?'
168.19 N then,   A then
171.1   N you.   A you,
171.25 N respect,   A respect
172.19 N friend   A freind
172.23 N it,   A it
172.32 N you   A you,
172.32 N mean,   A mean
174.13 N principal-and-interest
A principle-and-interest
174.21 N principal   A principle
174.26 N Frank?   A Frank.
174.31 N terrestrial   A terrestial
177.10 N it."   A it.
177.13 N Charlie."   A Charlie.
177.18 N him."   A him.
177.27 N it."   A it.
178.23 N heartlessness.   A heartlessness
183.14 N Talk,   A Talk,
185.22 N "At   A At
185.40 N him.   A him
188.44 N stone: A stone.
189.25 N that   A ihat
189.37 N Friend   A Friend,
191.26 N own.   A own?
194.5   N Trust? A Trust?"
194.5   N No   A "No
197.5   N up?   A up.
199.5   N hearts?"   A hearts?
199.29 N bald   A bold
205.2   N forms,   A forms
208.18 N bare   A bear
209.1   N white,"   A white,'
209.31 N only   A only more
209.37 N wisdom."   A wisdom.
212.7   N "nor   A nor
212.17 N boy;   A boy

THE RIVER†

The precise relationship that Melville intended between his prose fragment "The River" and *The Confidence-Man* is not known. The piece has an independent power to compel attention. It is probable that Melville wrote "The River" as part of *The Confidence-Man* and decided not to include it. Because it survives in a group of papers relating to *The Confidence-Man*, and because it reinforces motifs central to the narrative, "The River" warrants printing here.

Melville wrote "The River" on one side of two sheets of blue, ruled, machine-made paper that is designed to have the appearance of handmade, 'laid' paper. The manuscript is in the Houghton Library of Harvard University: MS. Am. 188 (384). It was the gift of Eleanor Melville Metcalf, Melville's granddaughter, in 1938.

The frequent occurrence of scarcely formed letters, contractions (letters or syllables omitted within a word), and transposed letters in the manuscript keep the words that Melville wrote from being legible at every point. Although it helps a transcriber to compare difficult spots with holograph passages that are similar but more legible, the transcriber still must make some guesses.

Elizabeth S. Foster presented a text of "The River" in her edition of *The Confidence-Man* (New York: Hendricks House, 1954), pp. 379–380. Edwin Fussell reprinted the greater portion of Miss Foster's text, questioned several of her readings, and offered an emendation in *Frontier* (Princeton: Princeton University Press, 1965), pp. 305–306. H. Bruce Franklin contributed a number of improved readings in his transcription, appended to his edition of *The Confidence-Man* (Indianapolis: Bobbs-Merrill Company, 1967), pp. 353–355.

Except where noted, Melville's contractions (e.g., Missippee = Mississippee) are silently expanded. I have followed Melville's spelling and punctuation. My intent in the notes is to display the author's work in the process of revision, to acknowledge differing readings of previous editors, and to offer a few explanatory notes by way of clarification.

ROBERT R. ALLEN

† Robert R. Allen transcribed and edited the manuscript of "The River" especially for publication in this Norton Critical Edition. The transcription is printed by permission of the Harvard University Library and Robert R. Allen.

The River

As the word Abraham means the father of a great multitude of men so the word Mississippee means the father of a great multitude of waters. His tribes stream in from east & west, exceeding fruitful the lands they enrich. In this granary of a continent this basin of the Mississippee must not the nations be greatly multi- 5 plied & blest?

Above the Falls of St: Anthony for the most part he winds evenly in between banks of flags or straight tracts of pine over marbley sands in waters so clear that the deepest fish have the visable flight of the bird. Undisturbed as the lowly life in its bosom feeds 10 the lordly life on its shores, the coronetted elk & the deer, while in the watrey forms of some couched rock in the channel, furred over with moss, the furred bear on the marge seems to eye his amphibious brothers. Wood & wave wed, man is remote. The Unsung tune, the Golden Age of the billow. 15

By his Fall, though he Rise not again, the unhumbled river ennobles himself now deepens now purely expands, now first forms his character & begins that career whose majestic serenity if not overborne by fierce onsets of torrents shall end only with ocean.

Like a larger Susquehanah like a long-drawn bison herd he hur- 20

Heading The River] underlined in MS; originally '*The Mississippi*', which is struck with a wavy line.
1 great] interlined with a caret; see note for line 2.
2 great] written over 'm'. Apparently Melville began to write 'multitude', writing 'great' over the completed initial letter, and currently interlining 'great', line 1.
8 evenly] first 'e' written over an 'o'; presumably Melville began to write 'over'.
8 straight] Foster reads 'through' and conjectures 'slight'. Franklin reads 'thight' (thick-set, dense).
8 pine] Foster conjectures 'trees' also.
8–9 marbley *Franklin*] Foster reads 'marbles' and conjectures 'marshes'.
9 visable] = visible.
10 lowly *Franklin*] Foster reads 'lonely' and conjectures 'lowly'.
11 lordly] Foster and Franklin read 'lonely'. Foster conjectures 'lowly' also.
12 watrey forms] Foster and Franklin read 'watery'. Foster reads 'form'.
12 couched] Melville first wrote 'couched', deleted it, interlined 'mossy', deleted it, and recalled 'couched' by underlining with dashes.
12–13 furred over with moss,] interlined with a caret.
13 the furred] 'the' written over '&'.
14 brothers] Foster and Franklin read 'brother'.
14 Unsung *Foster*] Franklin reads 'unsung'.
15 tune] Foster and Franklin read 'time'. Foster conjectures 'tune' also.
16 his] interlined with a caret after deleted 'the'.
16 Rise] Foster and Franklin read 'rise'.
17 deepens] emended from MS., which appears to have 'deepes'. Foster conjectures 'deeper' also.
18 character] MS. appears to have 'charter', but the occurrence of the same form of the word in other MS. fragments where the context certainly calls for 'character' supports expanding this contraction.
19 fierce] the 'f' is written over what appears to be an 'r'.
20 Susquehanah] emended from MS. 'Susquehanh.' Foster reads 'Susquehannah'; Franklin reads 'Susquehanha'.

ries on through the prairie, here & there expanding into archipelagoes cycladean in beauty, while fissured & verdant, a long China
Wall, the bluffs sweep bluly away. Glad & content the sacred river
glides on.

But at St: Louis the course of this dream is run. Down on it like 25
a Pawnee from ambush foams the yellow-jacked Missouri. The
calmness is gone, the grouped isles disappear, the shores are jagged
& rent, the hue of the water is clayed, the before moderate current
is rapid & vexed. The peace of the Upper River seems broken in
the Lower, nor is it ever renewed. 30

The Missouri sends rather a hostile element than a filial flow.
Longer, stronger than the father of waters like Jupiter he dethrones
his sire & reigns in his stead. Under the benign name Mississippi it
is in short the Missouri that now rolls to the Gulf, the Missouri
that with the snows from his solitudes freezes the warmth of the 35
genial zones, the Missouri that by open assault or artful sap sweeps
away fruit & field grass-yard & barn, the Missouri that not a tribu-
tary but an invader enters the sea, long disdaining to yield his
white wave to the blue.

21–22 archipelagoes cycladean] emended from MS., which appears to have 'archi-
plgoes cyclalean'.
22 &] Foster reads 'and'.
23 bluly] = bluely.
23 &] MS. repeats '&' from the right margin of one line to the left margin of
the next.
26 yellow-jacked] = discolored as by yellow fever (see Mathews, *Dictionary of
Americanisms*, where 'yellow jack' is a synonym for 'yellow fever'). Melville
wrote 'yellow-jacked' and may have connoted 'yellow-jacket'. Foster and
Franklin read 'yellow-jacket'. *Dictionary of American English* cites an early
occurrence of 'yellow jacket' transferring the sense of the insect's effect to
Indians: Doddridge, *Logan* (1823), "Why so large an encampment of
Indians? . . . Why do these Yellow-jackets come so near us?"
27 calmness *Franklin*] Foster reads 'calm'.
29 peace *Foster*] a conjectural reading. What appears to be an otiose stroke
precedes the 'p'. Franklin conjectures 'opium'. Foster conjectures 'green',
'prime', and 'dream' also.
29 broken *Foster*] Franklin conjectures 'trite'.
30 is it] Foster prints 'it is'.
30 ever] Foster conjectures 'e'er' also.
31 sends rather a] preceded by an undeciphered deletion; 'he' of 'rather' written
over undeciphered letters; 'a' preceded by 'an' wiped away.
32 Longer,] the 'o' written over an 'a'. Foster omits the comma.
34 in short] a conjectural reading; possibly 'no other [than]'.
35 snows] preceded by an undeciphered word ['warmer'?] deleted.
35 freezes] Foster conjectures 'frees' also.
35 warmth] Foster conjectures 'waters' also.
37 grass-yard] *OED* cross-references 'grass-yard' with 'green-yard' in sporting to
mean "a grass yard for hounds to take exercise in." Another meaning of
'green-yard' that *OED* lists seems more applicable in Melville's context: "an
enclosure for the reception of stray animals and vehicles; a pound." Mr.
James L. Harner contributed this reading. Foster and Franklin read 'grave-
yard'.
38 invader] a conjectural reading. Foster reads 'outlaw' and conjectures 'union'
and 'overlord'. Fussell reads 'murderer'. Franklin conjectures 'undermine'.

Backgrounds and Sources

ANONYMOUS

Arrest of the Confidence Man†

For the last few months a man has been travelling about the city, known as the "Confidence Man;" that is, he would go up to a perfect stranger in the street, and being a man of genteel appearance, would easily command an interview. Upon this interview he would say, after some little conversation, "have you confidence in me to trust me with your watch until to-morrow;" the stranger, at this novel request, supposing him to be some old acquaintance, not at the moment recollected, allows him to take the watch, thus placing "confidence" in the honesty of the stranger, who walks off laughing, and the other, supposing it to be a joke, allows him so to do. In this way many have been duped, and the last that we recollect was a Mr. Thomas McDonald, of No. 276 Madison street, who, on the 12th of May last, was met by this "Confidence Man" in William street, who in the manner as above described, took from him a gold lever watch valued at $110; and yesterday, singularly enough, Mr. McDonald was passing along Liberty street, when who should he meet but the "Confidence Man" who had stolen his watch. Officer Swayse, of the Third ward, being near at hand, took the accused into custody on the charge made by Mr. McDonald. . . . On the prisoner being taken before Justice McGrath, he was recognized as an old offender, by the name of Wm. Thompson, and is said to be a graduate of the college at Sing Sing. The magistrate committed him to the prison for a further hearing. It will be well for all those persons who have been defrauded by the "Confidence Man," to call at the police court, Tombs, and take a view of him.

EVERT A. DUYCKINCK

[The New Species of the Jeremy Diddler]‡

The Confidence Man, the new species of the Jeremy Diddler recently a subject of police fingering, and still later impressed into the service of Burton's comicalities in Chambers street, is excel-

---

† From the *New York Herald* (July 8, 1849). I am indebted to Johannes D. Bergmann for this selection.
‡ From the *Literary World* (August 18, 1849), 133. Presumably the introductory paragraph is by Melville's friend Evert A. Duyckinck. The asterisks are in the *Literary World* text. Paul Smith (1962) first pointed out the relevance of these paragraphs to *The Confidence-Man*.

lently handled by a clever pen in the *Merchants' Ledger*, which we are glad to see has a column for the credit as well as for the debtor side of humanity. It is not the worst thing that can be said of a country that it gives birth to a confidence man:—

"Who is there that does not recollect, in the circle of his acquaintance, a smart young gentleman who, with his coat buttoned to the throat and hair pushed back, extends his arms at public meetings in a wordy harangue? This is the young confidence man of politics. In private life you remember perfectly well the middle-aged gentleman with well-developed person and white waistcoat, who lays down the law in reference to the state of trade, sub-treasury, and the tariff—and who subscribes steadily to Hunt's excellent Magazine (which he never reads). This is the confidence man of merchandise. * * *

"That one poor swindler, like the one under arrest, should have been able to drive so considerable a trade on an appeal to so simple a quality as the confidence of man in man, shows that all virtue and humanity of nature is not entirely extinct in the nineteenth century. It is a good thing, and speaks well for human nature, that, at this late day, in spite of all the hardening of civilization and all the warning of newspapers, men *can be swindled*.

"The man who is *always* on his guard, *always* proof against appeal, who cannot be beguiled into the weakness of pity by *any* story—is far gone, in our opinion, towards being himself a hardened villain. He may steer clear of petty larceny and open swindling —but mark that man well in his intercourse with his fellows—they have no confidence in him, as he has none in them. He lives coldly among his people—he walks an iceberg in the marts of trade and social life—and when he dies, may Heaven have that confidence in him which he had not in his fellow mortals!"

ANONYMOUS

The Original Confidence Man in Town.— A Short Chapter on Misplaced Confidence†

He ["Samuel Willis"] called into a jewelry store on Broadway and said to the proprietor: "How do you do, Mr. Myers?" Receiv-

† From the *Albany Evening Journal* (April 28, 1855). Johannes D. Bergmann traced this quotation to the Albany paper; Jay Leyda had informed Elizabeth S. Foster of its reprinting in the *Springfield Republican* (May 5, 1855). The relevance of the article to Chapter 4 of *The Confidence-Man* is clear.

ing no reply, he added "Don't you know me?" to which Mr. M. replied that he did not. "My name is Samuel Willis. You are mistaken, for I have met you three or four times." He then said he had something of a private nature to communicate to Mr. Myers and that he wished to see him alone. The two men walked to the end of the counter, when Willis said to Myers, "I guess you are a Mason,"—to which Myers replied that he was—when Willis asked him if he would not give a brother a shilling if he needed it. By some shrewd management, Myers was induced to give him six or seven dollars.

T. B. THORPE

The Big Bear of Arkansas†

A steamboat on the Mississippi frequently, in making her regular trips, carries, between places varying from one to two thousand miles apart; and as these boats advertise to land passengers and freight at "all intermediate landings," the heterogeneous character of the passengers of one of these up-country boats can scarcely be imagined by one who has never seen it with his own eyes. Starting from New Orleans in one of these boats, you will find yourself associated with men from every State in the Union, and from every portion of the globe; and a man of observation need not lack for amusement or instruction in such a crowd, if he will take the trouble to read the great book of character so favorably opened before him. Here may be seen jostling together the wealthy Southern planter, and the pedlar of tin-ware from New England—the North merchant, and the Southern jockey—a venerable bishop, and a desperate gambler—the land speculator, and the honest farmer—professional men of all creeds and characters—Wolvereens, Suckers, Hoosiers, Buckeyes, and Corncrackers, beside a "plentiful sprinkling" of the half-horse and half-alligator species of men, who are peculiar to "old Mississippi," and who appear to gain a livelihood simply by going up and down the river. In the pursuit of pleasure or business, I have frequently found myself in such a crowd.

† This opening paragraph of Thorpe's most famous story is quoted here from its first publication in the *New York Spirit of the Times* (March 21, 1841). It was reprinted in Thorpe's *The Hive of "The Bee-Hunter"* (1854), as well as in contemporary periodicals. In a review of Francis Parkman's *Oregon Trail* in the *Literary World* (March 31, 1849), Melville described a Mississippi and Missouri steamer "crammed with all sorts of adventurers, Spanish and Indians, Santa Fé traders and trappers, gamblers and Mormons."

NATHANIEL HAWTHORNE

[A Satanic Beggar]†

While the merry girl and myself were busy with the show-box, the unceasing rain had driven another wayfarer into the wagon. He seemed pretty nearly of the old show-man's age, but much smaller, leaner, and more withered than he, and less respectably clad in a patched suit of gray; withal, he had a thin, shrewd countenance, and a pair of diminutive gray eyes, which peeped rather too keenly out of their puckered sockets. This old fellow had been joking with the show-man, in a manner which intimated previous acquaintance; but perceiving that the damsel and I had terminated our affairs, he drew forth a folded document and presented it to me. As I had anticipated, it proved to be a circular, written in a very fair and legible hand, and signed by several distinguished gentlemen whom I had never heard of, stating that the bearer had encountered every variety of misfortune, and recommending him to the notice of all charitable people. Previous disbursements had left me no more than a five dollar bill, out of which, however, I offered to make the beggar a donation, provided he would give me change for it. The object of my beneficence looked keenly in my face, and discerned that I had none of that abominable spirit, characteristic though it be, of a full-blooded Yankee, which takes pleasure in detecting every little harmless piece of knavery.

'Why, perhaps,' said the ragged old mendicant, 'if the bank is in good standing, I can't say but I may have enough about me to change your bill.'

'It is a bill of the Suffolk Bank,' said I, 'and better than the specie.'

As the beggar had nothing to object, he now produced a small buff leather bag, tied up carefully with a shoe-string. When this was opened, there appeared a very comfortable treasure of silver coins, of all sorts and sizes, and I even fancied that I saw, gleaming among them, the golden plumage of that rare bird in our currency, the American Eagle. In this precious heap was my bank note deposited, the rate of exchange being considerably against me. * * *

* * * Having already satisfied myself as to the several modes in which the four others attained felicity, I next set my mind at work

† From "The Seven Vagabonds," in *Twice-Told Tales* (Boston: James Munroe and Company, 1842), II, 174–175, 177–179. Melville knew the story from a copy of this edition given him by Hawthorne. Melville's use of "The Seven Vagabonds" had been pointed out privately by Harrison Hayford, but the first discussion in print seems to be that by Lang (1967).

to discover what enjoyments were peculiar to the old "Straggler,' as the people of the country would have termed the wandering mendicant and prophet. As he pretended to familiarity with the Devil, so I fancied that he was fitted to pursue and take delight in his way of life, by possessing some of the mental and moral characteristics, the lighter and more comic ones, of the Devil in popular stories. Among them might be reckoned a love of deception for its own sake, a shrewd eye and keen relish for human weakness and ridiculous infirmity, and the talent of petty fraud. Thus to this old man there would be pleasure even in the consciousness so insupportable to some minds, that his whole life was a cheat upon the world, and that so far as he was concerned with the public, his little cunning had the upper hand of its united wisdom. Every day would furnish him with a succession of minute and pungent triumphs; as when, for instance, his importunity wrung a pittance out of the heart of a miser, or when my silly good nature transferred a part of my slender purse to his plump leather bag; or when some ostentatious gentleman should throw a coin to the ragged beggar who was richer than himself; or when, though he would not always be so decidedly diabolical, his pretended wants should make him a sharer in the scanty living of real indigence. And then what an inexhaustible field of enjoyment, both as enabling him to discern so much folly and achieve such quantities of minor mischief, was opened to his sneering spirit by his pretensions to prophetic knowledge.

All this was a sort of happiness which I could conceive of, though I had little sympathy with it. Perhaps had I been then inclined to admit it, I might have found that the roving life was more proper to him than to either of his companions; for Satan, to whom I had compared the poor man, has delighted, ever since the time of Job, in 'wandering up and down upon the earth;' and indeed a crafty disposition, which operates not in deep laid plans, but in disconnected tricks, could not have an adequate scope, unless naturally impelled to a continual change of scene and society. * * *

NATHANIEL HAWTHORNE

[A Juvenile Salesman]†

To confess the truth, it is not the easiest matter in the world to define and individualize a character like this which we are now handling [i.e., the old apple-dealer]. The portrait must be so generally

† From "The Old Apple-Dealer," in *Mosses from an Old Manse* (New York: Wiley and Putnam, 1846), II, 161.

negative, that the most delicate pencil is likely to spoil it by introducing some too positive trait. Every touch must be kept down, or else you destroy the subdued tone, which is absolutely essential to the whole effect. Perhaps more may be done by contrast, than by direct description. For this purpose, I make use of another cake-and-candy merchant, who likewise infests the railroad depôt. This latter worthy is a very smart and well-dressed boy, of ten years old or thereabouts, who skips briskly hither and thither, addressing the passengers in a pert voice, yet with somewhat of good breeding in his tone and pronunciation. Now he has caught my eye, and skips across the room with a pretty pertness, which I should like to correct with a box on the ear. "Any cake, sir?—any candy?"

NATHANIEL HAWTHORNE

The Celestial Railroad†

Not a great while ago, passing through the gate of dreams, I visited that region of the earth in which lies the famous city of Destruction. It interested me much to learn that, by the public spirit of some of the inhabitants, a railroad has recently been established between this populous and flourishing town, and the Celestial City. Having a little time upon my hands, I resolved to gratify a liberal curiosity to make a trip thither. Accordingly, one fine morning, after paying my bill at the hotel, and directing the porter to stow my luggage behind a coach, I took my seat in the vehicle and set out for the Station-house. It was my good fortune to enjoy the company of a gentleman—one Mr. Smooth-it-away—who, though he had never actually visited the Celestial City, yet seemed as well acquainted with its laws, customs, policy, and statistics, as with those of the city of Destruction, of which he was a native townsman. Being, moreover, a director of the railroad corporation, and one of its largest stockholders, he had it in his power to give me all desirable information respecting that praiseworthy enterprise.

Our coach rattled out of the city, and, at a short distance from its outskirts, passed over a bridge, of elegant construction, but somewhat too slight, as I imagined, to sustain any considerable weight. On both sides lay an extensive quagmire, which could not have been more disagreeable either to sight or smell, had all the kennels of the earth emptied their pollution there.

"This," remarked Mr. Smooth-it-away, "is the famous Slough of

† From *Mosses from an Old Manse* (New York: Wiley and Putnam, 1846), II, 173–192.

Despond—a disgrace to all the neighborhood; and the greater, that it might so easily be converted into firm ground."

"I have understood," said I, "that efforts have been made for that purpose, from time immemorial. Bunyan mentions that above twenty thousand cart-loads of wholesome instructions had been thrown in here, without effect."

"Very probably!—and what effect could be anticipated from such unsubstantial stuff?" cried Mr. Smooth-it-away. "You observe this convenient bridge. We obtained a sufficient foundation for it by throwing into the Slough some editions of books of morality, volumes of French philosophy and German rationalism, tracts, sermons, and essays of modern clergymen, extracts from Plato, Confucius, and various Hindoo sages, together with a few ingenious commentaries upon texts of Scripture—all of which, by some scientific process, have been converted into a mass like granite. The whole bog might be filled up with similar matter."

It really seemed to me, however, that the bridge vibrated and heaved up and down in a very formidable manner; and, spite of Mr. Smooth-it-away's testimony to the solidity of its foundation, I should be loth to cross it in a crowded omnibus; especially, if each passenger were encumbered with as heavy luggage as that gentleman and myself. Nevertheless, we got over without accident, and soon found ourselves at the Station-house. This very neat and spacious edifice is erected on the site of the little Wicket-Gate, which formerly, as all old pilgrims will recollect, stood directly across the highway, and, by its inconvenient narrowness, was a great obstruction to the traveller of liberal mind and expansive stomach. The reader of John Bunyan will be glad to know, that Christian's old friend Evangelist, who was accustomed to supply each pilgrim with a mystic roll, now presides at the ticket office. Some malicious persons, it is true, deny the identity of this reputable character with the Evangelist of old times, and even pretend to bring competent evidence of an imposture. Without involving myself in a dispute, I shall merely observe, that, so far as my experience goes, the square pieces of pasteboard, now delivered to passengers, are much more convenient and useful along the road, than the antique roll of parchment. Whether they will be as readily received at the gate of the Celestial City, I decline giving an opinion.

A large number of passengers were already at the Station-house, awaiting the departure of cars. By the aspect and demeanor of these persons, it was easy to judge that the feelings of the community had undergone a very favorable change, in reference to the celestial pilgrimage. It would have done Bunyan's heart good to see it. Instead of a lonely and ragged man, with a huge burthen on his back, plodding along sorrowfully on foot, while the whole city hooted after him, here were parties of the first gentry and most respectable people in the neighborhood, setting forth towards the Celestial City, as cheerfully as if the pilgrimage were merely a summer tour. Among the gentlemen were characters of deserved eminence, magistrates, politicians, and men of wealth, by whose example religion could not but be greatly recommended to their meaner brethren. In the ladies' apartment, too, I rejoiced to distinguish some of those flowers of fashionable society, who are so well fitted to adorn the most elevated circles of the Celestial City. There was much pleasant conversation about the news of the day, topics of business, politics, or the lighter matters of amusement; while religion, though indubitably the main thing at heart, was thrown tastefully into the back-ground. Even an infidel would have heard little or nothing to shock his sensibility.

One great convenience of the new method of going on pilgrimage, I must not forget to mention. Our enormous burthens, instead of being carried on our shoulders, as had been the custom of old, were all snugly deposited in the baggage-car, and, as I was assured, would be delivered to their respective owners at the journey's end. Another thing, likewise, the benevolent reader will be delighted to understand. It may be remembered that there was an ancient feud between Prince Beelzebub and the keeper of the Wicket-Gate, and that the adherents of the former distinguished personage were accustomed to shoot deadly arrows at honest pilgrims, while knocking at the door. This dispute, much to the credit as well of the illustrious potentate above-mentioned, as of the worthy and enlightened Directors of the railroad, has been pacifically arranged, on the principle of mutual compromise. The Prince's subjects are now pretty numerously employed about the Station house, some in taking care of the baggage, others in collecting fuel, feeding the engines, and such congenial occupations; and I can conscientiously affirm, that persons more attentive to their business, more willing to accommodate, or more generally agreeable to the passengers, are not to be found on any railroad. Every good heart must surely exult at so satisfactory an arrangement of an immemorial difficulty.

"Where is Mr. Great-heart?" inquired I. "Beyond a doubt, the Directors have engaged that famous old champion to be chief conductor on the railroad?"

"Why, no," said Mr. Smooth-it-away, with a dry cough. "He was offered the situation of brake-man; but, to tell you the truth, our friend Great-heart has grown preposterously stiff and narrow in his old age. He has so often guided pilgrims over the road, on foot, that he considers it a sin to travel in any other fashion. Besides, the old fellow had entered so heartily into the ancient feud with Prince

Beelzebub, that he would have been perpetually at blows or ill language with some of the prince's subjects, and thus have embroiled us anew. So, on the whole, we were not sorry when honest Greatheart went off to the Celestial City in a huff, and left us at liberty to choose a more suitable and accommodating man. Yonder comes the conductor of the train. You will probably recognize him at once."

The engine at this moment took its station in advance of the cars, looking, I must confess, much more like a sort of mechanical demon that would hurry us to the infernal regions, than a laudable contrivance for smoothing our way to the Celestial City. On its top sat a personage almost enveloped in smoke and flame, which—not to startle the reader—appeared to gush from his own mouth and stomach, as well as from the engine's brazen abdomen.

"Do my eyes deceive me?" cried I. "What on earth is this! A living creature?—if so, he is own brother to the engine he rides upon!"

"Poh, poh, you are obtuse!" said Mr. Smooth-it-away, with a hearty laugh. "Don't you know Apollyon, Christian's old enemy, with whom he fought so fierce a battle in the Valley of Humiliation? He was the very fellow to manage the engine; and so we have reconciled him to the custom of going on pilgrimage, and engaged him as chief conductor."

"Bravo, bravo!" exclaimed I, with irrepressible enthusiasm, "this shows the liberality of the age; this proves, if anything can, that all musty prejudices are in a fair way to be obliterated. And how will Christian rejoice to hear of this happy transformation of his old antagonist! I promise myself great pleasure in informing him of it, when we reach the Celestial City."

The passengers being all comfortably seated, we now rattled away merrily, accomplishing a greater distance in ten minutes than Christian probably trudged over in a day. It was laughable while we glanced along, as it were, at the tail of a thunderbolt, to observe two dusty foot-travellers, in the old pilgrim-guise, with cockle-shell and staff, their mystic rolls of parchment in their hands, and their intolerable burthens on their backs. The preposterous obstinacy of these honest people, in persisting to groan and stumble along the difficult pathway, rather than take advantage of modern improvements, excited great mirth among our wiser brotherhood. We greeted the two pilgrims with many pleasant gibes and a roar of laughter; whereupon, they gazed at us with such woeful and absurdly compassionate visages, that our merriment grew tenfold more obstreperous. Apollyon, also, entered heartily into the fun, and contrived to flirt the smoke and flame of the engine, or of his own breath, into their faces, and envelope them in an atmosphere of scalding steam. These little practical jokes amused us mightily, and doubtless afforded the pilgrims the gratification of considering themselves martyrs.

At some distance from the railroad, Mr. Smooth-it-away pointed to a large, antique edifice, which, he observed, was a tavern of long standing, and had formerly been a noted stopping-place for pilgrims. In Bunyan's road-book it is mentioned as the Interpreter's House.

"I have long had a curiosity to visit that old mansion," remarked I.

"It is not one of our stations, as you perceive," said my companion. "The keeper was violently opposed to the railroad; and well he might be, as the track left his house of entertainment on one side, and thus was pretty certain to deprive him of all his reputable customers. But the foot-path still passes his door; and the old gentleman now and then receives a call from some simple traveller, and entertains him with fare as old-fashioned as himself."

Before our talk on this subject came to a conclusion, we were rushing by the place where Christian's burthen fell from his shoulders, at the sight of the Cross. This served as a theme for Mr. Smooth-it-away, Mr. Live-for-the-world, Mr. Hide-sin-in-the-heart, Mr. Scaly-conscience, and a knot of gentlemen from the town of Shun-repentance, to descant upon the inestimable advantages resulting from the safety of our baggage. Myself, and all the passengers indeed, joined with great unanimity in this view of the matter; for our burthens were rich in many things esteemed precious throughout the world; and especially, we each of us possessed a great variety of favorite Habits, which we trusted would not be out of fashion, even in the polite circles of the Celestial City. It would have been a sad spectacle to see such an assortment of valuable articles tumbling into the sepulchre. Thus pleasantly conversing on the favorable circumstances of our positions, as compared with those of past pilgrims, and of narrow-minded ones at the present day, we soon found ourselves at the foot of the Hill Difficulty. Through the very heart of this rocky mountain a tunnel has been constructed, of most admirable architecture, with a lofty arch and a spacious double-track; so that, unless the earth and rocks should chance to crumble down, it will remain an eternal monument of the builder's skill and enterprise. It is a great though incidental advantage, that the materials from the heart of the Hill Difficulty have been employed in filling up the Valley of Humiliation; thus obviating the necessity of descending into that disagreeable and unwholesome hollow.

"This is a wonderful improvement, indeed," said I. "Yet I should have been glad of an opportunity to visit the Palace Beautiful, and be introduced to the charming young ladies—Miss Prudence, Miss Piety, Miss Charity, and the rest—who have the kindness to entertain pilgrims there.'

"Young ladies!" cried Mr. Smooth-it-away, as soon as he could speak for laughing. "And charming young ladies! Why, my dear fellow, they are old maids, every soul of them—prim, starched, dry, and angular—and not one of them, I will venture to say, has altered so much as the fashion of her gown, since the days of Christian's pilgrimage."

"Ah, well," said I, much comforted, "then I can very readily dispense with their acquaintance."

The respectable Apollyon was now putting on the steam at a prodigious rate; anxious, perhaps, to get rid of the unpleasant reminiscences connected with the spot where he had so disastrously encountered Christian. Consulting Mr. Bunyan's road-book, I perceived that we must now be within a few miles of the Valley of the Shadow of Death; into which doleful region, at our present speed, we should plunge much sooner than seemed at all desirable. In truth, I expected nothing better than to find myself in the ditch on one side, or the quag on the other. But on communicating my apprehensions to Mr. Smooth-it-away, he assured me that the difficulties of this passage, even in its worst condition, had been vastly exaggerated, and that, in its present state of improvement, I might consider myself as safe as on any railroad in Christendom.

Even while we were speaking, the train shot into the entrance of this dreaded Valley. Though I plead guilty to some foolish palpitations of the heart, during our headlong rush over the causeway here constructed, yet it were unjust to withhold the highest encomiums on the boldness of its original conception, and the ingenuity of those who executed it. It was gratifying, likewise, to observe how much care had been taken to dispel the everlasting gloom, and supply the defect of cheerful sunshine; not a ray of which has ever penetrated among these awful shadows. For this purpose, the inflammable gas, which exudes plentifully from the soil, is collected by means of pipes, and thence communicated to a quadruple row of lamps, along the whole extent of the passage. Thus a radiance has been created, even out of the fiery and sulphurous curse that rests for ever upon the Valley; a radiance hurtful, however, to the eyes, and somewhat bewildering, as I discovered by the changes which it wrought in the visages of my companions. In this respect, as compared with natural daylight, there is the same difference as between truth and falsehood; but if the reader have ever travelled through the dark Valley, he will have learned to be thankful for any light that he could get; if not from the sky above, then from the blasted soil beneath. Such was the red brilliancy of these lamps, that they appeared to build walls of fire on both sides of the track, between which we held our course at lightning speed, while a reverberating thunder filled the Valley with its echoes. Had the engine run off the track—a catastrophe, it is whispered, by no means unprecedented—the bottomless pit, if there be any such place, woud undoubtedly have received us. Just as some dismal fooleries of this nature had made my heart quake, there came a tremendous shriek, careering along the Valley as if a thousand devils had burst their lungs to utter it, but which proved to be merely the whistle of the engine, on arriving at a stopping-place.

The spot, where we had now paused, is the same that our friend Bunyan—truthful man, but infected with many fantastic notions—has designated, in terms plainer than I like to repeat, as the mouth of the infernal region. This, however, must be a mistake; inasmuch as Mr. Smooth-it-away, while we remained in the smoky and lurid cavern, took occasion to prove that Tophet has not even a metaphorical existence. The place, he assured us, is no other than the crater of a half-extinct volcano, in which the Directors had caused forges to be set up, for the manufacture of railroad iron. Hence, also, is obtained a plentiful supply of fuel for the use of the engines. Whoever had gazed into the dismal obscurity of the broad cavern-mouth, whence ever and anon darted huge tongues of dusky flame—and had seen the strange, half-shaped monsters, and visions of faces horribly grotesque, into which the smoke seemed to wreathe itself,—and had heard the awful murmurs, and shrieks, and deep shuddering whispers of the blast, sometimes forming themselves into words almost articulate,—would have seized upon Mr. Smooth-it-away's comfortable explanation, as greedily as we did. The inhabitants of the cavern, moreover, were unlovely personages, dark, smoke-begrimed, generally deformed, with mis-shapen feet, and a glow of dusky redness in their eyes; as if their hearts had caught fire, and were blazing out of the upper windows. It struck me as a peculiarity, that the laborers at the forge, and those who brought fuel to the engine, when they began to draw short breath, positively emitted smoke from their mouth and nostrils.

Among the idlers about the train, most of whom were puffing cigars which they had lighted at the flame of the crater, I was perplexed to notice several who, to my certain knowledge, had heretofore set forth by railroad for the Celestial City. They looked wild, and smoky, with a singular resemblance, indeed, to the native inhabitants; like whom, also, they had a disagreeable propensity to ill-natured gibes and sneers, the habit of which had wrought a settled contortion of their visages. Having been on speaking terms with one of these persons—an indolent, good-for-nothing fellow, who went by the name of Take-it-easy—I called him, and inquired what was his business there.

"Did you not start," said I, "for the Celestial City?"

"That's a fact," said Mr. Take-it-easy, carelessly puffing some smoke into my eyes. "But I heard such bad accounts, that I never took pains to climb the hill, on which the city stands. No business doing—no fun going on—nothing to drink, and no smoking allowed—and a thrumming of church-music from morning till night! I would not stay in such a place, if they offered me house-room and living free."

"But, my good Mr. Take-it-easy," cried I, "why take up your residence here, of all places in the world?"

"Oh," said the loafer, with a grin, "it is very warm hereabouts, and I meet with plenty of old acquaintances, and altogether the place suits me. I hope to see you back again, some day soon. A pleasant journey to you!"

While he was speaking, the bell of the engine rang, and we dashed away, after dropping a few passengers, but receiving no new ones. Rattling onward through the Valley, we were dazzled with the fiercely gleaming gas-lamps, as before. But sometimes, in the dark of intense brightness, grim faces, that bore the aspect and expression of individual sins, or evil passions, seemed to thrust themselves through the veil of light, glaring upon us, and stretching forth a great dusky hand, as if to impede our progress. I almost thought, that they were my own sins that appalled me there. These were freaks of imagination—nothing more, certainly,—mere delusions, which I ought to be heartily ashamed of—but, all through the Dark Valley, I was tormented, and pestered, and dolefully bewildered, with the same kind of waking dreams. The mephitic gases of that region intoxicate the brain. As the light of natural day, however, began to struggle with the glow of the lanterns, these vain imaginations lost their vividness, and finally vanished with the first ray of sunshine that greeted our escape from the Valley of the Shadow of Death. Ere we had gone a mile beyond it, I could well nigh have taken my oath, that this whole gloomy passage was a dream.

At the end of the Valley, as John Bunyan mentions, is a cavern, where, in his days, dwelt two cruel giants, Pope and Pagan, who had strewn the ground about their residence with the bones of slaughtered pilgrims. These vile old troglodytes are no longer there; but in their deserted cave another terrible giant has thrust himself, and makes it his business to seize upon honest travellers, and fat them for his table with plentiful meals of smoke, mist, moonshine, raw potatoes, and saw-dust. He is a German by birth, and is called Giant Transcendentalist; but as to his form, his features, his substance, and his nature generally, it is the chief peculiarity of this huge miscreant, that neither he for himself, nor anybody for him, has ever been able to describe them. As we rushed by the cavern's mouth, we caught a hasty glimpse of him, looking somewhat like an ill-proportioned figure, but considerably more like a heap of fog and duskiness. He shouted after us, but in so strange a phraseology, that we knew not what he meant, nor whether to be encouraged or affrighted.

It was late in the day, when the train thundered into the ancient city of Vanity, where Vanity Fair is still at the height of prosperity, and exhibits an epitome of whatever is brilliant, gay, and fascinating, beneath the sun. As I purposed to make a considerable stay here, it gratified me to learn that there is no longer the want of harmony between the townspeople and pilgrims, which impelled the former to such lamentably mistaken measures as the persecution of Christian, and the fiery martyrdom of Faithful. On the contrary, as the new railroad brings with it great trade and a constant influx of strangers, the lord of Vanity Fair is its chief patron, and the capitalists of the city are among the largest stockholders. Many passengers stop to take their pleasure or make their profit in the Fair, instead of going onward to the Celestial City. Indeed, such are the charms of the place, that people often affirm it to be the true and only heaven; stoutly contending that there is no other, that those who seek further are mere dreamers, and that, if the fabled brightness of the Celestial City lay but a bare mile beyond the gates of Vanity, they would not be fools enough to go thither. Without subscribing to these, perhaps, exaggerated encomiums, I can truly say, that my abode in the city was mainly agreeable, and my intercourse with the inhabitants productive of much amusement and instruction.

Being naturally of a serious turn, my attention was directed to the solid advantages derivable from a residence here, rather than to the effervescent pleasures, which are the grand object with too many visitants. The Christian reader, if he have had no accounts of the city later than Bunyan's time, will be surprised to hear that almost every street has its church, and that the reverend clergy are nowhere held in higher respect than at Vanity Fair. And well do they deserve such honorable estimation; for the maxims of wisdom and virtue which fall from their lips, come from as deep a spiritual source, and tend to as lofty a religious aim, as those of the sagest philosophers of old. In justification of this high praise, I need only mention the names of the Rev. Mr. Shallow-deep; the Rev. Mr. Stumble-at-Truth; that fine old clerical character, the Rev. Mr. This-to-day, who expects shortly to resign his pulpit to the Rev. Mr. That-to-morrow; together with the Rev. Mr. Bewilderment; the Rev. Mr. Clog-the-spirit; and, last and greatest, the Rev. Dr. Wind-of-doctrine. The labors of these eminent divines are aided by those of innumerable lecturers, who diffuse such a various profundity, in all subjects of human or celestial science, that any man may acquire an omnigenous erudition, without the trouble of even learning to read. Thus literature is etherealized by assuming for its medium the human voice; and knowledge, depositing all its heavier particles—except, doubtless, its gold—becomes exhaled into a sound, which forthwith steals into the ever-open ear of the community. These ingenious methods constitute a sort of machinery, by which thought and study are done to every person's hand, without his putting himself to the slightest inconvenience in the matter. There is another species of machine for the wholesale manufacture of individual morality. This excellent result is effected by societies for all manner of virtuous purposes; with which a man has merely to connect himself, throwing, as it were, his quota of virtue into the common stock; and the president and directors will take care that the aggregate amount be well applied. All these, and other wonderful improvements in ethics, religion, and literature, being made plain to my comprehension, by the ingenious Mr. Smooth-it-away, inspired me with a vast admiration of Vanity Fair.

It would fill a volume, in an age of pamphlets, were I to record all my observations in this great capital of human business and pleasure. There was an unlimited range of society—the powerful, the wise, the witty, and the famous in every walk of life—princes, presidents, poets, generals, artists, actors, and philanthropists, all making their own market at the Fair, and deeming no price too exorbitant for such commodities as hit their fancy. It was well worth one's while, even if he had no idea of buying or selling, to loiter through the bazaars, and observe the various sorts of traffic that were going forward.

Some of the purchasers, I thought, made very foolish bargains. For instance, a young man having inherited a splendid fortune, laid out a considerable portion of it in the purchase of diseases, and finally spent all the rest for a heavy lot of repentance and a suit of rags. A very pretty girl bartered a heart as clear as crystal, and which seemed her most valuable possession, for another jewel of the same kind, but so worn and defaced as to be utterly worthless. In one shop, there a great many crowns of laurel and myrtle, which soldiers, authors, statesmen, and various other people, pressed eagerly to buy; some purchased these paltry wreaths with their lives; others by a toilsome servitude of years; and many sacrificed whatever was most valuable, yet finally slunk away without the crown. There was a sort of stock or scrip, called Conscience, which seemed to be in great demand, and would purchase almost anything. Indeed, few rich commodities were to be obtained without paying a heavy sum in this particular stock, and a man's business was seldom very lucrative, unless he knew precisely when and how to throw his hoard of Conscience into the market. Yet as this stock was the only thing of permanent value, whoever parted with it was sure to find himself a loser, in the long run. Several of the speculations were of a questionable character. Occasionally, a member of Congress recruited his pocket by the sale of his constituents; and I was assured that public officers have often sold their country at very moderate prices. Thousands sold their happiness for a whim. Gilded chains were in great demand, and purchased with almost any sacrifice. In truth, those who desired, according to the old adage, to sell anything valuable for a song, might find customers all over the Fair; and there were innumerable messes of pottage, piping hot, for such as chose to buy them with their birthrights. A few articles, however, could not be found genuine at Vanity Fair. If a customer wished to renew his stock of youth, the dealers offered him a set of false teeth and an auburn wig; if he demanded peace of mind, they recommended opium or a brandy-bottle.

Tracts of land and golden mansions, situate in the Celestial City, were often exchanged, at very disadvantageous rates, for a few years' lease of small, dismal, inconvenient tenements in Vanity Fair. Prince Beelzebub himself took great interest in this sort of traffic, and sometimes condescended to meddle with smaller matters. I once had the pleasure to see him bargaining with a miser for his soul, which, after much ingenious skirmishing on both sides, his Highness succeeded in obtaining at about the value of sixpence. The prince remarked, with a smile, that he was a loser by the transaction.

Day after day, as I walked the streets of Vanity, my manners and deportment became more and more like those of the inhabitants. The place began to seem like home; the idea of pursuing my travels to the Celestial City was almost obliterated from my mind. I was reminded of it, however, by the sight of the same pair of simple pilgrims at whom we had laughed so heartily, when Apollyon puffed smoke and steam into their faces, at the commencement of our journey. There they stood amid the densest bustle of Vanity—the dealers offering them their purple, and fine linen, and jewels; the men of wit and humor gibing at them; a pair of buxom ladies ogling them askance; while the benevolent Mr. Smooth-it-away whispered some of his wisdom at their elbows, and pointed to a newly-erected temple,—but there were these worthy simpletons, making the scene look wild and monstrous, merely by their sturdy repudiation of all part in its business or pleasures.

One of them—his name was Stick-to-the-right—perceived in my face, I suppose, a species of sympathy and almost admiration, which, to my own great surprise, I could not help feeling for this pragmatic couple. It prompted him to address me.

"Sir," inquired he, with a sad, yet mild and kindly voice, "do you call yourself a pilgrim?"

"Yes," I replied, "my right to that appellation is indubitable. I am merely a sojourner here in Vanity Fair, being bound to the Celestial City by the new railroad."

"Alas, friend," rejoined Mr. Stick-to-the-right, "I do assure you, and beseech you to receive the truth of my words, that that whole concern is a bubble. You may travel on it all your lifetime, were you to live thousands of years, and yet never get beyond the limits of Vanity Fair! Yea; though you should deem yourself entering the gates of the Blessed City, it will be nothing but a miserable delusion."

"The Lord of the Celestial City," began the other pilgrim, whose name was Mr. Foot-it-to-Heaven, "has refused, and will ever refuse, to grant an act of incorporation for this railroad; and unless that be obtained, no passenger can ever hope to enter his dominions. Wherefore, every man, who buys a ticket, must lay his account with losing the purchase-money—which is the value of his own soul."

"Poh, nonsense!" said Mr. Smooth-it-away, taking my arm and leading me off, "these fellows ought to be indicted for a libel. If the law stood as it once did in Vanity Fair, we should see them grinning through the iron bars of the prison window."

This incident made a considerable impression on my mind, and contributed with other circumstances to indispose me to a permanent residence in the city of Vanity; although, of course, I was not simple enough to give up my original plan of gliding along easily and commodiously by railroad. Still, I grew anxious to be gone. There was one strange thing that troubled me; amid the occupations or amusements of the fair, nothing was more common than for a person—whether at a feast, theatre, or church, or trafficking for wealth and honors, or whatever he might be doing, and however unseasonable the interruption—suddenly to vanish like a soap-bubble, and be never more seen of his fellows; and so accustomed were the latter to such little accidents, that they went on with their business, as quietly as if nothing had happened. But it was otherwise with me.

Finally, after a pretty long residence at the Fair, I resumed my journey towards the Celestial City, still with Mr. Smooth-it-away at my side. At a short distance beyond the suburbs of Vanity, we passed the ancient silver mine, of which Demas was the first discoverer, and which is now wrought to great advantage, supplying nearly all the coined currency of the world. A little further onward was the spot where Lot's wife had stood for ages, under the semblance of a pillar of salt. Curious travellers have long since carried it away piecemeal. Had all regrets been punished as rigorously as this poor dame's were, my yearning for the relinquished delights of Vanity Fair might have produced a similar change in my own corporeal substance, and left me a warning to future pilgrims. The next remarkable object was a large edifice, constructed of moss-grown stone, but in a modern and airy style of architecture. The engine came to a pause in its vicinity with the usual tremendous shriek.

"This was formerly the castle of the redoubted giant Despair," observed Mr. Smooth-it-away; "but, since his death, Mr. Flimsy-faith has repaired it, and now keeps an excellent house of entertainment here. It is one of our stopping-places."

"It seems but slightly put together," remarked I, looking at the frail, yet ponderous walls. "I do not envy Mr. Flimsy-faith his habitation. Some day it will thunder down upon the heads of the occupants."

"We shall escape, at all events," said Mr. Smooth-it-away; "for Apollyon is putting on the steam again."

The road now plunged into a gorge of the Delectable Mountains, and traversed the field where, in former ages, the blind men wandered and stumbled among the tombs. One of these ancient tomb-stones had been thrust across the track, by some malicious person, and gave the train of cars a terrible jolt. Far up the rugged side of a mountain, I perceived a rusty iron door, half overgrown with bushes and creeping plants, but with smoke issuing from its crevices.

"Is that," inquired I, "the very door in the hill-side, which the shepherds assured Christian was a by-way to Hell?"

"That was a joke on the part of the shepherds," said Mr. Smooth-it-away, with a smile. "It is neither more or less than the door of a cavern, which they use as a smoke-house for the preparation of mutton hams."

My recollections of the journey are now, for a little space, dim and confused, inasmuch as a singular drowsiness here overcame me, owing to the fact that we were passing over the enchanted ground, the air of which encourages a disposition to sleep. I awoke, however, as soon as we crossed the borders of the pleasant land of Beulah. All the passengers were rubbing their eyes, comparing watches, and congratulating one another on the prospect of arriving so seasonably at the journey's end. The sweet breezes of this happy clime came refreshingly to our nostrils; we beheld the glimmering gush of silver fountains, overhung by trees of beautiful foliage and delicious fruit, which were propagated by grafts from the celestial gardens. Once, as we dashed onward like a hurricane, there was a flutter of wings, and the bright appearance of an angel in the air, speeding forth on some heavenly mission. The engine now announced the close vicinity of the final Station House, by one last and horrible scream, in which there seemed to be distinguishable every kind of wailing and woe, and bitter fierceness of wrath, all mixed up with the wild laughter of a devil or a madman. Throughout our journey, at every stopping-place, Apollyon had exercised his ingenuity in screwing the most abominable sounds out of the whistle of the steam-engine; but in this closing effort he outdid himself, and created an infernal uproar, which, besides disturbing the peaceful inhabitants of Beulah, must have sent its discord even through the celestial gates.

While the horrid clamor was still ringing in our ears, we heard an exulting strain, as if a thousand instruments of music, with height, and depth, and sweetness in their tones, at once tender and triumphant, were struck in unison, to greet the approach of some illustrious hero, who had fought the good fight and won a glorious victory, and was come to lay aside his battered arms forever. Looking to ascertain what might be the occasion of this glad harmony, I perceived, on alighting from the cars, that a multitude of shining ones had assembled on the other side of the river, to welcome two poor pilgrims, who were just emerging from its depths. They were the same whom Apollyon and ourselves had persecuted with taunts and gibes, and scalding steam, at the commencement of our journey—the same whose unworldly aspect and impressive words had stirred my conscience, amid the wild revellers of Vanity Fair.

"How amazingly well those men have got on!" cried I to Mr. Smooth-it-away. "I wish we were secure of as good a reception."

"Never fear—never fear!" answered my friend. "Come—make haste; the ferry-boat will be off directly; and in three minutes you will be on the other side of the river. No doubt you will find coaches to carry you up to the city gates."

A steam ferry-boat, the last improvement on this important route, lay at the river side, puffing, snorting, and emitting all those other disagreeable utterances, which betoken the departure to be immediate. I hurried on board with the rest of the passengers, most of whom were in great perturbation; some bawling out for their baggage; some tearing their hair and exclaiming that the boat would explode or sink; some already pale with the heaving of the stream; some gazing affrighted at the ugly aspect of the steersman; and some still dizzy with the slumberous influences of the Enchanted Ground. Looking back to the shore, I was amazed to discern Mr. Smooth-it-away waving his hand in token of farewell!

"Don't you go over to the Celestial City!" exclaimed I.

"Oh, no!" answered he with a queer smile, and that same disagreeable contortion of visage which I had remarked in the inhabitants of the Dark Valley. "Oh, no! I have come thus far only for the sake of your pleasant company. Good bye! We shall meet again."

And then did my excellent friend, Mr. Smooth-it-away, laugh outright; in the midst of which cachinnation, a smoke-wreath issued from his mouth and nostrils, while a twinkle of lurid flame darted out of either eye, proving indubitably that his heart was all of a red blaze. The impudent fiend! To deny the existence of Tophet, when he felt its fiery tortures raging within his breast! I rushed to the side of the boat, intending to fling myself on shore. But the wheels, as they began their revolutions, threw a dash of spray over me, so cold—so deadly cold, with the chill that will never leave those waters, until Death be drowned in his own river—that, with a shiver and a heart-quake, I awoke. Thank heaven, it was a Dream!

CHARLES DICKENS

[The City of Eden]†

"Heyday!" cried Martin, as his eye rested on a great plan which occupied one whole side of the office. Indeed, the office had little else in it but some geological and botanical specimens, one or two rusty ledgers, a homely desk, and a stool. "Heyday! what's that?"

"That's Eden," said Scadder, picking his teeth with a sort of young bayonet that flew out of his knife when he touched a spring.

"Why, I had no idea it was a city."

"Hadn't you? Oh, it's a city."

A flourishing city too! An architectural city! There were banks, churches, cathedrals, market-places, factories, hotels, stores, mansions; wharfs; an exchange, a theatre; public buildings of all kinds, down to the office of the Eden Stinger, a daily journal; all faithfully depicted in the view before them.

"Dear me! It's really a most important place!" cried Martin, turning around.

"Oh! it's very important," observed the agent.

"But, I am afraid," said Martin, glancing again at the Public Buildings, "that there's nothing left for me to do."

"Well! it ain't all built," replied the agent. "Not quite."

This was a great relief.

---

† From *Martin Chuzzlewit* (New York, 1848), Chapter 21. Internal evidence shows that Melville used Dickens' novel (1843) in *Pierre*; Mrs. Metcalf (1953, p. 205) records a hilarious family anecdote that also testifies to Melville's knowledge of the novel during his years at Pittsfield.

"The market-place, now," said Martin. "Is that built?"

"That?" said the agent, sticking his toothpick into the weather-cock on the top. "Let me see. No: that ain't built."

"Rather a good job to begin with—eh, Mark?" whispered Martin, nudging him with his elbow.

Mark, who, with a very stolid countenance had been eyeing the plan and the agent by turns, merely rejoined "Uncommon!"

A dead silence ensued, Mr. Scadder in some short recesses or vacations of his toothpick, whistled a few bars of Yankee Doodle, and blew the dust off the roof of the Theatre.

"I suppose," said Martin, feigning to look more narrowly at the plan, but showing by his tremulous voice how much depended, in his mind, upon the answer; "I suppose there are—several architects there?"

"There ain't a single one," said Scadder.

"Mark," whispered Martin, pulling him by the sleeve, "do you hear that? But whose work is all this before us, then?" he asked aloud.

"The soil being very fruitful, public buildings grows spontaneous, perhaps," said Mark.

EGBERT S. OLIVER

Melville's Goneril and Fanny Kemble†

This character study in *The Confidence-Man* is indeed an interesting offshoot of Melville's robust genius. The character itself is worth contemplation; and the narrative episode in which this half-woman, half-devil is embodied is certainly not one of the less interesting parts of Melville's most unusual and least read book. However, the character Goneril takes on an added significance in being Melville's caricature of a widely known contemporary woman, the Shakespearean actress and dramatic reader, Fanny Kemble. Hence, Melville's use of the name *Goneril* had a double barb: it carried associations with Lear's violent and unfeminine daughter and it also related to the most widely discussed interpreter of Shakespeare's women of that generation.

Fanny Kemble was born into an English family of actors and actresses who had specialized in Shakespeare. When she went on

† From Egbert S. Oliver, "Melville's Goneril and Fanny Kemble," *New England Quarterly*, 18 (December, 1945), 489–500; the quotation is from 490–492. Reprinted by permission of the publisher and the author. This essay is also printed in Oliver's *Studies in American Literature* (New Delhi: Eurasia Publishing House, 1965).

the stage she captured London by storm. After several years of great popularity in England she acted in American theatres with equal success. She left the stage, however, to marry Pierce Butler, scion of an aristocratic, slave-owning Philadelphia family. Two daughters were born to the ill-matched couple, but domestic harmony never prevailed. As the perpetual family conflict quickened in intensity, the reasons for friction became more and more involved and far-reaching in scope, though they seemed largely to focus in quarrels over the two girls. Pierce Butler exercised his legal rights as a father to assume complete control of the children, even forbidding the daughters the privilege of speaking to their mother. Mrs. Butler returned to England and the stage, a result of the quarrels to which her husband bitterly objected. He did not want the wife of Pierce Butler to disgrace the family name by acting. He brought suit for divorce; his wife returned to America to contest the action. To provide for her livelihood during the litigation—so as not to be dependent upon her husband—, she began giving her tremendously popular Shakespearean readings.

Melville was in Boston for ten weeks early in 1849, where his wife, the daughter of Chief Justice Lemuel Shaw of the Massachusetts Supreme Court, had gone to give birth to their first child. Melville had ample time to read the newspapers, to absorb the gossip, and to attend Emerson's lectures and Mrs. Butler's readings. He did not entirely neglect his New York friends. Especially he kept in touch with Evert Duyckinck in chatty letters. "Mrs Butler too I have heard at her Readings," he wrote. "She makes a glorious Lady Macbeth, but her Desdemona seems like a boarding school miss.—She's so unfemininely masculine that had she not, on unimpeckable authority, borne children, I should be curious to learn the result of a surgical examination of her person in private. The Lord help Butler . . . I marvel not he seeks being amputated off from his matrimonial half."

This is Melville's earliest known comment on Pierce Butler's divorce trial. When he came to write his caustic caricature in The Confidence-Man seven years later, he had had ample opportunity to verify and extend his first impressions of Mrs. Butler. The various aspects of the divorce were sensational news in 1849. Mrs. Butler capitalized the notoriety with triumphant tours of readings. She made her home in Lenox, only about five miles from Arrowhead, near Pittsfield, where the Melvilles went to live in 1850. Thus Melville and the notorious lady were neighbors for the six years preceding the writing of The Confidence-Man, though much of this time Mrs. Butler was away on tour in the various states or in Europe. During the months of Melville's greatest intimacy with the Hawthornes at Lenox, Mrs. Butler was a visitor to the Haw-

thorne home on her horseback rides over the countryside.
At the very time Melville was at work on *The Confidence-Man,*
Mrs. Butler and her unfortunate domestic affairs were again recalled
to his mind. Pierce Butler had been granted custody of the two
daughters. In the spring of 1856, Sarah, the older daughter,
reached her majority and became free from the dominance of her
father. This daughter, just at her "coming out" age, and Fanny
Kemble—for thus, of course, she was known on the European
stage—fresh from the heady intoxicant of European theatrical
glory, met in Boston and went together to Lenox to plunge into an
active social whirl. Fanny Kemble's home in Lenox, "The Perch,"
became the gathering place for friends and admirers, young and
old. The robust, tireless Fanny organized games and dances in "her
own inimitable way," as one commentator observed. The newspapers made a great flurry of such society "copy."

JAMES HALL

Indian hating.—Some of the sources of this animosity.—Brief Account of Col. Moredock.†

The violent animosity which exists between the people of our
frontier and the Indians, has long been a subject of remark. In the
early periods of the hstory of our country, it was easily accounted
for, on the ground of mutual aggression. The whites were continually encroaching upon the aborigines, and the latter avenging their
wrongs by violent and sudden hostilities. The philanthropist is surprised, however, that such feelings should prevail now, when these
atrocious wars have ceased, and when no immediate cause of
enmity remains; at least upon our side. Yet the fact is, that the
dweller upon the frontier continues to regard the Indian with a
degree of terror and hatred, similar to that which he feels towards
the rattlesnake or panther, and which can neither be removed by
argument, nor appeased by any thing but the destruction of its
object.
In order to understand the cause and the operation of these feelings, it is necessary to recollect that the backwoodsmen are a peculiar race. We allude to the pioneers, who, keeping continually in
advance of civilization, precede the denser population of our country in its progress westward, and live always upon the frontier.
They are the descendants of a people whose habits were identically

† From James Hall, *Sketches of His-* (Philadelphia: Harrison Hall, 1835),
tory, Life, and Manners, in the West II, 74–82.

the same as their own. Their fathers were pioneers. A passion for hunting, and a love for sylvan sports, have induced them to recede continually before the tide of emigration, and have kept them a separate people, whose habits, prejudices, and modes of life have been transmitted from father to son with but little change. From generation to generation they have lived in contact with the Indians. The ancestor met the red men in battle upon the shores of the Atlantic, and his descendants have pursued the footsteps of the retreating tribes, from year to year, throughout a whole century, and from the eastern limits of our great continent to the wide prairies of the west.

America was settled in an age when certain rights, called those of *discovery* and *conquest*, were universally acknowledged; and when the possession of a country was readily conceded to the strongest. When more accurate notions of moral right began, with the spread of knowledge, and the dissemination of religious truth, to prevail in public opinion, and regulate the public acts of our government, the pioneers were but slightly affected by the wholesome contagion of such opinions. Novel precepts in morals were not apt to reach men who mingled so little with society in its more refined state, and who shunned the restraints, while they despised the luxuries of social life.

The pioneers, who thus dwelt ever upon the borders of the Indian hunting grounds, forming a barrier between savage and civilized men, have received but few accessions to their numbers by emigration. The great tide of emigration, as it rolls forward, beats upon them and rolls them onward, without either swallowing them up in its mass, or mingling its elements with theirs. They accumulate by natural increase; a few of them return occasionally to the bosom of society, but the great mass moves on.

It is not from a desire of conquest, or thirst of blood, or with any premeditated hostility against the savage, that the pioneer continues to follow him from forest to forest, ever disputing with him the right to the soil, and the privilege of hunting game. It is simply because he shuns a crowded population, delights to rove uncontroled in the woods, and does not believe that an Indian, or any other man has a right to monopolize the hunting grounds, which he considers free to all. When the Indian disputes the propriety of this invasion upon his ancient heritage, the white man feels himself injured, and stands, as the southern folks say, upon his reserved rights.

The history of the borders of England and Scotland, and of all dwellers upon frontiers, who come often into hostile collision, shows, that between such parties an intense hatred is created. It is national antipathy, with the addition of private feud and personal injury. The warfare is carried on by a few individuals, who become known to each other, and a few prominent actors on each side soon become distinguished for their prowess or ferocity. When a stage of public war ostensibly ceases, acts of violence continue to be perpetrated from motives of mere mischief, or for pillage or revenge.

Our pioneers have, as we have said, been born and reared on the frontier, and have, from generation to generation, by successive removals, remained in the same relative situation in respect to the Indians and to our own government. Every child thus reared, learns to hate an Indian, because he always hears him spoken of as an enemy. From the cradle, he listens continually to horrid tales of savage violence, and becomes familiar with narratives of aboriginal cunning and ferocity. Every family can number some of its members or relatives among the victims of a midnight massacre, or can tell of some acquaintance who has suffered a dreadful death at the stake. Traditions of horses stolen, and cattle driven off, and cabins burned, are numberless; are told with great minuteness, and listened to with intense interest. With persons thus reared, hatred towards an Indian becomes a part of their nature, and revenge an instinctive principle. Nor does the evil end here. Although the backwoodsmen, properly so called, retire before that tide of emigration which forms the more stationary population, and eventually fills the country with inhabitants, they usually remain for a time in contact with the first of those who, eventually, succeed them, and impress their own sentiments upon the latter. In the formation of each of the western territories and states, the backwoodsmen have, for a while, formed the majority of the population, and given the tone to public opinion.

If we attempt to reason on this subject, we must reason with a due regard to facts, and to the known principles of human nature. Is it to be wondered at, that a man should fear and detest an Indian, who has been always accustomed to hear him described only as a midnight prowler, watching to murder the mother as she bends over her helpless children, and tearing, with hellish malignity, the babe from the maternal breast? Is it strange, that he whose mother has fallen under the savage tomahawk, or whose father has died a lingering death at the stake, surrounded by yelling fiends in human shape, should indulge the passion of revenge towards the perpetrators of such atrocities? They know the story only as it was told to them. They have only heard one side, and that with all the exaggerations of fear, sorrow, indignation and resentment. They have heard it from the tongue of a father, or from the lips of a mother, or a sister, accompanied with all the particularity which the tale could receive from the vivid impressions of an eye-witness, and with all the eloquence of deeply awakened feeling. They have heard it perhaps at a time when the war-whoop still sounded in the distance, when the rifle still was kept in preparation, and the cabin door was carefully secured with each returning night.

Such are some of the feelings, and of the facts, which operate upon the inhabitants of our frontiers. The impressions which we have described are handed down from generation to generation, and remain in full force long after all danger from the savages has ceased, and all intercourse with them been discontinued.

Besides that general antipathy which pervades the whole community under such circumstances, there have been many instances of individuals who, in consequence of some personal wrong, have vowed eternal hatred to the whole Indian race, and have devoted nearly all of their lives to the fulfilment of a vast scheme of vengeance. A familiar instance is before us in the life of a gentleman, who was known to the writer of this article, and whose history we have often heard repeated by those who were intimately conversant with all the events. We allude to the late Colonel John Moredock, who was a member of the territorial legislature of Illinois, a distinguished militia officer, and a man universally known and respected by the early settlers of that region. We are surprised that the writer of a sketch of the early history of Illinois, which we published some months ago, should have omitted the name of this gentleman, and some others, who were famed for deeds of hardihood, while he has dwelt upon the actions of persons who were comparatively insignificant.

John Moredock was the son of a woman who was married several times, and was as often widowed by the tomahawk of the savage. Her husbands had been pioneers, and with them she had wandered from one territory to another, living always on the frontier. She was at last left a widow, at Vincennes, with a large family of children, and was induced to join a party about to remove to Illinois, to which region a few American families had then recently removed. On the eastern side of Illinois there were no settlements of whites; on the shore of the Mississippi a few spots were occupied by the French; and it was now that our own backwoodsmen began to turn their eyes to this delightful country, and determined to settle in the vicinity of the French villages. Mrs. Moredock and her friends embarked at Vincennes in boats, with the intention of descending the Wabash and Ohio rivers, and ascending the Mississippi. They proceeded in safety until they reached the Grand Tower on the Mississippi, where, owing to the difficulty of the navigation for ascending boats, it became necessary for the boatmen to land, and drag their vessels round a rocky point, which was swept by a violent current. Here a party of Indians, lying in wait, rushed upon them, and murdered the whole party. Mrs. Moredock was among the victims, and *all* her children, except John, who was proceeding with another party.

John Moredock was just entering upon the years of manhood, when he was thus left in a strange land, the sole survivor of his race. He resolved upon executing vengeance, and immediately took measures to discover the actual perpetrators of the massacre. It was ascertained that the outrage was committed by a party of twenty or thirty Indians, belonging to different tribes, who had formed themselves into a lawless predatory band. Moredock watched the motions of this band for more than a year, before an opportunity suitable for his purpose occurred. At length he learned, that they were hunting on the Missouri side of the river, nearly opposite to the recent settlements of the Americans. He raised a party of young men and pursued them; but that time they escaped. Shortly after, he sought them at the head of another party, and had the good fortune to discover them one evening, on an island, whither they had retired to encamp the more securely for the night. Moredock and his friends, about equal in numbers to the Indians, waited until the dead of night, and then landed upon the island, turning adrift their own canoes and those of the enemy, and determined to sacrifice their own lives, or to exterminate the savage band. They were completely successful. Three only of the Indians escaped, by throwing themselves into the river; the rest were slain, while the whites lost not a man.

But Moredock was not satisfied while one of the murderers of his mother remained. He had learned to recognise the names and persons of the three that had escaped, and these he pursued with secret, but untiring diligence, until they all fell by his own hand. Nor was he yet satisfied. He had now become a hunter and a warrior. He was a square-built, muscular man, of remarkable strength and activity. In athletic sports he had few equals; few men would willingly have encountered him in single combat. He was a man of determined courage, and great coolness and steadiness of purpose. He was expert in the use of the rifle and other weapons; and was complete master of those wonderful and numberless expedients by which the woodsman subsists in the forest, pursues the footsteps of an enemy with unerring sagacity, or conceals himself and his design from the discovery of a watchful foe. He had resolved never to spare an Indian, and though he made no boast of this determination, and seldom avowed it, it became the ruling passion of his life. He thought it praiseworthy to kill an Indian; and would roam through the forest silently and alone, for days and weeks, with this single purpose. A solitary red man, who was so unfortunate as to meet him in the woods, was sure to become his victim; if he encountered a party of the enemy, he would either secretly pursue their footsteps until an opportunity for striking a blow occurred, or, if discovered, would elude them by his superior skill. He died about four years ago, an old man, and it is supposed never in his life failed to embrace an opportunity to kill a savage.

The reader must not infer, from this description, that Colonel Moredock was unsocial, ferocious, or by nature cruel. On the contrary, he was a man of warm feelings, and excellent disposition. At home he was like other men, conducting a large farm with industry and success, and gaining the good will of all his neighbours by his popular manners and benevolent deportment. He was cheerful, convivial, and hospitable; and no man in the territory was more generally known, or more universally respected. He was an officer in the ranging service during the war of 1813–14, and acquitted himself with credit; and was afterwards elected to the command of the militia of his country, at a time when such an office was honourable, because it imposed responsibility, and required the exertion of military skill. Colonel Moredock was a member of the legislative council of the territory of Illinois, and at the formation of the state government, was spoken of as a candidate for the office of governor, but refused to permit his name to be used.

There are many cases to be found on the frontier, parallel to that just stated, in which individuals have persevered through life, in the indulgence of a resentment founded either on a personal wrong suffered by the party, or a hatred inherited through successive generations, and perhaps more frequently on a combination of these causes. In a fiction, written by the author, and founded on some of these facts, he has endeavoured to develope and illustrate this feeling through its various details.

MELVILLE AND THE TRANSCENDENTALISTS:

A Chronology

Melville's attitude toward individual Transcendentalists and Transcendentalism in general has been the cause of scholarly skirmishes and ambushes as well as occasional pitched battles. Some of the confusion arose because Egbert S. Oliver, who first demonstrated that Winsome and Egbert were portraits of Emerson and Thoreau, argued elsewhere—and much less persuasively—that "Bartleby" and "Cock-A-Doodle-Doo!" were both satires on Thoreau.[1] For an attempt to adjudicate, see, in the Bibli-

1. Besides Oliver (1946), in the Bibliography, see his "A Second Look at 'Bartleby,'" *College English*, 6 (May, 1945), 431–439; and "'Cock-A-Doodle-Doo!' and Transcendental Hocus-Pocus," *New England Quarterly*, 21 (June, 1948), 204–216. For valuable background on the kind of information Melville could have gained from Hawthorne, see Buford Jones, "'The Hall of Fantasy' and the Early Hawthorne-Thoreau Relationship," *Publications of the Modern Language Association*, 83 (October, 1968), 1429–1438—a model of contextual scholarship.

ography of this book, "Melville's Satire of Emerson and Thoreau: An Evaluation of the Evidence" (1970). The Chronology here is meant to be suggestive, not comprehensive. With his contacts in the New York publishing world, with the Boston social world, and with Concord through Hawthorne, Melville heard and read much about Emerson, Thoreau, and other Transcendentalists. Since two major items are from Jay Leyda's *The Melville Log*, the Chronology has been cast in the same format as the *Log*.

1847

CONCORD March 12. *Emerson writes to Evert A. Duyckinck, the editor of Wiley & Putnam's, asking him to consider "a book of extraordinary merit," Thoreau's "An* Excursion on the Concord & Merrimack Rivers." See *The Letters of Ralph Waldo Emerson,* ed. Ralph L. Rusk (New York: Columbia University Press, 1939), III, 384.

CONCORD May 28. *Thoreau writes to offer the manuscript to Duyckinck.* See *The Correspondence of Henry David Thoreau*, eds. Walter Harding and Carl Bode (New York: New York University Press, 1958), p. 181.

CONCORD July 3. *Thoreau sends the "Mss." to Duyckinck by express, asking Duyckinck to acknowledge receiving it. (Correspondence,* p. 184.)

CONCORD July 27. *Thoreau presses Duyckinck for an answer (and gets a negative one):*
It is a little more than three weeks since I returned my mss. sending a letter by mail at the same time for security, so I suppose that you have received it. If Messrs. Wiley & Putnam are not prepared to give their answer now, will you please inform me what further delay if any, is unavoidable, that I may determine whether I had not better carry it elsewhere—for time is of great consequence to me. (*Correspondence*, p. 184.)

NEW YORK July 31. *Melville, a former Wiley & Putnam author and now a friend of the editor, dines in the Astor House with Duyckinck.*

1848

NEW YORK October 31 or later. *In A* Fable for Critics (*New York: G. P. Putnam, 1848), p. 27 and pp. 29–30, James Russell Lowell characterizes Emerson and his imitators in a sensationally popular poem:*

> "But, to come back to Emerson, (whom, by the way,
> I believe we left waiting,)—his is, we may say,

A Greek head on right Yankee shoulders, whose range
Has Olympus for one pole, for t'other the Exchange;
He seems, to my thinking, (although I'm afraid
The comparison must, long ere this, have been made,)
A Plotinus-Montaigne, where the Egyptian's gold mist
And the Gascon's shrewd wit cheek-by-jowl co-exist * * *

"He has imitators in scores, who omit
No part of the man but his wisdom and wit,—
Who go carefully o'er the sky-blue of his brain,
And when he has skimmed it once, skim it again;
If at all they resemble him, you may be sure it is
Because their shoals mirror his mists and obscurities,
As a mud-puddle seems deep as heaven for a minute,
While a cloud that floats o'er is reflected within it.

"There comes [Channing],[1] for instance; to see him's rare sport,
Tread in Emerson's tracks with legs painfully short;
How he jumps, how he strains, and gets red in the face,
To keep step with the mystagogue's natural pace!
He follows as close as a stick to a rocket,
His fingers exploring the prophet's each pocket.
Fie, for shame, brother bard; with good fruit of your own,
Can't you let neighbor Emerson's orchards alone?
Besides, 'tis no use, you'll not find e'en a core,—
[Thoreau] has picked up all the windfalls before.["]

1849

BOSTON February 24. *Melville writes to Evert A. Duyckinck:*†
I have heard Emerson since I have been here. Say what they will,
he's a great man.

BOSTON March 3. *Melville writes again, defending himself from a
comment by the anti-Transcendental Duyckinck:*
Nay, I do not oscillate in Emerson's rainbow, but prefer rather to
hang myself in mine own halter than swing in any other man's
swing. Yet I think Emerson is more than a brilliant fellow. Be his
stuff begged, borrowed, or stolen, or of his own domestic manufac-

1. The bracketed names are supplied
from the manuscript. See Leon Howard, *Victorian Knight-Errant* (Berkeley: University of California Press,
1952), p. 262.
† This excerpt and the one following
are reprinted from the Duyckinck Collection, Manuscript Division, The New
York Public Library, Astor, Lenox and
Tilden Foundations, with the Library's
permission. The letters have been
published in *The Letters of Herman
Melville*, ed. Merrell R. Davis and
William H. Gilman (New Haven: Yale
University Press, 1960), pp. 77–80.
Three slight corrections have been
made from information generously supplied by Amy Puett.

ture he is an uncommon man. Swear he is a humbug—then is he
no common humbug. Lay it down that had not Sir Thomas
Browne lived, Emerson would not have mystified—I will answer,
that had not Old Zack's father begot him, Old Zack would never
have been the hero of Palo Alto. The truth is that we are all sons,
grandsons, or nephews or great-nephews of those who go before us.
No one is his own sire.—I was very agreeably disappointed in M^r
Emerson. I had heard of him as full of transcendentalisms, myths &
oracular gibberish; I had only glanced at a book of his once in Putnam's store—that was all I knew of him, till I heard him lecture.—To my surprise, I found him quite intelligible, tho' to say
truth, they told me that that night he was unusually plain.—Now,
there is a something about every man elevated above mediocrity,
which is, for the most part, instinctuly perceptible. This I see in
Mr Emerson. And, frankly, for the sake of the argument, let us call
him a fool;—then had I rather be a fool than a wise man.—I love
all men who *dive*.[1] Any fish can swim near the surface, but it takes
a great whale to go down stairs five miles or more; & if he dont
attain the bottom, why, all the lead in Galena can't fashion the
plumet that will. I'm not talking of Mr Emerson now—but of the
whole corps of thought-divers, that have been diving & coming up
again with blood-shot eyes since the world began.

I could readily see in Emerson, notwithstanding his merit, a
gaping flaw. It was, the insinuation, that had he lived in those days
when the world was made, he might have offered some valuable
suggestions. These men are all cracked right across the brow. And
never will the pullers-down be able to cope with the builders-up.
And this pulling down is easy enough—a keg of powder blew up
Block's Monument—but the man who applied the match, could
not, alone, build such a pile to save his soul from the shark-maw of
the Devil. But enough of this Plato who talks thro' his nose. To
one of your habits of thought, I confess that in my last, I seemed,
but only *seemed* irreverent. And do not think, my boy, that
because I, impulsively broke forth in jubillations over Shakespeare,
that, therefore, I am of the number of the *snobs* who burn their
tuns of rancid fat at his shrine. No, I would stand afar off & alone,
& burn some pure Palm oil, the product of some overtopping trunk.

—I would to God Shakespeare had lived later, & promenaded in
Broadway. Not that I might have had the pleasure of leaving my
card for him at the Astor, or made merry with him over a bowl of
the fine Duyckinck punch; but that the muzzle which all men wore

1. Heyward Ehrlich has pointed out
that Melville may have been paying a
compliment to his friend, since as the
New York-Dutch Duyckinck once
wrote to his brother, "Duyckinck
means *diving*,—that is to say seeking
the hidden pearls of truth—"; see "A
Note on Melville's 'Men Who *Dive*,'"
*Bulletin of the New York Public Li-
brary*, 69 (December, 1965), 661–664.
[*Editor's note.*]

on their souls in the Elizabethan day, might not have intercepted Shakspers full articulations. For I hold it a verity, that even Shakspeare, was not a frank man to the uttermost. And, indeed, who in this intolerant Universe is, or can be? But the Declaration of Independence makes a difference.—There, I have driven my horse so hard that I have made my inn before sundown.[2] I was going to say something more—It was this.—You complain that Emerson tho' a denizen of the land of gingerbread, is above munching a plain cake in company of jolly fellows, & swiging off his ale like you & me. Ah, my dear sir, that's his misfortune, not his fault. His belly, sir, is in his chest, & his brains descend down into his neck, & offers an obstacle to a draught of ale or a mouthful of cake. But here I am. Good bye— H. M.

NEW YORK September 22. *Duyckinck prints a two-page review of* Week *in the* Literary World. *For the most part he is kind to the book he had refused to publish, but he concludes with a complaint:*
The author, we perceive, announces another book, "Walden, or Life in the Woods." We are not so rash or uninformed in the ways of the world as to presume to give counsel to a transcendentalist, so we offer no advice; but we may remark as a curious matter of speculation to be solved in the future—the probability or improbability of Mr. Thoreau's ever approaching nearer to the common sense or common wisdom of mankind. He deprecates churches and preachers. Will he allow us to uphold them? or does he belong to the family of Malvolios, whose conceit was so engrossing that it threatened to deprive the world of cakes and ale. "Dost thou think that because thou readest Confucius and art a Confusion there shall be no more steeples and towers? Aye, and bells shall ring too and Bishops shall dine!"

1850

NEW YORK Spring or Summer? *Melville borrows* "Thoreaus Merrimack" *from Duyckinck, and—as Oliver argues—very possibly reads the following passages from* "Wednesday":
If one abates a little the price of his wood, or gives a neighbor his vote at town-meeting, or a barrel of apples, or lends him his wagon frequently, it is esteemed a rare instance of Friendship. . . . Most contemplate only what would be the accidental and trifling advantages of Friendship, as that the Friend can assist in time of need, by his substance, or his influence, or his counsel; but he who foresees such advantages in this relation proves himself blind to its real advantage, or indeed wholly inexperienced in the

2. Davis and Gilman point out that "Melville saw that he was approaching the end of the page and in order to make his final comments tightened the spacing."

relation itself. Such services are particular and menial, compared
with the perpetual and all-embracing service which it is. . . . We do
not wish for Friends to feed and clothe our bodies,—neighbors are
kind enough for that,—but to do the like office to our spirits. . . .

Friendship is, at any rate, a relation of perfect equality. It cannot
well spare any outward sign of equal obligation and advantage.

Nothing is so difficult as to help a Friend in matters which do
not require the aid of Friendship, but only a cheap and trivial service. . . .

NEW YORK *July or before. Melville reads* The Scarlet Letter, *and
presumably reads this passage in the introductory "Custom House"
essay:*

After my fellowship of toil and impracticable schemes, with the
dreamy brethren of Brook Farm; after living for three years within
the subtile influence of an intellect like Emerson's; after those wild,
free days on the Assabeth, indulging fantastic speculations beside
our fire of fallen boughs, with Ellery Channing; after talking with
Thoreau about pine-trees and Indian relics, in his hermitage at
Walden; after growing fastidious by sympathy with the classic
refinement of Hillard's culture; after becoming imbued with poetic
sentiment at Longfellow's hearth-stone;—it was time, at length,
that I should exercise other faculties of my nature, and nourish
myself with food for which I had hitherto had little appetite. Even
the old Inspector was desirable, as a change of diet, to a man who
had known Alcott.

PITTSFIELD *Late July or early August. Melville reads Hawthorne's
introduction to* Mosses from an Old Manse (*New York: Wiley and
Putnam, 1846*), *in which these passages occur:*

In furtherance of my design, and as if to leave me no pretext for
not fulfilling it, there was, in the rear of the house, the most
delightful little nook of a study that ever offered its snug seclusion
to a scholar. It was here that Emerson wrote "Nature;" for he was
then an inhabitant of the Manse, and used to watch the Assyrian
dawn and Paphian sunset and moonrise, from the summit of our
eastern hill. . . .

The site is identified by the spear and arrow-heads, the chisels,
and other implements of war, labor, and the chase, which the
plough turns up from the soil. You see a splinter of stone, half
hidden between a sod; it looks like nothing worthy of note; but, if
you have faith enough to pick it up, behold a relic! Thoreau, who
has a strange faculty of finding what the Indians have left behind
them, first set me on the search; and I afterwards enriched myself
with some very perfect specimens, so rudely wrought that it seemed
almost as if chance had fashioned them. . . .

The pond-lily grows abundantly along the margin; that delicious flower which, as Thoreau tells me, opens its virgin bosom to the first sunlight, and perfects its being through the magic of that genial kiss. He has beheld beds of them unfolding in due succession, as the sunrise stole gradually from flower to flower; a sight not to be hoped for, unless when a poet adjusts his inward eye to a proper focus with the outward organ.

PITTSFIELD Late July or early August? *Although he does not mention it in his review of Hawthorne's Mosses in* The Literary World *(August 17 and 24), Melville presumably reads "The Celestial Railroad," an allegorical satire on aspects of American optimism and progressivism, including Transcendentalism.*

LENOX September 3–6. *Melville visits the Hawthornes at their cottage by Stockbridge Bowl, after they learn he was the anonymous author of the review in* The Literary World.†

He was very careful not to interrupt Mr Hawthorne's mornings—when he was here. He generally walked off somewhere—& one morning he shut himself into the boudoir & read Mr Emerson's Essays in presence of our beautiful picture. In the afternoon he walked with Mr Hawthorne. He told me he was naturally so silent a man that he was complained of a great deal on this account; but that he found himself talking to Mr Hawthorne to a great extent. He said Mr Hawthorne's great but hospitable silence drew him out—that it was astonishing how *sociable* his silence was. (This Mr Emerson used to feel) He said sometimes they would walk along without talking on either side, but that even then they seemed to be very social.—[Sophia Hawthorne to her sister Elizabeth Peabody; the picture was an engraving of the Transfiguration, a gift from Emerson.]

LENOX September 5 or 6. *In the Hawthornes' "boudoir" Melville reads Emerson's Essays, perhaps reacting hostilely to passages like these from "Friendship":*

Friendship may be said to require natures so rare and costly, each so well tempered and so happily adapted, and withal so circumstanced (for even in that particular, a poet says, love demands that the parties be altogether paired), that its satisfaction can very seldom be assured. It cannot subsist in its perfection, say some of those who are learned in this warm lore of the heart, betwixt more than two. I am not quite so strict in my terms, perhaps because I have never known so high a fellowship as others. I please my imagination more with a circle of godlike men and women variously

† This item is reprinted from Jay Leyda, *The Melville Log* (New York: Gordian Press, 1969), 925, by permission of the publisher.

related to each other and between whom subsists a lofty intelligence. But I find this law of *one to one* peremptory for conversation, which is the practice and consummation of friendship. . . .

Let us buy our entrance to this guild by a long probation. Why should we desecrate noble and beautiful souls by intruding on them? Why insist on rash personal relations with your friends? Why go to his house, or know his mother and brother and sisters? Why be visited by him at your own? Are these things material to our covenant? Leave this touching and clawing. Let him be to me a spirit. A message, a thought, a sincerity, a glance from him, I want, but not news, nor pottage. I can get politics and chat and neighborly conveniences from cheaper companions. Should not the society of my friend be to me poetic, pure, universal and great as nature itself?

1851

LENOX and PITTSFIELD October 1850–November, 1851. *While they are neighbors, Melville and Hawthorne visit each other several times. They talk metaphysics, but they also gossip. In his old age Melville tells Theodore F. Wolfe an anecdote about Hawthorne's and his daughter Una's several-day (not a week-long) visit to the Melvilles in March, 1851:*

. . . Melville was often at the little red house, where the children knew him as "Mr. Omoo," and less often Hawthorne came to chat with the racy romancer and philosopher by the great chimney. Once he was accompanied by little Una—"Onion" he sometimes called her—and remained a whole week. This visit—certainly unique in the life of the shy Hawthorne—was the topic when, not so long agone, we last looked upon the living face of Melville in his city home. March weather prevented walks abroad, so the pair spent most of the week in smoking and talking metaphysics in the barn,—Hawthorne usually lounging upon a carpenter's bench. When he was leaving, he jocosely declared he would write a report of their psychological discussions for publication in a volume to be called "A Week on a Work-Bench in a Barn," the title being a travesty upon that of Thoreau's then recent book, "A Week on Concord River," etc. (*Literary Shrines*, Philadelphia, 1895, pp. 190–191.)

1852

CONCORD December 2. *On a day when Thoreau was apparently in the village, Melville visits the Hawthornes.*

1854

NEW YORK October. *Thoreau's Walden receives a four-page, two-*

column-per-page review in the issue of Putnam's Monthly Magazine *which contains Chapter 13 of Melville's* Israel Potter. *The reviewer prints long excerpts from "Economy" and enough of "Solitude" to appall the author of the chapter of* Moby-Dick *called "The Castaway." In the passage quoted, Thoreau declares that he has* "never felt lonesome"; "Why should I feel lonely? Is not our planet in the Milky Way?"

1862†

NEW YORK March 22. M *acquires two volumes by Ralph Waldo Emerson:* Essays. First Series *(Boston, 1847), &* Essays: Second Series *(Boston, 1844). In the* First Series M *marks in Essay IV, "Spiritual Laws," p. 126:*

[Each man] inclines to do something which is easy to him, and good when it is done, but which no other man can do. He has no rival. For the more truly he consults his own powers, the more difference will his work exhibit from the work of any other.

M's comment: True

His ambition is exactly proportioned to his powers.

M's comment: False

& *on p 133:*

The good, compared to the evil which he sees, is as his own good to his own evil. X

M's comment: X A Perfectly good being, therefore, would see no evil.—But what did Christ see?—He saw what made him weep.—However, too, the "Philanthropist" must have been a very bad man—he saw, in jails, so much evil.

M appends additional comment: * To annihilate all this nonsense read the Sermon on the Mount, and consider what it implies.

In Essay VII, "Prudence," M marks on p. 215:

Trust men, and they will be true to you; treat them greatly, and they will show themselves great, though they make an exception in your favor to all their rules of trade. X

M's comment: X God help the poor fellow who squares his life according to this.

& *on p 216:*

The drover, the sailor, buffets it [the storm] all day, and his health renews itself as vigorous a pulse under the sleet, as under the sun of June. X

M's comment: X To one who has weathered Cape Horn as a common sailor what stuff all this is.

In the Second Series (mistakenly inscribed "March 22, 1861") M

† This entry is reprinted from Jay Leyda, *The Melville Log* (New York: Gordian Press, 1969), pp. 648–649, by permission of the publisher. The x's and asterisk are Melville's device for keying his marginalia to Emerson's text.

marks in Essay I, "The Poet," p 20:

Also, we use defects and deformities to a sacred purpose, so expressing our sense that the evils of the world are such only to the evil eye. X

M's comment: X What does the man mean? If Mr Emerson travelling in Egypt should find the plague-spot come out on him—would he consider that an evil sight or not? And if evil, would his eye be evil because it seemed evil to his eye, or rather to his sense using the eye for instrument?

& on p 24:

As the limestone of the continent consists of infinite masses of the shells of animalcules, so language is made up of images, or tropes, which now, in their secondary use, have long ceased to remind us of their poetic origin. But the poet names the thing because he sees it, or comes one step nearer to it than any other. X

M's comment: X This is admirable, as many other thoughts of Mr Emerson's are. His gross and astonishing errors & illusions spring from a self-conceit so intensely intellectual and calm that at first one hesitates to call it by its right name. Another species of Mr Emerson's errors, or rather, blindness, proceeds from a defect in the region of the heart.

& on p 30–31:

Hence a great number of such as were professionally expressors of Beauty, as painters, poets, musicians, and actors, have been more than others wont to lead a life of pleasure and indulgence; all but the few who received the true nectar; and, as it was an emancipation not into the heavens, but into the freedom of baser places, they were punished for that advantage they won, by a dissipation and deterioration.

M's comment: No, no, no.—Titan—did he deteriorate?—Byron?—Did he.—Mr E. is horribly narrow here. He has his Dardenelles for his every Marmora.—But he keeps nobly on, for all that!

BENJAMIN FRANKLIN

[Confidence] †

Trusting too much to others' care is the ruin of many; for *In the affairs of this world men are saved, not by faith, but by the want of*

† From "The Way to Wealth," *The Works of Benjamin Franklin*, II, ed. Jared Sparks (Philadelphia: Childs & Peterson, 1840), 97–98. Melville's interest in Franklin at this time is clear from *Israel Potter* (serialized in *Putnam's*, July, 1854, to March, 1855, then published in book form). Franklin is portrayed in Chapters 7–12, with elaborate speculation upon his character. In Chapter 9 Israel Potter reads some of Franklin's sly wisdom in a copy of "The Way to Wealth."

it; but a man's own care is profitable; for, *If you would have a faithful servant, and one that you like, serve yourself.*

P. T. BARNUM

[The Mystified Barber] †

I made arrangements with the captain of the splendid steamer Magnolia, of Louisville, to take our party as far as the junction of the Mississippi and Ohio rivers, stipulating for sufficient delay in Natchez, Miss., and in Memphis, Tenn., to give a concert in each place. It was no unusual thing for me to charter a steamboat or special train of cars for our party. With such an enterprise as that, time and comfort were paramount to money.

The time on board the steamer was whiled away in reading, viewing the scenery of the Mississippi, etc. One day we had a pleasant musical festival in the ladies' saloon for the gratification of the passengers, at which Jenny volunteered to sing *sans ceremonie.* It seemed to us she never sang so sweetly before.

For the amusement of the passengers I related many anecdotes picked up in my travels, and gave them some of my own experiences. I also performed a number of legerdemain tricks, which pleased and surprised them.[1] One of the tricks consisted in placing a quarter-dollar upon my knee, covering it with a card, and then causing it mysteriously to disappear.

I found after the second day that the mulatto barber declined taking my money, assigning as his only reason that I was welcome to his services. The truth, however, soon leaked out. He had been a looker-on, by stealth, and his superstitious notions invested me with the powers of a league with the devil.

The next morning I seated myself for the operation of shaving, and the colored gentleman ventured to dip into the mystery. "Beg pardon, Mr. Barnum, but I have heard a great deal about you, and

† From P. T. Barnum, *The Life of P. T. Barnum Written by Himself* (New York: Redfield, 1855), pp. 333–335. Melville's interest in Barnum is well documented. In the summer of 1847 he wrote for *Yankee Doodle* a series of clumsily satirical letters on the Mexican War which made much use of the name and the promotional methods of the great American showman. (The clumsiness owes something to the fact that as an anti-war Democrat Melville was in the untenable position, aesthetically speaking, of satirizing a Whig general, Zachary Taylor, who was prof-

iting politically from the Democratic imperialistic war.) There is no proof that Melville read these pages, but the running heads might have caught his eye: "UP THE MISSISSIPPI."—"THE MYSTIFIED BARBER."—"FRIGHTFUL TRANSFORMATION."
1. I had performed them in that western and southern country, many years before, under very different circumstances. Sickness or desertion on the part of my employees in that line, repeatedly put me to the necessity of substituting myself in the legerdemain business [Barnum's note].

I saw more than I wanted to see last night. Is it true that you have sold yourself to the devil, so that you can do what you've a mind to?"

"Oh, yes," was my reply, "that is the bargain between us."

"How long did you agree for?" was the question next in order.

"Only nine years," said I. "I have had three of them already. Before the other six are out, I shall find a way to nonplus the old gentleman—and I have told him so to his face."

At this avowal, a larger space of white than usual was seen in the darkey's eyes, and he inquired, "Is it by this bargain that you get so much money?"

"Certainly. No matter *who* has money, nor where he keeps it, in his box or till, or anywhere about him, I have only to speak the words, and it comes."

The shaving was completed in silence, but thought had been busy in the barber's mind, and he embraced the speediest opportunity to transfer his bag of coin to the iron safe in charge of the clerk.

The movement did not escape me, and immediately a joke was a-foot. I had barely time to make two or three details of arrangement with the clerk, and resume my seat in the cabin, ere the barber sought a second interview, bent on testing the alleged powers of Beelzebub's colleague.

"Beg pardon, Mr. Barnum, but where is my money? Can you get it?"

"I do not want your money," was the quiet answer. "It is safe."

"Yes, I know it is safe—ha! ha!—it is in the iron safe in the clerk's office—safe enough from *you!*"

"It is *not* in the iron safe," said I. This was said so quietly, yet positively, that the colored gentleman ran to the office; and inquired if all was safe. "All right," said the clerk. "Open, and let me see," replied the barber. The safe was unlocked—lo! the money was gone!

In mystified terror the loser applied to me for relief. "You will find the bag in your drawer," said I—and *there* it was found!

In all this I of course had a confederate, and also in a trick which immediately followed. "Now," said I, "hand me a cent. I will send it to his Infernal Highness, and bring it back forthwith." A cent was handed me—I tossed it into the air, and it disappeared!

"Where will you have it returned?"

"Under this shaving-cup," was the answer. The cup was turned—and lo! the cent was there! The barber lifted it from the table, and instantly dropped it. It was scorching hot! "The devil has had it. It is hot yet," said the barber. It was another cent which my confederate had heated and slyly placed there a moment before.

"And now," continued I, "I will turn you into a cat, and change you back again directly."

"You can't do *that*," said the barber, but evidently with some suspicion of his own judgment.

"You shall see," I replied, solemnly. "You run only one risk," I continued: "if any thing happens to me, by losing remembrance of his Majesty's pass-word, or any thing of the kind, you will remain a black cat for ever. Are you ready?"

The barber fled in consternation, and was so seriously troubled, that Captain Brown feared he would jump overboard. On being informed of this extremity of the joke, I explained the whole thing to the subject of my fun.

"By golly!" said the barber, in the exultation characteristic of his race, "by golly! when I get back to New-Orleans I'll come Barnum over de colored people. Ha! ha!"

Reviews

His publishers here announce 'The Confidence Man' a new volume which he left behind him—a fine playful subject for a humorist philosopher.

—Evert A. Duyckinck to his brother George, from New York, November 18, 1856

Elizabeth has gone to Pittsfield to set her house in readiness to receive her husband whom she expects sometime in May. A new book by Herman called "The Confidence Man" has recently been published. I have not yet read it; but have looked at it & dipped into it, & fear it belongs [to] that horribly uninteresting class of nonsensical books he is given to writing—where there are pages of crude theory & speculation to every line of narritive—& interspersed with strained & ineffectual attempts to be humorous. I wish he could or would do better, when he went away he was dispirited & ill—& this book was left completed in the publisher's hands.

—Elizabeth's half-brother, Lemuel Shaw, Jr., to his brother, Samuel Shaw, from Boston, April 21, 1857

Allan Melville has just this moment sent me Herman's 'Confidence Man.' It is a grand subject for a satirist like Voltaire or Swift—and being a kind of original American idea might be made to evolve a picture of our life and manners. We shall see what the sea dog philosophy of Typee makes of it.

—Evert A. Duyckinck to his brother George, from New York, March 31, 1857

Albany Evening Journal†

HERMAN MELVILLE's new book, "*The Confidence Man, His Masquerade,*" is published this week by Dix, Edwards & Co., and may be had here of Sprague & Co. It is like his other recent works, a story in which the incidents and characters are chosen with a view to convey a theoretic moral, not a vivid, graphic delineation based upon real life, like "Typee" and "Omoo." MR. MELVILLE is so much more successful in simple narrative than in apologue, that we cannot but regret that he should devote his time and genius to the latter rather than the former. His reputation, however, would ensure the sale of the book, even if its merits were much less than they are.

Philadelphia North American and United States Gazette‡

A sketchy affair, like other tales by the same author. Sly humor peeps out occasionally, though buried under quite too many words, and you read on and on, expecting something more than you ever find, to be choked off at the end of the book like the audience of a Turkish story teller, without getting the end of the story.

New York Dispatch*

When we meet with a book written by Herman Melville, the fascinations of "Omoo" and "Typee" recur to us, and we take up the work with as much confidence in its worth, as we should feel in the possession of a checque drawn by a well-known capitalist So much greater is the disappointment, therefore, when we find the book does not come up to our mark. Mr. Melville cannot write badly, it is true, but he appears to have adopted a quaint, unnatural style, of late, which has little of the sparkling vigor and freshness of his early works. In fact we close this book—finding nothing concluded, and wondering what on earth the author has been driving at. It has all the faults of style peculiar to "Mardi," without the romance which attaches itself to that strange book. The Confidence

† *Albany Evening Journal* (April 2, 1857).
‡ *Philadelphia North American and*
United States Gazette (April 4, 1857).
* *New York Dispatch* (April 5, 1857).

Man goes on board a Mississippi steamboat and assumes such a variety of disguises, with an astonishing rapidity, that no person could assume without detection, and gets into the confidence of his fellow-passengers in such a manner as would tend to show that the passengers of a Mississisppi steamboat are the most gullible people in the world, and the most ready to part with their money. A deaf mute; a deformed negro; a Herb Doctor; a Secretary of a coal-mining company; a Collector for an Indian Charity, and a sort of crazy cosmopolitan philanthropist, are among the disguises he assumes; though why he appears in the character of a deaf and dumb man, we are unable to divine, unless to prepare the expected dupes for his extortions, and to exhort them to charity, by means of moral sentences written on a slate and held up to view; and what is intended by the rigmarole of the cosmopolitan, we find it impossible to surmise, being left quite in the dark, with the simple information that "something further may follow of this masquerade." In the last number of Putnam's Magazine, there is an article on authors, in which the genius of Melville is duly acknowledged, and his faults frankly spoken of. We noticed the article on the receipt of the Magazine. If he has not read it, Mr. Melville should read, and try to profit by it. It is not right—it is trespassing too much upon the patience and forebearance of the public, when a writer possessing Herman Melville's talent, publishes such puerilities as the Confidence Man. The book will sell, of course, because Melville wrote it; but this exceedingly talented author must beware or he will tire out the patience of his readers.

Boston Evening Transcript†

One of the indigenous characters who has figured long in our journals, courts, and cities, is "the Confidence Man;" his doings form one of the staples of villainy, and an element in the romance of roguery. Countless are the dodges attributed to this ubiquitous personage, and his adventures would equal those of Jonathan Wild. It is not to be wondered at, therefore, that the subject caught the fancy of Herman Melville—an author who deals equally well in the material description and the metaphysical insight of human life. He has added by his "Confidence Man" to the number of original subjects—an achievement for the modern *raconteur*, who has to glean in a field so often harvested. The plan and treatment are alike Melvillish; and the story more popularly eliminated [delineated?] than is usual with the author. "The Confidence

---

† *Boston Evening Transcript* (April 10, 1857). *"Knick."* indicates that this is a contribution from a New York correspondent, not that the review appeared in the *Knickerbocker Magazine*.

Man—His Masquerade"—is a taking title. Dix, Edwards & Co. have brought it out in their best style.—*Knick.*

Leader†

In this book, also,[1] philosophy is brought out of its cloisters into the living world; but the issue raised is more simple:—whether men are to be trusted or suspected? Mr. Melville has a manner wholly different from that of the anonymous writer who has produced "The Metaphysicians." He is less scholastic, and more sentimental; his style is not so severe; on the contrary, festoons of exuberant fancy decorate the discussion of abstract problems; the controversialists pause ever and anon while a vivid, natural Mississippi landscape is rapidly painted before the mind; the narrative is almost rhythmic, the talk is cordial, bright American touches are scattered over the perspective—the great steamboat deck, the river coasts, the groups belonging to various gradations of New-World life. In his Pacific stories Mr. Melville wrote as with an Indian pencil, steeping the entire relation in colours almost too brilliant for reality; his books were all stars, twinkles, flashes, vistas of green and crimson, diamond and crystal; he has now tempered himself, and studied the effect of neutral tints. He has also added satire to his repertory, and, as he uses it scrupulously, he uses it well. His fault is a disposition to discourse upon too large a scale, and to keep his typical characters too long in one attitude upon the stage. Lest we should seem to imply that the masquerade is dramatic in form, it is as well to describe its construction. It is a strangely diversified narration of events taking place during the voyage of a Mississippi river boat, a cosmopolitan philanthropist, the apostle of a doctrine, being the centre and inspiration of the whole. The charm of the book is owing to its originality and to its constant flow of descriptions, character-stretching [character-sketching?] and dialogue, deeply toned and skillfully contrasted.

Literary Gazette‡

We notice this book at length for much the same reason as Dr. Livingston describes his travels in Monomotapa, holding that its

† *The Leader* (London) (April 11, 1857).
1. Like *The Metaphysician*, which was reviewed just before *The Confidence-Man* as the first of "Three Works of Fiction," the third being D'Aubigné White's *Madaron*. [*Editor's note.*]
‡ *The Literary Gazette, and Journal of Archæology, Science, and Art* (London) (April 11, 1857).

perusal has constituted a feat which few will attempt, and fewer still accomplish. Those who, remembering the nature of the author's former performances, take it up in the expectation of encountering a wild and stirring fiction, will be tolerably sure to lay it down ere long with an uncomfortable sensation of dizziness in the head, and yet some such introduction under false pretences seems to afford it its only chance of being taken up at all. For who will meddle with a book professing to inculcate philosophical truths through the medium of nonsensical people talking nonsense —the best definition of its scope and character that a somewhat prolonged consideration has enabled us to suggest. A novel it is not, unless a novel means forty-five conversations held on board a steamer, conducted by personages who might pass for the errata of creation, and so far resembling the Dialogues of Plato as to be undoubted Greek to ordinary men. Looking at the substance of these colloquies, they cannot be pronounced altogether valueless; looking only at the form, they might well be esteemed the compositions of a March hare with a literary turn of mind. It is not till a lengthened perusal—a perusal more lengthened than many readers will be willing to accord—has familiarized us with the quaintness of the style, and until long domestication with the incomprehensible interlocutors has infected us with something of their own eccentricity, that our faculties, like the eyes of prisoners accustomed to the dark, become sufficiently acute to discern the golden grains which the author has made it his business to hide away from us.

It is due to Mr. Melville to say, that he is by no means unconscious of his own absurdities, which, in one of his comparatively lucid intervals, he attempts to justify and defend:—

> "But ere be given the rather grave story of Charlemont, a reply must in civility be made to a certain voice which methinks I hear, that in view of past chapters, and more particularly the last, where certain antics appear, exclaims: How unreal all this is! Who did ever dress or act like your cosmopolitan? And who, it might be returned, did ever dress or act like harlequin?
>
> * * *
>
> "If, then, something is to be pardoned to well-meant endeavour, surely a little is to be allowed to that writer who, in all his scenes, does but seek to minister to what, as he understands it, is the implied wish of the more indulgent lovers of entertainment, before whom harlequin can never appear in a coat too particoloured, or cut capers too fantastic." [157.20–158.16]

This is ingenious, but it begs the question. We do, as Mr. Melville says, desire to see nature "unfettered, exhilarated," in fiction [but] we do *not* want to see her "transformed." We are glad to see

the novelist create imaginary scenes and persons, nay, even characters whose type is not to be found in nature. But we demand that,
in so doing, he should observe certain ill-defined but sufficiently
understood rules of probability. His fictitious creatures must be
such as Nature might herself have made, supposing their being to
have entered into her design. We must have fitness of organs, sym-
metry of proportions, no impossibilities, no monstrosities. As to
harlequin, we think it very possible indeed that his coat may be too
parti-coloured, and his capers too fantastic, and conceive, moreover,
that Mr. Melville's present production supplies an unanswerable
proof of the truth of both positions. We should be sorry, in saying
this, to be confounded with the cold unimaginative critics, who
could see nothing but extravagance in some of our author's earlier
fictions—in the first volume of 'Mardi,' that archipelago of lovely
descriptions is led in glittering reaches of vivid nautical narrative—the conception of 'The Whale,' ghostly and grand as the
great grey sweep of the ridged and rolling sea.[1] But these wild
beauties were introduced to us with a congruity of outward accom-
paniment lacking here. The isles of 'Mardi' were in Polynesia, not
off the United States. Captain Ahab did not chase Moby Dick in a
Mississippi steamboat. If the language was extraordinary, the speakers were extraordinary too. If we had extravaganzas like the following outpouring on the subject of port wine, at least they were not
put into the mouths of Yankee cabin passengers:—

> "A shade passed over the cosmopolitan. After a few minutes'
> down-cast musing, he lifted his eyes and said: 'I have long
> thought, my dear Charlie, that the spirit in which wine is
> regarded by too many in these days is one of the most painful
> examples of want of confidence. * * *
>
> * * * But if wine be false, while men are true, whither shall fly
> convivial geniality? To think of sincerely genial souls drinking
> each other's health at unawares in perfidious and murderous
> drugs!' " [139.40–140.19]

The best of it is, that this belauded beverage is all the time what
one of the speakers afterwards calls "elixir of logwood."

This is not much better than Tilburina in white satin, yet such
passages form the staple of the book. It is, of course, very possible
that there may be method in all this madness, and that the author
may have a plan, which must needs be a very deep one indeed. Certainly we can obtain no inkling of it. It may be that he has chosen
to act the part of a mediaeval jester, conveying weighty truths
under a semblance antic and ludicrous; if so, we can only recommend him for the future not to jingle his bells so loud. There is no

1. This sentence seems defective. [*Editor's note.*]

catching the accents of wisdom amid all this clattering exuberance of folly. Those who wish to teach should not begin by assuming a mask so grotesque as to keep listeners on the laugh, or frighten them away. Whether Mr. Melville really does mean to teach anything is, we are aware, a matter of considerable uncertainty. To describe his book, one had need to be a Höllen-Breughel; to understand its purport, one should be something of a Sphinx. It may be a *bonâ fide* eulogy on the blessedness of reposing "confidence"—but we are not at all confident of this. Perhaps it is a hoax on the public—an emulation of Barnum. Perhaps the mild man in mourning, who goes about requesting everybody to put confidence in him, is an emblem of Mr. Melville himself, imploring toleration for three hundred and fifty-three pages of rambling, on the speculation of there being something to the purpose in the three hundred and fifty-fourth; which, by the way, there is not, unless the oracular announcement that "something further may follow of this masquerade," is to be regarded in that light. We are not denying that this tangled web of obscurity is shot with many a gleam of shrewd and subtle thought—that this caldron, so thick and slab with nonsense, often bursts into the bright, brief bubbles of fancy and wit. The greater the pity to see these good things so thrown away. The following scene, in the first chapter, for example, seems to us sufficiently graphic to raise expectations very indifferently justified by the sequel—

> "Pausing at this spot, the stranger so far succeeded in threading his way, as at last to plant himself just beside the placard, when, producing a small slate and tracing some words upon it, he held it up before him on a level with the placard, so that they who read the one might read the other. * * *
>
> * * *
>
> "Meanwhile, he with the slate continued moving slowly up and down, not without causing some stares to change into jeers, and some jeers into pushes, and some pushes into punches: when suddenly, in one of his turns, he was hailed from behind by two porters carrying a large trunk; but as the summons, though loud, was without effect, they accidentally or otherwise swung their burden against him, nearly overthrowing him; when, by a quick start, a peculiar inarticulate moan, and a pathetic telegraphing of his fingers, he involuntarily betrayed that he was not only dumb but also deaf." [2.7–3.42]

It will be seen that Mr. Melville can still write powerfully when it pleases him. Even when most wayward, he yet gives evidence of much latent genius, which, however, like latent heat, is of little use either to him or to us. We should wish to meet him again in his legitimate department, as the prose-poet of the ocean; if, however, he will persist in indoctrinating us with his views concerning the *vrai*, we trust he will at least condescend to pay, for the future, some slight attention to the *vraisemblable*. He has ruined this book, as he did 'Pierre,' by a strained effort after excessive originality. When will he discover that—

"Standing on the head makes not
Either for ease or dignity?"

New York Day Book†

We remember the quaint, curious story of "Typee," and how puzzled and interested we were over its pages. We do not think Mr. Melville has greatly improved, or else we have lost an interest in his rather queer way of telling a story. The present one, however, is a clever delineation of western characteristics, and will please many readers. Without being really a great or philosophical novelist, Mr. M. gives us pleasant delineations of nature, and a considerable insight into the springs of human action.

Burlington Free Press‡

The story of the chap who managed to diddle many out of their property lamenting their want of confidence in him till they were willing to prove its reality by trusting him with a watch, a gold pencil case or a five dollar bill, never to be seen again by their owners, has furnished the hint on which the volume is made up. In a jingle of traveller's incidents and stories, the confidence man and his dupes are presented under a great variety of masks. The reader finds himself amused with some of the presentations; but as a whole he will be apt to think there is rather too much of it. The world is not made up of cheats and their victims. The book will not add to the reputation of the author of "Omoo" and "Typee." For sale at Nichol's.

London Illustrated Times*

We can make nothing of this masquerade, which, indeed, savours very much of a mystification. We began the book at the beginning, and, after reading ten or twelve chapters, some of which

† *New York Day Book* (April 17, 1857).
‡ *Burlington* (Vermont) *Free Press,* April 25, 1857.
* *London Illustrated Times* (April 25, 1857).

contained scenes of admirable dramatic power, while others presented pages of the most vivid description, found, in spite of all this, that we had not yet obtained the slightest clue to the meaning (in case there should happen to be any) of the work before us. This novel, comedy, collection of dialogues, repertory of anecdotes, or whatever it is, opens (and opens brilliantly, too) on the deck of a Mississippi steamer. It appeared an excellent idea to lay the opening of a fiction (for the work is a fiction, at all events) on the deck of a Mississippi steamer. The advantage of selecting a steamer, and above all a Mississippi steamer, for such a purpose, is evident: you can have all your characters present in the vessel, and several of your scenes taking place in different parts of the vessel, if necessary, at the same time; by which means you exhibit a certain variety in your otherwise tedious uniformity. For an opening, the Mississippi steamer is excellent; and we had read at least eight chapters of the work, which opens so excellently, before we were at all struck with the desirability of going ashore. But after the tenth chapter, the steamer began to be rather too much for us; and with the twelfth we experienced symptoms of a feeling slightly resembling nausea. Besides this, we were really getting anxious to know whether there was a story to the book; and, if the contrary should be the case, whether the characters were intended—as seemed probable—not for actual living beings, but for philosophical abstractions, such as might be introduced with more propriety, or with less impropriety, floating about in the atmosphere of the planet Sirius, than on the deck and in the cabin of a Mississippi steamer, drinking, smoking, gambling, and talking about "confidence." Having turned to the last chapter, after the manner of the professed students of novels from the circulating library, we convinced ourselves that, if there was almost no beginning to the story, there was altogether no end to it. Indeed, if the negative of "all's well that ends well" be true, the "Confidence-man" is certainly a very bad book.

After reading the work forwards for twelve chapters and backwards for five, we attacked it in the middle, gnawing at it like Rabelais's dog at the bone, in the hope of extracting something from it at last. But the book is without form and void. We cannot continue the chaotic comparison and say, that "darkness is on the face thereof;" for, although a sad jumble, the book is nevertheless the jumble of a very clever man, and of one who proves himself to be such even in the jumble of which we are speaking.

As a last resource, we read the work from beginning to end; and the result was we liked it even less than before—for then we had at all events not *suffered* from it. Such a book might have been called "Imaginary Conversations," and the scene should be laid in Tartarus, Hades, Tophet, Purgatory, or at all events some place of which the manners, customs, and mode of speech are unknown to the living.

Perhaps, as we cannot make the reader acquainted with the whole plot or scheme of the work before us, he may expect us to tell him at least why it is called the "Confidence-Man." It is called the "Confidence-Man" because the principal character, type, spectre, or *ombre-chinoise* of the book, is always talking about confidence to the lesser characters, types, &c., with whom he is brought into contact. Sometimes the "Confidence-Man" succeeds in begging or borrowing money from his collocutors; at other times he ignominiously fails. But it is not always very evident why he fails, nor in the other cases is it an atom clearer why he succeeds. For the rest, no one can say whence the "Confidence-Man" comes, nor whither he is going.

The principal characters in the book are—

1. The "Confidence-Man" himself, whom, if we mistake not, is a melancholy individual attired in mourning, who distributes "Odes on Confidence" about the steamer, and talks on his favourite subject and with his favourite motive to everyone on board; but we dare not affirm positively that the "Confidence-Man" is identified with the man in mourning, and with the one who distributes "Odes on Confidence," or indeed with either—the character generally being deficient in substance and indistinct in outline.

2. A lame black man (we are sure there is a lame black man).

3. A misanthropic, unconfidential white man with a wooden leg, who denies with ferocity that the lame black man is lame.

4. A student who reads Tacitus, and takes shares in a coal company.

5. The President and Transfer Agent of the Rapids Coal Company, who declares his determination to transact no business aboard the steamer, and who transacts it accordingly.

6. A realist barber—who is moreover real—indeed almost the only real human being in the book, if we except, perhaps, the lame black man (for we still maintain he was lame in spite of the assertions of the white man with the wooden leg).

The description of the barber opening his shop on the deck of the steamer, hoisting his pole, and putting forth his label bearing the inscription "No trust!" is one of the best in the volume; and the scene in which he declines the suggestion of the "Confidence-Man" to the effect that he should shave on credit, one of the best scenes.

We should also mention an interesting conversation over a bottle of wine, in which one man receiving earnest assurances of friendship from another, ventures on the strength of it to apply for a loan, which is refused with insult—not a very novel situation, but in this case well written up to, and altogether excellently treated. Some of the stories introduced in the course of the work are interesting enough (that of Colonel John Murdock, the Indian-hater, for instance), and all are well told. The anecdotes, too, are highly amusing, especially the one narrated by the misanthrope regarding the "confidence-husband," as Mr. Melville might call him. A certain Frenchman from New Orleans being at the theatre, was so charmed with the character of a faithful wife, that he determined forthwith to get married. Accordingly, he married a beautiful girl from Tennessee, "who had at first attracted his attention by her liberal mould, and who was subsequently recommended to him, through her kin, for her equally liberal education and disposition. Though large, the praise proved not too much; for ere long rumour more than corroborated it—whispering that the lady was liberal to a fault. But though various circumstances, which by most persons would have been deemed all but conclusive, were duly recited to the old Frenchman by his friends, yet such was his confidence that not a syllable would he credit, till, chancing one night to return unexpectedly from a journey, upon entering his apartment, a stranger burst from the alcove. "Begar!" cried he; "now I *begin* to suspect."

In conclusion, the "Confidence-Man" contains a mass of anecdotes, stories, scenes, and sketches undigested, and, in our opinion, indigestible. The more voracious reader may, of course, find them acceptable; but we confess that we have not "stomach for them all." We said that the book belonged to no particular class, but we are almost justified in affirming that its *génre* is the *génre ennuyeux*. The author in his last line promises "something more of this masquerade." All we can say, in reply to the brilliant author of "Omoo" and "Typee" is, "the less the merrier."

Berkshire County Eagle†

"THE CONFIDENCE MAN"—by Herman Melville—is much praised in the English papers.—One[1] says of its picture of American society,—"The money-getting spirit which appears to pervade every class of men in the States, almost like a monomania, is vividly portrayed in this satire, together with the want of trust or honor, and the innumerable 'operations' or 'dodges' which it is certain to engender. We gladly hail the assistance of so powerful a satirist as Mr. Melville in attacking the most dangerous and debasing tendency of the age." We need not say to those who have read the book that as a picture of American society, it is *slightly* distorted.

† Lenox, Mass., *Berkshire County Eagle* (June 19, 1857).   1. *London Saturday Review* (May 23, 1857). [*Editor's note.*]

Cincinnati Enquirer†

Mr. Herman Melville has been well known for a dozen years past, both in this country and Europe, as the author of a number of tales, the most popular and best of which are stories of the sea, such as "Typee," "Omoo," and "Moby Dick." Of late years, Mr. M. has turned his attention to another species of composition more akin to the modern novel. "Pierre, or the Ambiguities," is an example of this; highly extravagant and unnatural, but original and interesting in its construction and characters. His last production, "The Confidence Man," is one of the dullest and most dismally monotonous books we remember to have read, and it has been our unavoidable misfortune to peruse, in the fulfillment of journalistic duty, a number of volumes through, which nothing but a sense of obligation would have sustained us. "Typee," one of, if not the first of his works, is the best, and "The Confidence Man" the last, decidedly the worst. So Mr. M.'s authorship is toward the nadir rather than the zenith, and he has been progressing in the form of an inverted climax.

† *Cincinnati Enquirer* (February 3, 1858), from the review of Melville's lectures on "Status in Rome." In the fourth sentence, "volumes through, which" should perhaps read "volumes, through which".

Criticism

"The Confidence Man" (1857), his last serious effort in prose fiction, does not seem to require criticism.
—Arthur Stedman in his Introduction to *Typee*, 1892

"My God, Movement, are you an authority on *The Confidence-Man* too?"
—Kiefer to Movement in Bernard Wolfe's
The Late Risers: Their Masquerade, 1954

CARL VAN VECHTEN

[The Great Transcendental Satire]†

Let us remember Melville's struggle for faith and the apparent collapse of his career as we approach "The Confidence Man," his last work in prose, save, perhaps, some fugitive magazine pieces and a privately printed book or two. It is not a novel, nor is it, as Frank Mather Jewett ingenuously suggests, a series of "middle-western sketches." Melville simply carried Brook Farm to the deck of a Mississippi steamboat as in "Mardi" he had carried Europe to the South Seas. Emerson is the confidence man, Emerson who preached being good, not doing good, behaviour rather than service. Why no one has heretofore recognized Melville's purpose in writing this book is a fact I cannot profess to understand. Perhaps some one has, but I can find no record of the discovery. Probably dozens of critics have been influenced by the misleading comments of their forebears into not reading the book at all. At any rate, here Melville has his revenge on those who accused him earlier in his career of transcendental leanings. This is the great transcendental satire. The work assumes the form of a series of dialogues, somewhat after the manner of W. H. Mallock's "The New Republic," ironic dialogues between the representatives of theory and practice, transcendentalism and reality, with the devil's advocate winning the victory. Emerson's fatuous essay on Friendship is required preparatory reading for this book. "If a drunkard in a sober fit is the dullest of mortals, an enthusiast in a reason-fit is not the most lively," is a good summing up of Ralph Waldo's "lofty and enthralling circus." Hawthorne may have been secretly pleased with this book, if he understood it, because Emerson confessedly had never been able to finish a book by the good Nathaniel. A recent commentator, H. M. Tomlinson, is content to say of it, in an otherwise glowing account of the genius of its creator. " 'The Confidence Man' is almost unreadable." I wonder if he cannot read the book with eager interest now that I have thrown this light upon it?

† From Carl Van Vechten, "The Later Work of Herman Melville," *The Double Dealer*, 3 (January, 1922); the quotation is from p. 19. Reprinted by permission of the Estate of Carl Van Vechten.

JAY LEYDA

[Melville's Allegorizing] †

Even the clearest symbols in these stories—and the example of process given[1] is the most explicit of these—are worked out neither as neatly nor with the well-oiled stage machinery that his immediate master in allegory sometimes displays. Taking the liberties of a poet whose special, perhaps unconscious mission is concealment, Melville's symbols slip away and elude one's keys. His most effective camouflage was also always his greatest artistic necessity—reality, the palpability with which all the greatest symbols continue to breathe beyond their year of publication. For him, as for Montaigne, "the Magazin of Memorie is peradventure more stored with matter, than is the store-house of Invention." As the Melville symbol is usually embedded in situation, the most tangible elements are elsewhere, in character and atmosphere: the reality and poverty of the Merrymusks and the Coulters, the pathos of the uncle in "The Happy Failure," and of Jimmy Rose. The intricate construction of "The Tartarus of Maids" had to be compounded of substance and the materiality of outer observation—and the machines and employees of the paper-mill he describes for his purposes were seen by him on his paper-buying excursions to Carson's "Old Red Mill" in Dalton, a sleigh-trip from Pittsfield.

Was this materiality employed as an aid or as a hindrance to the real meaning of these stories? Though some degree of communication is present in each artistic work (else the work would not have been brought into existence) much of these stories' materiality seems a minutely painted and deceptive screen erected across what is *really* taking place behind it—in Melville's mind. We are compelled to regard these stories as an artist's resolution of that constant contradiction—between the desperate need to communicate and the fear of revealing too much. In these stories the contradiction is expressed on various levels of tension—the fiercer the pull, the higher the accomplishment. There is also a level, closer to the surface, of *game*, for in "The Tartarus of Maids" Melville gives one the impression of seeing how close he can dance to the edge of nineteenth century sanctities without being caught. In this story the very audacity of the physiological symbolism was the author's

† From "An Introduction," in *The Complete Stories of Herman Melville* (New York: Random House, 1949), pp. xxvii–xxix. Reprinted by permission of the publisher.

1. Leyda refers to his account of "the whole compositional fusion of reality and symbol, subject and target" in Melville's "The Lightning-Rod Man." [*Editor's note.*]

best protection against discovery; the keenest of contemporary readers (with the possibly sole exception of his friend, Dr. Augustus Kinsley Gardner, the gynecologist) would not have dared admit to himself that anyone had been so bold in *Harper's* pages; the perceptive reader must have blamed his own imagination for what he found in Tartarus—which may have been part of Melville's intent. *Pierre,* in failing, had taught Melville how to guard his most wounding blows. No reader was warned that beneath the "humorous, magazinish" surfaces of "I and My Chimney" and "The Apple-Tree Table" lay even more painful layers of Melville's greatest fears—the twisted mind and the threatening backdrop of evil—and that his laughter in these stories was mighty bitter. The contemporary reviewer on *The Criterion* thought "The Encantadas" a "series of charming descriptions."

Though just as dangerous a game for biographers, these stories and their attitudes tell almost more than we care to learn of the writer himself in a period of his greatest anguish. As Keats said of Robert Burns, "We can see horribly clear in the works of such a Man his whole life, as if we were God's spies."

SAMUEL WILLIS

Private Allegory and Public Allegory in Melville[†]

The psychological motives Jay Leyda gives for Melville's use of personal allegory in some stories of the mid-fifties may also apply to his use of allegory in parts of *The Confidence-Man.* Elizabeth S. Foster treats the whole of the book as if it were written (like some of the tales) in "a kind of double-talk, that seems intended rather to darken than to illuminate meanings," or in "a cipher," or in "double-writing," where "it is quite possible that he intended no one to glimpse his shadow story."[1] She draws no distinction between the allegorical method of a story like "I and My Chimney" (where if Merton M. Sealts, Jr., is right about its dealing with his examination for insanity, Melville could hardly have wanted anyone to understand the meaning) and the method of *The Confidence-Man* (where, as John W. Shroeder shows, the meaning is revealed in precisely the way the meaning of "The Celestial Railroad" is and therefore should have been accessible to anyone who had understood the Hawthorne story). "The Celestial Railroad" and *The Confidence-Man* seem to differ not in allegorical method, for the

† Published here for the first time, by permission of the author.
1. Elizabeth S. Foster, Introduction to *The Confidence-Man* (New York: Hendricks House, 1954), pp. xvii–xix.

most part, but in degree of stylistic complexity. Unless one is prepared to call "The Celestial Railroad" a companion example of secret writing, it seems best to hold that only rarely does *The Confidence-Man* contain anything like the contorted personal allegory which scholars have found in several of the tales written just before it. If there is, say, any personal satire on Judge Hall based on information received from Evert A. Duyckinck, who had corresponded with Hall, then *that* is private writing; but the "Devil-in-disguise" allegory is public and conventional. One might even speculate that the passages of *The Confidence-Man* which seem most likely to contain personal allegory are among the earliest parts composed, perhaps leftovers a year or two old which Melville incorporated into his manuscript. Melville undoubtedly expected to deceive "the superficial skimmer of pages" (as he wrote of Hawthorne in "Hawthorne and His Mosses"), but he must have expected good readers, including Hawthorne himself, to understand the book.

LEON HOWARD

The Quest for Confidence†

I

While Melville was getting better physically and looking around for a new literary inspiration, he attended what the *Berkshire County Eagle* called "a startling novelty in this region"—a "fancy dress picnic" at which Lizzie carried off the honors in the character of "Cypherina Do-nothing" dressed in a costume of cyphers. As a convalescent from a "severe illness," he was merely an onlooker at the festivities, but Malcolm went dressed as Jack the Giant Killer, Augusta as a market woman of olden times, Mrs. Morewood as an old lady, Mrs. Ellen Brittain as a squaw, and J. E. A. Smith as a gray friar. Most of his local friends were there, and it was perhaps while engaged in the "sad business" of "holding out against a good time" that he began to meditate the conceit that "life is a picnic *en costume*" in which "one must take a part, assume a character, stand ready in a sensible way to play the fool." He had Shakespeare's authority for the notion that all the world was a stage on which one man in his time plays many parts, and he himself was of a mind to play the melancholy Jaques. He knew that to come to life's picnic "with a long face, as a wiseacre, only makes one a dis-

† From Leon Howard, *Herman Melville: A Biography* (Berkeley and Los Angeles: University of California Press, 1951), pp. 226–237. Reprinted by permission of The Regents of the University of California.

comfort to himself, and a blot upon the scene." But he had a desire to take the wind's liberty to blow on whom he pleased, speak his mind, anatomize the wise man's folly, and cleanse the foul body of the infected world if it would but patiently receive his medicine. From the union of this conceit and this desire was to come his next book. But before he began to write it he told another story of pride going before a fall which appeared as "Jimmy Rose" in *Harper's* for November, 1855, and related how a wealthy gentleman lost his fortune, retired from the world in misanthropic obscurity for twenty-five years, and then returned to his old haunts as a pathetically and desperately cheerful cadger of free meals. He was well enough in mid-September to take his mother on "a few days jaunt" to Gansevoort and Albany, bringing home with him on the eighteenth a copy of *Don Quixote* which was not entirely unrelated to his literary intentions. During his absence Judge and Mrs. Shaw had been visiting Arrowhead, where the judge entertained himself by making Malcolm a kite and perhaps leaving it for Herman to fly. The autumn seems to have passed without any difficulties. The statement of his *Israel Potter* account, which was finally sent on October 8, showed that three editions of the book had been published and 2,577 copies had been sold by July 1, earning the author $193.27 in royalties—a figure which had to be corrected to $241.58, in view of the fact that he was to receive twelve and a half per cent instead of what appears to have been the more customary ten. Although he seems to have spent much of his time sitting on his piazza and reading, Melville was feeling "pretty well again." He was able to brave a day of howling wind and snow on October 24 to call on his cousin Priscilla (who had taken a room in the village the year before), and three days later he went to Gansevoort to help watch by the bed of his uncle Herman's wife, who died on October 29. His mother and sister Frances remained at Gansevoort to keep house for their brother and uncle, and Herman came back home for a late autumn of meditation and another winter of his customary labors at his desk.

As he sat on his northern piazza in clear weather, smoking his pipe, reading Shakespeare, and gazing off at the distant mountains, his thoughts evidently went back to another period of his life in which he had also felt helpless in the grip of circumstances—and which, incidentally, was the only period he had not yet exploited in his writings. For the scene of the book he planned was laid on the sort of Mississippi River steamer he had taken home after his fruitless trip to Galena, fifteen years earlier, and just before he had shipped to the Pacific on a whaler. A river boat, crowded with the variegated specimens of humanity who moved up and down the Mississippi, offered an admirable stage for the masquerade of life;

and the "operators" or swindling confidence men supplied him with a type of character who played many roles while exposing the wise man's folly. "What fools these mortals be!" was his theme, but he called his book *The Confidence Man*.

Melville's somber recollection of his ill-adventured youth, however, did not lead him into another enterprise as deliberately reckless as that of signing up for a whaling voyage. *The Confidence Man* was almost certainly designed for serialization in *Putnam's Monthly*, which was publishing "Benito Cereno" in the last three issues of the year and was to publish "I and My Chimney" in March. The magazine had printed in May, 1855, a story called "The Compensation Office" which was not unlike the book Melville planned. It had satirized the manipulator of stocks and had made the point that the lonely wife, the high-minded clergyman, the disgusted writer, and the sorrowful maiden deserved no compensation for their miseries, because their self-centeredness had made them what Melville would have called "fools of virtue." He was not planning to stultify any representatives of society more "sacred" than these, and the novel and picturesque surroundings in which he expected to place his satire probably made him think of it as being especially "magazinish."

Certainly he did not plan the book as a novel. Like "The Compensation Office," it was a story "without any end" which could be continued as long as the boat moved down the Mississippi and new disguises could be invented for the confidence man. The river, the confidence man, and the theme provided the only continuity which ran through the book; and in an early appearance of the central character, disguised as a crippled Negro beggar, Melville had him prophetically allude to more disguises than he ever actually used. As a serial, designed for a magazine which was interested in picturesque sketches with a meaning to them, it was admirably planned: the confidence man could appear periodically in a new disguise, swindle a new group of characters or some of the same ones over again, and each time demonstrate the foolishness of mankind which could be gulled by appeals to a variety of impulses ranging from greed to goodness. It presented a cynical and melancholy view of humanity, and one of the most interesting characters in it was a peg-legged fellow who vehemently insisted that "looks are one thing, and facts are another" while trying to make his fellow travelers see the evil reality beneath the confidence man's disguise. The ghost of the commander of the *Pequod* still existed in his creator's mind; but in this book, for the first half at least, Melville was his own Ahab and the peg-legged man soon disappeared from its pages.

For once again in a book not unified by the continuity of his own adventures Melville changed his course before he had finished the work he had planned. In his last masquerade, the confidence man became a talkative figure in motley, and he remained in that role for the entire second part of the book, never becoming the "ge'mman as is a sodger" which the crippled Negro had led the reader to anticipate. The satire, instead of being directed at the gullibility of mankind, was turned against men of little faith. A misanthrope was told that the "notion of being lone and lofty is a sad mistake": men, in this respect, were "like roosters; the one that betakes himself to a lone and lofty perch is the henpecked one, or the one that has the pip." A character called Charlie Noble, who volunteered friendship and praised the press of the vine, proved to be afraid of the bottle and suspicious at heart. An Emersonian transcendentalist was shown to be cold toward humanity, and his practical disciple, ingeniously reasoning against the obligations of friendship, demonstrated how easy it was to keep "one eye on the invisible" and "the other on the main chance." But a suspicious nature offered no greater protection than a gullible one: the barber, whose very motto was "No Trust," was bilked in the end; and the book concluded with the discovery that the Biblical authority for his suspicions was not in "the True Book," which he cited, but in the Apocrypha, and with a brief scene indicating how readily a good man could be made uneasy by suspicion.

Had Melville conceived of his book as a balanced satire, playing off the material dangers of gullibility against the spiritual dangers of mistrust, he might have achieved a comedy comparable in its emotional and dramatic values to the tragedy of *Moby Dick*. He approached the delicate balance of the comic point of view early in the second part of the book when he had Frank Goodman, his man in motley, suggest that a spurious vintage might be better than no wine at all and draw an "extravagant" parallel to the effect that the society of falsehearted men might be preferable to a lone security from the wicked. Near the end, he achieved it, momentarily at least, when he had Charlie Noble argue that "there is no bent of heart or turn of thought which any man holds by virtue of an unalterable nature or will." "Even those feelings and opinions deemed most identical with eternal right and truth," he explained, "it is not impossible but that as personal persuasions, they may in reality be but the result of some chance tip of Fate's elbow in throwing her dice." There is a higher and lighter comedy in the conception of men made fools by fate and varying their foolishness from day to day than there is in the representation of men victimized by deceit—just as there is higher comedy in Shakespeare's *As You Like It* than in Ben Jonson's *Volpone*. But Melville did not have this balance in mind when he began writing *The Confidence Man*, and he did not give it a calculated balance in structure. The change of course observable in the book is more nearly explicable in terms of the author's life than in terms of his art.

Melville's worries about his health decreased while he was writing the book. Images and remarks born of his own troubles abound in the first part—the moroseness of "a criminal judge with a mustard-plaster on his back," fancies about "an invalid's easy-chair," the prescription of tincture of iron for the restoration of "lost energy," expressions of irritation at being "a gallipot" for doctors to "rinse" their "experiments into," the observation that "when the body is prostrated, the mind is not erect," and allusion to "the inglorious lockjaw" of a character's arthritic "knee-pans," references to "a crick in the neck" and to servility as a "spinal complaint," and, above all, a preoccupation with cripples. These, together with his meditations on the shortcomings of hired boys, disappeared from the latter section of the story. The attitude of the long-faced wiseacre, standing apart from life's masquerade, faded as the author's nagging worries about his illness dropped out of his mind.

The quality of detachment which Melville achieved during the winter was probably acquired by a conscious effort which was reflected in his short stories and sketches. "Jimmy Rose," written no later than September, 1855, had been an unhappy picture of the loss of human dignity under the impact of misfortune. "The Piazza," probably written not long before February 16, 1856, when he sent it to Dix and Edwards as an introductory piece for his collection of magazine tales, was of an entirely different tone. In it, Melville told the story of an imaginary adventure in late autumn, after he had recovered from his illness. While sitting on his piazza, he had noticed a flash of light in the distant mountains which could only come from a newly glazed window in that supposedly uninhabited region. Seeking out what he thought would be a princess in this distant fairyland, he discovered a wood burner's sister whose lonely amusement was to look down across the valley and think of the "happy one" who lived in the "marble" house she could see in the distance. The deceptively white house was his own, but he could not show the poor girl the "happy being" who lived there. Yet, "for your sake, Marianna," he could imagine himself saying, I "well could wish that I were that happy one of the happy house you dream you see; for then you would behold him now, and, as you say, this weariness might leave you." The story was a parable of what Melville called, in The Confidence Man, "the mystery of human subjectivity"; and, without resolving the mystery, it showed that by the middle of winter Melville was sufficiently free from his self-centered broodings to imagine how different his situation might appear to another person.

Related to "Jimmy Rose" and "The Piazza" were most if not

all of the stories incorporated into *The Confidence Man*. The first, the "Story of the Unfortunate Man," told of a good husband who was turned into a poverty-stricken wanderer by the inhuman behavior of a wife named Goneril, was as "black" as Shakespeare's *King Lear*, which obviously suggested it. The second, dealing with "A Soldier of Fortune," was almost as dark in its implications concerning a social order which let a murderer go free while keeping a material witness in jail until his health was ruined and he was left a cripple. The third, a retelling of Judge James Hall's tale of Colonel John Moredock, the Indian hater, was introduced by a chapter on "the Metaphysics of Indian-hating" which tried to explain such misanthropic behavior in terms of the frontiersman's experience and education. The fourth, a "Story of the Gentleman-Madman," was a retelling of the story of Jimmy Rose, with the hero of the new version merely affecting a misanthropic attitude out of sensitivity while he actually preserved his courage, made a new fortune, and reassumed his place in society as though nothing had happened. The bitterness implicit in each successive story decreased, and of the separate tales found in *The Confidence Man* only the fifth and last, the "Story of China Aster," was out of harmony with its position in the book. The longest of the separate tales, it told of a poor young candlemaker who was ruined by accepting a loan from a generous friend who afterward joined the Come-Outers and had the ungenerous side of his nature come out; and it is not impossible that it was written as a short story and inserted into the longer manuscript, as a contribution from the practical transcendentalist, when Melville felt his customary need to extend his narrative enough to make a book of respectable length.

As Melville's disposition softened during the course of the winter his reading also began to have a more humanizing effect upon his mind. For Shakespeare pervaded *The Confidence Man* as thoroughly as he pervaded *Moby Dick* and *Pierre*. The conceit of the world as a stage on which a man played various roles came from the familiar speech by Jaques in *As You Like It*, which Melville quoted, and the similar notion of a "fond pageant" showing "what fools these mortals be" was from *A Midsummer Night's Dream*. In addition to borrowing a name and the burden of a story from *King Lear*, he let his characters discuss or comment briefly upon Polonius in *Hamlet*, Autolycus in *The Winter's Tale*, and Jack Cade in *Henry VI*. *Cymbeline*, in a section from which he had taken a quotation for "The Piazza," supplied him with the name Fidele for the boat on which his action took place. But the reading reflected in these rather incidental allusions had a more profound effect upon him. "This Shakespeare is a queer man," he had Frank Goodman comment. "At times irresponsible, he does not always seem reliable. There appears to be a certain—what shall I call it?—hidden sun, say, about him, at once enlightening and mystifying." There was something of the same quality in Melville, especially in the second half of *The Confidence Man* when he had dropped the bystanding role of the melancholy Jaques and slipped into the story himself in the character of Touchstone. For when he let his confidence man drop the familiar disguises of the conventional swindlers and make motley his only wear, he began to "take a part, assume a character," and "in a sensible way to play the fool" as he had not been able to do before he reasoned and wrote himself out of his earlier despondency.

Frank Goodman, the man in motley, was a new sort of "Mississippi operator." Although a Machiavellian desire to match wits with the world remained a part of his character, he did not operate for money. He attempted to enlighten the world by serving as a touchstone to men's hidden faults. Whether he shed "the true light" his creator was unwilling to say. All the action of *The Confidence Man* was dated, like the signing of the master mason's report in "I and My Chimney," on April Fools' Day, and it was not supposed to be taken too solemnly. It was enough for Melville to have a character through whom he could discourse at large with the license permitted Shakespeare's fools or Cervantes' mad knight, Don Quixote, whose story he had brought home from Albany in September. If he was not free from worries about his health and economic prospects, he had recovered, for a while, his mental equilibrium; and he was inclined to celebrate it with exuberance.

Unfortunately for the success of Melville's high comedy, his exuberance made him careless. It is to be doubted that he knew, at times, whether he was writing ironically or enthusiastically. In a more elementary way, he was careless about identifying his speakers as they punned with ideas; and in one conversation he actually had one of the talkers inadvertently address himself. The book was too difficult to be taken lightly by readers, who have an inveterate tendency to confuse obscurity with either profundity or madness. Furthermore, not only was it incoherent in its emotional quality, but the aftertaste of its early bitterness inevitably affected the flavor of the second part of the story. Allusions to the Bible were as pervasive in the first half as allusions to Shakespeare were in the second; and Melville, with his habitual insensitivity to the reverential sensibilities of more orthodox minds, had seemed to be engaged in an ironic parody of the Sermon on the Mount and St. Paul's message of faith, hope, and charity. Against that background, even so commonplace a thing as a satire on Emerson might seem somehow sacrilegious. The loose serial construction, in general, was a mortal temptation to the author's worst faults of discursiveness. The artistic sophistication so necessary to any good comedy was simply lacking in *The Confidence Man*; and, although its readers were neither to look for nor consciously to miss such sophistication, its absence left a vacuum which they could not fill with any clear quality of understanding.

There is no evidence of any sort that Melville anticipated the failure of his new book or had any notion that it would be the last piece of prose fiction he was to publish during his lifetime. On the contrary, he seems to have been keeping a careful eye on his professional prospects. After a second reading of "Benito Cereno," just before it appeared in print, Curtis had decided that it was both "ghastly and interesting"; but he had no great hopes for the collection of stories Dix and Edwards were preparing to publish. "I don't think Melville's book will sell a great deal," he had advised them on January 2, 1856, "but he is a good name upon your list. He has lost his prestige, and I don't believe the Putnam stories will bring it up." Melville had greater expectations. Writing on January 7 for back numbers of the magazine in order that he could do his "share of the work without delay," he was vigilant to correct the tentative royalty agreement from twelve to twelve and a half per cent; and he did his proof-reading and made his verbal revisions carefully. It is unlikely, too, that he would have written "The Piazza" specifically as an introductory sketch for the volume had he not been optimistic about its success.

He also varied his usual procedure during a winter's work on one book by keeping up his magazine contacts. He did a sketch of the sea-going Portuguese from the Cape Verde island of Fogo for publication in *Harper's* for March, 1856, under the title "The 'Gees," and "The Apple-Tree Table, or Original Spiritual Manifestations" for *Putnam's* in May. The latter, however, was probably written less from a desire to preserve a literary connection than from the impulse of a mind lightened by the composition of "The Piazza" and the feeling of relief at getting a book off to press. For it was another study in human subjectivity, humorously developed from a passage he had found and marked in *A History of the County of Berkshire* which he had used for *Israel Potter*. It told of "a strong and beautiful *bug*" which "*eat*" its way out of an apple-tree table belonging to P. S. Putnam in Williamstown, presumably after developing from an egg deposited many decades before. Melville related the ticking sound accompanying its emergence to the fad for "spirit-rapping" which had swept the country some years before, but primarily he stressed its effect upon the members of the household who listened to it—a man given to midnight musings on Cotton Mather's *Magnalia*, his matter-of-fact wife, his two nervous daughters, and his superstitious Irish servant. The most humorously detached of all his tales, it indicates that he preserved his ability to escape from brooding melancholia throughout the latter part of the winter; and it also suggests that, in keeping the fictitious literary character and imaginary role he had created for himself in "I and My Chimney," he was looking forward to a continued career as a "magazinist."

Although his mental state during the spring did not prevent him from writing, his physical condition kept him from doing much active farming. On April 17 he began advertising half of his farm for sale and within a few weeks disposed of it to George S. Willis at the very good price of $5,500. The eighty acres he kept included some of his woodland, his orchard and pasture, and enough cleared ground for at least a garden and a turnip patch, but not so much as to make him dependent upon hired help except in case of severe illness. He also had $8,000 in the bank, which he seems to have begun transferring to a city bank or investing in stocks—for the tax rolls show that he declared $5,000 in money for 1857 and only his customary nest-egg of $1,000 in 1858, whereas the stocks which he first listed for local taxation in 1862 amounted in value to $6,548 and his cash to $1,500. Some of that, however, may have been speculative profit, since he had a note for $2,050 to pay off on May 1, 1856. Yet, like Jimmy Rose in the years of his misfortune, he seems to have held on to his capital regardless of how difficult it was for him to make a living. At the worst, his interest and dividends, with Elizabeth's small trust fund and their garden, could keep him in genteel poverty.

Poverty could hardly have begun to threaten his peace of mind, however, until after the middle of July when Augusta had finished making a printers' copy of *The Confidence Man* and the manuscript was ready to submit to a publisher. There are no records of its reception, but it was certainly not the kind of novel that Curtis would have called "extremely good" and it did not appear serially in *Putnam's Monthly*. Dix and Edwards were even hesitant about bringing it out as a book. They had printed 2,500 copies of the *Piazza Tales*, but the 1,047 copies sold by the end of August were only about three-fifths of the number required to pay expenses; and the firm, which may have already been in financial difficulties, not only assumed that the author would get no royalties until printing expenses had been paid but evidently wanted to wait and test the "fall market" before deciding whether Melville's name was good enough to carry a doubtful book. In any event, no agreement was signed for the publication of *The Confidence Man* until October 10.[1] During the period of delay and its inevitable nervous strain,

1. Evidence furnished by Watson G. Branch indicates that although Herman and Allan met with representatives of Dix, Edwards & Co. on October 10 the Melvilles were unable to come to an agreement with the publisher. Two un-

his family once more decided that too intensive an application to literature was ruining his health and that something should be done about it.

Herman's activities of the summer, however, were not those of a man in need of any particular attention. He spent his thirty-seventh birthday with his mother and uncle Herman at Gansevoort and for the next two weeks enjoyed a holiday away from home. Allan arranged to take his vacation at the same time, and on August 7 the two brothers went to Lake George on what their uncle called "an excursion of pleasure." Their friend Daniel Shepherd, Allan's former law partner and an author like Herman, joined them on their two-day jaunt; and after their return Herman relieved the quietness of Gansevoort by spending Tuesday and Thursday at Saratoga Springs, while Allan returned for a longer stay on Lake George. En route home by way of Albany on Saturday, August 16, he stopped off long enough to call upon his uncle Peter and take a midday meal with his family before taking the afternoon train to Pittsfield. Peter was anxious for him to return for a longer visit while the American Association for the Advancement of Science was meeting during the following week and reserved his "whole house" for his nephew, Lizzie, and the children. But for some reason—perhaps from Lizzie's reluctance rather than his own—he did not get back. He may have been worried and tired of writing, but he was neither rheumatic nor unsocial.

Elizabeth nevertheless continued to worry about him in her letters to Boston, and Judge Shaw began to turn over in his mind ways and means for breaking him of what had now become the vain habit of trying to make his living with his pen. The judge's daughter seems to have had no relish for a winter in the country with Herman shut up in his study, Mrs. Melville and the girls all away, and four small children and a big farmhouse to look after while she worried about making financial ends meet and about what she would do if her husband became bedridden. Herman was sensitive enough about the situation to be difficult at best, and, at his worst, he was probably impossible to deal with. How difficult Melville actually was, as a rule, no one can tell. He certainly was too independent to close up his house and move in upon his relatives with his large family, even if they would have had him: when he had lived with Allan and his mother after his marriage, he had always played host. He apparently was determined not to sacrifice

---

signed contract forms dated October 10 call for the manuscript to be delivered the next day, but it was not until October 28, after Herman had arrived in Scotland, that Allan signed the agreement on his behalf. It appointed November 1 as the date for delivery of the manuscript ready for printing and stated that the book was to be published on or before January 1, 1857. The latter date was passed over, apparently to allow arrangements to be made for simultaneous publication in England. [Leon Howard, 1971.]

his small claim on independence by spending the capital he had so slowly accumulated. He could be "sent abroad for his health" without losing his respectability, for that was a well-established convention in his own family and among his friends, and that seemed to be the only solution to the problem in a year when there was no political turnover to raise hopes for another government job.

Such was the solution probably pressed upon Judge Shaw by Elizabeth, who seemed already to have begun cultivating her lifelong habit of worrying audibly about Herman's health and nervous condition whenever she was secretly disturbed about her own situation. The expenses of a trip to the Mediterranean and the Holy Land, which Melville had sacrificed in 1849, could be borne by the judge as a "loan" against his daughter's future inheritance—just as he had treated his advances toward the purchase of the house in New York and the farm in Pittsfield. Judge Shaw was sympathetically disposed, but, before committing himself definitely, he briefed the case in a letter to Sam:

I suppose you have been informed by some of the family, how very ill, Herman has been. It is manifest to me from Elizabeth's letters, that she has felt great anxiety about him. When he is deeply engaged in one of his literary works, he confines him to hard study many hours in the day, with little or no exercise, and this specially in winter for a great many days together. He probably thus overworks himself and brings on severe nervous afflictions. He has been advised strongly to break off this labor for some time, and take a voyage or a journey, and endeavor to recruit. No definite plan is arranged, but I think it may result, in this that in the autumn he will go away for four or five months, Elizabeth will come here with her younger children, Mrs. Griggs and Augusta will each take one of the boys, their house at Pittsfield will be shut up. I think he needs such a change and that it will be highly beneficial to him and probably restore him.

The investment—for an "outfit" and traveling expenses—in Herman's health and Elizabeth's happiness would amount to something between fourteen and fifteen hundred dollars, and the "definite plan" had to be arranged through Allan as an intermediary. But with tactful handling Herman's sensitivity could be made to blossom into enthusiasm, and all the practical details were settled well before the end of the month.

With the prospect of spending the winter in her beloved Boston while Herman was taking a wholesome trip, Elizabeth could enter with spirit into Sarah Morewood's second fancy-dress picnic on September 3. She went as "the Genius of Greylock" with a hat of bird-nests and a dress decorated with leaves and pine cones, while Augusta covered herself with leaves and flowers and little Bessie took her first part in Berkshire festivities in the costume of Bo-Peep. Augusta probably spent most of the month working on a second copy of *The Confidence Man*, for Herman was expecting to sail on October 4 and hoped to sell the book abroad although no arrangements had yet been made for its publication at home.[2] On Saturday, September 27, he bade most of his family farewell and left for Gansevoort to deliver Stanwix, who was to stay with his grandmother, while Augusta remained behind to help close the house and get Elizabeth and the other children off to Boston. He stayed at home to talk with his uncle Herman while his mother and two of his sisters, Fannie and Kate, took Stanny to church on Sunday; and the next morning his uncle accompanied him as far as Saratoga Springs on his way to New York.

In the city, Melville was his old self. He sloughed off his four years of sensitive estrangement from Evert Duyckinck and spent the evening of October 1 with him, "fresh from his mountain" and "charged to the muzzle with his sailor metaphysics and jargon of things unknowable" as well as with good stories and lively comments upon books and people. It was "a good stirring evening," Duyckinck observed in his diary, "—ploughing deep and bringing to the surface some rich fruits of thought and experience." Melville enjoyed it, too, for he seems to have encouraged Allan to see that Duyckinck and Daniel Shepherd (who had recently published a novel called *Saratoga, a Tale of 1787*) were made acquainted with each other as soon as possible. The only restraint upon his spirits was his failure to come to any agreement with Dix, Edwards, and Company for the publication of *The Confidence Man*, for that was possibly the reason why he postponed his sailing for a week, getting a written agreement only on Friday, October 10, and delivering the manuscript the next morning just before his departure.[3]

The delay was not long enough to enable him to go to Boston, but it permitted him to run up to Gansevoort over Sunday in order to say good-bye once more to his mother and son before hurrying back to New York for "engagements" which prevented him from stopping in Albany. He may have had to confer with his publishers on Monday morning and make some last-minute changes in his book, for he did not go with Allan and Shepherd to call on Duyckinck Wednesday evening. But on Thursday evening he attended a

2. His wife's memoir says that when Melville sailed for London he took "manuscript books with him for publication there." However, Watson G. Branch's analysis of the variants between the first American and the first English editions shows that the English edition was set from proof sheets of the first American, whether or not Melville took a second manuscript with him. On March 20, 1857, Nathaniel Hawthorne on Melville's behalf signed a contract for publication of *The Confidence-Man* in London by Longman, Brown, Green, Longmans, and Roberts. No further details are available. [Leon Howard, 1971.]

3. See the note on p.294. [Leon Howard, 1971.]

298 · *John W. Shroeder*

farewell party given by Shepherd, with Duyckinck, Allan, and Robert Tomes (whose book on Panama Melville had bought the year before) as the other guests. They had "good talk," Duyckinck recorded, "Herman warming like an old sailor over the supper." He had got his passport, his book was at last going to be published, and over the seas lay Italy. Even the weather was wonderful—a "series of extraordinary fine days," according to Duyckinck's diary, "sunny, mellow, quiescent." On Saturday, October 11, his friends saw him off on the propeller steamer *Glasgow*, eagerly bound for Scotland, Naples, and points east.

When Melville left for Europe, he was in a state of mental excitability which his family and friends recognized but could not analyze, although it was rather clearly revealed in the unpublished manuscript of *The Confidence Man* that some members of the family had helped copy. He was still suffering from the conflict between the will to believe and the tendency to doubt which had provided the emotional tension observable in *Moby Dick* and *Pierre*. But the conflict no longer was represented by a skeptical assault on the will to believe. His skepticism had developed into cynicism, and, as a bystanding wiseacre, he had written the first part of his unpublished book from a point of view which portrayed all faith as folly. But in the second part he had shown himself to be skeptical of his own cynicism. He had no intellectual vantage point from which he could view life, consistently, either as a tragedy or as a comedy. As a writer and as a human being, he needed some sort of conviction in which to take refuge from his own moods; and he may have hoped, ironically enough, that whatever his trip might do for his health it might in some way restore his confidence.

JOHN W. SHROEDER

Sources and Symbols for Melville's *Confidence-Man*†

Melville criticism seems fated to a slow and uncertain growth. We have come a long way, to be sure, beyond the author who dismissed Melville as one among "several minor writers resident in the city or state of New York." But one chief fault we seem not to have corrected: it is perhaps not over-rash to say that this criticism

† John W. Shroeder, "Sources and Symbols for Melville's *Confidence-Man*," *PMLA*, Vol. 66 (June, 1951), pp. 364–380. Reprinted by permission of the Modern Language Association of America.

learns only reluctantly from what it has already accomplished. We know, for instance, that Melville's literary borrowings in such a work as *Moby-Dick* are worth close scrutiny; we also know that the allegory and the symbol lurk everywhere in Melville's pages. But our knowledge is not regularly put to use as a hypothetical principle for the examination of other works. Now I suggest that there is still a good bit to be done with these tools alone, and in this present paper I mean to try to do a part of it. I propose to identify and follow out certain of the sources and symbols which went into one of Melville's least-known works, *The Confidence-Man*.[1]

Nothing in particular happens in this book. The setting is the deck and cabins of a Mississippi steamer, the *Fidèle*, bound on the voyage down-river to New Orleans. On board the vessel, we are introduced to a number of figures: to a negro named Black Guinea, to a Mr. Roberts, a Mr. Ringman, a Mr. Goodman, a Mr. Noble, and various others. We are entertained with several debates and a few interpolated tales. Throughout the book rings the cry of "confidence," taken in both its main senses. Passengers approach other passengers with charitable schemes or demands for charity. There is a deal of talk and a deal of satire.

I think that this description is adequate to the surface of Melville's book. And if we are content to think that the book is nothing more than this surface, we will probably conclude that criticism has done well in letting this work slip out of sight. But we can, I think, set it down as law that Melville is never simply a writer of the surface.

The confidence-man, from whom our book takes its title, is a practiced shape-shifter; his existence is a succession of pious disguises. Among the characters which he assumes is that of collector of funds for the Seminole Widow and Orphan Asylum. The charitable operations of this gentleman are various. He has invented a "Protean easy-chair," designed to ease the torments of both body

1. Since writing the paper from which this present study grew, I have availed myself of an opportunity to read Elizabeth Foster's excellent unpublished dissertation, "Herman Melville's *The Confidence-Man*: Its Origins and Meaning." In several of my findings, large and small, Miss Foster has anticipated me; I have tried to credit her in my notes with the most important of these anticipations. Miss Foster is at present editing *The Confidence-Man* for the new uniform edition of Melville's works [uncompleted Hendricks House edition]; her introduction and notes for this edition, when published, will certainly prove a major stimulus in subsequent study and evaluation of this neglected book. I wish to add here that Miss Foster has been most gracious and helpful in discussing with me the question of our independent discoveries.

Among the other extant discussions of *The Confidence-Man* Nathalia Wright's and Richard Chase's are especially valuable. Miss Wright, however, whose insights concerning this work are many and excellent, makes no attempt to formulate a complete symbolic structure for the book as a whole—*Melville's Use of the Bible* (Durham, N. C., 1949), passim—and Mr. Chase's stimulating interpretation is marred by a number of factual inaccuracies—"Melville's Confidence-Man," *Kenyon Review*, XI (Winter 1949). 122–140: *Herman Melville: A Critical Study* (New York, 1949), pp. 185–209.

and conscience. While he was displaying this chair at the London World's Fair, the idea of the "World's Charity" came to him. The Charity, as he explains it (pp. 33–34),

is to be a society whose members shall comprise deputies from every charity and mission extant; the one object of the society to be the methodization of the world's benevolence; to which end, the present system of voluntary and promiscuous contribution to be done away, and the Society to be empowered by the various governments to levy, annually, one grand benevolence tax upon all mankind; . . . This tax, according to my tables . . . would result in the yearly raising of a fund little short of eight hundred millions; this fund to be annually applied to such objects, and in such modes, as the various charities and missions, in general congress represented, might decree; . . .

The project, he adds, "will frighten none but a retail philanthropist." The passage has a certain independent value as evidence of the confidence-man's character; it relates him to the misled and misleading reformers who figure so largely in Hawthorne's writings. And we need not stop with this suggested parallel. If we go directly to Hawthorne's sketch, "The Celestial Railroad," we can identify something that looks suspiciously like the origin of this scheme: "There is another species of machine for the wholesale manufacture of individual morality. This excellent result is effected by societies for all manner of virtuous purposes, with which a man has merely to connect himself, throwing, as it were, his quota of virtue into the common stock, and the president and directors will take care that the aggregate amount be well applied." This excerpt, it seems to me, is a window which opens between and connects two fictional worlds. Now that our attention has been directed to this source—which sometimes leads us through Hawthorne to *his* source in Bunyan's *Pilgrim's Progress*—a number of interesting parallels become manifest. And these should be of real importance in defining the symbolic setting within which the episodes of *The Confidence-Man* occur.

Hawthorne transferred the protagonist of his sketch from the Celestial Railroad to "a steam ferry boat," with the intention of sending him comfortably on to the Celestial City. And Melville, if my deductions are correct, transmuted this boat into the steamer *Fidèle*, combining his favorite symbol of the boat-as-world with Hawthorne's symbol of the vessel bound for Tophet. Occasional descriptive passages support this identification. Hawthorne's train passed through a dark valley, whose gloom encouraged certain melancholy imaginings in his hero: "As the light of natural day, however, began to struggle with the glow of the lanterns, these vain imaginations lost their vividness, and finally vanished with the first

ray of sunshine that greeted our escape from the Valley of the
Shadow of Death. Ere we had gone a mile beyond it I could well-
nigh have taken my oath that this whole gloomy passage was a
dream." Compare the order of events in the above quotation with
this passage from Melville: "The sky slides into blue, the bluffs
into bloom; the rapid Mississippi expands; runs sparkling and gurgling, all over in eddies; one magnified wake of a seventy-four. The
sun comes out, a golden huzzar, from his tent, flashing his helm on
the world. All things, warmed in the landscape, leap. Speeds the
dædal boat as a dream" (p. 65–66). And Melville's description of
Cairo, where "the old established firm of Fever & Ague is still settling up its unfinished business," is reminiscent of both
Hawthorne's Valley of the Shadow and Slough of Despond. There
is even one direct verbal echo. "The mephitic gases of that region,"
says Hawthorne, speaking of the Dark Valley, "intoxicate the
brain." At Cairo, Melville's "Don Saturninus Typhus . . . snuffs up
the mephitic breeze with zest."

The travellers on the Celestial Railroad stored their luggage and
bags away during the trip. Hawthorne's reference, of course, is to
the "heavy burden" dropped by the Wall of Salvation by Bunyan's
Christian. Both sources may have been in Melville's mind when he
wrote of a man in a cream suit (the first figure to appear in his
book) that "he had neither trunk, valise, carpet-bag, nor parcel"
(p. 1).

There is a gentleman aboard the *Fidèle* who represents the Black
Rapids Coal Company. The corporation has a sinister name, certainly; Hawthorne and Bunyan would have appreciated its allegorical possibilities. This particular confidence-man drives a thriving
trade. And the precise nature of his goods comes to the surface
when he refers to yet another stock for which there is no market:

> "You wouldn't like to be concerned in the New Jerusalem,
> would you?"
> "New Jerusalem?"
> "Yes, the new and thriving city, so called, in northern Minne-
> sota. . . . Here, here is the map," producing a roll. "There—
> there, you see, are the public buildings—here the landing—there
> the park—yonder the botanic gardens—and this, this little dot
> here, is a perpetual fountain, you understand. You observe there
> are twenty asterisks. Those are for the lyceums. They have lig-
> num-vitæ rostrums." (p. 43)

Further, the first settlement of this community was by "two fugitives, who had swum over naked from the opposite shore." It is a
little difficult to see how criticism has missed the references in this
passage. Perhaps it has been a case of misidentification; the settlement sounds vaguely like the Valley of Eden in Dickens' *Martin*

Chuzzlewit. From the description, too, it would be not impossible
to conclude that this is yet another cony-catching concern. But
there are fountains and gardens in Hawthorne which will be potentially helpful here. Speaking of the land of Beulah, Hawthorne
said: "The sweet breezes of this happy clime came refreshingly to
our nostrils; we beheld the glimmering gush of silver fountains,
overhung by trees of beautiful foliage and delicious fruit, which
were propagated by grafts from the celestial gardens." And Bunyan
will give us a source for our "lignum-vitæ rostrums" and for the
agent's "roll." Christian and Hopeful, his two fugitives, were told
that in the Celestial City they "shall see the tree of life, and eat of
the never-fading fruits thereof." And Christian, when he dropped
his burden, was given "a roll with a seal upon it," which he later
presented at the gate of the City. It is hard, certainly, to see why
criticism has not made more of all this. Richard Chase describes
the Black Rapids Coal Company as "a dubious or nonexistent
corporation."[2] I suggest, however, that the company, to Melville's
mind, was very palpably extant, just as was the New Jerusalem. The
parallels to Bunyan and Hawthorne—and more are still to
come—make of these concerns the polar opposites of the Fidèle's
universe.

The agent of the Seminole asylum, it will be recalled, first struck
on his plan for the World's Charity while at the London Fair. "I
will see," he claims to have said to himself, "if this occasion of
vanity cannot supply a hint toward a better profit than was
designed" (p. 33). The close association of the words "vanity" and
"fair" is evocative, especially when we remember the episode of the
Fair in Hawthorne's sketch. The motif occurs elsewhere; the deck
of the Fidèle, indeed, is like some "Constantinople arcade or
bazaar." There is a young fellow on the boat who once kept a
"toy-stand at the fair in Cincinnati"; he sold "more than one old
man a child's rattle" (p. 210). And a certain cosmopolitan, the
most striking of Melville's voyagers, capitalizes the word for us
during a discussion with another passenger:

> "Hands off!" cried the bachelor, involuntarily covering dejec-
> tion with moroseness.
> "Hands off? [the cosmopolitan is speaking] that sort of label
> won't do in our Fair. Whoever in our Fair has fine feelings loves
> to feel the nap of fine cloth, especially when a fine fellow wears
> it." (pp. 113–114)

Other parallels will occur to Melville's reader. The list of the "pilgrims" on the Fidèle—"Natives of all sorts, and foreigners; men of
business and men of pleasure; parlor men and backwoodsmen;

2. *Herman Melville*, p. 190. Miss Foster has noted the significant references
to Heaven and Hell in this passage.
See also Wright, p. 102.

farm-hunters and fame-hunters; ... English, Irish, German, Scotch, Danes; ... hard-shell Baptists and clay-eaters; grinning negroes, and Sioux chiefs solemn as high-priests" (p. 6)—may very well owe its accumulation of nouns to Bunyan's example: "And moreover, at this fair there is at all times to be seen jugglings, cheats, games, plays, fools, apes, knaves, and rogues, and that of every kind." "Here is the Britain-row, the French-row, the Italian-row, the Spanish-row, the German-row, where several sorts of vanities are to be sold." Or take the name of Melville's steamer, the *Fidèle*. Faithful was executed by the people of Bunyan's Fair.

At least one character, too, seems to cross from an earlier Fair to Melville's. At Hawthorne's: "Prince Beelzebub himself took great interest in this sort of traffic, and sometimes condescended to meddle with smaller matters. I once had the pleasure to see him bargaining with a miser for his soul, which, after much ingenious skirmishing on both sides, his highness succeeded in obtaining at about the value of sixpence." There is a miser given to precisely this same ingenious skirmishing on Melville's steamer. He purchases a box of herbs from a travelling doctor (whose relation to Prince Beelzebub will be treated subsequently):

> "Say a dollar-and-half. Ugh!"
> "Can't. Am pledged to the one-price system, only honorable one."
> "Take off a shilling—ugh, ugh!"
> "Can't."
> "Ugh, ugh, ugh—I'll take it.—There."
> Grudgingly he handed eight silver coins, but while still in his hand, his cough took him, and they were shaken upon the deck.
> One by one, the herb-doctor picked them up, and, examining them, said: "These are not quarters, these are pistareens; and clipped, and sweated, at that." (p. 90)

Even the distracting fashion in which Melville's actors suddenly disappear from sight may have been suggested by a passage from Hawthorne's dream-vision: "Amid the occupations or amusements of the Fair, nothing was more common than for a person—whether at feast, theatre, or church, or trafficking for wealth and honors, or whatever he might be doing, to vanish like a soap bubble, and be never more seen of his fellows; ..."

The value of these literary cross references is, I think, extreme. They act to locate the events of *The Confidence-Man* geographically and spiritually. The world of this book is a great Vanity Fair, situated on an allegorical steamboat which, presumably sailing for New Orleans (on the symbolic level, for the New Jerusalem of nineteenth-century optimism and liberal theology), is inclining its course dangerously toward the pits of the Black Rapids Coal Com-

pany. Aboard the vessel we have pilgrimaging mankind. And
among these pilgrims, the confidence-man is inordinately active;
the character and actions of this ambiguous figure must now claim
our attention.

The confidence-man, as I have noted before, is a shape-shifter; it
is never easy to pin him down and identify him. Let us seize upon
the handy figure of Black Guinea as a medium of introduction to
our confidence-man. Black Guinea is a negro, presumably crippled,
who begs about the deck (p. 7): "In the forward part of the boat,
not the least attractive object, for a time, was a grotesque negro
cripple, in tow-cloth attire and an old coal-sifter of a tamborine in
his hand, who, owing to something wrong about his legs, was, in
effect, cut down to the stature of a Newfoundland dog; . . ."
When we recall the black-white world of *Benito Cereno*—and
when we note that Guinea's tamborine is a "coal-sifter"—we are
apt to suspect a certain ominous quality in this negro; he may be
an inhabitant of the fiery pit. Whatever he is, however—and the
clues to his identity are not many—he is somehow related to the
confidence-man we are to meet. Asked whether he can produce any
witnesses who will certify his infirmity as real, he replies (p. 10):
"Oh yes, oh yes, dar is aboard here a werry nice, good ge'mman
wid a weed, and a ge'mman in a gray coat and white tie, what
knows all about me; and a ge'mman wid a big book, too; and a
yarb-doctor; and a ge'mman in a yaller west; and a ge'mman wid a
brass plate; and a ge'mman in a wiolet robe; and a ge'mman as is a
sodjer; . . ." This is a reasonably complete listing of the
confidence-man's masks. Several of these gentlemen appear, invoking confidence and fleecing the public. The man with the weed
exchanges a tale of personal misfortune for a friendly loan from a
merchant. The man in the gray coat (the Charity Agent) successfully solicits funds for the Seminole Asylum. The "ge'mman wid a
big book" proves to be the agent of the Coal Company. The
herb-doctor drives a good trade with the sick. The man with the
brass plate is the agent of a Philosophical Intelligence Office; he
breaks through the mistrust of a Missouri bachelor and receives, as
fee, money to provide the bachelor with a new hired boy. The identification of the other gentlemen on Guinea's list is more difficult.
Two pretended soldiers appear, but neither seems qualified to give
Guinea a recommendation. We are later introduced, too, to one
Charlie Noble (who has a violet vest) and to the cosmopolitan,
Francis Goodman, whose costume has something of the robelike in
it. I suspect, for reasons which I shall subsequently present, that
Noble is akin to the Charity agent, the Black Rapids agent, and
the man with the plate, and that Goodman is the confidence-man

raised to the highest power (though if this is the case, the long conversation which they hold together is rather difficult to explain). We cannot, it would seem, depend absolutely on Guinea's list; other evidence must be brought to bear in the task of unmasking the confidence-man.

The man with the weed is known as Ringman; the man with the book is Truman; the herb-doctor calls himself "the Happy Man"; the cosmopolitan, as we have noted, is named Francis Goodman. These fellows are apparently of the same allegorical family; Spenser's Sansfoy, Sansjoy, and Sansloy come immediately to mind as a kindred group. And this same surname-element of "man" occurs again in a highly significant passage. The cosmopolitan, late at night, startles the *Fidèle's* barber. The barber, however, quickly recovers from his fright:

"Ah!" turning round disenchanted, "it is only a man, then."
"*Only* a man? As if to be but man were nothing. But don't be too sure what I am. You call me *man*, just as the townsfolk called the angels who, in man's form, came to Lot's house; just as the Jew rustics called the devils who, in man's form, haunted the tombs. You can conclude nothing absolute from the human form, barber." (p. 193)

The hint is a good one; the confidence-man is pretty certainly not "only a man." Angel or devil, then, remain as the leading possibilities. And Melville, if we attend to him closely, will resolve the problem for us. Of the disguises voluntarily assumed by the confidence-man—of the masks of his masquerade—we have spoken. And the confidence-man is subject to yet another change—an involuntary metamorphosis— of which we must now speak.

While the man with the weed importuned the merchant for a loan, "a writhing expression stole over him" (p. 17). Later, while accosting yet another traveller, he is described as "sliding nearer," as "quivering down and looking up." The traveller seems under the man's spell; indeed, says Melville, the man "fascinated him" (p. 23). There is only one creature which writhes, quivers, looks up from below while speaking, and fascinates. And he is subsequently named. Later in the book (p. 75), an "invalid Titan" fells the herb-doctor with a blow, and cries at him: "Profane fiddler on heart-strings! Snake!"

Satan and his legions, according to Milton, are doomed to assume at certain periods the form of the reptile. The transformation was a favorite of Hawthorne's. And Melville pushes it to its limits. After the man with the plate has departed with the Missouri bachelor's money, the gulled Missourian finds time to wonder what species of being he has been dealing with: "Analogically, he couples the slanting cut of the equivocator's coat-tails with the sinister cast in his eye; he weighs slyboot's sleek speech in the light imparted by the oblique import of the smooth slope of his worn boot-heels; the insinuator's undulating flunkyisms dovetail into those of the flunky beast that windeth his way on his belly" (p. 113). Both Charlie Noble and Frank Goodman are subject to this reptilian change. Charlie, when asked by Frank for a loan, like "Cadmus glided into the snake" (p. 156). And Frank, later, while praising the "latent benignity" of the rattlesnake, is seen "to wreathe his form and sidelong crest his head, till he all but seemed the creature described" (p. 162). In the barber's shop, Goodman enchants that person by his "persuasive fascination—the power of holding another creature by the button of the eye" (p. 200). When we are told that a clergyman catches, in the expression of the Seminole Asylum agent, "something" which causes him uneasiness,[3] we do not have to exercise much speculative energy in order to discover what that something is. The legions of Satan, patently, are loose about the deck of the *Fidèle*.

Several traits act to set our cosmopolitan apart from the other confidence-men. His philosophical discourse, while basically like that of such fellows as Ringman and Truman in its refusal to recognize the dark side of the universe, is conceived in a freer spirit than is that of his underlings. He has powers of sorcery beyond those exercised by his fellows; he charms Charlie Noble with a tasselled pipe and a magic ring of ten half-eagles (p. 156). Finally, Melville permits him to talk at length with Noble, whose snake-metamorphosis I have already cited as evidence of demonism.

This cosmopolitan, I suggest, is related to that Prince Beelzebub (proverbially a much-travelled gentleman) who personally "took great interest" in the trade of Hawthorne's Vanity Fair. And certain of his comments are alarming; he protests a great love for humanity: "Served up à la Pole, or à la Moor, à la Ladrone, or à la Yankee, that good dish, man, still delights me; or rather is man a wine I never weary of comparing and sipping; wherefore am I . . . a sort of London-Dock-Vault connoisseur, . . . a taster of races; . . . smacking my lips over this racy creature, man, continually."[4] He declares to Charlie Noble that he has inspected the heart of the Missouri bachelor and "found it an inviting oyster in a forbidding shell." And Charlie himself pleads, in extenuation of his not smoking, that he "ate of a diabolical ragout at dinner" (p. 147). We need not go to the Fathers of the Church for this reference. Modern writers from Poe to C. S. Lewis have noted the Devil's

3. Page 29. Miss Foster has noted many of these events; her discussion of their import is admirable.

4. Page 115. Miss Foster has again anticipated me in assigning a diabolic character to the confidence-man.

fondness for the human soul as a dish. While we have Charlie Noble's dinner before us, it is helpful to remember that Poe's Pierre Bon-Bon offered his soul to the Devil as being particularly qualified for, among other things, a ragout. These implications, however, while amusing in themselves, do no more than aid in the identification of our symbolic personages. The question is not what the devil will do with the human soul when he gets it but how he gets it in the first place. How, we must inquire, does the confidence-man function in Melville's Fair?

The man with the brass plate represents himself to the Missouri bachelor as the agent of a Philosophical Intelligence Office. His Office, as he explains, engages, in a "small, quiet way," in the "careful analytical study of man, conducted, too, on a quiet theory, and with an unobtrusive aim wholly our own" (p. 104). The theory, he continues, he will not trouble to set forth at large. We must set it forth for him.

The most obvious point to be observed in all our various confidence-men is their continual invocation of confidence; they take money from their victims only on condition that the victims confide in them; the payment of cash, we might say, is only the visible symbol of the payment of confidence. And it is obviously a payment with a dark significance. The name Black Guinea— combining the Devil's color with a monetary unit—is interesting here; there is apparently a coinage which is especially prized by Prince Beelzebub. The Missouri bachelor (who has had such bitter experiences with hired boys that he has resolved to get a machine to do his work), his distrust lessened by the arguments of the man with the plate, agrees to admit "some faint, conditional degree of confidence" in the hired-boy the agent is to send him. He presents the agent with three dollars. Later, ruminating on his experience after the agent has gone ashore at a place called "the Devil's Joke," he finds that there is a sharp discrepancy between the guile exercised and the reward for it. "He revolves, but cannot comprehend, the operation, still less the operator. Was the man a trickster, it must be more for the love than the lucre" (p. 113). We are in a better position than was the bachelor; we are aware that it is not the transfer of money but the transfer of confidence which gives point to the Devil's joke. The analytical study of the Intelligence Office has been well adapted to the accomplishment of its "unobtrusive aim."

In Hawthorne's Fair, there was "a sort of stock or scrip, called Conscience, which seemed to be in great demand, and would purchase almost anything." In Melville's Fair the scrip is confidence; the demand is just as great and the penalty for its payment is, as in the other Fair, damnation. The scrip demanded by the confidence-man is confidence that the world has no dark side; that the boat is unerringly and necessarily bound for the Celestial City; that all the conscience requires is a Protean easy-chair or the medications of the herb-doctor.

The Missouri bachelor is the hardest nut that the confidence-man has to crack. The bachelor is theologically sound; the dark side of the universe is a part of his permanent vision. And we can profitably attend to certain of his views. The bachelor was continually pestered by the confidence-man. Before meeting the man with the plate, he found himself in the company of the herb-doctor. The doctor represents himself as having confidence in nature; he is, indeed, one of her "regularly authorized agents." This is not the sort of recommendation apt to pass with the bachelor, who earlier observed to the sick miser:

> "Natur is good Queen Bess; but who's responsible for the cholera?"
> "But yarbs, yarbs; yarbs are good?"
> "What's deadly-nightshade? Yarb, ain't it?" (p. 91)

There is nothing, says the bachelor, of which he is more suspicious than of nature. Nature carried away his ten thousand dollar plantation; Nature did her best to blind him. "Look you, nature!" he cries (p. 94), "I don't deny but your clover is sweet, and your dandelions don't roar, but whose hailstones smashed my windows?" In brief, the Missourian is very well aware that nature is cursed for man's sake; that the natural evil of the universe—an evil which the confidence-man attempts to conceal—represents to man a perpetual emblem of his fall and consequent perilous spiritual state.

The Bachelor's views on boys partake of a related theological concept. "Augustine on original sin," says he, "is my text book." He has had hired-boys of every nation and description. "No sir," he tells the man with the plate (p. 101), "No sir, . . . Don't try to oil me; the herb-doctor tried that. My experience, carried now through a course . . . of five and thirty boys, proves to me that boyhood is a natural state of rascality."

The arguments of the man with the plate, as we have seen, ultimately prevail with the bachelor. The agent persuades him that he can safely be confident; even a corrupt boy will in time become a sober, noble man. Goodness is latent in the corrupt boy just as the beard is latent in the boy's face: "supposing, respected sir, that worthy gentleman, Adam, to have been dropped overnight in Eden, . . . could even the learned serpent himself have foreknown that such a downy-chinned little innocent would eventually rival the goat in a beard? Sir, wise as the serpent was, that eventuality would have been entirely hidden from his wisdom." The confidence-man's mention of his master revives the bachelor's suspicions for a moment: "I don't know about that. The devil is very sagacious. To judge by the event, he appears to have understood man better even than the Being who made him" (p. 105). The Devil *is* very sagacious: the success of his agent is excellent witness to the power of his understanding. Our bachelor, like the other dupes at the Fair, finally pays over his confidence—renounces his vision of those qualities in man and the world which should perpetually recall his spiritual danger—and presumably finds himself damned. There is a certain hungry expectation in the cosmopolitan's discovery that this man's soul is an "inviting oyster."

The cosmopolitan engages only twice in the cony-catching which goes on aboard the *Fidèle*. In one instance, he persuades the barber to take down his "No Trust" sign; he then leaves the shop without paying for his shave. The other instance is a more crucial one. It provides the book's last chapter, whose title, "The Cosmopolitan Increases in Seriousness," is enough to alert us. The prince is about to take a hand in the business of his Fair.

"In the middle of the gentlemen's cabin," the chapter begins (p. 206), "burned a solar lamp, swing from the ceiling, and whose shade of ground glass was all round fancifully variegated, in transparency, with the image of a horned altar, from which flames rose, alternate with the figure of a robed man, his head encircled by a halo." The cosmopolitan, "Redolent from the barber's shop, as any bridegroom tripping to the bridal chamber might come, and by his look . . . seeming to dispense a sort of morning through the night," enters the cabin. He finds there "a clean, comely, old man," his head snowy as marble; this old gentleman is seated below the lamp and is studying the Bible.

The atmosphere, plainly, is highly charged with symbolism. I do not intend, indeed, to try to bring all of its symbols out. Richard Chase and Miss Nathalia Wright have written very well concerning some of the threads of meaning woven into this scene; I shall confine my own attention to a series of Biblical references which seem to have gone unnoticed. We must have one more hint before we settle down to them. Beyond the reaches of the lamp's rays, travellers sleep uneasily in their bunks. The conversation of the cosmopolitan and the old man occasionally disturbs one of them. When the cosmopolitan reads aloud the words of the Son of Sirach—"If thou be for his profit he will use thee; he will make thee bare, and will not be sorry for it. Observe and take good heed. When thou hearest these things, awake in thy sleep" (p. 208)—the sleeper, apparently obeying the admonition, inquires, "Who's that describing the confidence man?" And when the old gentleman explains to the cosmopolitan that the words of the Son of Sirach are apocrypha, the sleeper makes an important word-play (p. 209): "What's that about the Apocalypse?" And the Revelation of St. John will, I think, give us many of the hints we want. Here, for example, is a passage of possible relevance to the lamp and the old man:

> And I turned to see the voice that spake with me. And being turned, I saw seven golden candlesticks;
> And in the midst of the seven candlesticks, one like unto the Son of man, clothed with a garment down to the foot, and girt about the paps with a golden girdle.
> And his head and his hairs were white like wool, as white as snow; and his eyes were as a flame of fire. (i.12–14)

There is continual mention in the book of St. John the Divine, too, of the lamp, the robes, and the altar. And one altar (which has, of course, its counterparts elsewhere in the Bible) is particularly interesting: "And the sixth angel sounded, and I heard a voice from the four horns of the golden altar which is before God" (ix.13). And the cosmopolitan, that strange combination of bridegroom and morning radiance, must owe something to this passage (xxii.16-17): "I Jesus have sent mine angel to testify unto you these things in the churches. I am the root and the offspring of David, and the bright and morning star. And the Spirit and the bride say, Come." We should now be ready to recross the bridge between the Revelation of St. John and the cabin of the *Fidèle*. We must be careful in utilizing the evidence we have picked up. That the old gentleman is to be identified with the "Son of Man" is not likely. And earlier portions of the book act to negate any suspicion that the cosmopolitan has become Jesus. It is well to remember, in this connection, that Satan also was one of the sons of the morning; the coming of this present bridegroom portends a very different marriage from that of Christ and the Church. The primary function of Melville's references is to locate and define the action about to take place. The world, let us say, is now centered in the *Fidèle's* cabin, and Melville's own version of the Apocalypse is about to unfold before us. Again, as elsewhere in the book, the Devil works by the manipulation of confidence. A young boy enters the cabin; he is the fellow who kept a booth at the Cincinnati fair. Melville's description (p. 210) must be quoted: "All pointed and fluttering, the rags of the little fellow's red-flannel shirt, mixed with those of his yellow coat, flamed about him like the painted flames in the robe of a victim in *auto-da-fé*. His face, too, wore such a polish of seasoned grime, that his sloe-eyes sparked from out it' like lustrous sparks in fresh coal." Richard Chase likes this young fellow; he sees in him "the youthful, fiery Prometheus [who] tries to warn the Old God [the white-haired old man] that all is not well."[5] To

5. *Herman Melville*, p. 205.

Chase, the boy is the antagonist of the False Prometheus, who is represented by the cosmopolitan. There are several things wrong with Chase's symbolic identifications. The only persuasion exercised by the boy has as its object the instilling in the old man of confidence in several suspect objects of trade. He sells him a lock for his door; then he points out how a thief might evade the lock and sells him a money belt. He throws in, finally, a *Counterfeit Detector* which does not work. The lad seems to be in league with the cosmopolitan. He tries to sell that gentleman a lock (p. 211):

> "Excuse me, my fine fellow, but I never use such blacksmiths' things."
> "Those who give the blacksmith most work seldom do," said the boy, tipping him a wink. . . . But the wink was not marked by the old man, nor, to all appearances, by him for whom it was intended.

That "to all appearances" is a weasel-phrase; it is possible that the cosmopolitan did not catch the wink, but the very fact that there was a wink is enough to alert us. The description of this flaming lad, indeed—and we may add to it that his laugh disclosed "leopard-like teeth"—is pretty reasonable evidence that he is from the pit, called up by the cosmopolitan to aid in his project against the old man.[6]

The cosmopolitan first induces distrust in the old man and then quiets it. The ground, it appears, must be plowed before it can be planted. The old gentleman was instructed by his son, a careful man, to be certain that he has a life-preserver in his state-room. The confidence-man presents him with a chamber-stool. "In case of a wreck," he tells the old fellow, "barring sharp-pointed timbers, you could have confidence in that stool for a special providence." "Then," says the old man, "good-night, good-night; and Providence have both of us in its good keeping." Good-night, indeed. The old man, in the gloom of the cabin, inquires where his state-room may be; the cosmopolitan replies:

> "I have indifferent eyes, and will show you; but, first, for the good of all lungs, let me extinguish this lamp."
> The next moment, the waning light expired, and with it the waning flames of the horned altar, and the waning halo round the robed man's brow; while in the darkness which ensued, the cosmopolitan kindly led the old man away. (p. 217)

I cannot resist the temptation to find in the Revelation of St. John a possible origin for this last scene. In the City of God, writes

6. Again, the "sleeper" is helpful. When the lad laughs, the man in the bunk mutters: "The divils are laughing now, are they? . . . To bed, with ye, ye divils, and no more of ye" (p. 210). Miss Foster notes fully the significance of the many references to the Devil in the book.

John: "there shall be no night there; and they need no candle, neither light of the sun; For the Lord God giveth them light" (xxii.5). The point, of course, is that the old gentleman needs the candle and the sun above all other things. In the confidence-man's kingdom, the only light he is apt to find is the Miltonic "darkness visible."

Melville's book of the Apocalypse, it would seem, is more closely allied to the vision of Pope's *Dunciad* than to that of John's Revelation. The confidence-man has triumphed; he leads mankind, through an extinct universe, to his lightless kingdom. Or, to introduce a different set of symbols, the steamboat, filled with those who have confidence in herbs and easy-chairs, nature and boys, coal companies and Indian charities, counterfeit detectors and chamber-stools, has taken a direct course for the pit. Vanity Fair is sold out.

The *Confidence-Man*, manifestly, is a dark book. It ends, like *Pierre* and *Mardi*, in wreck. But it differs from these works in that its wreck symbolizes not Melville's inability to see but the result of his seeing perfectly well. *Moby-Dick*, too, ends in wreck, but there is something beyond; Ahab's destruction is objectified and balanced by the opposition to it of Ishmael's salvation. And in the same way, the triumph of the confidence-man is opposed and objectified, though apparently not negated, by an adversary of heroic proportions.

In the longest of the stories interpolated into the texture of our book, we are introduced to one Colonel John Moredock, an Indian fighter. The Colonel, we hear (p. 122), "hated Indians like snakes." Now hatred of the snake amounts to positive virtue in the cosmos of the *Fidèle*. And the Indian, I suggest, is coupled with the serpent in no accidental fashion. Let us follow the Indian for a little space.

The confidence-man, we recall, made an early appearance as the agent of the Seminole Widow and Orphan Asylum. If the Asylum has, as it must, affinities to the Coal Company, the doctor's herbs (the doctor calls himself a "true Indian doctor"), and the Intelligence office, the advantages of bestowing charity on the Red Man become very dubious indeed. We are later (p. 51) told the tale of Goneril, a strange woman given to eating clay, gifted with the "evil-touch," and possessed by a "calm, clayey, cakey devil." Goneril's figure is "Indian"; her health is "like a squaw's." Whatever else is to be said of this woman, the savage element in her nature is arresting.

We are to meet more of this imagery. At a houseless landing, two transient figures come aboard the *Fidèle*. One is an "invalid Titan in homespun"; the other, "a puny girl, walking in moccasins, not improbably his child, but evidently of alien maternity, perhaps Creole, or even Camanche." The child is clad in an Indian blanket. Melville, at one point, describes the invalid father as bowing over with pain "like a mainmast yielding to the gale, or Adam to the thunder" (p. 73). Let us take this last hint as a workable theory. The couple might very well be Adam and Eve, cast out of Paradise. Eve may properly be considered as being both Adam's daughter and a child of "alien maternity." And her apple will turn up later in the book. The cosmopolitan and Charlie Noble drink and smoke together for several chapters. When they call for wine, it is brought to them in "a little bark basket, braided with porcupine quills, gayly tinted in the Indian fashion" (p. 139) And when they call for cigars, they come in "a pretty little bit of western pottery, representing some kind of Indian utensil": "Accompanying it were two accessories, also bits of pottery, but smaller, both globes; one in guise of an apple flushed with red and gold to the life; and, through a cleft at top, you saw it was hollow. This was for the ashes" (p. 146). Eve's fruit has become one of Sodom's apples.

The book supplies, we may say, a running system of Indian-images related to concepts, situations, and persons connected with the theological doctrines of human guilt and damnation. It is interesting to note that the Puritans could account for the Indian only by supposing him to be a descendant of Satan. And another link in this long chain is useful. In one of the several chapters which deal with Moredock, Melville tells the story of the Wrights and the Weavers, a little band of frontiersmen from Virginia. After a long and bloody period of hostility with the Indians, the survivors of the group contrived a treaty with Mocmohoc, the enemy chief. Their pact stipulated that the whites would never be expected to enter the chief's lodge together: "Nevertheless, Mocmohoc did, upon a time, with such fine art and pleasing carriage win their confidence, that he brought them all together to a feast of bear's meat, and there, by stratagem, ended them. Years after, over their calcined bones and those of all their families, the chief, reproached for this treachery by a proud hunter whom he had made captive, jeered out, "Treachery? pale face! 'Twas they who broke their covenant first, in coming all together; they that broke it first, in trusting Mocmohoc" (p. 129). This chief certainly is the confidence-man in one of his more open disguises; those critics who incline to think that the confidence-man is Christ—doing good by stealth to man's spirit—should profit by this passage. Mocmohoc's words will stand very well as the motto of Ringman, Truman, Goodman, and the rest.

The ill-fated feast of bear's meat has its symbolic implications. The agent of the Black Rapids Coal Company confesses that his stock has recently undergone a slight devaluation. This depression of the stock he assigns to "the growling, the hypocritical growling, of the bears." "Why," he says, "the most monstrous of all hypocrites are these bears" (p. 41). They are "hypocrites in the simulation of things dark"; they thrive on depression; they are, indeed, experts in the wicked art of creating depression: "scoundrelly bears!" When we make the proper allowance for the speaker, it becomes evident that the bear is the distrustful man; the man who has no confidence in the false, bright side of things; the only man in Melville's universe who has a sporting chance against snakes, Indians, and confidence-men.

The Missouri bachelor was "somewhat ursine in aspect"; he sported "a shaggy spencer of the cloth called bear's-skin" (p. 91). He growled at the man with the plate like "Bruin in a hollow trunk" (p. 104). The confidence-man, as we know, finally took in this bear, just as he took in the Wrights and the Weavers. But there is a mythic figure of whom the bachelor is but a weakened type. He is the dedicated "Indian-hater." The confidence-man cannot trap him. Charlie Noble, who tells the tale of Colonel Moredock to the cosmopolitan,[7] says that he once, having come to a house where the Colonel was sleeping, slipped up into the loft to catch a sight of the hero; the Colonel, however, vanished at his approach.

The Indian-hater is a rarity. Such souls, says Melville, quoting Pope, peep out but once an age. His dedication is a religious one; his is "the solemnity of the Spaniard turned monk." His salvation is a completely individual matter: "The backwoodsman is a lonely man. He is a thoughtful man. He is a man strong and unsophisticated. Impulsive, he is what some might call unprincipled. At any rate, he is self-willed; being one who less hearkens to what others may say about things, than looks for himself, to see what are things themselves. If in straits, there are few to help; he must depend upon himself; he must continually look to himself. Hence self-reliance, to the degree of standing by his own judgment, though it stand alone" (p. 125). The value of individualism and isolation for the achievement of spiritual vision is one of the most interesting things to emerge from this book. The Prince is well aware that they provide a way out of his Fair. Goodman, conversing with the Missouri bachelor, praises the graces of sociability; only remorse, he says, can drive man to "that awful sin of shunning society." The bachelor answers that remorse does nothing of the kind. Cain founded the first city; the pickpocket especially enjoys having his fellows about him.

The Indian-hater is the world's only remedy against the confi-

7. "Hate Indians?" exclaims the cosmopolitan. "Why should he or anybody else hate Indians? *I* admire Indians" (p. 122).

dence-man; a severe disease calls for a strong purge. Like Ahab, the Indian-hater is an isolated hunter; like Ahab, he is little given to kneeling; like Ahab, he is grave, "as is not unusual with men of his complexion, a sultry and tragical brown." But unlike Ahab, the Indian-hater has succeeded in locating Evil in its real home; there is no distortion in his vision of spiritual reality.

"Something further," wrote Melville at the conclusion of his book, "may follow of this Masquerade." This may or may not represent both spiritual prophecy and a statement of future creative intent. Whatever the case, *The Confidence-Man* is complete within the limits which it proposes to itself. It is, certainly, complete in the same sense that *Pilgrim's Progress* and "The Celestial Railroad" are complete. And if we are determined to classify it as to kind, it is by reference to these two allegorical visions of the state of man's soul that we must make our classification.

The reader who knows his Melville will be aware that I have ignored certain crucial problems connected with his book. I have not attempted to identify the man in cream colors—the deaf-mute—with whom the novel begins. I have not offered any explanation as to why Noble and Goodman, if both are from the pit, should unknown to one another carry on their long conversation. I have not attempted to unriddle the tales of Goneril, Charlemont, and China Aster.[8] For these problems I have no answers. But this is not to say that there are no answers, nor is it to say that these characters and passages are mere random digressions. No critic has yet satisfactorily explained why Melville, in *Moby-Dick*, apparently decided to drop the important character Bulkington overboard shortly after introducing him. No critic has satisfactorily accounted for the presence of the cassock chapter in *Moby-Dick*. Criticism, in these cases, must be content to explain as much as it possibly can and then rest in the faith that it will in time arrive at a level of interpretation which will resolve these questions.

With these reservations in mind, I am ready to suggest that *The Confidence-Man* is one of the most valuable of the works in Melville's canon. It does not, of course, attain to the depth and imaginative energy which distinguishes *Moby-Dick*. But where *Moby-Dick* itself is often uncertain of its direction—where *Moby-Dick* sets out on false trails and perhaps unrelated mental voyages—*The Confidence-Man* establishes a single, though complex, aim and follows that aim through with what is, for Melville, remarkable fidelity. There are many reasons why *Moby-Dick*, imperfect though it sometimes is, should command our critical preference. But among

8. For a recent interpretation of this episode, see D. G. Hoffman's "Melville's 'Story of China Aster'," *AL*, XXII (May 1950), 137–149.

Melville's other writings—among such things as the incoherent *Mardi*, the ranting *Pierre*, the frigid *Billy-Budd—The Confidence-Man* stands as a hale and well-proportioned giant.

WATSON G. BRANCH

The Mute as "Metaphysical Scamp"†

The nature of the mute whose advent on April Fool's Day opens Herman Melville's *The Confidence-Man* has puzzled many critics. The crux seems to be the problem of whether or not the mute is an avatar of the Confidence Man.

Miss Elizabeth Foster, in her introduction of the book (1954), presents the most reasoned case for the mute's *not* being an avatar (p. l–li):

> The first advertiser of Christianity, the lamblike man, differs from those who follow him in that he commits no wrong, except perhaps unintentionally in softening victims for subsequent swindlers, and in no way, except to some people through his oddity, suggests that he is an impostor. Upon him the stigmata of the true Christian, and even of Christ himself, are patent. His message is Love. His white and "lamb-like" appearance is stressed; he seems "singularly innocent," gentle, helpless, and harmless. Though banged and nearly overthrown by some of the porters, though jeered and buffeted by his fellow-Christians, he remains meek, gentle, dreamy. In this world he is, "in the extremist sense of the word, a stranger."

Miss Foster relates this position to what Melville had written regarding Christianity in earlier books, and in *Moby-Dick* and *Pierre* she finds Melville presenting God as an enigma: "God is unknowable. If He hears us, He gives no sign. The Voice of our God is Silence. That is why the lamblike man is deaf and dumb." This strangeness and isolation reflect the "forever unreconcilable difference between the order of heaven and the order of earth." The mute sleeping at the foot of the ladder reminds her of the resurrection of God's promise to Jacob. She contrasts the mute and the crippled Negro in the next scene as representatives of Christ and Antichrist.[1] While admitting that the placard describing the

† Published here for the first time, by permission of the author.
1. Most other critics who agree with Miss Foster that the mute is not an avatar of the Confidence Man also see him as Christ or a Christ-figure. See Rosenberry (1955), p. 153; Miller (1959), p. 104; Gross (1959), pp. 303–304; and Humphreys (1962), pp. 104–106. Some critics see him as Christ or a Christ-figure but still believe that he is an avatar. See Chase (Winter 1949), pp. 124–125; Fiedler (1949), p. 494; Thompson (1952), pp. 303–305; and Magaw (1966), pp. 88–92. Cawelti (1957), p. 285, holds that the mute is an enigma. Oates (1962), p. 123, calls him a "symbolic representation . . . of a heavenly ethic." Porte (1969), pp. 157–159, sees him as a "mordant self-portrait" of Melville as a writer of romances.

impostor from the East suggests that the mute might be one of the swindlers, Miss Foster differentiates between him and the subsequent avatars: "he is innocent of fraud; he is unequivocal; he is not on the Negro's list of Confidence Men" (p. li).

Many critics, without examining the problem in detail, simply assume in their interpretations of the book that the mute is the first avatar, but H. Bruce Franklin (1963) answers Miss Foster directly (p. 159):

> Since the lamb-like man's message prepares the flock of fools for many later fleecings, he is at the very least an unwitting accomplice to fraud, and "unequivocal" hardly describes this mysterious figure. And is it safe to say that he does not appear on the list which Professor Foster elsewhere finds so defective?

The answer to Miss Foster's three-point position needs to be expanded, and some of Franklin's "eight pieces of circumstantial evidence which indicate that the lamb-like man is probably the first avatar of the Confidence Man" (p. 155) are helpful in this regard.

He is innocent of fraud. Even Miss Foster admits that the mute may "unintentionally" soften the Confidence Man's victims with his message of charity. As Nathalia Wright said (1949), *The Confidence-Man* is unique among Melville's books in its presentation of the Gospel and St. Paul as "a deceiving and misleading message" (p. 124). In Chapter 8 the narrator notices that the charitable lady, soon to be swindled out of twenty dollars by an avatar of the Confidence Man, holds the Bible, "her finger inserted at the xiii. of 1st Corinthians, to which chapter possibly her attention might have recently been turned, by witnessing the scene of the monitory mute and his slate."

None of the avatars can be proven guilty of fraud in any single encounter with a victim. The repetition of the actions that are possible swindles and the selfsameness of the Confidence Man through all his disguises expose the fraud.[2] Melville's irony and equivocal language help in this exposure. In regard to Miss Foster's contention that the mute is alone in his innocence, it should be noted that the cosmopolitan "commits no wrong" in his dealings with Charlie, Mark Winsome, Egbert, or the old man who appears in the last chapter—and he is before the reader much longer than the mute.

He is unequivocal. The diversity of opinion regarding the mute's nature would indicate that he is indeed equivocal. As Miss Foster herself concedes, the placard hints at the possibility of his being an avatar. His strangeness and otherworldly nature makes him mysterious. Again the language indicates that first appearances may be deceptive, as, for example, in Melville's play on the word "fleece,"

---

2. One critic refuses to acknowledge any guilt on the part of the Confidence Man. See Drew (1964).

used in describing both the mute and his successor, the Negro cripple, and later in characterizing the actions of confidence men. The ambiguous nature of the color white—so important to the mute's appearance—was examined earlier by Melville in "The Whiteness of the Whale" in *Moby-Dick.* In a footnote to that chapter he wrote of the polar bear, "the irresponsible ferociousness of the creature stands invested in the fleece of celestial innocence and love."[3]
He is not on the Negro's list of Confidence Men. Franklin argues rather unconvincingly, through the etymology of the word "vest" and a tortured treatment of the Negro's description in dialect of the subsequent avatars, that the mute is indeed on the list by virtue of his cream-colored clothing, which supposedly identifies him as the "ge'mman in a yaller west." More probably he is *not* on the list, and one reason might be that Melville wrote Chapter 1 and those sections of Chapter 2 concerning the mute *after* he had written Chapter 3 with the list outlining his plan for the subsequent disguises of the Confidence Man. While all the avatars from the Negro cripple to the man from the Philosophical Intelligence Office recommend and vouch for each other while talking to their victims (many of whom are fleeced by more than one avatar), the mute is excluded from this series and is mentioned only once in the book after Chapter 2, that being the instance in Chapter 8 noted above. The Confidence Man is indisputably the center of focus of every chapter in the book from Chapter 3 on, except Chapter 23 when Pitch meditates at Cairo over his duping by one of the "metaphysical scamps" he has encountered. Logically the Confidence Man would be at the center of Chapters 1 and 2 as well.

Certainly the character who has his advent in so grand a manner on the first page of a book entitled *The Confidence-Man: His Masquerade* should be the Confidence Man himself. Also a pattern exists, at least in the first half of the book, in which each avatar is replaced by his successor and no two avatars are on stage at the same time. So when the mute falls asleep in the forward part of the boat and disappears, "not unlikely, waked up and landed," he is replaced by the Negro cripple, who appears in the forward part of the boat at the beginning of Chapter 3.

Were she persuaded that the mute is the first avatar of the Con-

3. Also in regard to *Moby-Dick*, an interesting parallel can be drawn between the mute's boarding a ship at St. Louis and Jonah's boarding one at Joppa. According to Father Mapple, " 'So disordered, self-condemning is his look, that had there been policemen in those days, Jonah, on the mere suspicion of something wrong, had been arrested ere he touched a deck. How plainly he's a fugitive! no baggage, not a hat-box, valise or carpet-bag,—no friends ac-company him to the wharf with their adieux.' " Jonah, the stranger, tries in vain " 'to look all ease and confidence.' " The sailors, feeling that he is " 'no innocent,' " comment aloud on him, and one " 'runs to read the bill that's stuck against the spile upon the wharf to which the ship is moored, offering five hundred gold coins for the apprehension of a parricide, and containing a description of his person.' "

fidence Man, then Miss Foster might answer affirmatively the questions she posed regarding Melville's attitude toward the mute: "Does he mean to include the lamblike man among the impostors and thereby to imply that the very founding of Christianity was an expression of the universal malignity towards man? that God, though in an absolute sense unknowable, is in an effective and human sense evil?" Yet accepting the mute as an avatar of the Confidence Man does not necessarily lead to this dark conclusion. If, as such critics as John W. Shroeder (1951), Miss Foster, and Hershel Parker (1963) argue, the Confidence Man is the Devil (or one of his followers), a most appropriate way to have the Devil begin his April Fool's Day masquerade on the ship-microcosm is to have him appear as a Christ-figure preaching a sermon from the New Testament. The point may as some have said be both satiric and tragic—satiric of the nominal Christians who reject a Christ-like message, and tragic in that Christianity is dead, extinguished like the solar lamp in the last chapter.

WARNER BERTHOFF

[Ponderous Stuttering in Chapter 5]†

In the sparer style of Melville's prose after *Moby-Dick* and *Pierre*, individual words and phrases are less conspicuously thrust forward. They seem less exploratory, less (literally) provocative. We feel that Melville is no longer so consistently following their lead into the possible meanings and openings-out of the material in hand. Except as part of a general effort toward exact definition, the diction in this later work does not attract attention to itself. The distinction of the language is now a distinction of controlling intelligence, of right judgment and completed understanding. Single words are still potent— "penal" and "penitential" in "The Encantadas," along with the suggestive concreteness of "clinker" and "scar" as names for the blighted landscape; or the superb epithet "motionless" for the first appearance of Bartleby; or the whole rather stiff and angular vocabulary of specification in *The Confidence-Man* and *Billy Budd*—but they serve more to crystallize governing impressions than to search out new meanings. They function now like signals; like "apparitions," as Professor Mayoux nicely describes them; like standing mirrors of the realities they denote.

† From Warner Berthoff, *The Example of Melville* (Princeton: Princeton University Press, 1962), pp. 165–166.

The effort is simply to be precise, to give right names. A language of denomination, it might be called, and it has its own perils. When some right word or determinative name is not forthcoming, a kind of ponderous stuttering can set in—as in the first long paragraph of Chapter 5 of *The Confidence-Man*, with its proliferation of "may" and "might" and "seemed" and "appeared" and "perhaps" and "sometimes" and "not wholly" and "seldom very," without one firm verb or noun. Scrupulousness of that sort is likely to be self-defeating, even for a writer with great and grave things to say. There is always some use, stylistically speaking, in a capacity for small talk. But the instance is a freakish one; it is not for the most part in matters of language that *The Confidence-Man* falls short of its highest promise.

R. W. B. LEWIS

[Goneril and the Man with Gold Sleeve-Buttons: The Prose in Chapters 12 and 7]†

The whole tone, purpose and strategy of *The Confidence-Man* are in those sentences,[1] with their parade of notations and counter-notions, and the final flurry of phrases that modify, hesitantly contradict, and then utterly cancel one another out, leaving not a rack of positive statement behind. Goneril is in fact repellent: flat-chested, with a baked face and matted hair, heavily made-up, moustached and prickly-looking; *or is she?* As her physical actuality is blurred and dissolved by Melville's prose, we belatedly remember that Goneril probably does not even exist, but is simply an invention of the Confidence Man himself in his guise as "the man with the weed."

Or take Melville's analysis of the gentleman with the gold sleeve-buttons in Chapter 7. He had, Melville tells us with a straightforward air, the "very good luck . . . to be a very good man"; although, Melville adds, he could not perhaps be called righteous, and righteousness was indeed—St. Paul is cited as the authority—a quality superior to goodness.[2] Still, Melville goes on, the gentleman's goodness, if falling short of righteousness, should even so not be regarded as a *crime*; or anyhow (pressing the argument onward) not a crime for which the poor fellow should be

† From R. W. B. Lewis, Afterword to *The Confidence-Man* (New York: Signet, 1964), 265. Copyright © 1964 by R. W. B. Lewis. Reprinted by arrangement with The New American Library, Inc., New York, from the Signet Classic Edition.
1. Lewis refers to the second paragraph of Chapter 12. [*Editor's note.*]
2. This is not precisely the "apostolic preference" attributed to Paul. [*Editor's note.*]

sent to jail, since after all he might have been innocent of it. This is mental and moral sabotage. Amid all those pre-Jamesian qualifiers and circlings, Melville is of course insinuating that the gentleman with the gold buttons is not good at all, that his alleged goodness is no more than willful, self-protective innocence, thus reinforcing an earlier hint that the gentleman was the kind who refused to dirty his hands in the dilemmas of ethical choice, and was moral brother to history's most notorious hand-washer, "the Hebrew governor"—Pontius Pilate. Before Melville's prose is through with him, this very good man is lumped with those responsible for the crucifixion of Christ; and Melville has delivered himself of a very searching moral insight.

ELIZABETH S. FOSTER

[Melville's Revisions of Chapter 14]†

Any reader who observes the changes that Melville made from verson to version will see some of the reasons why the novel is obscure. It is immediately apparent that Melville's fear of wounding religious sensibilities was a real one and strong enough to account for his having buried his religious allegory pretty effectively in his novel. For example, Melville liked the following sentence well enough to carry it over intact (except for a shift to the subjunctive) from B to D, but he deleted it before publication: "So that the worst that can be said of any author in this particular, is that he shares a fault, if fault it be, with the author of authors." He gradually softened the following sentence until the first part was gone altogether and the second reduced to the word "contrasts": "And it is with man as with his maker: what makes him hard to comprehend is his inconsistency." Also, he finally stuck out every phrase or sentence in D which makes a clear assertion of his agnosticism, e.g.: "And possibly it may be in the one case as the other [human nature and the divine nature], that the expression of ignorance is wisdom . . ." He deleted a ringing sentence which says that sooner or later Nature "puts out every one who anyway pretends to be acquainted with the whole of her, which is indispensable to fitly comprehending any part of her." (Melville capitalizes "Nature" throughout D, but not "author of authors.")

Furthermore, the style that Melville invented or evolved for the expository parts of this novel desiderates understatement, underem-

† From Elizabeth S. Foster, ed., Appendix to *The Confidence-Man* (New York: Hendricks House, 1954), pp. 375–377.

phasis, litotes, and complexity that looks like simplicity. As we see him in his revisions moving always in these directions, and away from the loose structure, open clarity, and directness of his earliest versions of passages, we watch many ideas growing less and less obvious. Let us look in a general way at these revisions.

If any testimony were needed that artistry, taste, and genius presided at the composition of this novel, it could be found in the consistency with which Melville's tireless revision pushed towards one wished-for, clearly defined, and hitherto uncreated style, the style proper to the mood and matter of his unique novel.

In revision Melville tended to expand first, and later to contract. He expanded by pausing to emphasize or clarify a point * * *; by adding new material or allowing the old to ramify; and by adding qualifying words and phrases which almost invariably softened or weakened the meaning (e.g., "still be" becomes "still run the risk of being," and "fare . . . as" becomes "fare . . . something as"). He shortened in two ways: he cut out whole sentences and passages, almost every one of which would have been considered sacrilegious or infidel by many of his contemporaries; and with unsparing hand he pruned away superfluous words and predications.

Some of Melville's revisions of diction show him groping for the exact word. A very great many of them show him carefully converting statement to understatement: "proof sufficient" becomes "proof presumptive" and finally "some presumption"; "is" becomes "may prove"; "prove otherwise" becomes "prove not so much so"; "always" becomes "mainly"; "many characters" becomes "no few characters"; "is" becomes "would seem"; "it would" becomes "it ought to"; "a fatal objection" becomes "an adequate objection"; "always varies" becomes "subject to variation"; "are bound to" becomes "may." Only once or twice does Melville make his language stronger in revision: "different" becomes "conflicting"; "excluded" becomes "excluded with contempt."

In keeping with this hushing of the voice, this meticulous moderation of thought, this elegant avoidance of vulgar emphasis in language, is the toning down of color, of metaphor and simile: the sequestered youth is described first as "pine green," and then merely as "at fault" upon entering real life; a comparison of inconsistent characters with some of the beasts in Revelation is deleted. Only those comparisons are finally retained which are, not fanciful or decorative, but as functional as an axle.

The same consistency of purpose is seen in Melville's syntactical revisions. By combining sentences, shrinking predication, subordinating, he not only achieves a classical economy and purity but also diminishes the emphasis that some of his thoughts enjoyed while they stood alone; compare the last sentence of the fourth paragraph below, the next-to-last of the sixth, and their counterpart in the text of the novel (at the end of the fourth paragraph there). His favorite method of achieving understatement by subordination, an achievement which may be seen in the sentence just mentioned, is to set main thoughts on relative grounds by tucking them into the terms of a comparison and then to put the whole upon even more minor and tentative grounds by introducing it with "Upon the whole, it might rather be thought, that . . . ," or "Which may appear the less improbable if it be considered that. . . ." Thus the very syntax abets the hinting and whispering which are the language of this novel.

The other object or end of Melville's syntactical revisions was tension, tautness, strength in sentence structure. He increased parallelism regularly and periodic structure frequently from revision to revision as he combined and reduced sentences. He reversed the terms of comparisons, sometimes to make them conform better to the logic of the context, but often to gain suspense and climax, as in the next-to-last paragraph. The sentences, particularly the balanced and periodic ones, uncoil like springs, with a lithe, inexorable, cool precision. But this relentless movement of the sentence is half hidden beneath the mild language, the hesitating modifications, and emerges at the period with the shock of wit. In his revisions we may see Melville with infinite pains achieving in his sentences that fine ironic contrast and tension between mildmannered, leisurely surface and stern dialectic beneath, which is the mode of his novel.

* * *

HERSHEL PARKER

The Metaphysics of Indian-hating†

Even the closest student of *The Confidence-Man* admits that it "still keeps many, or most, of its secrets."[1] A reader can still share the sense of discovery which informed this paragraph by Sedgwick:[2]

> There is interpolated in *The Confidence-Man* a strange story, the point of which, I believe, has escaped notice. I refer to the

† From *Nineteenth-Century Fiction*, 18 (September, 1963), 165–173. Copyright © 1963 by The Regents of the University of California. Reprinted by permission of The Regents.
1. *The Confidence-Man* (New York, 1954), p. xlvi, edited by Elizabeth Foster. All references to Miss Foster's Introduction and Notes will be to this edition and will be given in parentheses within the text.
2. William Ellery Sedgwick, *Herman Melville: The Tragedy of Mind* (Cambridge, 1944), p. 190.

story of Colonel Moredock, the Indian-hater, followed by a discussion of the genus "Indian-hater" and the metaphysics of Indian-hating. The allegory here is so transparent that it needs no comment. The point to which it leads is important; to my way of thinking it is the most important thing in the book.

But today the critic of the Indian-hater section cannot be as confident as Sedgwick that the point has escaped notice. Both Elizabeth Foster (p. xci) and Nathalia Wright[3] have agreed that the section is the crux of the book, and the "transparent" allegory has evoked a good deal of comment.[4] In this paper I will survey the arguments of the three major critics of the Indian-hater chapters, John W. Shroeder,[5] Roy Harvey Pearce,[6] and Miss Foster, and point out some unresolved difficulties. Then, often working from their findings, I will interpret the story in terms of the opposing elements of the allegory and in relation to a theme recurring in all of Melville's novels. The Indian-hater story, as I read it, is a tragic study of the impracticability of Christianity, and, more obviously, a satiric allegory in which the Indians are Devils and the Indian-haters are dedicated Christians, and in which the satiric target is the nominal practice of Christianity.

If Shroeder has not "let more light into this book than any other critic," as Miss Foster says (p. xlii), certainly his use of literary cross-references "to locate the events of The Confidence-Man geographically and spiritually"[7] is the most illuminating criticism besides her own. Briefly as Shroeder treats the Indian-hater chapters, he indicates convincingly the diabolic nature of the Indians and the god-like character of the Indian-hater. Colonel Moredock, says Shroeder, "has succeeded in locating Evil in its real home; there is no distortion in his vision of spiritual reality."[8] But I would quarrel with Shroeder's conclusion that the only hope in this "dark book" is that "the triumph of the confidence-man is opposed and objectified, though apparently not negated, by an adversary of heroic proportions"[9]—that is, by Moredock. And I suggest that Shroeder, while accurately formulating the terms of the allegory, has missed the ironic inversion of accepted values which is the basis of Melville's gigantic satire.

Pearce's article amounts to a general contradiction of Shroeder's conclusions. He denies that the Indians "are symbols of satanism," and argues from Melville's attitude toward real Indians that he

3. *Melville's Use of the Bible* (Durham, 1949), p. 56.
4. Sedgwick's discussion of the passage does not justify the use of the word "allegory."
5. John W. Shroeder, "Sources and Symbols for Melville's *Confidence-Man*," *PMLA*, LXVI (June, 1951), 363–380. [Bracketed page numbers are to the reprinting in this Norton Critical Edition.]
6. Roy Harvey Pearce, "Melville's Indian-hater: A Note on a Meaning of *The Confidence-Man*," *PMLA*, LXVII (December, 1952), 942–948.
7. Shroeder, p. 368 [p. 303].
8. *Ibid.*, p. 379 [p. 315].
9. *Ibid.*, p. 376 [p. 312].

does not use the Indian symbolically in *The Confidence-Man*.[1]
Pearce submits "that there is nothing but distortion in the
Indian-hater's vision of spiritual reality," and denies that Moredock
"functions as a kind of hero."[2] The artistic function of Melville's
version of the Indian-hater story—a version in which hatred is
called a "devout sentiment" and the hater is praised—"is to be too
violent a purge, a terrible irony." In Pearce's reading there is hope
neither in the blind confidence of some of the passengers of the
Fidèle nor in Moredock's blind hatred: "The blackness is
complete."[3]

Although agreeing with Pearce that the Indian-hater is in no
sense a hero (p. 340), Miss Foster finds that "in the Indian-hater
chapters the Indian embodies allegorically a primitive, or primal,
malign, treacherous force in the universe" (p. 314). Unlike Pearce,
she distinguishes between Melville's attitude toward real Indians
and his use of them as symbols (pp. 339–340.) She takes exception
to Pearce's "blackness": "Melville, though a pessimistic moralist in
this novel, is not, I take it, a despairing one. Like many another
moralist and writer of comedy, he is concerned to point the dangers
of both extremes" (pp. 340–341).[4] Reading the section as one of
Melville's warning qualifications of "the cynicism and materialism
of the main argument" [*i.e.*, "No Trust"] (p. lxix), she concludes
that Melville "gives us an unforgettable picture of a society without
faith or charity. . . . This is the alternative if we jettison charity—a
world of solitary, dehumanized Indian-haters" (p. lxx).

Despite Miss Foster's tactful mediation between Shroeder and
Pearce and despite her own interpretation, major problems remain.
Neither Pearce nor Miss Foster has adequately explored the implications of Shroeder's evidence that the Indians are diabolic. Nor has
enough been made of the likelihood that in an allegory as carefully
structured as *The Confidence-Man* the antagonist of the satanic
Indians might be in some way religious. Then, Pearce's disgust at
the praise accorded Moredock (disgust shared by any reader of the
Indian-hating story as a literal narrative) has not been reconciled
with Shroeder's claim that Moredock is the heroic adversary of the
Confidence Man. The solution lies, I suggest, in taking the episode
as allegory, as Shroeder and Miss Foster do, and in carefully identifying the elements of that allegory. Melville's opposition of the

1. But Melville also uses race symbolically in "Benito Cereno," written at
the time *The Confidence-Man* was
begun and related to the Indian-hater
story by verbal echoes (such as "apos-
tatize," "Senegal") which build into
thematic echoes (such as the impossibility that the diabolic nature change:
the "Papist convert" Francesco is a
mulatto, and the half-breed in the Indian-hater story threatens, "Indian
blood is in me" [p. 129]).
2. Pearce, p. 942.
3. *Ibid.*, p. 948.
4. Miss Foster's moderate position is
in accord with the last stanza of "The
Conflict of Convictions" and with Melville's injunction in the second sketch
of "The Encantadas": "Enjoy the
bright, keep it turned up perpetually if
you can, but be honest, and don't deny
the black."

Indian-hater and the Indian constitutes, I believe, a consistent allegory in which Christianity is conceived as the dedicated hatred of Evil at the cost of forsaking human ties, and in which most of the human race is represented as wandering in the backwoods of error, giving lip-service to their religion but failing to embody it in their lives. The allegory is a grotesquely satiric study of the theme which Miss Foster calls the most obvious in the novel, "the failure of Christians to be Christian" (p. liii,) and in the vein of *Mardi* and *Pierre* it is a study of the practicability of Christianity as Jesus preached it.

Both Shroeder and Miss Foster offer evidence for the identification of the allegorical significance of the Indians. Demonstrating that snakes in *The Confidence-Man* are associated with the Devil as in Genesis, *Paradise Lost*, and Hawthorne's works, Shroeder argues cogently that the coupling of the Indian and the snake at the outset of the Indian-hater story is a deliberate guide to the diabolic nature of the Indians.[5] Never definitely calling the Indians Devils, Miss Foster observes that in Mocmohoc "readers will have recognized a type of the Confidence Man" (p. lxvii). She also suggests the possibility that "the Indian is something not so much sub-human as extra-human" (p. lxvii), and that by giving Indian containers for their wine bottles and cigars to the cosmopolitan and Charlie (the ordinary Mississippi confidence man who tells the Moredock story), "Melville meant to remind the reader that they are the Indians of the argument" (p. lxxii). The same function, I would add, is served by Melville's having the cosmopolitan ironically call his pipe a "calumet"—a peace pipe (p. 131). Miss Foster agrees that Shroeder "demonstrates beyond question the diabolic and mythic nature" of the Confidence Man (p. xlii,) but she does not pursue the allegorical associations of the Indians with Devils. Yet if the Confidence Man is associated with snakes and *is* the Devil, while Indians are associated with snakes and at least one Indian is "a type of the Confidence Man," then in Melville's allegorical geometry the Indians are Devils also.

Recognizing the Indians as types of the Devil of Christian literary tradition, we should reasonably expect the Devil's antagonist to be an earnest Christian. But Moredock, who dedicates his life to killing, hardly fits the ordinary conception of a follower of Jesus. The cosmopolitan (the last avatar of the Confidence Man) makes

5. Shroeder, pp. 376–377 [312]. Melville's knowledge of the Puritan identification of Indians with Devils is adequately attested by his reference in *Moby-Dick* (Chapter 27) to the "superstitions of some of the earlier Puritans" which might almost lead one to half-believe the Indian Tashtego "to be a son of the Prince of the Powers of the Air." For evidence of Melville's interest in Cotton Mather's *Magnalia* during the composition of *The Confidence-Man* see "The Apple-Tree Table" in *Putnam's Monthly* for May, 1856. In the *Magnalia*, Mather frequently calls Indians both Devils and snakes.

the obvious objection in professing himself unable to believe that a man so loving to his family could be so merciless to his enemies (p. 136). Pearce in a similar spirit rejects Shroeder's interpretation of Moredock as the man who has located Evil in its real home. But repugnant as it is, the logic of the opposition demands that we see Moredock as a Devil-hating Christian, though one who does not live up to all of Jesus' commands. The outrageous irony that has escaped notice is that it is when Moredock is murdering Indians that he is Christian and when he is enjoying the comforts of domestic life that he is apostatizing.

Before seeing how the dedication to Indian-hating is described in terms of dedication to Christianity, one must dispose of the cosmopolitan's ironic objection that some parts of Charlie's story do not hang together: "If the man of hate, how could John Moredock be also the man of love?" Considering the familiarity with the Bible which he displays elsewhere, the cosmopolitan should be aware that there is ample biblical authority for being both a man of hate and a man of love. In Amos 5:15 the duality is stated baldly: "Hate the evil, and love the good." Psalm 139, from which Melville quotes earlier (p. 59), is also explicit about the duty to hate: "Do not I hate them, O Lord, that hate thee? and am not I grieved with those that rise up against thee? I hate them with perfect hatred; I count them mine enemies." In this tone Melville's Father Mapple cries: "Woe to him whom this world charms from Gospel duty! Woe to him who seeks to pour oil upon the waters when God has brewed them into a gale!" Father Mapple in his peroration is as implacable as Moredock: "Delight is to him, who gives no quarter in the truth, and kills, and burns, and destroys all sin though he pluck it out from under the robes of Senators and Judges." There is a darker side of Christianity, as Melville is careful to remind us by the cry of "church militant!" when the Methodist minister shakes the one-legged man till his timber-toe clatters "on the deck like a nine-pin" (p. 11), by the mention of Torquemada, the Spanish inquisitor general (p. 49), and by the references to Jesuits (p. 79), to Loyola (p. 108), and to "a victim in *auto-da-fé*" (p. 210).

Once we accept Melville's ironic view of Christianity as the practice of Devil-hating, we are ready to follow the similarity of the dedication to Indian-hating to the dedication to Christianity. Keeping in mind the word "Metaphysics" in the title of Chapter xxvi, we can see the significance of the religious references like "guilty race," "monk," and "cloistered" in Melville's description of how the Indian-hater *par excellence* comes to his resolution (p. 130):

An intenser Hannibal, he makes a vow, the hate of which is a vortex from whose suction scarce the remotest chip of the guilty race may reasonably feel secure. Next, he declares himself and settles his temporal affairs. With the solemnity of a Spaniard turned monk, he takes leave of his kin; or rather, these leave-takings have something of the still more impressive finality of death-bed adieus. Last, he commits himself to the forest prime-val; there, so long as life shall be his, to act upon a calm, clois-tered scheme of strategical, implacable, and lonesome vengeance.

Later in the conversation (p. 148) Charlie's allusion to Matthew 19 (or Mark 10) emphasizes the similarity of the dedication of the Indian-hater to the way Jesus would have one begin a life as His follower. The whole of the passage just quoted from should be read in the light of Jesus' words to the rich young man, and to His disciples after the young man has gone sorrowfully away, especially the command to dispose of worldly possessions and the reward promised to "every one that hath forsaken houses, or brethren, or sisters, or father, or mother, or wife, or children, or lands, for my name's sake." Moreover, there is a parallel to the Christian's being, as Paul says (Romans 6:2), "dead to sin."

Throughout Charlie's story theological terms are employed to describe the "devout sentiment" of Indian-hating. We are told (p. 131) that there is

a species of diluted Indian-hater, one whose heart proves not so steely as his brain. Soft enticements of domestic life too often draw him from the ascetic trail; a monk who apostatizes to the world at times. . . . It is with him as with the Papist converts in Senegal; fasting and mortification prove hard to bear.

According to Charlie, Judge Hall "would maintain that there was no vocation whose consistent following calls for such self-containing as that of the Indian-hater *par excellence*" (p. 131). Here Melville is using "vocation" in its literal and theological sense of "calling."[6] Where in Melville's source the real James Hall says that Moredock watched the murderers of his mother for more than a year before attacking them, Melville alters the account to stress Moredock's solitude, for "upwards of a year, alone in the wilds" after his dedication (p. 133).[7] Melville has already made the judge declare that the backwoodsman is "worthy to be compared with Moses in the Exodus" (p. 126). Now he emphasizes Moredock's role as religious leader by making him on one occasion seek the

6. "Vocation" in Melville is usually not merely a synonym for "profession." See *The Confidence-Man*, pp. 108, 153; for more ambiguous uses, pp. 1, 178.
7. The reader who has been made con-stantly aware of the Pauline epistles by the allusions to I Corinthans 13 may well recall Paul's semi-legendary retreat to the Arabian deserts shortly after his conversion. For the meager biblical source, see Galatians 1:17. It should be noted that for "murder" (p. 134, line 1) one should read "num-ber." [Emended in this edition.—*Edi-tor's note.*]

murderers "at the head of a party pledged to serve him for forty days." Here Melville has added to Hall's account the biblical number for times of purgation and preparation—forty. It is Melville (or his storyteller Charlie) who gives Moredock a retributive spirit that speaks like God's "voice calling through the garden" (p. 133). In Charlie's story Moredock's manner of being benevolent (p. 134) is in accord with Jesus' command in the Sermon on the Mount (Matthew 6:3): "But when thou doest alms, let not thy left hand know what thy right hand doeth." And, apropos of Moredock's refusal to seek high political office, Judge Hall (according to Charlie) says (p. 135) that the Colonel

> was not unaware that to be a consistent Indian-hater involves the renunciation of ambition, with its objects—the pomps and glories of the world; and since religion, pronouncing such things vanities, accounts it merit to renounce them, therefore, so far as this goes, Indian-hating, whatever may be thought of it in other respects, may be regarded as not wholly without the efficacy of a devout sentiment.

Leaving such vanities behind, the dedicated Indian-haters inhabit the moral wilderness which, as Miss Wright says, is "the symbolic scene of mature experience throughout Melville."[8] The Indian-hater *par excellence* is nearly fabulous, a soul "peeping out but once an age" (p. 131). The lesser Indian-hater like Moredock either backslides to domestic life or, desperate from the loneliness which his ascetic vow has imposed, "hurries openly towards the first smoke" (p. 131) and embraces the Indian Devil. For as the pamphlet in *Pierre* has it, efforts at the absolute imitation of Christ may often involve the idealist in "strange, *unique* follies and sins."[9] Those still less devoted, the inhabitants of the fringes of the moral wilderness, the backwoods, are "diluted Indian-haters" who give nominal allegiance to the religious ideals realized (if at all) only by the Indian-hater *par excellence*. They teach their children the traditional hatred of the Indian as Eve teaches her children enmity to the serpent (p. 126; for an allusion to the curse in Genesis see p. 113), and they join in community disapproval of the adversary (p. 126) without ever applying the religion of Indian-hating, or Devil-hating, to their ordinary lives. To repeat Sedgwick's phrase, almost without irony, the allegory is transparent.

8. Wright, p. 56.
9. *Pierre*, ed. Henry A. Murray (New York, 1949), p. 250. See pp. 103–105, 125 for Pierre's dedication, which is in crucial ways like that of the Indian-haters. See also p. 252: when the "Enthusiast to Duty" despairs at the impossibility of fulfilling his vow, "he is too apt to run clean away into all manner of moral abandonment, self-deceit, and hypocrisy (cloaked, however, mostly under an aspect of the most respectable devotion); or else he openly runs, like a mad dog, into atheism." The consequences of the Indian-haters' vows are strictly comparable.

With the basic allegory of Indian Devils and Devil-hating Christians established, the story can be interpreted coherently.[1] We are spared Pearce's revulsion at the literal story and can appreciate the grisly humor in Melville's outrageous distortion of our habitual way of thinking of Christianity. For in a book in which the Devil comes aboard the world-ship to preach Christianity as an April Fool's joke, it is apt that the best haters be the best Christians. The story of the Weavers and the Wrights can be recognized as not simply a piteous tale of frontier betrayal and violence, but as a warning against making a "covenant" with the Devil (p. 129). The "moral indignation" of the Indians who claim to be maligned (p. 127) is wryly comic, especially since the "Supreme Court" to which is left the question of whether Indians should be permitted to testify for themselves is, within the allegory, the Last Judgment.[2] Any reading of the section with the terms of the allegory in mind will reveal other elements in Melville's mordantly comic study of the discrepancy between the Christianity that Jesus preached and that which nominal Christians practice.

It is not surprising that the reviewers of *The Confidence-Man* in 1857 did not understand the allegory. As Miss Foster shows (pp. xviii-xix), Melville in the mid-1850's habitually concealed his darker meanings from a public unwilling or unable to face them. It is more surprising that the point of the story has "escaped notice" among modern readers, for it is altogether characteristic of Melville. The "failure of Christians to be Christian" is satirized in each of his novels from *Typee* to *Billy Budd, Sailor,* and the tragic impracticability of Christianity is dramatized at length in *Mardi* and *Pierre.* Perhaps readers of the Indian-hater chapters have been, in the pamphlet's word, too "horological" to acknowledge biblical

---

1. This reading does not solve every formal difficulty. While it relates the meaning of the section to that of a major theme in this book and Melville's other works, it does not account for the story's function in the plot. It is presumably a well-chosen gambit in Charlie's nefarious strategy for duping the cosmopolitan, whom the application of the story is designed to flatter. Pitch is (p. 135) "a sort of comprehensive Colonel Moredock, who, too much spreading his passion, shallows it." Moredock, the Pitch figure in the story, is a failure in that he is not, according to Hall's distinctions in Charlie's story, an Indian-hater *par excellence,* for while retaining his antipathy to Indians, Moredock retreats from his struggle in order to establish a family. A difficulty is that no one would want to claim that Charlie is aware of the allegorical meaning of his story or of the true identity of his new companion. It is easy to see why Miss Foster (p. lxviii) calls the views in the story "orphan." In view of Melville's cavalier interpolations into his manuscripts, it may well be wrong to look for a New-Critical aptness of story to storyteller or relevance of dramatic situation to plot as a whole. [Hershel Parker, 1971].

2. This instance of Melville's habit of choosing elaborate legal equivalents or opposites for the Last Judgment may be compared with the cosmopolitan's decision (p. 163) to leave the accountability of the rattlesnake not to "the Court of Common Pleas, but to something superior." Other examples are Elijah's "Grand Jury" (*Moby-Dick,* Chapter 21), and Captain Vere's "Last Assizes" in *Billy Budd, Sailor,* eds. Harrison Hayford and Merton M. Sealts, Jr. (Chicago, 1962), p. 111.

authority for single-minded hatred of Evil, or to acknowledge the Christlikeness of forsaking family and property for religion. The final irony may be that for modern readers able to accept Melville's darkest meanings Christianity is so "diluted" that they have become insensitive to his satire and, more appallingly, have lost his apprehension that the impracticability of Christianity is tragic.

MERTON M. SEALTS, JR.

[The Dialogue in Chapter 30]†

A look at the movement of Melville's skillful rhetoric through these tightly structured speeches discloses the intensely serious thrust behind the humorous extravagance. When the comic Noble makes his increasingly fatuous remarks about the forward march of geniality, the witty Goodman, pretending to agree, not only caps each successive point on Noble's own level but at the same time transforms their verbal exchange into a series of increasingly serious jabs at prevalent contemporary assumptions about "the advance of the humanitarian spirit" and "the progress of Christianization." His inference, obvious to the clear-eyed reader, is that "the whole world" is just about as likely to turn genuinely Christian as it is to become truly "genialized": "In a word, as the progress of Christianization *mellows those in manner whom it cannot mend in mind*, much the same will it prove with the progress of genialization" (emphasis added). "Geniality" in this immediate context is actually Melville's rhetorical stalking-horse for an exposure of the pretensions of humanitarianism and religion, conceived in terms of the prevailing nineteenth-century faith in inevitable "progress" that so frequently drew his fire. This point once established, the function of "geniality" in *The Confidence-Man* as a whole is further illuminated. When the dealer in "confidence" assumes geniality as his mask, it becomes the exact equivalent of such other humbugs as the superficial piety and charity he displays elsewhere in the book. And when passengers aboard the *Fidèle* cannot resist playing the confidence-game, both its operators and their gullible victims get out of it about what they both deserve.

† From Merton M. Sealts, Jr., "Melville's 'Geniality,'" in *Essays in American and English Literature Presented to Bruce Robert McElderry, Jr.*, edited by Max F. Schulz with William D. Templeman and Charles R. Metzger (Athens, Ohio: Ohio University Press, 1967), pp. 3–26; the quotation is from p. 16. Reprinted by permission of the publisher. The particular speeches analyzed here occur late in Chapter 30.

ALLEN HAYMAN

["Reality" in Chapter 33]†

What Melville was getting at in this chapter can be seen, I think, by taking as a gloss the distinction that Hawthorne made between the novel and the romance in his famous preface to *The House of the Seven Gables* in which Hawthorne made it clear that his fiction was not a transcript from everyday life but rather an interpretation of or a comment upon that life. The actualities of the everyday world were less important than what they signified. In Melville's words, then, the aim of Hawthorne's romance was to "present another world" but "one to which we feel the tie." Although Melville and Hawthorne testified that they knew what growing numbers of literary men of their day were demanding of fiction—that it give a faithful and accurate portrayal of everyday life—they both declined the gambit.

Harry Levin has noted that the concept of realism "profited from Daguerre's epoch-making invention, which entered the public domain in 1839,"[1] and definitions of realism often refer to the writer's photographic accuracy in the representation of material. The realistic novelist deals with the surface of life, with what could actually happen, with—in a word—*actuality*. Melville's fiction, as he asserted in Chapter 33 of *The Confidence-Man*, is primarily concerned not with actuality, but with *reality*, with, indeed, "more reality, than real life itself can show." A writer concerned with this heightened reality is mainly interested not in the circumstantial events of daily experience, the surface of life, but rather in what lies beneath the surface, the meaning of the surface—the meaning of life, or as much of it as the writer can apprehend. That is, Melville distinguished between what may be called actuality, on the one hand, and reality, on the other. Actuality—superficial verisimilitude—is what the realistic writer deals with; reality is the concern of a writer like Melville who searches for Truth, what Melville called in the *Mosses* essay the "intuitive Truth," "those short, quick probings at the very axis of reality." This is what he admired in Shakespeare and discovered with a shock of recognition in his compatriot, neighbor, and fellow-novelist, Nathaniel Hawthorne. I

† From Allen Hayman, "The Real and the Original: Herman Melville's Theory of Prose Fiction," *Modern Fiction Studies*, 8 (Autumn, 1962), 211–232; the quotation is from pp. 220–221. Reprinted by permission of *Modern Fiction Studies*, © 1962, by the Purdue Research Foundation, Lafayette, Indiana.

1. "What Is Realism?" *Comparative Literature*, III (Summer, 1951), 196–197.

take Melville's heightened reality to be the equivalent of Hawthorne's "truth to the human heart," which, as Hawthorne insisted, had little to do with surface accuracy. Both of these writers probed deeper into experience than did the realistic novelist. They examined men's innermost beings—their souls, if you will—rather than their daily experiences—except as those experiences affected men's souls.

ELIZABETH S. FOSTER

[Emerson in *The Confidence-Man*]†

Anyone in the nineteenth century waging war against optimistic philosophy must of course sooner or later single out for particular attack its great American champion, Ralph Waldo Emerson. Accordingly, Melville brings Emerson aboard the *Fidèle*, perhaps in the herb-doctor, certainly in the mystic Mark Winsome and his practical disciple Egbert, whom the cosmopolitan next encounters.[1] Using Winsome and Egbert as his targets, Melville fires a few derisive volleys at the Emersonian metaphysics; and against the Emersonian ethics, especially Emersonian individualism, he empties the arsenal of his scorn.

In splitting Emerson's philosophy between Winsome and Egbert, whom I take to be its metaphysics and its ethics respectively, or perhaps better the abstract philosophy and its practical effect, Melville was dramatizing a dualism in Emerson that has been generally commented on from Lowell's *A Fable for Critics*

† From Elizabeth S. Foster, Introduction to *The Confidence-Man* (New York: Hendricks House, 1954), pp. lxxiii–lxxix, lxxxi–lxxxii.

1. Miss Foster's insistence that Winsome and Egbert are portraits of two sides of Emerson has been a major stumblingblock to later critics. She granted Oliver only three "telling points" in his identification of Egbert with Thoreau (1946): the fact that "Thoreau *was* a disciple of Emerson," "that Egbert's disquisition on friendship is very close in idea to some passages" from Thoreau's *Week*; and that "Winsome and Egbert are about as far apart in years as Emerson and Thoreau" (p. 351). She insisted that "Emerson was certainly not Thoreau's 'sublime master' in the 1850's"—a point that is perhaps accurate but that is altogether anachronistic, according to a great deal of contemporary testimony. Admitting that Lowell, at least, thought Thoreau was a disciple of Emerson's, she rejected the relevance of that fact by arguing (p. 352) that "the difference between Winsome and Egbert, however, is not so much the difference between an originator and a disciple as between a mystic and a practical man, between the man of theory who confines himself to words and the man of action who puts that theory to work." (She recognized that in view of Thoreau's practical application of Emerson's principles her own point could support Oliver's thesis.) In denying that Winsome and Egbert are characterized as originator and disciple, Miss Foster ignored the chapter title where Egbert is conspicuously described as a disciple, as well as Winsome's benevolent introduction of him as "Egbert, a disciple." Evidence as well as elegance seem to be on Oliver's side. See Parker (1970). [*Editor's note.*]

(1848) to the present; and Lowell implies that he was not the first
to see it. The *Fable* says that Emerson's is

> A Greek head on right Yankee shoulders, whose range
> Has Olympus for one pole, for t'other the Exchange;
> He seems, to my thinking (although I'm afraid
> The comparison must, long ere this, have been made),
> A Plotinus-Montaigne, where the Egyptian's gold mist
> And the Gascon's shrewd wit cheek-by-jowl coexist . . .;

and the recently published *Emerson Handbook*, by Frederic Ives
Carpenter, stresses almost throughout its length the "two sides to
Emerson's face and philosophy"; it quotes from Bliss Perry "as perhaps the first to emphasize the actual embodiment of this dualism
in the physical lines of Emerson's face" (in *Emerson Today*):

> His features were slightly asymmetrical. Seen from one side, it
> was the face of the old school, shrewd, serious, practical. . . .
> Seen from the other side, it was the face of a dreamer, a seer, a
> soul brooding on things to come, things as yet very far away.

The three main heads under which Mr. Carpenter discusses Emerson's ideas are "The Ideal and the Real," "Transcendental Ideal-
ism: Mysticism," and "Yankee Realism: Pragmatism." The "two
sides" which these heads suggest are precisely those caricatured in
Winsome and Egbert respectively. Parallels between the details of
the Emersonian portrait in Chapters 36–41 of *The Confidence-Man*
on the one hand and descriptions of Emerson by biographers and
comments by Melville himself on the other will be brought out in
the notes to those chapters.

Further evidence that Melville intended the mystic Winsome
and his practical disciple Egbert to be different aspects of the same
person, or of the same philosophy, comes from a piece of manuscript, a very early draft of "Titles for Chapters," which seems to
represent a jotting down of ideas in the early stages of inventing
the story.[2] The second of these titles is "The practical mystic," and
it could apply to no one except Egbert-Winsome.

This splitting was partly suggested, no doubt, by Emerson's frequent explanation that the role of the poet and philosopher should
be, not participation in active and fragmentary reforms, but the
generation of a moral atmosphere that would encourage each man
to elevate his own nature, and also in Emerson's own reluctance to
enter the practical reforms which his beliefs encouraged. Speaking
of the taint of burlesque in the active representatives of virtue,
Emerson had written: "Yet we are tempted to smile, and we flee

2. The editors and the author of the
"Historical Note" in the Northwestern-
Newberry Edition of *The Confidence-
Man* hold, on the contrary, that these
draft titles were written after most or
all of the book was completed. [*Editor's
note.*]

from the working to the speculative reformer, to escape that same slight ridicule."[3] Melville's overt splitting of the Emersonian philosopher into the working and speculative reformer enabled him to say very earnestly that, though the metaphysics might be dismissed as moonshine, the practical ethics were operative and were charged with moral danger to mankind.

Melville is sweeping in his criticism of Emerson, and he is as severe as it is possible for one to be who loves "all men who *dive*" no matter what they bring up from the depths of thought. His marginalia in his copies of Emerson's works reiterate his tribute to the nobility of Emerson's aim and of much of what Emerson had to say. But the satiric portraits of Winsome and Egbert are unrelieved by any such acknowledgment, for they embody only the faults of Emerson's mind and thought.

The satire, through Winsome, of a number of Emersonian traits is corroborated by direct comments on Emerson in Melville's letters and marginalia. Winsome is aloof, icy-cold, shrewdly opposed to philanthropy; his disciple will have " 'a head kept cool by the under ice of the heart.' " In his copy of Emerson's essay "The Poet," beside the passage beginning "Language is fossil poetry," Melville wrote:[4]

> This is admirable, as many other thoughts of Mr. Emerson's are. His gross and astonishing errors & illusions spring from a self-conceit so intensely intellectual and calm that at first one hesitates to call it by its right name. Another species of Mr. Emerson's errors, or rather blindness, proceeds from a defect in the region of the heart.

Winsome's oracular, pedantic incoherencies about the Egyptians, Proclus, and Plato recall an early impression of Melville's, expressed in a letter to Evert Duyckinck, that Emerson was full of "transcendentalisms, myths & oracular gibberish," a "Plato who talks thro' his nose."[5] Winsome does not respond to the cosmopolitan's conviviality, and prefers to keep his love for wine, he says, " 'in the lasting condition of an untried abstraction.' " In the same letter to Duyckinck, Melville wrote:

> You complain that Emerson tho' a denizen of the land of gingerbread, is above munching a plain cake in company of jolly fel-

3. "The Transcendentalist," *Complete Works of Ralph Waldo Emerson*, Centenary Edition (Boston, 1903–1907), 12 vols.; I, 355.
4. Melville's copies of Emerson's *Essays . . ., Essays: Second Series . . ., Poems . . .,* and *The Conduct of Life . . .,* all annotated by Melville, are in HCL-M. Most of Melville's direct comments on Emerson have been published in William Braswell, "Melville as a Critic of Emerson," *American Literature*, IX (1937), 317–334; and F. O. Matthiessen, *American Renaissance, passim.* Although these marginalia were written after *The Confidence-Man,* they are consonant with Melville's earlier impression of Emerson.
5. Boston, 3 March 1849; NYPL-D; printed in Thorp, *Herman Melville,* pp. 371–373.

lows, & swiging [sic] off his ale like you & me. Ah, my dear sir, that's his misfortune, not his fault. His belly, sir, is in his chest, & his brains descend down into his neck & offer an obstacle to a draught of ale or a mouthful of cake.

Melville frequently repeated such strictures. It is part of his comment on Emerson that Emerson kept many human goods, from ale to friendship, " 'in the lasting condition of an untried abstraction.' "

But it is when Winsome and Egbert discourse on self-reliance and friendship that Melville trains his artillery on Emerson. Emerson's primary ethical doctrine of self-reliance is based upon his optimistic belief that "all nature is the rapid efflux of goodness executing and organizing itself," and that the individual therefore shares in the self-existence of the Deity; in "Self-Reliance" he says:[6]

> . . . we inquire the reason of self-trust. Who is the Trustee? What is the aboriginal Self, on which a universal reliance may be grounded? . . . The inquiry leads us to that source, at once the essence of genius, of virtue, and of life, which we call Spontaneity or Instinct. We denote this primary wisdom as Intuition. . . . We lie in the lap of immense intelligence, which makes us receivers of its truth and organs of its activity.

Emerson does not, of course, close his eyes to evil. But serene in his faith that "the nature of things, the eternal law" will balk wickedness and transform it in the end, Emerson urges self-reliance in spite of the evil in the Napoleons of the world. "We like to see everything do its office after its kind, whether it be a milch-cow or a rattlesnake," he says.[7] Winsome expresses admiration for the rattlesnake, implying that it would be a desirable experience to change personalities with one, " 'to sting, to kill . . . and revel for a while in the carefree, joyous life of a perfectly instinctive, unscrupulous, and irresponsible creature.' " This, Melville is saying, is your self-reliance, a reliance upon the rattlesnake spirit of nature, " 'perfectly instinctive, unscrupulous, and irresponsible.' " If you think that there is a universal benevolence that nullifies this poison, you delude yourself criminally; in the name of an unwarranted optimism you have encouraged man to revert to the jungle. Winsome indeed says, or implies through his questions, that people are not morally accountable, since rattlesnakes are not.

What Melville had called non-benevolence in describing Plinlimmon in *Pierre* is the concomitant of Emerson's intense individualism. To Emerson the relation between man and man is important only in its bearing on the relation between man and God. Friend-

6. "Circles," *Works*, II, 31; "Self-Reliance," *Works*, II, 63–64.

7. "Napoleon; or, The Man of the World," *Works*, IV, 235.

ships and loves are steps by which the soul mounts, he says in several places; in "Circles" he puts it thus:[8]

> The continual effort to raise himself above himself, to work a pitch above his last height, betrays itself in a man's relations. We thirst for approbation, yet cannot forgive the approver. The sweet of nature is love; yet if I have a friend I am tormented by my imperfections. The love of me accuses the other party. If he were high enough to slight me, then could I love him, and rise by my affection to new heights. A man's growth is seen in the successive choirs of his friends. For every friend whom he loses for truth, he gains a better.

Melville mocks such individualism with acrid humor. Egbert says that he agrees with his sublime master Winsome, " 'Who, in his Essay on Friendship, says so nobly, that if he want a terrestrial convenience, not to his friend celestial (or friend social and intellectual) would he go,' " because " 'for the superior nature, which on no account can ever descend to do good, to be annoyed with requests to do it, when the inferior one, which by no instruction can ever rise above that capacity, stands always inclined to it—this is unsuitable.' " One should choose one's friends, says Egbert, as one chooses one's mutton, " 'not for its leanness, but for its fatness,' " and this is not vile prudence but the means of preserving the delicacy of friendship. For one ever to help his friend, or to lend him money—that would violate the delicacy of the relation. No true friend will ask it, as no true friend will, in platonic love, require love-rites. Emerson had written in "Friendship":[9]

> We chide the citizen because he makes love a commodity. It is an exchange of gifts, of useful loans; it is good neighborhood; it watches with the sick; it holds the pall at the funeral; and quite loses sight of the delicacies and nobility of the relation.
> The condition which high friendship demands is ability to do without it.

The most heartless part of this creed, according to Melville, is that it treats the individual as if he were morally responsible for what is inevitable, blandly ignores the inconsistency, and shrugs its shoulders over his suffering. A man who wants help, says Egbert, has a defect and so does not deserve help. There is "always a reason *in the man*, for his good or bad fortune," said Emerson, "and so in making money."[1] Since nature labels her harmful creatures, putting rattles on rattlesnakes, says Winsome, it is the victim's own fault if he is destroyed; and " 'for a man to pity where nature is pitiless, is a little presuming.' "

8. *Works*, II, 307.
9. *Works*, II, 205, 208.

1. *Works*, VI, 100.

In merging Emerson's ethics with the doctrines of economic individualism as he does in Egbert, Melville was not going beyond his text. A. C. Kern has demonstrated Emerson's commitment to *laissez-faire* economics.[2] The consanguinity of Emerson's philosophy with this school of thought is reasonable, since both derive from a common concept of natural law. Emerson could fit his concurrence with "the dismal science" into his serene optimism because he was sure of the goodness and beauty of the universal laws and because his scorn of materialism made it easy for him to overlook the suffering due to material causes.

But after Egbert has told the story of China Aster to prove " 'the folly, on both sides, of a friend's helping a friend' " with a useful loan, the cosmopolitan declares that he has had enough of this " 'inhuman philosophy,' " and takes his leave. * * *

It came naturally to Melville's mind to think of Christ when he wanted an opposite pole from some of Emerson's ideas. Emerson wrote: "The good, compared to the evil [which a man sees], is as his own good to his own evil"; Melville commented: "A Perfectly Good being therefore would see no evil.—But what did Christ see? He saw what made him weep—To annihilate all this nonsense read the Sermon on the Mount, and consider what it implies." Melville read in a book by William Alger that

> even the kindly Emerson illustrated the temptation of the great to scorn the commonalty, when he speaks of "enormous populations, like moving cheese,—the more, the worse"; "the guano-races of mankind"; "the worst of charity is, that the lives you are asked to preserve are not worth preserving"; "masses! the calamity is the masses; I do not wish any shovel-handed, narrow-brained, gin-drinking mass at all."

Melville's notation was: "These expressions attributed to the 'kindly Emerson' are somewhat different from the words of Christ to the multitude on the Mount.—Abhor pride, abhor malignity, but not grief and poverty, and the natural vices these generate."[3] This antinomy—Christian brotherly love, that suffereth long and is kind, that seeketh not her own, the helping hand and the feeling heart, this on the one hand, and on the other, Emersonian individualism, which is, after all, only a rarefied form of enlightened self-interest—this antinomy is central to *The Confidence-Man* and perhaps, as we have seen, primary. It is a more sardonic, a more mordant, version of the contrast between chronometrical and horological ethics in *Pierre*. In the morning a lamblike man appealing to men to love their neighbors; in the evening—in the nineteenth

2. "Emerson and Economics," *New England Quarterly*, XIII (1940), 678–696.

3. These passages and marginalia are quoted in Matthiessen, *American Renaissance*, pp. 184, 401 f.

century—a practical mystic teaching men, in effect, to love themselves.

So inhuman have Winsome and Egbert shown themselves that the cosmopolitan begins to look like the true champion of magnanimity and benevolence after all. Melville's quiet reminder, at the end of the scene with Egbert, that the cosmopolitan is playing a role is hardly clear or strong enough to dethrone him now in the reader's sympathy. A number of readers have been blinded, even to his dubious performance in the ensuing scenes, by the dazzle of his humane sentiments in this one. Melville wrote the cosmopolitan's lines about the helping hand and the feeling heart and about the troughs and crests of vicissitude with an eloquence that came from his own heart. But it is clear that he does not intend, by making the Emersonian individualist seem worse than the Confidence Man, to whitewash the latter, but rather to underline the inhumanity of the former. That the philosophy of Mark Winsome, the practice of the Mississippi swindler, and the machinations of our "metaphysical scamps" the Confidence Men, all tend to the same end, an atomistic world of trustless, loveless misanthropes, should not be obscured by the cosmopolitan's bland, benevolent mask.

BRIAN HIGGINS

Mark Winsome and Egbert: "In the Friendly Spirit"†

Taking Mark Winsome as a portrait of Emerson, Elizabeth S. Foster (1954) declares that the antinomy of "Christian brotherly love" and "Emersonian individualism" ("which is, after all, only a rarefied form of enlightened self-interest") is central to, and perhaps primary to, the meaning of *The Confidence-Man* (p. lxxxii). She sees *The Confidence-Man* as "a more sardonic, a more mordant, version of the contrast between chronometrical and horological ethics in *Pierre.*" For that part of the Winsome-Egbert episode which treats of the propriety of a friend's helping a friend, Miss Foster's linkage of ideas is especially pertinent, for an awareness of the pervasive Christian references in the episode is essential to an understanding of its satiric intention, while a knowledge of Plinlimmon's Pamphlet in *Pierre* makes all the clearer the nature of Winsome's and Egbert's offenses.

Along with *Pierre*, *The Confidence-Man* is a study of the practicability of biblical Christianity. Throughout the book, beginning

† Published here for the first time, by permission of the author.

with the contrast between the words on the mute's slate and the
words on the barber's sign in Chapter 1, Melville constantly uses
the teachings of the New Testament as a critical touchstone for the
words and actions of his characters. In the course of the Winsome-
Egbert chapters the reader sees ever more clearly that, judged by
the standards of absolute Christianity, the teachings of Winsome
and Egbert are culpably lacking, though by the standards of the
world they may be eminently commonsensical. The Christian context is established unobtrusively, but with good comic effect, early
in the exposition of the practical side of Winsome's philosophy
(Chapter 37, "The mystical master introduces the practical disciple."). Blandly drawing Winsome in, the cosmopolitan asks him if
the study of his philosophy "tends to the same formation of character with the experiences of the world." Winsome replies:

> "It does; and that is the test of its truth; for any philosophy
> that, being in operation contradictory to the ways of the world,
> tends to produce a character at odds with it, such a philosophy
> must necessarily be but a cheat and a dream."

His statement may at first sound reasonable, but given Melville's
habitual unfavorable contrast of "this world" with another world of
more absolute values, it must be recognized as insidious.[1] By implication Winsome is airily dismissing Christianity, along with any
other philosophy "in operation contradictory to the ways of the
world." Melville clearly enough designed Winsome's teachings to
oppose those of the New Testament so persistently that biblical
passages would be evoked to provide a silent judgment on Winsome's pronouncements. The Winsome vs. Christ opposition furnishes a chief source of humor for the episode in the dramatic
irony of Winsome's and Egbert's cool sense of the viability of their
own views and the reader's consciousness of the unstated but criti-
cally operative ethic which damns them.

Winsome's philosophy, as relayed through Egbert, is finally
reduced in Chapter 41 to "the folly, on both sides, of a friend's
helping a friend."[2] The contrast with the teachings of the New

1. It is, moreover, too complacent.
Compare Winsome's attitude with that
of the "earnest, or enthusiastic youth"
in *Pierre* who discovers the disparity
between what "good and wise people
sincerely say" about the world and
what the New Testament says about
it: "unless he prove recreant, or unless
he prove gullible, or unless he can find
the talismanic secret, to reconcile this
world with his own soul, then there is
no peace for him, no slightest truth for
him in this life." Winsome's conclusion
that "mouth and purse must be filled"
is hardly the talismanic secret Melville
had in mind.

2. While the identification of Winsome
with Emerson is demonstrable enough,
the justness of Melville's harsh portrait
is open to question. There are passages
in Emerson's essay on "Friendship"
which quite contradict what Egbert
says. In contrast to Egbert's celestial
relationship, Emerson's friendship can
serve terrestrial ends: "It is for aid
and comfort through all the relations
and passages of life and death." While
Egbert speaks of the "delicacy" of
friendship, Emerson does "not wish to
treat friendship daintily, but with
roughest courage." When friends "are
real, they are not glass threads, or

Testament could not be more obvious or specific, for Jesus commands his followers: "Give to him that asketh thee, and from him that would borrow of thee turn not thou away" (Matt. 5:42). Clearly, from this New Testament point of view, where the man that has two coats is told to "impart to him that hath none" (Luke 3:11), arguments about the delicate nature of friendship scarcely justify Egbert's denial of the Christian injunction to give. In fairness to Egbert, he would not completely deny relief to a friend, if that friend renounced the friendship and applied "only as a fellow-being":

> "Take off your hat, bow over to the ground, and supplicate an alms of me in the way of London streets, and you shall not be a sturdy beggar in vain. But no man drops pennies into the hat of a friend, let me tell you. If you turn beggar, then, for the honor of noble friendship, I turn stranger."

The circumstances under which this hypothetical aid is to be given hardly redound to Egbert's credit, and the New Testament again furnishes the relevant criticism: Egbert's hypothetical giving is Pharasaical. Gospel generosity has no prescribed limits, as in the unconditional command in Luke 6:30: "Give to every man that asketh of thee; and of him that taketh away thy goods ask them not again." Furthermore, Egbert's contemptuous alms-giving is opposed to the spirit as well as the letter of the New Testament, violating the passage first suggested by the message of the mute from I Cor. 13:3:

> And though I bestow all my goods to feed the poor, and though I give my body to be burned, and have not charity, it profiteth me nothing.

Egbert is oblivious or indifferent to the Christ who is ministered to when one ministers unto the least of one of his brethren. His refusal to lend even to a friend is a grotesque inversion of Jesus' injunctions to lend to anyone, not merely "to them of whom ye hope to receive" (Luke 6:34).

A further fault with Winsome's philosophy in the hands of Egbert is that, in its exaltation of friendship above worldly considerations such as helping a friend in need, it degenerates into a worldliness worse than the one it would avoid. In asserting a celes-

---

frostwork, but the solidest thing we know." But there are also in the essay passages assertive of a high sense of self which could easily be interpreted not as a refining to sublimity but as a refining away of friendship. The inconsistencies are not irreconcilable, but without a fairly elaborate defense there is more than sufficient in the essay to create a Winsome from, and one can easily enough see the way in which the essay could represent for Melville that aspect of "non-benevolence" in "Emerson's intense individualism" (Foster, p. lxxvii) and an insidiously paradoxical view of man which exalts him yet treats him without charity.

tial relationship which can be elevated and sustained above worldly considerations, Egbert is on the surface a counter to Melville's Plinlimmon who deprecates the introduction of the celestial into terrestrial situations. In fact, Egbert's views on friendship become so inextricably mixed with mercenary considerations—the avoidance of relationships likely to prove an embarrassment for pecuniary reasons, the elaborate defense against giving a loan—that Egbert appears ultimately like nothing so much as Plinlimmon's horological average son-of-man who mixes his Christianity with prudential considerations of worldly practicality. Plinlimmon considers that "the God at the Heavenly Greenwich" does not "expect common men to keep Greenwich wisdom in this remote Chinese world of ours; *because such a thing were unprofitable for them here*" (italics added). He proposes that men be given a horological (or terrestrial) substitute to chronometrical (or celestial) teaching, "while still retaining every common-sense incentive to whatever of virtue be practicable and desirable" (from a horological point of view, of course). Plinlimmon's final judgment on the teachings of Christ is this:

> so far as practical results are concerned—regarded in a purely earthly light—the only great moral doctrine of Christianity . . . has been found (horologically) a false one. . . .

The joke with Plinlimmon is that he introduces worldly considerations as a criticism of a teaching which explicitly denies the validity of such considerations, a teaching which denies the worth of the world and counsels men to reject it in favor of something higher.

Egbert is guilty of a similar confusion of the worldly and the unworldly in his account of the beginning of his friendship with Frank—a not injudicious beginning, on his part, for he first weighed Frank's favorable points, not the least of which, he tells Frank, "were your good manners, handsome dress, and your parents' rank and repute of wealth." He chose his mutton "Not for its leanness, but its fatness." Egbert's intention was to "preserve inviolate" by these means "the delicacy of the connection":

> "For—do but think of it—what more distressing to delicate friendship, formed early, than your friend's eventually, in manhood, dropping in of a rainy night for his little loan of five dollars or so? Can delicate friendship stand that?"

Apart from the irony of Egbert's strange delicacy, there is the same confusion of the celestial and terrestrial, the same consideration of the celestial from a terrestrial point of view that is characteristic of the Pamphlet. Both here and in his earlier account of loans as "unfriendly accommodations" Egbert demonstrates the misplacing of reason, prudence, and worldly considerations that marks Plinlimmon's treatment of the Sermon on the Mount.

There are also links between Winsome and the Pamphlet, as in the mystic's assertion that any philosophy contradictory to the ways of the world is "a cheat and a dream." Here Winsome denies, in effect, the validity of Christianity for the same reasons given by Plinlimmon:

> Few of us doubt, gentlemen, that human life on this earth is but a state of probation; which among other things implies, that here below, we mortals have only to do with things provisional. Accordingly, I hold that all our so-called wisdom is likewise but provisional. . . .

Winsome's words are also similar to Plinlimmon's advice that "in things terrestrial" a man "must not be governed by ideas celestial." A particularly specific link between Winsome and Plinlimmon is the mystic's reference to Francis Bacon: "Was not Seneca a usurer? Bacon a courtier? and Swedenborg, though with one eye on the invisible, did he not keep the other on the main chance?" In the Pamphlet, which seems indebted to a number of Bacon's essays, Bacon is a type of worldly practicality. For Melville, Bacon represented the commonsensical, pragmatic, expedient, nominal Christian—the same kind of Christian Melville was satirizing through Plinlimmon. It is obviously appropriate that Bacon be mentioned approvingly by Winsome, who in his own way shares the same characteristics.[3] Winsome's insistence on his being "a man of serviceable knowledge" and a "a man of the world" again brings him within the terms of the Pamphlet and its satirical intention. Likewise the joke against Egbert that "he might, with the characteristic knack of the true New-Englander, turn even so profitless a thing [as mysticism] to some profitable account," and the insistence on Egbert as the *practical* disciple, serves to keep before us the Pamphlet's frame of reference and its satire on precisely this practicality and profitableness and serviceability.

While knowledge of Plinlimmon's Pamphlet is not essential to an understanding of the Winsome-Egbert episode, an acquaintance with Melville's satiric intention in that document enables us to see more readily the nature of his satire in the episode and the standpoint from which he is condemning Winsome and Egbert. As a corollary, the episode demonstrates the similarity of the terms in which Melville was thinking in 1852 and four years later when he wrote *The Confidence-Man.*

3. There is further irony in Bacon's thought being by implication balanced against his practical actions as a man of the world, when for Melville Bacon's philosophy represents the essence of worldliness. It is a neat little joke against Winsome that he should pick on Bacon for an example, at least by implication, of unworldly vision in his writings.

HARRISON HAYFORD

Poe in *The Confidence-Man*†

Among the fictional passengers on the steamboat *Fidèle* in Melville's *The Confidence-Man*, as among the characters in most of his other books, the presence of certain historically real persons has been recognized or suspected. In some of his works, real people, personal acquaintances or public figures, appear under their own names. In this book only two do so: Colonel John Moredock, the Indian-hater, and Judge James Hall, to whom the story of Moredock's career is rightly ascribed. But other real persons seem more or less recognizable under fictional names. Like the Confidence Man in his masquerade, they can be spotted by conspicuous details of their physical appearance, of their previous careers, and of their known attitudes and philosophies.

Aside from the Confidence Man himself, who has been taken to be such varied figures as the Yankee Peddler, Brother Jonathan, Uncle Sam, Orpheus, Christ, and (most plausibly) the Devil,[1] three other characters have been identified with real persons. Of these, the least successfully disguised is Mark Winsome, a "practical mystic," unmistakably Ralph Waldo Emerson in his physical features and philosophical views. Several critics have seen through the disguise.[2] A single critic has challenged the identity of two other figures. In Goneril, reported as the mannish and inhuman wife of the Man-with-the-Weed, this critic sees Melville's version of his neighbor Fanny Kemble. And in Egbert, Mark Winsome's acknowledged and practically successful disciple, the same critic sees Thoreau.[3] The most thorough critic of the book, however, questions both of these identifications sharply, pointing out salient unshared and contrary characteristics.[4] Still, suspicions may linger

† From *Nineteenth-Century Fiction*, 14 (December, 1959), 207–218. Copyright © 1959 by The Regents of the University of California. Reprinted by permission of The Regents.

1. Richard Chase, *Herman Melville* (New York, 1949), p. 188 *et passim*. Chase argues that the figure is a composite. Identification as the Devil (or perhaps one of his legion) is made by John W. Shroeder, "Sources and Symbols for Melville's *Confidence-Man*," *PMLA*, LXVI (June, 1951), 363–380; it is further developed by Elizabeth S. Foster (ed.), *The Confidence-Man* (New York, Hendricks House, 1954), pp. xlvi ff.

2. Egbert S. Oliver, "Melville and the Idea of Progress" (unpublished dissertation, University of Washington, Seattle, 1939); also "Melville's Picture of Emerson and Thoreau in 'The Confidence-Man,'" *College English*, VIII (November, 1946), 61–72. Foster, pp. lxxiii ff. F. O. Matthiessen, *American Renaissance* (New York, 1941), p. 472, n. 1. See n. 38 below.
3. Egbert S. Oliver, "Melville's Goneril and Fanny Kemble," *NEQ*, XVIII (December, 1945), 489–500; "Melville's Picture of Emerson and Thoreau . . .," pp. 68–72.
4. Foster, pp. 311–314, 351–352.

in the wary reader of this book where by definition no person, word, thought, or deed can be taken at fixed value.

Though the likelihood has thus been established that the masquerade aboard the *Fidèle* may include not alone that "metaphysical scamp" the Confidence Man, but also avatars of various persons, as yet no critic has suspected the identity of a certain passenger who appears only briefly. That passenger seems to me clearly enough to be Edgar Allan Poe. At least he seems to be as much Poe as any of the fictional figures in Melville's books can be said to be the actual persons from whom Melville drew them.

This passenger, who is given no name, appears in the midst of the conversation in which the Confidence Man, in his final disguise as the Cosmopolitan, is engaged in exposing the "incoherencies" in the philosophy of Mark Winsome (Emerson), while Mark Winsome, the practical mystic, is attempting to warn the Cosmopolitan that another passenger is a confidence man. The figure whom I take for Poe, and his reception by the Cosmopolitan and Winsome, are presented in this brief scene in chap. 36:

> Fortunately, to arrest these incoherencies, or rather, to vary them, a haggard, inspired-looking man now approached—a crazy beggar, asking alms under the form of peddling a rhapsodical tract, composed by himself, and setting forth his claims to some rhapsodical apostleship. * * * As for his adroitly playing the madman, invidious critics might object the same to some one or two strolling magi of these days." [167.7–168.11.]

Identification of the figure of this thumbnail sketch as Poe depends upon striking similarities between it and numerous eyewitness descriptions of Poe's appearance. These similarities lie in details of physique, of dress, and of manner, details which were repeatedly selected by various acquaintances and observers during the 1830's and 1840's as the salient points of Poe's personal appearance.

The points of physique assigned to this sad figure by Melville focus on his "slender frame," which "appeared the more so from the broad, untanned frontlet of his brow, tangled over with a disheveled mass of raven curls, throwing a still deeper tinge upon a complexion like that of a shriveled berry." Poe was regularly described as "slight" or "slender";[5] his broad brow and "raven" hair were almost always remarked, especially after publication of "The Raven";[6] and a number of reports commented on some sort

5. Mary E. Phillips, *Edgar Poe The Man* (Philadelphia, 1926), II, 930. Hervey Allen, *Israfel* (New York, 1934), pp. 276, 459, 658. (Citations in this and following footnotes are not exhaustive.)

6. John J. Moran, M.D., *A Defense of Edgar Allan Poe . . .* (Washington, 1885), pp. 63, 82. Phillips, II, 1101, 1440. Allen, pp. 276, 283, 459, 658. Arthur Hobson Quinn, *Edgar Allan Poe* (New York, 1941), pp. 461, 623.

of disproportion between his upper and lower parts. A description of him in 1843, for example, states: "Poe was a slight, small boned, delicate looking man, with a well-developed head, which at a lance, seemed out of proportion to his slender body."[7] Chivers wrote of him, as in 1845:

> His forehead was broad . . . , looking, from the peculiar conformation of his head, a good deal higher and broader than it really was. His hair was dark as a raven's wing. His form was slender. . . . His neck was rather long and slender, and made him appear, when sitting, rather taller than he really was.[8]

C. F. Briggs, in his *Tom Pepper* caricature (1847), maliciously rendered him as "a very small man, with a very pale, small face, which gave to his head the appearance of a balloon. . . ."[9] As to Poe's coloring, the "complexion like that of a shriveled berry" of Melville's figure finds (at least so far as the suggested *texture* goes) no counterpart in descriptions of Poe, who is always described as "pale."[1] His paleness corresponds, however, to the "untanned frontlet" of Melville's figure; and the "sallow" or "olive" coloring sometimes ascribed to Poe may be what Melville was thinking of as "that of a shriveled berry."[2]

In detail of dress this figure and Poe are identical in a major peculiarity. That is the "frock coat, buttoned up to the chin." Several observers of Poe were struck by the same sartorial oddity. In the early 1830's, already, "He always wore a black frock-coat buttoned up."[3] Similarly in 1833, ". . . his frock coat was buttoned up to the throat."[4] Between 1844–1847, his coat was "generally buttoned up close."[5] Describing Poe as he looked on his last journey, in 1849, Mrs. Shelton said, ". . . he always wore his coat well buttoned up to his throat covering much of his person."[6] And the conductor of the train which took him to Baltimore testified to the same detail: ". . . his coat was buttoned up close to his throat."[7] One gathers, from the repeated comments upon it, by both intimates and strangers, that this was a conspicuous idiosyncrasy of Poe's dress. Several portraits illustrate it.[8]

7. Allen, p. 459.
8. Richard Beale Davis (ed.), *Chivers' Life of Poe* (New York, 1952), pp. 53–54.
9. Harry Franco [C. F. Briggs], *The Trippings of Tom Pepper* . . . (New York, 1847), I, 159. Melville was acquainted with Briggs and owned this volume. See Perry Miller, *The Raven and the Whale* (New York, 1956), chap. iv, 168 ff., for discussion of this satire and its relation to Poe, Melville, and the Duyckinck circle, at which much of its animus was directed; Miller suggests a general connection between *The Confidence-Man* and the metropolitan literati (p. 339).

1. *The Poetical Works of Edgar Allan Poe, with an Original Memoir* [by C. F. Briggs] (New York, 1859), p. 36. Phillips, II, 1045, 1243, 1425, 1440. Allen, pp. 276, 459. Quinn, pp. 461, 635.
2. Davis, p. 57. Allen, p. 276. Phillips, II, 1417, 1503.
3. Allen, p. 277.
4. Allen, p. 283.
5. Phillips, II, 930.
6. Moran, p. 61.
7. Moran, p. 60.
8. See reproductions of various portraits. Phillips, II, frontispiece, 894, 998, 1019, 1339, 1419. Allen, pp. 300, 492. Quinn, frontispiece, pp. 574, 622.

Other details of clothing involve its condition and the manner of
wearing it. That Poe ever went around with his coat literally "tattered" or his clothing actually "ragged" is asserted in no description
I have seen; but several do refer to his clothes as "well worn"
(1848) or the like.⁹ From all accounts Poe was never, like this
figure, "dirty" in person or apparel. Quite to the contrary, there are
many remarks that in dress he was "neat"; and credit is given for
this not only to the care of Mrs. Clemm but as well to his own fas-
tidiousness.¹ Briggs, however, in the *Tom Pepper* caricature, has it
that "He was dressed primly and seemed to be conscious of having
on a clean shirt, as though it were a novelty to him."² This detail
of dirtiness may therefore be regarded either as casting doubt upon
the identification with Poe, or, what seems to me quite likely, as
dictated not so much by fact as by the contrast Melville is drawing
for thematic purposes between the fellow's apparel and his manner.
Though his apparel is beggarly, his manner has "no touch of vulgarity," is "not unrefined," even suggests "picturesque Italian ruin
and dethronement," and his courtesy is worthy of a viscount. That
is, the fellow's idea of himself, his confidence in self, ignores
(appropriately to the general thematic irony of the book) his actual
plight. Observers of Poe do not miss the same contrast. In 1843
"He was then *un homme blessé*, seedy in his appearance and
woebegone. He . . . begged me to lend him 50¢ to obtain a meal.
. . . Though he looked the used-up man all over—still he showed
the gentleman."³ In 1848, to a boy upon chance encounter, he
seemed "a gentleman of distinguished bearing but somewhat seed-
ily attired," and on the same occasion a woman to whom he was a
stranger thought him "a person evidently in needy circumstances
from his attire."⁴ Another observer who met him in the same year
wrote:

> He was unmistakably a gentleman of education and refinement
> with indescribable marks of genius in his face of marble white-
> ness. He was dressed with perfect neatness; but one could see
> signs of poverty in the well-worn clothes, though his manner
> gave no consciousness of the fact.⁵

So consistently is Poe's manner described as "gentlemanly" and
"courteous" that no specific quotations seem called for to establish
the similarity of his deportment to that of Melville's figure.⁶ The
heightening, in Melville's description, of these qualities, from the
negatively concessive "no touch of vulgarity" and "not unrefined"

9. Phillips, II, 1296, 1299. Allen, p.
283.
1. Moran, p. 61. Davis, pp. 53, 57.
Phillips, II, 1299. Allen, pp. 285, 459.
2. Briggs, *Trippings* . . ., I, 159.
3. John Hill Hewitt, *Recollections of*
Poe (Atlanta, 1949), p. 19.
4. Phillips, II, 1296–1297.
5. Phillips, II, 1299.
6. Phillips, II, 930, 1239, 1296, 1299,
1446, 1449, 1453. Allen, pp. 283, 332.
Quinn, pp. 570, 623.

to nobility and "dethronement," finds its counterpart in reported impressions of Poe's aspect, which employ similar romantically-freighted terms.[7] And of course Poe himself, in the narrative *personae* of many of his tales and poems, had projected his own image repeatedly as a man of high birth cast down, dethroned in fortune and in reason. Poe's fanciful claims of noble ancestry soon led biographers to credit him, curiously enough, with precisely the "picturesque Italian" origin suggested in the "look" of Melville's figure.[8]

Three details of appearance and attitude attributed to Melville's figure remain: his "haggard" mien, "inspired" look, and attitude of "resentful pride" and "cracked disdain." All three are repeatedly matched in descriptions of Poe. The haggardness coincides with the "paleness" and "used-up" mien already adduced. Many observers attested to the genius evident in his aspect. As to his pride and disdain, such reactions of rejected merit evidently were manifested in Poe's expression. As Chivers would have it:

... he was the Incarnation of the Greek Prometheus chained to the Mount Caucasus of demi-civilized Humanity, with the black Vulture of Envy, feeding on his self-replenished heart, while upon his trembling lips, sat enthroned the most eloquent persuasion alternating with the bitterest, triumphant and Godlike Scorn.[9]

One who in 1848 urged him to modify the "pantheistic" closing of *Eureka*, noted in his facial reaction a "look of scornful pride worthy of Milton's Satan. . . ."[1] Another observer in his last year remarked his look of mingled "scorn and discontent."[2]

So, too, of the epithets "crazy" and "cracked." Poor Poe's erratic behavior from 1845 on, in New York, whatever its causes, certainly justified the label of madness which many applied to it in his last two or three years. (These were years, 1846–1849, when Melville would have heard much, and seen at least something, of Poe in New York literary circles.) More than once Poe himself so described and excused episodes susceptible of scarcely any other diagnosis.[3] A cursory reading of Poe's painful letters, or only those addressed to Melville's friend and patron, Evert Duyckinck, would document Poe's enforced practice of "asking alms," under whatever proud form and protestation—often enough under that of "peddling" literary wares "composed by himself."[4]

Indeed, if at all persuaded by the identities of physique, dress,

7. Davis, p. 53 ff. Moran, p. 82, See n. 24 above.
8. James A. Harrison, "Biography," *Complete Works of Edgar Allan Poe* (New York, 1902), I, 3–4. Phillips, I, 3–4. See comment by Allen, p. 679. Quinn, p. 13.
9. Davis, pp. 55–56.

1. Phillips, II, 1265.
2. Phillips, II, 1265, 1440, 1446, 1458, 1517. Allen, pp. 459, 473–474, 660. Quinn, p. 477.
3. John Ward Ostrom (ed.), *The Letters of Edgar Allan Poe* (Cambridge, 1948), I, 300; II, 356, 360, 402, 455.
4. *Letters, passim.*

manner, and attitudes, between Melville's figure and Poe, one looks beyond them for further correspondences between the two in Poe's history, one must think immediately of Poe's *Eureka.* Delivered in 1848 as a lecture at the New York Society Library, of which Melville was a member though he did not attend the lecture, this "tract" or "prose poem," as Poe preferred to call it, was well described by one who did attend as "a rhapsody of the most intense brilliancy." As Poe delivered it, said this listener, "He appeared inspired, and his inspiration affected the scant audience almost painfully. He wore his coat tightly buttoned across his slender chest; his eyes seemed to glow like those of his own raven. . . ."[5] Soon afterwards, offering it to G. P. Putnam for publication, Poe declared, according to Putnam, "I have solved the secret of the universe." Putnam—like the Cosmopolitan and unlike Mark Winsome—accepted the "pamphlet," advanced Poe "alms" of $14 (extracting a receipt and signed promise "not to ask or apply for any other loans or advance from said Putnam in any way"), and printed it in a small edition.[6] But Winsome-like reviewers rejected the prose-poem pamphlet—or so it rightly or wrongly seemed to its proud and scornful author. Still, to raise money for his projected literary review, Poe, like Melville's "crazy beggar," went about the country (New York, Providence, Richmond, Norfolk) as a "strolling" lecturer. A parallel exists, aptly enough.

But why should Melville represent Emerson as rejecting Poe? At this point, so far as my own conjectures carry me, the parallel to Poe's history ends. One might recall Poe's career-long quarrel with Boston, with "Frogpondium," with transcendentalism; one thinks of his Boston reading fiasco of 1845 and the ensuing newspaper tilts. Yet little reason could Melville have to saddle Emerson with any of the onus of all this. Emerson's rejection of Poe, in his famous epithet "the jingle man," occurred later, in 1860 in a conversation with Howells.[7] At this point, I can only suppose, the reference passes to another plane, that of the dialectic of ideas Melville is satirically developing.

Quite evidently, it seems to me, Melville utilized Poe's physical appearance, his dress, his personal manner, and something of his psychology. Beyond this, he included an aspect of Poe's actual history: his "asking alms under the form of peddling a rhapsodical tract." He fixed on an allowable if somewhat ironic classification of Poe as in some sort of a fellow-magus to Emerson. In taking this

5. Phillips, II, 1256–1257. The listener was Maunsell B. Field, who reported his memory of the lecture and of Putnam's account to him of Poe's visit, in *Memoirs of Many Men . . .* , (New York, 1874), p. 224. By his account Putnam "lent Poe a shilling to take him home to Fordham. . . ." Field

was acquainted with Melville (pp. 201–202).
6. Phillips, II, 1258 ff. Quinn, p. 539 ff.
7. W. D. Howells, *Literary Friends and Acquaintance* (New York, 1911), p. 63.

much of Poe, he left out conspicuous aspects of Poe's full character and life: his notable career as editor, critic, and poet; but he also excluded some of Poe's notorious personal failings. Of his writings, only *Eureka*, his rhapsodical prose-poem, is allowed him. Poe's settled and oft-voiced contempt for transcendentalism, at least of the Frogpondian variety, is suppressed. The picture of Poe is not complete; it is limited by Melville's purpose in this book.

One can only speculate as to why Melville should have brought in an image of Poe at all. It seems doubtful to me that he intended the portrait to be recognized or meant it as a comment in public. An initial reason for his using Poe would lie no doubt in Melville's habitual practice, perhaps a necessity of his creative method, of writing from experience, observation, and reading, rather than from pure invention. The greater part of his characters seem to have originals, not all of whom he intended or wished to be recognized. In reply to the request of R. H. Dana, Jr., to be told the identity of the officers of the *United States* represented in *White-Jacket*, Melville wrote to him:

> I am very loath to do so, because I have never indulged in any ill-will or disrespect for them, personally; & shrink from any thing that approaches to a personal identification of them with characters that were only intended to furnish samples of a tribe. . . .[8]

Melville's literary method always involved this curious combination of recognizable fact and identity with generalized "truth."

In *The Confidence-Man*, as in *White-Jacket* and in the satirical section of *Mardi*, the actual persons brought into the fiction were used as available and appropriate embodiments of relevant ideas and attitudes, not simply as themselves. So among type-exponents of various brands of "confidence," Melville arraigns a facsimile of a conspicuous confidence-philosopher, Emerson. Among type-exponents of resistance to "confidence" he introduces (from the pages of Judge Hall) the historical Colonel John Moredock. In each case he exercises his right to exaggerate and select. He fixes only upon aspects of Emerson's philosophy relevant to his theme: upon its inconsistency, chiefly, of "mystic" and "practical" elements;[9] its high pretensions, couched in Neoplatonic mumbo-jumbo,[1] in contrast to its real lack of a touchstone of knowledge; and to its actual standard of cold, shrewd, Yankee cuteness. He omits, deliberately, the quality he admired in Emerson on first hearing him lecture in 1848 ("I love all men who dive. . . ."), and much which he still found "admirable," in spite of objectionable

8. Jay Leyda, *The Melville Log* (New York, 1951), I, 374; also 317, 367.
9. Foster, pp. 334 ff.

1. Merton M. Sealts, Jr., "Melville's Neoplatonical Originals," *MLN*, LXVII (February, 1952), 84 ff.

qualities, when he read and marked his essays in the 1860's.[2] He misrepresents the habit of the actual Emerson, too, in picturing him as rejecting a beggarly fellow-transcendentalist while endorsing "a well-dressed commercial-looking" disciple. Emerson's benevolent encouragement of his entourage of what Hawthorne disgustedly called "bores of a very intense water" was notorious—to the point indeed of obscuring Thoreau's independent merits from those who discounted Emerson's generous commendations. Rather than any acts of the man Emerson, it is the epistemological incoherency and the ethical pragmatism of Emerson's teaching that Melville dramatizes.

The context calls for Winsome-Emerson first to reject an impractical brand of "transcendentalism" and then to endorse a commercially successful one. The fact that personally Emerson had not publicly rejected a disciple would forestall the use of any actual follower of his at this point. But what figure might come to Melville's mind as a sad specimen of a crackbrained exponent of a rhapsodical apostleship, who had gone begging and been despised as a madman and scoundrel? Not inconceivably Poe.

What attitude toward Poe does the passage reveal? The answer must be qualified in several ways. First, for the reasons already given, one cannot assume that Melville saw the actual Poe only in the light in which he presented some of his attributes here, where not all of whatever he may have known or thought of him was to the purpose. Then, one has to be careful in drawing any conclusion from the response of either the Cosmopolitan or Winsome. The Cosmopolitan's courteous response, his purchase of the pamphlet, his promise of "much satisfaction in its perusal," his reproach to Winsome for not sympathizing with the "poor fellow," and his innuendo that if the fellow be playing the madman certain others are said to be doing the same—all of these constitute a gambit which serves the Cosmopolitan's purpose in exposing Winsome. None of them commits the Cosmopolitan to a favorable attitude on his own part. The purchase and promise are equivocal (he gets rid of the beggar thereby—and what will be the real nature of his "satisfaction" in perusing the pamphlet?). His "tones kind and considerate" may reflect not real courtesy and consideration but tactics calculated to show up Winsome's lack of these qualities. Similarly with his purchase of the pamphlet, again: by purchasing it he can rebuke Winsome for inconsistency in not being willing to purchase the sort of thing he himself peddles and expects others to buy. And, clearly enough, the reproach of lack of sympathy is simply an innuendo identifying Winsome as one who should have "fellow-feeling" for the "shatter-brain," not as a fellow being—such humanity is beyond him—but as a fellow peddler of claptrap, though of a different brand. This is made clear by the scarcely concealed jibe that "As for his adroitly playing the madman [which Winsome deduces from his "damning peep of sense"—just what damns Winsome] invidious critics might object the same to one or two strolling magi of these days." The implication is that Winsome-Emerson only plays at his own madness, to get money; he has sense enough not to act on his philosophy in any way damaging to health, wealth, common sense, or clean clothes.

As to Winsome's response, in the full context of the work Melville apparently expects the reader to regard with some favor those who refuse to be taken in by peddlers of phony philosophies of confidence. Clearly the "crack-brain" is, however sincerely, peddling such a philosophy. So evidently Winsome deserves some credit for not "buying" it—if not for his discourtesy or for the cold and curious logic of his justification. The overarching irony, of course, is that while Winsome, himself a kind of confidence man, is warning the Cosmopolitan against another passenger as a confidence man (quite correctly) and refusing to buy a pamphlet from the crack-brain whom he at least suspects of being another confidence man, he is all the time talking to the chief of confidence men—even, it may be, to the Devil himself—whom he does not suspect at all.

One cannot, then, judge Melville's attitude toward the Poe-figure simply by choosing between the attitudes of the Cosmopolitan and Winsome, though these must be taken into account. Neither the Cosmopolitan's courtesy and at least manifest sympathy, nor Winsome's perception (which the Cosmopolitan tacitly shares) of the fellow's insanity and possible charlatanism can be rejected. It is safe to say that Melville endorses both.

Beyond this, one can derive something more of Melville's attitude from the fact that the set description of the "crack-brain" is stated by him as narrator. The narrator's statement is unconditioned by the point of view of either of the principals in the scene but all the same it is controlled by the general style and tone of the book. That style is one of pointed brevity and stringency, to serve the tone of highly involuted and noncommittal irony. So far as we can deduce or disengage anything Melville is saying about Poe from this complex structure, it may be safe to list these points. There is at bottom an accurate enough description of Poe's personal mien and manner. There is an epitome description of his end plight, about as Melville would have seen and heard of it between 1846–1849. There is a dismissal of his pretensions to reason, to having solved the secret of the universe—a flat dismissal of these as madness which even his own glimmering of reason at times saw through. There is some admiration for his demeanor, his pride and quiet self-respect (though pride and respect for what, and how soundly based, after all?). And finally, in keeping with the book's feeling of unsentimental sympathy and near despair for mankind, there is an austere pity for the poor man, a pity which can go side by side with such a summarily objective view of the actuality of a shattered fellow being.

If this attitude seems to display inhumanity toward poor Poe, one must suppose that Melville was well enough aware of similarities to himself in the picture. He had looked straight at his own situation and seen it as one not far removed indeed from that of this crack-brain. He too had sought the secret of the universe, had entertained fantasies of himself as a "dethroned" noble, and felt scorn and disdain rise within him as the coldly complacent world rejected the offerings of his genius. He had verged upon madness, had been accused of it in the public prints and examined for it by private doctors at the behest of his family. He had declared that he would "never surrender."[3] In the end he had not lost his own sanity, or his sense of proportion and of reality. If he had looked upon Poe with a straight and honest gaze, and seen what was there, he had looked upon himself in the same way.

HERSHEL PARKER

"The Story of China Aster":
A Tentative Explication†

At the start "The Story of China Aster" seems plainly enough an allegory of the artist as light-giver, parallel to the allegory of writer as seedsman in "The Tartarus of Maids." Apparently the only specific comment on this double-meaning yet printed is Edwin Fussell's passing reference (1965) to the "rather transparent parody of Melville's disastrous literary career." Fussell must have noticed that China Aster the candle-maker is in the business of giving light to the world, just as a writer is. His candles sell slowly, yet he has stores enough of them to light up a whole street. In a parallel fashion, in the fifties, when his books were selling poorly, Melville could have lighted up a whole street with, say, copies of Typee, or perhaps with unpublished—or even unwritten—stories, although these last possibilities seem unlikely. China Aster's friend Orchis, the shoemaker, is in the business of keeping men from contact with

3. Merton M. Sealts, Jr., "Herman Melville's 'I and My Chimney,' " AL, XIII (May, 1941), 142–154. [Reprinted with slight changes in The Recognition of Herman Melville, ed.

Hershel Parker (Ann Arbor: University of Michigan Press, 1967), pp. 237–251.—Editor's note.]
† Published here for the first time.

reality. As Melville explains in Shakespearean puns, Orchis has a "calling to defend the understandings of men from naked contact with the substance of things." A contrast is not explicit, but presumably one should think of China Aster's own light-giving vocation: his function is to *reveal* reality, not to protect men from it. Orchis urges China Aster to change his business tactics: "You must drop this vile tallow and hold up pure spermaceti to the world." The "vile tallow" could refer to the short stories that Melville had begun to write in the fifties, for, ambitious as a few of them are, stories like "The Happy Failure," "The Fiddler," and "The 'Gees" are products of an energy obviously less than that apparent in *Moby-Dick*. The injunction to hold up pure spermaceti may well be a suggestion that Melville turn again to ambitious sea-fiction, or even specifically to write another whaling story like *Moby-Dick*. As Melville said in one of his few comments on *Moby-Dick* (tucked into his essay on Hawthorne's *Mosses*): "You must have plenty of sea-room to tell the Truth in." The vats into which China Aster's wisdom may have been spilled stand in the allegory for Melville's inkwells, one could argue. Later the comment that China Aster's "candles per pound barely sold for what he had paid for the tallow" may be an oblique admission that Melville's stories hardly sold for enough to pay for the paper they were written on. Through all this, Orchis's function is simply to be a crass stooge, giving all sorts of glib advice on regaining an audience; China Aster is an infinitely subdued and defeated version of Melville.

How far-fetched is all this? Does it become irresponsible if one pushes farther, as Fussell does in the sentence mentioned above? His whole sentence is this: "Hawthorne, I conjecture, is Orchis, or Doleful Dumps, in 'The Story of China Aster,' a rather transparent allegorical parody of Melville's disastrous literary career and of its relation to Hawthorne's." Is this merely based on the long-exploded notion that there was some dramatic estrangement between Melville and Hawthorne? How similar to Orchis *is* Hawthorne? Even if one agrees that the lines of an allegorical interpretation have been properly drawn, will he agree that the whole story is a consistent allegory? or even that it is consistently allegorical? More important, what is Melville's attitude toward what he was writing? Is the story, as might seem likely, an embittered *cri du coeur*? Is it, quite the contrary, a *jeu d'esprit*? And after all, does the allegory, if any, conflict with the narrative function of the story, where Egbert (in the role of Charlie) tells it as evidence as to the danger of accepting a loan?

I am not at all sure that the proper way to proceed is to rigorously work out an allegorical interpretation of the rest of the story. Further autobiographical elements are hard to identify, if they are present at all. What of China Aster's uncle, the blacksmith, who refused a loan with a nobly independent speech? No uncle on Melville's mother's side would have needed a loan, and the uncle on his father's side would never have refused one. Unless it is a wry look backward at the perennially borrowing Uncle Thomas Melvill, it can have no autobiographical bearings. One could possibly account for the "little memorandum" that Orchis has China Aster make (it turns out to be a "note for one thousand dollars on demand") as a fantastic allusion to the legal documents Melville had signed at various times when he was borrowing from Shaw against his wife's inheritance. Like China Aster's father, who died in a poorhouse, Melville's father died deeply in debt. Certainly it could be said of Allan Melvill that "he had no business to be in business." Like Orchis, Judge Shaw took a trip to Europe (in 1853, at a time when such a trip might have been most beneficial to Melville himself, then chronically ill). Just as China Aster might have been able to settle his accounts and earn money as a journeyman, "a paid subordinate to men more able than himself," Melville might have been more successful doing what he steadfastly refused to do in his more ambitious days—becoming a hack-writer of reviews on demand from Duyckinck or another editor. When China Aster wants to re-establish himself, he borrows six hundred dollars from a rich old farmer, at the cost of inducing his wife to sign a bond surrendering a prospective inheritance if he failed. One could suspect some oblique allusion to the T. D. S. who loaned Melville $2050 in 1851, or perhaps to the Harpers, who had made him advances against his books. China Aster's wife has a saying: " 'China Aster,' she would say, 'is a good husband, but a bad business man!' " Melville's wife later complained to Catherine Gansevoort (*Log*, p. 729): "Herman from his studious habits and tastes being unfitted for practical matters, all the *financial* management falls upon me." She had firm opinions about indebtedness, as another letter to Catherine shows: "I have never forgotten what I have heard my father tell us so often—'Always be *precise* about money matters to the *smallest* Sum' and 'never forget the smallest debt'—not so much for your creditors sake as your own" (*Herman Melville: Cycle and Epicycle*, pp. 219–220).

None of these parallels seems as conclusive as the opening parallels between China Aster's and Melville's roles as lightgivers in poverty, but there is at least the possibility that Melville was working into the story oblique, distorted, or even perverse versions of incidents from his own life. If he was doing this, he probably relied on his ability to make the parallels remote enough so they would never be discovered by the ones most likely to resent them. Any real-life versions of incidents in "The Story of China Aster" are probably irrecoverable now. And even if the story is a fantasy in which Melville indulges in self-pity and in wry attacks on his wife, his in-laws, and other relatives, a mock-autobiography in which he portrays himself as more innocent and more defeated than he ever was in fact, it may still have been written not out of agony but out of humor. As I suggested before, it may be more *jeu d'esprit* than *cri du coeur*.

Nor does this autobiographical explication begin to exhaust the story. In the vein of *Israel Potter*, it is a re-examination of the Franklinesque virtues of Industry, Frugality, and Prudence. It is also rather obviously satiric of the Transcendental respect for private impulses, best epitomized in "Self-Reliance," where Emerson replies to the suggestion that " 'these impulses may be from below' " by declaring: " 'They do not seem to me to be such; but if I am the Devil's child, I will live then from the Devil.' " Orchis joins the Transcendental-like Come-Outers, whose distinctive practice is to bring their hidden thoughts and emotions out into the open and to indulge in a "free development" of their inmost natures. Old Plain Talk speaks for Melville: "if some men knew what was their inmost natures, instead of coming out with it, they would try their best to keep it in, which, indeed, was the way with the prudent sort." Stylistically, the story is interesting as an experiment in maudlinity. Egbert (in his role as Charlie) warns the Cosmopolitan—the Devil—that he cannot repeat China Aster's incidents without "sliding" into the style of "the original story-teller." He continues: "I forewarn you of this, that you may not think me so maudlin as, in some parts, the story would seem to make its narrator." This is partly Melville's usual device for avoiding the demands of consistency in his interpolated stories, but in this case it may conceal Melville's use of a source. None has been discovered, but the piece is in genre a tract, perfectly suitable to being passed out by a Temperance organization. Finding a source just might allow one to speculate sensibly about whether Melville wrote the story with Egbert in mind as an appropriate narrator (with some allegorical relevance to Thoreau's own rehashes of Franklin) or whether he simply saw at some stage of the composition of the book a chance to use a story he had written without a thought of putting it into *The Confidence-Man*.

HOWARD C. HORSFORD

Evidence of Melville's Plans for a Sequel to *The Confidence-Man*†

When Melville broke off *The Confidence-Man* with the abrupt words, "Something further may follow of this Masquerade," he was

† Howard C. Horsford, *American Literature*, 24 (March, 1952) 85–89. Re-   printed by permission of the author and Duke University Press.

ill, tired, and close to a breakdown. While the integrity of *The Confidence-Man* has not been without defenders, some scholars have not unreasonably assumed that this statement was really an empty gesture of placation for an unresolved and inconclusive ending to the book, and that Melville was too bitter and disillusioned to carry on even in this bitingly ironic vein.[1]

Actually, there is some evidence to indicate that either view may need qualification. We know from various letters of the family that Melville was very ill during the summer of 1856 as he wrote *The Confidence-Man*. One of the more important of these letters is that of Melville's father-in-law, Judge Lemuel Shaw, to his son, Samuel, who had gone to Europe in the spring of that year. It is dated Boston, September 1, 1856, and reads, in part:

> I suppose you have been informed by some of the family, how very ill Herman has been. ... He has been advised, strongly, to break off this labor for some time, take a voyage or a journey. ... No definite plan is arranged [?] but I think it may result in this, that in the autumn he will go away [?] for four or five months. ...[2]

This letter alone would seem to indicate that Melville stopped writing on the novel, not because he could find nothing more to say, nor because he was too bitter and disillusioned to continue, nor yet because he was completely satisfied with its form as it stood, but because he was forced to by his own desperate health and the insistence of his family and doctors.[3]

At any rate, Melville did go away in the autumn for, not four or

---

1. F. O. Matthiessen, in his *American Renaissance* (London and New York, 1941), p. 412, stated flatly: "Melville was so far from having imagined a conclusion for *The Confidence-Man* that he could only break it off as a distended fragment." See also *ibid.*, p. 492, or, for other instances, Newton Arvin, *Herman Melville* (New York, 1950), pp. 211–212, 232; Lewis Mumford, *Herman Melville* (New York, 1929), pp. 252–253; and for a more equivocal statement, Geoffrey Stone, *Melville* (New York, 1949), pp. 233–234. *The Confidence-Man*, for various reasons, has been defended by, among others, Jean Simon, *Herman Melville, marin, métaphysicien et poète* (Paris, 1939), p. 437; and Richard Chase, *Herman Melville* (New York, 1949), pp. 205–206.

2. In the Lemuel Shaw Collection, Massachusetts Historical Society, Boston, Massachusetts. I am indebted to Mrs. Eleanor Melville Metcalf for confirming my reading of her great-grandfather's very difficult handwriting. A longer extract from this same letter is included in Jay Leyda's *The Melville Log* (New York, 1951), II, 521.

3. The best evidence of Melville's health and state of mind at this time is in Nathaniel Hawthorne's entry in his English notebooks for November 20, 1856. The "intervening day" mentioned in this quotation is November 12: "Melville has not been well, of late; he has been affected with neuralgic complaints in his head and limbs, and no doubt has suffered from too constant literary occupation, pursued without much success, latterly; and his writings, for a long while past, have indicated a morbid state of mind. So he left his place at Pittsfield, and has established his wife and family, I believe, with his father-in-law in Boston, and is thus far on his way to Constantinople. I do not wonder that he found it necessary to take an airing through the world, after so many years of toilsome pen-labor and domestic life, following upon so wild and adventurous a youth as his was. I invited him to come and stay with us at Southport, as long as he might remain in this vicinity; and, accordingly, he did come, the next day, taking with him, by way of baggage, the least little bit of a bundle, which, he told me, contained a night-shirt and

five, but nearly eight months. Just before sailing for Scotland on
October 11, 1856, he evidently delivered one copy of the novel
manuscript to his American publishers, Dix and Edwards, while
with him he seems to have taken another copy for English
publication.[4]
Now, in the journals which Melville kept of his trip to Europe
and the Near East during the winter of 1856-1857, there appears
more positive evidence of what his intentions about this novel were,
evidence that is obscured in the published version of the journals.
When Raymond Weaver edited the manuscript, he did so, apparently, from a transcript made by Mr. Gerald Crona, a graduate student at Columbia University.[5] Under the entry for Sunday, April 5
(in Venice, where Melville is describing his guide, Antonio), this
printed version reads:

> My Guide. How I met him, & where. Lost his money in 1848
> Revolution & by travelling.—Today in one city, tomorrow in
> next. Fine thing to travel. When rich, plenty compliment. How
> do you do, Antonio—hope you very well, Antonio—Now Anto-
> nio no money, Antonio no compliment. Get out of de way Anto-
> nio. Go to the devil, Antonio. Antonio you go shake yourself.
> You know dat Sir, dat to de rich man, de poor man habe always
> de bad smell? You know dat Sir?
> Yes, Antonio, I am not unaware of that. Charitably disposed.
> Old blind man, give something & God will bless you [Will give,
> but doubt the blessing]. [Antonio good character for com.
> man][6]

An examination of the original manuscript shows, however, that

a tooth-brush. He is a person of very
gentlemanly instincts in every respect,
save that he is a little heterodox in the
matter of clean linen.
He stayed with us from Tuesday till
Thursday; and, on the intervening day,
we took a pretty long walk together,
and sat down in a hollow among the
sand hills (sheltering ourselves from
the high, cool wind) and smoked a
cigar. Melville, as he always does,
began to reason of Providence and fu-
turity, and of everything that lies beyond human ken, and informed me that
he had "pretty much made up his mind
to be annihilated"; but still he does
not seem to rest in that anticipation;
and, I think, will never rest until he
gets hold of a definite belief. It is
strange how he persists—and has per-
sisted ever since I knew him, and probably long before—in wandering to-
and-fro over these deserts, as dismal
and monotonous as the sand hills amid
which we were sitting. He can neither
believe, nor be comfortable in his unbelief; and he is too honest and coura-

geous not to try to do one or the
other. If he were a religious man, he
would be one of the most truly religious and reverential; he has a very
high and noble nature, and better
worth immortality than most of us."
(*The English Notebooks*, ed. Randall
Stewart [New York, 1941], pp.
432-433.) [*Editor's note.*]
4. Leyda, *The Melville Log*, II, 525.
Whether or not Melville negotiated directly with the English firm, Longman,
Brown, Green, Longmans, and Roberts,
is not clear, but it was Nathaniel
Hawthorne who signed the contract
with the firm on behalf of Melville,
March 20, 1857, while Melville was in
Italy (*ibid.*, II, 560). The novel was
published in America and England at
the end of March and the beginning of
April, 1857.
5. *Journal up the Straits, October 11,
1856—May 5, 1857*, ed. with an in-
trod. by Raymond Weaver (New York,
1935), p. xxix.
6. *Ibid.*, pp. 157-158 (Melville's
brackets).

the last sentence in brackets clearly reads, "Antonio good character for Con. Man." The whole context that I have quoted makes it certain that "Con. Man" can only be an abbreviation for *Confidence Man.* Thus, six months after Melville had last set pen to the manuscript of the story, and even as the novel was being issued, he seems to have been still planning to continue the "Masquerade," observing and collecting material for it.

Were this a unique instance, the significance would be questionable at best. But it is not. The manuscript of the journal shows evidence of considerable revision. In addition to the regular pen-and-ink entries, made contemporaneously with the events recorded, there are markings, revisions, and additions, made in ink, black lead pencil, and a kind of reddish-brown drawing pencil. These changes were made for a variety of purposes, some, I think, as he prepared material for the lecture he gave in 1857-1858, "Statuary in Rome," some for what seems to have been one or more projected books or articles,[7] many as he meditated the material for *Clarel.* These changes, then, seem to date all the way from 1857 to early in the 1870's.[8] Now in this same passage which I have quoted above, there is such an addition which Weaver (or Mr. Crona) missed altogether and which does not appear in the published version of the *Journal.*[9] In the space between the paragraphs quoted above, Melville added something later, in black pencil: "(For Con. Man)."

Of several other entries which suggest, though not as explicitly as the two above, that Melville was keeping *The Confidence-Man* in mind, both as he traveled, and for some indefinite time afterwards, the clearest occurs in the third manuscript volume. In a series of random jottings suggested by Constantinople, Melville noted (in ink):

[Pera, the headquarters of ambassadors, and where also an unreformed diplomacy is carried on by swindlers, gamblers, cheats, no place in the world fuller of knaves.]

In the left margin, written in black pencil, is: "For the Story." To this, Weaver's note is, "I cannot discover that this projected story

7. My reasons for thinking so are elaborated in the introduction to an edition of these journals which I have prepared. [*Journal of a Visit to Europe and the Levant,* October 11, 1856–May 6, 1857 (Princeton; Princeton University Press, 1955).] It is clear enough, in any case, from the correspondence Melville had with the newly founded *Atlantic Monthly,* that during the latter part of 1857, he contemplated prose writing of some sort. See J. H. Birss, "Herman Melville and the 'Atlantic Monthly,'" *Notes and Queries,* CLXVII, 223–224 (Sept. 29, 1934).

8. The analysis of the changes which leads me to this conclusion is too detailed to be included here, but in part it depends upon a correlation of the additions and revisions in the journal with *Clarel,* especially Volume II. Mr. Walter Bezanson of Rutgers, who has done a great deal of work with *Clarel,* assures me that the latter volume was substantially written in the late 1860's and early 1870's.

9. Leyda, *op. cit.,* II, 566, reprints the original entry correctly, but disregards the addition.

survives."[1] But in view of the two other explicit references to *The Confidence-Man*, I think it not at all improbable that both the original jotting and the penciled note refer to his last novel. Though these and other pencilings cannot be dated with precision, they point at the very least to the summer of 1857, after Melville's return from abroad, and after the publication of the novel. It seems evident, then, that Melville had by no means dropped the idea of *The Confidence-Man* when he sent the manuscript off to his publishers in the fall of 1856. Rather, all through the trip he was probably keeping his eye open for further material for a sequel. His frequent wandering among the crowds in the cities, and in the fashionable promenades of Naples, Rome, Florence, and London had more purpose than simply the absorption of local color. Considering the failure of his American publishers in 1857, and the not very enthusiastic reception accorded *The Confidence-Man*, I suppose that Melville did not entertain plans for a sequel much later than the summer or perhaps early winter of 1857, by no means as late as 1870. That he considered a continuation at all would seem to indicate neither that he was destitute of ideas nor that he regarded the work as it stands to be complete.

1. *Op. cit.*, p. 39 and n. 2. R. S. Forsythe, in his review of Weaver's edition (*American Literature*, VIII, 85–96, March, 1936), advanced the theory that this might refer to one of three titles advertised by Dix and Edwards, a theory which, Mr. Bezanson has informed me, Forsythe later privately abandoned when he discovered that the attribution to Melville was due to the garbled form of the advertisement.

An Annotated Bibliography

A glance through Melville criticism [on *The Confidence-Man*] would reveal on the part of his most sympathetic expounders a series of frank misreadings and evasions of the cagiest and most transparent sort.
—Leslie A. Fiedler, 1949

Notwithstanding the enormous volume of critical commentary on Melville's works during recent years, only a few students of *The Confidence-Man* seem to have grasped the book's significance as a document reflecting Melville's characteristic attitudes; and no one, apparently, has fully clarified its complex and devastating meaning.
—Walter Dubler, 1961

Well over a decade ago Elizabeth S. Foster, herself one of the leaders in the trend she described, asserted that Melville's *The Confidence-Man* was, at last, being rescued from "the dust of neglect and the murk of obscurity." Professor Foster apparently means by "obscurity" simply ignorance, both of the novel and its general significance. If, however, "rescue" means general agreement regarding a demonstrable reading of *The Confidence-Man*, then it is questionable whether the diverse critical comment on this novel has appreciably reduced its "obscurity."
—Edward Mitchell, 1968

The criticism of *The Confidence-Man* is so snarled that nothing can be gained, least of all clarity, by adding one more argument.
—Sidney P. Moss, 1968

WATSON G. BRANCH

An Annotated Bibliography

This bibliography lists in chronological order all the significant twentieth-century commentary on *The Confidence-Man*. The annotations are basically descriptive, but in view of the unusual nature of the criticism of the book, evaluations have often been ventured. The standard biographical sources (besides Leon Howard's 1951 study, listed below) are Jay Leyda, *The Melville Log* (New York: Harcourt, Brace, 1951; reissued with a new supplement, New York: Gordian Press, 1969); Merrell R. Davis and William H. Gilman, eds., *The Letters of Herman Melville* (New Haven: Yale University Press, 1960); and Eleanor Melville Metcalf, *Herman Melville: Cycle and Epicycle* (Cambridge: Harvard University Press, 1953). Most of the known reviews of *The Confidence-Man* are discussed in Hugh W. Hetherington, *Melville's Reviewers* (Chapel Hill: University of North Carolina Press, 1961); but see the annotation below. Hershel Parker, ed., *The Recognition of Herman Melville* (Ann Arbor: University of Michigan Press, 1967), prints four contemporary reviews not included in this Norton Critical Edition.

1919

Mather, Frank Jewett, Jr. "Herman Melville," *The Review*, 1 (August 9, 1919, and August 16, 1919), 276–278, 298–301. Finds only "middle-western character sketches" and "numerous tidbits of irony and wit" amid the "somewhat dreary wastes" of the briefly noted *CM*.

1921

Weaver, Raymond M. *Herman Melville, Mariner and Mystic*. New York, 1921. Passim. *CM* dismissed in passing as "a posthumous work" written after "the last glow of Melville's literary glamour" in *The Piazza Tales* had sunk into "blackness and ash."

1922

Van Vechten, Carl. "The Later Work of Herman Melville," *The Double Dealer*, 3 (January, 1922), 9–20. In short comments on *CM*, declares that the book is neither a novel nor what Mather called "sketches" but, instead, "the great transcendental satire" in which "Emerson is the confidence man."

1923

[Brooks, Van Wyck]. "A Reviewer's Notebook," *The Freeman*, 7 (May 9, 1923), 214–215. The book condemned as "an abortion" and "the product of a premature artistic senility," in which Melville's attempt at satire was, except at moments, "lost in a fog of undirected verbiage."

1926

Freeman, John. *Herman Melville.* London, 1926. Pp. 62–63, 140–144. Calls the book "an abortion" and finds the basis for this "vainest of satires" in Melville's "sense of personal failure." The meaning of the masquerade on the *Fidèle* ("a world in little") judged to be "hopelessly obscure."

1929

Mumford, Lewis. *Herman Melville.* New York, 1929. Pp. 247–255. Divines in the "unfinished" *CM* "indirect revelations of Melville's own life" and "pathological allusions" reflecting his state of mind. Rating Freeman's criticism beside the point and Mather's not more accurate, interprets the Confidence Man's masquerade in this "companion" to *Gulliver's Travels* as Melville's "own bitter plea" for support and as the representation of man's "sweetness and morality," which had become for Melville "the greatest of frauds."

1937

Braswell, William. "Melville as a Critic of Emerson," *American Literature,* 9 (November, 1937), 317–334. Declares Van Vechten's theory "unfounded" and proposes curtly that after *Pierre* "Melville apparently did not express himself in print on either Emerson or the Transcendentalists as a school." However, does see *CM* as a severe satire on man's supposedly innate goodness.

1938

Thorp, Willard. *Herman Melville: Representative Selections, with Introduction, Bibliography, and Notes.* New York, 1938. Pp. xi–cxxix. In brief comments on *CM*, discusses chapters 14, 33, and 44 as an exposition of Melville's theory—one at variance with mid-nineteenth-century views—of what constitutes reality in fiction. The "nadir" of Melville's "disillusionment" is thought to be reflected in the misanthropy of *CM*, which was written with "grim detachment." Understands the book as "an allegory of man's life journey, like *Pilgrim's Progress* or Hawthorne's 'The Celestial Railroad.'"

Winters, Yvor. *Maule's Curse.* Norfolk, 1938. Pp. 82–85. Seminal study finding the theme of the allegorical *CM* "identical" with that of *Pierre*: "that the final truth is absolute ambiguity, and that nothing can be judged." The Winsome-Egbert episodes seen as a "very biting commentary" on Emerson and the practical implications of his philosophy. Declares that the book is "unsatisfactory as philosophy" and "tediously repetitious as narrative" but the prose is "crisp and hard, and in a few passages the comment is brilliant." Mumford's notion that *CM* came out of a period of insanity called "absurd."

1939

Simon, Jean. *Herman Melville: Marin, Métaphysicien et Poète.* Paris, 1939. Pp. 430–442. Argues that Melville makes his hero "un expérimentateur," who adopts diverse attitudes to test his fellow men and finally meets deception everywhere. Seeing the book as a series of dialogues (as in Plato and others), either comedic or philosophic, judges its form to be damaged by Melville's inability to escape the narrative demands of the romance. Winsome called "un portrait" of Emerson.

1941

Matthiessen, F. O. *American Renaissance.* New York, 1941. Pp. 409–412, 472, 491–493. Concludes that Melville, as an outsider, was unable to present a realistic picture of the Mississippi or the West, and that because of intense mental suffering during this period of his life he could not keep the satire under control nor could he imagine a conclusion for the book. The structure of this "distended fragment" is deemed "no more than a manipulated pattern of abstractions," but the style is "hard and decisive." Tentatively identifies Winsome as Emerson.

1943

Braswell, William. *Melville's Religious Thought.* Durham, 1943. Pp. 30, 72, 115–117. Short comments on *CM*, declaring that Melville "presents religion in a very cynical light" and "was without pity in portraying men as contemptible or ridiculous." Jest about Providence in last chapter "reminds one of some of Swift's vulgar humor."

1944

Sedgwick, William Ellery. *Herman Melville: The Tragedy of Mind.* Cambridge, Mass., 1944. Pp. 187–193. Like Thorp, regards *CM* as marking "the nadir of disillusionment" Melville sank to after *Pierre.* A sensitive reading that makes undeveloped assertions about the book's overelaboration and too-patent ingenuity, about the "savage indignation" and "spiritual anguish" at its core, and about the Dantesque visual imagery. Finally, by a paradoxical reading, sees the Indian-hating tale as an affirmation of love, which is called "the primal reality."

1945

Watters, R. E. "Melville's 'Sociality,' " *American Literature,* 17 (March, 1945), 33–49. Approaches *CM* briefly from the point of view of a "head-heart antithesis" and ventures the conjecture that there is "no evidence at all that in any of his guises the Confidence Man defrauds anybody."
Oliver, Egbert S. "Melville's Goneril and Fanny Kemble," *New England Quarterly,* 18 (December, 1945), 489–500. Builds a convincing, though not unimpeachable, case for the identification of Goneril and the famous actress, with interesting contemporary descriptions of Fanny Kemble and her apparently ambiguous character.

1946

Oliver, Egbert S. "Melville's Picture of Emerson and Thoreau in 'The Confidence-Man,' " *College English,* 8 (November, 1946), 61–72. Convincing though imperfectly documented presentation of the theory that Melville was picturing Emerson in the character of Mark Winsome, but the case for Egbert's being a picture of Thoreau is not so well done.

1947

BOOK

Brooks, Van Wyck. *The Times of Melville and Whitman.* New York, 1947. Pp. 164–169. This later view finds a suggestion of Hawthorne in the ambiguity of *CM.* The book's "opaqueness" now blamed on Melville's "obvious inability" to draw characters vivid enough to support his thought.

ARTICLE

Chase, Richard. "An Approach to Melville," *Partisan Review,* 14 (May–June, 1947), 285–294. In one paragraph declares *CM* to be "a great book": not a "fragment" or a "chaotic cry of despair," but a "book of folklore" that makes a perceptive study of the American character. The Confidence Man is another "false Prometheus," in this case "a do-gooder, a Progressive in fact, and an emotional-intellectual-spiritual cutpurse."

1948

Fuller, Roy. Introduction to *CM.* London, John Lehmann, 1948. Pp. v–xiii. Credits Winters with putting Melville's novels in their "proper perspective" and follows his interpretation of *CM.* Also sees "a little humour, much irony" in this satire, a work that is ambiguous because "the eighteenth-century reasonable man has disappeared." Praises Melville's "single-mindedness" in developing his theme.

Finds similarities to Kafka and contrasts Melville to English Victorians because he was "neither Christian nor radical."

1949

BOOKS

Chase, Richard. *Herman Melville, A Critical Study.* New York, 1949. Pp. 185–209. Both this chapter and Chase's 1949 article (see below) are provocative, though inaccurate, treatments which develop fully declarations made in the 1947 Chase article and attempt to draw specific correspondences between *CM* and American folklore. Both end with pæans for the new liberalism of the 1940's.

Stone, Geoffrey. *Melville.* New York, 1949. Pp. 228–234. Routine interpretation.

Wright, Nathalia. *Melville's Use of the Bible.* Durham, 1949. Passim. In a brief treatment of *CM* relates its theme—"distrust of men"—to the wisdom books of the Bible, and discusses the many Biblical allusions. Sees Biblical base for the book's structure and style. Finds *CM* unique among Melville's works in presenting the Gospels and St. Paul as "a deceiving and a misleading message".

ARTICLES

Chase, Richard. "Melville's Confidence Man," *The Kenyon Review*, 11 (Winter, 1949), 122–140. For annotation see Chase's 1949 book, listed above.

Hillway, Tyrus. "Melville and the Spirit of Science," *The South Atlantic Quarterly*, 48 (January, 1949), 77–88. Traces Melville's apparently changing attitude toward nature, deciding near the end of the article that in *CM* Melville makes an explicit attack "upon those who persist in counting upon the goodness of nature."

Howe, Irving. "The Confidence Man," *Tomorrow*, 8 (May, 1949), 55–57. Socioeconomic interpretation of the book, seeing the Confidence Man as "the Salesman *par excellence*" in this attack of Melville's "on the American ethos and character." Very critical of the book's form: "a dialectical Punch-and-Judy show." Review of Lehmann edition.

Beverley, Gordon. "Herman Melville's Confidence," *The Times Literary Supplement*, 2493 (November 11, 1949), 733. Short letter to the *TLS* making the undocumented assertion that *CM* displays, especially in its conclusion, "a splendid picture of true confidence in the Universe and in Man."

Fiedler, Leslie A. "Out of the Whale," *The Nation*, 169 (November 19, 1949), 494–495. Says Chase's "ambitious and sensitive reading [of *CM*] is marred only by being basically wrong," and then proclaims an equally idiosyncratic reading that the Confidence Man, rather than being a villain, is Christ, who has learned from sad experience in this world to "*bamboozle* us into belief." Finds book's "primary ambiguity" based in Melville's own lack of definite beliefs.

Redman, Ben Ray. "New Editions," *Saturday Review of Literature*, 32 (November 26, 1949), 28. Generalized praise in the form of a review of the Grove Press edition (1949) that counsels the reader not to be baffled by *CM* but simply to enjoy the book.

1950

BOOKS

Arvin, Newton. *Herman Melville.* New York, 1950. Pp. 211–212, 232, 246–252. Criticizes the book for failing to be expressive of what Arvin felt made Melville great ("his sense of the tragic"). Argues that Melville had lost confidence in nature and in man and saw only the "lurking treacheries," which resulted in an infidel, nihilistic book: the "unendurably repetitious" *CM*.

Pommer, Henry F. *Milton and Melville.* Pittsburgh, 1950. Passim. Briefly identifies allusions to Milton in *CM* and draws parallels between the book and *Paradise Lost*.

ARTICLES

Kazin, Alfred. "On Melville as Scripture," *Partisan Review*, 17 (January, 1950), 67–75. A review of Chase's book attacking him for reducing *CM* to myth or folklore. Claims Melville's book expresses his "unappeasable fury against the human situation."

Hoffman, Dan G. "Melville's 'Story of China Aster,' " *American Literature*, 22 (May, 1950), 137–149. Unconvincing application of Chase's folklore thesis to the China Aster tale. Attempts to "link" the tale to the rest of the book.

1951

BOOKS

Howard, Leon. *Herman Melville: A Biography*. Berkeley, 1951. Pp. 226–239. Suggestive, but sometimes conjectural, explanation of *CM*'s composition, substance, and publication, seen in terms of Melville's life and other works.

Mason, Ronald. *The Spirit Above the Dust: A Study of Herman Melville*. London, 1951. Pp. 198–207. Reviews earlier criticism. Sees *CM* not as satire but as "the spontaneous, almost artless outcry of an affronted spirit" against materialism, with the Bible as "a saving grace never finally repudiated."

ARTICLES

Shroeder, John W. "Sources and Symbols for Melville's *Confidence-Man*," *Publications of the Modern Language Association*, 66 (June, 1951), 363–380. Like Thorp, sees parallels to "The Celestial Railroad" and *Pilgrim's Progress*, and goes on to attempt a point-by-point comparison. Detailed examination of Indian-hating tale, proposing that the Indian-hater has "no distortion in his vision of spiritual reality" and is the only hope against the Confidence Man. Credits Elizabeth Foster's dissertation for anticipating several of his independent findings, especially on the Satanic nature of the Confidence Man; finds Miss Wright's interpretation limited and Chase's inaccurate.

Nichol, John W. "Melville and the Midwest," *Publications of the Modern Language Association*, 66 (September, 1951), 613–625. Relates western imagery in *CM* to Melville's 1840 Galena trip and to the actual geography of the Mississippi region.

1952

BOOKS

Baldini, Gabriele. *Melville o le ambiguità*. Milano, 1952. Passim. Brief sections on *CM* derived generally from American critics, especially Matthiessen and Arvin.

Thompson, Lawrance, *Melville's Quarrel with God*. Princeton, 1952. Pp. 296–328. Attempts to fit *CM* into the thesis that Melville was trying to expose God as an unjust Practical Joker, this time through the "crafty indirections" of irony and allegory. Inaccuracy regarding details of the book spoils provocative discussions such as that of narrative point of view.

ARTICLES

Sealts, Merton M., Jr. "Melville's 'Neoplatonic Originals,' " *Modern Language Notes*, 67 (February, 1952), 80–86. Mostly about *Mardi*, but does state that Melville's reference to Proclus in *CM* shows his "hostility to certain characteristics of Transcendentalism" and that Mark Winsome is a Transcendentalist "satirically portrayed."

Wright, Nathalia. "The Confidence Men of Melville and Cooper: An American Indictment," *American Quarterly*, 4 (February, 1952), 266–268. Unpersuasive effort to draw close parallels between *Homeward Bound* and *CM*, and particularly between Steadfast Dodge and Frank Goodman.

——. "Form as Function in Melville," *Publications of the Modern Language Association*, 67 (June, 1952), 330–340. Briefly discusses the three chapters on the art of fiction (Chapters 14, 33, and 44), relating them to the putative organic form "embodied" in Melville's book.

Horsford, Howard C. "Evidence of Melville's Plans for a Sequel to *The Confidence-Man*," *American Literature*, 24 (March, 1952), 85–89. Careful and prudently balanced presentation of the evidence supporting the possibility that Melville might have planned a sequel to *CM*.

Pearce, Roy Harvey. "Melville's Indian-Hater: A Note on a Meaning of *The Confidence-Man*," *Publications of the Modern Language Association*, 67 (December, 1952), 942–948. Rejects Shroeder's position that the Indian-hater has undistorted vision: "blind hatred" is as bad as "blind confidence," and, therefore, the "blackness is complete" in *CM*. Cites earlier American works about Indian-haters, comparing Melville's Moredock story with its original by Judge James Hall. Partially rewritten and combined with two other essays under the title "The Metaphysics of Indian-Hating: Leatherstocking Unmasked," in Pearce's *Historicism Once More* (Princeton: Princeton University Press, 1969), pp. 109–136.

1953

BOOK

Feidelson, Charles, Jr. *Symbolism and American Literature*. Chicago, 1953. Pp. 207–212. Brief but suggestive treatment of *CM* and its major symbols. Finds Melville committed to "the problematic method" in presenting conflict of faith and no trust, which leads to a *modus vivendi* based on inconsistency.

1954

BOOKS

Foster, Elizabeth S. Introduction to *CM*. New York, Hendricks House, 1954. Pp. xiii–xcv. By far the best and most thorough single study of *CM*, despite the unconvincing nature of several of the conclusions based on the excellent collection of information pertaining to the book. Contains careful, if somewhat oversympathetic, analyses of *CM*'s satire, allegory, themes, structure, and composition. Stresses Satanic nature of the Confidence Man and centrality of Indian-hating tale. Reviews earlier criticism. Also extremely valuable are this edition's Explanatory Notes (pp. 287–365). Studies surviving manuscript drafts in Appendix (pp. 373–392).

1955

BOOK

Rosenberry, Edward H. *Melville and the Comic Spirit*. Cambridge, Mass., 1955. Pp. 141–184. Compares *CM* and *Tristram Shandy*, reading each "as a mordant but whimsical gambol with ideas and personalities, to which progressive characterization, dramatic tension, and even narrative consequence are irrelevant". Analyzes carefully Melville's themes and his artistic method (the mixing of bright and dark in the "ambiguity of humor") during the mid-1850's. Like Oliver, argues that Winsome and Egbert are "sharply focused" caricatures of Emerson and Thoreau for the purpose of satirizing their ideas. Places Melville in tradition of the frontier humorists.

ARTICLES

"The Misanthrope." Anon. rev., *Time Magazine*, 65 (March 7, 1955), 114, 116, 118. Superficial comments in a review of the Hendricks House edition.

O'Connor, William Van. "Melville on the Nature of Hope," *University of Kansas City Review*, 22 (December, 1955), 123–130. Optimistic reading of *CM* as an expression of Melville's hopefulness. Alleges that the Confidence Man is "like most men, partly a con-man and partly a philanthropist."

1956

BOOKS

Baird, James. *Ishmael*. Baltimore, 1956. Passim. Discusses very briefly Melville's creation of primitivistic symbols in relation to his attitude toward Indians and his Orientalism and animism in imagery in *CM*.

Miller, Perry. *The Raven and the Whale*. New York, 1956. Pp. 338–339. Places *CM* in context of Melville's supposed relationship to the American national literary movement.

1957

ARTICLES

Botta, Guido. "L'ultimo romanzo di Melville," *Studi Americani*, 3 (1957), 109–
131. Routine discussion of *CM* except for the suggestion that Melville created
a new mode of characterization, not seen again until Expressionism and Piran-
dello, in which the Confidence Man is "un complesso di personaggi," a micro-
cosm showing the inconstancy and ambiguity of humanity, and a total representation of Man.
Kaplan, Sidney. "Herman Melville and The American National Sin: The Meaning
of 'Benito Cereno,' " *The Journal of Negro History*, 42 (January, 1957), 11–
37. Brief, unsuccessful attempt to read *CM* as a part of Melville's supposed
expression in his writings of his position regarding the black man and slavery.
Cawelti, John G. "Some Notes on the Structure of *The Confidence-Man*," *American Literature*, 29 (November, 1957), 278–288. Sees *CM* as a "paradigm of
reality," a reality that is itself ambiguous. Claim for structural analysis based
on study of "incomplete reversals"—in characterization, incident, idea—which
leave the reader with no foundation for interpretation of the action. Examines
the three chapters on the art of fiction and several of the tales told by the
characters.

1959

BOOKS

Bewley, Marius. *The Eccentric Design: Form in the Classic American Novel*.
New York, 1959. Pp. 191–219. Sees in a brief examination of *CM* "the relaxa-
tion of form" (because of the book's ambiguity, which is the "negation" of
form) and a "denial of life." The Confidence Man is thought to be "appearance
drained of all reality," a mask with nothing behind it.
Honig, Edwin. *Dark Conceit: The Making of Allegory*. Evanston, 1959. Passim.
Brief, sometimes abstruse comments on those aspects of *CM* that are seen as
relevant to this analysis of allegory as a genre.

ARTICLES

Miller, James E., Jr. "*The Confidence-Man:* His Guises," *Publications of the
Modern Language Association*, 74 (March, 1959), 102–111. Traces themes of
CM through earlier works and sees parallels between the Confidence Man and
confidence men of earlier books, like Riga, Cuticle, and sometimes society as
a whole. Distinguishes *CM* from other works almost solely on the basis of its
mode of "comic allegory," which controls the structure. Argues unpersuasively
that certain "ruggedly honest individuals"—the wooden-legged man, the Titan,
Pitch, Winsome, and Egbert perceive intuitively the Confidence Man's dia-
bolical nature and oppose it, but only the last two are able to defeat him.
Gross, John J. "Melville's *The Confidence-Man:* The Problem of Source and
Meaning," *Neuphilologische Mitteilungen*, 60 (September 25, 1959), 299–310.
Routine interpretation that focuses on the problem of the mute and makes the
unconvincing assertion that Joseph Glanvill's *The Vanity of Dogmatizing* is
Melville's "source" for this character.
Hayford, Harrison. "Poe in *The Confidence-Man*," *Nineteenth-Century Fiction*, 14
(December, 1959), 207–218. Expands from an identification of Poe as the
original for the peddler of the rhapsodical tract in *CM* into a fruitful study of
Melville's mode of composition, creation of character, and style.

1960

BOOK

Bowen, Merlin. *The Long Encounter: Self and Experience in the Writings of Herman Melville*. Chicago, 1960. Passim. Brief discussions of themes and character types in *CM*. Taking a position like Thompson's (1952), asserts that an
"unprincipled and chameleon-like God" in the guises of the Confidence Man
toys with mankind throughout the bitter masquerade.

ARTICLES

Reeves, Paschal. "The 'Deaf Mute' Confidence Man: Melville's Imposter in Action," *Modern Language Notes*, 75 (January, 1960), 18–20. Tenuous claim that the model for the mute was an impostor who pretended to be Melville during the 1850's and who is the subject of two letters (quoted in the article) of a Fayetteville, N.C., family.

Weissbuch, Ted N. "A Note on the Confidence-Man's Counterfeit Detector," *Emerson Society Quarterly*, No. 19 (II Quarter 1960), 16–18. Factual study that relates Melville's counterfeit detector of the *CM*'s last chapter to the banknote problem and to actual counterfeit detectors.

Rosenberry, Edward H. "Melville's Ship of Fools," *Publications of the Modern Language Association*, 75 (December, 1960), 604–608. Calls "the ship of fools" a "paradigm" for *CM* as the tradition developed from Brant's *Das Narrenschiff* through Burton, *Cock Lorell's Boat*, and Jonson. Finds in *White-Jacket* the immediate antecedent for the morality figure of the Confidence Man and for the ship-microcosm of the *Fidèle*. Qualifies earlier support of Shroeder's case for "The Celestial Railroad" and *Pilgrim's Progress* as sources for Melville's book.

1961

BOOKS

Finkelstein, Dorothee Metlitsky. *Melville's Orienda.* New Haven, 1961. Pp. 40–41. Claims that a certain allusion in *CM* has the *Arabian Nights* as its source.

Hetherington, Hugh W. *Melville's Reviewers: British and American, 1846–1891.* Chapel Hill, 1961. Pp. 255–264. Excerpts, often inaccurately, from contemporary reviews of *CM* known in 1961. Quoted citations and summary comments do not always reflect substance of the reviews.

Hoffman, Daniel G. *Form and Fable in American Fiction.* New York, 1961. Pp. 279–313. Focuses on question of genre, considering Melville's special use of the literary streams that flow into *CM* from such diverse sources as Hawthorne's stories, the picaresque satiric romance, Mather's *Magnalia*, and traditional American humor. Declares *CM* a "book of brilliant fragments" but a "failure" of overall form. Stresses Melville's "ironical" viewpoint.

Perosa, Sergio. Introduction to *L'uomo di fiducia.* Venezia, Neri Pozza, 1961. Pp. ix–xxxiv. Borrows much from American critical opinion, especially from James Miller's article, including his hint concerning Northrop Frye, which Perosa follows to his own conclusion that *CM* is an "anatomia." Also argues that *CM* has much in common with morality plays.

ARTICLES

Anderson, David D. "Melville and Mark Twain in Rebellion," *The Mark Twain Journal*, 11 (Fall, 1961), 8–9. Factually inaccurate and unsuccessful attempt to associate Melville's and Twain's visions regarding appearance and reality.

Male, Roy R. "The Story of the Mysterious Stranger in American Fiction," *Criticism*, 3 (Fall, 1961), 281–294. Examines *CM* as one of several works of American fiction with a "mysterious stranger" as protagonist, attempting to delineate similarities in action, characterization, and theme.

Dubler, Walter. "Theme and Structure in Melville's *The Confidence Man*," *American Literature*, 33 (November, 1961), 307–319. Imposition on *CM* of "the motif of the tragic flaw," which is made applicable through strained readings of textual details. Sees structure as neat dialectic, but with only an implied synthesis: the norm of the golden mean between tragic excesses.

1962

BOOKS

Berthoff, Warner. *The Example of Melville.* Princeton, 1962. Passim. Provocative and thoughtful observations regarding *CM*'s action, structure, and style.

Humphreys, A. R. *Melville.* London, 1962. Pp. 102–110. Cursory treatment of the book.

Miller, James E., Jr. *A Reader's Guide to Herman Melville.* New York, 1962. Pp. 170–192. Contains essentially the same material as his 1959 article.

ARTICLES

Smith, Paul. *"The Confidence-Man* and the Literary World of New York," *Nineteenth-Century Fiction,* 16 (March, 1962), 329–337. Provides background material for analysis of *CM*'s position regarding Emerson and Christianity and offers convincing evidence that confidence men were "a contemporary phenomenon" in mid-nineteenth-century America.

Oates, J. C. *"Melville and the Manichean Illusion,"* *Texas Studies in Literature and Language,* 4 (Spring, 1962), 117–129. Like Simon, sees the Confidence Man as hero testing his ideal in the world, but unclearly presents the Confidence Man's role as that of the dreamer-author of the events that take place in the book. Irresolute regarding the relevance of Manicheanism to *CM.*

Hayman, Allen. "The Real and the Original: Herman Melville's Theory of Prose Fiction," *Modern Fiction Studies,* 8 (Autumn, 1962), 211–232. Informative study of Melville's theory of the art of fiction, with special attention, like Thorp, to *CM*'s three chapters on the subject.

1963

BOOKS

Franklin, H. Bruce. *The Wake of the Gods: Melville's Mythology.* Stanford, 1963. Pp. 153–187. Declares *CM* to be "Melville's most nearly perfect work," explaining it in terms of Hindu myth. A suggestive approach that breaks down, however, when too-exact correspondences are proposed, based on the apparent assumption that Melville consciously constructed the book upon the framework of this mythic material. Reasons that the mute definitely is the first avatar of the Confidence Man.

Hillway, Tyrus. *Herman Melville.* New York, 1963. Pp. 119–122. Routine analysis except for the allegation that the three chapters on the art of fiction show Melville's "growing preference for scientific realism as against imaginative romanticism."

ARTICLES

Seelye, John D. "Timothy Flint's 'Wicked River' and *The Confidence-Man,"* *Publications of the Modern Language Association,* 78 (March, 1963), 75–79. Focuses not on *CM* but on a Melville manuscript fragment ("The River"), which is considered by many critics to be a discarded section of the book. Draws many parallels, none absolutely convincing, between the fragment and Flint's writings on the Mississippi.

Hall, Joan Joffe. *"Nick of the Woods:* An Interpretation of the American Wilderness," *American Literature,* 35 (May, 1963), 173–182. Like Pearce, notes Indian-haters in American literature before Melville and goes on to compare *Nick* and the Indian-hating tale.

Parker, Hershel. "The Metaphysics of Indian-hating," *Nineteenth-Century Fiction,* 18 (September, 1963), 165–173. Summarizes the arguments of Shroeder, Pearce, and Miss Foster regarding the Indian-hating tale, pointing out unresolved difficulties. Analyzes the tale as "a tragic study of the impracticability of Christianity, and, more obviously, a satiric allegory" aiming at "the nominal practice of Christianity."

McCarthy, Paul. "The 'Soldier of Fortune' in Melville's *The Confidence Man,"* *Emerson Society Quarterly,* No. 33 (IV Quarter 1963), 21–24. Following James Miller, argues unconvincingly that the Soldier of Fortune is on the Black Guinea's list and is "a disciple of the Devil."

1964

BOOKS

Bernstein, John. *Pacifism and Rebellion in the Writings of Herman Melville.* The Hague, 1964. Pp. 147–164. *CM* not important to Bernstein's thesis because "pacifism and rebellion do not play an integral role in the novel," and therefore the treatment of Melville's book is routine and derivative.

Cohen, Hennig. Introduction to *CM.* New York, 1964. Pp. ix–xxiv. Routine in many areas, but argues that the meaning of *CM* is determined by response of secondary characters to the Confidence Man, alleging that "specific geographical identifications" of some of these characters is possible. States that Melville's "talents lay in the direction of extension, elaboration, involution, diversity, and digression."

Lewis, R. W. B. Afterword to *CM*. New York, Signet, 1964. Pp. 261–276. Suggestively calls *CM* the first of a new genre in American fiction—the comic apocalypse, which comprises "the continuing antiface of the American dream." [See Lewis's "Days of Wrath and Laughter" in his *Trials of the Word* (New Haven, 1965).] Finds the prose of *CM* "self-erasing" in that it presents no positive statement. Proposes that the Confidence Man is an embodiment of the archetypal figure of the trickster god—like Hermes, but more sinister. Also sees the Confidence Man as "Everyman as All-men" and as "not the bringer of darkness" but the revealer of "the darkness in ourselves."

ARTICLE

Drew, Philip. "Appearance and Reality in Melville's *The Confidence-Man*," *ELH, A Journal of English Literary History*, 31 (December, 1964), 418–442. Attacks earlier criticism by distorting the "received view" of *CM*. Ignores internal evidence in making many assertions: for example, there is "no evidence" that all the "confidence-men" are disguises of one man; and the Confidence Man represents true charity and has Melville's sympathy. Argument essentially based on refusal to see irony or allegory, except social, in the book.

1965

BOOK

Fussell, Edwin. *Frontier: American Literature and the American West*. Princeton, 1965. Pp. 303–326. Reduces *CM* to a book about the West and the Indian, who "was the crucial and intractable fact of American history." Alleges that Melville asks the book's readers "to discriminate the genuine from the false through identifying the genuine with the West," not the "false-front, travesty West" but "the real West" as defined by this critic and supposedly represented by Pitch. Declares, therefore, that "reversing perspective, or involuted irony, is the chief formal principle" of *CM*.

ARTICLES

Grauman, Lawrence, Jr. "Suggestions on the Future of *The Confidence-Man*," *Papers on English Language & Literature*, 1 (Summer, 1965), 241–249. Review and criticism of earlier interpretations of *CM*.

Ishag, Saada. "Herman Melville as an Existentialist: An Analysis of *Typee, Mardi, Moby Dick*, and *The Confidence Man*," *The Emporia State Research Studies*, 14 (December, 1965), 5–41. Section on *CM* generally routine treatment except for comparisons to the Theatre of the Absurd and to Existentialistic thought.

1966

BOOK

Grube, John. Introduction to *CM*. New York, Airmont, 1966. Pp. 7–9. Short, unscholarly introduction.

ARTICLES

Magaw, Malcolm O. "*The Confidence-Man* and Christian Deity: Melville's Imagery of Ambiguity," *Explorations of Literature, Louisiana State University Studies*, 18 (1966), 81–99. Builds upon earlier criticism, but sees the Confidence Man as a "God," mythical in his own right, "whose many-colored masks are the fantastic projections of the minds of those men who unconsciously turn to dreams and illusions to give themselves identity." Like Miss Wright, attempts to relate all eight avatars to Christ. Cites Melville's technique as "eclectic," a technique that leads to ambiguity.

Karcher, Carolyn Lury. "The Story of Charlemont: A Dramatization of Melville's Concepts of Fiction in *The Confidence-Man: His Masquerade*," *Nineteenth-*

Century Fiction, 21 (June, 1966), 73–84. Draws a tenuous relationship of Charlemont to Christ and to the mute and the man with gold sleeve-buttons in an attempt to show that the characters "redefine" each other, a process that is deemed part of Melville's "revelatory technique" in *CM*.

Tuveson, Ernest. "The Creed of the Confidence-Man," *ELH, a Journal of English Literary History*, 33 (June, 1966), 247–270. Irresolute discussion of the Confidence Man's putative role as a prophet of the creed of confidence, "a jesuit of the new religion" for mid-nineteenth-century America as well as for the passengers on the *Fidèle*.

1967

BOOKS

Franklin, H. Bruce. Introduction to *CM*. Indianapolis, Bobbs-Merrill, 1967. Pp. xiii–xxvii. Essentially the same position expressed in *CM* section of his 1963 book, but with added introductory material and annotations and a discussion of the relationship of "fiction" and "reality" and Melville's "fictive realities."

Guetti, James. *The Limits of Metaphor: A Study of Melville, Conrad, and Faulkner*. Ithaca, 1967. Pp. 136–139. Brief attempt to apply thesis regarding the "failure of imagination" to *CM*. Sees the book's tone as one of "extended confusion" founded on the "tenuous dichotomy" of trust and distrust. *CM* said to exhibit a world "totally without meaning."

ARTICLES

Lang, Hans-Joachim. "Ein Argerteufel bei Hawthorne und Melville: Quellenuntersuchung zu *The Confidence-Man*," *Jahrbuch für Amerikastudien*, 12 (1967), 246–251. Starting from Daniel G. Hoffman's hint regarding similarities in structure between *CM* and Hawthorne's "The Seven Vagabonds," develops a convincing case for the "old 'Straggler' " of this tale being a source for the Confidence Man. Also cites resemblance in presentation of the "Welt als Bühne" in the two works.

Sealts, Merton M., Jr. "Melville's 'Geniality.' " *Essays in American and English Literature Presented to Bruce Robert McElderry, Jr.*, edited by Max F. Schulz. Athens, Ohio, 1967. Pp. 3–26. Studies Melville's attitudes toward "geniality" and discusses his artistic uses of the concept.

Seltzer, Leon F. "Camus's Absurd and the World of Melville's *Confidence-Man*," *Publications of the Modern Language Association*, 82 (March, 1967), 14–27. Suggestive effort to apply Camus' Existentialistic theories to *CM* is vitiated by imposition of moral and ethical values on the book. Finally resorts to routine interpretation.

1968

BOOKS

Dryden, Edgar A. *Melville's Thematics of Form: The Great Art of Telling the Truth*. Baltimore, 1968. Pp. 149–195. Provocative interpretation based for the most part on careful, though sometimes over-ingenious, readings of the text, especially the three chapters on the art of fiction. States that *CM* "presents a world where the real and fictitious are indistinguishable and interchangeable," and that the creative artist himself is a confidence man. Argues that the book's structure is "obviously Biblical." Convincing development of Miss Foster's suggestion that Burton's *Anatomy* is important to *CM*. Following the hint of R. W. B. Lewis, proposes to identify the boy peddler with Hermes, but uncompellingly expands this reading to include the Cosmopolitan as Apollo.

Maxwell, D. E. S. *Herman Melville*. London, 1968. Pp. 68–87. Standard comments on *CM*, with long extracts.

Seelye, John. Introduction to *CM*. San Francisco, Chandler, 1968. Pp. vii–xl. Informative comparison of material in *CM*—"a work of unadulterated satire"—with "mid-century American themes" appearing in contemporary magazines and books. Examines earlier criticism and contemporary reviews.

ARTICLES

Travis, Mildred K. "Spenserian Analogues in *Mardi* and *The Confidence Man*," *Emerson Society Quarterly*, No. 50, Supplement (First Quarter, 1968), 55–58.

374 · Watson G. Branch

Claim that *CM* "seems to have its origin" or "source" in Spenser's "Mother Hubberds Tale" supported only by a single, most tenuous similarity.

Mitchell, Edward. "From Action to Essence: Some Notes on the Structure of Melville's *The Confidence-Man*," *American Literature*, 40 (March, 1968), 27–37. Routine article except for declaration that it is "an impossibility" to define the "*essence*" of the Confidence Man or his victims, the book's "two basic types of characters," distinguishable only "in terms of their function."

Sumner, D. Nathan. "The American West in Melville's *Mardi* and *The Confidence-Man*," *Research Studies*, 36 (March, 1968), 37–49. Takes the same basic approach to *CM* as does Fussell (1965), the only important difference being in his treatment of Moredock, who represents mythically, as Pitch does really, the "only hope for America," a hope symbolically extinguished when the cosmopolitan puts out the solar lamp at the book's end.

Moss, Sidney P. " 'Cock-A-Doodle-Doo!' and Some Legends in Melville Scholarship," *American Literature*, 40 (May, 1968), 192–210. Not primarily on *CM* but argues that Melville never satirized either Emerson or Thoreau. See Parker (1970) for an evaluation of the evidence adduced by Oliver (1946), Foster (1954), and Moss.

Swanson, Donald R. "The Structure of *The Confidence Man*," *CEA Critic*, 30 (May, 1968), 6–7. Superficial, derivative examination of *CM*'s structure.

1969

BOOKS

Berthoff, Warner. "Herman Melville: *The Confidence-Man*," in *Landmarks of American Writing*, ed. Hennig Cohen. New York, 1969. Pp. 121–133. An impressionistic survey of *CM*, which finds the "command to charity" in Chapter 1 inviolable ("No mere pattern of words can put down the force of true charity"). Disputes Miss Foster's "apocalypse-minded" interpretation of the Confidence Man's character and ventures an optimistic reading in which the Confidence Man presents the image of a way of life: "engaged watchfulness." Argues that the cosmopolitan's leading away of the old man in Chapter 45 is an "act of kindness" which gives the book "a hopeful, benignant ending after all."

Porte, Joel. *The Romance in America: Studies in Cooper, Poe, Hawthorne, Melville, and James*. Middletown, 1969. Pp. 155–170. The search for unity in the five authors examined results in a contrived explication of *CM* as "a lecture with illustrations . . . on the theory and practice of romance," containing "a bizarre portrait of the artist as a gay Devil." Like Oates, sees the book as the dream of the mute, who is a "mordant self-portrait" of Melville as romancer. Includes improbable allegations; for example, Goneril "is in fact slyly described as a transvestite homosexual."

ARTICLES

Baim, Joseph. "The Confidence-Man as 'Trickster,' " *American Transcendental Quarterly*, No. 1 (First Quarter, 1969), 81–83. Unsuccessful effort to apply hurriedly some terms (and occasionally some principles) of modern psychology to the character of the Confidence Man. Contains serious misreadings of the text.

Brouwer, Fred E. "Melville's *The Confidence-Man* as Ship of Philosophers," *Southern Humanities Review*, 3 (Spring, 1969), 158–165. Follows Miss Foster's explication of philosophical positions presented in *CM* and argues for specific identification of guises of the Confidence Man—from the man with the weed to the Philosophical Intelligence Office man—with individual "antagonists" of Hobbes's theories.

Bach, Bert C. "Melville's Confidence-Man: Allegory, Satire, and the Irony of Intent," *Cithara*, 8 (May, 1969), 28–36. Starting from Miss Foster's view of *CM* as allegory and satire, examines the three chapters on the art of fiction (14, 33, 44) in an attempt to show "the subtle manner in which Melville employs ironic self-depreciation" to establish his theory of characterization.

Bergmann, Johannes Dietrich, "The Original Confidence Man," *American Quarterly*, 21 (Fall, 1969), 560–577. Presents, with extensive documentation, a convincing case that the "Original Confidence Man," a swindler who was first in the news in New York City in 1849 and who reappeared in Albany in 1855, was "an important source" for Melville's Confidence Man.

Turner, Frederick W. III. "Melville's Post-Meridian Fiction," *Midcontinent American Studies Journal*, 10 (Fall, 1969), 60–67. A cursory reading of *CM* from an anthropological point of view, marred by factual errors.

Bowen, Merlin. "Tactics of Indirection in Melville's *The Confidence-Man*,"

Studies in the Novel, 1 (Winter, 1969), 401–420. Claims that the "non-digressive digressions"—the interpolated tales and the three chapters on the art of fiction—are "among Melville's tactics of indirection," introduced with "deliberate awkwardness" to force the modern reader to consider their "deeper implications": the "dark truth" and "heresy" implied is that the Confidence Man is God. Agrees with Parker (1963) that "condemnation of the Indian-hater has been based on general moral grounds with little or no reference to the specific evidence set forth in the book." Like Shroeder (1951), sees Pitch (with Mordock as his heroic extension) as the representative of Melville's best hope to oppose the Confidence Man.

Brodtkorb, Paul, Jr. *"The Confidence-Man:* The Con-Man as Hero," *Studies in the Novel*, 1 (Winter, 1969), 421–435. Concludes that *CM* presents Melville's theory about the inconsistency of human behavior: "there is finally no such thing as *character*" and "posing, role-playing" is the fundamental human condition. Like Drew (1964), argues for admiration and respect for the cosmopolitan because he "most clearly and emphatically demonstrates his comparative purity of heart and the gratuitous basis of his actions."

Seelye, John. " 'Ungraspable Phantom': Reflections of Hawthorne in *Pierre* and *The Confidence-Man*," *Studies in the Novel*, 1 (Winter, 1969), 436–443. In an attempt to find the "link between autobiography and fiction" in *CM*, argues that in the encounter between the cosmopolitan and Charlie, "Melville was commenting ironically upon his failure to establish an ideal communion of souls" with Hawthorne.

1970

BOOKS

Pops, Martin Leonard. *The Melville Archetype.* Kent, Ohio, 1970. Pp. 162–168. Brief, superficial treatment of *CM* that declares the book nihilistic but "beyond bitterness and, therefore, curiously serene" rather than expressive, like *Pierre*, of "Melville's own sexual crises and metaphysical doubts," though Orchis, in the China Aster tale, is seen as the incarnate "well of sexual energy, now polluted and poisoned," so that "he is a betrayer of sperm."

Seelye, John D. *Melville: The Ironic Diagram.* Evanston, 1970. Pp. 117–130. Unconvincing presentation of *CM* as "another of Melville's diminished quests" and one of his two (with *Israel Potter*) attempts at the picaresque novel. Contains undeveloped assertions on various aspects of the book, usually stated in terms of antithesis, irony, or paradox. Pitch called the "ethical ideal" in the book.

Seltzer, Leon F. *The Vision of Melville and Conrad.* Athens, Ohio, 1970. Passim. Cites *CM* occasionally in comparing the two authors' skepticism, nihilism, prose technique, and concepts of the nature and behavior of man. Sees the Confidence Man as "a person who, without faith in himself, has learned how to exploit his nihilistic awareness most satisfyingly by betraying others to repose their faith in him."

ARTICLES

McCarthy, Paul. "Affirmative Elements in *The Confidence Man*," *American Transcendental Quarterly*, No. 7, Part 2 (Summer, 1970), 56–61. Argues that "the prevailing mood of gloom and futility in *The Confidence-Man* is lightened somewhat by the writer's treatment of various characters," especially Pitch and the boy peddler. Emphasizes only the positive or "affirmative" aspects of these "half-dozen or so" characters and their actions.

Parker, Hershel. "Melville's Satire of Emerson and Thoreau: An Evaluation of the Evidence," *American Transcendental Quarterly*, No. 7, Part 2 (Summer, 1970), 61–67. Passages omitted in printing, with consequent garbling of the sense, are listed on a page tipped into the hard bound copies of this issue of *ATQ*, published as *Studies in the Minor and Later Works of Melville*, ed. Raymona E. Hull. Hartford, 1970. An examination of Melville's satire of Emerson and Thoreau that supports most of Oliver's arguments (1946) as they apply to *CM* and takes issue with Miss Foster (1954) and especially Moss (1968) regarding their denials that Melville could be satirizing Thoreau in *CM*. Cites substantial evidence, some of it overlooked or ignored by the earlier critics, "about Melville's possible and certain knowledge of Thoreau," and relates that evidence to the characterization of Thoreau as Egbert in *CM*. Printer's omissions, especially on p. 66, disguise the extent to which this article constitutes a defense of Oliver (1946).

1971

PAMPHLET

Costner, Martha Izora. *Goldsmith's* CITIZEN OF THE WORLD *and Melville's* THE
CONFIDENCE-MAN. Comanche, Okla., 1971. A thirty-five page pamphlet, mimeo-
graphed. An unpretentious but well-informed study. Through carefully mustered
parallels, makes a plausible case for Melville's indebtedness to Goldsmith;
convincingly demonstrates that Miss Foster's study of Melville's eighteenth-
century sources needs to be supplemented.

NORTON CRITICAL EDITIONS

ANDERSON *Winesburg, Ohio* edited by Charles E. Modlin and Ray Lewis White
AQUINAS *St. Thomas Aquinas on Politics and Ethics* translated and edited by
Paul E. Sigmund
AUSTEN *Emma* edited by Stephen M. Parrish Second Edition
AUSTEN *Mansfield Park* edited by Claudia L. Johnson
AUSTEN *Persuasion* edited by Patricia Meyer Spacks
AUSTEN *Pride and Prejudice* edited by Donald Gray Second Edition
BEHN *Oroonoko* edited by Joanna Lipking
Beowulf (the Donaldson translation) edited by Joseph F. Tuso
BLAKE *Blake's Poetry and Designs* selected and edited by Mary Lynn Johnson and
John E. Grant
BOCCACCIO *The Decameron* selected, translated, and edited by Mark Musa and
Peter E. Bondanella
BRONTË, CHARLOTTE *Jane Eyre* edited by Richard J. Dunn Second Edition
BRONTË, EMILY *Wuthering Heights* edited by William M. Sale, Jr., and Richard Dunn
Third Edition
BROWNING, ELIZABETH BARRETT *Aurora Leigh* edited by Margaret Reynolds
BROWNING, ROBERT *Browning's Poetry* selected and edited by James F. Loucks
BURNEY *Evelina* edited by Stewart J. Cooke
BYRON *Byron's Poetry* selected and edited by Frank D. McConnell
CARROLL *Alice in Wonderland* edited by Donald J. Gray Second Edition
CERVANTES *Don Quixote* (the Ormsby translation, revised) edited by Joseph R. Jones and
Kenneth Douglas
CHAUCER *The Canterbury Tales: Nine Tales and the General Prologue* edited by
V. A. Kolve and Glending Olson
CHEKHOV *Anton Chekhov's Plays* translated and edited by Eugene K. Bristow
CHEKHOV *Anton Chekhov's Short Stories* selected and edited by Ralph E. Matlaw
CHOPIN *The Awakening* edited by Margo Culley Second Edition
CLEMENS *Adventures of Huckleberry Finn* edited by Sculley Bradley,
Richmond Croom Beatty, E. Hudson Long, and Thomas Cooley Second Edition
CLEMENS *A Connecticut Yankee in King Arthur's Court* edited by Allison R. Ensor
CLEMENS *Pudd'nhead Wilson and Those Extraordinary Twins* edited by Sidney E. Berger
CONRAD *Heart of Darkness* edited by Robert Kimbrough Third Edition
CONRAD *Lord Jim* edited by Thomas C. Moser Second Edition
CONRAD *The Nigger of the "Narcissus"* edited by Robert Kimbrough
CRANE *Maggie: A Girl of the Streets* edited by Thomas A. Gullason
CRANE *The Red Badge of Courage* edited by Donald Pizer Third Edition
DARWIN *Darwin* selected and edited by Philip Appleman Second Edition
DEFOE *A Journal of the Plague Year* edited by Paula R. Backscheider
DEFOE *Moll Flanders* edited by Edward Kelly
DEFOE *Robinson Crusoe* edited by Michael Shinagel Second Edition
DE BALZAC *Père Goriot* translated by Burton Raffel edited by Peter Brooks
DE PIZAN *The Selected Writings of Christine de Pizan* translated by Renate
Blumenfeld-Kosinski and Kevin Brownlee edited by Renate Blumenfeld-Kosinski
DICKENS *Bleak House* edited by George Ford and Sylvère Monod
DICKENS *David Copperfield* edited by Jerome H. Buckley
DICKENS *Hard Times* edited by George Ford and Sylvère Monod Second Edition
DICKENS *Oliver Twist* edited by Fred Kaplan
DONNE *John Donne's Poetry* selected and edited by Arthur L. Clements Second Edition
DOSTOEVSKY *The Brothers Karamazov* (the Garnett translation) edited by Ralph E. Matlaw
DOSTOEVSKY *Crime and Punishment* (the Coulson translation) edited by George Gibian
Third Edition
DOSTOEVSKY *Notes from Underground* translated and edited by Michael R. Katz

DOUGLASS *Narrative of the Life of Frederick Douglass, an American Slave, Written by Himself* edited by William L. Andrews and William S. McFeely
DREISER *Sister Carrie* edited by Donald Pizer Second Edition
Eight Modern Plays edited by Anthony Caputi
ELIOT *Middlemarch* edited by Bert G. Hornback
ELIOT *The Mill on the Floss* edited by Carol T. Christ
ERASMUS *The Praise of Folly and Other Writings* translated and edited by Robert M. Adams
FAULKNER *The Sound and the Fury* edited by David Minter Second Edition
FIELDING *Joseph Andrews with Shamela and Related Writings* edited by Homer Goldberg
FIELDING *Tom Jones* edited by Sheridan Baker Second Edition
FLAUBERT *Madame Bovary* edited with a substantially new translation by Paul de Man
FORD *The Good Soldier* edited by Martin Stannard
FORSTER *Howards End* edited by Paul B. Armstrong
FRANKLIN *Benjamin Franklin's Autobiography* edited by J. A. Leo Lemay and P. M. Zall
FULLER *Woman in the Nineteenth Century* edited by Larry J. Reynolds
GOETHE *Faust* translated by Walter Arndt, edited by Cyrus Hamlin
GOGOL *Dead Souls* (the Reavey translation) edited by George Gibian
HARDY *Far from the Madding Crowd* edited by Robert C. Schweik
HARDY *Jude the Obscure* edited by Norman Page
HARDY *The Mayor of Casterbridge* edited by James K. Robinson
HARDY *The Return of the Native* edited by James Gindin
HARDY *Tess of the d'Urbervilles* edited by Scott Elledge Third Edition
HAWTHORNE *The Blithedale Romance* edited by Seymour Gross and Rosalie Murphy
HAWTHORNE *The House of the Seven Gables* edited by Seymour Gross
HAWTHORNE *Nathaniel Hawthorne's Tales* edited by James McIntosh
HAWTHORNE *The Scarlet Letter* edited by Seymour Gross, Sculley Bradley, Richmond Croom Beatty, and E. Hudson Long Third Edition
HERBERT *George Herbert and the Seventeenth-Century Religious Poets* selected and edited by Mario A. DiCesare
HERODOTUS *The Histories* translated and selected by Walter E. Blanco, edited by Walter E. Blanco and Jennifer Roberts
HOBBES *Leviathan* edited by Richard E. Flathman and David Johnston
HOMER *The Odyssey* translated and edited by Albert Cook Second Edition
HOWELLS *The Rise of Silas Lapham* edited by Don L. Cook
IBSEN *The Wild Duck* translated and edited by Dounia B. Christiani
JAMES *The Ambassadors* edited by S. P. Rosenbaum Second Edition
JAMES *The American* edited by James W. Tuttleton
JAMES *The Portrait of a Lady* edited by Robert D. Bamberg Second Edition
JAMES *Tales of Henry James* edited by Christof Wegelin
JAMES *The Turn of the Screw* edited by Robert Kimbrough
JAMES *The Wings of the Dove* edited by J. Donald Crowley and Richard A. Hocks
JONSON *Ben Jonson and the Cavalier Poets* selected and edited by Hugh Maclean
JONSON *Ben Jonson's Plays and Masques* selected and edited by Robert M. Adams
KAFKA *The Metamorphosis* translated and edited by Stanley Corngold
LAFAYETTE *The Princess of Clèves* edited and with a revised translation by John D. Lyons
MACHIAVELLI *The Prince* translated and edited by Robert M. Adams Second Edition
MALTHUS *An Essay on the Principle of Population* edited by Philip Appleman
MANN *Death in Venice* translated and edited by Clayton Koelb
MARX *The Communist Manifesto* edited by Frederic L. Bender
MELVILLE *The Confidence-Man* edited by Hershel Parker
MELVILLE *Moby-Dick* edited by Harrison Hayford and Hershel Parker
MEREDITH *The Egoist* edited by Robert M. Adams
Middle English Lyrics selected and edited by Maxwell S. Luria and Richard L. Hoffman
Middle English Romances selected and edited by Stephen H. A. Shepherd
MILL *Mill* selected and edited by Alan Ryan

MILL *On Liberty* edited by David Spitz
MILTON *Paradise Lost* edited by Scott Elledge Second Edition
Modern Irish Drama edited by John P. Harrington
MORE *Utopia* translated and edited by Robert M. Adams Second Edition
NEWMAN *Apologia Pro Vita Sua* edited by David J. DeLaura
NEWTON *Newton* edited by I. Bernard Cohen and Richard S. Westfall
NORRIS *McTeague* edited by Donald Pizer Second Edition
Restoration and Eighteenth-Century Comedy edited by Scott McMillin Second Edition
RICH *Adrienne Rich's Poetry and Prose* edited by Barbara Charlesworth Gelpi and
Albert Gelpi
ROUSSEAU *Rousseau's Political Writings* edited by Alan Ritter and translated by
Julia Conaway Bondanella
ST. PAUL *The Writings of St. Paul* edited by Wayne A. Meeks
SHAKESPEARE *Hamlet* edited by Cyrus Hoy Second Edition
SHAKESPEARE *Henry IV, Part I* edited by James L. Sanderson Second Edition
SHAW *Bernard Shaw's Plays* edited by Warren Sylvester Smith
SHELLEY *Frankenstein* edited by Paul Hunter
SHELLEY *Shelley's Poetry and Prose* selected and edited by Donald H. Reiman and
Sharon B. Powers
SMOLLETT *Humphry Clinker* edited by James L. Thorson
SOPHOCLES *Oedipus Tyrannus* translated and edited by Luci Berkowitz and
Theodore F. Brunner
SPENSER *Edmund Spenser's Poetry* selected and edited by Hugh Maclean and
Anne Lake Prescott Third Edition
STENDHAL *Red and Black* translated and edited by Robert M. Adams
STERNE *Tristram Shandy* edited by Howard Anderson
STOKER *Dracula* edited by Nina Auerbach and David Skal
STOWE *Uncle Tom's Cabin* edited by Elizabeth Ammons
SWIFT *Gulliver's Travels* edited by Robert A. Greenberg Second Edition
SWIFT *The Writings of Jonathan Swift* edited by Robert A. Greenberg and William B. Piper
TENNYSON *In Memoriam* edited by Robert H. Ross
TENNYSON *Tennyson's Poetry* selected and edited by Robert W. Hill, Jr.
THACKERAY *Vanity Fair* edited by Peter Shillingsburg
THOREAU *Walden and Resistance to Civil Government* edited by William Rossi
Second Edition
THUCYDIDES *The Peloponnesian War* translated by Walter Blanco edited by Walter Blanco
and Jennifer Tolbert Roberts
TOLSTOY *Anna Karenina* edited and with a revised translation by George Gibian
Second Edition
TOLSTOY *Tolstoy's Short Fiction* edited and with revised translations by Michael R. Katz
TOLSTOY *War and Peace* (the Maude translation) edited by George Gibian Second Edition
TOOMER *Cane* edited by Darwin T. Turner
TURGENEV *Fathers and Sons* translated and edited by Michael R. Katz
VOLTAIRE *Candide* translated and edited by Robert M. Adams Second Edition
WASHINGTON *Up from Slavery* edited by William L. Andrews
WATSON *The Double Helix: A Personal Account of the Discovery of the Structure of DNA*
edited by Gunther S. Stent
WHARTON *Ethan Frome* edited by Kristin O. Lauer and Cynthia Griffin Wolff
WHARTON *The House of Mirth* edited by Elizabeth Ammons
WHITMAN *Leaves of Grass* edited by Sculley Bradley and Harold W. Blodgett
WILDE *The Picture of Dorian Gray* edited by Donald L. Lawler
WOLLSTONECRAFT *A Vindication of the Rights of Woman* edited by Carol H. Poston
Second Edition
WORDSWORTH *The Prelude: 1799, 1805, 1850* edited by Jonathan Wordsworth,
M. H. Abrams, and Stephen Gill